The Real Katie Lavender

The Real Katie Lavender

ERICA JAMES

First published in 2011 by Orion Books,
an imprint of The Orion Publishing Group Ltd
Orion House, 5 Upper Saint Martin's Lane
London WC2H 9EA

An Hachette UK Company

1 3 5 7 9 10 8 6 4 2

A CIP catalogue record for this book
is available from the British Library.

ISBN (Hardback) 978 1 4091 3081 9
ISBN (Export Trade Paperback) 978 1 4091 3082 6

Typeset by Deltatype Ltd, Birkenhead, Merseyside

Printed in Great Britain by Clays Ltd, St Ives plc

www.orionbooks.co.uk

To Edward and Samuel
for continuing to keep me on my toes.

Acknowledgements

I'm grateful to a number of lovely people who helped me with various aspects of this novel and as ever I'm responsible for anything I may have twisted to suit my purposes.

Thank you to Samuel and Rebecca for their Brighton insight.

Thank you to my 'fraud expert' who wants to remain anonymous on the grounds that it might not look good for him to be so clued up on such things!

Lastly, posthumous thanks to Michael Jones for sharing with such enthusiasm his beloved Henley-on-Thames with me, as well as introducing me to Tony and Gloria and their stunning garden. Henley won't be the same without him.

Chapter One

At the age of thirty, Katie Lavender believed she was better equipped than most when it came to receiving bad news. She had coped with the death of her mother a year ago, and with her father's death three years before that, and as a result she was convinced there was little anyone could do or say that could shock her.

Which was why, when she was summoned that hot June Friday morning to the executive producer's office and offered a redundancy package of derisible generosity, and politely informed that there would be no need for her to show up for work next week, she had merely nodded her consent and closed the door after her.

During her walk of shame back to her desk she was acutely aware that nobody in the open-plan office area was looking at her. Never had she seen such industrious activity as her colleagues studiously avoided catching her eye. For the past week Stella Media Productions had been rife with rumours that numbers would have to be cut, and it looked like Katie had been the first to be given the chop. Look on the bright side, she told herself; better to be a trailblazer than a mindless follower.

Her mobile was ringing when she got to her desk. 'A job offer already,' she said cheerfully as Daz raised his head from behind his computer and glanced over at her. He gave her a sickly half-hearted smile of what she supposed was comradely support.

The voice in her ear belonged to a man. 'Is that Miss Lavender? Miss Katie Lavender?'

'It is,' she said.

'My name is Howard Clifford, of Tyler, Robinson and Clifford. I'm sorry I wasn't around yesterday to take your call when you telephoned, and I hope this isn't an inappropriate moment to speak with you, but I shall be out of the office for most of next week and I didn't want to miss you again.'

She recalled the solicitor's letter that was in her bag and which had arrived in the post yesterday morning before she'd set off for work. The letter had puzzled her for most of the day, especially as she had never heard of Tyler, Robinson and Clifford. It had been very clear: she was to make contact with a Mr Howard Clifford at her earliest convenience so that an appointment could be made for her to visit him in his office in Fulham. 'That's all right,' she said. 'What is it you want to talk to me about?'

'I'd rather not say on the telephone. It would be much better for you to come to my office. I don't suppose you're free today, are you?'

'It's my lunch break in an hour's time. And since I've just been made redundant, I don't see why I can't take an extended break.' Daz's head bobbed up from behind his computer again, then disappeared just as quickly.

'I'm sorry to hear that, Miss Lavender,' Howard Clifford said. His voice sounded unexpectedly kind. Then he was all business again. 'I'll see you at one o'clock, then. You have the address, don't you?'

With thunder rumbling overhead, and a strike in full swing on the underground, Katie hailed a cab on the corner of Portland Street and took out her mobile to ring her mother.

No sooner had she got the phone in her hand than she caught her breath and her heart squeezed. A year had passed and yet she could still forget that Mum was dead. That she could never talk to her again. Never again could she share a moment like this with her. She felt the hot prickle of tears at the backs of her eyes and the all too familiar panicky tightness

2

forming in her throat, the feeling that she couldn't breathe. She put a hand to her mouth and concentrated on breathing. Slow and steady. Slow and steady.

When she was sure she wasn't going to cry and embarrass herself in front of the cab driver, she wondered what people would think if they knew that she still had her mother's contact details on her phone. Would they think it was a bit weird? A bit macabre? She had thought she might remove them when the first anniversary of Mum's death had passed – a symbolic act to prove she had moved on and was coping well – but she hadn't been able to do it. She simply couldn't part with that link to her mother. And the only reason she didn't still have her father's contact details was because she'd lost the mobile she'd had at the time and when she'd replaced it, she had forced herself not to add his name to the address book. She had felt so guilty doing that.

She took a long and steady breath and phoned her closest friend, Tess.

'*Redundant!*' Tess shrieked down the line. 'That's outrageous! How dare they? How bloody dare they? What did Ian say?'

'I haven't spoken to him yet. You're the first I've told.'

The fact that she hadn't told Ian before Tess spoke volumes, but if her friend was thinking what Katie suspected she was thinking, she had the decency not to say anything. Just lately Tess had made a couple of comments about Ian that suggested she thought he wasn't right for Katie – the remarks had coincided with Katie thinking much the same.

'Do you want to meet for lunch?' Tess asked.

'I can't, I'm on my way to meet a solicitor.'

'What for? You're not thinking of suing for wrongful redundancy or something, are you?'

Katie explained about the letter.

'How mysterious,' Tess said. 'You don't suppose it's some unfinished business with your mum's will, do you?'

'I wouldn't have thought so. Mum's solicitor was the same

as Dad's in Guildford, and anyway everything was sorted out some months ago.'

'Well, call me later and tell me all. And don't worry about getting another job; with your experience you'll soon be fixed up.'

Katie ended the call and stared out of the side window of the cab. Would she be fixed up soon? As grateful as she was for her friend's optimism, she knew the job market wasn't exactly overflowing with opportunities for people like her right now.

She had been at Stella Media for two and a half years. Following several years of gofer-style jobs, she had joined the company as a production secretary and climbed the media ladder all the way to the dizzy heights of production coordinator. Her days mostly revolved around reminding everybody else what, when and how they should be doing something. It was difficult to pinpoint precisely where it had all gone wrong, but gone wrong it had.

When she had been at school, she had dreamt of being a human-rights lawyer. She had imagined herself defending the weak and the poor, of changing the world, of making a difference. Then when her A levels hadn't panned out as well as she'd needed to study law, she had hit upon the idea of changing the world through the medium of television; she would change the way people thought and behaved by becoming an award-winning documentary-maker. She would be involved in groundbreaking projects that were dark and gritty and life-affirming and full of integrity. With a degree in media studies, she embarked upon her crusade with all the zeal of a newly converted missionary, only eventually to wind up working for a production company that churned out television programmes that pulled in good ratings but totally shamed her. As popular as some of the programmes had been, they were hardly the award-winning programmes she wanted to be associated with. Stella Media's big success stories were *My Ugly Best Friend* and *My Fat Best Friend* – the premise being that so-called best friends nominated those closest to them to undergo drastic cosmetic surgery or to be starved within an inch of their miserable lives. *Too Big for Your Boots* had also done relatively good business – a quiz show that revolved around participants being humiliated and cut down to size with cruel glee. It was essentially car-crash telly with everyone on a journey or living the dream. One more bloody journey, one more bloody dream and Katie would take a stick to the lot of them.

Things had not turned out the way she had planned, she thought tiredly as she stared through the window at the gloomy, thundery sky. Especially now she had been made redundant. Apparently Stella Media, with the well of creative ideas having run dry, would somehow manage without a production coordinator for the foreseeable future. Frankly Katie wouldn't trust any of them to blink without a reminder in their diaries.

She could probably get temporary work as a production assistant as a short-term measure, but she wasn't so sure she could bring herself to do it, because now that she had allowed herself to think the unthinkable, she realized she was bored with wiping programme-makers' bottoms. Where was the sense of fulfilment and satisfaction in that?

Tyler, Robinson and Clifford was wedged in between an interior-design shop with a glittering chandelier in the window and an antiquarian bookshop.

Katie had pictured Howard Clifford with short iron-grey hair and a pinstripe suit, and for extra effect a red silk hand-kerchief in his breast pocket, but he was nothing of the sort. She guessed he was in his mid-forties, his hair was a sandy-blond colour and there wasn't a pinstripe or silk handkerchief in sight. His suit was a dark shade of blue; its jacket was hanging lopsidedly on the back of his chair, a tie poking out of a pocket, a Marks and Spencer label just visible. With his shirt open at the neck and his sleeves rolled up to his elbows, he was as informal as his office was chaotic, with files, folders, law books and papers covering every available surface. There was a cricket bat propped against a filing cabinet and a lone well-worn trainer next to it. On the windowsill behind the desk was a framed photograph of two young grinning children peering out of a Wendy house; they both had the same sandy-blond hair as he had. At odds with all this was his voice, which was the same as it had been on the phone, extremely courteous and very proper.

'Please, Miss Lavender, sit down. May I offer you a cup of tea or coffee?'

As tempting as the offer was, she didn't want anything to delay the purpose of her visit. 'No thank you,' she politely declined.

'Then to business,' he said briskly, sidestepping a three-foot-high tower of files and going round to his side of the desk. He sat down and reached for an envelope next to a computer that was decorated with a collection of yellow Post-it notes. 'I've been instructed to give this letter to you to read,' he said. 'The original instructions were given to this firm thirty years ago and the matter became my responsibility ten years ago when I joined the firm. Accordingly I've been informed that I must leave you alone whilst you read the letter.'

Genuinely mystified and not a little alarmed, Katie watched him leave the room. When the door was closed, she opened the envelope and took out four sheets of cream notepaper. She recognized her mother's expressive handwriting at once; the flamboyant flourishes of the pen strokes that had been Fay Lavender's character all over. Sadness clutched at Katie's heart. She took a deep steadying breath and began reading.

My dearest Katie,

This is the hardest thing I've ever had to do, but I know that it is absolutely the right thing to do.

If my instructions have been followed properly you will be reading this a year after my death. The reason for

*this is that I hope that you'll be over it and will be strong
enough now to take the shock of what I'm about to tell
you.*

*There's no way to dress this up other than to come
right out with it. The truth is, your father, who was
the best father you could ever have had, and who loved
and cherished you, was not your biological father. Your
biological father and I made a pact the moment I knew
I was pregnant with you that he would have nothing to
do with me ever again or interfere in any way with your
upbringing. In return, he made me promise to carry out
just one wish on his behalf; it was something I was in no
position to deny him. But I shall leave that to Howard
Clifford to explain to you, or whoever else has been
entrusted with the task.*

*Let me say straight away that your father knew about
the affair, as brief and as reckless as it was, and he
somehow found it in his heart to forgive me. He said
he did so because he loved me. I just hope you can find
it in your heart to forgive your father and me for our
deception.*

*If you do think less of me for what I did, and I
wouldn't blame you if you did, I hope you will never
think less of your father. He was such a good man – a
wonderful husband and an adoring father. I made a
promise to him that you would never know the truth
whilst he was still alive, and I held firm to that promise.*

*You're probably wondering why I feel it's important
now for you to know the truth after all these years. My
justification is simple: the only reason you'll be reading
this letter is because your father and I are no longer
around, and I hate the thought of you being alone in the
world and not having anyone – by that I mean family
– to look out for you. I want you to meet your biological
father – in the hope that he's still alive when you read this
– along with any other children he may have had. You*

*always did want to have a brother or a sister; remember
how you used to write to Father Christmas to bring you
a baby sister? Sadly your father and I could not make
that wish come true for you. Much to your father's
disappointment, it turned out he couldn't actually have
children, maybe that's why he treasured you the way he
did.*

*Please, my darling girl, forgive me for any pain and
distress you feel as a consequence of reading this letter.*
With all my love,
Mum.

*PS What happens next is up to you, Katie. I have given
very clear instructions to Howard Clifford, who will be
dealing with this matter, and he will help you all he can.*

When she had finished reading, Katie sat very still and
stared unseeingly ahead of her.

A knock at the door made her start. Behind her Howard
Clifford came in; he was carrying a tray of tea things. In her
stunned state, she focused all her concentration on the flowery
teapot, the matching small milk jug with the chip in the rim,
the sugar bowl and the two cups and saucers. Anything but
think of what she'd just read.

'I thought you might have changed your mind about something to drink,' he said.

She nodded, unable to speak

'Milk?'

She nodded again.

'Sugar?'

She shook her head.

She put her mother's letter down in front of her on the
cluttered desk and with trembling hands she took the prof-
fered cup and saucer. She suddenly shivered, as though a rush
of cold air had entered the room. She watched the solicitor
swivel his chair and open a filing cabinet behind him. After

a few seconds of rustling he pulled out a packet of chocolate fingers. 'My weakness,' he said, passing her the packet.

She shook her head and took a long wobbly intake of breath. And to think she had believed herself impervious to shock. Finally able to speak, she said, 'I take it you know the exact contents of my mother's letter?'

'Yes. Drink your tea and then I'll tell you the rest.'

'The rest?'

'Your tea,' he said firmly.

Dazed, she did as he said.

When he seemed to be satisfied with how much she'd drunk, he passed her the packet of chocolate fingers again. This time she took one, and while she nibbled on the biscuit, he sat back in his chair, his elbows resting on the arms.

'When you were born, your biological father set up a trust fund for you. That fund can now be released and accessed by you.'

'What kind of trust fund?'

'The kind that represents a considerable amount of money.'

She swallowed. 'Can you define *considerable?*'

He smiled, leant forward, slipped on a pair of glasses and opened a file to his right. He turned a couple of pages, paused, then said, 'As of yesterday, that fund was worth seven hundred and fifty-eight thousand pounds and sixteen pence exactly.'

Chapter Two

With no real grasp of what she was feeling, only that her brain seemed to have seized up and she was numb, Katie made her way to Victoria station. Why bother returning to work when she didn't have a job to go back to?

She caught the first available train to Brighton and sat in the stifling carriage with her face turned to the grimy window. The sky had finally cracked open and it had started to rain, a real deluge. When the window became too opaque with dirt and rain to see through, she looked at the two middle-aged women sitting opposite her. Flushed with the airless heat, and fanning themselves with magazines, they were happily discussing the spoils of a successful shopping expedition. It sounded as if they'd been hunting down outfits for a wedding; all they had left to find were the right handbags. Next to Katie was a man playing solitaire on his laptop. There was an unpleasant whiff of cigarettes and BO coming off him. How ordinary and familiar it all seemed.

But ordinary wasn't how she felt. She felt as though her world had been blown apart, shattered into a million pieces that could never be put back together again. This morning she had left home ready for the normal kind of Friday, cheerfully taking her seat on the usual crowded commuter train in the full and happy knowledge that the end of the week had almost arrived, that Slackerday and Slumberday lay ahead – as she and Tess had renamed their favourite days of the week. But now nothing was as it had been when she'd woken up. Nothing made sense. Nothing felt real. What if she closed her eyes and fell asleep? Would she wake up and find that today had been a dream? First losing her job and then ... and then this bombshell.

Her mobile rang. She saw that it was Tess and that she had tried ringing earlier. She switched the phone off. She couldn't speak to anyone at the moment. Not even Tess. She hoped her friend would forgive her.

She closed her eyes. Immediately she was back in Howard Clifford's untidy office. He was explaining to her in his kind but firmly matter-of-fact way that in accordance with the instructions Tyler, Robinson and Clifford had received, the trust fund was hers whether she wanted to get in touch with her biological father or not; there were no strings attached, the two things were not related. An unfortunate choice of word, she had thought.

'But why should I now suddenly be entitled to it?' she had asked. 'What's significant about now?'

'Only one person could make the decision as to when you received the money, and that was your mother. She came to see me shortly after your father died, that is to say when Desmond Lavender died, and lodged instructions with this firm that a year after her death, whenever that took place, I was to give you the letter you've just read, along with details about the trust fund. She didn't want you to know about the fund while your father – Desmond – was still alive.'

'What if I had died before her?'

'The fund would have been closed and the money given to a charity of your mother's choosing.'

'What if I don't want the money?'

'That's entirely your prerogative. But if I were you, Miss Lavender, I'd think very carefully before looking a gift horse in the mouth.'

If I were you, Miss Lavender ...

The question was: who was she? Who was Katie Lavender? One minute she was the daughter of Fay and Desmond Lavender with thirty years of memories and certainties behind her, and now those years meant nothing; every single one of them had been a lie. Dad hadn't been her father and Mum hadn't been the woman Katie had believed her to be.

The telephone was ringing when she let herself in. The answering machine picked up the call. It was Ian. She made no effort to lift the receiver. 'Hi, Katie,' she heard him say in his jaunty trouble-free voice. 'I tried your mobile but it wasn't switched on. Just wanted to let you know there's been a change of plan; I won't be flying back tonight after all as I'm now at the airport on my way to Dubai. Berlin's been fun. I know I've said it before, but you'd love it, we must come here for a long weekend some time. I'll call you tomorrow. Bye.'

If anyone were to ask Katie what exactly it was that Ian did for a living, she'd be hard-pressed to say. Accountancy was his background, and as far as she knew he was a project manager and spent a lot of time travelling round Europe, and more recently the Middle East and Manila in the Philippines. What he actually did was a mystery to her. He spoke about his work a lot, especially the office politics that went on, something that really excited him, but if she were honest, and she wasn't proud of this admission, she frequently tuned out whenever he started talking about his work. Frankly, it just sounded so dull. Tess had once joked that Ian secretly worked for MI6, that his job for a major German bank was a cover. It didn't seem very likely.

But as the day had so far taught her, nothing was as it seemed.

She put the kettle on and went upstairs to change out of her work clothes. Back down in the kitchen again, she made herself a cup of tea and took it outside to the rain-washed and now sun-filled garden. The air had been cleared of all its earlier oppressive mugginess, and as she wiped the wooden chair and table dry, she breathed in the heady smell of warm damp earth.

The small walled garden had been Mum's pride and joy.

She had thrown all her energy into making it even more beautiful than it already was, freely admitting that it was her way of turning her grief and mourning for Dad into something creative and positive. Katie had inherited her mother's green fingers, and after her death she had willingly assumed the mantle of responsibility for the garden. As with so many things, it was a way to feel close to Mum.

Moving here after Dad's death had been her mother's way of starting a new life. Tired of living in the country, she had wanted to be in a town, to have everything on the doorstep and be surrounded by people of all ages and backgrounds. Katie had helped her organize the sale of their old house in Midhurst, and together, whilst scouring the internet, they'd found this small but perfectly formed two-bedroomed terraced house with its south-facing garden. The previous owners had converted the third bedroom into a large and lavish bathroom and extended the kitchen into something equally lavish with French doors opening on to the walled garden. Originally, when she had decided that Brighton would be her new home, Mum had been adamant that she wanted a sea view, that nothing else would do, but when she'd seen this garden with its walls dripping in wisteria blooms and a fig tree offering a corner of welcome shade on a hot day, she had changed her mind. And anyway, if you stood on a chair in either of the two bedrooms, you could see the sea. You could certainly hear the seagulls; their insistent cries were as constant as the ebb and flow of the tide.

If Dad's sudden death had taken them by surprise – he'd died of septicaemia as a result of, of all things, food poisoning – Mum's death had been even more of a shock. She had been knocked over by a car. Witnesses had said she'd simply stepped into the road without looking where she was going. The driver – a forty-six-year-old man with his young family in the car with him – had been distraught, so the police told Katie. He'd repeatedly claimed he'd had no way of avoiding Fay. There had been no reason to disbelieve him. Fay had been rushed to hospital with a serious head injury. The medical staff had had to put her into a coma in order to operate, and whilst the operation was a success, she never came out of the coma. She died four days later.

With no other relatives on hand – neither of her parents had had any brothers or sisters – it had been down to Katie to arrange the funeral and to deal with the subsequent formalities. Her decision to leave London and move into her mother's house and commute to work from Brighton had surprised her friends, particularly Tess. But it had made sense. Rather than leave the house empty whilst waiting for probate to be sorted out, it was better for it to be occupied. Also, Tess and her boyfriend, Ben, were getting more serious about their relationship, and Katie had known that it was only a matter of time before they would want to find somewhere to live together. With Katie happy to move out, Ben could then move in. It was the ideal arrangement.

It was late one evening when travelling back to Brighton on the train from Victoria that Katie had met Ian. He'd been in the seat next to her, and after apologizing for knocking his foot against hers they'd got talking. She had recognized him as a regular commuter, and the next morning she'd spotted him on the platform. He came over and chatted and they got on the train together. Things just naturally progressed. A drink. A meal. A film. A night spent together. A weekend spent together. It was all very easy. All very comfortable. It was what Katie had needed in the aftermath of losing her mother. Nothing too dramatic, just the warmth and security of someone who cared. Someone who was happy to be there when she needed a sure and steady shoulder to lean on now and then. Five years older than her, he was reliably dependable; he knew how to fix a leaky tap or how to coax the boiler into working when she couldn't.

But recently Ian had started talking about them following Tess and Ben's example and moving in together, and since she had the larger house, it made sense, as he had pointed out, for him to move in with her. After all, as he had also pointed out, he already spent more time in her place than his own.

Not for the first time, Katie had to admit that too often she drifted into relationships that she then found difficult to get out of. Another thing that she did, quite unconsciously, was to adopt the likes and dislikes of a boyfriend. It was as if with each new partner she became a different person. For instance Ian was a big U2 fan. Katie had never liked the band or their music. She especially disliked their constant save-the-planet posturing. Couldn't they do it quietly? Couldn't they save the planet without banging on about it? She should have told Ian this the very first time he had played one of their CDs. But because she hadn't, because she'd been too polite ten months ago when they'd met to be honest with him, he now believed her to be as big a fan as he was.

Honesty. It was the bedrock of a relationship. Of any relationship.

So why the hell hadn't her parents been honest with her? Why the deceit? Between them they'd made a mockery of her life. How could they do that? She let out a cry of frustration and blinked back hot stinging tears as the jumble of bewildered hurt and anger that had been mounting inside her sparked and flared. How could her mother have done this to her? How could one of the people she had trusted most in the world ambush her like this and rob her of everything she had thought was true? The contents of that awful letter had taken away her past. Her identity, too. She had nothing left that mattered. Nothing.

She suddenly felt achingly alone.

Chapter Three

What happens next is up to you, Katie, her mother had written.

It was Saturday morning, not yet twenty-four hours since the world had changed for ever for her, and what exactly was she supposed to do next? For now, all she wanted to do was pull the duvet up over her head and stay there until her wish came true: that yesterday had never happened, that she still had her job and her parents were still the people they'd always been.

She had spent most of the night trying to sleep, and when she did manage to drop off she'd dozed fitfully, tormented with dreams that had her hunting the house for things she couldn't find or driving a car that had no brake pedal and a windscreen she couldn't see through. She had also dreamt she was back at school, as an adult, but having to sit her GCSE maths exam. No prizes for guessing the obvious, that she was seriously rattled.

So come on, Mum, she thought as she lay in bed staring through the gap in the curtains at the blue sky beyond and listening to the screech of seagulls, just what am I supposed to do next? How did you imagine the scenario would play out?

Downstairs in the kitchen, and stuffed in a drawer where she couldn't see it – out of sight, out of mind supposedly – was an envelope that Howard Clifford had given her. It contained the address of a firm of solicitors who could make contact with her biological father if she so wished. She hadn't opened the envelope and didn't know when she would be able to do so. Or if she ever would. What was to be gained from it? Only more confusion. Only more betrayal. Because apart from her own feelings, what of the feelings of his family? If he had children of his own, how would they react to her showing up out of the blue? And his wife – if he had one – what if she had no idea that he'd fathered another child? What if Katie had been conceived while he'd been married?

Now she did pull the duvet up over her head. It was all too awful to contemplate. She felt angry with her mother for putting her in this position. Why couldn't she have kept quiet? Why had she felt the need to mess things up for the rest of Katie's life? For that was what she had done. Much as Katie would like to pretend that envelope in the kitchen drawer didn't exist, she couldn't. It was going to taunt her for ever. It already was. *Open me*, it was whispering to her. *Open me and take the next step.*

The telephone by the side of the bed rang. Katie briefly considered letting the answering machine deal with it, but with her mobile still switched off and knowing that it was probably Tess wondering why on earth she hadn't returned her calls, she picked up the receiver.

'So you are still alive!' Tess exclaimed. 'I've been worried sick. Why've you switched your mobile off?'

'I'm sorry.'

'And so you should be. I was about to call the police. Just think how embarrassing that would have been if they'd turned up at your door with a battering ram and burst in on you.' Tess was laughing now, and her lightness cheered Katie. 'So what's going on? Why the Greta Garbo routine?'

'It's a long story.'

'You're not beating yourself up over being made redundant, are you? And don't think I'm trivializing it, but you mustn't take it personally. It's about numbers, that's all. You'll find a much better job, just you see.'

'It's nothing to do with that. It's something far worse.'

'Worse? You're not having a relationship emergency, are

you? What's Ian done? Because I'll tell you now, if he's—'

'Tess, hit the off switch and give me a chance to speak, will you?' She explained about her visit to Howard Clifford and her mother's letter.

When she'd finished, and with uncharacteristic restraint, Tess said, 'Oh my God, you must be in bits. Is Ian there with you?'

'He doesn't know anything about it. He's on his way to Dubai. Though by now he's probably there.'

'OK, here's what we do. I come down there and spend the weekend with you. You can't be on your own with this whirring around inside your head. You need to do something to take your mind off it.'

'Don't be silly. I'm fine.'

'Yeah, right, that's why you've been incommunicado, sitting there all on your own fretting yourself silly. Now look, I'm not going to take no for an answer, I'm coming down. And before you whinge about Ben, he's busy working on some big project that should have been finished days ago, so he won't even notice that I'm not here.'

'Tess, listen to me: I'm fine. I just need to think it through on my own. I don't want to make a massive drama out of it.'

'But it is a big drama. You've just discovered that your father wasn't your father.'

It took a while to convince her friend not to come rushing down from London to hold her hand, that she had a million and one things to keep her busy, including an appointment at the hairdresser's, and after she came off the phone Katie felt exhausted. She dragged herself out of bed, showered, dressed and went downstairs. Realizing that her hair appointment was in fifteen minutes, she grabbed an apple for her breakfast and flew out of the house.

For the last ten years there had only been one person who she'd trusted to cut her hair. His name was Zac and she'd followed him from salon to salon when he'd been in London.

He now owned his own place in Brighton. He'd made a good name for himself in the two years since he'd moved here, and his clients included a growing number of A-list London refugees. He also just happened to be Tess's older brother.

Waiting for him to finish blow-drying the hair of a majorly funky-looking man who was displaying more leather about his person than a Bank Holiday DFS sofa sale, Katie sipped the skimmed latte one of the Saturday girls had brought her from the coffee shop next door and stared at her reflection in the mirror in front of her.

She had hated the colour of her hair when she'd been a child; it had earned her a clutch of clichéd nicknames, such as Ginger Nut, Carrot Top and Annie, as in Orphan Annie. When she was sixteen her parents allowed her to alter it, and after a couple of disastrous attempts with DIY kits in the bathroom, she reinvented herself as a strawberry blonde. When she was twenty and Zac started cutting her hair, he persuaded her to do away with colouring it and to embrace not only the true vibrant colour mother nature had given her, but its natural curl and wave. Ever since that day she had grown to love the rich chestnut of her hair, and trusted Zac's judgement and opinion implicitly.

She continued to scrutinize her reflection, taking in the paleness of her complexion, the bluey-grey, almost violet, of her eyes and the wide set of her cheekbones. Her hair was loose and stopped halfway down her back. She had always been told that she'd inherited her colouring from her mother's great-grandmother – a woman Katie had never met; nor had she ever seen a photograph of her. Now she couldn't help but think that that had been a lie, and that maybe her colouring came from her biological father.

She put down her coffee and leant forward to look at her reflection more closely, as if she would suddenly spot something that had always been there but which she'd never noticed before. She felt that if she stared hard enough, something would leap out at her and make her realize the

19

blindingly obvious, that she wasn't the person she'd always believed herself to be. On the outside she looked the same, but as irrational as it sounded, on the inside she already felt very different.

She scooped up her hair in her hands, pulled it tight to the back of her head and slowly turned her face to the right, then to the left. She repeated the movement. Then did it again and came to a decision. A big, symbolic decision.

Zac was horrified. 'I'll do no such thing for you, darling!'

'It's *my* hair,' Katie asserted.

'It's more than just hair, it's your crowning glory, and I'll play no part in destroying it.'

Katie frowned. 'Oh brilliant! Trust a gay man to give a master class in how to overreact.'

He pouted and put his hands on his hips. 'Trust a gay man to give a master class in common sense, more like it!'

'But you won't be destroying it, you'll be restyling me. Come on, Zac, I'm stuck in a time warp here. I've had this look for years; it's time for a change.'

'If it ain't broke, don't try fixing it is my maxim. What's more, it's a classic look you have. It's your signature feature. Audrey had her eyebrows, Marilyn had her luscious curves and you, Katie Lavender, have your heavenly hair.' He ran his fingers through it as though this would convince her he was right.

'It's only hair,' she muttered.

Zac shuddered and rolled his eyes. 'Only hair,' he repeated, a hand now pressed against the ruffles of his white open-necked shirt – although technically it was probably a blouson. 'Only freakin' hair. Look about you, Katie. Is this the kind of establishment where we treat hair as being *only* hair? I'm shocked at you, darling. You'll be saying next oh, what the heck, it'll grow back.'

For the first time since yesterday, Katie laughed. 'Are you telling me it won't?'

'But something as dramatic as you're suggesting, going from long to pixie-short like Emma Watson – damn that girl! – can sometimes induce such a shock in the structure of the hair, it might never be the same again.'

'I know the feeling,' Katie said darkly.

'Sweetheart,' he said, leaning down so that his head was level with hers and he was meeting her gaze in the mirror, 'you need to think about this some more. I'll get the style books and Mandy will fetch you another coffee and maybe a slice of carrot cake, and you can see if there's a less drastic style that takes your fancy.'

'But drastic is what I want. I feel like living dangerously. I want to be edgy.'

'Edgy?' He straightened up and laughed. 'Darling Katie, you're as edgy as an After Eight mint. And who wants to be edgy when they can be as sweet and adorable as you? What does Tess say about this? And dear old Ian for that matter? Though I suspect he wouldn't notice if you grew an extra head.'

'What do Ian or Tess have to do with me changing my hair?' she snapped with exasperation and suddenly feeling stupidly close to tears. 'It's my hair, I'll do what I want with it.'

Zac sucked in his cheeks and raised his hands in mock surrender. 'And pray tell, which side of the royal bed did Princess Touchy get out of this morning?'

'I could always go to another salon,' she murmured.

He gasped. 'Bitch! Traitorous bitch!'

'Who's a bitch?'

They both turned. 'Tess!' they exclaimed together. 'What are you doing here?'

Tess kissed her brother on the cheek, dumped a large bag on the floor, sat in the chair next to Katie and grinned. 'Sorry, Katie,' she said. 'I know you told me not to come down, but I was already on the train when I phoned. Call it a sixth sense or something, but I was worried when I couldn't get hold of you. You're not cross, are you?'

Katie smiled, but before she could say anything, Zac said, 'Clearly there's something going on here that I don't know about. Would anyone care to put me in the picture?'

In the end, and after he had been put in the picture, Zac and Tess talked Katie out of doing anything drastic with her hair, and she reluctantly opted for what she'd originally made the appointment for, a trim and blow-dry.

She and Tess then went for lunch and a quick blast around the shops, ending up at Beyond Retro, where, to feed her ongoing *Mad Men* fixation, Tess bought herself a classic sixties figure-hugging short-sleeved dress with a viciously nipped-in waist. She also bought a Don Draper-style fedora for Ben to add to his ever-growing hat collection. To Katie's amusement, they were as bad as each other, neither having grown out of messing about with the dressing-up box.

Back at the house, Katie opened a bottle of wine and they made themselves comfortable in the garden. With the sun high in the cloudless sky, it was a perfect summer's day. Katie was glad that Tess had taken matters into her own hands and come down for the weekend. It was so typical of her. She had been the most wonderful of friends, fantastically supportive and always so generous with her time. Although when Mum had died, Tess and Zac had had family troubles of their own to deal with – their mother was undergoing a course of chemo for breast cancer, from which, thank goodness, she had since made a full recovery. It had been a horrendous time for them all and was probably why Katie had leant on Ian to the extent she had when he'd come into her life.

She and Tess had been friends since they'd met at a fancy-dress party in Freshers' Week at university; along with many others, they'd been unimaginatively dressed as nuns. The only difference between them was that Tess, for some strange reason, was sporting a moustache of stupendous proportions. In their second and third year they'd lived in a house together with two other friends, and when they'd graduated they'd moved to London and shared a flat with Zac until they'd found a place of their own. For the last four years Tess had worked for a PR agency – her current clients included an ex-MP trying to put his involvement in the expenses scandal behind him and forging a new career for himself as a TV commentator, a past *X Factor* winner, and a celebrity chef with a new TV series and accompanying book to push. She always made her work seem fun and there were any number of interesting tales to share – she'd told plenty over lunch – but Katie knew, just as with any job, it was hard grind at times.

That was why Katie appreciated Tess giving up her weekend to be here. She had done exactly what she'd said she would: she had distracted Katie. In fact she had done such a good job, Katie could almost kid herself that yesterday had been a totally normal day.

But just articulating that thought was enough to set her off again. And whether or not it was the wine they'd drunk that was giving her the courage, she stood up abruptly and went inside the house to the kitchen.

She rejoined her friend in the garden. 'Will you do something for me, Tess?' she said.

Tess opened her eyes. She stretched languidly. 'It's nothing too energetic, is it?'

'Nothing very taxing at all. It's a silly thing, and I could easily do it on my own but I'd rather you were here when I did it.'

Tess sat up straighter. 'This is about yesterday, isn't it?'

Katie nodded. She sat in the chair next to Tess and put the envelope on the table in front of them. She gave it a tap and said, 'It contains the name of my biological father and how to make contact with him.'

Tess sucked in her breath. 'OK, so no biggie, then.'

Katie smiled. 'No biggie at all.'

She picked up the envelope and opened it. She unfolded the sheet of paper and smoothed it flat on the table so that Tess could read it with her. It didn't take them long to discover what they were both looking for.

Katie's biological father's name was Stirling Nightingale.

Chapter Four

Monday morning, and sweeping out through the gates of his riverside home at Sandiford, some six miles from Henley-on-Thames, Stirling Nightingale was on his way to work.

He couldn't put his finger on why, but he couldn't get his mind to settle on the day ahead. Normally when he got behind the wheel of his Aston Martin and set off early to beat the traffic, his thoughts were instantly clear and focused. Today, for instance, he should be thinking about the two client meetings he had that morning followed by a strategy meeting after lunch. But try as he might, his thoughts kept being sidetracked by a sense that something wasn't right.

What was it? What was his brain trying to flag up? Was there something important he'd forgotten?

He was a stickler for detail and getting things right, and was frequently telling those who worked for him that the devil was in the detail. He ran through a mental checklist of work-related things he might have overlooked, but nothing came to mind. Next he tried home-related matters, in particular important family dates. It wasn't his wife's birthday, he knew that much. Gina's fifty-sixth birthday had been last month and he'd taken her to Paris for the weekend. As for their wedding anniversary, he was off the hook there, as that had been a week after Gina's birthday, when they'd celebrated thirty-four years of marriage.

Thirty-four years, it didn't seem possible. If they were both to be brutally honest, neither could say with a hand on their heart that it had been three and a half decades of wedded bliss, but they'd been happy enough. Wasn't that all anyone could hope for? Especially in this day and age, when it was damn near a miracle to stay married to the same person this long.

Confident that he hadn't made an oversight regarding his wife, he turned his thoughts to his children, Rosco and Scarlet. Again he drew a blank. Rosco's thirty-second birthday had been back in February and Scarlet's had been in April, when on her twenty-ninth birthday she had announced she was pregnant.

He smiled at the thought of Scarlet – from the way she was carrying on, you'd think she was the first woman to experience pregnancy. His mother had said much the same in private to him yesterday afternoon when he'd gone to help hang some pictures for her.

When his mother had first mentioned that she thought it was time for her to move out of the house she had lived in for over half a century, Stirling had been surprised but hugely relieved. He and his brother had often talked about which of them was going to be brave enough to suggest to Cecily Nightingale – the archetypal matriarch – that it was time for her to live somewhere more manageable. Stirling had been all for her moving in with him and Gina at Willow Bank; they had plenty of room, after all, and who knew, that day may yet come to pass.

For now, though, Cecily had swapped a rambling five-bedroom cottage with two acres for a two-bedroom second-floor flat that was part of an exclusive development of retire-ment homes. The glossy brochure that had sold her the idea of South Lodge had described the set-up as being ideal for those wanting their own luxury self-contained home but secure in the knowledge that support and care was available if required. South Lodge boasted several acres of beautifully landscaped gardens and a number of communal facilities; they included a library complete with computers, an indoor swimming pool and a croquet lawn. There was also a regular shuttle bus to and from the centre of Henley just two miles away.

From the day she moved in, just before Easter, Cecily confessed that she wished she'd done it years ago. She had made plenty of friends with her neighbours – most of whom were younger than her, but all of whom were in the same boat, having reached an age when they wanted to take things a little easier, and most importantly didn't want to be a nuisance to their families. Or as Cecily put it, she didn't want her family to become a nuisance to her.

Of all the important family dates Stirling had to remember, Cecily's ninetieth birthday was the one there was absolutely no danger of forgetting. It was next Saturday and the celebrations, thanks to Gina, were all in hand. As was to be expected, Cecily had said she didn't want any fuss, but she should know the family better than that; there wasn't a chance in hell of letting such a momentous occasion slip by without a great fuss being made of her.

He pulled into the car park of the modern three-storey office building that was home to Nightingale Ridgeway Investments and parked alongside his brother's bright red Porsche. It was a family joke amongst the younger members, including Neil's son, Lloyd, that he was too old for such a car, but let's face it, the Porsche 911 Turbo S Cabriolet was a beautiful piece of machinery, and why shouldn't Neil have precisely what he wanted?

It was as he was looking at Neil's personalized number plate that something in Stirling's head stirred. It was, he realized, the 'something' that had been nagging at him. And it was something that Cecily had said yesterday afternoon about Neil. She had asked Stirling if he thought Neil was all right. He registered now that he hadn't answered his mother's question; he'd been distracted by his mobile going off – it had been Scarlet talking excitedly about something she and Charlie wanted to discuss with him.

He had a pretty good idea of the sort of thing Scarlet and Charlie wanted to talk to him about, and the thought made him shake his head with wry acceptance. The pair of them were two of a kind; they were inherent dreamers. Some might say they made a dangerous combination, but what wasn't in doubt was that they loved each other. Charlie might not have been Stirling's first choice for his daughter, but if the boy made her happy, then that was good enough for him.

Charles Rupert Benton-Norris, to give him his full name, was the youngest son of John and Caroline Benton-Norris. The Benton-Norrises were a family steeped in history; they could trace their lineage all the way back to the Plantagenets. Yet whilst they were property-rich, they were cash-poor, and the great pile they lived in was literally crumbling to dust around them. Gina always dreaded an invitation to Wilton Park; the place was as draughty as a barn and colder than a morgue. Stirling had once felt something brush against his foot at a dinner party, only to find a mouse nibbling at his shoelaces when he'd looked under the table. His startled reaction had provoked laughter from his hosts. There'd been no embarrassment on their part, not even an apology, just a joke about their idle pack of hounds not doing enough to keep the rodent population down.

Taking the lift up to his office on the third floor of the building they shared with two other businesses – a firm of accountants and an insurance broker – Stirling's thoughts returned to his brother and the question Cecily had asked yesterday afternoon about him.

One thing he and Neil had always been able to count on was their mother's knack for spotting a potential problem long before anyone else did. Stirling hoped in this instance that Cecily's antenna for trouble was off-beam. The last thing he and Neil needed right now, as co-owners and joint managing directors of Nightingale Ridgeway Investments, was for one of them to lose focus. These were tough times. Businesses the length and breadth of the country were fighting for survival, and theirs was no exception. It had been bad enough last year but they'd started this year knowing that the outlook was bleaker still and that very likely next year wouldn't be much better. Which, on a personal level, meant he and Neil hadn't been able to pay themselves their usual dividend for the last eighteen months. It was basic maths, if targets weren't met and profits were down, the dividend couldn't be paid. They'd never known a time like it. Not as prolonged at any rate.

The downturn in the market had hit just as they'd started negotiations to buy out another investment management company. They'd been considering the move for some while and had high hopes for the future, but the recession had put an end to their plans and they'd reluctantly withdrawn their interest. Rosco had been particularly disappointed, having seen himself as playing a pivotal role in the newly formed company. With a law degree and an MBA in business management, he was impressively book-smart and already an asset to the firm, but just occasionally he displayed a clumsy eagerness to move too fast. But that wasn't surprising; Rosco was young and in a tearing hurry to get on. Stirling had been the same at that age. Even so, he believed his son needed reining in now and then; he needed to learn to temper his ambition with a little more life experience. Dynamism was all very well, and Rosco had plenty of that, but there was no substitute for an equal measure of coal-face know-how.

Maybe all fathers thought that of their sons. Perhaps if Stirling had wanted to follow in his own father's footsteps and be a heart surgeon, his father might have always doubted his capabilities. It was the same in the animal kingdom: the male lion – the head of the pride – never accepts his cub has come of age.

He stepped out of the lift and smiled at the analogy. He hoped he'd never have to fight his own cub.

The day flew by, and at the end of it, when Stirling had dealt with the last phone call and given the last instruction to Joanne, his highly efficient personal assistant of fifteen years, and ordered her to go home to her husband, he slipped some papers into his briefcase to read later that night and walked along the deserted carpeted corridor to Neil's office.

After the strategy meeting had broken up, he'd asked Neil if he could have a word with him when they'd finished for the day. It seemed to him that Neil was definitely not his usual self. He'd been visibly distracted during the meeting they'd chaired together, and at one point, when Rosco had been asking him a direct question, he'd appeared not to hear and Rosco had jokingly tapped the table and asked if anyone was at home. Neil had quickly pulled himself together, but not before Stirling had caught the troubled expression that flickered across his brother's face.

Cecily had been right, he concluded, there most certainly was something wrong with Neil. Usually his brother was one hundred per cent on the ball; nothing got past him, and he'd be the first to rap someone's knuckles during a meeting if they weren't paying strict attention.

Neil's office door was closed, and out of courtesy – his brother might have a client with him – Stirling knocked and waited. There was no reply. He pressed the handle down and pushed the door open. There was no sign of Neil; the office was empty.

Frowning, Stirling took the lift downstairs. Out in the car park, he saw that his brother's Porsche was gone. Had Neil simply forgotten about meeting him after work? Or – as unlikely as it sounded – was he avoiding him?

Chapter Five

He drove home and tried ringing Neil from his car. The call went straight to voicemail. He left a message: 'Hey, what happened to our chat after work?'

A matching pair of Range Rovers was parked on the drive at Willow Bank. Nobody had told him that Scarlet and Rosco were coming to dinner. Not that his family had to report in to him with their every movement, and anyway, his children were welcome to visit any time they wanted.

He found everyone outside on the terrace, a glass jug of Pimm's on the table. 'Hello, darling,' his wife greeted him from her chair. 'We decided that since it's such a lovely evening, we'd have dinner out here. That OK with you?'

He kissed her cheek. 'Of course.' He went over to his daughter and kissed her. 'How's my favourite grandchild coming along?' he asked.

'Still making me throw up,' she said with a grimace.

Rosco laughed. 'Just wait till it's born, then you'll really know what throwing up's about. You'll be covered in the stuff. And a lot more besides.'

Scarlet threw a pistachio nut at her brother. 'Don't be so gross, or I'll make sure you get covered in more than your fair share of whatever is going.'

Stirling moved round the table to where Charlie was standing awkwardly to attention, waiting to shake hands with him. You'd think that after two years of being married to Scarlet he would have realized there was no need for him to be so formal, but no matter how many times it had been pointed out to him, not just by Stirling but by Scarlet, he still insisted on doing it, and as a consequence, Stirling was forced to go along with the tiresome charade. 'Charlie?' he said affably. 'How's things?'

'Fine, sir,' Charlie said, pumping away at Stirling's hand, 'just fine. And you?'

It was the same response every time. It didn't matter if they'd only seen each other twenty-four hours ago; they went through the same awkward exchange. Extricating his hand, Stirling excused himself. 'Give me five minutes to change and I'll be back.'

'Twenty minutes and supper will be ready,' Gina called after him as he disappeared inside the house. 'I'm doing your favourite, medallions of pork. And there's a bottle of that Chianti you really like already open for you.'

Passing through the kitchen, he poured a large glass of the Chianti and took it upstairs with him. He stood at the open window of the bedroom and looked down on to the garden and the river beyond, fringed with willow trees. It was a view that never failed to give him the most satisfyingly intense pleasure. He often considered it to be one of the finest views in England, if only because it was so very English. He loved the river; he loved the constancy and the innate sense of nature's life force flowing through it. He stood for a moment longer, drinking his wine, enjoying the view and listening to the happy animated chatter of his family floating up to him. Not for the first time, he thought how lucky he was. He had everything in life he wanted. How many could say that? Mind you, he'd worked damned hard for it. He and his brother. Together, and from scratch, they'd created a highly successful business. He still couldn't believe his luck at times. Although he knew very well that luck had nothing to do with it. It was guts, determination and hard graft that got you to the top of the pile. And kept you there.

He changed out of his suit, put on a pair of jeans and a faded Rolling Stones T-shirt from the band's last European tour – he and Neil had gone to Twickenham to see them – and went back downstairs.

They had just settled into the meal when Scarlet said, 'Dad, Charlie and I have come up with this brilliant idea.'

Rosco snorted and rolled his eyes. 'Here we go.'

'Oh yes?' Stirling said, ignoring Rosco. 'Is that what you wanted to talk to me about?' The last time Scarlet and Charlie had had a brilliant idea, it had not only fallen flat, but he'd lost the money he'd put in to help get the business off the ground. And when he said 'off the ground', he meant it quite literally – the brilliant idea had been to offer hot-air balloon trips, their target audience being the romantically inclined who wanted to surprise their loved one with a proposal they'd never forget. They'd called the company Sweep Your Intended Off Their Feet. An old school chum of Charlie's had been involved, a chum who had recently been on a course to learn how to fly hot-air balloons.

Sadly, it never took off – again, quite literally – as they'd had such a run of bad weather they could never actually get the balloon in the air. The only time they did, it was blown miles off course until it finally thudded to the ground in the middle of a farmer's cornfield. The couple on board had been so terrified by the experience they had threatened to sue, and it was only when Stirling had stepped in and calmed the waters with a gift of considerable generosity by way of compensation that they backed off.

But as bizarre as some of Scarlet's 'brilliant ideas' were, Stirling always listened. He badly wanted her to succeed with something, to have something of her very own. Academically she had never been in the same league as her brother, and after muddling her way through university, switching courses after her first year and later flunking her finals, she moved to London and flitted from one job to another, usually reception work, where a pretty face and long blonde hair could be put to good use.

When she and Charlie got married, they moved out of London and set up home in the house that Charlie had inherited from a great-aunt who'd died the previous year. Woodside was a ramshackle Edwardian property in a poor state of repair, which Charlie, with the help of yet another chum, was supposed to be doing up – he hadn't got very far with it.

Scarlet put down her knife and fork and laid a hand on Charlie's forearm. She beamed at Charlie and then at Stirling. 'We just know you're going to love what we've come up with, Daddy.'

Rosco groaned. 'Give me your wallet, Dad, I'll keep it safe for you.'

'Oh do shut up, Rosco!' Scarlet pouted.

'Now, now, you two,' Gina intervened, 'no squabbling, not on such a perfect summer's evening.'

From her silky tone, Stirling suspected that Gina had been complicit in arranging the evening with Scarlet, making it as perfect as she could, cooking his favourite supper dish, remembering which wine was currently his preferred choice, in short setting the scene for a buttering-up session. She probably hadn't bargained on Rosco joining them, though. As with most siblings, there was always an element of argy-bargy between Rosco and his sister. Usually Rosco was overtly dismissive of anything she tried her hand at, and if Stirling was to be brutally honest, he had to admit that his son had a point, Scarlet did flit like a butterfly from one dream to the next, convinced that she was on the verge of greatness. The caveat was always that 'greatness' needed a helping hand; in particular, her father's helping hand.

'Ignore your brother, Scarlet,' he said encouragingly. 'Tell me about this idea you and Charlie have come up with.'

'We want to turn Woodside into a sort of sanctuary, a place where people can come and detox and de-stress themselves. We'll run courses on all sort of things, like ... like ...' She looked to Charlie for help.

34

'Er ... like yoga and er ... massage and stuff.'

'You mean a healing centre?' asked Rosco, an eyebrow raised.

'Yes, exactly,' Scarlet said.

'A sure-fire winner if ever I heard one.'

'Please don't be sarcastic, Rosco darling,' Gina said.

'Actually I'm not being sarcastic; I'm being serious. There are enough fools out there clamouring for precisely this kind of claptrap; it'll be money for old rope, like taking candy from the proverbial baby.'

Scarlet turned her face to Stirling. 'What do you think, Daddy? Do you like the sound of it?'

'It sounds very interesting,' he said. 'How much research have you done?'.

'Oh, none,' she said brightly. 'We only came up with the idea on Saturday. Isn't that right, Charlie?'

Charlie nodded.

'We wanted to see what you thought of it before we went any further,' she continued. 'So what do you think? And be honest.'

Scarlet always said 'be honest', and the sad truth was, Stirling never was. Bottom line was, he couldn't refuse her anything. 'Well,' he said carefully, unable to bring himself to admit that funds were a little low right now, 'the first thing that strikes me is that Woodside is going to need an awful lot of work doing to it. Have you thought how much time, money and effort that's going to take? And of course, if there are any major structural changes to be made, you'll have to have planning permission, and that always takes time. And before any of that takes place, you'll need permission for change of use.'

Scarlet wrinkled her nose. 'You sound like you're pouring cold water on the idea.'

'Not at all. I'm just ensuring that you know what you're letting yourself in for. You know I'll help you all I can.'

Her face lit up. 'Really?'

'Of course. Don't I always?'

She went to him and gave him a hug. 'You're the best! The absolute best! I told Charlie you wouldn't let us down. Charlie, didn't I say Daddy wouldn't let us down?'

Charlie nodded and looked embarrassed as Scarlet proceeded then to hug him. This was the reason Stirling could never say no to his daughter. He loved to see her happy. He loved to see that joyful expression on her face. Admittedly there had been a period of adjustment when he'd had to accept that she was all grown up and it wouldn't always be him who made her happy, that it would be a rival for her affections who did that, but he'd never harboured any feelings of jealousy or animosity towards his son-in-law. Charlie just wasn't that kind of a man. It would be like kicking a puppy.

'So,' Rosco said, 'if we could put this delightful love-in to one side, maybe someone could pass me the wine. By the way, Dad, what the hell was the matter with Uncle Neil today? He was all over the place. The lights were on, but there was definitely no one at home.'

Later that evening, when everyone had gone and Gina was tidying the kitchen, Stirling wandered down to the riverbank, glass of whisky in hand. He followed the herringbone-brickwork path that cut the broad sweep of lawn in two and which was lit every ten feet by glowing solar-powered lamps. He sat in the dark on the wooden bench Lloyd – Neil's son – had made for him. It was positioned right next to the boathouse where his treasured motorboat was kept. The *Lady Cecily* was a thirty-foot slipper stern launch built in the fifties, and Stirling had bought it for himself nine years ago for his fiftieth birthday. It had been a restoration project, and he'd kept to the original style of the boat, with the traditional Lloyd Loom chairs at the helm and bench seats aft along with two smaller child seats. The varnished mahogany cabinets had needed some work doing to them, but they'd come up a treat. In one he stowed wine glasses, and the other was specially lined with stainless steel and a drain put in so that bottles of wine, champagne or beer could be kept on ice. No two ways about it, it was a boy's dream of a riverboat!

He sipped on his whisky, savouring its rich peaty smell and satisfyingly smooth taste. He heard rustling in the undergrowth and stayed very still: the night shift was about its business. Minutes passed.

Eventually he pulled his mobile out of his pocket. It was gone eleven o'clock, but he knew his brother of old; like him, Neil rarely went to bed before midnight. They often chatted on the phone late at night. Occasionally, when they were really busy, it was the only chance they got to catch up properly with each other.

Just as it had before, his call went straight to voicemail. This time he didn't leave a message; he ended the call and dialled the landline at The Meadows. It rang and rang, until finally Pen's sleepy voice sounded in his ear; he'd obviously woken her. He apologized and asked if Neil was there.

'Why would he be here?' She sounded confused, which wasn't an uncommon occurrence. Frequently she was so absorbed in what she was doing, it took her a few moments to adjust when somebody disturbed her. Things also had a habit of slipping her mind. In contrast, when it came to her great passion in life – her garden at The Meadows – she was razor-sharp. She devoted her every waking thought and ounce of energy to it. A lot of husbands would have resented playing second fiddle to a garden, but Neil never had; he'd always said he was proud of what Pen had achieved. Three times now the garden had featured in various glossy magazines, and last year it had made a brief appearance on the television. Currently Pen was getting it ready to open to the public to raise money for the local hospice. She did it every year, and made a good deal of money. Whatever funds she raised, Neil always bumped things up with his own generous contribution.

Why would he be here? Stirling silently repeated. Because

he's your husband and lives there, was his first thought. His second was very different. Some inner instinct told him to tread warily. 'Sorry, Pen,' he said, 'it's a bad line. What did you say?'

'I said why would you think he was here when you must know that he's spending the night at a hotel at the airport to catch an early flight tomorrow morning.'

'An early flight,' Stirling echoed, as if he'd known this all along.

'Yes, he got a last-minute booking to go off on another of his Greek sailing holidays. Now where did he say he was going? South Ionian, or was it North? Sorry,' she said vaguely, 'you know what I'm like, in one ear and out the other when I'm getting ready for an open day.'

The inner instinct again told him to tread warily. 'Of course,' he said. 'I forgot all about that. How stupid of me. But he'll be back for Cecily's party, won't he?'

'Oh yes, I'm sure he said all he wanted was a few days away. He wouldn't miss Cecily's ninetieth birthday. Not for anything.'

'Of course he wouldn't. I'm sorry to have disturbed you.'

'That's all right.' She laughed. 'It makes a change for someone else in the family to have the memory lapse.'

He laughed too. 'It's my age, Pen. Sorry again that I woke you. I'll see you soon. Bye.'

Stirling ended the call and pushed his mobile back into his pocket. He drained his glass of whisky and stared thoughtfully and not without a frisson of foreboding into the darkness. What was Neil up to?

More to the point, where was he?

Chapter Six

When Ian returned from his trip to Dubai, Katie waited twenty-four hours before sharing her news with him. First she explained about being made redundant and then she told him about going to the solicitor's office.

Afterwards he kept saying that he couldn't believe she hadn't told him straight away or that she was behaving as calmly as she was. 'If I found out something like that I'd be furious,' he said over and over. 'I don't think I'd ever forgive my parents for keeping something so important from me.'

He also, rather irritatingly, kept going on about the trust fund. Just as she hadn't mentioned it to Tess straight away – only deciding to do so after they'd opened the envelope and learnt the name of her father – she had omitted to tell Ian anything about it. But in bed last night she let something slip, and out it all came.

He was astounded, and at one point he punched the air. 'Bloody hell!' he laughed. 'I've bagged myself a trustafarian!' His reaction shocked her.

'You've done no such thing,' she retorted.

He kissed her and said, 'I'm only joking. You'll always be the same old Katie to me, even if you are loaded.'

'I'm not loaded,' she said. 'The money's not mine, and I'm never going to touch it.'

'You're joking?'

'Look at my face. Am I laughing?'

'But Katie, this is an answer to a prayer for you. You've just been made redundant; you need that money. It couldn't have come at a better time. You could use a fraction of it to live off and tuck the rest away somewhere safe.'

'What are you suggesting, that I stash the best part of three-quarters of a million quid under the mattress?'

'Don't be daft. I mean invest it. Then it would be there ticking away nicely until you need it.'

'There's an awful lot of ticking and tucking you suddenly want me to do. And anyway,' she added, 'I don't need anything. Especially not conscience money. I'd rather give it all to charity than touch a penny of it myself.'

She'd then switched off her bedside lamp and turned her back on him in what could only be described as a marked manner.

He had been sensible enough not to pursue the subject further then.

But now, the following day and back from work, he was trying to convince her that she shouldn't make any hasty decisions.

They were in the kitchen. Sitting at the table, he was going on about her entitlement to the trust fund, at the same time checking something on her laptop whilst she cooked supper.

Cooking was stretching it; she was assembling food, emptying packets of M&S prawns and salad on to plates. She'd spent the day gardening, trying to distract herself from the madness that was inside her head. Ian had got it wrong when he said she was taking it all so calmly. She wasn't. She was angry, and that anger was growing exponentially. It didn't help to recall how Mum had often said that she was like Dad, that she had the capacity to hide her feelings better than most people.

'Shall we eat outside?' she asked, when her culinary skills had concluded and she was throwing away the plastic bags into the appropriate recycling bin.

'Give me two seconds,' he said, without looking up from her laptop. 'I think I've found something.'

'I didn't know you were looking for anything.'

He smiled and tapped his nose.

Curious, she went over to see what he was looking at. It took her a couple of seconds to home in on what was of such interest to him on the screen. 'What are you doing?' she asked. Although it was damned obvious what he was doing.

'I've found your father,' he said. He looked up at her, his expression triumphant. 'And it was dead easy. All I did was—'

'All you did was totally disregard my feelings,' she snapped. 'Did I ask you to go snooping about on the internet? No! In fact I seem to recall very clearly that I said I wasn't interested in knowing anything about him. Which bit of that did you not understand?'

He put his arm around her waist. 'Katie,' he said, 'you can't just ignore him. You're trying to un-know something and you can't. He's real. He's very much out there; your flesh and blood. Don't you want to know him, or know anything about him, just a little?'

She wriggled out of his embrace. 'No,' she said. 'Until a few days ago, I didn't even know he existed. Why should I suddenly care about him? He's never cared about me, has he?'

Ian frowned. 'He created that fund for you. It's a hell of a lot more than most men would do in that situation. You have to give him credit for that. And from what I can see here,' he pointed at the laptop screen, 'he's not short of a bob or two. He and his brother run a very successful business. There's even a mention of them in the *FT*.'

'I don't care if he's been mentioned in *Heat* magazine or *The Beano*, I don't have to give him credit for a thing. And I'd appreciate you not telling me what I should or should not do.' She heard the telltale break in her voice, giving away the fact that her inner anger bunny was itching to be let loose. Then she saw the wounded look on Ian's face and breathed in deeply, forcing herself not to argue, worried that if the conversation escalated further, she might well take out her confusion and anger on him. And she knew that wasn't fair; he didn't deserve that. 'Now stop going on about it,' she said more reasonably, 'and come and have your supper.' She sounded more in control now, but also like she was reprimanding a naughty child.

They ate in the garden, in silence, until finally Ian cracked. Just as Katie knew he would.

'I'm sorry,' he said. 'I didn't mean to upset you. I honestly thought I was helping. I thought that perhaps once you knew more about him, you might start to view things differently. Hand on heart, aren't you at all curious? And don't forget, it's what your mother wanted. She made that very clear in her letter.'

Katie knew it had been a mistake to let Ian read her mother's letter. She put down her knife and fork. 'I hope you're not going to say something silly like I must respect the wishes of a dying woman,' she said. 'Because that wasn't the case. Mum wrote that letter when she was fit and well, ages before she had the accident.'

'Does that change anything? It was still something she wanted you to do when the time was right.'

Katie looked at him. 'You've changed your tune, haven't you? Talk about a U-turn. At first, when you were putting yourself in my shoes, you were practically beating your chest with scandalous shock. Now, ever since last night, you're pushing me into the arms of a stranger. What's changed?'

Ian shrugged. 'I've had time to think about it, I suppose. I'm looking at it more objectively, putting my emotions to one side.'

'You're sure that's what it is? You wouldn't, for instance, be swayed by the idea of all that money?'

He leant back in his seat, his eyes wide. 'That's a terrible thing to say!'

'Isn't it just?' she said.

His face flushed. 'You're accusing me of something, Katie, and I don't like it. I'm only thinking of you.' He pursed his lips. Then: 'I thought I knew you; I thought you were level-headed and warm-hearted, but now I'm not so sure. I've never seen you like this before, so cold and accusatory. I have to say, it doesn't suit you.'

'What? You expected me to be pathetically flaky, rushing to throw myself into the arms of a man who had sex with my mother thirty years ago, crying "Daddy, oh my daddy!" like that fool of a girl in *The Railway Children*?'

'I'd expect you at least to have an open mind. And not bite my head off for trying to help.'

'Well, boo-bloody-hoo, I'm sorry to disappoint you,' she said stiffly. 'Though what else could you expect when you're doing such a bang-up job of annoying me? But if you do really want to help me, there is something you can do.'

His expression brightened. 'What's that?'

'You can leave me in peace with my cold and accusatory self. Because you know what, I don't need anyone else messing up my life right now.'

Chapter Seven

The next morning, Saturday, and after sleeping well for the first time in a week, Katie woke with a clear sense of purpose and resolve.

She hated to admit it, but Ian had been right last night. She *was* curious. But she would no more admit that to him than she would tell anyone what she was about to do. With Tess and Ben away in Barcelona for a long weekend, she felt she had free rein to do as she pleased, that while the cat was away, the mouse would play. Not that she was answerable to her best friend, but undoubtedly Tess would have something to say on the subject, and Katie didn't want to explain herself or her actions.

She knew that as plans went, it was on the woolly side, but in the circumstances it was the best she could come up with. If it came to nothing, what would it matter anyway? She suddenly felt that she had to do something; she had to be pro-active and stop sitting around griping and feeling angrily sorry for herself. Her energy might be better put to use by looking for a job, but right now that didn't feel such a priority.

So with the satnav fired up, a map on the passenger seat and the information she had printed off from her computer, she was on her way to Henley-on-Thames, or more precisely, to a village called Sandiford, which was about three miles from Henley.

Thanks to Ian's snooping on the internet, she had Stirling Nightingale's business address but not his home address. However, Ian wasn't the only one to play at being Sherlock

Holmes; after some digging around on her laptop whilst she'd been eating breakfast, she had discovered that the wife of Stirling Nightingale's brother was a serious gardener, and that her garden had featured in several magazines. It had even popped up in an episode of *Gardener's World* several years ago for a feature about newly created gardens. From what Katie had seen online, it looked beautiful.

With The Meadows as her destination, she figured that as joint MDs of Nightingale Ridgeway Investments, the two men wouldn't live that far apart, and on that basis one would lead to the other. She had ruled out tracking down Stirling Nightingale at his work address for the simple reason that it was the weekend and he wouldn't be there. And now that she had made a decision, she didn't want to wait until Monday.

She had no intention of blundering in on Stirling Nightingale. Quite the contrary. If it was possible, she wanted to observe him from a safe distance, to see what kind of a man he was. Again, she didn't really know how she would manage to do that, but she would cross that bridge when she came to it. She had seen several photographs of him online, along with his brother, but they were artificially posed – typical examples of corporate portraiture. They told her nothing about him. He was merely a tanned, silver-haired man in a suit. He could be anyone. Certainly he bore no resemblance to her. She could detect nothing in his face that she recognized, nothing that suggested he had passed on any of his genes to her.

With a plan of action now securely fixed in her brain, some of her anger had cooled. She wanted to believe that she was beginning to think more rationally, but she suspected that she had grown tired of being angry. It didn't suit her temperament. She wasn't one of those people who thrived on drama and high emotion; she needed a steady equilibrium to her life. Some might say that was a boring way to live, but she had always been that way. Over the years, friends had described her as being rock-solid and dependable, the one they could turn to in a crisis. She hadn't liked it last Saturday when Zac had described her as being sweet and adorable and as edgy as an After Eight mint; he had made her sound dull.

Being cool-headed was, she knew, what had enabled her to cope with the deaths of her parents. When Dad had died, she had put her own grief to one side and helped her mother through hers. Then when Mum had died last year, she had had no choice but to keep it together and cope. What was the alternative?

Undoubtedly her emotions had got the better of her last night with Ian. She had been anything but sweet and adorable. She had been horrid. She really shouldn't have spoken to him in the way she had, or insisted that he leave. He had only been trying to help her; she could see that now. But it was as if all the tensions of the last week had collided and found a release in being cruel to him. She should ring him later and apologize.

The village of Sandiford was the last word in picture-postcard perfection: it was *Midsomer Murders* territory with a dash of *Vicar of Dibley* thrown in. Immaculate thatched cottages rubbed shoulders with Georgian and Victorian houses, and the narrow lanes were lined with overblown cow parsley and a generous sprinkling of buttercups. Ignoring the satnav, which was instructing Katie to prepare to take the next right, she turned into the car park of a thatched pub called the Riverside, the front of which was decked out with overflowing wall troughs and hanging baskets – petunias, lobelia, busy Lizzies, nasturtiums and geraniums cascaded in a blaze of colour. There was a sign declaring that wholesome food was served all day. That was handy, because she was starving and it was late afternoon, long past lunchtime.

In the cool, dimly lit interior of the pub, she was greeted with a cheery smile from the woman behind the bar and enough boating paraphernalia to make her think she was in a chandlery. There were coils of ropes behind glass cases, oars crossed and attached to the beamed walls and ceiling. Shiny copper lanterns hung from hooks and photographs of boats and strapping young rowers, mostly black and white, adorned what wall space was left. Above a cavernous fireplace there was a glass case containing a very large and very dead fish of some sort. Painted and varnished to a high sheen, it had a beady eye that would probably follow Katie round the bar if she put it to the test. Actual customers seemed to be somewhat thin on the ground. Perhaps the fish didn't make for good company.

The woman behind the bar took Katie's order of a smoked salmon and cream cheese sandwich, poured her a glass of wine and pointed her in the direction of the beer garden, saying that her sandwich would be brought out to her shortly.

Outside it was a very different matter: the garden was thrumming with customers. With only a few tables free, Katie picked the smallest one and repositioned the umbrella so that she wasn't in the full glare of the sun. She could see why everyone was sitting outside in preference to the gloomy bar: the attractive lawned garden sloped gently down towards the river, where a variety of boats were neatly moored along the towpath. In the shade of a willow tree, its branches dipping into the water, a man and two small children were surrounded by a mob of persistent ducks. The children were flinging bits of bread at the ducks with nervous excitement, their arms moving with sudden jerky movements, their laughter shrill. The setting was as perfect as the weather, and despite the reason she was here, Katie felt herself relax. It really was a perfectly sublime summer afternoon with a hot sun shimmering in a hazy blue sky.

Her sandwich duly arrived, and as she hungrily tucked in, Katie scanned the other tables. It wouldn't be beyond the realms of possibility for Stirling Nightingale to be here. For all she knew, this could be his local pub. But as far as she could see, there was no one at any of the tables who resembled the man she'd seen on her computer.

The man who was her father ...

47

Her *biological* father, she corrected herself. No matter what transpired, Dad would always be her real father.

As a child, you never really think about how much your parents love each other, but Dad must have loved Fay to an extraordinary extent to forgive her for what she'd done, and then to pretend to the world that the child she'd conceived with another man was his own.

How difficult had it been for him? Had there been a time when he'd struggled to like Katie, never mind bond with her? She would never know. And that saddened her, because now that the seed had been sown, she didn't know if she would ever be able to rid herself of the doubt. All she could do was rely on the memories she had of her father. A patient and quiet undemonstrative man, he had always been someone to whom she could turn. If she'd been upset over something that had happened at school, he would be the one to calm her and make her realize that it was nothing more than a storm in a teacup. He was always able to get things in perspective for her.

Mum, on the other hand, was the sparky one of the two. When the mood took her, she was her very own localized storm in a teacup, who could whip up a commotion in seconds flat and out of nothing. Dad had joked that she ran on high-energy fuel and didn't have a brake pedal. They were opposites in just about every way, but as everyone said of them, they made a great team. Not just as husband and wife, but as business partners. For more than twenty-five years they had jointly run an antiquarian bookshop, and for a couple who lived and worked together, Katie couldn't recall a single heavy-duty argument between them. Maybe that was because Dad wasn't the argumentative type. He never let things get to him.

After Dad's death, Mum had carried on running the bookshop, but as she later admitted to Katie, her heart was no longer in it without Dad. What had once been a great source of pleasure, a real labour of love, became a millstone around her neck, and within a year she had sold up. That was when she moved to Brighton, to start a new life. Albeit a tragically short new life.

Behind the wheel of her car again – it was a yellow Mini Cooper that had once belonged to her mother, and which Katie had nicknamed the Custard Cream – she switched the satnav back on. She wondered whether by tracking down her biological father, she was also about to start a new life.

Was this what her mother had wanted for her?

The white-painted gate to The Meadows was open, and practising aloud what she was going to say, Katie turned into the drive and followed the pretty tree-lined sweep of it to the front of the white house. It was gracefully proportioned and perfectly symmetrical, with two columns either side of a front door that was painted a very dark shade of blue. A Volvo estate was parked in front of the double garage, which gave her hope that somebody was at home.

She rang the doorbell and tried to contain her nerves.

When nobody responded, she rang the bell again, this time for longer.

But still nobody came.

She had come this far; she had no intention of giving up so easily. She walked round to the side of the house on the gravel path and called out, 'Hello, anyone at home?'

Still no response.

She pressed on through a dappled tunnel of laburnum whilst continuing to call out. She stepped into a courtyard where the walls were covered in variegated ivy and water gently played from a fountain in the farthest corner, its base surrounded by a bed of lush hosta plants. It was very tranquil, a cool and restful oasis.

Opposite her was a small arched wooden door; it was only about four feet high, and there was a sign on it that read: 'Open Me'. Feeling a bit like Alice in Wonderland, she self-consciously turned the metal handle, bent down and went through.

And again like Alice, she found that she'd stepped into another world, a beautiful and enchanting world. After the shade of the courtyard, she blinked at the brightness of the sun and teased out the impact of what she was seeing. In front of her was an immaculate stretch of perfectly striped, luxuriant green lawn that was flanked by two deep borders and enclosed by soft-hued brick walls covered in a scrambling rose the colour of clotted cream. The borders were stunning, planted with delphiniums, lupins, hesperis, alliums, aquilegia and poppies – all the flowers that Katie's mother had adored, and which in turn had become favourites for Katie. She walked to the middle of the lawn and slowly turned round, looking back at the small wooden door through which she'd entered, as if not really believing it would still be there. It was truly spellbinding.

'Can I help you?'

She spun round at the sound of a woman's voice, fully aware that if this was the owner of the house – Mrs Penelope Nightingale – she had every right to be angry, to accuse Katie of trespass. But pushing a wheelbarrow and dressed in a loose-fitting top and jeans that were rolled to just above her ankles, with off-white canvas shoes on her feet and a large-brimmed hat on her head, the woman didn't look angry, just enquiring. She actually looked quite a nice woman, down-to-earth, with an open and friendly expression. On the shortish and dumpy side, she wasn't at all what Katie had expected. She had dreaded a gentrified gorgon of a woman, one of those tall, haughty horse-faced types prone to wearing headscarves. Although, of course, Katie had yet to establish whether this was the owner. Maybe she was a gardener who worked here.

'The garden isn't open to the public yet,' the woman said in a pleasantly low and rich husky voice, when Katie still hadn't replied.

'Um ...' Oh hell, she'd forgotten what she was supposed to say. She'd been so blown away by her surroundings, her mind had gone blank, every carefully chosen word of her ruse gone from her head.

'That's all right,' the woman said, letting go of the wheelbarrow. 'People are always turning up at the wrong time. I'm quite used to it. You need to come back a week today, next Saturday.'

Katie tried to pull herself together. 'I did ring the bell,' she began. 'I rang it several times.'

The woman laughed. 'Sorry. Once I get stuck in, there's no chance of me hearing it. But as I said, you'll have to come back next weekend.'

'Um ... it's not the garden I've come about,' Katie said. 'It's ... I'm looking for Mr Stirling Nightingale. I have a delivery for him. This is his address, isn't it?'

The woman tipped the brim of her hat back and wiped her face with her forearm. 'I'm glad I'm not the only one who gets things muddled up,' she said. 'I'm afraid you've come to the wrong Nightingale house; Stirling, my brother-in-law, lives less than a mile away at Willow Bank. You can't miss it; just follow the river in the Marlow direction and take the turning after the church.'

So she *was* the owner. 'Thank you. Thank you very much. I'm sorry to have troubled you.'

'Think nothing of it. Glad to be of help. Can you find your way out on your own?'

'Oh yes, don't worry about me.' Katie reluctantly turned to go, but didn't quite manage it. It was the strangest thing, but she suddenly felt intoxicated by the magical beauty of the garden, overcome with the feeling that she had fallen under some kind of spell here. It made her want to stay, to wander round some more and lose herself in this beguiling paradise. 'You have an amazing garden,' she said, somehow finding her voice. 'I've never seen anything like it. It has a very special feel to it. My ... my mother would have loved it.'

The woman smiled. A real smile of genuine warmth. 'Then come back next Saturday and have a proper look. This is only a fraction of what there is to see. You'll have to pay an admission charge, but it's all in a good cause, for the local hospice.'

'Thank you,' Katie said again. 'I'd love to come back and see it properly.'

'The gate opens at ten thirty.'

Katie smiled. 'I look forward to it.'

Nice girl, Pen thought to herself as she went to fetch a spade. Not the usual kind of delivery person, though. Usually it was a man, and if they couldn't get an answer, they just shoved a card through the letter box. Good of her to go to so much trouble. One thing was certain: Pen had to do something about having a new doorbell installed. For ages now Neil had been on about getting one of those special devices that could make itself heard for miles around.

On the subject of Neil, she thought how odd it was that she hadn't heard from him since he'd gone sailing. It was very unlike him. He always phoned home at least once when he was away. She had mentioned it to Lloyd yesterday when he'd called from New Zealand, and he'd agreed that it was odd but had reached the same conclusion as she had: that it was probably something simple, such as being out of mobile range. Still, so long as Neil was enjoying himself, that was all that counted. He worked so hard; he deserved some fun.

But he was cutting it fine for Cecily's party. Perhaps his flight home had been delayed. She looked at her watch. Gracious! How did it get so late? She would have to get her skates on. Abandoning the idea of doing any more gardening, she hurried back up to the house.

Katie drove out of The Meadows. What was she thinking? What madness had she just experienced? Imagining herself falling under the spell of a garden; how had that happened? And why had she mentioned her mother?

Chapter Eight

Gina was frequently told that no one could organize a party better than she could. Naturally she brushed the compliment aside with an appropriately modest shrug, but secretly she believed it to be true. She put the success of anything she organized down to being highly meticulous and with a keen eye for detail. She was an inveterate list-maker and never approached anything without painstaking preparation. Rosco and Scarlet liked to tease her about it. 'Oh, there goes Mum with one of her lists,' they'd laugh. 'We could wallpaper the whole house twice over with the lists she's written over the years.'

It was just as well that she was as thorough as she was, because no one else in the family was capable of doing what she did. Whilst it couldn't be disputed that Pen had cornered the market when it came to green fingers, nobody in their right mind would count on her to arrange a picnic with shop-bought sandwiches, much less coordinate a party. Thankfully Pen was good-natured enough to admit her failings and was invariably the first to congratulate Gina on a job well done and to apologize for not doing more to help; without fail she would promise to do more next time. Always quick to quash these offers of assistance, Gina would reassure her sister-in-law that she wasn't to give it a moment's thought, that Pen had enough on her plate as it was.

Armed now with her A4-sized Filofax, she put a tick against Floral Arrangements. The florist had left no more than a few minutes ago and the house was already fragrant with the

53

heady perfume of old English roses, freesias and early sweet peas – Cecily's favourite flowers. The arrangements had been placed in the hallway, the sitting room and the conservatory. Later, when it was dark, candles and flaming torches would be lit on the terrace.

This surprise party for Cecily was to be held in the garden, but once the temperature dropped, the older guests would very likely be drawn inside the house. Sadly for Cecily, many of her contemporaries were long since dead, but – and behind her back – her newly made friends from South Lodge had been invited. Taxis would be fetching them thirty minutes after Stirling had collected his mother, the plan being that she would think she was coming here for a quiet family dinner to celebrate her birthday. Gina hoped that the South Lodge crowd, with their memories and faculties not quite as sharp as they had once been, wouldn't give the game away.

It was hard to imagine there ever being a time when Cecily wouldn't be around; she was very much a key member of the family, and still most assuredly had plenty to say on what went on. In the early years of her marriage, Gina had been convinced that her mother-in-law didn't approve of her. When she had voiced this concern to Stirling, he had laughed and said she was being ridiculous. All these years on, Gina still got the feeling that Cecily had to force herself to like her. Their conversations were superficial and stiffly polite, as if they'd only just met and couldn't get beyond making small talk. In contrast, Cecily and Pen were completely natural around each other. Gina had repeatedly told herself that the effortlessness of their relationship was down to their shared love of gardening. But she wasn't so sure. She was convinced it went deeper.

She wasn't so bothered about being treated differently herself, but she did object to partiality when it came to the grandchildren. It irked her that Lloyd was so clearly his grandmother's favourite. But then Lloyd, as they all knew, was a special case. Not that anyone was supposed to talk about that. Heaven forbid. Like Pen, he had the same laid-back and affable temperament, but beneath it there was a core of steel. If he didn't want to do something, you couldn't make him do it, not for anything. Gina frequently wondered if Neil wasn't just a little disappointed in him. He must have expected more of his only son and occasionally he surely must have wondered why Lloyd hadn't turned out more like Rosco; after all, as cousins, they'd had the exact same advantages and opportunities.

With only a couple of months separating them in age, the two boys had attended the same schools and had both gained places at Cambridge. Rosco had read law and graduated with a 2.1 and Lloyd had opted for philosophy and graduated with a first. It had seemed horribly unfair to Gina, knowing just how hard Rosco had worked, that he hadn't been rewarded with a first, especially when Lloyd downplayed his own achievement, claiming it was a fluke.

Whereas Rosco had always had a very clear idea about his future – Cambridge followed by business school before joining Nightingale Ridgeway – Lloyd hadn't had a clue what he wanted to do. After Cambridge, he had messed about for a few years doing voluntary work in some godforsaken eastern European country, and when he returned to England he'd helped his mother with the initial transformation of the garden at The Meadows and then announced his intention to start up a business making bespoke garden furniture. All that expensive education and he wanted to be no better than a carpenter! 'Just like Christ,' Rosco had teased his cousin. 'Next you'll be saying you can walk on water.'

To Gina's astonishment, Lloyd had made a go of his business. Some of his garden furniture was too wacky for her taste – a touch too much Mad Hatter's Tea Party in style – but he seemed content enough muddling along playing the part of callus-handed artisan to the tune of his parents' praise.

Of course they'd say they were proud in public, but in private it had to be otherwise. Or at least for Neil: Pen would

55

probably argue that all she wanted was for their son to be happy, but fathers had a different relationship with their sons; they had different expectations. Unquestionably that was true of Stirling and the poles-apart-way he treated Rosco and Scarlet – Scarlet could get away with murder, but not so her brother.

A daddy's girl right from the word go, Scarlet had openly hero-worshipped her father throughout her childhood. She still did. In turn, Stirling had tolerated her legendary tantrums and her capricious nature with fond indulgence. When Charlie had come along and shown himself to be serious about Scarlet, Gina had doubted that Stirling would be able to stand aside and accept that a greater being had eclipsed him. Amazingly he had.

Things had been quite different with Rosco. From an early age he had been taught by Stirling to do his best, that anything less was not acceptable. Lucky for Stirling, then, that Rosco had been born with a blistering sense of determined ambition. He cut his first tooth nearly a full month before most babies did, he sat up early, and he talked and walked early. As one paediatrician had described him, he had been a high-achieving baby and toddler. He had been hard work, though, and all too often Gina had been exhausted and nightmarishly near the end of her tether. Oh how she had envied Pen! It was the only time she had ever been jealous of her sister-in-law. Slow to talk and walk, as if he really couldn't be bothered, Lloyd had been such an easy, placid baby. She could remember how he would sit on his own, propped up by cushions and seemingly fascinated by nothing but a tiny ball of fluff. In contrast, Rosco was toddling about on his sturdy legs, demanding to be played with and screaming at the top of his voice if anyone dared to ignore him. One was a thinker, the other a doer was how the family had described the two boys. Gina had felt the slight of the labels; she had thought it disparaged Rosco, casting him as an empty-headed bull in a china shop and Lloyd as some great philosopher.

All these years later, it was plain for all to see that Rosco had easily outperformed his cousin. Gina would never admit this to anyone, but she firmly believed that genes always won out. Rosco's genes were of an indisputable pedigree, but with Lloyd, well, who knew their origin?

Another thought she would never openly voice, not even with Stirling, was that the up side of Lloyd not wanting to work for the family firm was that the way was clear for Rosco to take over the running of things one day. In her opinion, this was exactly how it should be. Lloyd didn't have the same drive that Rosco did, and had he joined Nightingale Ridgeway, he would only have been a hindrance. In exactly the same way as Pen's help in arranging a party could only ever be a tiresome interference.

The caterers had arrived forty-five minutes ago, and deciding she had given them sufficient time to unload the van, Gina went through to the kitchen to see how they were getting on.

She was informed of a small hitch, nothing for her to worry about, they assured her; the problem would be resolved. She viewed this assertion with unease. Unexpected problems were anathema to her. She simply didn't countenance things not going perfectly to plan.

Chapter Nine

Admittedly Katie hadn't started the day with too much of a plan, other than to go with the flow and see what transpired, but things were beginning to get crazily out of hand.

It had all started when she'd had that funny turn in Penelope Nightingale's garden. If she closed her eyes and imagined herself back at The Meadows, she could relive that lovely spellbinding sun-filled moment when for a couple of brief minutes she had felt wonderfully happy and worry-free. It was extraordinary that a garden could have that effect on her.

If that wasn't surreal enough, now she was dressed in a white blouse and a black skirt that was mortifyingly too short for her long legs. Her hair was tied back in a ponytail and she looked every inch a waitress. Which, funnily enough, was what she was expected to be.

When she'd left The Meadows, she had followed the road – just as that nice woman had instructed – and in no time she was parked at the end of a drive beside an open gate with a sign bearing the name Willow Bank. At the sight of it she had suddenly lost her nerve. What on earth was she doing? What did she plan to do? Waltz in and introduce herself as Stirling Nightingale's daughter? *There, you old devil, bet you didn't see that coming, did you?* Or maybe he did. Maybe, once he'd agreed to Mum's terms and had got on with his life pretending the affair had never happened, he had lived in constant fear of a child turning up out of the blue and putting a spanner in the works of his carefully ordered life. Was that what she wanted to do? To disrupt the equilibrium of his life just as her mother's letter had done to hers?

Shamefully, a part of her had wanted to do exactly that, and knowing that it was wrong, she had driven away from the house to take stock.

An hour later, after driving round the beautiful countryside and walking along the towpath of the river, she had decided to rework the ruse she had used earlier, but with a twist. She would go back to Willow Bank and pretend she had a delivery for a Mr Neil Nightingale. If she hit lucky and it was Stirling Nightingale who answered the door, it would give her the opportunity to satisfy her curiosity, to meet her father in the flesh. She would do that and then she would leave. The only problem she could foresee, given that she didn't actually have anything to deliver, was if she was told that she could leave the parcel at Willow Bank and they would make sure it was passed on to Neil Nightingale. If that happened, she would have to say something about it being company policy that the recipient signed for it in person. Improbable to anyone with half a brain, but the best she could come up with in the circumstances.

But when she had returned to the entrance to Willow Bank, she had found herself caught up in a cavalcade of taxis. What was going on? A party? Again her nerve was in danger of running out on her, but there was no way she could turn around: another taxi had driven in after her, and so resigned to pressing on, she had stopped in the only available space, alongside a small cream-coloured van with the words *Elite Caterers* written on the back of it. No sooner had she registered the words than a heavy-set woman wearing a striped blue and white apron appeared beside her car. Katie had lowered the window and the woman had spoken in a breathless rush. 'Thank goodness you made it, and at such short notice! We were beginning to panic. The agency was my last resort. I told them not to worry, that I had a uniform here for you. We always have a selection of spare skirts and blouses in case of accidents. You've just got time to change and then it's action stations.'

She should have said there and then that the woman had got it wrong, that Katie was no more a waitress than she was Lady Gaga booked as the entertainment act. But she hadn't. She had seized her opportunity – nobody ever noticed a waitress at a party; it would be the perfect way to observe Stirling Nightingale at close quarters. And feeling like an undercover agent, she told herself that if it all went wrong – that when the real replacement from the agency arrived – she would say there must have been a mix-up.

Luckily she had worked as a waitress in her student days, and so a heavily laden tray of glasses or canapés posed no problem for her. There was only one other waitress, and as the heavy-set woman – whose name was Sue – explained, they had fifty-six guests to serve. Sue had a sidekick called Merrill, and as Merrill handed Katie a tray of filled champagne flutes, she definitely seemed the calmer of the two women.

The other waitress – Dee, who looked about seventeen – was already on duty in the hall, handing guests a glass of champagne or a non-alcoholic drink as they arrived and pointing them in the direction of the garden. Katie's first job was to replace Dee so that she could return to the kitchen for another tray of drinks. Left on her own in the hallway, she was so absorbed in her task, she had almost forgotten why she was here. It was only when Dee returned and there was a lull in arrivals and the girl discreetly pointed out Mrs Nightingale as she crossed the hall towards the kitchen that Katie reminded herself of the reason she was putting herself through this charade. 'What about Mr Nightingale?' she asked. 'Where's he?'

'Probably with his mother, it's her birthday party. She's ninety today. Not that you'd think so. I mean, she's clearly old, but she just looks old as opposed to ancient. I mean, ninety, it's just too awesome. I can't imagine ever living that long.'

'Have you worked for the family before?'

'Loads of times. Uh-oh, Mrs Nightingale's on her way over. Smiley face on. Sue and Merrill insist on that.'

'Dee, there are only a few guests yet to arrive,' Mrs Nightingale said, 'so you can start serving the canapés in the garden now.' The woman abruptly switched her gaze from Dee to Katie, and the length of her skirt, or rather the lack of it. 'You must be the replacement from the agency. Thank you for coming.'

Mrs Nightingale's voice was so crisply authoritative and regal, Katie felt compelled to curtsy. She restrained herself, and unable to think of a suitable reply, widened her smile then watched the woman – *her biological father's wife* – walk away, straight-backed and supremely composed. A cool customer and no mistake. It was hard to pin an exact age on her, but Katie decided she had to be in her mid-fifties. Tall and slim with silvery blonde hair (probably not entirely natural), cut into a sleek bob that flattered her face perfectly, she was wearing an elegant off-the-shoulder dress the colour of coral. She could not have been more different to Katie's mother. Had that been Mum, she would have had a jumbled, windswept look about her, and more than likely would have bumped into someone or knocked something over as she walked away. Mum's mind had always been elsewhere, working on at least half a dozen things at the same time. It was doubtless what had caused her to step out into the road that day into the path of the oncoming car.

Slim, cool and composed were not words one would ever have used to describe Mum. For as long as Katie could remember, her mother had battled with her weight. But then, as she had constantly joked, it wasn't much of a battle, since she had no willpower when it came to fresh bread and French cheese and a glass or two of red wine. And as for chocolate and cream cakes, she had been a total pushover. She hadn't ever been really overweight; she just had what Dad had called a cuddlesome body. Before her father's death had impacted on their lives and become a grim reality, Mum had joked about dying with a chocolate eclair in her hands, saying it would be the ideal way to go.

Mrs Stirling Nightingale didn't look like the sort of woman who ate too many eclairs. Unlike Mum, who had had an Oscar Wilde approach to life – she could resist everything but temptation – she appeared to be a very disciplined woman. The sort of woman who liked things just so. How would she react if she discovered that her husband's past wasn't as squeaky clean as she had always thought it was?

There again, it was possible that her husband might have confessed his affair in order to make a clean break of things. Admitting to an affair was one thing, though; confessing that he'd fathered a child? That was altogether different.

But there was no more time to ponder the imponderables; there were chicken satay and mini frittata canapés to serve. And Stirling Nightingale to run to earth. Katie wanted to get the measure of the man who had betrayed his marriage and this coolly composed woman; the man for whom Mum had betrayed her own marriage.

Stirling was worried. There was still no sign of Neil.

Pen had phoned earlier when he'd been on his way to collect his mother to say that Neil hadn't arrived home. Despite his own growing alarm, Stirling had done his best to allay Pen's concerns, saying that he had probably just got delayed somewhere. 'But why hasn't he been in touch?' she'd asked. 'I hadn't realized until now, but it's five days since I last heard from him.'

It was a reasonable concern. 'Perhaps he's misplaced his mobile,' Stirling had responded calmly. 'We've become so dependent on them these days, we're completely lost without them. Don't worry, just get yourself here for Cecily's big night. And Pen, let's not worry Cecily with this, let's keep it between ourselves. I'll tell her Neil's been held up, because I'm sure that's exactly what's happened. OK?'

Now, as he slipped away from the party and shut himself in his study, he decided to ring Lloyd. Lloyd was in New Zealand for a friend's wedding, and it would be early there, just after seven in the morning, but it was possible he might have heard from his father.

Lloyd's mobile rang and rang until finally Stirling heard his nephew's voice. Thankfully he didn't sound sleepy. 'Sorry if I kept you,' Lloyd said. 'I was in the shower. How's the party going? I spoke to Granza last night. She sounded great and was looking forward to a quiet dinner with you all. How's the surprise going down?'

Stirling glossed over his response and then casually asked, 'Have you heard from your father?'

'No. Why, what's wrong?'

'Nothing's wrong.'

'Are you sure about that? Because if I'm reading this right, you've just left Granza's party to ask me very specifically if I've heard from Dad. What's going on? It's not Mum, is it? Is she ill? Has she had an accident?'

Stirling knew he had to be honest with Lloyd. 'Pen's fine. It's just that we're both worried. It's your father, he ... he seems to have disappeared. He told Pen he was going sailing in Greece, a last-minute thing, but didn't mention anything to me about the trip. On top of that, he hasn't been in touch all week. I've left countless messages on his mobile, but he hasn't got back to me. It's not like him. Did you know he was going sailing?'

'No, I didn't. Have you checked with the flotilla company?'

'I don't know which one he used this time round, so this afternoon I checked with as many as I could find online, and not one of them has any record of a booking with him for this week.'

'What the hell's he playing at?'

'I have no idea. I'm worried, Lloyd. Why would he miss Cecily's ninetieth birthday? What would make him do that?'

'I can't think of a single reason. It's so out of character it doesn't make sense.'

'Then the only conclusion I can reach is that something's happened to him. I think we have to consider getting in touch with the police to report him as missing.'

'What does Mum say about that?'

'I haven't mentioned the police to Pen, I didn't want to make her any more anxious than she already is.'

'I wish she'd called me.'

'You know your mother; she doesn't like to make a fuss. I haven't discussed it with anyone else either.'

'What do you want me to do? John and Emma's wedding is tomorrow; as best man I don't feel I can just leave them in the lurch, but I could fly back as soon as it's over.'

'Let's speak again tomorrow. For all we know, Neil could be tearing up the drive in that Porsche of his as we speak.'

'If that's the case, give him a huge piece of my mind for putting you and Mum through all this worry.'

'Trust me, that's what I fully intend to do.'

Words of bravado, Stirling conceded when he rang off. He knew in his guts that his brother wasn't going to be here tonight. Moreover, he knew with every fibre of his being that something was seriously wrong. It had started that day when Cecily had voiced her concern for Neil. Recalling her question, he now had to admit that he was fooling himself if he thought he could lie to her as to why Neil hadn't made it back for her party this evening. It was fair enough Lloyd missing it unavoidably because he was best man at his friend's wedding, an event that had been planned more than a year ago, but what possible excuse could Neil have? Other than a delayed flight. For the sake of not spoiling the evening, Stirling knew that Cecily would go along with whatever explanation he gave her, but once the curtain came down on the party, she would want to know what was really going on. Wouldn't they all?

*

Having spent most of the afternoon at the office, Rosco was running late. He was in a state of shock. Every time he thought about the implications of what he'd discovered, he shuddered with disbelief. How could it have happened? And what if they dug deeper and discovered this was just the tip of the iceberg? It was unthinkable.

He turned into Willow Bank and slammed on the brakes behind a yellow Mini. He switched off the engine and thought about what he should do. It wasn't the right time or place, but he had to speak to his father. He had to do it tonight. It couldn't wait. They would have to figure out how they were going to keep a lid on this. If it went public, it would cause them no end of harm. Worst-case scenario, and not beyond the realms of disbelief, they might never recover from it. Financial institutions of any kind had to be whiter than white these days; the faintest whiff of something dodgy and the tainted reputation stayed for ever.

He was out of his Range Rover and locking it when another car appeared at the end of the drive. It was Pen's Volvo. His heart sank. How the hell was he going to look her in the eye? Nothing else for it, he would have to find a way to avoid his aunt. He quickly walked round to the back of the house as though he hadn't seen her.

Guests were everywhere; some were seated on the terrace, some were drifting about the garden, some were down by the riverbank. Which made Dee and Katie's job all the more difficult as they had so much ground to cover. And all the while she was scurrying around with trays of canapés and drinks, and worrying that the real waitress from the agency would arrive, she was keeping an eye out for Stirling Nightingale.

Maddeningly, she was spoilt for choice with potential candidates – there were plenty of grey-haired, prosperous-looking men here; he could be any one of them. To make matters worse, the mental picture she had of him from the internet had begun to fade from her memory. She had asked Dee to

65

point him out to her, and the girl had vaguely thought he was inside the house. 'Why are you so keen to know?' she had said with a frown. Not wanting to attract suspicion, Katie had smiled and said, 'Oh, you know, just curious. It's quite some set-up here, isn't it?'

Her voice low, Dee said, 'The Nightingales are loaded. *Seriously* loaded.'

That much Katie had worked out for herself. As F. Scott Fitzgerald had said, the rich are different, and that difference was abundantly apparent at Willow Bank. Edwardian in style, no expense had been spared in its decoration or furnishings. It was lavish, but stylishly positioned on the right side of extreme good taste.

As to who the party had been thrown for, that was easy to figure out. Mrs Nightingale senior was seated at the head of the large wooden table on the terrace. In front of her on the table was a pile of unopened presents. Chatting happily with guests, and dressed in a navy-blue dress with white trim, a simple pearl necklace at her throat, she looked a very elegant lady. Her hair was white and stylishly swept to the back of her head, held in place with a tortoiseshell comb. Her face was soft and lightly made-up, and her eyes were bright and alert. Dee was right: Mrs Nightingale senior didn't look her age.

So far Dee had worked the terrace, but since she was currently occupied elsewhere, Katie approached the table with a tray of smoked-salmon blinis. She was suddenly struck by the thought that she was actually related to this elderly woman. It was the weirdest feeling.

'Thank you,' the old lady said as she helped herself to a blini. She was one of the few guests actually to make eye contact with Katie. 'You girls are doing a splendid job taking care of us this evening,' she said. 'The food, as ever, is delicious.' Her voice was measured and clear-cut, but not so much as to be unfriendly.

Katie smiled. 'Thank you.' And before she knew what she was doing, she added, 'Happy birthday.'

The old lady smiled, and for a moment it seemed to Katie that the woman's bluey-grey gaze intensified. Was it her imagination – or her paranoia – but was she being scrutinized? Then the moment was gone and the woman looked away, her attention caught by a strident voice. 'Happy birthday, Granza!'

Moving on to serve the other guests, Katie observed a good-looking man about the same age as her approach the table – a confident, well-dressed man who liked an entrance, she thought, as everyone watched him embrace the old lady.

'You're late, Rosco,' she chided him good-humouredly.

'Sorry,' he said. 'I'm a terrible grandson, I know. But you love me anyway, don't you, Granza?' Something about him didn't ring true for Katie; it was as if he was putting on a performance.

'You're growing on me,' the old lady said, flicking a dismissive hand against his shoulder.

He laughed, then spotted Katie. 'Any chance of a glass of wine?' he asked, at the same time reaching for a blini and putting it straight in his mouth.

'Certainly, sir,' she replied. 'Red, white or rose?'

With an unsubtle cocky glance at her legs, he took a napkin from the tray she was carrying and wiped his mouth. 'Red,' he said.

Red, *please*, you arrogant sod, she thought as he turned his back on her and resumed chatting to his grandmother. He was so utterly self-possessed, his every gesture giving off a grating sense of entitlement. Then, with a jolt that brought her up short, she realized he had to be one of two things; her cousin or a half-brother.

'Do you know where Dad is?' she heard him say as she finished serving the seated guests and turned to go inside the house to fetch him his glass of wine.

So preoccupied was she with her thoughts that she turned the corner in the hallway too fast and went smack into a couple of guests. She let out a startled cry and the empty metal tray dropped to the floor with a deafening crash. 'I'm so sorry,' she said as she bent to pick it up, along with the scattered paper napkins.

'Are you all right,' the man said as he hunkered down beside her to help.

'I'm fine, sir.'

He put the napkins on the tray and they both stood up. That was when the photograph that had faded from her memory returned with total clarity, and she realized she was finally face to face with Stirling Nightingale.

Chapter Ten

Not only was Katie face to face with her biological father, but she was being stared at by the woman she'd met that afternoon at The Meadows. Standing next to Stirling Nightingale, the woman was looking at Katie as if registering that there was something familiar about her. More than anything Katie wanted to draw out this encounter with Stirling Nightingale for as long as possible, to gain more than just a passing observation of him. But not if it would give his sister-in-law the chance to realize where she had seen her before. So with her head down, she mumbled another apology and shot off to the kitchen.

With both Sue and Merrill busy loading more trays of food into the oven, and no sign of Dee, Katie grabbed a glass and filled it with red wine. With her heart pounding fit to burst and her hands shaking, she had to concentrate hard on what she was doing. She took a deep steadying breath. Her natural inclination was to run, to escape before she was found out: Penelope Nightingale had definitely recognized her.

But she couldn't run. She hadn't gone to this much trouble for a mere two-second exchange with her biological father. She couldn't leave here without gaining a better insight into the man. Into him *and* his family. And anyway, what was she risking by continuing with the subterfuge? So what if she got caught out and ended up having to explain herself? That was Stirling Nightingale's problem, not hers. She was perfectly innocent in the whole thing. She had done nothing wrong. Impersonating a waitress was hardly a crime, was it?

Feeling calmer, she took the glass of red wine and went back outside to find the person who'd asked for it.

There was no sign of him on the terrace with his grandmother – an attractive blonde girl seemed to have taken his place – but after scanning the garden, she located him down by the boathouse. He wasn't alone; he was with Stirling Nightingale.

She was a short distance from the boathouse when the two men moved so they were partially hidden by a screen of weeping-willow branches. With their backs to her, they had no idea she was there. Something about their body language and the intensity of the exchange between them made Katie hesitate; whatever they were discussing was apparently for no one else's ears. Her curiosity irresistibly roused, she flattened herself against the side of the boathouse so there was no danger of her being spotted.

'You're wrong. You have to be mistaken.'

'Dad, I'd give anything to be wrong but I'm not. I double-checked; I swear it. What I want to know is why. Why did he do it? I mean, how much money did he need, for God's sake?'

'I still think there has to be an explanation.'

'There is, it's called defrauding the company.'

'Don't be flippant!'

'Dad, face up to it, Uncle Neil's had his hand in the till and has been stealing from clients. And not just small amounts; he's stolen almost—'

'He wouldn't! Rosco, I know my brother. He would never steal from anyone. It's got to be someone else who's been doing it and has deliberately made it look like Neil's responsible.'

'How do you explain his disappearance, then? Coincidence? And let's not forget his strange behaviour just before he fell off the radar. Didn't I say to you that he wasn't himself?'

Stirling shook his head. He felt sick. Sick in the pit of his stomach. He wanted to defend his brother, wanted to do it till his dying breath, but instinct was telling him that there was an appalling chance that Rosco was right.

Irrationally he felt angry with his son. If Rosco hadn't played tennis that morning and overheard a snippet of conversation in the club bar between one of Neil's clients and an accountant from High Wycombe with whom Rosco had had dealings in the past, he would never have done what he did next, which was to drive straight to the office and check through Neil's client files. Why hadn't Rosco come to him first? And why couldn't he have kept this to himself tonight? Why did he have to go and spoil Cecily's party? Oh God, how would Cecily react to the news?

'Let's not jump to any hasty conclusions,' he said. 'There's got to be a reasonable explanation for what you've found and for why Neil's not here.'

'There is, it's staring us right in the face. He's helped himself to a ton of money that doesn't belong to him and then buggered off with it. And worse still, he's left us to clear up the shit he's left behind.'

'Don't you dare talk about my brother like that!' Stirling exploded. 'Not when you don't have any real proof. All you've got—'

'Dad, listen to me. You have to forget that Neil's your brother. You've got to look at this objectively. As for proof, take my word for it, it's there. I'm talking irrefutable proof.' He took a folded piece of paper out of his pocket and passed it to Stirling. 'As I said earlier, I checked and I double-checked and for no other reason than I didn't want it to be true.'

With a sense of dread, Stirling forced himself to take the sheet of paper, but before he managed to read what was printed on it, a sneeze had them both turning round.

'Who's there?' demanded Rosco. His voice, as thunderous as the crack of a whip, made Stirling jump.

A girl stepped out from the side of the boathouse; it was the pretty red-haired waitress who had bumped into him in the hall. From nowhere he had the feeling that they'd met before this evening. There was something in the eyes and the cheekbones. Very probably he had seen her at some other party like this where she'd been serving drinks and food. With such a distinctive look, she was the sort of girl anyone would remember.

'Your wine,' she said to Rosco.

Rosco made no effort to take it from her. 'Were you listening to our conversation?' he asked abruptly. Stirling was taken aback at the forceful tone of his son's voice.

'Certainly not,' she replied indignantly. Her expression suggested she might like to throw Rosco's wine at him.

'I'm sure you weren't,' Stirling said smoothly. He slipped the piece of paper in his hand into his pocket and, taking the glass from the tray she was carrying, gave it to his son. The world might be about to come crashing down on them, but Stirling would be damned if he was going to allow Rosco to take out his mood on an innocent girl. There again, he thought, as he watched her march across the lawn back up to the house, she looked more than capable of taking care of herself.

'Stroppy cow,' muttered Rosco.

'She was hardly that. And you were extremely rude to her.'

Rosco took a mouthful of his wine. 'Given the sensitive nature of what we were discussing, I had every right to be suspicious of her. You know as well as I do, we can't afford for a word of this to get out. If she did hear anything, we have to hope she's as thick as two short planks and didn't understand what she was hearing.'

'She didn't look stupid to me,' Stirling said. 'Far from it.'

Rosco frowned. 'What the hell's wrong with you, Dad? Why are you defending some nobody of a waitress when we've got the mother of all messes on our hands to deal with?'

His son was right. What the hell was wrong with him? Neil. He had to focus on Neil and what may or may not be true about him. But for all Rosco's insistence, he simply couldn't believe his brother had been embezzling clients' money. Then from across the lawn he saw Gina hurrying towards him. She looked worried. Very worried.

'Darling,' she said breathlessly, 'there are two police officers here. They won't say exactly what they've come about, other than it's something to do with Neil. They want to speak to Pen, but I think you should be there with her, don't you? Scarlet's with her on the terrace.'

The three of them hurried back up to the house. Oh Neil, thought Stirling, just what the hell have you done?

Chapter Eleven

Dee burst into the kitchen. 'Guess what! There are two police-men with Mr Nightingale in his study. Well, actually, it's a po-liceman and a policewoman. They looked dead serious. What do you think's going on?' She giggled. 'It's like something off the telly. Just think; somebody could have been murdered! How cool would that be?'

'Not cool at all,' Sue huffed as she put the finishing touches to a tray of mini profiteroles and passed it to Katie. 'And don't you go gossiping in front of the guests. Just remember, whatever's going on, it's none of our business.'

Back outside, dusk was falling into night. Circulating the garden and terrace with the profiteroles, Katie's mind was racing. Putting together the scraps of conversation she'd overheard and the arrival of two police officers, it didn't take a lot to work out that something was seriously up. Talk about cupboards and skeletons! Just what kind of a family was she related to? And as for that obnoxious Rosco Nightingale, how could she have any DNA in common with someone like that? Someone who she now knew was her half-brother. She'd clearly heard him call Stirling, Dad.

Stirling had taken charge. Having instructed his wife and Rosco and Scarlet to go back to the party and pretend noth-ing untoward was happening – under no circumstances was Cecily to suspect that anything was amiss – he was now standing beside Pen, who he had seated behind his desk. Sitting opposite them were the two police officers. Detective

Inspector Rawlings was the senior of the two. He had coarse grey hair and an unfortunately long and beaky nose, and had just finished explaining that they'd been to The Meadows but, finding no one at home, a neighbour had suggested they try Willow Bank, knowing that Penelope Nightingale was here for a party. The other officer, Detective Sergeant Fisher – the seemingly silent note-taking sidekick – was a chunky woman in her early forties.

'When did you last see your husband, Mrs Nightingale?' Detective Inspector Rawlings now asked.

Immediately Pen looked flustered. 'Um ... oh, I think it was Monday.'

'You *think*? Or you know?'

'Um ... it was definitely Monday. Yes, of course it was. I'm sorry.'

'So Monday was the last time you saw him. Have you spoken in the days since?'

'No. He's been away.'

'Away? Where?'

'Sailing. He's on a sailing holiday. Somewhere in Greece.'

'You're sure about that?'

Stirling intervened. 'Please, can you get to the point of why you're here? Why exactly are you asking about my brother?' He braced himself for the worst: that the clients with money missing from their portfolios had gone to the police and an investigation was under way.

'A body has been found in the river at Medmenham, and we have every reason to believe that it's your husband's body, Mrs Nightingale.'

Pen gasped and put a hand to her mouth. 'No. Not Neil!'

Stirling swallowed. 'How do you know it's Neil?' he asked.

'A Porsche 911 registered in the name of Mr Neil Nightingale was found nearby, along with his mobile phone and a wallet containing his driving licence. This is never an easy process,' Rawlings went on, 'but we need someone to formally identify the body.'

Stirling placed his hands on Pen's shoulder. 'I'll do it,' he said. 'There's no need for you to go through that, Pen.'

'But it can't be Neil,' she murmured. Her face was pale and dazed, her eyes moist. 'Not Neil. He's away sailing. He's ...' Her words trailed off.

'We strongly believe it is your husband, Mrs Nightingale, otherwise we wouldn't be here.' Rawlings paused. 'We don't think his death was an accident.'

Pen let out another gasp. She shook her head. 'But it has to be an accident. He must have fallen in. Or it's not him at all and this is all a terrible mistake.'

Rawlings just stared at her.

Stirling could have punched the man. Did he have no feelings? Was he so inured to the job that he could be so insensitive? He cleared his throat. 'Why do you think Neil's death wasn't an accident?'

'Until a post-mortem is carried out, we can't be one hundred per cent sure, but we have reason to believe it was suicide because of what we found in the car: an empty bottle of sleeping pills, a half-consumed bottle of whisky and a note.' Rawlings paused. 'So you can see why we've reached the conclusion we have.'

Pen began to cry. 'It can't be true. I don't believe it. Not Neil.'

Stirling desperately wanted to hang on to the hope that it wasn't Neil's car that had been found, that it was some other poor devil's body waiting to be identified. But he knew in his bones it was false hope. Call it a sixth sense but he knew his brother was dead.

He swallowed. *Dead.* For the love of God, what the hell had been going on in Neil's head lately? And why hadn't any of them noticed the change in him? How could everything have been going on right under their noses without them realizing?

The woman police officer spoke for the first time. 'Mr Nightingale, can you think of any reason why—'

'No more questions,' Stirling said decisively. 'I think you should go now. I'll be happy to speak to you tomorrow morning, but for now I think you should show us the respect we deserve and leave us to deal with the shock of ...' His voice faltered and he blinked hard. 'Of my brother's death,' he managed to say. 'If indeed it is my brother's body you've found.'

The two police officers had the decency to know a dismissal when they heard one and got to their feet. 'As I said before,' Rawlings said, when he was at the door and Stirling had opened it for him, 'we'll need someone to identify the body. I'll ring you in the morning to make an appointment for you to attend the mortuary.'

'I was right! There has been a murder!' If she'd been excited earlier, now Dee was practically beside herself.

They all stopped what they were doing and stared at her. 'Don't talk nonsense,' Merrill said, smoothing down her apron. 'Of course there hasn't been a murder.'

'So why was Mr Nightingale told he'd be needed to identify the body? I heard them talking. They were in the hall. Mrs Nightingale was there as well, and she'd been crying. It wasn't like I was eavesdropping; I just happened to be passing.'

Sue and Merrill exchanged looks. 'Which Mrs Nightingale?' asked Sue.

'Penelope.'

Katie kept quiet. Penelope Nightingale, the woman from The Meadows. She felt a pang of sadness for her. Katie knew all about losing someone she loved. She knew how it felt to receive the kind of news nothing ever prepared you for.

Sue said, 'You don't suppose it's her husband who's died, do you, Neil Nightingale?'

Merrill pulled a face. 'If it's not him, I hope it isn't the son. That would be too awful.'

They both looked at Dee again. 'Did you actually hear the word murder used?' asked Sue.

Dee frowned as if trying to remember exactly what she'd overheard. 'No,' she said shortly, 'but if it isn't murder, why would the police be involved?'

'It could be an accident,' Sue suggested.

'Whatever's happened,' Merrill said, 'it's not for us to worry about. Our priority is, if there's been a sudden death in the family, where does that leave us? Is there still a party to cater for or is it over?'

Stirling Nightingale's wife suddenly appeared in the doorway of the kitchen. If she had heard what they'd been saying, her expression gave nothing away. 'We're ready for the champagne and birthday cake now,' she said crisply. 'We'll have it on the terrace.'

An ice-cool customer that one, thought Katie; a family tragedy and not a flicker. But then it was a cool family altogether if they were going ahead with the birthday celebrations as if nothing had happened.

Cecily was eager for the party to be over. She was tired of the charade. She wanted to know what Stirling was keeping from her. Just because she was ninety, it didn't mean she'd become senile overnight. If anyone had lost their power of reasoning it was Stirling for imagining she didn't know something was terribly wrong. Neil wasn't here, and now suddenly Pen had gone missing. And if Rosco and Scarlet fussed over her any more, she would give them a piece of her fully functioning mind. Their patronizing manner always annoyed her, and tonight it made her long for Lloyd's quiet, unpretentious company. There was a refreshing honesty to Lloyd's character that she had always enjoyed and respected. She wished he was here now.

Meanwhile, and because she knew her elder son so well – that he would go to extraordinary lengths when it came to her well-being – she would play along with his pretence that despite the obvious, there was nothing wrong and they were all having a jolly good time.

At the sound of a collective '*Ooh!*' she looked up to see one of the young waitresses walking carefully towards her; it was the pretty one who had earlier wished her a happy birthday. She was carrying a large birthday cake ablaze with an embarrassing number of candles. In the dark, the light cast from the candles illuminated the girl's face with a soft radiance, making her pale skin glow like alabaster and her eyes shine. With her chestnut hair and delicate features, she was an extremely eye-catching young woman. Funnily enough, Cecily's hair had been that exact same colour when she'd been young – before age had taken its toll and turned it white. Her eyes too had been the same colour as those of the girl, but they also had faded with age.

When the waitress placed the cake in front of her on the table, Cecily was reminded how she had felt before, that there was something familiar about this girl. But it was a familiarity that went beyond simple recognition; this was a feeling of something being woken deep within her, something that made her want to reach out to the girl. Puzzled, and ignoring the crowd of guests that had now gathered round the table, she stared intently at the waitress, scrutinizing her violet-blue eyes, her cheekbones and the pale pink of her lips. Then all at once, she experienced a moment of crystalline understanding: it was as if she was looking in the mirror at her young self. She was so struck by the realization that she impulsively put a hand out to the girl and touched her lightly on the arm, as though checking to see if she was real. 'What's your name?' she asked.

The girl's face flushed. 'Katie,' she murmured.

'Katie what?'

'Um ... just Katie.'

'You must have a surname.'

An unmistakable look of alarm passed through the girl's eyes. But then her chin jutted out. 'It's Lavender,' she said. 'Katie Lavender.'

Cecily froze. 'How old are you?'

But her question was lost in the commotion of Stirling and Gina appearing at her side and everyone singing 'Happy Birthday' to her. And as if she had never been there, the girl had vanished.

When the singing came to an end and she had blown out the candles and made the first cut in the cake, and the other waitress had taken it away to be portioned for the guests, Cecily pushed herself out of her chair and got to her feet. 'Stirling,' she said urgently, 'I have to speak to you.'

He looked worried. Which further confirmed her suspicions that he was hiding something important from her. 'It's not about Neil,' she said impatiently, 'and whatever it is that you're trying to hide from me. This is a different matter altogether: you have to speak to that waitress.'

He glanced anxiously about him and she suddenly saw that he looked more than worried. He looked awful, as though he was strained to the point of collapse. 'Which one and why?' he asked absently. 'Has she done something wrong?'

Cecily dismissed his question with a wave of her hand. 'Find the pretty red-haired waitress and ask her what her name is. Ask her how old she is and why she's here. And then later, when everyone has gone, you must tell me exactly where Neil is.'

Chapter Twelve

Stirling had no idea what Cecily was talking about, but one thing he did know was that he couldn't keep up the pretence any longer.

Only the faintest of hopes that the police had jumped to the wrong conclusion, that it hadn't been Neil's body found in the river, had given him the strength to carry on with his mother's birthday party. But just as he had known that Rosco's revelations about the missing client money were true, his instinct was – that sixth sense – telling him that Neil was indeed dead. He knew it with absolute certainty. He knew too that life was never going to be the same again. It wasn't just a brother he had lost; he had lost his oldest and closest friend. So why then was he trying to compartmentalize Neil's death for the sake of appearances? What sort of unthinking bastard did that?

'Stirling? Whatever is the matter? You look quite ill.'

He swallowed the painful lump in his throat and held firm. He would not let himself become unglued. 'Let's go inside the house,' he murmured, putting a hand to his mother's elbow. He concentrated on walking. One step. Then another. And then another.

He closed the door of his study and led Cecily to the two comfortable armchairs either side of the empty fireplace, steeling himself for one of the hardest, if not the hardest thing he'd ever have to do in his life. Cecily had never had favourites when it came to him and his brother, but Neil had always had a special place in her heart, just as Lloyd did.

He told her first about Rosco's discovery in the office.

She made no reaction, merely listened attentively, sitting bolt upright, her hands on her lap, as if knowing there was worse to come. Then he told her about the police and the reason for their visit. He heard the quiet catch of her breath and she closed her eyes for a very long time. Stirling watched her carefully.

'I knew,' she said, when finally she looked at him again. 'I knew something was wrong. He wasn't happy. When I last saw him I sensed he was at odds with himself. I asked him if everything was all right, but he wouldn't open up to me. I should have tried harder. If only I had. If only ...' She closed her eyes once more.

'If anyone should be saying that, it's me,' Stirling said. He knelt at her side, covered her hands with his. 'I should have realized he was going through some kind of hell. I just don't understand why he didn't turn to me. Didn't he trust me? Didn't he think I'd help ...' He broke off, unable to continue. The lump in his throat had returned; it was made of anger and bewilderment. Why? Why hadn't Neil come to him? It hurt him acutely that his brother hadn't confided in him. Then he did what he hadn't done since he'd been a small boy. He rested his head in his mother's lap and wept. For a while he wasn't conscious of anything other than the feeling that he would never recover from this. He thought he knew what it was like to feel real sorrow – he'd experienced that when his father died more than ten years ago – but this was different. The desolation was all-consuming. It was unbearable.

Gradually he became aware of Cecily's hands on his head and neck, gently stroking him as she had when he'd been a boy. He was shocked how easily he had reverted to being that child in need; shocked also at his selfishness. He should be the one soothing and consoling her; she had lost a son. He pulled himself together, dug out a handkerchief from his trouser pocket, blew his nose, wiped his eyes. 'I'm sorry,' he said, his voice a rasp.

'What for? For being human? Don't ever apologize for that. Where's Pen?'

'She wanted to go home, but I insisted she stayed here. She's upstairs lying down.'

'We must go to her. She mustn't be alone. Have you telephoned Lloyd?'

His mother's composure and clear thinking shouldn't have surprised him, but it did. But maybe she was doing what he had done earlier when he had slammed the door shut on his emotions by throwing himself into being practical. Perhaps he should be firm and say that she must stay the night here, too, so that when her grief hit her she wouldn't be on her own. 'I haven't called Lloyd, not yet. I just wanted to get through this party for your sake. I didn't want anything to spoil your evening.'

She shook her head. 'How many times have I told you, Stirling, you don't have to carry the world on your shoulders. Not everything is down to you. Who else knows about Neil?'

'At the moment, only you, Pen and me. All Gina, Rosco and Scarlet and Charlie know is that something has happened that I'll tell them about after the party.'

'Does Pen know about the missing client money?'

'No. And I don't want her to. She doesn't need to know any of that.'

She gave him a severe look. 'That might not be your decision to make.' She rose stiffly from the chair. 'Let's go up and see Pen. Then perhaps you should get Gina to tell the guests the party's over, that I'm not feeling well. And while you're doing that, I shall call Lloyd. That's if Pen hasn't done so already.'

It felt all wrong, his mother taking command of the situation, but once more he should have known better, that she would be the strong one. She always had been.

The net was closing in on Katie. Any minute and the whole crazy charade was going to blow up in her face. Merrill had just taken an apologetic call from the girl who was supposed to have filled in for the original waitress; apparently she'd been involved in a car shunt in Marlow and had spent the evening at A & E. Fortunately she hadn't been badly hurt, but it had left Merrill and Sue wondering how Katie had ended up here. Thinking fast, Katie had suggested that the agency had got itself in a muddle and booked two girls by accident. The lie seemed to have satisfied them, however Katie didn't think she could fool Cecily Nightingale so easily. But then part of her hadn't wanted to fool the old lady; that was why she had given her real name when pushed. She had thought there was little likelihood of the name meaning anything to Cecily Nightingale – after all, what were the chances of her knowing that her son had had an affair with Fay Lavender all those years ago? – but the expression on her face had left Katie in no doubt whatsoever that it had.

So where did that leave Katie? Should she sneak away whilst no one was looking? Not easy given that Merrill was outside loading boxes of dirty crockery and cutlery into the van, which was parked directly in front of Katie's car.

But to stay was to risk the consequences of the old lady's reaction to her name. Was her reticence to take flight based on a desire to be found out? Was that it? Did she want Stirling Nightingale to acknowledge she was his daughter? She really hadn't come here to pick a fight or to hurt anyone. It was lucidity she had been seeking, a light thrown on to this newly revealed dark corner of herself.

That aside, it would be nice to stick it to that Rosco character by announcing she was his half-sister. She imagined his horror and her saying, 'Yeah, I thought that would wipe the arrogant sneer off your face.'

As satisfying as the thought was, there was a more altruistic side to her reluctance to leave at once. The grief that the family would go through tugged at her heart; it made her want to know that Pen Nightingale would be all right. The poor woman had been so nice to Katie this afternoon, little knowing that she was being lied to. Katie didn't feel good about that. Not good at all.

There had been no sign of the woman during the cutting of the cake, and Katie wondered where she was. Had she gone home? Wherever she was, Katie hoped she had someone with her. She remembered how she had been alone at the hospital when the medical staff had decided to take her mother off the life-support machine. It had been the right thing to do, to leave her with her mother in those last moments, but to be alone, entirely alone, at a time like that was brutal; it wasn't something you could ever forget.

She had watched her mother die. She had held Fay's hand, part hoping her mother could feel her last touch, but terrified that she could because that would mean it had been wrong to switch off the machine that had kept her alive. She had lain on the bed alongside her mother's still body and stroked her cheek, tears running down her own. Later the nurses had found her like that and had gently pulled her away.

No, that wasn't something you could forget.

With a heavy heart, she carried on with the task she'd been assigned, that of making coffee while Dee was passing round plates of birthday cake. Over by the draining board a large electric urn was hissing and bubbling.

Coming into the kitchen with a tray of dirty glasses, Sue said, 'I've just been informed that the party's over, so I wouldn't bother putting any more cups out; just keep enough for the family. Apparently Cecily Nightingale isn't feeling so good and guests have been asked to go home. Where's Merrill?'

'She's outside loading stuff into the van. What's wrong with Mrs Nightingale? It's not anything serious, is it?'

The woman shrugged. 'I don't think so.'

Left on her own again as Sue went out to the van, Katie began stacking the unwanted cups and saucers. What an evening it was turning into for the family.

'I wonder if I could trouble you for some tea?'

She spun round at the sound of a man's voice. It was Stirling Nightingale. But he barely resembled the confident and smiling man she had bumped into previously. His eyes were red-rimmed and his expression stricken; a handkerchief was poking out from his trouser pocket. He looked tired and shaken, like a man who had fought to stay in control in the aftermath of receiving bad news but had lost the battle. Katie felt a wave of sympathy for him. More than that, she realized she cared about this stranger. Was it a genetic thing? Was she programmed to feel something for this person she had only just met?

'Tea,' she repeated, her heartbeat accelerating wildly. 'Of course. Any particular type?' she asked, wondering where on earth the tea was kept.

'Earl Grey, please. You'll find it in the cupboard above … Here, let me get it for you.'

He came over and stood just a few feet away from her. Close up, she could see the excruciating strain in his eyes. One way or another he was having a hell of an evening. Suddenly her deceit sickened her; the last thing he needed right now was a secret love child turning up on his doorstep. She took the box of tea bags from him.

He was staring at her intently, his brow drawn. 'I keep getting the feeling that we've met before,' he said. 'Have we?'

'No,' she said, turning her back to him and scanning the kitchen for a teapot. 'This is my first time here.'

'Maybe at another party where you've waitressed?'

Before she could reply, he said, 'For some reason my mother said I should speak to you, that I should ask you what your name is.'

'Really?'

'She also suggested that I should ask you why you're here.'

No flies on the birthday girl, then. 'Um … I'm here by accident,' she said, turning round to face him. She almost cheered herself for her choice of words. If he and her mother hadn't had an affair, she most certainly wouldn't be here! 'Just helping out,' she added. 'I stepped in at the last minute for someone else. Can you show me where there's a teapot?'

He opened another cupboard and handed her a blue and white Spode pot. 'So what is your name?'

Should she lie to him? One simple lie and this moment would stop. She would make his tea and he would leave her alone. But then all he had to do was speak to his mother and he would know. Lavender wasn't a common surname. He would hear it and know in a blink of an eye who she was. Stalling, she put two tea bags into the pot and went over to the hot-water urn. 'How's your mother?' she asked. 'I heard she wasn't feeling very well.'

'She's ... she's tired. It's been a long day for her. Thank you for asking.'

Katie found a tray and put the teapot on it. 'How many cups do you need?'

'Three should be enough. You still haven't answered my question.'

Katie turned her eyes on him. She forced herself to look beyond the strain in his face and saw a striking and distinctive man. Tall, well dressed and giving the impression of leading an active and healthy lifestyle, he probably still had the power to make any woman look twice at him. His silver-grey hair was thick and short and neatly cut. His eyes were brown, and despite the weight of sadness in them, they met her gaze with a compelling potency.

'You really do look familiar,' he said, when still she hadn't answered him.

She thought of the letter her mother had written, and the reason she had done it.

'My name's Katie,' she said at last. 'Katie Lavender. You knew my mother. Fay Lavender. I'm your daughter.'

Chapter Thirteen

Stirling stared and stared at her. What was she doing here? What was she doing in his house working as a waitress? Numb with shock, he didn't know how to react or what to say. First his brother. Now this. He felt he would stay numb for the rest of his life.

Years ago, he had often thought about this moment, but never had he pictured it quite like this. He had imagined something more carefully planned, a situation – rightly or wrongly – that he would have felt in control of. This wasn't at all how he'd envisaged their meeting. For a start, he had imagined a boy: a son. The arrangement he'd had with Fay was that she would never tell him what sex of child she gave birth to. 'It's better that you never know,' she had said. Despite his initial refusal to agree to this, he had eventually given in to her wishes and had promised he would never pursue the matter, that he would leave her alone to get on with her life. She had begged him not to renege on his promise, claiming that a clean break was the only way either of them would be able to cope.

The girl was the first to speak. 'I only came here to check you out,' she said. 'I didn't intend to announce who I was. I just wanted to see what kind of a man you were.'

Her frankness forced Stirling to say something. 'You're not catching me at a good time,' he said.

'I know. I gather someone's died.'

He frowned. 'How do you know that?'

'The other waitress heard you talking to the two police

officers who were here. Is it a member of your family?'

'My brother.' He flinched at hearing himself declare so casually that Neil was dead. You don't know for sure yet that he's dead, he wanted to shout back at himself. He could be alive. It could all be a terrible mistake.

'I'm sorry,' she said. 'Was it an accident?'

Stirling cleared his throat. 'It's ... it's possible that he killed himself.'

'Oh, how awful for him. And for you and his family. Did you have any idea he might do something like this?'

Her concern was like a punch to his chest. He caught his breath. 'Not a clue.'

There was a silence between them. He simply didn't know what else to say.

'I haven't come here to cause trouble for you,' she said. 'I'll leave you in peace; it'll be as if I've never been here.'

He swallowed. 'Is that what you want?'

'It's probably what you want, isn't it?'

'I ... I don't know.' He rubbed at the back of his neck. 'I'm sorry, I'm not really thinking straight.'

'I understand. Can I ask you something?'

'Go ahead.'

'Does your family know about me?'

'No. My relationship with Fay was a secret.'

'Except that can't be true, can it? Your mother reacted quite strongly to my surname when she asked me what it was. And as you said, it was she who told you to talk to me.'

He almost smiled. 'My mother is an exceptionally intuitive woman.'

'And she never once let on to you that she suspected something?'

'All I was aware of at the time was that she knew Fay and I had been close for a brief period. You know, the more I look at you, the more I realize you remind me not just of Fay but also of my mother when she was young. How is Fay? Does she know you're here?'

'She died a year ago. It was very sudden. A road accident.'

'God, I'm sorry. And your father?'

'He died three years ago.'

'Do you have any brothers and sisters?' Please God, he thought, having put his foot in it twice already, don't let them be dead as well.

She shook her head. 'I'm an only child. But I have some very good friends. They're like family to me.'

The clatter of footsteps and voices had them both turning towards the back door. The two women who ran the catering business came in, then stopped in their tracks when they saw him. 'Everything all right, Mr Nightingale?' one of them asked. To his shame, he could never remember their names. Beryl and Lou, was it?

'I ... I came for some tea,' he replied awkwardly, feeling he had to justify his presence in his own kitchen. 'Perhaps ... perhaps Katie could bring it up when it's ready? I'll be upstairs with my mother in the guest room, third door on the left,' he added, looking directly at Katie.

He left the kitchen, knowing that he'd probably just made himself look obnoxiously high-handed by not offering to wait a few minutes longer so he could take the tea himself. But asking her to bring it up was the only way he could think to talk to her again without arousing suspicion.

Out in the hall, his wife was saying goodbye to a group of guests. When they'd gone, she stopped him at the foot of the stairs. He knew what was coming, knew too that Gina would feel slighted that he hadn't been honest with her straight away. The truth was, he hadn't been able to bring himself to utter the words. Strange then, that he had been able to do it just now in the kitchen. Thinking of the extraordinary encounter with that girl – *his daughter* – and the precarious position in which her appearance put him, his heart began to race.

'Stirling,' Gina hissed, 'I've done what you asked, told people that Cecily's not well and that the party's over, but will you now kindly tell me what is really going on? Why were those police officers here? And where have Cecily and Pen disappeared to? Have they gone home?'

A vein in his head began to throb. He inhaled deeply, then let out his breath in one long rush. 'The police were here because a body has been found at Medmenham and they think it's Neil's. They think it's suicide. That he drowned himself.'

'Suicide? Neil? But that can't be right. Neil wouldn't do something like that. It's absurd. He's a good swimmer, he wouldn't be able to drown himself.'

'It looks like he did. The police said there were pills and alcohol in the car.'

'But why?'

Stirling felt he knew why, but again he couldn't bring himself to say the words. Instead, he said, 'We'll have to wait and see.'

'I don't understand why you kept this from me,' she said with a frown. 'Why didn't you tell me the truth?'

'I didn't want you to worry,' he lied.

She tutted. And then her expression softened, as if only now grasping the reality of what he'd told her. 'I'm so sorry, Stirling,' she said. 'Neil was so much more than just a brother to you.' She put her arms out to comfort him, but he stepped away, rested a hand on the newel post of the stairs. He suddenly felt he couldn't bear to be touched.

'Would you do your best to get rid of anyone who still hasn't left,' he said. 'Please don't say anything about Neil; it'll come out soon enough. For now it's private, a family matter. If you need me, I'll be upstairs with Pen and Mum.'

'Of course, darling. Leave everything to me.'

He forced himself to smile his gratitude, to show he appreciated her support. His wife had always been so competent and steadfast. Admittedly she could be a little cold around the edges, but he'd always been able to rely on her to do the right thing. Though God knew how she would react to the news that currently he had a secret illegitimate daughter standing in their kitchen who he'd fathered in the early years of their marriage.

He took the stairs slowly, his legs weary and leaden. In the space of a few short hours his life had been turned upside down, and he had absolutely no idea how he was going to contain not just the fallout of Neil's death and the fraud Rosco had uncovered, but the consequences of the child he'd never known showing up. She had said she hadn't come here to cause trouble, but one thing he was convinced of: trouble most assuredly lay ahead.

He knocked on the door of the guest room, and at his mother's response, he went in. She and Pen were sitting on the window seat, the curtains drawn. Pen was on the telephone; she wasn't crying any more. Cecily got up and came over to him. 'She's talking to Lloyd,' she said. 'Where's the tea?'

'On its way. The waitress you told me to talk to is bringing it,' he added.

They stared at each other.

'And?' Cecily said meaningfully.

'How did you know about me and Fay?' he asked without preamble, his voice low so that Pen wouldn't hear.

'Later,' she said. 'We'll discuss that later. Do you know what you're going to do about the girl?'

'That's up to her, isn't it?'

Cecily's eyes narrowed. 'You've gone all this time without acknowledging her; it would be an act of great wickedness to continue doing so now.'

'What about Gina? What do I say to her?'

'The truth. Which she'll have to learn to live with. Rosco and Scarlet, too. But I tell you this: I for one won't pretend she doesn't exist. She's my granddaughter, and for the little time I still have left on earth, I want to get to know her.'

'I didn't pretend she didn't exist,' he said defensively. 'I didn't wilfully turn my back on her. It was Fay who wanted me to have nothing to do with the baby. She insisted on that; she wanted a clean break for the sake of her marriage.'

There was a soft knock at the door. Stirling opened it, guessing who it would be. He was right.

'Your tea,' she said.

He took the tray from her. He didn't want her waiting on him. Bad enough that he'd had to treat her as a waitress down in the kitchen just now in front of those two women. 'Come in,' he said.

She glanced warily into the room. She didn't look as confident as she had downstairs.

Cecily moved forward. 'Come in,' she repeated. 'We won't bite you.'

From the window seat, Pen ended her call with a strained goodbye. She said, 'Lloyd says he'll be on the first plane he can get a seat on.' She looked at Stirling holding the tray of tea things, then at who had brought it. She tilted her head to one side, just as he had seen her do a million times before when she was trying to remember something. 'Aren't you the girl who came to my house this afternoon?' she asked. 'What are you doing here?'

Not knowing what Pen was referring to, Stirling put the tray down on the ottoman at the end of the bed and said, 'Let me pour you some tea, Pen.'

From behind him, and without answering Pen, Katie said, 'I'll leave you to it, then.'

Stirling turned round quickly, knocking one of the cups with his hand. 'No! Not yet.' He righted the cup in its saucer. 'How will I be able to contact you?'

'Maybe you need time to decide if you really want to,' she replied evenly.

'Don't be ridiculous,' Cecily cut in. 'Of course he's going to want to get in touch with you. And if he doesn't, I most certainly do. Do you live in the Henley area?'

'I live in Brighton.'

'So where are you staying tonight?'

'I planned to drive home. That was before I got roped in to being a waitress for the evening. None of this was supposed to happen. I'm really sorry. I'm sorry now that I came. It was a mistake. But I was curious. I just wanted to see what you

93

looked like.' She looked over at Pen. 'I'm really sorry about your husband.'

'Stirling,' Cecily said, 'we can't have Katie driving back to Brighton when it's so late. She must stay here with us.'

'And how the hell do I explain that to Gina?'

'When I say *us*, I mean *me*. I have a perfectly serviceable spare room. She can stay there with me.'

'But Mum, I want you to stay here tonight. I don't want you on your own.'

'I won't be on my own if Katie accepts my invitation.'

'I'm quite capable of driving home.'

'I'm sure you are,' Cecily said, 'but I think tonight of all nights, I'd like the company.'

'But you don't know me from a bar of soap.'

'All the more reason for us to get better acquainted.'

'Mum, are you sure?'

'When am I never sure of a thing, Stirling? Now please get on and pour that tea before it's stone cold and is neither use nor ornament.'

'I know I'm not myself right now,' Pen said, her voice fluttery with tired confusion, 'but would someone explain to me what's going on?'

Nothing else for it, Stirling thought: time to take the bull by the horns. He knew if he didn't, his mother would do so anyway. At least he could trust Pen to keep a secret. 'Pen,' he said, 'this is Katie Lavender. She and I have just met for the first time this evening. She's my daughter from an affair I had thirty years ago. But you mustn't breathe a word of this to anyone, not yet at any rate.'

'Oh my,' Pen said.

'Oh my, indeed,' he echoed.

Chapter Fourteen

A habitual early riser, Cecily woke a little after six o'clock the following morning.

Through her bedroom wall she could hear the faint sound of her neighbour's television. Every morning Marjorie, also an early riser, started her day watching one of those energetically upbeat breakfast news programmes. Cecily preferred the radio; she liked her news to be succinct and to the point, clearly enunciated and intoned with just the right amount of gravitas. She found it patronizing when it was wrapped in a sugary coating of shallow lifestyle twaddle. Who needed a fashion tip first thing in the morning?

The South Lodge community tom-toms would probably be thrumming with activity this morning as to why the party had been wound up the way it had last night, and doubtless Marjorie would knock on Cecily's door later. It was comforting and reassuring when people were concerned, but too much concern was never a good thing. When the time was right, explanations would be made, but for now Cecily wanted her friends and neighbours to leave her alone.

All that mattered now was her family. It was all that had ever mattered to her. In particular her sons' health and happiness; anything else was a bonus. Long ago she had learnt that even in the happiest lives there could be periods of great sadness and anxiety. And often concealed. Even though she had recently begun to feel that Neil was keeping something from her, something important, not once had she thought he was so tormented that he would believe ending his life was the answer to whatever was troubling him. Had she had the merest inkling of his intentions, she would have moved heaven and earth to drag him back from the brink. But the sad truth was, once a person had decided on a course of self-destruction, there was very little anyone could do to prevent that fateful step being taken.

Last night Stirling had been quick to blame himself for not seeing the signs, but he was wrong to do so. She would have to make sure she disabused him of that impulse before it took root too deeply. He was no more to blame than she was.

Right from the word go, from the day she and her husband had brought Neil home with them, Stirling had looked out for his brother. He would run and tell her the second Neil started to cry for his feed. He would watch over him if Cecily had to answer the telephone or deal with someone at the door. He would help fold the terry nappies and patiently soothe Neil if he was fractious. Neil's eyes would follow his brother round the room, and just as soon as he was able to crawl and then subsequently walk, he would tag along wherever Stirling went. Another child might have felt threatened or misplaced by the arrival of a younger sibling, but not Stirling; he loved his brother. One bedtime, when Stirling was four and they'd just celebrated Neil's first birthday, Stirling said, 'We're lucky to have Neil, aren't we, Mummy?' She had kissed him and said, 'Yes, we are. But then your daddy and I are lucky to have both of you.'

'But Neil is different, isn't he?' Stirling had said. 'He's special.'

'You're both special, and don't you forget it.'

As they grew older, there was never any rivalry between them, Stirling had been too confident in his own ability to feel threatened by a younger brother, and in turn Neil had admired his older brother too much to want to do anything that would annoy him. People often commented how exceptionally well they got on, and that bond continued through their teens, their twenties and beyond. Right up until now.

That was why Stirling was taking Neil's death so hard.

Perhaps it was that bond that had been Neil's final undoing. Perhaps the guilt of his actions – taking money that wasn't his – meant there was no way back, that he would never be able to face Stirling again. But Cecily knew that Stirling would have forgiven Neil for anything. And in a heartbeat. He would have found a way to put things right.

But why had Neil been taking money from clients' accounts? What had possessed him to do such a thing? Maybe if they could get to the bottom of that, they might find a way to comprehend what had pushed him to the point of no return.

Tossing aside the bedclothes, Cecily swung her legs out of bed, placed her feet on the soft carpeted floor and sat bolt upright, stretching her back.

Ninety years old, she thought. Ninety. She had outlived her husband and countless friends, but to outlive her younger son went against the natural order of things. It was wrong. It wasn't meant to be like this. Thank God she still had Stirling. And Pen, and Lloyd. They were the three people who now meant the most to her. Gina she tolerated, as she did Rosco and Scarlet. Maybe she would love Scarlet and Charlie's child. Maybe.

The commonly held view was that blood was thicker than water; however, Cecily violently disagreed with this. To believe such nonsense made an insulting mockery of her love for Neil. And for Lloyd. It pained her to ask herself the question, but had Neil felt less loved than Stirling? She would stake her life on her having loved the two boys equally – fiercely and constantly – yet was there a possibility that Neil imagined that the strength of her love for him was exaggerated in some way, a subconscious overcompensation on her part? She hoped not. She hoped that in his last moments he knew that he was loved, no matter what he'd done. But wouldn't that have made his final moments crueller still? To know too late that he would be forgiven? Tears filled her eyes. Oh Neil, why? Why didn't you come to me? Didn't I repeatedly tell you when you were a child that I would always be there for you? You only had to ask.

In her mind's eye, she pictured Neil as a small baby, help-less and vulnerable, entirely dependent on her for his survival. If she thought very hard, she could imagine the weight of that baby in her arms, even the smell of him. He'd been consider-ably underweight at birth, but within weeks she had got him to what had been considered his correct weight. He had been such a loving and rewarding baby.

For some years she and her husband had tried to start a family, and just when they were on the verge of giving up and considering adoption, Cecily had discovered she was pregnant with Stirling. Overjoyed with his arrival, they vowed they would make their family complete by adopting. Their hearts were set on giving an unwanted child the chance of a life it would otherwise be denied. The odds then seemed to be stacked against them, as they went through a series of heartbreaking disappointments – young mothers who had agreed to give up their baby for adoption but who changed their minds at the last minute. Her sadness aside, Cecily had felt no anger or animosity towards those young girls, only a bittersweet understanding as to why they had realized at the eleventh hour that the baby they had given birth to was wholly precious. Then finally they were blessed with a baby boy. It had been Stirling who had named him, and to this day they didn't know where he'd got the name from. But Neil was Neil from then on, and he fitted into their family as if he had always been meant to be a part of it.

So no, Cecily had no truck with blood ties being stronger than any other kind. Adoption went so much deeper than mere bonds of blood.

And yet, she had instantly felt something towards the girl who was now sleeping in her spare room. How to explain that? How to explain that mysterious feeling of knowing her? Of feeling a connection? And not just because she had recognized her younger self in the girl. It had been a far more profound feeling than mere recognition.

Katie Lavender. It was an interesting name. It conjured up a creative and generous-hearted temperament, a girl of steady and even temper. In comparison, Scarlet could only ever be a flighty, self-centred individual, and Rosco a dynamic, ambitious young tyke. While Lloyd's name suggested a young man thoroughly at ease with himself. Which was Lloyd all over. He knew just who he was and understood exactly what was important in life.

At this late stage in Cecily's own life, was Katie Lavender one last blessing for her? Was she to lose a much-loved son but be given a new granddaughter?

When Katie had been persuaded to accept the invitation to stay the night with her at South Lodge, and long after the last of the guests had been rounded up and sent home in their taxis, the two of them had quietly slipped away whilst Gina and Rosco and Scarlet were talking to Charlie and his parents. Katie had driven the short journey, and other than Cecily giving her directions, they hadn't talked in the car, but once they'd arrived, and after Katie admitted that she hadn't eaten anything that evening and Cecily had rustled up a sandwich and a slice of cake that Marjorie had made for her yesterday, they had sat in the kitchen and talked. Katie had said straight away how sorry she was about her son. 'I know what it's like to lose people you love,' she'd said, 'how much it hurts.'

There had been a genuine look of empathy and sadness in her face, and Cecily had wanted to know more, if only to distract herself from thinking about Neil. Katie had then explained that both her parents were dead, her mother had died only a year ago. She had then told Cecily about being summoned to the solicitor's office out of the blue last week, and that being the first she knew that her father hadn't been her biological father. She had also mentioned about a trust fund Stirling had set up for her. At least he had done the right thing there, Cecily had thought. Although, of course, money couldn't make amends for everything.

'Did you know my mother?' Katie had asked.

'Just a little,' she had replied. 'Fay was Stirling's PA. If ever I had cause to ring him at work, I often spoke with her. There were times, too, when I met her in the office.'

'I never knew that my parents lived in Henley,' Katie had said with a frown.

'They didn't. As far as I can remember, they lived in or near Maidenhead. In those days that was where Stirling and Neil had their office.'

Cecily had gone on to say how she had guessed there was more than just a work relationship between Stirling and Fay Lavender. There was a rapport between them that was unmistakable. And then, a chance in a million, she had seen them one day. She had been visiting a friend in Reading for lunch and spotted them in a restaurant together. The thing that had struck her most was how right they looked together. Stirling had had a hand to Fay's chin and was about to kiss her; it was such a tender gesture. She had never seen him like that with Gina.

'Do you think they loved each other?' Katie had asked.

'You'd have to ask Stirling that,' she had said.

Up and dressed and in the kitchen with Radio 4 on, Cecily thought now about that question. She had always been sure that as fleeting as their relationship had been, Stirling had loved Fay. Had things been different, Cecily would have preferred Fay as her daughter-in-law instead of Gina. Gina had been one of those young, beautiful women who drew men to her, like bees and the proverbial honeypot. She would have been the girl at school with whom everyone wanted to be friends, the one all the boys dreamt of asking out. In other words, she had been a catch. Stirling's temperament in those days had been to strive to have the best of things in life, and Gina would have epitomized the best wife he could have, the perfect partner to support him in his plans for the future. But as beautiful and intelligent as she was, as excellent a homemaker and hostess as she was, she hadn't been a soulmate; Cecily had known that from the word go. That, perhaps, had been what Stirling had found in Fay.

Not once had Cecily felt it was her place to say anything to her son. Everyone had secrets, and she hadn't seen any reason why she should poke about in Stirling's. The only time she had felt inclined to let him know that she knew about him and Fay was when he suddenly wasn't his usual patient self, and he began spending longer and longer at the office, all at a time when Rosco was proving to be an exceptionally demanding baby and Gina was struggling to cope and probably longing for the days when she had been an air stewardess and travelled the world in the company of well-behaved first-class passengers. Sensing trouble, Cecily had stepped in and helped to take the pressure off Gina – it was the only time Gina had ever accepted help from her. Stirling's change in behaviour, Cecily later realized, had coincided with Fay handing in her notice. Now Cecily wondered if that was when Fay discovered she was pregnant and ended the affair with Stirling. Had he been devastated? Had he ever confided in Neil? Had that been a secret between the two of them? Was that why it hurt so much for Stirling that Neil hadn't been able to reciprocate and turn to him when he needed help?

Katie woke to find herself tangled in a long, flower-sprigged cotton nightdress. It was new, and still had the price tag on when Cecily gave it to her last night. 'An unworn Christmas present,' she'd said, snipping off the tag, 'and not what you're used to, I'm sure. Rosco gives me the same thing every year. I prefer silk, so much nicer against the skin, don't you think? I usually donate the wretched things to Help the Aged, but this one slipped through the net.'

Katie didn't normally bother with wearing anything in bed – occasionally she'd put on an old T-shirt if she was cold – but for the sake of propriety, she had worn the nightdress just in case she needed to get up for the toilet in the middle of the night.

As she wriggled around in the large double bed with its intricately carved mahogany headboard, trying to straighten out the nightdress, she felt like a small child again, cosseted in an older person's world.

It was funny to think that Cecily was officially her grandmother. The grandparents she had grown up with had all died. For most of her childhood Fay's mother had nursed her husband through Parkinson's. When he'd died, and imagining that she was now free to live an easier life, she had booked a cruise on the Nile, something she had dreamt of doing ever since Katie could remember. But two days before she was due to leave, she had a stroke and died three weeks later. On Dad's side of the family, his mother had died when he'd been a teenager and then his father had dropped dead of a heart attack during Katie's first year at university. He'd gone to the doctor's surgery with chest pains, and whilst he'd been in the waiting room he'd simply let out a sudden gasp, slipped off his chair and died.

All in all, Katie felt as if she had encountered more than her fair share of death. Worse than that, she was beginning to think she attracted it. Within hours of arriving here, the grim reaper had tiptoed up behind her and whispered in her ear, 'Coo-ee, remember me, old friend?' Admittedly she hadn't known the man who'd died, but technically he had been her uncle.

Cecily seemed to be taking his death well, but Katie knew better than most that appearances could be deceiving. Cecily was very likely being strong for the family, just as Katie had done for her mother when Dad had died. Katie didn't know what it felt like to lose a brother or a sister, but last night Cecily had said that Neil had been Stirling's best friend, so the thought of Tess or Zac dying was the closest she could get to imagining how awful the loss must be for him.

And what about Ian? she thought guiltily as she stared at

the gap in the curtains where sunlight was streaming through. Does he not get a mention? How would she feel if he died today? Sad. Yes, she'd definitely be sad. But perhaps mostly because she felt guilty about how she had treated him the other evening. She regretted now the way she'd taken her shock out on him. He really hadn't deserved that.

She slid to the edge of the bed and reached down to the floor where her handbag lay. She fished out her mobile, which she'd put on to silent mode whilst working last night. She had four text messages and all from Tess. The first two were to say how fantastic Barcelona was. The next was to ask where she was and why hadn't she replied. The last message was: CALL ME!

She switched the phone off. As close as she was to Tess, she didn't feel able to explain to her just what she'd got into here. Come to that, she didn't know herself what she'd got into and what the outcome would be.

Her first dilemma of this new and strange day was: should she stay on for a while as Cecily had mentioned last night, or should she get going straight after breakfast? It didn't feel right to stay when the family was in the midst of such a terrible tragedy. The death of a loved one was difficult enough at the best of times, but the aftermath of a suicide was far harder to bear for those left behind because seldom could anyone make sense of it.

Although in this instance, given the conversation she had overheard between Stirling and his son, the man's death could be rationalized to a certain extent. It would be a lot for the family to come to terms with.

A knock at the door had her turning away from the window. 'Yes,' she said, sitting up.

Cecily came in, fully dressed and instantly putting Katie to shame that she was still lazing in bed. 'Tea,' the old lady announced. 'I hope I didn't wake you.' She carefully placed the mug on a coaster on the bedside table, a faint tremble to her liver-spotted hand causing the tea to quiver in the mug.

'Not at all,' Katie said. 'Anyway, I should be up. I should be going.'

'You keep saying that, that you should be going. Are you always in such a hurry to leave a place you've scarcely set foot in?'

'No, but in the circumstances I'm sure you have better things to do than take care of a tiresome house guest.'

The old lady slowly lowered herself to sit on the edge of the bed. 'Katie,' she said, 'you are not a tiresome house guest, you are my granddaughter and I'd really like us to get to know each other better. I'm not a fanciful woman, prone to irrationality, but I believe you turning up here at a time of crisis for this family was meant to be. I really feel that you've come into our lives for a reason.' She patted Katie's hand. 'And now you think I'm a dotty old dear, don't you?'

Katie smiled. 'No one would ever think that of you. Least of all me.'

Cecily smiled too. But it was a fleeting smile shot through with great sorrow. 'Drink your tea and then we'll have some breakfast,' she said.

By the time she had emerged from the shower and was dressed, Katie could smell bacon.

'I love this kitchen,' Cecily said as with a wooden spatula she indicated the chair Katie had sat in last night. 'In my old house I had an enormous and very draughty kitchen and was forever toing and froing. This is so wonderfully compact. And so lovely and warm. As one ages, one becomes stupidly resistant to change, but I freely admit I should have moved to a smaller place years ago.'

Katie said, 'That's what Mum did when Dad died. She needed a fresh start.'

Cecily put their plates of bacon and scrambled eggs on the table and sat down. 'We all do at some stage in our lives. How about you, do you need a fresh start, Katie?'

It was a good question. And one Katie thought about

before answering. 'Well,' she said at last, 'I've just been made redundant, I've found out the man I thought was my father wasn't and I think the relationship with my boyfriend has run its course. We had a big argument before I came here. But the thing is, he was there for me after my mother died, he helped me a lot. I'll always be grateful for that. Which makes me feel bad for arguing with him. Though really it was only a matter of time before we argued about something and had a bust-up. Better to argue about something important than something petty.' She took a breath, realizing that she had admitted more to this woman than she had to Tess. With Tess, she always felt she had to defend Ian. 'So,' she said, 'probably the answer is yes, yes I do need to make a fresh start.'

Cecily passed her the salt and pepper. 'As I said earlier, you've been led here for a reason.'

They were tidying the kitchen when the phone rang. Cecily went to answer it. 'Hello, Stirling,' Katie heard her say. And then, 'Of course she's been no bother ... What sort of bother were you expecting her to be? ... Yes, I should imagine she can hear every word of this conversation, she's standing no more than twelve feet away from me.' Cecily glanced over at Katie. Then, adopting a more serious tone, she said, 'How's Pen this morning? ... That's good ... And what about identifying Neil's ... Neil's body? I really think we should spare her that, don't you? ... *No!* I don't want you doing it alone. I shall come with you ... Stirling, I'm not going to argue with you. Now, what time do we need to go?'

Chapter Fifteen

Stirling had barely slept; he'd been kept awake by the same thought buzzing like a trapped bluebottle inside his head: how could he protect his brother's reputation?

If – when – word got out, not just about his death, but about the missing client money, the memory of Neil would forever be tarnished. He didn't want that for his brother and he didn't want it for Pen and Lloyd or Cecily. He wanted Neil to be remembered for being the man he'd always been, funny, generous, warm-hearted and loyal. That had been the real Neil, that was how he had to be remembered.

Earlier, dead on seven o'clock, Rosco had called him, not on the landline but on his mobile so as not to disturb the rest of the house. Stirling had been downstairs in the kitchen making himself a cup of coffee when his mobile rang – his wife had still been asleep upstairs, and with no noise coming from the spare room, he'd hoped Pen was also sleeping. He had been glad of his son's company, even on the phone. He'd needed someone to talk to.

But the conversation with Rosco hadn't helped. It had made him feel worse. Far worse. Since sharing the news of Neil's death late last night when the party was over with Rosco and Scarlet and Charlie, Rosco – in his own words – had had time to think about the consequences. The upshot was, Rosco's main concern was that the reputation of Nightingale Ridgeway was in danger of being destroyed. 'Dad, I don't think you understand the seriousness of what Neil's done. This could ruin us.'

Stirling had told him not to exaggerate, that they'd find a way to sort things out.

'Are you kidding?' Rosco had fired back. 'He defrauded clients and committed suicide! How can you sort that out? This can only ever escalate. What the hell had that bloody man been thinking? Shit! If he wasn't already dead, I'd kill him myself!'

That was when Stirling had lost it. 'That *bloody man*, as you call him, was your uncle! He was my brother and I never want to hear you talk about him that way again. You'll show some respect. Do I make myself clear?'

'OK, OK, I'm sorry,' Rosco had capitulated, 'but I just hope you're not underestimating the situation. We have to keep this mess under our control. If we don't, we'll have clients leaving us in their droves. On top of everything else, it's a disaster!'

For the first time ever, Stirling felt proprietorial. Who was Rosco to dictate how things should be done at Nightingale Ridgeway? He and Neil had created the company; it was theirs. Whatever Rosco believed, the company was not his. Not yet at any rate.

Rosco's parting words were, 'I'll check in with you later. When you're back.' There had been no word of encouragement from him. No word of sympathy about the grim task ahead for Stirling that day – identifying the body of his brother. Had Rosco always been so unthinking? Stirling had asked himself when he'd gone outside to the garden to drink his coffee.

He still felt annoyed by the conversation as he drove through the gates of South Lodge, passing the shuttle bus that was on its way into the centre of Henley with a full load of elderly passengers. In the past when anything had bothered him, Stirling had always turned to Neil. The realization that he would never be able to do that again sliced through him with the swiftness of a dagger blow. What did people do when they lost someone who meant so much to them? How did they ever get over it?

He thought of Katie. How had she coped with losing her

parents in such quick succession? Who had she turned to? The friends she had mentioned last night who were like family to her?

He sighed. Family. Katie deserved her place in the Nightingale family now, but what would be the consequences of him instigating that? Thirty years ago he had wanted to take that risk; it had seemed a risk worth taking because he had wanted to have Fay permanently in his life. He had offered to leave Gina to be with her, but Fay had refused to listen, saying she wouldn't be responsible for destroying his marriage along with her own. Despite everything, and as much as it pained Stirling, she had said she loved her husband and couldn't bring herself to hurt him by leaving him. 'Let me go,' she'd begged. 'Let me disappear completely from your life.' And he had. He'd done it because he'd loved her. Just as her own husband had loved her and had been prepared to forgive her the affair. She'd had no choice but to tell Desmond about their relationship and the baby she was carrying, she'd explained to Stirling; she couldn't stay married without being completely honest with him. Stirling had always admired her for that. She had been capable of more honesty than him.

But now he was going to have to be honest. And who knew what the price would be? The manner in which he delivered the news to his family would be key. It was vital that he kept the damage limitation to a minimum. Damage limitation – two words he never thought would mean so much to him.

Not long after Fay ended their affair, she and her husband moved away, just as she'd said they would. Stirling had had no idea where they went, but in the twelve months that followed, he couldn't stop thinking about the child he would never know. Somewhere in the world, there was a part of him that was living and breathing. It nearly drove him mad. But then Gina told him she was pregnant again, and he knew he had to forget Fay and their child and concentrate on his own family. He threw himself into that and the business. Gradually he surfaced from the madness and accepted that this was the life he was meant to have. When Scarlet was born, he promised himself he would never do anything again that would jeopardize his family. It was a surprisingly easy promise to keep, because every time he looked at his beautiful baby daughter, he felt a powerful surge of tender love for her. There were times when he held her and was moved to tears, knowing that had he left Gina, Scarlet would never have been born and he would have been denied such a joyful gift. There were other times when he didn't think he deserved such happiness.

Occasionally he would wonder what he would do if, in years to come, the child he had created with Fay turned up on his doorstep. How would he react? He alternated between fear of discovery and losing the happy equilibrium of his life, and wanting it to happen so that his curiosity would be satisfied. When eighteen years had passed; he wondered then if he would get a knock on the door or a telephone call. But there had been nothing, and part of him was relieved. His secret was still safe. Three years later, when their child would be twenty-one, he wondered again if this would be the time he or she would appear. But nothing.

He then reasoned that either Fay had never told their child the truth, or he or she knew but had decided not to look for him. Which wasn't any different to Neil having no interest in meeting his birth mother, something he never did. 'What's the point?' he'd once said with a shrug. 'What would we have to say to each another?'

Now and then Stirling had entertained the idea of his unknown son or daughter discreetly getting in touch and the pair of them arranging to meet in secret and instantly getting along, both happy with the secrecy of the relationship.

Had it been cowardly and selfish of him to want to do everything on his own terms, to have his child only partially in his life, to conduct a secret father-and-child relationship so that his family wouldn't be hurt and that no one would think badly of him for having strayed in his marriage? Cake and eat it was the shameful and only conclusion to that question.

Cecily greeted him with a hug and a reprimand. 'You haven't slept, have you?'

'Not much,' he conceded, gripping her tightly, wanting to communicate the depth of his feelings, that he appreciated she was the kind of tough and spirited woman she was, that she wouldn't let him go through the impending ordeal alone.

She led him through to the sitting room. He saw Katie on the balcony looking out at the landscaped gardens. The morning sun was on her and she looked radiant, almost unearthly. For a moment all he wanted to do was stand and stare. Her loose hair fell almost to the small of her back, it was thick and full of waves and curls, and in the sunlight it blazed with a vibrancy that defied description. Certainly he wasn't capable of doing it justice. But he knew from old photographs that Cecily's hair had once been that same length and eye-catching colour. His father had often joked that it was a miracle he was alive, as the first time he'd set eyes on Cecily – as a medical student in Oxford and when he'd had a thing about the Pre-Raphaelites – he'd been so entranced by her hair he'd fallen off his bicycle on Magdalen Bridge and had been lucky to break only an arm.

On the balcony, Katie turned, and when she saw Stirling she gave him a hesitant half-smile. Something inside him stirred. His daughter. His and Fay's daughter. He couldn't understand now how he hadn't known straight away who she was when he'd first seen her last night. But then he supposed he had known on a subconscious level, because he'd had the strongest feeling they'd met before.

She stepped inside and they moved slowly towards each other. How should he greet her? What was the etiquette here? An awkward and formal handshake? Or a casual and inadequate 'hi'? He knew what he wanted to do and that was to hug her, but was that appropriate?

The moment was lost with a ring at the doorbell. 'I expect

that will be Marjorie, wanting to know how I am,' his mother said.

Whilst Cecily was out in the hall, he said, 'This feels awkward this morning. I don't know how to be around you.'

'I feel the same way,' she said. 'Perhaps we shouldn't worry too much. For now you have more important things to think about. How's your sister-in-law?'

'She's gone back to The Meadows.'

'To the comfort of her garden,' Katie said quietly.

It was a statement, not a question. It surprised him. 'You know about Pen and her garden?'

'It's a long story and I was about to tell you it last night, but that was when your wife came in.'

'Yes,' he said, remembering Gina's face as she took in the scene. Katie had, to his gratitude, quickly resumed her role as a waitress and said that if there wasn't anything else, she'd leave them to their tea. 'So tell me now,' he said.

'Well, I knew from the internet about a Mrs Penelope Nightingale who had a garden that she opened to the public, so I went there yesterday pretending I had a delivery for you and had inadvertently got the wrong address. I feel awful that I lied to her to find you. She seems such a lovely person.'

'She is, and I'm sure she'll forgive you for the small white lie you told her.' A thought occurred to him. 'Do you have anything planned for today?' he asked.

'Not really. Other than going home to Brighton.'

'Do you have to go today? Could you bear to stay on a little longer?'

'Your mother wants me to, but I feel I'm imposing, what with everything that's going on.'

'If I said I wanted you to stay, would you?'

Again the hesitant half-smile and a gentleness in her expression. An expression that reminded him of her mother. 'On the understanding that I make myself useful,' she said.

'In that case, I can think of something very useful you could do for me.'

The first thing Katie did was to drive into Henley. If she was going to stay the night again, she needed a few essential items, such as a change of underwear and maybe a top, and some toiletries and a basic make-up kit.

With everything she needed in two bags on the back seat of her car, she negotiated the one-way traffic system of the town. She drove along the river until she came to a set of traffic lights by a bridge. Across the road she saw a pub called the Angel on the Bridge. She wondered idly what it was like, recalling Dee referring to it last night as her favourite pub in Henley.

She had felt a little guilty continuing with the pretence last night while saying goodbye to Dee, but what else could she do? One word about her being Stirling's daughter to a gossip like Dee and the whole of Henley would know about it! As soon as Sue and Merrill had finished loading up the van and had tidied the kitchen, they gave Dee and Katie their wages – both of them now changed out of their waitress uniforms – and drove off with Dee following slowly behind on her bicycle, her rear light flickering in the dark. If they'd wondered why Katie wasn't leaving at the same time, they hadn't said anything. Back inside the house, Stirling had reappeared with Cecily for her to take home, having sneaked her away while the rest of the family were occupied elsewhere.

The traffic lights changed from red to green and she turned left over the bridge, following the sign for Sandiford, where Pen Nightingale was expecting her at The Meadows. Katie had been instructed to walk round to the back of the house, just as she had done yesterday.

'It was sweet of Stirling to think I'd like the company,' Pen said to Katie, kicking off her gardening shoes at the back door and leading the way to the kitchen in her bare feet, 'but I'm sure you must have better things to do with your time than babysit me.'

Watching her go over to the sink to wash the dusty soil from her hands, Katie thought how she must have taken refuge in her garden the minute she had returned. There was no mistaking that her husband's death had aged her overnight. Her face was pale and drawn, her eyes red and puffy, and her voice was huskier than it had been yesterday, probably hoarse from crying. For all that, she was giving a good performance of a woman seemingly now in control of her emotions.

'I don't think babysitting was quite what Stirling had in mind for me, Mrs Nightingale. I think he wanted you to make use of me.' Actually what Stirling had as good as said was that he thought Katie might provide a useful distraction for his sister-in-law.

The woman dried her hands on an old towel. In comparison to Willow Bank, the kitchen here had not been updated in many years; everything had definitely seen better days. The cream-coloured cupboards were knocked about in places, with the paintwork chipped and marked, and a large dresser taking up most of a wall from floor to ceiling was home to an untidy library of gardening books and horticultural magazines. There wasn't a cookery book to be seen on the cluttered shelves. On the pine table in the centre of the kitchen was a hand-written poster advertising the open day for the garden next Saturday. Presumably that would have to be cancelled now.

Her hands dried, she hooked the towel over the back of a chair. 'Please, call me Pen. What kind of use of you did Stirling have in mind?'

'He thought I could help you in the garden.'

She gave Katie a wary look, as if contemplating the horror of a clumsy novice wrecking her pride and joy. 'Do you know anything about gardening?'

'A bit.' Katie explained about her mother's love of gardening and how it had rubbed off on her. She described the small courtyard garden back in Brighton. 'Mum was a good teacher and I like to think I'm a good student. I know I'm still learning.'

Pen nodded thoughtfully as if satisfied with Katie's response. 'Yes. Well.' She cleared her throat. 'That's what a true gardener would say. We never stop learning, there's always something new to find out.' She filled the kettle and put it on the Rayburn. She then straightened her back, drew in her breath and exhaled with a shudder that seemed to come from the very depths of her being. She turned to stare out of the window, her expression intensely sad. A heavy silence swept into the kitchen and for a long, long moment it was as if she had forgotten anyone else was there. But as though suddenly snapping back into the here and now, she looked at Katie, her eyes pools of anguish. 'I still can't get over the fact that you're Stirling's child, that he had an affair. Have you always known he was your father?'

Katie shook her head and told her story all over again. When she'd finished, and when she had apologized for her deception yesterday, Pen said, 'I wouldn't be surprised if a love child of Neil's pops up in the coming days.' Her words had no bitterness to them, just a weary echo of sad acceptance.

'Why do you think that?'

Tears filled Pen's eyes. 'Because I wasn't a good wife to him. I put all my energy and passion into that.' She pointed at the beautiful garden through the window. 'I always convinced myself that he didn't mind. But he must have minded. I didn't put him first. Not even second. I neglected him. And now he's dead and I can never say how sorry I am. He killed himself because of me. I made him so unhappy. He must have been suffering inconceivable agony.' Her face contorted and she began to cry.

Katie went to her. 'Please don't think that,' she said inadequately. 'I'm sure it wasn't you who made him unhappy. It's never just one thing that makes a person do what he did.'

The poor woman sagged heavily against her and sobbed.

Oh dear, thought Katie. Stirling had been right when he

said he didn't think Pen should be left on her own today. But as a stranger to this poor distraught woman, how could she possibly help her?

How long, she wondered, before the son arrived home from New Zealand?

Chapter Sixteen

All around him people were buckling up and preparing themselves for the eleven-hour journey ahead.

It was almost midnight, and finally Lloyd was on his way.
Or he would be providing there wasn't another hold-up. The
flight had already been delayed by two hours with a fuelling
problem. The captain had just assured them the problem had
been fixed and they would be ready for take-off in the next
twenty minutes.

Lucky to have got the last available seat, Lloyd was wedged
in between a rake-thin woman who was fidgeting nervously
and a hulk of a teenage boy with a scalped head and two
large diamond studs in his ear lobes. At odds with the chilly
weather they would soon be leaving behind them, the boy was
wearing the biggest and baggiest shorts Lloyd had ever seen
and a loose-fitting vest top. His bare arms and legs sported
a range of tattoos – decorative Chinese characters that most
likely didn't say what he thought they did. In the row of seats
behind him, Lloyd could hear an overly loud man telling a
fellow passenger about the Pilates classes he attended. He had
clocked the man when he'd sat down: a leathery grey-haired
hippie type sporting a goatee and a ponytail. Not even in the
air yet, and already Lloyd was heartily sick of the sound of
the man's voice and had to fight the urge to tell him to shut
the hell up.

Since receiving the call from his mother, Lloyd had allowed
himself only to deal with the immediate problem of finding
a flight, packing and saying goodbye to his friends – not just

John and Emma, whose wedding it had been, but the group with whom he'd flown out. They'd all planned to stay on to explore Wellington, then drive down to Christchurch and back up to Auckland before flying home. Lloyd had managed to keep the news of his father from John and Emma, saying only that a family emergency required him to leave – he hadn't wanted their wedding day to be marred by death. They were currently on their way to Bali for their honeymoon. He'd tell them the truth when the time was right.

But now with nothing to occupy him – only counting down the hours from here to Singapore and then on to Heathrow – time stretched dauntingly ahead for Lloyd. With nothing to do, there would be no avoiding the shock of his father's death and the big question: why? Why had he done it?

With no sign yet of the plane taxiing to take off, he took out his mobile to send his mother one last message, to put her mind at rest that he really would be on his way soon. He'd spoken to her earlier to see how she was, and she'd said that she was back at home now. Which meant she was probably distracting herself in the garden.

One look at the screen of his mobile and he saw that he'd received a text message; it was from Rosco and it was worryingly long. He read it, and then because he simply couldn't believe it, he read it again.

But still he didn't believe what he was reading. It had to be a mistake; his father wouldn't have done that. Fraud? Taking clients' money? Not in a million years. Not Dad. Dad wouldn't take a toothpick from a restaurant.

He sat back in his seat, stunned. What the hell had been going on in his father's head lately? And why the hell did it have to be Rosco to tell Lloyd about it?

You probably know by now that your dad had been embezzling clients' money, Rosco had written. *It explains why he took the easy way out and killed himself, but not why he took the money in the first place. Any ideas?*

Choking anger took hold of Lloyd. Only Rosco could behave with such obscene insensitivity. Not a word of sympathy for the death of a member of the family, a man Rosco had known all his life. No thought given to the fact that this was Lloyd's father who had died. Rosco could have been referring to a stranger.

Anger was good, Lloyd told himself. Anger would get him through the journey. It would get him home, and then he'd beat the shit out of his cousin. Yeah, he'd do that the minute he was back. First he'd thrash the arrogance out of him. Then the superiority. Followed by his condescension. And none of it would be personal. Nothing personal at all. Not much.

Lloyd was known within the family for being steady and easy-going, but when push came to shove, he could shove with the best of them. It was all a matter of who was doing the pushing against him. And it wouldn't be the first time he and Rosco had had a falling-out.

'I'm sorry, sir, you're going to have to switch that off now.'

He looked up at the smiling stewardess and nodded polite acquiescence. When she'd moved further down the aisle, he quickly sent Rosco a message. *Thanks for your support in this difficult time,* he wrote. *Mum and I appreciate it.* He hit send. Oh yeah, he was royally pissed off.

The stewardess was heading back his way. He switched off his mobile and stuffed it in the inside pocket of his leather jacket, only then to realize he had wasted the opportunity to send a message to his mother. Now he'd have to wait until they landed in Singapore.

The plane was moving at last. The fidgety woman to his left was fidgeting even more. A nervous flyer. Lloyd hoped she wouldn't be hitting the drinks trolley too heavily to calm her nerves. A fidgety tipsy woman would start talking, and he was in no mood to talk.

He closed his eyes. Had his mother known about the fraud when she'd phoned with the news that Dad was dead? Had she deliberately kept it from him, wanting to spare him that extra burden of shock? He doubted it. She would have wanted to share the worst with him. So if Mum genuinely didn't know about it, there was only one reason why that would be, and that was probably Stirling's doing. He would be protecting her. It would be so typical of him.

Lloyd wished now that he'd spoken to Stirling to get the full story. And Granza. Granza would know what was what. Nothing slipped under the wire with her. She was one of the sharpest people he knew. Age had not dulled her senses; if anything, time had honed them to make her almost supernaturally intuitive. If anyone had noticed anything different about Dad, it would be her.

To his shame, Lloyd hadn't spotted a change in his father's behaviour, but then for the last six months, since the article about his garden furniture had appeared in the *Sunday Times* lifestyle magazine, he'd been so inundated with commissions he'd barely had time to draw breath. Had it been anyone else's wedding in New Zealand, he wouldn't have found the time to go. But because John – his oldest and closest friend, who had met and fallen in love with a girl he'd met on holiday in Wellington and had decided to settle there with her – had asked him to be his best man, there was no way he could say no.

And now he would always be left to wonder whether, had he not been so wrapped up in his own affairs, and had he not gone to New Zealand, his father might not be dead.

A meal and a film later and with the cabin lights lowered, he slept. He dreamt of his father. He was on his own, sitting on the riverbank at home in the sunshine, smiling his usual relaxed smile. And then the sky darkened, and fully clothed he slowly waded into the cold water. First it came up to his waist, then his chest, then his neck, and then he was gone, the inky-black water swallowing him up. Lloyd appeared on the bank, not as he was now, a grown man, but as a boy. He called to his father: 'Dad, where are you?' Like something out of a horror film, a hand suddenly shot through the surface of the black water. 'Help me!' Lloyd heard his father call. 'Help me, Lloyd.' 'I'm coming, Dad. I'm coming.' But try as he might, Lloyd couldn't move. He was stuck to the riverbank, his feet sinking in the squelching mud. 'Swim, Dad!' he shouted. 'Swim! You can do it.' 'I can't,' his father cried. 'Lloyd, you have to help me!'

He woke with a jolt, his heart crashing wildly. The stewardess who had earlier asked him to switch off his mobile was hovering in the aisle, a concerned expression on her face. 'Are you all right, sir?' she asked.

'I was dreaming,' he said, embarrassed. Oh God, had he called out in his sleep? Had people heard him?

She smiled and offered him a plastic cup of water from the tray she was carrying.

He took the cup. 'Thank you.'

When she'd gone, he turned to his right. The tattooed hulk was fast asleep, his mouth open. To his left, the fidgety woman had a pair of headphones plugged into her ears and with her eyes closed she was moving her head in time to whatever music she was listening to.

Too strung out now to sleep, Lloyd checked his watch: five and a half hours until Singapore. Five and a half long hours until he could speak to his mother. And, more importantly, Stirling.

Chapter Seventeen

Had she been a coward not to go with Stirling and formally identify Neil's body? Would this be something else that she would always regret?

It still didn't seem possible that Neil could be dead. If only it could be a ghastly nightmare from which she would suddenly wake up. Breathless with relief, she would turn over and there, the other side of the bed, would be Neil, snoring and muttering in his sleep. He'd always been a snorer and a mutterer. Most of what he'd said was incoherent, a babble of one-sided conversation. Often she had teased him about it, and he had laughed that one day his so-called babbling would be decoded and would be found to solve the mysteries of the universe that had for centuries eluded the world's greatest minds.

She would give anything now to hear Neil muttering in his sleep. To hear his laughter one more time. To see that carefree smile of his. To take pleasure in his support and encourage-ment for the latest idea she'd had for her beloved garden. He had never really shared her love of gardening, but he had enjoyed the results, and had given her free rein to transform the two acres here when they'd moved to The Meadows seven years ago. 'Do whatever you like, Pen,' he'd said as, glass of wine in hand, they'd wandered round the existing and unimaginatively laid-out garden in the evening sun. 'I trust you completely to make a stunning success of it.'

'It won't be cheap,' she'd warned him when they'd come to a stop and watched a riverboat passing by. 'Not for what I have in mind. I'll need help as well.'

'Spend whatever is necessary. I just want you to be happy here.'

Tears filled Pen's eyes as she heard Neil's words so clearly in her head. She remembered how touched she'd been. She was a lucky woman, she had thought at the time. The passion may have fizzled out of their marriage, but they had something far more important and lasting between them: they had loving companionship and a wealth of shared experiences. And they had Lloyd, who was unquestionably the absolutely best aspect of their marriage.

She wished Lloyd was here now. He wouldn't be able to make Neil alive again, but he would be a reassuring presence when all else felt frighteningly unreal. Perhaps it was that absence of reality that made her hang on to the hope that it was all a mistake. That it hadn't been Neil's car that had been found. That it had been another man who had taken his life, and another wretched family left to come to terms with the death of a loved one. Was that selfish of her to wish such an awful thing on another family if it would spare her own?

And wasn't there a real possibility that it might not be Neil's body that Stirling had gone to identify? Someone might have stolen the car and his wallet. A simple case of mistaken identity. That was why it was so important, she understood now, that as grim as the task was, it had to be done. One had to be sure.

She closed her eyes, willing Stirling to return with the news that it wasn't Neil. She was clutching at straws, but so long as there was doubt, there was hope. Even if it didn't make sense.

She patted the earth around the euphorbia she'd just planted, then stood up and heeled it in more firmly. She wondered if Katie was doing exactly as she'd asked her to do. She seemed a capable enough girl. She also seemed wise beyond her years.

Stirling's love child. What a thought. And what a cat amongst the pigeons that was going to be when it came out.

Poor Gina, it was going to be a dreadful shock for her.

When Pen had broken down in the kitchen earlier, having said to Katie that she wouldn't be surprised if it turned out Neil had done the same as Stirling, she had not uttered the words lightly. It stood to reason in so many ways that he would have had an affair, because she hadn't provided him with the one thing he'd badly wanted – a child of his own.

After repeated miscarriages, she had finally been forced to accept the advice of the doctors that she would never be able to carry a baby full term. That was when she and Neil decided to adopt. She had always thought that there was something satisfyingly right about Neil, having been adopted, becoming an adopter himself. Yet as happy as they were as a family with Lloyd at the centre of it, in later years it had become a recurring thought for her that Neil might look elsewhere for sexual fulfilment. If he had, she would have accepted the situation, knowing that it was her fault, because sex, unless it was to create a baby, had lost its interest for her. She had done her best to please him, but when she hit an early menopause, it was game over; she didn't even have the will to pretend any more. Neil never forced the issue; he was too patient and considerate a man to do that. If he had had an affair, he'd been extraordinarily discreet about it. She liked to think that had she discovered he'd been quietly seeing another woman, she would have accepted it as a necessary part of their marriage. She could have borne it so long as nothing ever changed between them.

The ground nicely compacted around the euphorbia, she picked up the watering can and watered the plant in. Nurturing the plant, that was what she was doing. Tending to it like a helpless baby.

Was it wrong of her to be out here in the garden? Would people think it disrespectful? Hard-hearted, even? But what else could she do? She had to do something to keep busy, to keep her mind from plunging down into that place from which she feared she might never return. So to hell with what people thought; activity was what sustained a person during a time like this. What did it matter if there were those who would think she didn't care? They would be wrong.

No doubt she would garner more sympathy if she was to weep and wail at the top of her voice and beat her breast and rend her garments as they did in some countries. Did they still rend their garments these days, or was that just in the Bible? One thing she did know: people didn't go in for that sort of thing here in Henley-on-Thames.

The absurdity of the thought immediately made her think of sharing it with Neil later. But like a jagged shard of glass piercing her heart, she knew there would be no sharing anything ever again with Neil. He was dead. Of course he was. She had been fooling herself to hope otherwise. How she would miss him. How she would miss sharing a joke with him over something she'd forgotten or misunderstood. But most of all, she would miss his kindness and gentle understanding of her. A sob burst out of her and she felt the strength drain from her body, and very slowly, as if she was being deflated like a balloon, she sank to her knees. She wrapped her arms around herself and gave in to the raw agony of the pain, letting it overwhelm her, letting it suck the very breath out of her.

'Oh Neil,' she cried, 'what am I going to do without you?'

Having completed the task she had been set, a test as much as anything, she suspected, Katie went in search of Pen to see what else she could do.

She found Pen kneeling on the grass, her head lowered as if in prayer. She was rocking backwards and forwards in a scarily rhythmic motion, at the same time emitting an awful wailing sound. Katie knelt beside the woman and pressed a hand to her shoulder.

'Pen,' she said, feeling wholly inadequate. 'Is there a friend I can call for you? A friend who could come and be with you?'

Seemingly unaware of Katie's touch or her voice, Pen continued keening and rocking.

'Pen,' Katie repeated, this time louder. 'There must be someone. What about Stirling's wife, can I ask her to come?'

When Pen still didn't seem to hear and her teeth began to chatter, Katie stood up. What on earth should she do? Call a doctor? She regretted now listening to Pen in the kitchen after she'd blamed herself for her husband's death; she should have been firm with her and insisted she rest. She must have cried for about five minutes, then just as suddenly as the tears had started, they'd stopped. She'd wiped her eyes, blown her nose and said briskly, 'Sorry about that, I don't know what came over me. I'm OK now. I'm fine. Thank you. Let's go into the garden and see if there's something I can find for you to do.' To hear her apologize for breaking down and then witness her valiant attempt to appear normal had been heart-rending.

It was just as harrowing now to see her in this agony of grief. Katie hated to see anyone upset. Tears were infectious. She'd found that with Mum. But she'd never seen her mother like this. Was it possible Mum had kept the worst of her grief hidden from Katie? She pictured her mother crying alone, and it saddened her so much she had to get a hold of her emotions. If she started crying, she'd be of no use to anyone.

But how to help Pen?

Once more she knelt on the grass alongside the poor distraught woman and placed both of her hands on her shoulders, deciding she would remain here like this, however long it took, until Pen was all cried out.

Please don't let it be him ... Please let it be anyone but Neil.

Stirling had clung on to the hope with such determination, he had almost convinced himself that it would be true, that when the sheet was pulled back and he was asked if it was his brother, he would shake his head and say that whoever the poor sod was, he had never seen him before in his life.

But the hope had been in vain. His voice choked, he had

formally confirmed that it was his brother. Cecily had been at his side. With great tenderness she had stroked Neil's cheek and kissed his forehead. They were told that his appearance – the swollen and wrinkled skin marked with cuts and bruises – was consistent with drowning; that his body would have sunk and been bumped along the surface of the river bed before resurfacing.

They were led away to an office and it was explained to them that a more exact time of death would follow, but for now they were working on the theory that Neil's body had been in the river for two days, and that death had been caused by asphyxia by drowning. Stirling listened in a daze, hearing the words but not really taking them in. Coroner. Post-mortem. Inquest. What did any of it matter? Neil was dead. That body he had just identified really was his brother's.

Tea in polystyrene cups was brought to them, and he was asked if he could think of any reason why his brother might have taken his life. They had obviously done some digging, for now Detective Inspector Rawlings was asking about Nightingale Ridgeway. Were there any problems at work? Had there been any disagreements? He felt Cecily stiffen at his side. 'Please,' he said, putting his untouched tea on the desk between him and the police officer, 'this has been a very distressing ordeal for my mother. I'd like to take her home now.'

Rawlings looked at him. 'Just one more question. Do you know a woman called Simone Montrose?'

'No,' Stirling replied tiredly.

'Only she was the last person your brother spoke to on his mobile, which we found in his car. Phone records show that he spoke with her regularly. Are you sure the name doesn't mean anything to you? To either of you?'

Chapter Eighteen

Simone Montrose hadn't stopped crying since the police-woman had called her on her mobile. That was more than three hours ago.

Recognizing his number, she had happily assumed it was Neil, but hearing a woman's voice, she had been instantly on her guard. In the two years since their affair had begun, she had always dreaded his wife discovering that he'd been unfaithful and ringing 'the other woman' to vent her feelings.

But the woman at the other end of the line hadn't been an aggrieved wife; she had been a police officer, and she was hoping Simone might be able to help her. The woman had asked if she knew a Mr Neil Nightingale.

Simone hadn't known how to answer. To say no would look odd, in as much as the policewoman was clearly ringing her on Neil's mobile. Which meant she knew Simone's number was listed in the phone's list of contacts. Instead of answering the question, and suddenly concerned that something had happened to Neil, that he'd been involved in an accident – she hadn't heard from him in a couple of days, and now a police officer was in possession of his mobile – she'd said, 'Can you tell me what this is all about, please?'

And then the world was turned upside down for Simone. 'Mr Neil Nightingale has been found dead,' the policewoman had said bluntly, 'and we're trying to piece together his final movements. We believe you might have been one of the last people he spoke to. According to his mobile, that was Thursday morning. How did he seem to you?'

'How did he seem?' she'd repeated, her voice hollow. 'What do you mean?'

She couldn't remember much more of the conversation thereafter, other than that suicide was mentioned. *I must not cry*, she'd told herself as she fought to stay in control whilst the woman droned on. *I must not cry*. To cry would give the police officer more information than was necessary. She was a friend. An acquaintance who was saddened to hear of the death of Neil Nightingale. Saddened. Not devastated. Not heartbroken. None of those things. She owed it to Neil not to break down. At all costs she must not give their relationship away. But she realized that the police, if they hadn't checked already, would know from the phone records that Neil called far too often for her to be *just* a friend.

Now, as she lay on her bed – the linen that smelled so redolently of Neil after he'd stayed with her last week – the thought ripped through her that he would never call her again, or lie in this bed with her again. She felt desolate, her heart torn from her ribcage. 'Oh Neil,' she cried aloud, her shoulders and chest heaving with renewed sobbing, 'you can't be dead. We had everything planned. We had a life together to look forward to.'

Chapter Nineteen

They drove to The Meadows in silence. What could either of them say after what they'd just gone through? Could either of them ever forget seeing Neil in that dimly lit, eerily silent room? Save for the bloating, save for the discoloration, he had at least looked at peace. Or was that wishful thinking on Stirling's part? At peace or not, Stirling regretted agreeing to Cecily coming with him. No mother should be subjected to such an ordeal. Although he was kidding himself if he thought he could have prevented it. Cecily was a force of nature when she set her mind to do something.

'And you're sure you can't think of anything that might have been troubling your brother?' Rawlings had tried one last time when they were leaving. 'There's always something,' the man had added. Of course there bloody well is! Stirling had wanted to shout back at him. People don't kill themselves without good reason. The way Rawlings kept asking the question, it was as if he knew that Stirling was hiding something.

But sooner rather than later, Stirling would have to be honest with Rawlings. If he wasn't, and if at a later date anyone suspected a cover-up, or even an attempt at a cover-up, the shit would really hit the fan. But before he spoke to Rawlings again, he had to be one hundred per cent sure that Rosco was right, that Neil was guilty of the unthinkable. He had to check the client files personally. Only then would he be utterly convinced.

But how could Rosco have got it wrong? There were often occasions when his son could act like the proverbial bull in a china shop, but there wasn't a chance in hell of him getting something as important as this wrong. As Rosco had said, he'd checked and he'd double-checked, because he didn't want to believe what he'd overheard and then discovered.

Putting aside all the emotions involved, it was of paramount importance that Nightingale Ridgeway could not be accused of trying to cover up anything as serious as client money being embezzled. In their industry, this was as bad as it got. For the good of the company, Stirling would have to report Rosco's findings to the police. And the Financial Services Authority. He wished wholeheartedly that it wasn't necessary.

'Stirling, I know what you're thinking,' Cecily said, breaking into his thoughts.

He took his eyes off the road momentarily and looked at her. 'You do?'

'What Neil did was wrong. You mustn't fall into the trap of also doing the wrong thing. You must put things right, no matter how difficult or potentially hurtful.'

'I know. I'm going to go to the office later, and when I've seen for myself what he did, then ... then I'll ...' His voice broke and he gripped the steering wheel hard. 'It feels such a betrayal. How can I do this to him? How can I tell the world what he's done?'

'He would have known this would have been the outcome,' she said gravely. 'He may have acted stupidly, but he wasn't stupid.'

'What are we going to tell Pen?'

'The truth. All of it. He killed himself because he knew the full extent of what he'd been doing was about to be exposed and he couldn't see a way out.'

'Do we tell her about Simone Montrose?'

'Yes. She's not as fragile as you think. It's all going to come out anyway, and it would be an insult to keep her in the dark; she's not a child. We have to brace ourselves for the worst, Stirling. Once the inquest takes place, the local press will get hold of the story. If they haven't already. Suicide is always newsworthy, especially when it's someone who was as well known locally as Neil was.'

Stirling groaned. 'Which means the nationals might also pick up the story.'

'Yes,' she said simply.

He turned into the driveway for The Meadows. Parked alongside Pen's car was the now familiar sight of a yellow Mini. He came to a stop and switched off the engine. He suddenly felt very tired. 'You must be disappointed with us,' he said morosely.

'With whom?'

'Neil and me. We've let you down. First I betrayed my marriage vows all those years ago, and now it looks as if Neil has been doing the same thing. You must have hoped for better from us.'

She turned and faced him, the strength of her gaze belying her age. 'My love for you and Neil has always been unconditional; I've never judged either of you, and I'm certainly not about to start doing so now. When are you going to tell Gina about Katie?'

He shook his head wearily. 'God only knows.'

'I suggest you do it soon. Get it over and done with. Get everything out in the open.' She paused. 'Katie's a lovely girl, you know. You should consider yourself extremely lucky that she found you.'

Right now, Stirling felt far from lucky. He felt like a condemned man.

They found Pen and Katie outside; they were sitting in the coolness of the courtyard, it was one of Stirling's favourite parts of Pen's amazing garden. It was very peaceful, very calming. Almost as if Pen had planned it, it was the perfect place for him to deliver the news she would be dreading.

When Pen saw them, she rose unsteadily to her feet and with puffy, bloodshot eyes looked anxiously at Stirling.

He went to her and held her close, if only so that he didn't have to look at the suffering in her face when he said the words. 'I'm so sorry, Pen,' he said gruffly, her head resting against his shoulder. 'So very sorry. I'm afraid it was Neil.'

She clung to him. 'I hoped ... I hoped so much it wouldn't be ... that it would be ...' Her words trailed off and she gulped back a sob.

With tears in his own eyes, he led her to the chair she'd been sitting in; Katie stood up so that he could take the chair next to it. He heard her quietly offer to make everyone a drink. When it was just him and Pen and his mother in the courtyard, he said, 'Pen, there's no easy way to tell you this, but we think we know why Neil killed himself.'

'It was because of me, wasn't it?'

He frowned. 'How could you think that?'

'Did he leave a note? I mean another note, other than the one the police found in his car. The one that just said he was sorry. Did he leave something that makes sense of what he did?'

Her words came at Stirling in a breathless rush. A rush of hope. 'No, Pen, there's no other note. Not yet, at any rate. But ... the thing is, it's possible that he was taking money from some of his clients.'

'Taking money? What do you mean, *taking*?'

'Stealing.' He swallowed. 'Defrauding clients.'

She shook her head. 'That's not possible. Why would he do that? We had enough money. More than enough. Why would he want more?'

'I don't know, Pen. None of this makes sense to me either.'

But the trouble was, slugging it out inside his brain was the realization that it was all beginning to make perfect sense. The woman called Simone Montrose was very likely the reason Neil had been siphoning money off from his clients. She had somehow ensnared him into not only a secret double life, but an extravagant lifestyle that required funding. Whoever the woman was, Stirling hated her. He hated her for what she had made his brother do, and for the pain they were all now going through. Almost certainly she was one of those scheming women who could wrap a man around her little finger and make him do whatever she wanted.

Looking at the distress in Pen's face, Stirling wasn't brave enough to tell her about Simone Montrose. Not now. Perhaps when Lloyd was here, when she had him to comfort and support her.

His mobile rang. He stood up and moved away to take the call: it was Rosco. 'It's started, Dad. As I warned you. I'm at the house with Mum and we've just had a local reporter on the phone.'

'Oh hell!'

'You're going to have to make sure Pen doesn't answer the phone at The Meadows. Where are you now?'

'With Pen.' He lowered his voice. 'Your grandmother and I have just got back from identifying Neil's body.'

'And?'

'It was him.'

Katie appeared in the courtyard with a tray of drinks. Stirling watched her go over to Cecily and Pen. He saw the compassion in her face as she offered Pen the tea she'd made. Twenty-four hours ago, all this girl had wanted to do was snatch a glimpse of the man she'd learnt was her father, and now here she was taking care of two bereaved strangers.

'Dad? Are you still there?'

'Sorry, the line went a bit crackly for a moment,' he lied. 'Look, I'm going to go to the office now. I need to see with my own eyes what you found out yesterday.'

'You still don't believe me?'

'Like I say, I need to see it for myself.'

'I'll meet you there.'

'No. I want to do this alone.'

'Then what will you do?'

'If it's as you say it is, then we have to report it to the police and the FSA. We can't cover this up, Rosco. You understand that, don't you? If we do, we'll be complicit and we'll be crucified by the FSA and anyone else who wants to take a shot at us.'

'I get it, Dad. No need to spell it out for me.'

'Tell your mother I'll be home later. I've no idea what time.'

Stirling let himself in at the office. The building was empty, as it should be on a Sunday. He remembered the day he and Neil signed the lease on the place, how excited they'd been. And how proud. 'Here's to the big time,' they'd said over a celebratory glass of champagne.

He took the lift up to the third floor and opened the door to Neil's office. He hesitated on the threshold. What would happen to this office after today? Would it become a crime scene? Would Neil's computer and all his files be taken away as evidence? He felt sick. If only he could go through the client files and find that the irregularities Rosco had discovered were nothing more sinister than sloppy typos – a misplaced zero here, a misplaced decimal point there.

He sat in his brother's chair behind his desk. He placed the palms of his hands flat on the desk and took a deep breath. Then he switched on the computer, and whilst it came to life, he distracted himself by thinking of Katie. He'd been tempted to ask her to come with him, just so that he could spend some time alone with her in the car. But her presence here would have been inappropriate. Before leaving The Meadows, he'd thanked her for spending the day with Pen and apologized for not being able to talk to her properly. He tried to explain that there was so much he wanted to say but couldn't right now. She said she understood, that he wasn't to worry about her, she just wanted to know if there was anything more she could do to help. She said that she'd been worried about Pen, that she had been in a terrible state earlier. For a moment he had been overwhelmed by her thoughtfulness and had wanted to hug her. It seemed impossible, given the magnitude of his grief and shock, but her presence was a consolation to him.

An hour later, he sat back in Neil's chair and rubbed his eyes.

It was true, exactly as Rosco had said. Over a period of fourteen months, Neil had siphoned off the best part of a million pounds. He'd been clever with it, bloody clever, but the evidence was there once you knew what you were looking for. The portfolios that he'd targeted were all new additions to the company and of a kind that were bulky and well spread over a wide spectrum of investments. He had been paying client cheques and transfer payments into a bank account that wasn't actually a Nightingale Ridgeway account, but one called Nightingale Ridgeway Finance Inc. From there he had been siphoning off a percentage from each sizeable payment made, which was then presumably transferred into another account – an account that would have to be traced. The bulk of the money, that he hadn't touched, was then paid into the official Nightingale Ridgeway account, and – Stirling was surmising here – if any of the clients had queried why they weren't getting as good a return on their investment as they might have hoped for, Neil would have blamed it on the recession, the fact that the market was performing badly. Experience told Stirling – and this never failed to surprise him – that a lot of clients didn't even bother to check how their investments were going in the short term. Their trust in the fund manager was implicit.

Admittedly none of the clients who Neil had targeted would go hungry as a result of his dishonesty, but this absolutely wasn't the point. These clients had trusted Nightingale Ridgeway, and Neil had abused their trust for his own ends.

Stirling knew what people would say – what and where were the safety procedures to prevent something like this? How could it have been allowed to happen? The simple answer was: who the hell would have thought a founding director of a prestigious investment management company like Nightingale Ridgeway would need watching?

Having printed page after page of damning evidence, he stared at it bleakly. How could you do it, Neil? How could you look yourself in the face of a morning?

But that was exactly what had gone wrong, hadn't it? In the end, Neil hadn't been able to face himself or anyone else.

Stirling nearly jumped out of his skin at the sound of his mobile ringing on the desk. He hoped it wasn't Rosco again.

His heart sank.

It was Lloyd.

Chapter Twenty

From the landing window, Gina watched her husband's car pass through the open gate at the end of the drive. Countless times before she had stood here and watched Stirling leave for work. Usually – so long as there hadn't been some silly disagreement between them over, say, Scarlet or Rosco – they waved goodbye to each other. But not today. Today Stirling hadn't looked back up at the house.

Never before had she seen her husband so worried or so introverted. Or so unreachable. Never before had she felt so locked out. He'd come home late last night, having gone to identify Neil's body in the morning and then spent the rest of the day at the office. His face drawn and grey, he'd looked awful when he'd been getting ready for bed. It had frightened her just how much he'd changed in so short a time.

She still couldn't believe how disgracefully Neil had behaved. How could he have put the family in this invidious position? Such wanton and deplorable selfishness. As Rosco had said, killing himself was perhaps the only decent thing he could have done; it did at least spare them the impossible task of forgiving him. Or feigning forgiveness. Because one thing Gina knew with great certainty: she would never be able to bring herself to absolve Neil for his appalling conduct.

She didn't know how she was ever going to face her sister-in-law again. Surely Pen must have had an inkling as to what Neil was up to? You couldn't be married to someone for over thirty years and not notice a change in their manner, not when the level of deception was of such magnitude. But there again, this was Pen – Pen wouldn't notice a hurricane blowing the roof off her house, not unless it landed on her precious garden.

She turned away from the window angrily. If Pen had been a better wife and kept an eye on her greedy husband, none of this would be happening. And inevitably it was going to get a lot worse. For them all. They'd had a taste of what was to come with those two reporters haranguing them on the telephone yesterday. Rosco had firmly informed them that no one had anything to say on the matter. After a brief call to Stirling, he had then called Scarlet to impress upon her and Charlie that they mustn't speak to anyone about Neil's death. Heaven only knew what Charlie's parents would think.

Katie was making good time; she would be back in Brighton within the hour. She felt as if she had been away for several weeks instead of just a few days. She had experienced a real twinge of sadness saying goodbye to Cecily and Pen. Cecily had wanted her to stay on for longer so she could meet Lloyd. 'He's your cousin, after all,' she had said, 'and I'm sure the two of you will hit it off.'

'I don't think now is the right time for him to be forced into being sociable with me,' Katie had replied gently.

She had to admit, though, that she was intrigued to meet her cousin. She had slept in his old bedroom last night. Remnants from his childhood were in evidence on the shelves, including a classic school photograph hanging on the wall above a mahogany chest of drawers. Somewhere amongst the rows of grinning faces, surly faces and downright weird faces, there was one that she assumed had to belong to Master Lloyd Nightingale. Going by the date that was printed beneath the photograph and the fact that she knew he was thirty-two – two years older than her – she reckoned that she was looking for a boy of sixth-former age. She had scanned the faces along the back two rows of blazer-clad boys. One stood out from the rest. Chin tilted up, a superior expression on his face, he oozed confidence and was a dead ringer for none other than Rosco Nightingale. Did that mean the two boys – the cousins – had attended the same school together? She had hunted for another face that bore a resemblance, but hadn't been able to find one. But then cousins didn't necessarily resemble each other, did they? Nor had she been able to find anyone who looked like Pen, and not having met Neil Nightingale, she had no idea what to look for from his genetic perspective. There had been plenty of family photographs around the house downstairs but with so much going on she hadn't had a chance to look at them.

Yesterday evening, when Stirling had returned from his office, he had asked Katie and Cecily to stay the night with Pen. Discreetly taking them aside so that Pen couldn't hear, he had quietly said that he'd spoken to Lloyd, who had asked for someone to stay with his mother until he got there; he was hoping to arrive at The Meadows by lunchtime the following day – today. 'It's useless persuading her to come and stay with Gina and me,' Stirling had explained. 'She would much rather be here. But I don't want her to be alone.' When Katie had tactfully suggested that Pen might prefer just having Cecily with her, the old woman had put a hand on her arm and said, 'Pen likes you, stay here for her. Besides, I like having you around. You're good for both of us.' So Katie had agreed to stay for another night, but again only if she could be useful. With Pen ready to drop with emotional exhaustion, she had made it her job to rustle up something for them to eat – cheese on toast had been the best she could manage from the limited contents of the fridge.

It had been a warm night, and Katie had slept with the windows open and the curtains back. She had left Cecily's unwanted flower-sprigged nightdress at South Lodge and had slept in an old T-shirt she had found in the airing cupboard when looking for sheets to make up beds for her and Cecily. It had seemed unlikely that the T-shirt was Pen's, and unless her husband had been a fan of the band Gorillaz, it probably belonged to their son.

During breakfast, when Katie had announced that it really was time for her to leave, Cecily had taken all her contact details, double-checking she had got them right by repeating them twice over, and then made Katie promise that she would call her the minute she was safely back in Brighton. It was kind of sweet having someone fussing over her like that.

Before she'd left The Meadows, she had called Tess just as she and Ben were about to board their flight back from Barcelona. Conveniently it meant that Tess couldn't berate her for too long. 'Where on earth have you been?' she had demanded. 'I've been worried sick about you.'

'I went to see my biological father,' Katie had said.

'OMG! And?'

'And I'll tell you all about it later, when you're back.'

'You better believe you will! Oh, and just so as you know, Ian's been making a pain of himself. He's been driving me nuts with all his calls. You know, I could almost think he really cares about you. He said you had a big bust-up, that you told him to sling his hook.'

'I didn't actually say it quite like that, but I made it clear I didn't want him around at the moment.'

'Oh hell, I'm going to have to go. I'll ring you tonight, and don't, whatever you do, switch your mobile off again.'

On the outskirts of Brighton now, Katie contemplated why she hadn't called Ian as she thought she would and why she had ignored his attempts to ring her last night and early this morning. It wasn't because she was still angry with him; she wasn't. It wasn't even that she didn't want to have to admit to him that he'd been right, that contacting her biological father had been the right thing to do, which in turn would mean admitting that she'd been wrong. No, it wasn't any of that. She just didn't know what to say to him. But she couldn't hide from him for ever; she would have to resolve the situation with him.

Meanwhile, things were going to seem a bit flat and dull when she got home. With everything that had been going on, she felt as if she'd been living someone else's life these last few days. She had made her decision to return home when she had woken this morning. She had looked out of the bedroom window at Pen's beautiful garden, and seeing it bathed in golden sunlight beneath a soft milky-blue sky, she had felt there was a very real danger that if she didn't leave today, she might never leave.

Before she'd left, she had done one last thing to help out: she had found the nearest supermarket and stocked up on comfort food. She knew from experience that cooking and eating was a chore at times like this, and so she'd selected a range of tempting snacks, the kind of food that had helped her to regain her own appetite – ready-made soup, a nice loaf of wholemeal bread, a selection of cheese, tubs of hummus and taramasalata and olives, pre-cut crudites, cherry tomatoes, eggs, crisps, and a cooked chicken. She'd also selected two large chocolate cakes and a tub of ice cream for those in need of a sugar rush.

Pen had given her a fragile smile and waved her off with Cecily. 'You'll come again, won't you?' Cecily had said. 'When things aren't so awful.'

'If I'm invited.'

'Don't be so ridiculous, of course you're invited. Any time you want.'

'Say goodbye to Stirling from me.'

'He'll be in touch, I'm sure.'

At the house in Cavendish Terrace, Katie gathered up the mail from the doormat and walked through to the kitchen. She dumped her bag on a chair, sifted through the mail and, finding nothing of interest, put it on the table to deal with later. She looked about her and was gripped abruptly by how alone she felt. It was absurd, but she was suddenly homesick for The Meadows – for the house and garden, but most especially for Cecily and Pen. In the short time she had known the two women, she had grown fond of them. She hadn't really had a chance to get to know Stirling, but she felt she could be fond of him as well; he seemed a caring sort of man. For the first time, she wondered what it might have been like to grow up with him as her father. Guilt slapped at her. How could she betray Dad with such a thought?

She opened the door on to the garden to let some fresh air in, and then went over to the shelf where she kept one of her favourite photographs of her parents. She picked up the frame and looked at her mother. She tried to imagine Fay with Stirling, but couldn't. They were chalk and cheese. She studied her father's face, searching it for something that might tell her what he had really thought of his wife sleeping with another man and conceiving a child that wasn't his. How had he borne it? Was that what true unconditional love was? The ability to forgive and love a person no matter what? She thought of Pen's raw grief. She too must have loved her husband very much.

She realized with a small flutter of regret that she had never been in love to that extent. Ian was kind and loving, he was dependable and supportive, and he'd said he loved her – she had even said that she loved him – but she wasn't so sure that she really had. She had simply grown used to him. She had enjoyed having him around. Until recently. Recently he had begun to annoy her.

Dad used to say that if you truly loved someone, you loved that person for their faults, and that only when the faults became greater than the sum of your love did it mean the relationship had no future. Not until now did Katie understand that he had been speaking totally and utterly from the heart.

She placed the photograph back on the shelf, put the kettle on and then remembered her promise to ring Cecily as soon as she was home. She dialled the number for The Meadows – Cecily had said she would remain there for the rest of the day – and listened to the ringing tone. As the tone continued, she pictured Cecily and Pen outside in the garden, oblivious to the telephone ringing. She was about to give up and call back later when a voice said, 'Please leave us alone. We have nothing to say.'

The voice belonged to a man. A softly spoken man. He sounded tired. There was a clunk in her ear and then the line went dead.

She debated what to do. Whoever had answered the phone at The Meadows – possibly Pen's son – must have assumed that she was a nuisance reporter.

But she'd promised Cecily she would ring.

She dialled again. This time the phone was answered straight away, and before whoever was at the other end of the line had a chance to say anything, Katie said, 'I'm not a reporter. I just want to leave a message for Cecily. Can you tell her I'm back in Brighton now.' Her words tumbled out of her in such a hurry, she wondered if they'd made sense.

There was a pause. 'What name shall I give?'

'Katie. Katie Lavender.'

There was the sound of voices in the background, followed by the muffled rustling of a hand covering the mouthpiece of the receiver. Seconds passed and then: 'Katie, is that you?'

It was Cecily. 'Yes. I'm sorry if I'm disturbing you, but you did say you wanted me to let you know when I was back.'

'And I'm very grateful that you have.'

'Was that Pen's son I just spoke to?'

'Yes. He's only been here an hour and already he's had to deal with half a dozen calls. Neil's death was in the *Financial Times* this morning. Only a small piece, but heaven only knows how it got there so fast.'

'What about the local newspaper?'

'That's not out until Friday. Then the whole of Henley will know.'

'I'm sorry. Perhaps you should put the answering machine on; that way you can field the calls. How's Pen?'

'Better for Lloyd being here.'

'That's good. Well, I'd better let you get on.'

After a brief pause, Cecily said, 'Katie, I want you to know that you're welcome to stay with me any time you want. You're a member of this family, and as far as I'm concerned, the sooner everyone knows that, the better.'

'That's kind of you, but Stirling needs to do this in his own time. I'm not going to rush him. It's important that he knows it was a spur-of-the-moment thing me showing up at his house. I only wanted the chance to see what kind of a man he was. It was never my intention to cause him any trouble. I tried explaining that to him; I hope he believes me.'

'And that's very much to your credit, my dear. You can accuse me of bias if you like, but in my opinion he's a good man who always strives to do the right thing.'

Lloyd had never felt so wired yet at the same time so ready to crash. He hadn't slept at all during the flight from Singapore to Heathrow. How could he after speaking to Stirling?

But sleep would have to wait. For now he was hungry and needed something to eat. With Pen and Cecily both sitting at the kitchen table, he opened the fridge hoping he'd find something more useful than a carton of milk and an out-of-date yoghurt. His father had often joked that Pen could live happily off air for a week. In return she would laugh and say, 'Yes, and I'd still put on weight.' His chest tightened at the thought of his parents' easy, light-hearted rapport.

When he saw the contents of the fridge, his surprise must have shown. Pen said, 'We have Katie to thank for that.'

Reaching into the fridge for the pre-cooked chicken, he said, 'Who's Katie?' He didn't get an answer, but was aware of some nervous glances being exchanged between his grandmother and Pen. '*So*,' he said meaningfully, 'who is she?'

Still nothing from them both.

He put the chicken on the table. 'I assume she's the girl who phoned earlier to speak to you, Granza. So what's the big deal about her?'

His grandmother looked serious. 'Lloyd, you have to promise not to breathe a word of this to anyone.'

He sighed. 'Oh God, what now?'

'Do you promise?'

'Yes, I promise,' he said tiredly. In his sleep-deprived state, he didn't think he had the energy to be shocked by anything more.

When his grandmother and Pen had finished explaining, he sat down heavily. 'Bloody hell! I wouldn't like to be in her shoes when Rosco and Scarlet find out about her.'

'I don't care what they think,' Cecily said stoutly. 'She's a lovely girl.'

Pen nodded in agreement. 'She couldn't have been more helpful. I'm ... I'm afraid I rather fell apart, and she was very sweet with me. I hope you don't mind, but she slept in your old room last night.'

'Of course I don't mind.' He leant forward and rested his hand on top of his mother's. 'I'm just glad you had someone here to look after you. She sounds nice.'

Cecily smiled. 'She is. You'll love her. You really will.'

Time would tell on that score, Lloyd thought. He doubted very much that his cousins would welcome this girl with open arms. More likely they would view her as a threat, an interloper. After all, that was how they'd always viewed him, a trespasser on the hallowed ground of the name of Nightingale. A name, in their eyes, that was now about to be dragged through the mud as a result of his father's actions.

The thought was enough to kill off his appetite. He stood up abruptly, banging his leg against the table. 'I need to speak to Stirling,' he said. 'I need to know if he's informed the police about Dad, and what he ...' His words trailed away. He couldn't bring himself to say the words out loud. Fraud ... embezzlement ... He still couldn't believe his father had done it. What possible motive could he have had? Was there something Stirling hadn't told him?

Chapter Twenty-one

The Church of St Oswald's in Sandiford was packed.

It was to be expected, Rosco thought bitterly. They were here in their sickening droves to be a part of the show, to satisfy their perverse curiosity. Not content with reading about it in the newspapers and on the internet, they wanted their own take on the speculation that was currently rife, and to witness for themselves how the family was bearing up. The regatta was on this week, and odds on most of the two-faced sticky-beaks here would head straight for the river afterwards, and with the champagne flowing would mull over what they'd just seen and heard with prurient delight.

When Lloyd had informed him how the funeral was to be carried out – that it would be a full church service, followed by drinks, open-house style, at The Meadows – Rosco had argued vehemently with Dad over it. He'd said they should make it as quiet an affair as they could; it should be private, family only. The last thing they should do was draw attention to themselves. But Dad had disagreed. He'd said that the decision wasn't his, it rested entirely with Pen and Lloyd, and that he for one had no intention of burying his brother in a half-hearted fashion in an attempt to hush things up.

Fat chance of anything being hushed up with the kind of comments being posted on the internet. Accusations were being fired at them left, right and centre. *Who else was in on the fraud at Nightingale Ridgeway?* one anonymous writer had asked. *How can the company ever be trusted again?* said another. *Where there's brass, there's a thieving bunch of con artists!* someone else had written.

According to the Reverend Roger Batley – the minister leading this charade – Neil had been a devoted family man and loved by all. No mention then that the entire firm would be tainted with the same shade of his sleazy dishonesty. The whole performance was a travesty, and it made Rosco's blood boil. The minister was now harping on about forgiveness. Unbelievable!

Forgiveness! He had to be joking. Neil had been a lying, cheating bastard. Why should they be expected to forgive him for that? Rosco was tempted to yell at the top of his voice, 'This is all a load of crap! If the man had kept it in his trousers, he wouldn't have been stealing from clients!'

When his father had told him that the police had evidence that Neil had had a mistress on the side – not that Dad had used those words, he'd said something about there having been another woman in Neil's life, as though that made it almost respectable and less sordid – the picture was complete for Rosco and the final nail was driven home in his uncle's coffin. The bastard had been stealing from clients to feather a love nest with some tart on the make. That was the long and the short of it.

He didn't know how Pen and Lloyd had taken the news of this other woman, but to all intents and purposes they were carrying on here today as if Neil had led a life of perfect rectitude and had slipped away in his sleep, called by the blessed angels themselves. Was there anyone here today displaying a genuine emotion?

In need of something to take his mind off the drivel he was being forced to listen to – Lloyd was now at the front of the church and giving a reading – Rosco looked at the stained-glass window behind the altar and took in the vision of the crucifixion in all its gruesome glory. It made him hope that in those final moments before death had claimed him, his uncle had known real fear and regret and had suddenly changed his mind and wanted to live, only to realize that it was too late. Rosco didn't believe in God, or any kind of god for that matter, but he believed in justice. And in his opinion, it would be wholly just if in Neil's last seconds he had suffered.

It had been hell at work since Dad had formally informed the police that irregularities had come to light with various clients' accounts. The full weight of the police force, including a team from the Economic Crime Unit, had promptly descended on the offices, and clients were then informed of what was going on, as well as all members of staff. Everyone had been stunned. Neil's office had been taped off, and computers, files and anything else deemed to be potential evidence taken away.

That was the day they'd heard the results of the post-mortem on Neil's body – death had been caused by asphyxia by drowning – and several days later, the inquest was held. It lasted no more than a few minutes, its purpose seemingly to state the obvious: that Neil Nightingale was dead, and that his body could be released for burial. They were told that the inquest was now adjourned until a later date, when all the necessary evidence and information had been gathered. Only then would a formal verdict be given as to the hows and whys. Again, as though it wasn't bloody well obvious. The man had killed himself as a result of knowing he was about to be found out, hadn't he? What more was there to say?

Rosco turned his head to his right, where his mother sat. Still and composed and dressed in a simple black suit and cream silk blouse, she looked as elegant as ever. Dad was sitting the other side of her, his head lowered. To Rosco's left, and with her eyes closed, Scarlet was stroking her swelling bump through the fabric of a black and white halter-neck dress. Fiddling with a cufflink in his shirtsleeve the other side of Scarlet was Charlie. Charlie's parents had excused themselves from attending on the grounds of a clash of dates, a prior and long-standing engagement up in Scotland. Lucky them.

Across the aisle, Granza, looking as regal as ever, was sitting bolt upright next to Pen. Now back in his seat, Lloyd was holding Pen's hand. Them and us, thought Rosco. But hadn't it always been thus? He and Scarlet had known from an early age that they had to fight to get a look-in from their grandmother. She had never actually said in so many words that Lloyd was her favourite, but she didn't need to; it was there in her every word and gesture. Their mother had known it too. He'd often heard her complaining to Dad that it just wasn't fair the way Cecily treated Lloyd so differently. Dad's stock reply was that Cecily was the most fair-minded person he knew. Which, when you thought about it, was an interesting response, because maybe Dad believed Cecily was being fair in favouring Lloyd.

The final hymn sung, Dad and Lloyd, along with the other pall-bearers, were now hefting the coffin on to their shoulders and carrying it the length of the church. Rosco hadn't been asked to help with this task. Nor had he offered. The sight of a single tear running down his father's solemn face as he slowly passed had Rosco looking away.

Itching to escape the crush of pity, Pen let out a small sigh of relief. The worst was over. The service had come to an end. People were now standing around chatting soberly amongst themselves in the graveyard in the sunshine.

Everyone had been very kind to her, but how much sympathy and carefully measured words was she expected to take? How much of it was even genuine? How many of these so-called mourners, once she was out of earshot, would say something bad about Neil? And there was plenty of bad stuff they could say if they had a mind to.

On the day that Lloyd had come back from New Zealand, Stirling had arrived at The Meadows in the evening and, looking ominously ill at ease, had told them that he had yet more bad news for them. He'd said that the police suspected Neil had been having an affair. 'I'm so sorry to be the one to tell you,' he had said, his gaze switching nervously between her and Lloyd.

'Suspect or know?' Lloyd had asked.

'They have phone records and they've spoken to the woman herself.'

'Do you know who it is?' Pen had asked quite calmly.

'Her name is Simone Montrose. I've never heard of her. I certainly never heard Neil mention her.'

It was quite plausible that she had been mad with grief, but when Stirling had said it, the first thing Pen had thought was, oh, what a nice name.

'I wouldn't be at all surprised if she's responsible for what Neil did,' Stirling had said, with more force to his voice than was normal for him. 'She will have put him up to it. It would have been all her idea.'

Pen had hugged Stirling fiercely, knowing that he was trying to make Neil sound less guilty. She'd said, 'You know as well as I do, no one could make Neil do anything he didn't want to do.'

Stirling had rubbed his eyes hard. 'He was always the same: once he decided on something, there was no stopping him.'

'So how do we find out more about Simone Montrose? We'll need to invite her to the funeral.'

He had stared at her in horror. 'You can't be serious?'

'If Neil loved this woman, then I owe it to him to give her the opportunity to mourn him in the proper way.'

'But Pen, how can you be so ... so reasonable, when in all probability – and I'm sorry to be so blunt – it looks very like Neil was taking the money because he was planning to leave you for this other woman?'

'We don't know that for sure,' she'd replied firmly. 'And maybe I'm still numb with shock, but what harm could it do to let her come? And what's wrong with being reasonable? Isn't that what you want Gina to be when you tell her about Katie?'

He hadn't said another word on the subject after that.

If Lloyd had been shocked, angry or disappointed by this

latest revelation about his father, he had kept it to himself. Which was so typical of him.

For her part, she was all shocked out. And all cried out. The only thing that had the power to upset her now was what was printed in the newspapers. But so long as she remained in ignorance of what was being written, she could survive.

She had made the mistake initially of wanting to know every word of what was being said, and would drive into Henley each morning to buy a whole raft of newspapers. She hadn't gone to the newsagent she'd always used, but to the supermarket in the hope of being anonymous. Admittedly the story had become smaller as the days dragged by, but when Lloyd found her crying at the kitchen table over a piece in the money section of the *Telegraph* – they'd printed a photograph of Neil that made him look like a criminal – he got rid of every newspaper she'd brought into the house and made her promise she wouldn't buy any more.

It had been good having Lloyd living back at home with her, but she knew the arrangement couldn't go on for ever; he had to return to his own house and get on with his life. But he'd been a great comfort to her. At night, when neither of them could sleep, he'd sat with her going through the photograph albums, remembering all the good times they'd had as a family. 'It wasn't all lies, was it?' she'd said to him one night. 'It was only latterly that he hid things from us. The rest of it was all true.'

Pen didn't have a clue what Simone Montrose looked like. Other than the picture she had created in her head of an elegant and sophisticated young woman. A career woman. A perfectly groomed woman who knew her way round clothes, who could dress for any occasion with style and panache. She would have her hair and nails done regularly at an expensive salon, and she would always smell of perfume. Probably something alluring and sensual. She would have petite feet that would never be seen in anything other than a pair of four-inch heels. And she would move gracefully at all times. She would be perfect.

But apart from Gina, Pen hadn't spotted anyone amongst the mourners who fitted that description. Perhaps Simone hadn't come, had thought her presence inappropriate. Or maybe she hadn't really loved Neil. Looking out for Neil's mistress – there, she'd said the word, if only inside her head – had not really been a top priority for her during the service. Saying goodbye to Neil had been the only thing on her mind throughout the proceedings, praying for him mostly. In common with so many people, she only prayed when she was in urgent need. She'd prayed on her knees for a child all those years ago, and Lloyd had been given to her. She had thanked God so fervently and so regularly afterwards that she began to imagine God was getting a little tired of constantly hearing from her, and so she'd stopped. Only to resume in earnest again when Lloyd had been five years old and had been rushed into hospital with appendicitis. She was bothering God again three years later when he had fallen from a tree he had been climbing with Rosco and had managed to knock himself unconscious. She had prayed when he left home for university. She had prayed when he went overseas to work for that charity. Now here she was making yet more demands, begging for Neil to be allowed to be at peace. Suicide was still considered to be a sin by some. Such blindly prejudiced judgement was more of a sin to her way of thinking. She hoped that God had moved on, that he wouldn't hold it against Neil that he'd taken things into his own hands and killed himself.

Lloyd was magically at her side, his hand touching her arm lightly. 'Time to make a move now, Mum,' he said softly. 'We need to go back to the house.'

She'd lost track of where she was, and suddenly saw afresh the open hole and the coffin that lay at the bottom of it. Lloyd had helped her choose the coffin. It was from their mid-range of caskets, the man at the undertaker's had explained in a murmured, deferential tone that was so low and quiet that she'd had to ask him several times to repeat himself.

'Just a few more moments, Lloyd,' she said.

'Do you want me to stay with you?'

She shook her head. 'See to everyone else.' She watched him walk away, saw him say something to Stirling and Gina, and then returned her attention to the polished mid-range casket that contained her husband's body. She thought of the clothes she and Lloyd had chosen for Neil to wear – a dark charcoal suit he'd had made last year, a pale blue shirt and a favourite pink and silver silk tie. She hoped he approved.

She regretted now that she hadn't gone with Stirling to identify Neil's body. Regretted too that she hadn't been brave enough to go with Lloyd to view the body at the undertaker's when it had been taken there after the post-mortem had been carried out. Laid to rest, they called it, the body made all neat and tidy and reassuringly presentable, as if it had never been touched by a scalpel, much less by death.

She should have gone, if only so she could have said goodbye to him properly. But she hadn't wanted to see him that way for fear of being haunted for the rest of her life by the memory of his cold, inert body. She was paying for that decision now. That and not telling him how much she still loved him. She hadn't expressed her love for him in a long while. It was a mistake too many people made. One always thought there would be time to say all the things one wanted to say. But life didn't play fair. And once that chance was gone, it was gone for ever.

Had Neil doubted her love? Was that why he had found someone else and had begun to think about leaving her, as Stirling seemed to think was the case? As indeed the newspapers were hinting at. How had they got their story? she wanted to know. Where did they get their information? Did they hang about the police station waiting for interesting titbits to come their way? Or were they guessing? So far they had spoken in vague terms of another woman being involved, and probably that was merely to spice the story up to sell more copies. Surely they had no actual evidence?

Her breath suddenly became short, and there was a tightness in her chest. She fought the tears that were threatening to destroy her self-control. Only moments ago she had thought the worst was over; now she feared the worst might be yet to come. Back at the house, she would have to face everyone; she would have to exchange more than just a polite nod in response to offers of condolence. The mood of the guests would have picked up a beat; in turn she would be expected to do the same. People much preferred backbone and spirit to an embarrassing scene. A widow could dab her eyes decorously with a glass of dry sherry in her hand, but a hysterical weeping widow was just plain awkward.

She wasn't used to being in the limelight, but today she couldn't have been more centre stage. She hated to think that people would be trying to imagine how she felt about Neil. Was she angry? Had she known? Did she want revenge on this other woman?

None of which was the case.

Even though Neil had always been popular and well known in the area, Pen hadn't expected such a large turnout today. Friends and neighbours had filled the church, along with people from the hospice that she raised money for. Work colleagues and long-standing clients had come – though understandably, not the ones Neil had stolen from. There were also his sailing friends, about twenty of them, and a lot of other people Pen had never set eyes on before. She was concerned she wouldn't have enough energy to make the right responses to them all. *Thank you for coming ... I'm glad you could make it ... It was good of you to travel so far ...* How many times could a person say thank you and sound sincere? Should she even worry about such a thing when she knew that not everyone here was being genuine? There would be those amongst the guests who would be revelling in the scandal, perversely cheered by the downfall of a successful man, all too ready to call him a criminal.

There had been some cruelly barbed letters sent to the editor of the local newspaper. One local man had gone so far as to say that Neil's deception – not just of the clients he'd robbed, but of those who'd known and trusted him – epitomized everything that was wrong in today's society: the dishonest-self-seeking-snatch-and-grab-winner-takes-all mentality that was depriving the world of all its ethical values. It so happened that the writer of the letter had approached Neil at a charity ball last year and, bold as brass, had asked for a contribution towards funding his daughter to go trekking through Costa Rica on her gap year. Would he now be returning Neil's generous donation? Pen wondered.

'I'm sorry to disturb you, but—'

Pen started violently. So lost in her thoughts, she had been oblivious to the approach of one of the guests. She turned and found herself staring into the tear-filled eyes of an attractive dark-haired woman. Pen knew at once who it was. She swallowed and opened her mouth to speak, but nothing came out.

'I'm sorry,' the woman repeated. 'My name is Simone Montrose, and I just wanted to thank you for letting me come here today. It means ... it means a lot to me.' She put a handkerchief to her mouth and stifled a sob.

Pen automatically opened her arms wide. 'Oh, you poor thing,' she said.

The other woman didn't hesitate; she sank into Pen's embrace and cried without restraint.

'It's all right,' Pen soothed. 'You'll get through this. We both will.'

Chapter Twenty-two

Gina was horrified. She simply could not believe what Pen had done. Admittedly, grief could make a person behave strangely, but in this instance Pen was making an embarrassing spectacle of herself. And worse, she was dragging the family through yet more shame and humiliation. Hadn't they suffered enough already?

Just as unbelievable, Stirling had been party to the decision to allow that disgusting woman to attend the funeral. Giving his consent for Neil's tart to parade herself in front of everyone was so beyond the realms of respectable behaviour that it made her question Stirling's state of mind. Really, what could he have been thinking? He should have put his foot down. He should have asserted himself as head of the family. But no, he had deferred to some kind of fraternal nonsense that this was what his brother would have wanted. What rubbish! As if Neil would have wanted them to meet his mistress. But no wonder Stirling had kept quiet about it before today. Had he told her in advance, she would have refused to come.

She had just been suggesting to Stirling that it was time to walk the short distance to The Meadows when Rosco had joined them and asked if they knew who the woman was who was crying with Pen at the graveside. Gina had noticed the woman earlier – she had arrived alone and didn't seem to know anyone else – but other than that, she hadn't given her any more thought. Frankly, all she'd been interested in was getting this awful day over and done with, and with as much haste and dignity as was possible. Something in Stirling's manner, the way he'd stared at Pen, who seemed to be comforting the other woman, made her repeat Rosco's question. And as if it was the most normal thing in the world, he'd said, 'Her name's Simone Montrose and she's the woman Neil was having an affair with.'

'*What?*' both she and Rosco had said in horrified unison.

'Now isn't the time,' he'd said, and promptly walked away, colliding with Scarlet and Charlie. He hadn't stopped, not even to apologize to them. Gina had wanted to chase after him, but Rosco had held her back. 'Let him go,' he'd said. 'We don't want to cause a scene and give the gawpers anything else to gossip about.'

Now, at The Meadows, and with all the guests in the garden, she and Rosco, along with Scarlet and Charlie, had collared Stirling inside the house and forced a full explanation out of him.

'So now you know as much as I do,' he said as they stood in the middle of Pen's sitting room. 'This is what Pen wanted. Because she believes it's what Neil would have wanted.'

Gina stared at her husband. The whole situation was too sordid for words. 'You should have stopped this ridiculous circus of a funeral,' she said. 'You should have told Pen it wasn't appropriate. She would have listened to you.'

Stirling didn't want to be having this conversation. He couldn't stand to see the disdain in the faces of his wife and children. Why could they not be as understanding and accepting as Pen and Lloyd?

He could have lied to them, of course. He could have simply said he didn't know who the woman was. But that would have flown in the face of his true feelings. To lie would give the message that he was ashamed of his brother for his infidelity. But how could he condemn Neil, when he had done the very same thing thirty years ago? Moreover, how would he have wanted Fay to be treated if he had died during their affair?

When Pen had made it clear she was serious about wanting to invite Simone Montrose to the funeral, he had offered to contact her on his sister-in-law's behalf. He had got the necessary contact details from Detective Inspector Rawlings and made the call. He'd been nervous about speaking to her, anxious that he might lash out and blame her for what Neil had done. But as Pen had said, no one ever made Neil do something he didn't want to do. It soon became apparent whilst talking to Simon Montrose that she was deeply shocked and bewildered by Neil's suicide. Her voice strained with emotion, she told him that the police had questioned her for some time about their affair, and had scrutinized her bank and savings accounts, obviously checking for any trace of the embezzled money. 'I had no idea what he was doing,' she told Stirling. 'You have to believe me. I still can't take it in. All he ever said to me was that he was making investments for the future.' She had been tactful enough, Stirling noted, to phrase it as *the* future and not what it surely was, their *shared* future.

'Why didn't you take control of today, Dad?'

Stirling looked at his son. 'Control?' he repeated. 'A funeral isn't about seizing control; it's about commemorating the life of a loved one, of saying a final goodbye and sharing the moment with those who were close to that person.'

Rosco rolled his eyes. 'In normal circumstances, yes. But this isn't a normal situation.'

'It's still your uncle who's died and my brother I've just had to bury. That's what's important here.'

'Dad, you're behaving as if Neil did nothing wrong.' This was from Scarlet. 'He stole from clients. He lied to Auntie Pen. He lied to us. He wasn't the man we thought he was. How can you expect us to forget the awful things he did?'

'And how can you forget all the times he played French cricket with you? How he taught you kids to sail when we all went on holiday to Corfu together? How can you forget the magic shows he put on for you when you were little? Or,

Scarlet, the time your mother and I were away and you were staying with him and Pen and he rushed you to the hospital when you'd cut your finger?'

'That was in the past and has no bearing on the present,' asserted Rosco.

'Rosco's right,' Charlie said.

Furious, Stirling glared at his son-in-law. 'Keep out of this, Charlie. When I want your opinion, I'll ask for it.'

Charlie's jaw dropped. He looked like he'd just been punched.

'Stirling!' Gina exclaimed. 'What's got into you? Why are you behaving like this?'

Never had he felt such anger before. 'I'll tell you what's got into me,' he said, his voice raised. 'It's the shock of discovering how shallow my family is, knowing that all you care about is keeping up bloody appearances. You should be ashamed of yourselves. What's more, I'm proud of Pen and Lloyd for the way they're handling Neil's death. And I'm doubly proud that they're standing by him despite every evil word that's being said or written about him.'

'They're in denial,' Rosco said contemptuously. 'Any fool can see that. They're desperately hanging on to the man they thought Neil was, refusing to believe the evidence of their own eyes. It's as I said before: the past has no bearing on the present.'

Stirling had heard enough. He wouldn't listen to any more self-righteous, judgemental arrogance from his son. He badly wanted to make him understand that life wasn't the clear-cut race he believed it to be. 'So let me get this straight, Rosco,' he said. 'According to you, the past is the past. It's only where we are now that matters? Is that what you're saying? Just as in a court of law, if someone is being tried for a current crime, his previous crimes should not be referred to? Is that your position?'

Gina tutted with impatience, but Rosco stared back at him steadily. 'Yes,' he said. 'That's as good an analogy as any.'

'Come on, Dad,' said Scarlet. 'You know that Rosco's only speaking the truth, that what Uncle Neil did was wrong. I mean, he broke the law, you can't ignore that.'

'I break the law every day I get in my car and drive too fast. Does that mean you should view me differently?'

'Now you're just being absurd.'

Stirling rounded on Rosco. 'No, I'll tell you what's absurd. It's listening to this rubbish from you lot. Neil was family. He was my brother. Why does that not mean anything to you?'

'For pity's sake, Stirling, listen to yourself. You sound almost as mad as Pen. Just accept that Neil wasn't the man you thought he was. Somewhere along the line he changed and lost perspective on what was right and what was wrong.'

'Mum's right,' Rosco said. 'We have to judge him on the man he became, not the man he was. Besides, we might never have known the real Neil. Maybe there was always this darker side to his nature just waiting to have its moment. He wasn't a true Nightingale, after all.'

'Oh, now I've heard everything!' Stirling exploded. 'You're saying that because Neil was adopted, he was a criminal waiting to happen. Thank God your grandmother isn't here to witness this appalling disloyalty. You should be ashamed of yourselves. But how about I give you something to really test your loyalty? Although since you seem to think one's past behaviour isn't relevant, you should be able to take it perfectly on the chin when I tell you – Rosco and Scarlet – that you have a sister. More accurately, a half-sister called Katie who is two years younger than you, Rosco.'

He turned to his wife. Her eyes were wide and she suddenly looked very pale. 'But as that was all in the past,' he said savagely, 'thirty years ago to be precise, you're not going to hold it against me, are you?'

'Is this some kind of sick joke?' Gina said.

'You think I'm in the mood to crack jokes on a day like today? Now that truly would be sick.'

'But, Dad, it can't be true. You wouldn't do something like that. You just wouldn't.'

'I'm afraid I did, Scarlet.'

He didn't see Gina's hand coming. But he felt it hard against his face.

Chapter Twenty-three

Cecily had come inside the house to look for Stirling. Hearing voices coming from the sitting room, she had crossed the hall and was about to push the door further open – it was ajar by a couple of inches – when she hesitated and shamelessly eavesdropped.

Anger scorched through her at what she heard. How dare Rosco be so breathtakingly rude about Neil! If he were younger, she'd march in there and box his ears. Just as she'd once done when she'd come across him goading Lloyd when they'd been small boys. 'You're not a real member of this family,' Rosco had told Lloyd. 'And nor is your dad. You don't have the same blood as us.'

Stirling sounded incandescent now. She couldn't ever recall him being so angry. She wanted to go in there and back him up, but he was more than capable of fighting his own battles. Then she heard him saying something that had her putting a hand to her mouth. No, Stirling! Not that. Not now. Then she heard the unmistakable sound of a slap.

This could not go on. It was time to intervene. But no sooner had she put a hand out to the door than it was thrown wide open and Gina appeared in the doorway. Her face drained of colour, she glared at Cecily. 'What kind of a mother are you to have raised two such awful sons?' Not waiting for an answer, she pushed past and hurried away. Next came Rosco and Scarlet with Charlie in tow. They didn't speak to her. They barely looked at her.

Cecily stepped into the room and saw Stirling standing

alone. He looked ineffably wretched. 'How much did you hear?' he asked.

She went to him. 'Enough to know that you said what needed saying.'

He shook his head. 'I didn't mean to tell them ... not like that. But I couldn't bear to hear them disparaging Neil the way they were.'

'I'm proud of you for sticking up for him. I wanted to come in and join forces with you, but you were managing quite well without my interference.'

'But I've hurt them. Particularly Gina. And the awful thing is, I did it deliberately. The red mist came down and I wanted to puncture their intractable certainty.' He went over to the window and ran his hands through his hair. 'What if they never forgive me?'

'That was always going to be a risk.'

'I could have lessened the risk, though. Now they'll hate Katie before they've even met her. They'll regard her as the enemy.'

'Oh, Stirling, that was inevitable as well. But in time, when emotions have settled down and everyone is thinking straight again, then Scarlet and Rosco will want to get to know their half-sister.'

'I wish I had half your confidence.' He sighed heavily. 'How's Pen coping?'

'She's doing well. Lloyd is watching over her like a hawk. They'll be glad when today is over.'

'Did you meet Simone Montrose?'

'No. I didn't get a chance. She didn't come back here. Which was perfectly correct of her, don't you think?'

'I suppose so. Though I'm beginning to lose track about what constitutes a good idea now.'

'What was she like?'

'Hard to say. In common with us, she was probably not at her best.'

*

Now at home in Oxford, Simone was curled up on the sofa with a box of tissues at her side, holding a framed photograph of Neil. She had taken the picture two years ago, when they'd met on a flotilla sailing holiday in the Greek islands. She had never sailed before, but the friends she'd gone with had sworn that they'd teach her all she needed to know, that it would be a piece of cake. They had also claimed it would be the ideal way for her to meet new people and, who knew, maybe have a little fun in the form of a holiday romance.

There had been six boats in the flotilla, and she had met Neil the first evening of the trip, when they had anchored in the village harbour of Meganisi and, as a group, gone for dinner at a nearby taverna. Purely by random chance, she and Neil had sat next to each other, and she had enjoyed his company enormously, but hadn't for a second considered him holiday romance material. Besides, he was married. She'd spotted his wedding ring straight away and during the course of the meal he had spoken often of his wife and son. She had felt happy and relaxed in his presence, which counted for a lot. Having been on her own for more than four years, she was tired of either being fixed up by well-intentioned friends or being hit on by men who assumed she must be so desperate she'd go to bed with anyone.

But Neil hadn't hit on her; he had been highly entertaining and had made everyone laugh around the table, not just her. As the days drifted by, they found themselves gravitating towards each other for lazy picnic lunches on sandy beaches and boisterous evenings spent in tavernas. By the end of the holiday, she knew that something special had passed between them, something life-changing. He had felt it too, and very quietly, when they'd been swimming in the sparkling clear Ionion water on the last day of the holiday, he had admitted he wanted to see her again when they were back in England. 'I shouldn't be putting you in this situation,' he'd said, 'and I want you to know I've never done anything like this before. I never thought I was capable of cheating on my wife, but the thought of not seeing you again is making me feel ill.'

A week later, on her forty-fifth birthday, he came to see her in Oxford. She gave him a brief tour round the college where she worked as an art restorer, and then he drove her out for lunch at Le Manoir Aux Quat'Saisons, where he surprised her with a present: a double-strand pearl necklace. It wasn't until he drove her home and she invited him in that he kissed her. Until then, there had been no real physical contact between them. For her part, it had been a blessed relief when his mouth had touched hers. They didn't go to bed until a fortnight later. It had felt so natural between them, as though they'd known and understood each other's bodies for a long time.

Whilst the sex between them was always good, it wasn't what their relationship was founded on. It was the easy and honest rapport between them that they cherished the most. He told her about his marriage: how he loved his wife, but as a brother would love his sister – there hadn't been anything physical between them for many years, but he cared deeply about her well-being. In turn, she told him about her eight-year marriage: how she had reluctantly ended it when she faced up to the sad truth that her husband's drinking would destroy them both if she stayed. She told Neil things she had never shared with anyone else. Not even her closest friends.

They spoke almost every day on the telephone, and before she knew it, she was completely in love with him. And he with her. That was when she tried to break it off with him. She suddenly saw the futility of being in love with a man she could never have to herself. He was devastated and begged her to reconsider. But she held firm. A fortnight later, he came to see her and told her he was making plans to change his life so that he could be with her. He said the one thing he had to do was make sure that his wife would be financially secure for the rest of her life, and just as importantly, he wanted to secure their future together. He spoke of investments he was putting in place. He spoke of being a free man one day and asking her to marry him. He begged her to be patient, to put her trust in him.

And she did. She wanted to spend the rest of her life with this man, so why not be patient? Why not help him through this difficult period in his life so they could then be together?

Fresh tears filled her eyes and rolled down her cheeks as she recalled the last time she'd seen Neil, when he'd surprised her by coming to stay for three whole days and nights, something he'd never done before. On his last night with her he'd been on edge, pacing the floor in the kitchen, unable to settle. She had never seen him like that. 'Drop everything and run away with me,' he'd suddenly said. She'd laughed and replied, 'I can't, I have a hair appointment tomorrow.' He'd grabbed hold of her hands and said, 'I'm being serious. Come on, let's do it. Let's take a boat and spend the rest of our lives sailing round the Mediterranean. What's to stop us?' God help her, she'd laughed again and changed the subject by taking him upstairs to her bed. The next morning, he'd woken early, kissed her goodbye and promised to call her. That was the last time she saw him. He must have known then that what he'd set in motion was about to catch up with him.

How had she not suspected that something was dangerously wrong with him, that he'd set himself on a course from which there was no way back? And why hadn't she simply agreed to run away with him? Wouldn't that have been better than the guilt she now had to live with? She held the framed photograph to her heart. 'Oh Neil,' she murmured, 'it's all my fault. If only we had never met, you'd still be alive.'

She gulped to try and stem the flow of tears. But it was no good, and once again she was sobbing uncontrollably, just as she had at Neil's graveside.

Neil had frequently said that his wife was one of the most kind-hearted people he knew, and after today, Simone knew that he hadn't been exaggerating. The woman had been extraordinarily generous towards Simone, had shown her immeasurable compassion and understanding.

She had met the son, only briefly, and while he had been guarded, she sensed in him the young man that Neil had been so proud of. There had been no hostility from him, or his mother, which was what she had dreaded. She had feared that she had been invited to attend the funeral merely so that the family could emotionally corner her and hold her responsible for Neil's death. But they hadn't. Not even Neil's brother, who she knew from their telephone conversation, when he'd explained that his sister-in-law had suggested she come to the church for the service, and had found talking to her extremely difficult.

She had recognized him straight away when she had entered the church, from photographs Neil had shown her. He had been shaking hands with a group of mourners, and seizing her chance when he'd been momentarily alone, she had plucked up her courage and discreetly introduced herself. She had asked him to pass on her thanks to Neil's widow for allowing her to come, and had then moved off quickly so that he didn't have an opportunity to respond. During the service, she had watched him transfixed as he'd given the eulogy for his brother and then when he had helped to carry the coffin out of the church.

Partway through the burial ceremony, she had felt his eyes on her, and when she'd met his gaze, he hadn't looked away. There hadn't been anything defiant in his expression, just an intense look of scrutiny. He'd probably been wondering what sort of loathsome woman she was to have an affair with a married man.

Let him think what he wants, she thought now. What did it matter? She would never see any of Neil's family again, so why beat herself up over what they might think of her?

Chapter Twenty-four

'They do have food in Brighton, you know.'

'I'm well aware of that.'

'So why the food parcel, Granza?'

'I don't like turning up empty-handed or putting anyone to any trouble. And for your information, Mr Smarty-Pants, this is a hamper, and we're going to surprise your cousin with a picnic.'

Lloyd took the hamper from his grandmother and placed it carefully on the back seat of his car. Then, after helping her into the passenger seat, he settled himself behind the wheel and drove out through the gates of South Lodge.

A month had passed since his father's death, and occasionally there were moments when Lloyd felt that life seemed almost normal. Usually this was when he was absorbed in his work, when he was focused entirely on the piece of wood he was planing, sanding or staining and there was music playing on the radio in the workshop, and Adam and Pete were engaged in their customary good-natured banter, usually arguing over whose turn it was to make the coffee.

Then there were times when it all came crashing down on him again, and he struggled to make sense of anything that had come to light. The latest, and needlessly cruel turn of events was that the hospice for which Mum had so generously raised money had written to say they felt they could no longer accept her donations from the garden open days she put on at The Meadows. Tainted money, was the implication. After everything Mum and Dad had done for them, could they be more short-sighted? Or more hurtful? Lloyd doubted it.

He hated the position his mother had been put in. She deserved to be treated better; she had done nothing wrong. And didn't she have enough to contend with, without the bank and building society freezing the joint accounts she'd had with Dad? And then the will was still to be read. They were in a state of limbo. It was a nightmare. And all of Dad's doing.

Increasingly Lloyd felt like raging against his father for the mess he'd left behind him. Then he'd feel guilty at the strength of his anger and tell himself that anger wouldn't help, and it certainly wouldn't bring his father back, which he wanted more than anything. Nor would it give him the answers he needed. At night, when he couldn't sleep, his head spun with myriad questions. Always he wanted to know why his father hadn't left them a proper note, not just to explain why he'd done what he had, but something personal for them – a tangible goodbye, a final communication of love and assurance. A one-worded note saying 'sorry' wasn't enough. He and Mum needed more. He had discussed the absence of a proper note with Stirling and Cecily, and between them, the only explanation they could come up with was that perhaps if Dad had started to write such a letter, it would have torn him apart and he wouldn't have been able to go through with killing himself. He'd needed to keep it impersonal. Almost anonymous. They would never know for sure if that was the case, but one thing Lloyd was sure of was that he would go mad if he didn't find a way to resign himself to never knowing the truth.

Today was what you could call another day in search of the truth: he was on his way to meet his newly discovered cousin for the first time.

Cecily had called him yesterday morning, and after she'd established he didn't have anything planned for today – Saturday – she had asked him if he would drive her down to Brighton. She'd then explained that she wanted to see her granddaughter – Katie Lavender – again. He had to admit that he was intrigued to meet her. And if she was at all interested in his opinion, he'd tell her that she would be better off having nothing to do with the family; that she should run as fast as she could in the opposite direction.

Following Stirling's explosive announcement at Dad's funeral, the hairline crack in the family that had always existed had been blown asunder. That night, at Gina's insistence, Stirling moved out of Willow Bank and booked himself into the Hotel du Vin in the centre of Henley. As soon as Lloyd had got wind of this, he'd suggested that his uncle stay with Pen. Pen had been only too happy with the idea, and Stirling had accepted the offer, saying, 'It'll only be for a short while, just until everyone calms down.'

A calm didn't seem likely to be on the cards for any time soon. Stirling had no sooner unpacked his case at The Meadows than Scarlet and Charlie moved in with Gina. It was always possible that Gina was genuinely so devastated that she needed the company and support of her daughter, but Lloyd suspected the move had more to do with colours being nailed to the mast in a blatant display of solidarity. He wouldn't be at all surprised if it turned out that Rosco had put Scarlet up to it. His cousin could never resist a divisive manoeuvre; it was in his blood.

And blood would be very much at the heart of Rosco's machinations. Rosco had never really accepted Lloyd as his equal, due to the simple fact that he wasn't a true Nightingale – just as his father hadn't been – but now there was a stranger in their midst who most certainly had a legitimate claim on the name. No guesses for how that was going down with Rosco.

And just as Neil had been cast as the villain of the family, so now had Stirling, and with allegiances firmly declared and a schism of enormous proportions in place, it was difficult to imagine how family accord could ever be reinstated. Not with Gina talking about divorce.

Lloyd glanced at his grandmother in the passenger seat and

said, 'Do you think Gina really will go through with divorcing Stirling?'

Cecily tutted. 'No. But for now, she's making her feelings very clear by punishing him in the only way she knows how. I'm not without sympathy for her; I do understand that she'll be feeling horribly betrayed. It was wrong what Stirling did when he had that affair with Katie's mother, but on the other hand, he's been an excellent husband and father ever since. If he hadn't loved Gina and Rosco and Scarlet, he would have left them a long time ago, wouldn't he? I predict she'll make a bit more noise and bluster for a while yet, but the reality is, she's not the kind of woman to want to make do with half of what she currently has.'

'You mean financially?'

'Exactly so. Stirling has provided her with an extremely comfortable lifestyle. When was the last time Gina had to worry about the cost of anything? If she divorces Stirling – and let's assume she gets half of what they have by way of money and assets – it's still only half. Why settle for half a cake when you can have the whole thing?'

'For your self-respect?'

Cecily laughed. 'A very high ideal, but not one to which a certain type of woman is prepared to subscribe.'

Lloyd had always admired his grandmother for her candour, so he said, 'Can I ask you a personal question, Granza?'

'Of course.'

'You're one of the most observant people I know; did you ever suspect that Dad was having an affair?'

'No. But I did wonder from time to time if he was tempted.'

'Mum told me the other day about ... well, you know ... that things weren't entirely ... um ... not entirely that good in the bedroom, and ...' He couldn't go on. Discussing his parents' sex life was not a regular line of conversation to have with anyone, let alone his grandmother.

'No need to be coy,' she said, in her typically no-nonsense

171

voice. 'Pen told me a long time ago that she had lost interest in sex. It happens in many marriages. That's why I wondered whether your father might be tempted to stray.'

'You sound as if it's perfectly reasonable to do so.'

'Not perfectly reasonable, but understandable. I wouldn't have endorsed such behaviour, but neither would I have censured it. Lloyd, are you angry with your father?'

The question took him by surprise, and he hesitated before answering. 'Yes,' he admitted reluctantly.

'That's to be expected. Promise me you won't feel guilty about it, though. Anger is all part and parcel of the grieving process. Especially when it's suicide.'

Indicating and putting his foot down to overtake a car towing a caravan, he said, 'How about you, Granza, do you feel angry?'

'Only at those who seem intent on making things worse for us.'

Lloyd knew exactly to whom Cecily was referring. The latest news to be reported in the press was that the police investigation had successfully tracked down the missing clients' money to several accounts in the Cayman Islands. Spurious stories had then followed, claiming that this was where Neil had planned to escape, along with changing his identify. Oh, and he was going to do it with a woman. A lover. As far as Lloyd was aware, there was no rock-solid evidence to support these claims – other than that the family knew of Simone Montrose's existence – but even he had to admit that he could no longer say anything with any certainty about his father.

For legal reasons the located money couldn't be returned straight away to the clients, and so Stirling had personally made good the debts from his own pocket. This also had been reported in the press, but was given no more than a line or two of coverage. Plainly, even in the serious newspapers, it was far more interesting to fill the column inches with dubious speculation.

Stirling had come in for a good deal of scrutiny, the

implication being that he must have been in on the scam, and to his knowledge he had been followed to and from the office on three different occasions. It was for this reason, so Cecily had told Lloyd, that he had decided not to visit Brighton, for fear of dragging Katie into the mire. It wasn't difficult to picture just how much the press would love to get hold of the story of a love child suddenly popping up in Stirling's life.

Not for the first time, Lloyd wondered just how involved Katie Lavender would want to become with the Nightingale family. Based on what she had seen and heard so far, she had to be questioning if she had done the right thing in making contact.

Unless, of course, she had made contact because her motives were not as innocent as she'd claimed, just as Rosco had speculated on the phone the other day when he'd been in touch to instruct Lloyd to keep an eye on Cecily and Pen. 'Your mother and Granza are vulnerable right now to any sob story going,' he'd said, 'and since you're closest to them, it's your job to keep an eye on them. And let's face it, what evidence do we have that this girl is telling the truth? She literally walks in off the street and claims to be the result of some fling Dad had thirty years ago. I mean, come on, she could be anyone trying a number on us.'

Lloyd hadn't mentioned the conversation with Rosco to either his mother or Granza, knowing that nothing would have insulted his grandmother more. There was no one more in control of her faculties and emotions than Cecily Nightingale.

As to what Katie Lavender's motives might be, for now Lloyd was prepared to give her the benefit of the doubt if only because he was more inclined to trust the opinion of his mother and grandmother than that of a hot-headed, bigoted cousin.

Katie was a bag of nerves. She had spent the morning in a demented frenzy of tidying and dusting and vacuuming. When the phone rang, just as she was giving her all to a particularly stubborn bit of limescale on the kitchen tap, she gave a little start.

'Hey, Katie, how's it going?'

'Oh, it's you again, Tess. What do you want now?'

'I just wanted to know if they'd arrived yet.'

'If they had, I wouldn't be talking to you, would I?'

'Hey, what's with all the uptightness?'

'I'm not uptight. I'm just busy.'

'Busy doing what?'

'Cleaning the house.'

'Why?'

'Because I've got visitors coming. As well you know.'

'Do you clean when I visit you?'

'No, I have to clean *after* you've gone. You're the messiest person I know. A complete slob.'

'I'm hurt. Deeply hurt. And the way you're going on, anyone would think you had royalty visiting. Have you laid down a red carpet and put rose petals in the loo for them?'

'Don't be stupid. I just want to make a good impression.'

'Why?'

'Because I want them to like me.'

'I thought you said that you and Cecily hit it off like a regular pair of old muckers. The way you were going on about her, I was beginning to feel jealous, like you'd swapped me for a new best friend.'

'Keep me talking on the phone any longer and I *will* trade you in for another best friend. Oh my God, I've just spotted a humongous cobweb!'

'Calm down, will you? So what if you've got a cobweb, what's the worst that can happen: you'll be reported to the Serious Grime Unit? Hey, that was a joke, girlfriend.'

'Save it for someone who's got time to appreciate your special brand of humour. I'll ring you later, when they've gone.'

'You promise?'

'Hand on heart.'

She was standing on a chair with a duster on the end of a wooden spoon, trying to reach the cobweb above the French doors, when the telephone rang again. She clambered down grumpily. 'Tess, if you think this is funny, I'll bloody well kill you!'

There was a silence at the other end of the line.

'I'm warning you, one more joke about royalty and rose petals and I'll be on the next train to London to burn your entire collection of Johnny Depp scrapbooks! What's more, I'll make you watch! Now will you leave me in peace so I can deal with the mother of cobwebs.'

'Um ... I think you might be mistaking me for someone else.'

'Oh. Who are you?'

'I'm your cousin, Lloyd.'

Katie gulped. So much for making a good impression. 'Er ... Hello. I'm sorry about shouting at you. I thought you were a friend.'

'That's OK. Do you shout at all your friends?'

'Only the really annoying ones. Is there a problem? Aren't you coming?'

'No, everything's fine. According to the satnav, we'll be with you in about twenty minutes. Cecily just wanted me to let you know that we're running early. She has a thing about not inconveniencing people and wanted to make sure it would be all right for us to turn up earlier than expected.'

'Earlier is good for me.'

'Excellent. I'll let you get back to your cobwebs, then.'

Cheeky devil, she thought as she put the phone down and climbed back up on to the chair. He'd better not turn out to be anything like that arrogant pig Rosco.

The cobweb dealt with, she washed her hands, brushed her hair and took a deep breath. She wasn't at all nervous about seeing Cecily again, but Lloyd was a different kettle of fish. An unknown quantity, he would be here today to size her up and report back to his cousins. And having just yelled at him, she hadn't exactly done herself any favours, had she? Still, his approval wasn't really that important.

Who was she kidding? As she'd just said to Tess, it was important to her that she was liked, for which read *approved of*. Cecily and Pen liked and approved of her, as did Stirling. Well, she thought he did. Although given what he now had to deal with, he may well be having second thoughts about her.

She had been surprised how disappointed she'd been when Stirling had phoned to explain that he didn't think he ought to meet up with her again just yet. She understood his reasons and was touched by his concern to protect her, but at the same time there was a small part of her that felt excluded. Rejected, even. She couldn't really explain it, but she wanted to feel a part of his problems. She didn't want to feel an outsider.

And hadn't she caused some of those problems? She had sent a card to Cecily after the funeral, hoping, within the few lines she'd written, to strike the right chord of formality that she felt the situation warranted, and had received a long letter two days later in which Cecily told her everything that had gone on at the funeral and afterwards. Katie had been appalled to read about Stirling and his wife, that he was now staying with Pen, and Gina was breathing fire about divorce. She felt horribly responsible. This was all her fault. Cecily had written, *Now, Katie, I don't want you to blame yourself for the consequences of Stirling's announcement. He alone is responsible for his actions. You're not to worry. He and Gina will find a way to sort this out.* She had finished her letter by asking if she could visit Katie in Brighton.

But Katie *was* worried. That was why she had been up since seven, frantically spring-cleaning the house. Classic displacement activity. She didn't want to be viewed by her cousin as being responsible for destroying Stirling's marriage.

Before the day she'd lost her job and visited the solicitor's office in London, she had begun to feel as if she was moving on from the death of her parents and was once more back in control of her life. But following that fateful meeting with Howard Clifford, everything had changed, and once again she was at the mercy of circumstances over which she had no control. The simplest thing to do would be to walk away from the Nightingales and not get involved. It would be so much easier to get on with her life as though she had never read that letter from her mother.

But how could she do that? How could she effectively put the genie back in the bottle? It just couldn't be done. She had to go through with what she had started. Or rather, what her mother had started. Fay had wanted her to meet Stirling, and despite everything, she was glad she had.

Two things she wasn't so happy about were her continued lack of employment, and Ian. She was circulating her CV like crazy, but the job market had all but dried up. She had never been unemployed before, and the lack of purpose to her days didn't suit her.

As for Ian, he had been devastated when she'd invited him for dinner and broken it to him that she thought it would be better if they didn't see each other any more. She had assumed he would have seen it coming, that it wouldn't have been a big shock. He hadn't, though. 'But we haven't spoken for almost a fortnight,' she'd reasoned. 'Surely you must have thought that was a bad sign?'

'I was giving you your space,' he'd said. 'I didn't want to crowd you.' He'd looked like a wounded puppy, and she'd hated herself for hurting him. 'Please, I know it's been a difficult time for you,' he'd continued, 'and you're probably feeling really confused about everything, but we've been good together, haven't we?'

She was confused about a lot of things, but the one thing she saw with great clarity was that she couldn't be with Ian any longer. 'Cruel to be kind,' both Tess and Zac had told her. 'End it properly. No ambiguity.'

But they weren't the ones staring into the face of a wounded puppy. 'Ian,' she'd said, 'I'll always be grateful to you. You were wonderful to me when my mother died—'

'No!' he'd said, his voice raised to an embarrassing pitch. 'I don't want your gratitude. I want *you*. I want the Katie I knew before you found out about your father. You've been different ever since.'

'Maybe you're right. Maybe I have changed. So if that's true, wouldn't you be better off finding someone new?'

She'd willed him to accept it was over between them, not to make it any more difficult than it already was. He'd shaken his head and said, 'Did you ever really love me, or was I just a convenient shoulder for you? And be honest with me. Don't lie.'

But she had lied. 'I loved you, Ian. I really did.'

'But you don't now.'

'No.'

'Do you know why? Was it something I did? Or something I didn't do?'

Just go, she'd wanted to say. Stop making this so difficult. But she supposed he was driven by his analytical brain searching for some logical reason for why they were breaking up. 'It wasn't anything you said or did, Ian,' she said. 'We just ran our course. It happens. And often for no particular reason, other than a thing has come to a natural end. Unfortunately relationships aren't based on logic. If they were, they would be a lot easier to get right.'

He'd stared at her as if she was speaking a foreign language, and then had left a few minutes later. She had tried to give him a no-hard-feelings hug at the door and suggest that they stay in touch as friends, but he'd shrugged her off and said he'd collect his things the next day. He'd be grateful if she could bag them up ready for him.

She had hurt him badly, and that upset her.

A ring at the doorbell instantly put Ian out of her mind. She took a deep breath and went to open the door.

Chapter Twenty-five

Katie could hear Cecily talking, and she was vaguely aware of gabbling back a reply, something inane about the journey, but she was having what Tess called a shocky moment. A shocky moment was when you saw someone or something that made your spine tingle and you suddenly wanted to dance and laugh and cry all at the same time. It had happened to Tess when she'd met Ben.

But it shouldn't be happening to Katie in her tiny hallway. Hell no! Lloyd was her cousin. But he was so cute. Tall and exceptionally well built, with strong, clear-cut features, he was dressed in jeans with a navy-blue T-shirt and a black well-worn leather jacket. Loaded with just the right amount of nonchalance – any more and it would look forced – his hands were pushed into the pockets of his jeans, causing his shoulders to hunch slightly. The ends of his brown collar-length hair were lightened by the sun and his eyes were blue – intensely blue, for the record. Normally she didn't go for blue eyes. Not her thing. But in this instance she was prepared to make an exception.

Except he was her cousin, she reminded herself. Cousin, cousin, *cousin*! But man o man, he'd got the look perfectly tuned. He was Captain Divine from Planet Awesome.

She realized that he was speaking and holding out his hand towards her. 'Hello, Cousin Katie,' he said.

She had to think what to do. She tried to smile, but couldn't quite manage it. 'Er ... hello, Cousin Lloyd,' she said, taking his lead and his hand, the palm of which she had sufficient wits to note was warm and rough and callused. She remembered Cecily mentioning something about him making upmarket garden furniture for a living.

Letting go of her hand, he looked about him, particularly, for some weird reason, up at the ceiling. 'Good work with the cobwebs,' he said. 'Not a one to be seen.'

Her face prickled and she gave a nervous, unconvincing laugh.

'Lloyd, whatever are you talking about?' This was from Cecily.

'A small joke,' he said, 'and perhaps not a very funny one.'

'I should think it isn't. Now why don't you see if you left your manners in the car along with the hamper?'

He smiled, clicked his heels together and made a salute. 'I'll be right back.'

Cecily gave him an airy wave of her hand, 'Tiresome boy, be off with you.' There was affection in her voice. 'Katie, darling, it's such a beautiful day, shall we go and sit outside in the garden?'

Composing herself, Katie said, 'Please don't expect too much, it's only small.'

'Bigger than my balcony, I'll wager. Lead on, lead on! Ooh, it's perfectly charming. What a clever girl you are to keep it looking so nice.'

'That's what comes of having too much time on one's hands.'

'Still no job?'

'Unfortunately not,' she replied whilst offering Cecily the most comfortable chair, in the shade of the magnolia tree.

'Something will turn up before too long, just you see.' Cecily took her time to get settled into the seat, first removing her silk scarf and lightweight coat and passing them to Katie, then placing her handbag neatly beside her well-shod feet.

'I certainly hope so,' Katie said with feeling.

'Perhaps you're not looking in the right direction. Ah,

Lloyd, there you are. Isn't Katie's garden lovely? One of your benches would be right at home here, don't you agree?'

He cast his gaze around the small space and nodded. 'Green fingers like Cecily and my mother,' he said. Then, looking directly at Katie, he added, 'That must be why they've spoken so highly of you.'

'With or without the green fingers, Pen and I would have taken to Katie,' Cecily said curtly. 'Now then, are you going to stand there all day with that hamper, Lloyd, or are you going to do something useful with it?'

He smiled. 'Having given the matter my full consideration, I think I'll just stand here and annoy you all day, Granza.'

She laughed. 'And what a fine job you're doing of that already.'

'Years of experience, that's what makes me the expert I am.' He placed the hamper on the table, undid the straps and lifted the lid. 'Lunch care of Cecily Nightingale,' he announced. He turned to Katie. 'You haven't spent the morning cooking for us, have you?'

'No,' Katie answered with a wry smile. 'The cobwebs took up all of my time. I planned to take you out somewhere for lunch.'

'Then unplan that arrangement right away,' Cecily said, 'and we'll have a picnic here in the garden. What could be better? And will one of you kindly tell me what all this non-sense is about cobwebs?'

Just about everything Stirling did these days, he imagined how it would look through the eyes of a journalist intent on caus-ing trouble. An innocent trip on the river in his boat could be made to look like the actions of a man flaunting his wealth with a couldn't-give-a-shit attitude. The caption would read, *While others bear the brunt of his brother's deception and greed, Stirling Nightingale sails blithely on.* To ensure there was no danger of that happening, he hadn't been out in his treasured slipper launch in over a month. Nor had he driven his Aston Martin at his usual lick in case he was caught for speeding and it was turned into a newsworthy misdemeanour. He felt he had to watch his every step, not just for his family's reputation but for Nightingale Ridgeway's reputation; for its very survival.

Since Neil's funeral, they had lost nearly a dozen clients, including one of their biggest investors. Stirling had written to every single client, from the biggest to the smallest, assuring them that something like this could never happen again, that procedures had been put in place. He also informed them that all the missing monies had been recovered and that he'd personally refunded what had been taken from the portfolios. It seemed to have stemmed the flow of haemorrhaging clients, and he could only hope it would continue to do so. Perhaps those who hadn't left were taking the view that lightning wouldn't strike twice in the same place.

Even the state of his marriage had found its way into the newspapers. God knew how. But since it had rapidly become common knowledge that he had moved out of Willow Bank – you couldn't keep something like that secret in a small place like Sandiford – it was probably someone in the village who had been coerced by some hack or other into divulging the titbit that he was staying with his brother's widow. He really would have thought that journalists had more important things to write about. But then it was the summer; it was open season for superficial news stories. Which was why he was keeping his distance from Katie for the time being. He badly wanted to see her again, but he didn't want to risk compounding the situation.

Gina and Rosco and Scarlet had said some hurtful things about Katie. He could understand their anger and in particular Gina's sense of betrayal, and he could tolerate them venting their feelings towards him, but what he couldn't do was stand by and listen to any attacks made on Katie. Sadly his defence of her had only further enraged them. Thank God he hadn't said anything about the trust fund he'd set up all those years ago; that would certainly add fuel to the fire. For now, that had to remain a secret between him and Katie and Cecily.

He put down the glass of water he'd ordered and looked at his watch: still five minutes to go. He'd got here early, ostensibly so that he could make sure he hadn't been followed – he was beginning to feel he was a character in a spy novel – but mainly so that he would have time to gather his thoughts. He had believed this to be a good idea last night; now he wasn't so sure. Could she really tell him anything he didn't know already?

What more was there to add to what they now assumed to be the case, that Neil had taken the money because, like Stirling, he'd been facing a sharp and sudden drop in income for the foreseeable future due to the continuing downshift in the economy? For Stirling it wasn't a serious problem, not being able to pay himself the usual dividend, but for Neil, planning to start a new life with Simone and at that time provide generously for Pen, it must have been a disaster. Impatient to be with Simone, had he looked at his client portfolios and thought he could simply borrow from them during the difficult period and then return the money when times were good again? Stirling wanted to believe that his brother fully intended to pay back the money, but he couldn't be sure of it.

One thing he was sure of, based on what had since come to light, was the client who Rosco had overheard talking with his accountant that day at the tennis club had been in touch with Neil regarding a query about a discrepancy in his investments. It was that phone call, Stirling now believed, that made Neil realize he was about to be found out and which led him to take his life several days later.

He glanced nervously round the dining area of the Old Parsonage. He hadn't been to the hotel here in Oxford in a long time; nothing seemed to have changed in the intervening years. To his relief, there didn't seem to be anyone remotely interested in him, overtly or otherwise. The other diners comprised a mix of well-dressed couples and American tourists, all engrossed in their own conversations and meals.

He returned his attention to his newspaper. He'd lost count of how many times he'd tried to read the same article on the front page, not a word of which he had taken in. He forced himself to concentrate, determined this time to master it.

He'd read for no more than a minute or two when he heard a softly pitched woman's voice saying his name. He looked up, straight into the face of Simone Montrose. He got to his feet. After a moment's hesitation, they shook hands. He pulled out a chair for her.

'Thank you,' she said.

He sat down again and swallowed. He cleared his throat. 'Is this as awkward for you as it is for me?'

'Very awkward. I nearly didn't come.' She gave a tremulous smile. 'You're quite like him, you know.'

'People often used to say that, they called it our simpatico mindset. Which wouldn't be at all remarkable for blood-related brothers, but since Neil was adopted, the similarity was all the more incredible. My mother says it's what happens when people spend a lot of time together: they mirror each other's mannerisms and speech patterns. The body language merges.'

'But perhaps only if the bond is a strong one; if there's real affection between two people. You and Neil were extremely close, weren't you? He was always talking about you. You were hugely important to him.'

From nowhere, a wave of unbearable grief swept over Stirling. Lately the pain had lessened; it had become sub-merged beneath a layer of something else: anger. He was angry that Neil hadn't confided in him. Angry that he had not been honest with the one person in the world with whom he should have been totally honest. But sitting here with Simone Montrose, the woman who had been such a closely guarded secret in Neil's life, and hearing her talk about Neil, her voice low and full of sadness, his anger was stripped away to expose his grief in all its painful purity once more. To steady himself, he tidied his newspaper away and reached for a menu. 'Shall we choose and then order?'

They neither spent long deliberating over what to eat or drink, and with their food quickly ordered, along with a glass of wine, Simone was the first to resume the conversation. 'How's Neil's widow?' she asked.

'Coping.'

'Does she know that you're here in Oxford, that you wanted to see me?'

'Yes. I didn't want to keep something like this from her. One way or another, there's been enough secrecy in the family. It's time to be totally honest now.'

'That's easier said than done in my experience. We lie all the time, even with those we love. I lied to Neil when I said I didn't want him to leave Pen. Of course I wanted him to leave her. I wanted him for myself, but I went through the motions of trying to be the understanding mistress.'

He found himself wincing. 'I don't think you should use that word.'

'Which word?'

'*Mistress*. It doesn't seem appropriate.'

'But that's what I was. It's how your family will always regard me.'

'Some might, but not all. I certainly don't want to.'

Their drinks arrived and when the waiter left them, Simone said, 'What do you want, Stirling? Why did you want to see me again?'

'This may sound strange, but I feel I owe it to Neil to make sure you're all right.'

She raised an impeccably arched eyebrow in surprise. 'That's very kind of you. But entirely unnecessary. I shall be all right. Eventually.'

He neither pushed the offer of his help nor felt slighted by her firm rebuttal. As she sipped her wine, he tried to observe her without appearing to do so. His memory of her from the funeral – as sketchy as most of his memories were from that day – was quite different to the woman he was looking at now. Then, she'd been a spectral presence amongst the mourners. There had been a frailness to her, a sort of insubstantial bearing to the way she'd held herself. He could remember thinking as he'd watched her when Neil's coffin had been lowered into the ground that all it would have taken was one puff of wind for her to be swept away. He thought now that that might have been some kind of subconscious wishful thinking on his part. But now, sitting across the table from her, he saw a stronger and more substantial woman. For a start, she was taller than he recalled, and younger. He wasn't usually very good at guessing a woman's age, but he put her in her early forties, perhaps forty-four at a push. Her hair was long and dark and perfectly straight, and seemed to accentuate her height and slender build. There were faint lines around her almond-shaped eyes and a tight pensiveness to her face – wholly understandable, given the awkwardness of the situation – but he could see all too clearly that she was an attractive and elegant woman. There was a dignity and considered intelligence to her bearing, which suggested to him that she was a person who didn't rush into things lightly. He tried to imagine how she had got herself into an affair with Neil, but failed. Their waiter reappeared with their food; they'd both ordered the poached salmon on a bed of leeks. Alone again, Stirling steeled himself for what he wanted to say next. 'I'd like you to help me,' he said.

'How?'

'I want to know more about the Neil you knew. You must have seen a different side to him, one that I, and the family, didn't know about.'

'And with that knowledge, you then think you'll be able to make sense of what he did?'

Stirling nodded. 'The Neil I knew wouldn't have stolen money and then killed himself.'

'Who knows what anyone is capable of doing when confronted with a difficult choice?' she said at length.

'Meaning he'd made up his mind to leave Pen but wanted to do it in the kindest way possible? I'm sorry, but that doesn't explain why he appeared to undergo a complete character change.'

'I agree with you. And I'm sorry to say this, but you've had a wasted journey today, because I can't throw any more light on what Neil did than you can. Don't you think I've thought of little else? Why, why, *WHY*? It's all I think of. It's the last thing I think of when I fall asleep at night and the first thought that I wake up to. If I knew the answer, don't you think I would have told you or the police?'

Hearing the tension in her voice, Stirling said, 'I'm sorry. Please, I didn't mean to insinuate that you were holding anything back. It's just that there has to be an answer somewhere. And I thought that since the two of you were so close, in a way that maybe he wasn't with Pen, he might have shared something with you he couldn't share with anyone else. I know that's what I did when I had an affair many years ago.'

Her eyes widened. 'I didn't know that. Neil never mentioned it.'

'He didn't know about it. No one did. In fact, it's only just come to light.' He wiped his mouth with his napkin and told her about Katie, and his reckless announcement the day of Neil's funeral and how Gina and his children had reacted.

'Goodness. You've had quite a load to carry recently, haven't you? And your daughter – Katie – how is she now going to fit into your life?'

'That's a good question. I want to get to know her, but only once things have calmed down.'

'What about her mother, will you meet up with her again?'

'Sadly that's not possible. She's dead. Along with Katie's father – the man who brought her up as his own. She doesn't have any other family.'

'But now she has you.' Simone looked thoughtful. 'I know

187

what it's like to be alone. My mother died many years ago and my elderly father is now in a care home and most of the time he doesn't know who I am. I have no brothers or sisters.' She paused. 'I know it sounds selfish, and I'm too old really, but I wish I'd had a child with Neil.'

'That was something Pen always regretted she wasn't able to do. Not that that means she loves Lloyd any less than if she'd given birth to him herself, she doesn't. You knew that Lloyd was adopted?'

'Yes. And it was the same for Neil: he was always talking about his son, he was immensely proud of him. I hope Lloyd knows that.'

'I think he does. Did my brother ever talk about adoption? Lloyd's or his own? I've been wondering recently ...' He broke off, suddenly uncomfortable at voicing what had been going through his head in the last few weeks.

'Go on,' she urged.

He drank some of his wine. 'Did Neil ever talk about his birth parents? With us he didn't, but that might have been because he thought we'd be hurt if he did, as though we might have felt he was rejecting us after all this time.'

The diners at the table nearest theirs were on the move, scraping chairs back, gathering bags. When they'd gone, Simone said, 'There was a conversation we had not long before Easter. We'd gone for a walk in Christchurch Meadows and I remember thinking at the time that he wasn't his normal self, he was unusually quiet and introverted. We found a bench and sat down for a while. It was a lovely day.' Her gaze slid away from Stirling's and a sadness clouded her eyes, as if touching the memory of that day was causing her pain. He waited for her to continue. She did, although her gaze remained fixed on some faraway point through the window, where shafts of sunlight shone through the glass. 'We'd just been watching a young mother stop to tie her son's shoelaces, and the girl was patiently explaining to the little boy – he must only have been about four – how to do it when Neil asked me what I thought of him as a person, and did I think I really knew him. He then started saying a person couldn't know who he was if he didn't know where he was from. I disagreed with him, and we debated the subject for some minutes until he grew tired of it and suggested we carry on with our walk down to the river.'

'So he did hanker to know?'

'It was the only time I ever heard him talk that way.'

'Do you think it's possible he wanted to track down his real family?' Stirling felt the sting of his words as soon as they left his mouth. It was the sting of jealousy. He didn't want Neil to have another family. He didn't want to share him with real blood brothers and sisters. Because to do that would make Stirling feel second best. But was that what Neil had always felt? Second best? Somehow not quite a proper Nightingale? And was that how Lloyd felt at times?

'I have no idea,' Simone answered. 'He never raised the matter again.'

Stirling fell quiet. He pushed his plate away, unable to finish his meal. 'Simone,' he said after a long silence, 'do you think Neil was experiencing some kind of breakdown?'

She shook her head. 'He may have lost his way a little, but a breakdown, no, I can't go along with that.' She put a hand out to him. 'Stirling, I know it's hard, but we may have to accept that we'll never know what drove Neil to do what he did.'

'I don't think I can do that.'

'I'm not sure I can either, but I'm frightened that if I don't, if I keep blaming myself for the part I played in his death, I'll go mad. I can see you doing the same thing: you're beating yourself up because you didn't spot that he was on the verge of killing himself; you weren't able to stop him. And I'm convinced that's not what Neil would have wanted.'

Stirling felt the coolness from Simone's hand on his. She was now looking straight at him, her eyes filled with tears. 'If only he'd left a note,' he murmured. 'If he had just done that one small thing, I'd be able to ...' His words got stuck in his throat and he lowered his head. 'I'm sorry,' he said when he'd dug around inside his jacket pocket for a tissue and composed himself. 'I feel such a fool. Losing it like this.'

'Don't apologize,' she said. 'Come on, neither of us is hungry. Let's pay the bill and go for a walk.'

Chapter Twenty-six

Gina knew what she was doing but she couldn't stop herself. She didn't want to.

She hadn't come here to The Meadows spoiling for a fight, but now she was more than ready for one. She had called in on the off chance to speak with Stirling about a financial matter, only to be told by Pen that he'd gone to Oxford to see Simone Montrose. And then, in one of her typical and infuriatingly throwaway remarks, Pen had said that Lloyd and Cecily had gone down to Brighton to see ... to see that wretched girl. Gina couldn't bring herself to say the girl's name, not even in her head.

From then on everything about her sister-in-law annoyed her and made her want to grab hold of the useless woman and shake her hard. Stop being so bloody wet and pathetic, she wanted to shout at her. And if Pen said just once more, with regard to Gina's decision to divorce Stirling, that they were all under a lot of stress right now, that it wasn't the time to make any hasty decisions, or that time was a great healer, then Gina would do something very hasty that no amount of time would ever heal. Stirling had betrayed her in the worst possible way. Their whole marriage had been a lie. And Stirling would pay for that. But could she make Pen understand? No. Because the silly woman wasn't listening to her. She was far more interested in wandering round the garden deadheading her precious roses, forcing Gina to follow her like some stupid dog.

'Pen,' she said, her exasperation reaching boiling point.

'please, will you stop what you're doing and listen to me properly.'

No reply.

'*Pen!*'

Pen stopped what she was doing and looked round in surprise. 'Why are you shouting at me?'

'Because you weren't listening to a word I was saying and it was the only way I could attract your attention.'

'I *was* listening to you. Of course I was. You were saying you couldn't understand why Stirling would want to talk to Simone Montrose, and I've already told you, he said he wanted to ask her some questions about Neil.'

'Oh, for heaven's sake, I'd moved on from that. I was saying how appallingly insensitive Cecily is being by going down to Brighton to see that ... that girl, and trust her to involve Lloyd and ... Oh, what's the point in trying to make you understand when you're doing what you always do, avoiding anything you don't want to confront by disappearing into your silly little world. Honestly, Pen, you're nothing but a child sometimes and I for one have had enough of it.'

Pen looked startled. 'Gina, whatever is the matter with you? Why are you getting yourself so worked up over me?'

'If you'd been listening, you'd know!' Gina could hear her voice getting shriller and shriller, but she made no effort to control it. She didn't want to control it. She wanted to let rip. 'If you weren't so self-absorbed, you'd realize this family is falling apart and it's all your fault.'

'My fault?'

'Yes, your fault! If you had been a better wife, none of this would have happened. If you hadn't been so obsessed with this garden, Neil wouldn't have felt so neglected and needed to look elsewhere.'

Pen's jaw dropped. For what felt like for ever she stared mutely at Gina. Then her face crumpled and the secateurs dropped from her hands. She turned and walked very quickly back up the garden towards the house.

Finally, thought Gina with grim satisfaction, she had got her sister-in-law's attention and provoked a reaction. A genuine reaction.

She caught up with Pen in front of a large stone trough of sweet peas; with great care Pen was weaving the tender shoots up the frame of willow supports. She looked as if she didn't have a care in the world. Except on closer inspection Gina could see that her hands were shaking. 'Damn!' Pen suddenly cursed. She had forced one of the stems too much and it had snapped off. She whipped round and faced Gina. 'I don't understand why you feel the need to attack me so personally and so vociferously. What have I ever done to you?'

If Pen was expecting her to climb down and apologize, she had another think coming. 'For years we've all played along with your wafty, head in the clouds, airy-fairy act; well, let me tell you, we're all heartily sick of it. And as for that ridiculous farce of a funeral you put us through, you could not have made yourself look more stupid. No one in their right mind would have done what you did. It was sheer madness, not to say horribly offensive to the rest of us, for you to invite Neil's mistress. I don't think I'll ever forgive you for putting us through that shameful day.'

'I did it for Neil.'

'For Neil?' Gina exploded. 'For Neil? Really, Pen, just how dim are you? Neil was planning to leave you for that woman!'

'I understand why you're angry,' Pen said calmly. Annoyingly calmly. 'You're angry with Stirling and you're taking it out on me.'

'Oh well done, Pen, that's your great thought for the day, is it? Of course I'm angry with Stirling. But I'm far angrier with you. You could have stopped all this from happening.'

'How exactly?'

'If you'd had your eye on the ball you would have known what Neil was up to.'

'And what's your excuse for not knowing what Stirling was up to thirty years ago?'

Gina sucked in her breath. 'That's different. We'd only been married a few years.' Immediately she regretted what she'd said, it sounded as if she was defending Stirling, and nothing could be further from her mind.

'It may have taken place just a couple of years into your marriage,' Pen came back at her, 'but you still have to ask yourself why he did it. At least I know why, as you put it, Neil looked elsewhere, and I have to say it's none of your business. Perhaps you should consider the adage that people in glass houses really shouldn't throw stones.'

At that, and seeing that at last Pen was showing she had some fight in her, Gina couldn't resist playing her trump card. A trump card that would hurt as no other could. 'At least I gave my husband children. Unlike you.'

Pen stared at her steadily. 'I think you'd better go now,' she said.

'Don't worry, I wouldn't dream of staying a second longer. I'm just glad that at last we've been honest with each other.'

'I had no idea you despised me so thoroughly, Gina. You should have got this off your chest years ago.'

'You're right, I should have, but for the sake of the family, I kept quiet.'

'You don't think that for the sake of the family, during this particularly difficult time, it wouldn't have been better to continue with the pretence that you liked me?'

'I've had enough of pretending. And I'd seriously advise *you* to stop pretending you're some kind of middle-aged Pollyanna and acquaint yourself with the real world. You're on your own now, Pen. There's no more good old Neil to protect you. It's time to stand on your own two feet. Unless, of course, you're planning to replace Neil with Lloyd and rely on him for everything. But how soon before he grows sick of your stifling dependence on him and ends up hating you?'

'Please go, Gina. I'll tell Stirling you called in to see him. Can I pass a message on?'

'Don't bother. He'll be hearing from my solicitor soon enough.'

Alone in the garden, Pen closed her eyes. Her body was stiff and ached with the effort of trying not to shake. Gina was just being irrational, she told herself. She's furious with Stirling. Lashing out at the first and easiest target. She didn't mean what she said. Of course she didn't.

As if it was now safe to do so, Pen opened her eyes. She let out the breath she'd been holding in and wrapped her arms tightly around her body. All her life she had taken every possible step she could to avoid conflict of any sort. She hated arguments and disagreements. She had witnessed too many with her warring parents when she'd been a child. Their eventual divorce had come as a relief to her; naively she'd imagined that the fighting would then be over with. But she'd been wrong. They had kept up the arguments, most of which revolved around whose turn it was *not* to have her for the school holidays. Their busy schedules – her father had been a diplomat and her mother had been what could only be described as a socialite with a ferociously busy diary – had dictated that she attend boarding school. She hadn't minded a bit, she had loved school; it was the holidays she had dreaded, knowing that she would be the cause of yet more conflict and hostility. She had done her best to be as unobtrusive a child as she could, and it was a habit she had taken on through to adulthood, always wanting to keep the peace, never to be the cause of a disagreement or get involved in one.

But with Gina just now, she had come as close as she'd ever come to a full-blown fight, not just to rant and rave, but to cause actual bodily harm to her sister-in-law. At every accusation Gina had made, she'd had to force herself with superhuman strength not to react. Had she given in to her feelings, she would have lost all control.

The knowledge of that frightened her. It made her realize that her emotions were balanced on a knife edge. One more push, and who knew what she might be capable of.

Chapter Twenty-seven

'I'd say the day was an unqualified success. What do you think?'

Brighton was behind them now and they were on the A23 heading towards Horsham. Lloyd had known when they'd set off this morning that Cecily was keen for him to approve of his newly discovered cousin. He was about to reply when Cecily said, 'I wanted you to meet the real Katie as soon as possible, because I wanted to nip in the bud any preconceived ideas you might have been forming about her, given that with their pernicious and pejorative tosh, Gina and co. are branding her as some sort of devil child. Especially Rosco.'

'Since when have any of my opinions coincided with Rosco's?'

'I know that, but I'm on a mission to ensure the poor girl is given a fair chance. As any right-thinking person would agree, the circumstances of her birth are no fault of hers. So what did you think of her? You seemed to be getting along very well. She was understandably a little on edge when we arrived, but that's no wonder, since she would have known you would be putting her under the microscope.'

Lloyd thought of the obvious bond he'd witnessed between his grandmother and Katie, how surprisingly natural they'd been around each other. But he knew of old that if Cecily took to a person, she would develop an instant and easy rapport with them; there would be no standing on ceremony with her.

In contrast, there had been an initial guardedness from

Katie towards him, but gradually she had relaxed and been funny and quick-witted. Yet at the same time, there was a serious and sensitive side to her. When she had offered him her condolences regarding his father, her words had been frank and sincere and said without any hint of awkwardness on her part. He had respected her for that. Too frequently of late when people spoke to him of his loss – was there a more inadequate word for what he was going through? – he'd been subjected to stultifying embarrassment or insulting artifice.

'I think she makes an excellent addition to the family, Granza,' he said, choosing his words with care. 'It should be fun having her around, although Rosco is likely to make her life hell and I wouldn't wish that on anyone.'

'You don't think she's more than capable of taking care of herself? And Rosco? Just as you do?'

He nodded. 'Fair point.'

'You like her, then?'

'I believe we've established that.' He turned and smiled at his grandmother. 'I'm officially a fan. She's great. Really great.'

'Good. I'm glad. Because I have every intention of us seeing a lot more of her.'

'No complaints from me on that score.'

Rosco couldn't believe what he was hearing. What the hell was his father playing at? Going to Oxford to meet Uncle Neil's mistress? Was he mad?

It was becoming rapidly clear to him that certain elements of the family were losing their grip on reality and were deliberately – if not downright maliciously – pulling in the wrong direction, and to the detriment of those around them. Which included Cecily and Lloyd getting all chummy with the product of Dad's affair. How did they think Gina was supposed to cope with that? It beggared belief. Looking at the highly agitated state of his mother as she sat knocking back a second gin and tonic in the conservatory with Scarlet, who was drinking some kind of lemon and ginger concoction, he wished Dad was here to see the damage he was inflicting.

Rosco didn't think he would ever come to terms with his father's infidelity and the grotesquely cavalier way he'd told them about it. It still sickened him to recall the expression on his father's face that day of the funeral; it was as if he had taken malevolent delight in shocking them with the announcement. In that moment, Dad had turned into a stranger.

Increasingly Rosco was becoming concerned that his brother's death might have affected Dad more than they had originally thought. What if it was making him unwell? *Mentally* unwell? And what if he wasn't in a fit state to make important decisions at work? What then? Rosco knew the answer, and if it was necessary, he would take that step to safeguard the company. There could be no woolly behaviour or illogical uncertainty; too much was at stake. They had to be seen to be totally back in control, a united front with nothing to hide. There had been enough whispering and gossiping going on in the last month amongst the staff, not just in relation to Neil, but now about Stirling and his marriage. As yet nobody seemed to know about Katie Lavender, and Rosco hoped it would remain that way. For the sake of appearances, he made damned sure that whenever anyone was around them, he and Dad appeared to be in perfect harmony. But when they were alone, it was a stretch for him to be civil to his father. His father knew it, too.

He went over to the wine rack and picked out a bottle of red wine. As he uncorked it, he listened to Scarlet through the open doors between the kitchen and conservatory; she was talking about the child she was carrying and all the stress this situation was putting on it. He rolled his eyes. The baby would know stress all right when it was born. Having a mother like Scarlet would not be an easy ride. Always trying to put herself at the centre of any drama, she was about as consistent and reliable as the weather. She could happily claim black was white one day and then swear with breathtaking conviction that she'd said no such thing the following day.

At the moment, of course, she was baby-centric, and unless a thing related directly to her and her baby she wasn't interested. But the Dad and Katie Lavender situation was very much of interest to her. She had been stunned to learn of their half-sister and swore she would never accept her as such.

When it came to Mum divorcing Dad, Rosco knew that his sister was secretly against the idea. Oh yes, she wanted Dad to be punished for what he'd done to them, but deep down Scarlet – the poster girl for Daddy's girls the world over – loved him and didn't want their parents to split up. Neither did Rosco. He knew what would happen if they did go through with it. Scarlet would have given birth by then and would have turned into the Mumzilla from Hell, and he would be left to shoulder the burden of taking care of their mother. The slightest problem and he would be expected to deal with it. It had happened to a friend of his – during the divorce and thereafter the friend's mother practically lost all ability to think or do anything for herself. Rosco didn't want that for his mother. Or for himself. A far worse scenario would be if Gina married again. If that happened, they'd have a stranger meddling in their affairs, and that was something Rosco would never countenance.

These were two very good reasons why he needed to get Scarlet on side; he needed her to start thinking clearly and to stop stirring up their mother by going on and on about how awful Dad had been. With her help he believed he could bring about a reconciliation between their parents, as well as a way to get rid of Katie Lavender from their lives for good. He was all for his mother showing her anger and disgust at what Dad had done, but she could turn this to her advantage if she used her head. All it would take was a simple ultimatum and Dad would be brought back into line. And three cheers to that, he thought, raising his wine glass in the air.

*

On the B4009 and heading towards Watlington, Stirling was stuck in traffic – ahead of him there was a set of temporary lights and a sign for roadworks. With Fauré's Requiem playing on the car's CD player, he felt boundless and detached from all that was going on around him. He was tempted to pull over, close his eyes and give in to the feeling of unexpected calm he was experiencing.

It was the first time since Neil's death that he hadn't felt like his heart was racing or that he was continuously swimming against the tide with a heavy load on his back. Sleep had become a rarity for him, and most mornings he woke exhausted, as though he hadn't slept at all, his head fuzzy, his legs and arms leaden. It was a monumental effort to drag himself out of bed, but then once he was up and showered, his mind became a maelstrom of anxious activity and his body was flooded with adrenalin. It was an exhausting state to be in.

But with the top back on his car, the sun shining down on him, the music soaring, he felt so relaxed he could almost believe he didn't have a care in the world. The thought was so ludicrous he wanted to laugh out loud. He couldn't help but wonder if this was a sign he was on the brink of losing his mind. But given the choice, he'd rather be happily out of his mind than sane and consciously having to endure another day · of this nightmare.

He pondered why he was feeling this lightness of spirit. It was possible that Simone had something to do with it. Being with her had made him feel connected to Neil in a way that no one else did, not Pen, not Lloyd, not even Cecily. She had told him how she and Neil had met, how initially it had been nothing more than a relaxed and easy friendship, neither one of them knowingly pushing it to be anything else.

That was how it had been for Stirling with Katie's mother, Fay. A natural friendship had developed between them from the first day she had started working for him. A clichéd affair with his secretary could not have been further from his thoughts, and he'd been shocked rigid when he realized that his feelings for her were tipping into something dangerously inappropriate. He tried to alter his behaviour towards her, to put some distance between them. He considered asking her to leave, planning in his head how he would go about it, but when it came to it, he couldn't go through with the plan; the thought of never seeing her again was too much, and so he found himself crossing the line he never thought he would.

At no stage did Fay make a move on him; it was, as Simone had described the situation with her and Neil, a natural coming together of two people intensely and profoundly attracted to each other. When something as strong as that happened, when love was involved, all sense of right and wrong no longer existed. For that brief time with Fay he was happier than he'd ever been; she'd made him feel something he hadn't known he could feel.

He couldn't say that he'd ever been unhappy in his marriage to Gina, and he was convinced that had he not met Fay, he would never have strayed, but Fay had been that special one-in-a-million woman who had had the power to completely change his life.

Just as Simone had done to Neil.

The sound of a horn beeping impatiently from behind him had him moving forward. Twenty yards later the queue of traffic ground to a halt once more.

Thirty years on, and Fay still had the power to change his life. She had bequeathed him a gift like no other. When the time was right, he was looking forward to getting to know Katie better. He hoped that by then Rosco and Scarlet would be over their shock and would accept that Katie was a very real part of him, and therefore a part of the family.

He didn't know what to think about Gina. He understood completely her saying she couldn't bear to be in the same room as him, and that she wanted a divorce – it was a classic knee-jerk reaction to his betrayal – but was it really what she wanted in the long term? For now he was prepared to go along with whatever she said or did, if only so as not to antagonize her yet further.

He had told Simone all this as they'd walked through the park in Oxford and strolled down to the river. They had stood for a moment on a bridge to watch the amusing spectacle of some inept punting going on below them, and she had asked him what it was he actually wanted. 'Do you want to stay married?' she had asked.

'I don't know,' he had replied with more candour than he could have owned up to with anyone in his family. 'It's all I feel I know. It's all that I'm familiar with.'

'Is that enough?'

'Again, I don't know.'

'Do you love Gina?'

'I don't *not* love her, if that makes any sense.'

Simone had looked directly at him, unnervingly so. 'It makes perfect sense. But you still have to decide if that's enough.'

He had found her company surprisingly refreshing, and for a couple of hours he had known a fleeting moment of peace.

The cars in front of him were moving again, and he pressed down on the accelerator. He drove the rest of the journey back to Sandiford as though returning to the battlefield with fresh purpose and intent.

Chapter Twenty-eight

It was Saturday morning of the August Bank Holiday weekend and Cecily was sitting on her balcony drinking her first cup of tea of the day. From a cloudless blue sky, the sun was shining brightly. The day promised to be good. Cecily was glad. For Pen's sake, she wanted everything about the weekend to go well.

After the disgraceful behaviour of those perfidious turn-coats on the hospice committee and their refusal to accept any more contributions from Pen's garden open days, Cecily had urged Pen to find another charity to raise funds for during the Bank Holiday weekend. She knew from experience – when her own husband died fifteen years ago – that keeping busy was a vital part of battling one's way through the debilitating loneliness and sense of everything being utterly pointless. It didn't solve anything, but it did distract the mind sufficiently to be an effective tonic.

As luck would have it, no sooner had Cecily made the sug- ·
gestion than a good cause landed in their laps. Although the Reverend Roger Batley probably wouldn't think it was lucky that St Oswald's had recently been inspected by the church structural boys and found wanting in the roof department. But thank God Roger was a robust, old-style, no-nonsense man of the cloth who was more than happy to take a donation from Pen. Stirling and Lloyd had backed the idea whole-heartedly and so a plan was drawn up. It had been just the thing to distract Pen, to give her a new sense of purpose and drive.

With The Meadows open to the public for the whole of

the Bank Holiday weekend, the next few days were going to be busy. Doubtless more than just garden lovers would come; there would be an element of local nosy parkers rolling up to have a snoop round the garden of a man who had committed fraud and then suicide. When Cecily had warned Pen of this, Pen had said, 'Let them come and gawp. So long as they pay their entrance fee, let them poke and pry as much as they want.' Cecily had never felt more proud of her daughter-in-law. Too often, because she was so easy-going, people were inclined to underestimate and dismiss Pen, but she had backbone aplenty, and had been proving it ever since Neil's death.

As Cecily knew it would, life had begun to settle down and a degree of normality had crept back into their lives. Thankfully the press had backed off, bored with a story that was now *sub judice*, and this meant that Stirling was able to devote time to establishing a meaningful relationship with Katie.

Obviously this wasn't going down too well in certain quarters, but sooner or later Rosco and Scarlet were going to have to accept that they had a half-sister. Sibling rivalry was one thing, but spiteful prejudice was another. Cecily knew that initially, when emotions were running high, Rosco and Scarlet had refused point-blank to meet Katie. Then they'd softened their view and said they'd consider it. But whenever Stirling proposed a meeting, they had always found some reason or other as to why they couldn't make that date or time. Shame on them. Didn't they realize how churlish this made them look?

Her cup of tea finished, Cecily roused herself and went back inside to make her breakfast.

At Willow Bank, breakfast in the garden was proving to be yet another master class in the art of how to punctuate a long awkward silence with an equally awkward burst of meaningless small talk.

Drinking their coffee and hiding behind their newspapers

of choice – *The Times* for Stirling and the *Mail* for Gina – they were currently perfecting a long awkward silence. They were conducting themselves in this painfully strained fashion because they were trying too hard to act as if everything was perfectly normal between them, as though, if they pretended hard enough, they could convince themselves that the events of the last few months had never taken place. Tiptoeing round each other with agonizing care, neither one of them was saying what they were really feeling. The tension was getting to Stirling, to the point where he almost welcomed a full-blown argument to clear the air and for them to behave how they used to.

Last week, and much to his surprise, Gina had withdrawn her threat of divorce and had given Stirling the go-ahead to return to Willow Bank. At the same time Scarlet and Charlie had moved back to their own place, which perversely had disappointed Stirling. Having them around might have acted as a human shield, a buffer between him and Gina. But they'd been eager to go home, as they wanted to start work on preparing the nursery for the baby. Their idea to turn Woodside into some kind of therapeutic retreat had gone on hold – probably never to see the light of day again – as Charlie had gone into business with yet another old school friend. Stirling had only a vague idea what work it was: something to do with website design. He had apologized to Charlie for the way he'd spoken to him the day of Neil's funeral, and Charlie being Charlie had shrugged the apology off, saying he hadn't given it another thought.

Actually, Stirling wasn't sorry for his loss of control that day. Nor was he sorry for Katie's existence. Whilst he was sensitive to Gina's feelings, he was not going to fall into the trap of repeatedly apologizing for what he'd done thirty years ago. To do that would be to insult Katie.

An exaggerated tut from the other side of the table, followed by a newspaper being vigorously rustled, had him looking up. 'Something wrong?' he asked.

Gina closed the pages of the newspaper, put it down on the table and met his gaze with a cool stare. 'Oh, just another story about a husband betraying his wife.'

'Oh,' he echoed. Not knowing what else to say, he returned his attention to the article he'd been reading – a blatantly biased attack on the government by the Institute of Fiscal Studies.

Dangerous seconds passed.

Listening to the sound of doves cooing from the roof of the summer house, he waited for the telltale rustle of Gina picking up her newspaper again.

Nothing.

Was this how it was going to be from here on? he wondered. Watching. Listening. Being perpetually on his guard. He lowered his paper and risked a glance. Gina was staring straight at him. The coolness had gone from her gaze, and in place was a look of disgusted disbelief. 'You really were going to just sit there and not say anything, weren't you?'

He carefully folded his newspaper and put it to one side on the table. 'What do you want me to say? What could I possibly say that would be right in your view?'

Her eyes flared. 'I want you to react, damn you. I want you not to sit there as if you're made of stone.'

'Even though that's how I feel?'

She frowned. 'How can you talk about how you feel? What about me? What about how *I* feel? Don't you ever think of that?'

It wasn't his intention, but he knew he was giving off an air of detached indifference. He softened his voice. 'Tell me how you feel, then. Because unless you do, unless I know what you're really thinking, we're never going to be at ease with each other again.'

She bristled. 'You sound as if I'm at fault. As if I'm to blame.'

'I didn't say that.'

'It jolly well came across that way.'

He paused and chose his words with care. 'Wouldn't you say that in some respects we're both at fault for the way we're behaving now?'

'No I wouldn't! And I resent that you could accuse me of any such thing. Honestly, Stirling, I used to think of you as being a decent, fair-minded and understanding man. How wrong could I have been!' She got up abruptly. 'And you can forget about me coming with you to The Meadows. I've changed my mind.'

'Fine!' he snapped, his patience gone. 'You be as irrational and as difficult as you want. Just don't expect me to indulge you like a spoilt child.'

The colour rose to her cheeks. 'Irrational!' she repeated hotly. 'You think *I'm* being irrational? What a joke! It's not me who's been unfaithful. It's not my sordid deception that has turned our marriage into a sham. My God, you and your brother, what a pair you make!'

He struggled to keep his voice level. 'Keeping something from you doesn't make me irrational, Gina. For once, why don't you calmly ask yourself why I kept it from you?'

'I've asked myself that time and time again. And the only answer I've come up with is that you were a coward.'

'And that,' he said slowly, 'is the most astute observation you've made about what I did. You're right, I was a coward, and have continued to be so all these years, but I'm not prepared to carry on being one any more. Which is why I want you to come to The Meadows with me today.'

'For God's sake why?'

He steeled himself. 'Katie will be there and I want you to meet her. And before you dismiss the idea out of hand, put yourself in her shoes. How easy is this for her? If she has the courage to face you and Rosco and Scarlet, don't you think you could display the same courage?'

Gina stared at him. '*She* is going to be there at The Meadows? My God, you're unbelievable. What were you going to do, spring her on me when I was least expecting it? "Oh Gina, let me introduce you to my illegitimate daughter." Was that what you had in mind?'

'Don't be so melodramatic. I was hoping you'd meet her on your own and anonymously, and form an impartial opinion.'

'And then what did you think would happen? That she and I would magically form some kind of conveniently happy-ever-after mother-and-daughter bond?'

'All I'm asking from you is an open mind. Is that really too much to expect?'

'In the circumstances, yes it is.'

'Now who's being a coward?'

Her expression hardened. 'What a piece of work you've turned into.'

Chapter Twenty-nine

Katie and Pen had been up since six o'clock working in the garden. They hadn't bothered with breakfast, and now, at nine thirty, with Lloyd calling out that he'd made them something to eat, they didn't need telling twice.

Sitting in the courtyard, Katie tucked in with hungry relish to the bacon sandwich Lloyd had given her. 'Mmm ... sublime,' she said, wiping the butter from her lips. 'Cousin Lloyd, can I just say, as of now, you're my favourite person in all the world?'

He passed her a mug of tea. 'You may indeed.'

'He's a dab hand with a loaf of soft white bread and a packet of bacon,' Pen said. 'Always has been.'

'I do have other culinary masterpieces in my repertoire.'

'Such as?' Katie asked.

'I'll have you know I make an excellent Thai chicken and coconut curry.'

'Really? You've gone even further up in my estimation. I should have roped you in to help me with the baking.'

'Ah, now that wouldn't have been such a smart move. I have what one might describe as limited baking experience.'

Pen laughed. 'Remember that cake you made for my birthday when you were ten years old?'

'How could I not remember when you and Dad never let me forget it? My God, the joke went on for years!'

'He overdid the baking powder, Katie, and the cake literally exploded. I was cleaning the oven for days afterwards.'

Lloyd shrugged. 'And as a result of being emotionally

scarred by parents who wouldn't let me forget my one little mistake, baking and I never became the brothers-in-arms we were meant to be. It's a wonder I ever ventured into the kitchen again after such ritual abuse.'

'But we're glad you did, especially as you make such first-class bacon sandwiches. Now then,' Pen said decisively, 'I must get on.'

'Slow down, Mum, you haven't even drunk your tea.'

She stood up, mug in hand. 'I'll take it with me.'

'If you don't need me for anything in the garden, Pen,' Katie said, 'I'll make a start on getting the refreshments ready.'

'I'll give you a hand,' Lloyd offered. 'What time do the others arrive?'

'Speedy Sue promised she'd be here just before the gates open at eleven, and Posh Pam said it would be shortly after eleven thirty when she showed up; she has to take her granddaughter for her horse-riding lesson.'

When Katie and Lloyd were alone and gathering up the plates and mugs to take inside, Katie said, 'Speedy Sue and Posh Pam; do you and your mum call them that to their faces?'

'No,' Lloyd said with a laugh. 'Dad gave them the nicknames a long time ago. Sue acquired hers after she'd got done twice for speeding in as many weeks, and Pam, well, she's just uber-posh and has a voice that would make Brian Sewell think he ought to take elocution lessons. They're both keen gardeners themselves and have always helped Mum with the open days.'

In the kitchen, and while Lloyd tidied away the breakfast things, Katie started ferrying cakes from the larder and laying them out on the kitchen table. Since arriving here three days ago, she had done nothing but bake and help Pen in the garden – she had another stash of cakes in Pen's chest freezer for tomorrow and the day after. In years gone by, Pen had only laid on tea and coffee and shop-bought biscuits as refreshments, but at Cecily's suggestion, and on the basis that

Katie would organize it all, cakes were now being offered as an extra way to raise money.

It was something Katie had helped her mother do for the annual summer fete in the village where she'd grown up. The cake stall had easily been the busiest of all the stalls. They would usually have everything sold within the first hour and then they'd be free to help on the plant stall, which Dad ran and which was mostly stocked with cuttings from their garden.

The day Cecily and Lloyd had visited her in Brighton, and at Cecily's request, Katie had shown them some old photographs of her as a child. One photograph in particular had caught Cecily's eye – a picture of Katie wearing a chef's hat and grinning like an idiot for the benefit of the camera as she held up a large mixing bowl whilst stirring the contents with a wooden spoon. Katie had explained how she had been helping her mother prepare for the village fete. This, she supposed, explained why a few days later Cecily phoned and asked if she had any plans before and during the Bank Holiday weekend. She was beginning to learn that Cecily was a wily old girl.

When she had all the foil and cling-film-wrapped cakes set out on the kitchen table and work surfaces, Lloyd said, 'That's a lot of cake; do you really think we'll sell them all?'

'Breaking news, Cousin Lloyd! We'll be lucky to have the plates left after the feeding frenzy is over.'

He gently flicked a hand towel at her. 'Are you always going to call me Cousin Lloyd?'

She hesitated. Something in his tone confirmed her suspicion that he was tired of the joke. Trouble was, it was her way of reminding herself not to get any funny ideas about him. She could not go around fancying a cousin. No, no, no, it was too *ee-uw* for words.

In the time since she'd last seen him in Brighton she had managed to convince herself that he really wasn't that cute, but then last night when he'd turned up for dinner and to help with the garden, she had had the same reaction to him as before. *SHOCKY MOMENT! SHOCKY MOMENT!* her tingling body had squealed, wanting suddenly to dance around the room. With admirable restraint she had greeted Lloyd with a small smile and a polite 'hi'. He had mirrored her greeting exactly. Which had helped immensely to call her overexcited body to heel. But really, he had no business being so attractive. 'I rather like the formality,' she said lightly, in response to his question, 'especially as I've never had the pleasure of knowing a cousin before.'

There was a quiet intensity to him as he stared back at her – it was an integral part of him she was coming to know. She'd noticed also that he sometimes had a way of looking at her that was slightly unsettling, as if he was trying to figure something out about her. She saw a muscle tense at his jaw and he looked as if he was about to say something but then seemed to think better of it. 'I don't know how Cecily persuaded you to come here,' he said in an abrupt change of tone, 'but I know my mother really appreciates your help. As do I.'

'Well I don't think you need me to tell you what a persuasive force Cecily is,' she said with a laugh. 'Plus being here gives me the opportunity to see Stirling again.'

'Even so, it's still good of you to come and muck in like this.'

'To be honest, I'm enjoying myself. And it's good to see your mother looking so much better.' She glanced at the wall above the cooker. 'Right, Cousin Lloyd, we're up against the clock here; we need to get the tables organized in the pavilion.'

'Already done,' he said. 'I did that earlier.'

'With tablecloths?'

'Is there any other way?'

'In that case, let's get these cakes rocking and rolling!'

Ten minutes later they had everything in place. The pavilion was a spacious hexagonal structure of glass and teak that could comfortably seat thirty people. 'This is where we've always had Christmas lunch,' Lloyd said, looking about him.

'We had underfloor heating put in a while back and Dad used to …' He stopped short. He pushed his hands deep into his pockets and hunched his shoulders. Katie had seen him do this a few times now, usually when he was uncomfortable about something. The first time was when he came to Brighton with Cecily. He'd done it twice last night, once when Rosco had phoned him on his mobile and then again later in the evening when he'd been saying how cross he'd been at the way the hospice committee had treated his mother.

'That will happen a lot,' Katie said to him gently. 'You'll find yourself happily talking about your father one minute, and the next, the pain of a memory will wrap itself around you and stop you in your tracks.'

He blinked. Then swallowed. 'Earlier in the courtyard while we were having breakfast I mentioned him without a flicker, but here …' He blinked again. 'It just hit me that he won't be with us at Christmas. It won't be the same.' He dropped his shoulders to a more relaxed position. 'How long was it before you stopped getting these … these flashes?'

'I still get them. For Mum *and* Dad. Less than I used to, but the thing is, I don't want the ache to stop entirely. It's a connection, a way of still feeling close to them both.'

He nodded, opened his mouth to say something, but faltered. He suddenly turned away from her, but not before Katie saw that his eyes were dark and glistening. Her throat clenched with the understanding of what he was going through. She put a hand on his shoulder. He breathed in sharply. 'I'm OK,' he said, his back to her. 'Really, I'm OK.' He took another deep breath.

She didn't say anything, but with her hand still on his shoulder she felt a tremor running through him and knew that it was taking all his energy to stay in control, to master his emotions. She wondered if he had allowed himself to cry over the death of his father. Perhaps not. Perhaps he had been too busy being the strong one for Pen. Just as she had done with Mum when Dad had died.

When he slowly turned to face her, she felt the compulsion to comfort him, to put her arms around him. He tensed at her touch, then responded by holding on to her, but cautiously, as if she were made of glass and might shatter if he pressed her too tightly.

Seconds passed and then he spoke. 'You're the first person to say something that makes sense to me. People talk about closure, about time being a healer, but I don't want closure. I don't want to forget Dad. I want to feel connected to him still.'

She lifted her head and looked up into his eyes; they were almost black, the pupils were so large. 'Without meaning to, people talk a lot of rubbish. Forget what they say. OK?'

He nodded. 'Thank you,' he murmured.

His embarrassment was all too acute, and all of a sudden she was conscious of the tautness of his body against hers and the rhythmic thud of his heartbeat. She let go of him and with a hesitant smile said, 'It's what any good cousin would do. Come on, we'd better get a move on. We've still got all the cups and saucers to organize.'

Nothing like the mundane to bring things back down to earth, she thought.

Or to crush the shamefully uncousin-like feelings she harboured for him.

Lloyd fell silently in step beside Katie as they walked back up to the house. Two thoughts were battling it out inside his head.

Dad and the extent of how much his death still hurt when he was least expecting it.

And Katie. *It's what any good cousin would do.*

He didn't want her as a cousin and he wanted very much that she would stop treating him as one. Because technically they weren't cousins. Which made his feelings for her OK, didn't it?

But what if that was the only way she wanted to view him?

Odds on it was. Why else would she keep calling him Cousin Lloyd?

Only one way to find out. He'd have to clarify the situation for her.

'Come on, Scarlet, I thought we'd got this sorted on the phone last night. We'll do it together, a united front and all that. I'm not asking you to like her. We're going to show our faces and be polite. That's all.'

'I just don't think I can do it.'

'Look,' Rosco said patiently, 'we can't go on hiding from her; it gives entirely the wrong impression, as if we're scared of her. If we meet her, we get Dad off our backs and we'll have done our duty and it will be an end to it.'

'Don't you understand anything, Rosco? There will never be an end to it!'

Scarlet's voice had risen sharply, shattering the quiet of the morning and further annoying Rosco. His small garden over-looking the river was his private oasis, it was where he liked to start his weekend when the weather was warm enough, sitting here on his own, drinking his coffee, pondering what he'd do to amuse himself. He didn't appreciate his routine being disrupted by an unplanned visit from his flaky sister. Nor did he appreciate her stomping about the small area of wooden decking he'd only recently had restained. It was why he was so resolutely single: he couldn't abide the constant mood swings, the never knowing what would happen next. In his experience girls always became hysterical and clingy, and without fail they always wanted to change things. He preferred to dip in and out of relationships at his convenience.

'She's his daughter and she's always going to be around from now on,' Scarlet continued with her rant. 'Look how she's practically moved in with Pen.'

'Pen's a soft touch, you know that as well as I do. She'd take anyone in.'

'And how soon before she's invited to our family occasions?' Scarlet rattled on as though Rosco hadn't spoken. 'There'll be no escape from her. Just you see, Daddy will ask for her to be at Baby's christening.'

Rosco shuddered at the way Scarlet now referred to the child inside her. Why the hell did women change into these ridiculous beings just because they were pregnant? A girl in the office had gone the same way. Before she announced she was pregnant she had seemed reasonably grounded, but then overnight she changed into a simpering idiot intent on sharing every intimate detail of her pregnancy with anyone who was fool enough to ask how she was. She grew forgetful too, made no end of mistakes and blamed it on her hormones. It had been a relief when she'd left to have the baby: no more sickening baby talk and no more making allowances for her sloppy work.

God only knew what Scarlet was going to be like when she had the child. But that was in the future. Now his immediate problem was convincing her that they had to stand as one and make it very clear to Katie Lavender how they regarded her. He thought of it as Plan B.

Plan A – his original plan to bring their father to his senses – had been put on hold. He'd been about to share it with his mother when out of the blue she had announced she wasn't going to divorce Dad after all. He had been so relieved at the news that it had seemed eminently more sensible on his part to leave well alone, to let his parents sort things out for themselves.

He changed tack with his sister. 'Aren't you just the littlest bit interested?' he tried. 'If only to see what she's like?'

Scarlet flicked at her hair. 'I vaguely remember her from Granza's party. But why would I take any notice of her? She was just a waitress.'

Rosco also had a vague recollection; his was of noticeable

attitude and equally noticeable legs. 'If we don't agree to meet her, she'll think we're petty,' he pressed on, 'or worse, scared of her. You're not scared, are you, Scarlet?' He knew all too well how to play on Scarlet's insecurities. He'd always been able to do it; ever since they were children it was how he'd got her to do exactly what he wanted.

She looked at him sharply. 'What do you mean?'

He came and stood next to her on the edge of the decking, where she was watching a moorhen nosing around in the undergrowth on the riverbank. He put his arm around her. 'I know it's difficult for you, Scarlet; you've always been Dad's little princess, and now there's potentially a new princess on the block trying to muscle in. It's understandable that you'd feel threatened. I just want you to know that I'm in this with you and I won't let anyone hurt or upset you. As far as I'm concerned, you'll always be the number one girl in this family.'

Her face crumpled and tears filled her eyes. 'Oh God, Rosco, you always understand me so well, don't you? Even Charlie doesn't appreciate how difficult I'm finding this. He doesn't see that I'm terrified Daddy will think she's better than me, that ...' Her voice trailed off as she gave in to a full-blown sob.

'Hey, hey, hey,' he soothed. 'That's not going to happen.' He held her close and tucked her head under his chin, hoping that she wouldn't blub too much over his shirt. 'That's not going to happen,' he repeated, 'and don't forget you're carrying Dad's first grandchild. No one else can top that.'

She sniffed loudly. 'When you put your mind to it, you can sometimes be a surprisingly nice brother,' she said.

'I do my best. So how about we turn up at The Meadows, you and me together, and show this girl what we're made of, eh?'

She sniffed again and pushed herself away from him. 'OK,' she said.

'And think how proud Dad will be of you,' he said, slamming home his ace.

Having undergone a U-turn in his thinking, he was almost looking forward to showing up at The Meadows to support Pen's open day. There was some sport to be had in meeting their half-sister. There were points to be scored.

Let the games begin.

Chapter Thirty

Just as Katie had predicted, they'd been rushed off their feet. The queue for refreshments had been relentless, and with only thirty minutes to go until the garden would be closed, they were left with just half a dozen scones and two slices of ginger cake. Since it was unlikely there would be any new arrivals, Lloyd had gone off to do a head count of those already admitted and still wandering the garden.

From the comments Katie had heard throughout the day, the opening had been a big hit. The quality of the refreshments had frequently been remarked upon, and many regulars to The Meadows had said what a welcome addition it was to have something decent to eat and drink and Pen should seriously consider opening the garden more often. Katie was glad for Pen that things had gone so well, and glad too that she was a part of it.

Wondering whether she could risk slipping away to take a tray of used crockery up to the house, she saw Stirling coming towards her across the lawn. He was wearing a cream linen suit with a panama hat, and she, once again, thought how striking he looked. He'd been here for most of the day, pitching in wherever help was needed as well as charming Cecily's fellow female oldsters from South Lodge, settling them at the tables in the shade, taking their tea and cake orders and generally making a fuss of them. He was the most relaxed Katie had seen him. Yet she knew he had little to be relaxed about. Whilst he was back with his wife, things – according to Lloyd – were far from normal between them. The fact that

Gina wasn't here today with Stirling told its own story, and knowing that she was the reason for the woman's absence was weighing heavily on Katie's conscience. But what could she do to rectify things? How could she heal the rift? Other than disappear entirely from Stirling's life? But could she do that now?

'Looks like the show's winding down,' Stirling said. 'Anything I can do to help?'

'What would you rather do, take these up to the house or stand in for me while I do it?'

He eyed the heavily laden trays and smiled. 'Trick question, eh?' He took one and pretended to stagger beneath its weight. 'I'll be back for the other in a minute.'

Katie watched him go. She still hadn't got used to thinking of him as her father. Would she ever? Did she need to? But if she didn't, what did that make him? A friend? A sort of uncle? It was all too vague. Relationships – of any kind – had to be clearly defined; it was what laid the foundations and set the parameters. But it was early days, she reminded herself. Apart from occasionally speaking on the phone and exchanging emails, she and Stirling really hadn't had much of a chance to get to know each other. Hopefully that could now happen.

From across the lawn she spotted a pair of late arrivals – a couple whose appearance had just dramatically reduced the average age of the visitors that day. Clearly pregnant and dressed in a white drop-waisted dress with spaghetti straps, the girl wore a floppy-brimmed hat that hid her face. The man – presumably her husband – was busy talking into a mobile phone, and he too had his face partially hidden, in his case with a pair of aviator sunglasses. Intrigued, Katie watched them as they came to a stop on the sweep of lawn that gave them the best view of the area of garden sloping gently down to the river. The man ended his call, said something to his wife, and as one they turned their heads, taking in the garden. It was then, just as they both looked towards the pavilion, that Katie realized who they were.

Not husband and wife. But brother and sister.

Rosco and Scarlet.

Uh-oh.

They exchanged a brief word, and with one hand placed in the small of his sister's back, Rosco seemed to push Scarlet in the direction of the pavilion.

I can do this, Katie told herself as they drew near.

She shot a panicky glance towards the house, hoping for Stirling to appear. Why hadn't he told her they might show up? No, second thoughts: he'd done the right thing in not telling her; she'd only have spent the day worrying.

There was no sign of Stirling.

She then looked to her right, further down the garden, hoping to see Lloyd galloping to her rescue.

I do not need rescuing, she scolded herself in disgust. Since when had she turned into such a pathetic wimp? She had coped with far worse than this before. She was the absolute real deal when it came to coping. Just let them try to intimidate her. And so pretending she hadn't noticed them, she busied herself with sweeping up cake crumbs.

An eternity passed, and then: 'And this must be none other than the person we've heard so much about recently, Katie Lavender.'

She looked up, polite smile firmly in place. 'Hello,' she said, feigning ignorance for a nanosecond as to whom she was facing. If Rosco could put on a performance of laughable fakery, so could she. 'Oh,' she then said, as if recognition had dawned, 'and you must be Rosco and Scarlet who I've heard so much about.' She put her hand out, noting that Rosco was working the whole alpha-male thing to death – sunglasses tipped back on his head, chest out, jaw set, smart-arse smile plastered across his self-assured face. He was looking at her hand, as though considering whether to shake it or not. She would have expected nothing less from him and so kept her hand resolutely outstretched. He'd shake it or she'd use it to whack the bejeezus out of him.

'But of course we've met before, haven't we?' he said with an affected drawl, finally, and briefly, shaking her hand. 'The night of my grandmother's birthday party, when you were waitressing for us. Now here you are again waiting on us.'

Nice put-down, she thought. And so tempting to return the compliment. 'Yes,' she said simply. She turned to Scarlet. She didn't bother to try and force a handshake from her; no point in pushing her luck. From beneath the brim of her hat, the girl looked at Katie with an artful do-I-give-a-shit look. Ooh, so slap-worthy. 'It's good to meet you both properly,' Katie said, adding with just a hint of emphasis, 'at last.'

'We've been busy,' Rosco said. 'It's been a difficult time for the family.'

'I know,' she said. 'You have my sympathy. It must have been an awful shock for you all.'

'Yes, we're still trying to come to terms with what Uncle Neil did.'

'And with Daddy telling us about *you*.'

This was from Scarlet. 'Yes, I would expect that was quite a shock for you both,' Katie said, trying her best to sound friendly.

Scarlet leant over the table. 'You have no idea what we think or feel, so don't waste your breath.' Her eyes flashed dangerously – they were blue, but icily blue, not the soft sky-blue of Lloyd's eyes. 'And just because you've wormed your way in with Pen and Lloyd,' she went on, 'don't imagine for one minute you can do the same with us. You might think you're family, but you're not. And you never will be. As far as Rosco and I are concerned, you don't exist. So why don't you go back to wherever you're from and leave us alone?'

A cheery voice rang out. 'Rosco! Scarlet! You made it.' It was Stirling. 'I'd given up on you. And I see you've met Katie. Excellent.' He rubbed his hands together. 'Excellent,' he repeated. He was talking much too fast. A sure sign, even to Katie's ears, that he wasn't feeling anywhere near as cheerful as he was making out.

'Yes,' Rosco said, his hand pressing at the small of his sister's back, 'we were just getting to know one another. Now we'd better go and find Auntie Pen.' He gave his sister a little shove. 'We really must congratulate her on her hard work. I don't think I've ever seen the garden looking so good.' Leaving Stirling looking awkwardly on, they moved off quickly.

When they were out of earshot, Stirling said, 'How did that go?'

Katie tried to give him a smile of encouragement – that sure, everything was hunky-dory and in apple-pie order – but she couldn't quite manage it. 'Let's just say the ice has been broken,' she said evasively.

Lloyd had been ordered by Pen to take Katie out for dinner. Apparently she not only deserved it but was in need of a change of scene. This was news to Katie, but she was more than happy to go along with the arrangement. As was Lloyd. But only once it had been established that Speedy Sue and Posh Pam were spending the evening at The Meadows with Pen. 'Don't you worry about us,' Speedy Sue had said. 'We three witches will cook something up in our cauldron for supper. Off you go.'

They had walked to the Riverside, the pub where Katie had stopped for lunch the first time she'd come to Sandiford. Lloyd had booked ahead and they had a table with an uninterrupted view of the river. It was a beautiful warm evening, the kind of evening when everything felt in harmony, and with their food ordered and a bottle of smooth plummy red wine chosen, they sat back and relaxed. A boat came into view. Low in the water and stylishly streamlined, it looked very classy. 'That's a smart boat,' Katie said, imagining herself all glammed up and sitting in the back of it with a glass of champagne.

'You have excellent taste,' Lloyd replied.

'It looks like something out of a film.'

He smiled. 'It's a slipper launch, and to my mind it's one of the best crafts on the river. Mighty pricey, though. Stirling has one. You should get him to take you out in it.'

'Just so long as Rosco and Scarlet don't want to join us. Knowing how fond they are of me, the first opportunity they got, they'd push me overboard.'

'Hey, don't go all paranoid on me now.'

She laughed. 'Not paranoid, just stating a fact. They hate me.'

He raised his glass. 'Welcome to the club.'

'Goodness, I hope the membership is exclusive. I don't want to be a member of just any old club. Do you have a boat? Is it de rigueur to have one if you live here?'

'Not de rigueur at all. But I do have an old rowing boat, which I keep at Mum's. I haven't used it in a long while. No time these days.'

'Are you a rower? I mean a proper rower?'

'Not competitively, if that's what you mean. I did a bit when I was younger, and then at college. But I wasn't in the same league as some of the guys there. I didn't have the same hunger as they did.'

'And Rosco? I bet he was a killer rower?'

Lloyd shook his head. 'Rosco never really got into it, for the simple fact he's not a team player.'

'And you are?'

'When I want to be, yes.'

Their food arrived, and after they'd sorted themselves out with napkins, salt and pepper and topped up their glasses, Katie said, 'Thank you for bringing me here. It's lovely.'

He shrugged. 'Not like I had a choice.'

'Thanks a bunch!'

He laughed. 'I was on the verge of suggesting it anyway but didn't want to leave Mum on her own. How's the duck?'

'Delicious. And your steak?'

'As good as ever.'

'Do you eat here a lot?'

'Not especially. Just now and then. Actually, I used to work here as a teenager. Then when I was old enough I worked behind the bar.' He smiled. 'It was a good way to meet girls.'

Curious, just as she'd been from the moment they'd met, Katie said, 'So, Cousin Lloyd, what's your situation, then?'

He looked at her blankly.

'What's your dating situation currently? Anyone on the scene? Or behind the scenes, maybe? A secret lover, for instance.' She realized her gaffe too late: his jaw tightened and he looked away.

'I'm sorry,' she said, appalled. 'Me and my monster big mouth, we go back a long way.'

He drank some of his wine, then slowly put his glass down. 'It's OK, it's me, I'm being overly sensitive.'

'The hell you are! It's me being a total idiot. But seriously, I am sorry.'

'No need to turn into a serial apologist; once was quite enough. And as for my situation, there's no one on the scene currently. There was last year but it fizzled out.'

'I know the feeling. And there's been no one since then?'

'Nope.'

'Why's that, then? The girls round here don't know a good thing when they see it, or are you too picky?'

An eyebrow raised, he said, 'You're making the assumption that I'm straight.'

She tutted and wagged a finger at him. 'My friend Zac has taught me all I need to know on that score. Trust me, I'd know if you were gay, and you're not, Cousin Lloyd.'

He put a piece of steak into his mouth, chewed on it slowly, then said, 'Can I ask you something?'

She shook her head. 'Sorry, the game doesn't work that way. Only I'm allowed to ask questions.'

'That doesn't sound very fair.'

'Who said anything about fairness?'

'I don't think this change-of-scene idea is working out too well. I liked you better back at home. You played nicely then.'

She smiled and flung her arms out either side of her. '*Ta-daar!* Meet the real Katie Lavender!'

He smiled too. 'Pleased to meet you, Miss Katie Lavender. Great name, by the way.'

'Nightingale is also pretty good.'

'Strictly speaking you're a Nightingale as well. Miss Lavender-Nightingale. Or would you prefer Miss Nightingale-Lavender?'

'Neither. I'm a Lavender through and through.'

'Don't you think there's anything of Stirling in you?'

The question caught her unawares. 'I don't know. I suppose that's what I want to find out. You see, as soon as I knew about him, I felt different about myself. I suddenly didn't feel like I was *me* any more. I came here to find him, to see if getting to know him would resolve that feeling.'

'And has it?'

'No. No it hasn't. I still feel confused. I like him, I like him more than I expected to, but I don't know what he could ever be to me.'

'Perhaps it's too soon to know. You've scarcely had a chance to get to know him. You have to give it longer.'

'You're right. Patience isn't one of my strong suits, I guess. And I don't like things out of kilter. I like everything to be neat and tidy. I'm naturally very organized.'

He smiled.

'You don't think I am?'

'Oh no, I know you're a neat-freak. I saw your house in Brighton, remember? And I've seen the way you cook, you're constantly cleaning up after yourself. No, I was smiling because Stirling is exactly the same. He's the most obsessively organized person I know.'

She thought about this, recalling how Mum and Dad used to tease her for always tidying after them – neither of them could ever put anything away. As a young child she would spend ages lining up her toys, straightening the books on the shelf above her bed and keeping her wardrobe and chest of drawers in order.

'So who do you most take after?' she asked. 'Pen or your father?'

'I'm probably more like Pen; I have her creative flair rather than Dad's business acumen. But I believe who we are is a mixture of genes and the influence of our surroundings in our formative years.'

'Sitting on the fence regarding the nature versus nurture debate, then?'

'I wouldn't say that, I ...' He broke off. 'Is that your mobile?'

'Sorry, yes.'

She bent down to her bag on the grass at the side of her chair and fished out her phone. 'It's my friend Tess,' she said. 'She can wait.'

'No, go ahead. It's fine.'

'I'm busy,' Katie greeted Tess, who she could scarcely hear above the eardrum-bursting racket of what sounded like a chainsaw hacking its way through sheet metal. She then remembered Tess and Ben were going to a gig in a pub in Brixton tonight to support a mate of Ben's who played bass guitar in a newly put together band. 'How super-annoying and inconsiderate of you to be busy,' Tess yelled back at her.

'Not as annoying or inconsiderate as you. I'm having dinner with my cousin.'

'As in, Lloyd the Gorgeously Divine Cousin?'

Katie turned her head away from the table in the hope Lloyd wouldn't hear Tess's voice shrieking down the line as the band continued to kick up a storm. 'Did you ring for any reason other than to deafen me?'

'Hey, I'm ringing with glad tidings: expect the posse to arrive tomorrow. That's me, Ben and Zac, in case you've forgotten your old friends.'

'You're really coming?'

'You doubted me? I'm hurt.'

'And I'm surprised and touched.'

'Ah, *sweet*. Anyway, we'll be saddling up after breakfast, whenever that is, and moseying into town around lunchtime. Save some cake for me. See you!'

Her mobile now switched off and back in her bag, Katie said, 'You didn't hear any of that, did you?'

The corners of Lloyd's mouth twitched. 'You mean apart from the bit about the gorgeously divine cousin?'

She fought back a colossal blush. 'Tess always speaks like that. She works in PR.'

'So are we Nightingales to be put under the microscope tomorrow?'

'No more than I've been constantly under it.'

'Touché. More wine?'

'Please.' She held out her glass, praying her deadpan expression wouldn't slip. *Just wait till she got hold of Tess!*

Another boat appeared and chugged slowly by. It wasn't anything like the sleek craft they'd seen earlier. It was a noisy old tub of a boat with what seemed to be a shambolic lean-to affair tacked on the back with a plastic corrugated roof, through which poked a crooked chimney. A shaggy-haired man wearing a black and white spotted neckerchief was drinking from a can of beer whilst casually steering the boat one-handed. Sitting at the prow was a dog that looked so comically alert, Katie could almost have believed it was navigating for the man. For a moment the boat and its occupants were perfectly silhouetted against the sun, which was dropping low in the roseate sky. When they were no longer in sight, Katie said, 'You wanted to ask me something earlier. What was it?'

He suddenly looked awkward. He pushed the sleeves of his shirt further up his arms, revealing tanned forearms and muscles that were absurdly well defined. She'd seen his arms before and had thought in passing how strong they looked, but sitting here like this, so close, she was observing them anew. And not in a good way. Oh dear God, not in a good way at all. She really had to get a grip on herself. This could not go on. But then she recalled the careful way he'd held her that morning when she'd been comforting him, and she felt a shameful longing to feel his arms wrapped around her again. Wrenching her gaze away, she glanced up to his face and found he was giving her one of his quietly unsettling looks. 'Um ... it's this whole cousin thing,' he said.

'What about it? Don't you like having a new cousin in your life?' Oh hell, he'd guessed, hadn't he? He knew that she was riddled with shamefully inappropriate thoughts about him and he wanted to make damned sure she stopped having them. Like the idiot she was, she'd given herself away with those stupid questions about whether or not he was seeing anybody. And if that wasn't bad enough, Tess had then gone shooting her mouth off. She should never have told Tess about him. And she definitely should not have told her how hot he was.

'What if I wasn't your cousin?' he said.

'But you are.'

His blue eyes met her gaze with such an intensity, she held her breath. 'Did you know that my father was adopted?'

'No.'

'So no one's mentioned that to you? Not Cecily or Stirling?'

She shook her head.

'And what about me being adopted; has anyone mentioned that to you?'

'*You?* You're adopted?'

'So you see, we're not cousins at all. We're not the least bit related. Not in the sense of being blood-related.'

She let her breath out. 'Does that mean I can't call you Cousin Lloyd any more?'

'It means a lot of things.'

It certainly does, she thought.

Chapter Thirty-one

It was dark when they left the Riverside and started walking back to The Meadows.

Instead of retracing their steps on the road, Lloyd had assured her the moon was bright enough to light the way for them along the towpath, that they would be quite safe. He'd been right. The moon, so fat and round it looked too heavy to stay up in the star-pricked sky, illuminated the path like a theatrical effect. Katie was sure that without the silvery light, the darkness would have been complete. It was another world here, such a contrast to Brighton and London, where it was never truly dark. It was also eerily quiet, and she felt hyper-sensitively alert to everything around her, picking up on the slightest rustle in the undergrowth, the crack of a twig under-foot, even her own breath. She was aware too that the air, still and quiet and rich with the earthy smell of the riverbank, was thunderous with the silence between her and Lloyd.

Lloyd who was suddenly no longer her cousin.

His announcement should have had her cheering. But it hadn't. From the moment he'd explained that they weren't related, she hadn't known how to be around him any more; she had become cripplingly self-conscious of her every word and gesture. She didn't even trust herself to look at him properly.

The rest of the meal had been utter torment, with Katie unable to string more than two words together. He must have sensed the change in her – well, let's face it, he'd have been hard-pressed to miss it – because he too had then struggled to find anything to talk about. And all the while, her head had been crammed full of questions about his adoption, none of which she could put into actual spoken words; it was as if she'd lost the power of speech. When he'd suggested they leave, she'd agreed only too readily.

Alone now on the towpath, following the gentle curve of the river, its slick surface shining like quicksilver, she was desperately trying to make sense of her reaction to what he'd said.

'Katie?' His voice cracked the stillness like a gun being fired.

She forced herself to reply, but kept her eyes steadfastly on the path. 'Mm?'

'You OK?'

'Just thinking.'

'Anything you want to share?'

'Not particularly.'

'You sound cross.'

'I'm not cross.'

He slowed his step. 'I am.'

She slowed as well. 'Why?'

'Because I've ruined the evening for us.'

'No you haven't.'

'You're a terrible liar.' When she didn't respond, he put a hand on her arm and came to a stop, making her do the same. 'One minute we were having a fun evening, and then everything changed when I told you I wasn't your cousin. You've been quiet ever since. And you haven't looked at me either. Not once.'

'I'm just tired, that's all.'

'I don't believe you. I think you're upset by what I said. Why won't you look at me?'

She reluctantly raised her gaze. In the glowing light of the moon, she saw that the pallor of his face had acquired a luminosity that darkened his eyes, and in those liquid pools of darkness she could see that he looked completely wretched.

Witnessing his misery – knowing she was the cause of it – she longed to put her arms around him, to kiss that pain away from his face. So why not do exactly that? She had done it this morning, hadn't she? Not the kissing bit, obviously, but the arms bit she'd managed well enough. And now she knew they weren't cousins, there was nothing wrong in the way she felt about him, was there? She could touch him with total impunity. But she couldn't. She just couldn't. And the stupid thing was, she didn't know why. She felt so horribly confused.

He shoved his hands in his pockets. 'Look, I told you what I did because I didn't want there to be any ambiguity between us.'

'Did you think there was before?'

He stared down at the ground. 'For me there was. I can't speak for you. All I wanted to do was to make things clear between us. I wanted clarity. It's important to me.'

'What kind of clarity are you talking about?'

'The kind that says I don't want you to think of me as your cousin.' He looked up, and she heard a soft exhalation of breath escape from him. 'The kind that says there are things I want to do with you that I can't so long as you view me as a cousin.'

She stared back at him. And very slowly, as if the moon itself was shining a light on the jumble of her thoughts, she was no longer confused. 'What sort of things?' she murmured, her heart fluttering.

'For starters, I'd like to kiss you.'

'For starters,' she repeated, unable to stop herself from smiling. He looked so very serious.

'OK, you're smiling. That's a good sign, right? You're not about to run off screaming into the night?'

Her smile widened and she started to laugh.

'OK, laughing isn't so good. When a girl laughs at a bloke, that's usually a bad sign.'

'Says who?'

'Says every bloke who's ever been turned down.'

'I haven't turned you down.'

'But you're about to. That's a nervous laugh I'm hearing. It's the sound of a girl trying to find the right words to say she doesn't want to be kissed. Given the circumstances, who could blame you? I mean, this is all a bit left of field, one minute you think we're related, and the next I'm coming on to you. It's too bloody weird, isn't it?'

'You have absolutely no idea what you're talking about,' she said. She closed the gap between them and tilted her face up to his. 'Lloyd, would you kiss me, please? *For starters.*'

He swallowed. 'You're sure you want me to? I don't want you doing a fakey number on me out of sympathy. There's only so much humiliation I can take.'

She reached for one of his hands, pulled it from his trouser pocket and kissed his palm. 'I swear it won't be a sympathy snog. It will be the real thing. I'll put my every genuine feeling into it.'

His eyes stayed on her face. He put his hand to her cheek and with his other hand drew her closer still, then kissed her on the mouth. His lips were warm and soft and seemed instantly familiar to her. He kissed her for a very long time, his arms wrapped around her, his body pressed against hers. 'No, don't stop,' she said when he eventually broke away.

'I need oxygen,' he said. 'You've taken my breath away.'

'And that's just for starters,' she said with a laugh.

He laughed too. Then suddenly they were both laughing hard. She had no idea why. She doubted he did either. They were laughing so hard they were leaning against each other for support. It was a moment of utter madness. But it felt good, as if all the tension of the last hour was being drawn out of her. Her sides aching, she straightened up and took a step backwards, only to miss her footing on something round and solid on the ground. In the time it took her to process the information that she was in danger of losing her balance, Lloyd's weight had added to the momentum of her stumble and down they went. They landed with a thud in the long grass, with Lloyd lying on top of her. 'Are you all right?' he asked anxiously.

'I think so,' she gasped. 'Just a bit winded. Better that than in the river and soaked to the skin. Do you knock all the girls off their feet when you kiss them?'

'I promise you, you're the first.' He shifted his weight, but made no move to get up. Lying on his side, he smoothed her hair away from her face. 'You're sure you're OK? Nothing broken?'

'I'm fine. Really. What made you laugh?'

'I don't know. Everything just got to me.'

'And is that what you do when things get too much? You laugh?'

'It's never happened before. Blame it on the full moon. Why were *you* laughing?'

'I think it was the relief. I've been feeling so confused about you.'

'The cousin thing?'

'Yes.'

'Well, now we don't need to worry about that, do we?' He smiled and lowered his head until his lips were almost touching hers. He seemed to hover there for an age, his mouth so tantalizingly close, they were breathing the same air. When their lips met, he stroked her cheek, then her neck, sending shock waves of tingling desire running through her.

But their kissing was rudely interrupted by what sounded like a hippopotamus charging through the undergrowth. When a duck popped out from behind a bush on the river-bank, they both laughed. 'I didn't think ducks were nocturnal creatures,' Katie remarked after it had given them no more than a cursory glance and waddled off.

'Perhaps he's on his way to a late-night assignation,' Lloyd said, 'or returning home from one.'

'Do you think we ought be going?'

'No. Let's stay here and talk. Unless you're cold?'

'Not at all. I could stay here all night.'

He smiled and rolled on to his back, his right hand holding her left. They lay in companionable silence on the soft, dry grass, gazing up at the sky, where the moon and stars felt close enough to touch. It was such a perfect night.

'I'm glad you got rid of all that ambiguity,' Katie said.

He squeezed her hand. 'Me too. It was driving me crazy. I realized after meeting you down in Brighton that I had to make things clear, but adoption isn't something I generally talk about when I meet someone for the first time. "Oh hi, I'm Lloyd and I'm adopted." How creepy would that be? And I know I asked you earlier if anyone had told you about it, or about Dad being adopted, but I didn't really think Mum or Cecily or Stirling would have mentioned it. Again, it's just not something that comes up in casual conversation. Unless you're Rosco, and feel the need to drive the point home. But that's a different matter altogether. And then you seemed so pleased to have a cousin – an actual proper relative – and I was worried you'd be disappointed if I took that away from you.'

'What made you change your mind?'

'I decided this morning that I had to be honest with you; the situation was becoming way too weird for me. Originally I'd planned just to say we weren't related and leave it at that, to see how things might progress between us, but then you went all quiet on me and I had to know why, and then I just blurted everything out.'

She sat up. 'I'm sorry I did that. The thing is, I knew I was attracted to you but I felt it was wrong. And yeah, I know that some people don't have a problem with first cousins getting it together, but it didn't feel right to me. Too taboo. I kept wishing you weren't my cousin. And that felt wrong too. I really had no idea how you felt about me. You hid it well.'

'As did you. So why *did* you go so quiet?'

'Because I was confused. I think I needed to recalibrate my brain. One minute you were my cousin and therefore off limits, and the next you were a guilt-free zone, a virtuously tempting skinny latte. Except my brain was struggling to keep up.'

'I've been called many things, but never a skinny latte.' He pulled her back down beside him, placing her head on his shoulder, his arm around her. It felt nice.

After a small silence, she said, 'Do you know who your biological parents are? Have you ever tried to contact them?'

'No on both counts.'

'Why not?'

'Because I've never felt the need to do so. And I couldn't do it to Mum. Even though she'd be her usual understanding self, I know it would hurt her deep down. No one – not even a birth mother – could have been a better mother to me.'

'How old were you when you were adopted?'

'Six days. And I was five years old when Mum and Dad told me I was adopted.'

'And you've never been the slightest bit intrigued about your birth parents?'

'Not sufficiently to make me want to meet them.' He put his hand under her chin and tilted her face up to his. 'But that's not to say I don't understand why you wanted to meet Stirling. We're all different. You did what you needed to do. I just don't need to figure out who I am; I know who I am. I always have. It was the same with Dad. He never had the urge to dig around in the past either. Not so far as I'm aware, anyway. But who knows what was really going on inside his head.'

Chapter Thirty-two

Lloyd woke to the sound of doves cooing through the open window and the shower being used in the bathroom next to his bedroom. It wouldn't be his mother in there; she had her own en suite. Which meant it had to be Katie. In a flash, he was hit with the image of her naked body just the other side of the wall. OK, he didn't actually know what her body looked like undressed, but he could imagine. Oh yes, he could do that all right.

It was gone two when they had eventually got back home. The hall light had been left on for them, and creeping quietly upstairs, they had stood for an awkward moment on the landing outside the open door of his bedroom. To invite her in, or not to invite her in, that was the question. She had settled the matter for him by whispering good night and kissing him on the cheek. And with hindsight, it had been the right thing to do. What was the hurry? Well, other than the obvious. But he could wait. Contrary to his behaviour last night, he could be patient when required.

Walking home, he'd shared with Katie how, at first sight and totally unexpectedly, he'd been drawn to her, and how in the following days and weeks, when they'd been in contact by email, that attraction had grown. Looking back on the emails he'd written to her, he could have easily referred to his being adopted in one of them, but the strange thing was, he simply wasn't very practised at telling people that Pen and Neil weren't his birth parents. He could probably count the number of people he'd told on the fingers of one hand.

He opened his eyes; sunlight streamed into his old bedroom. Seldom did he sleep with the curtains drawn, a habit from childhood. He picked up his watch from the bedside table: seven fifteen. He should get up. His mother was probably already out in the garden, making sure it was as perfect as it had been yesterday. He was proud of her for her extraordinary strength, and especially for her capacity for forgiveness. How many widows in the same situation would cope as well as she was? He wasn't sure he would be so forgiving if the woman he loved did the same to him.

Cecily had been right to encourage Pen to open the garden for the Bank Holiday weekend – it had given her something positive and enjoyable to focus on – but Lloyd was worried what would happen when it was all over. In the early years, when Mum had opened the garden for the hospice, she had gone through a period of let-down afterwards. To avoid this happening again, Dad came up with the bright idea of taking her on holiday after each event. Last year he'd taken her to the Languedoc to visit the gardens in the region. They'd gone on a short cruise on the Canal du Midi and sampled the wines of the area. Lloyd could vividly recall how happy they'd seemed when he'd collected them from the airport. But Dad couldn't have been happy, could he? He must have been faking it.

If Lloyd thought too much about the desperate state his father had been reduced to, a knot of guilt tightened in his stomach. Why hadn't he noticed that he was in such a mess? Had he been so absorbed with getting his business off the ground that he had missed the signs? Try as he might, he couldn't think of anything that could be classed as a sign. Dad's medical records showed no evidence that he'd visited the doctor for any stress or depression-related problems; only that he had complained of an apparent inability to sleep as he used to – something that Lloyd and Pen had had no knowledge of. A prescription for sleeping pills had been made out for him the week before his death; combined with what had been found on his computer – he had actually Googled how

239

best to go about killing himself – his intent had been chillingly clear. Just as chilling was the matter-of-fact site he had visited, which had gone into considerable detail about consuming just the right amount of alcohol and pills, get it wrong and you'd vomit the pills back up and survive. Never had Lloyd been more shocked at what you could research online.

In one of her emails to him, Katie had said that as sad and shocking as it had been to lose her parents, she had at least been able to make sense of their deaths, whereas with suicide it had to be one of the hardest things to understand. She was right. Lloyd could say the words – his father had killed himself because he realized he was about to be outed for fraud and couldn't face the consequences – but it didn't help one little bit, because whilst it explained everything, it explained nothing.

He heard the shower being switched off next door. He pushed the duvet back decisively: time to get a move on. He went and stood at the window. Down in the garden, his eyes following a trail of footprints on the dew-sodden grass, he saw his mother on her knees, gathering rose petals that had dropped on the lawn overnight. He wondered how she would feel once this weekend was over. What would she have then to keep her busy and distract her from thinking of Dad?

Perhaps he should offer to take her away like Dad used to. But how would he spare the time? He was already behind with a commission, and though the customer wasn't hounding him for the table and chair set that had to be shipped to Dubai, it bothered him that he wasn't on top of things.

It bothered him more, though, that he could be so selfish. After everything Mum had done for him, the least he could do was find the time to help her through the coming months.

Stirling was doing his best to keep the peace, but Gina didn't seem to want peace; she seemed much more inclined to pick a fight, and over the most insignificant of things – he'd prepared a grapefruit for her when she'd wanted watermelon ... he'd made her coffee when she'd wanted tea ... he was wearing a shirt she'd never liked ... he'd switched the radio on too loudly. He couldn't do anything right.

He knew very well that these trivial irritations didn't form the real basis of her antagonism; they were merely symptoms of what was actually upsetting her, and so, wisely, he was biting his tongue and waiting for the storm to pass.

With breakfast cleared away, he went upstairs to find Gina and tell her that he was off to help at The Meadows. He also wanted to check that she didn't have any plans for tonight. If not, he thought he'd take the *Lady Cecily* out. He hadn't used the boat in nearly three months – the last time had been with Neil, when they'd gone on one of their evening jaunts. The thought had occurred to him that it would be nice to take Katie for an evening cruise. He could put a small picnic together and have some proper time alone with her. Not that he'd tell Gina that.

He had hoped to be able to spend some time with Katie yesterday, but it hadn't been possible. From start to finish the day had been hectic. He had been assigned the job of standing at the gate taking the entrance money – the job Neil had always done – and towards the end of the afternoon, he'd asked Posh Pam to take his place so he could chat with Katie for a while.

Rosco and Scarlet's appearance had taken the wind out of his sails, though. Whilst he'd been eager for them to meet Katie, he'd also dreaded it. He understood why they might view her as a threat, but he'd known that the only way for them to accept the situation and come to terms with it was to meet her. He'd wanted to believe that once they had, they'd put things into perspective and would want to get to know her better. For all Rosco's light-hearted manner yesterday, Stirling suspected the brief exchange with Katie hadn't gone too well. Why else would he and Scarlet have slipped away without saying goodbye? He'd wanted to ring them both later in the evening but hadn't had the nerve.

He found Gina upstairs in their bedroom; she was standing at the window talking on the telephone. It sounded like she was bringing to an end a heated conversation with Scarlet. He made his presence known just as she clicked the phone off. She turned on her heel, her face tight. Immediately the air was tense between them.

'That was Scarlet,' she said, indicating the phone in her hand.

'I gathered so.'

'She was telling me how she and Rosco gave in to your bullying and finally agreed to meet that bastard child of yours yesterday afternoon.'

He strained not to rise to the bait. 'I didn't insist. I asked them to meet Katie.'

'Liar! You bullied them into doing it!'

'I did no such thing. I would never do that. All I did was ask if they would take the time to meet their half-sister while she was staying with Pen.'

'Do you have any idea of the pressure you're putting your children under? Do you?'

'We're all under pressure. This is not an easy situation. But overreacting will only make things worse.'

She breathed in deeply, pursed her lips. 'I don't want Rosco and Scarlet having to go through another afternoon like yesterday. Do you have any idea how upset Scarlet is? Do you even care that she was so distraught last night that she couldn't sleep? Have you given a moment's thought to what all this stress could be doing to her baby, to your grandchild? Do you even care?'

'I care enormously,' he said gravely. 'And I resent that you could accuse me otherwise.'

'Then prove to me that you care. I don't want you to see that girl again. Nor do I ever want to hear her name mentioned again in my presence. Do you understand?'

'I can't turn my back on Katie. What kind of a man would that make me?'

'You should have asked yourself the same question thirty years ago when you were screwing the girl's mother – what kind of man were you to do that?'

There was a cold, implacable defiance to Gina that he'd never seen before. In contrast, he could feel himself vibrating with a hot rage. Very carefully he said, 'I've told you I'm sorry, Gina.'

'Sorry isn't enough.'

He sucked in a ragged breath. 'Why is it that Pen can forgive Neil for all that he did, but you can't forgive me something I did thirty years ago? If you can't do that, then there's really no point in us staying together.'

'I'll forgive you if you do as I ask. You have to promise you'll never see that girl again.'

'I can't do that.'

Her voice was steely. 'I'm asking you to choose your family or a girl you barely know. It can't be that difficult, surely?'

The rage was squeezing his chest so hard he could barely breathe. 'Don't do this, Gina.'

She gave him a sour look. 'I just did.' Very calmly, she replaced the phone in its cradle on his side of the bed and walked out of the room.

Chapter Thirty-three

Stirling tore up the drive. He shot out on to the road and put his foot down. How the hell could Gina expect him to make such a choice? It was inhuman of her. He was appalled she could be so cold-blooded.

He braked hard at the entrance to The Meadows, but instead of turning in, he remained on the road and stared at the open-day poster on the gate. He couldn't do it. He couldn't stand at that gate for the day putting on a cheerful and welcoming smile. The last thing he wanted to do was let Pen down, but he just couldn't face it. Politeness would be beyond him.

He put his foot on the accelerator and drove on, fast, the hedgerows thick and high, flashing by in a blur of green. He knew it was wrong to drive when he was so pumped up, but he didn't care. The sensible thing to do would be to turn around and go home, to take his boat out on the river, to let the water soothe and calm him, clear his head. But he didn't want to be calmed or soothed. He wanted speed. He wanted ferocity. And aggression. He wanted six litres of snarling engine to meet his fury head-on and take him away from here. A one-way ticket to oblivion. That was what he needed.

He had never been a big drinker, never smoked or taken drugs. He'd always stayed the course of sense and reason, of doing the right thing. The only time he'd done anything remotely crazy and spontaneous was when he'd fallen for Fay. Since then, he'd anchored himself firmly in clear-headed judgement, of being reliable and prudent, of always putting his family first. Over the years, he'd carefully erected extra-high safety rails around himself, and the creation of the ultra-sensible and careful man he strived to be was complete when his father died and he unintentionally, but inevitably, became head of the family. Now he wanted to do anything but the right thing. He wanted to break out and be reckless. To throw off the constraints of his life. To be wildly out of control. And to hell with the consequences!

Was this how Neil had felt?

He drove on. Faster. And more furiously.

'Another ten minutes,' Lloyd said, 'then we'll try ringing him.'

'It's so unlike Stirling not to be on time,' Pen said. 'You can usually set your watch by him.'

'Not to worry, I'll go on the gate until he gets here.'

This was from Speedy Sue. The five of them – Katie, Lloyd, Pen, Speedy Sue and Posh Pam – were in the pavilion, where Katie was setting out the plates of cakes. 'Perhaps he's overslept,' she suggested.

Lloyd shook his head. 'That's one thing he never does.'

'I expect he's just got stuck on the phone with someone,' Pen said.

'Well, wherever he is,' Posh Pam said in her schoolmistressy voice, tapping her watch, 'it's five minutes to eleven, so to your posts!'

Katie exchanged a smile with Lloyd. 'I'll help you unwrap the cakes, shall I?' he said when the others had gone.

It was the first time they'd been alone this morning, and the atmosphere between them was loaded with conspiratorial caution. They had decided that what had passed between them last night would, for the time being, remain a private matter. Katie was glad. She had trodden on enough toes since her arrival in Sandiford without further antagonising the Nightingale family. Who knew what they would make of her and Lloyd hooking up? No, it was a difficult situation, and one that needed careful handling. She hadn't said anything to Lloyd, but she had woken this morning troubled by doubts. She hoped there would be a chance later to talk properly with Tess when she arrived with Ben and Zac.

Stirling didn't know what kind of a reception he was going to get, if any; after all, she might not be at home.

He found her house, having remembered where it was when he'd dropped her off the last time he was here, and parked directly opposite in the one-way street. He stowed his mobile in the glove compartment – he'd switched it off earlier when he'd stopped for petrol. He didn't want anyone to contact him.

Out of the car, he looked up at the terraced house. It was nicely painted, white stucco, with a dark blue wooden door with three steps leading up to it from the pavement. There were window boxes outside the two upstairs windows, and they contained the palest of creamy-yellow flowers. The houses either side were equally well cared for.

He lifted the brass knocker on the door, gave it a firm but what he hoped was a polite knock. If he'd been here earlier, when he was going through the worst of his anger and frustration, he might have banged the door knocker hard.

The door opened and Simone Montrose looked back at him. Her surprise was unconcealed.

'I was just passing,' he said.

She tilted her head slightly. 'Really?'

'Clearly I'm lying. May I come in?'

'I suppose you better had.' She stepped aside so he could enter. 'I'm afraid the house isn't very tidy. It's been a busy week.'

He followed her through to the kitchen, which looked immaculately tidy – even to his demanding standards – and opened on to a conservatory and a long, thin garden. Everything in the kitchen was white, with chrome or stainless-steel accessories. The only colour was provided by a row of white pots containing pink and mauve orchids. There was classical music playing. Bach's Mass in B Minor. It was a particular favourite of his.

'Coffee?' she said. 'I was about to make myself a cappuccino.'

He nodded. 'I'll have the same. Thank you.'

She had the identical coffee machine he had treated himself to last Christmas. He suddenly pictured his brother here in this light and airy kitchen, sitting at the glass-topped table, drinking coffee or enjoying a glass of wine and a meal. It was very different to life at The Meadows. Much as he loved Pen, Stirling would never cope on a permanent basis with her carefree attitude to housekeeping.

The coffee made, Simone said, 'Shall we go outside?'

Again he nodded.

He took off his jacket and they sat at a circular marble-topped table; there were only two chairs. Settled side by side, she said, 'Why are you here, Stirling?'

'I didn't know where else to go. I couldn't think of anyone I could talk to. Someone who would understand. Someone who won't judge me or think I'm mad.'

She looked at him steadily. 'Why do you think I'm the right person?'

'Because you hardly know me and will have very little in the way of preconceived ideas about me.'

She smiled. 'Very well. What's on your mind?'

He told her how Gina had presented him with an ultimatum this morning.

When he fell quiet, she said, 'And if you had to make that decision right now, your wife or Katie, what would you do?'

He glanced away, down the garden. On the parched lawn, beneath a lilac tree, a blackbird was poking about in the curled-up leaves. The bird looked like it had lost something and was determined to find it. 'God help me,' he said, 'but right now I'd choose Katie.'

'A girl who is practically a stranger, over your family?'

'But Katie is my family as well. I want to do the right thing by her. I owe it to her. What would she think of me if I rejected her now? She doesn't have anyone else. And I keep thinking of Fay. What would she think if I didn't stand by Katie? She's our daughter.'

'Perhaps you all need a cooling-off period. Katie would understand that, wouldn't she? A few months without any pressure, and maybe Gina would have a change of heart.'

'But if Gina loved me, would she put me through this? Would she force me to make a decision I'd always regret?'

'I can't speak for your wife, but I would think she's trying to make you demonstrate your love for her, isn't she?'

He shook his head. 'I don't feel I can love someone who would do that. Could you?'

She gave him a soft smile. 'This isn't about me.'

'But you think I'm wrong to consider putting Katie first?'

'Stirling, I'm not saying that at all. I'm just asking you questions and giving you the opportunity to answer honestly, and without the fear of being judged. Isn't that why you came here? Because you thought you could trust me?'

He nodded, suddenly tired. 'You're right. I do trust you. And yet I barely know you.'

'That's often the way it goes. Shall I make us some lunch?'

'I don't want to intrude.'

She stood up and gave him that soft smile again. 'You're not intruding. It's nice to have your company.'

'Really?'

'Don't look so surprised. If I didn't like you, Stirling, I wouldn't have invited you in.'

'Strictly speaking, I invited myself in.'

'I could have shut the door in your face.'

'I'm pleased you didn't.'

While Simone made a chicken Caesar salad, Stirling opened a bottle of white wine from the fridge – it was the most she would allow him to do. He watched her carefully chopping

248

and slicing, her movements neat and meticulous. Dressed in a light grey long flowing skirt and a white sleeveless top, her feet bare and her dark hair tied in a loose ponytail, she looked a totally different woman to the one he'd met at Neil's funeral, and different again to the woman with whom he'd had lunch at the Old Parsonage. She seemed to have a different guise for every time they met.

'Glasses are in the cupboard to your right,' she said.

He fetched them and poured the wine. 'So how are *you*?' he asked.

'Oh, you know, taking each day as it comes. I keep waiting for …' She stopped what she was doing, the knife she'd been using to chop the chicken poised in mid-air.

'For what?' he prompted.

Her shoulders slumped and she put the knife down. She turned to face him. 'For the emptiness and loneliness to stop,' she said, so quietly he almost didn't hear her. 'I feel so very alone.'

He knew exactly what she meant. He was surrounded by people all the time – at work and at home – but he felt isolated. Cut off and adrift. 'I feel it too,' he said.

'I know. I sensed it the first time we spoke on the telephone.'

'You did?'

'And again at the funeral.'

He took a step towards her. 'There's nobody I can talk to. I'm supposed to be the strong one in the family, the person everyone turns to. I can't bother my mother, or Pen. Or Gina; she's in her own world of pain right now. I've hurt her and she's furious. She's lashing out at me, and I deserve it. I know that. But it doesn't make it any easier to bear. Some days I want to throw my head back and howl like a wild animal. Just let it all out. Today I wanted to lose control completely. I want to be reckless and to hell with the consequences. Does that sound crazy? Do I sound crazy?'

Tears filled her eyes and she shook her head. 'I feel like that nearly all the time.'

The empathy she had, that she truly understood, ripped through him. They stared at each other, and then with absolute sureness, they moved at precisely the same moment. They were in each other's arms, his mouth was on hers and she was kissing him back. It was a mutual need and they gave in to it with an explosion of energy. He wanted her and she wanted him. It was as simple as that. She was unbuttoning his shirt, tugging it from his trousers. Desire surging through him, he started to undo his belt. 'No,' she said breathlessly.

Oh God, he thought, she's changed her mind.

But she hadn't.

'Not here,' she murmured. She pulled him towards the door.

It was half past one, and the lunchtime rush for tea and cake was in full swing. It was even busier than yesterday, and Katie was grateful for Lloyd's help.

There was still no sign of Stirling, and no response from his mobile. Katie couldn't lay claim to knowing the man well, but he struck her as being the reliable sort, not the type to let people down at the last minute, especially not Pen, who he was clearly extremely fond of. Lloyd had rung Willow Bank and had got very short shrift. Essentially the reply had been that Gina didn't give a damn where 'that man' was; as far as she was concerned, he could go to hell.

Just as there was a lull in people wanting refreshments, and whilst Lloyd was taking a tray of used crockery up to the house to put in the dishwasher, Katie looked across the garden and saw Tess, Ben and Zac. They were dressed in what presumably they thought was garden-party chic, their inspiration taken from what appeared to be *The Great Gatsby*. Tess was wearing a divine floaty marshmallow-pink silk dress with a pair of cream Mary Janes, and perched on her shoulder was a lacy parasol, which she was twirling playfully with her gloved hands. The boys were both done up as Jay Gatsby, in cream suits, ties, striped shirts, braces and caps. They must have spent hours, if not days, trawling the vintage clothes shops to nail the look. And nail it they had. They looked beautiful. They caught sight of Katie and broke out with waves and smiles and a squeal from Zac. Picking their way through the groups of people, who were all staring, they rushed towards her. Katie felt unaccountably pleased to see them.

Stirling woke up. It took him a few seconds to realize where he was and that he wasn't alone. Simone was asleep, her long naked body curved into his, her hair, loose now, forming a curtain between her back and his chest.

He needed the bathroom, but didn't want to move and risk waking her. Lying perfectly still, he thought how good it would be to stay here. Nobody knew where he was. Nobody could bother him. He felt he had run away, had escaped to somewhere safe. The thought puzzled him. He'd never needed to feel safe before. Was that because he'd never felt vulnerable before? Did everyone experience that sensation at some time in their lives?

He thought about what he had done. In one single step he'd betrayed his wife – again – and his brother.

Reckless.

Wildly out of control.

Consequences.

He didn't give a damn. He and Simone had both craved what they had done. It had been mutually beneficial, because while their bodies had been joined with an unstoppable and powerfully physical force, their minds had known a respite of peace. They had been cleansed for brief moments of their grief, their loneliness expunged.

Their lovemaking had not been an act of gentle tenderness; it had been an explosively fierce and fervent coming together. The strength of her need for him had made him feel alive and invincible. She had aroused in him a passion he'd never known

251

before. Good God, he'd done things with her he'd never done before! Almost sixty, but not too old to learn a new trick or two, he thought wryly.

But what now? Would she feel embarrassed at what they'd done? Ashamed even? Would it be better if he slipped away so she wouldn't have to face the awkwardness? Would that be the behaviour of a gentleman? Or a despicable coward?

Chapter Thirty-four

'He's pure yummy angel cake, darling. I could happily take a bite out of him. And have you noticed his hands and arms? I bet he could crack walnuts with no more than a tap of one of his big manly knuckles.'

Tess flicked her brother on the nose. 'Back in your playpen, Zac, let the grown-ups talk.' She turned to Katie. 'Come on, while Ben and Lloyd are inside ordering the food, 'fess up. What is it you wanted to tell us that you couldn't when he was around earlier? You're not still stressing about Stirling being a no-show, are you? We can always suss him out another time.'

Although Katie was disappointed her friends hadn't been able to meet him, she shook her head. 'No, it's nothing to do with Stirling.' She glanced over her shoulder to check there was no danger of being overheard. They were in Henley, at the Angel on the Bridge, and with its decking area directly overlooking the river, Katie could see why it was such a popular pub. Early evening, and the place was packed, which meant that her friends, still dressed in their garden-party Gatsby gear, had garnered the maximum amount of attention on their arrival – a state of affairs that had pleased Zac, who liked nothing more than a good audience, the more captive the better.

Satisfied that it was safe to talk, Katie faced Tess and Zac across the table. 'Lloyd isn't my cousin,' she said simply.

'So what is he?' Tess asked. 'God, he's not your brother, is he?'

'We're not related. He was adopted. So was his father. There's no blood tie. None whatsoever. And we've—'

Tess and Zac spoke at the same time. 'And you've what?'

Katie blushed. 'And last night, once he'd explained he wasn't really my cousin, we … we kissed.'

Again Tess and Zac spoke as one. '*Kissed?*'

Katie gave them the edited highlights of what had taken place on the riverbank. She also told them about the alarming shocky moment she'd experienced when she'd first set eyes on Lloyd in Brighton, something she'd deliberately withheld from Tess until now.

'How divine,' Zac cooed. 'It's *soooo* romantic.'

'But is it?' Katie asked. 'How will the rest of the family react? I can see all sorts of problems ahead. And if I'm really honest, there's still a part of me that's concerned what people will think; you know, that technically we'll always be defined as cousins.'

Tess wrinkled her nose. 'Technically defined? What kind of language are you speaking these days?'

'You know what I'm saying. How others will see us.'

'Since when have you ever worried about what others think of you?'

'Zac's right. Which means there's something else that's bothering you. What is it?' Tess's expression intensified, a sure sign that her intuitive radar had just cranked up a gear.

'OK, it's this,' Katie said. 'What if we do get seriously involved and then it all goes wrong and we end up hating each other?'

'What, like you and Ian?'

Katie frowned at Zac. 'I don't hate Ian.'

'Well I do. He was disgustingly homophobic.'

'He wasn't!'

Tess nodded. 'He was, Katie. You just never saw it. He nearly cacked himself once when Zac put his arm around him.'

Katie was shocked. 'What else didn't I notice about him?'

Zac shrugged. 'Nothing much, just that he was a creepy

twat. We were terrified you'd marry him. But I had it all planned: when the time came, I'd have been up on my feet in the church with a long list of just causes and impediments. I'd have stormed the altar and refused to get down until you came to your senses.'

Katie laughed. 'Oh Zac, you're such a headcase. But I do love you. Why did you never say anything?'

'You wouldn't have listened. You wanted to believe in Ian. And at the time, you seemed to need him more than you needed us.'

Once more Katie was shocked. 'Never! That's never going to happen. I'm always going to need you two in my life.'

Tess clapped her hands impatiently. 'Hey, people! We're getting off track here. Stay focused. Why would it be so awful for you to try a relationship with Lloyd and for it to go wrong? It's the risk we all take.'

'But he and I are members of the same family, a family, strange as it might seem, that I want to be a part of. So how would we face each other if we fell out badly?'

'Ah ... good point.'

'And there's something else. Something I have personal experience of. Lloyd has recently lost his father, and he'll be going through the grieving process for some time yet. Look how I turned to Ian when Mum died. And then what happened when I was over the worst of my grief: I realized the relationship had run its course and dumped him. I'm not proud of that. I don't want to be a convenient distraction for Lloyd, someone he'll shrug off when he doesn't need me any more as a crutch.'

Zac whistled. 'You're assuming a hell of a lot, sweetheart. Just because that was your experience with Ian, it doesn't mean it's a one-size-fits-all situation.'

'I hate to say it twice in one conversation,' Tess said, 'but Zac's right. You're doing what you always do, overanalysing people. Don't try and think for Lloyd; let him do his own thinking.'

'Take it from me,' Zac said, 'from what I've seen of him, the boy looks plenty big enough to think for himself.'

'You're such a lech, brother dear.'

He laughed. 'You know me: if the bonnet fits, I'll wear it.'

'But seriously, Katie, what if Lloyd's the one? He did give you a shocky moment, after all. Why not give it a go? You don't have to rush things.'

'For what it's worth, I think it's fate.'

Katie laughed. 'You say that every time you meet somebody new, Zac.'

'Just because it doesn't work out doesn't mean it wasn't meant to be. Uh-oh, the object of our mutual desire is heading this way. No, strike that, he's *striding* this way. God, I love a man who strides.'

Stirling was still in Oxford.

Five hours ago, he had got as far as sneaking into the bathroom to get dressed, and when he'd returned to the bedroom for his shoes, he'd found Simone sitting up in bed, hugging the duvet to her. 'Are you running away to hide from your own shame or to spare me mine?' she had asked.

He'd sat down heavily on the bed, hanging his head. 'Both,' he'd said.

'Then don't. Let's be perfectly adult about this, shall we? Otherwise we'll be in a worse mess than we were before.'

'I don't regret what we did,' he'd said, lifting his eyes.

'Nor do I. Which is why I don't want you to run off.'

'I have to go sometime.'

She'd smiled. 'I'm not going to hold you captive. How about that lunch I was making for us?'

'What an extraordinary woman you are.'

'Thank you.'

They'd eaten lunch and somehow – wordlessly – they'd ended up in bed again. It had been less frantic second time around. But no less exhilarating.

'I should go,' he said now, when once more they were dressed and downstairs.

'Yes, you should.' She passed him his jacket.

'I won't bother you again like this,' he said when he was at the door. 'I won't become a nuisance to you.' He kissed her lightly on the cheek. 'Goodbye.'

'Goodbye, Stirling. Drive carefully.'

She had already closed the door when he started the car and pulled away from the kerb. He felt churlishly disappointed not to get a wave from her.

From the landing window Simone looked down on the street as Stirling drove off. She touched her cheek where he'd just kissed her. Don't, she warned herself. Just don't.

She turned from the window and went to her bedroom and stripped the bed. She took the bedding downstairs to the kitchen, stuffed it into the washing machine, tipped powder into the tray and pressed the button. 'There,' she said aloud as water began gushing. 'All trace of him gone. As if it had never happened.'

She went back upstairs, removed her clothes and stepped into the shower. 'Though your sins are like scarlet, they shall be as snow,' she quoted a little sadly to herself.

Chapter Thirty-five

Stirling had not told an out-and-out lie to Gina in years. Not since his affair with Fay. In the intervening years he might have fudged the truth once or twice, usually to cover a surprise he'd arranged for his wife, but the need for an ugly, bare-faced, back-covering lie had not occurred.

Until now.

But telling Gina he'd gone to Oxford to see Simone Montrose – even if he kept quiet about what they'd actually done – didn't strike him as being a smart move. Justifying his visit by saying something like he owed it to his brother to make sure his mistress was coping was hardly going to cut the mustard with Gina in her current frame of mind. 'So you care more about Neil's tart than you do about my feelings, do you?' he imagined her throwing back at him.

Yet the newly revealed reckless side to him was almost daring him to go down this route. Why not stir things up some more by hurling another grenade into the battlefield? Why was he always striving to keep the peace, to be so bloody reasonable?

It was late when he entered the village of Sandiford. He slowed his speed as he drew level with St Oswald's, where they'd had Neil's funeral and where Neil was buried in the churchyard. On the noticeboard against the flint wall there was a poster advertising the open weekend at The Meadows in support of the church roof fund. For the first time that day, guilt hit him: he'd let Pen down. He would have to make amends.

But before that, there was something he now felt compelled to do.

He left the car on the road and in the dark carefully followed the path round to the side of the church, his footsteps crunching on the gravel in the shadowy hush. He passed the lofty stone monument for which he'd always had a secret affection. Late Victorian and robustly sentimental, it was of an angel; with her eyes closed and her hands clasped in humble supplication, she was praying on one knee atop a three-foot-high plinth. What he'd always liked about the statue was the surprisingly sensual nature of the angel's feet; they were bare, and the toes were long and slender. As he observed those elongated toes now, they evoked the unsettling memory of Simone's bare feet.

He pressed on slowly towards Neil's grave, just as the moon shot out from behind a cloud.

He came to a stop in front of the last plot in a row of the recently deceased. It was still without a headstone and looked obscenely fresh and new. There were flowers attractively placed in a pretty china vase and the scent of sweet peas, roses and sprigs of lavender was palpable in the still night air. Doubtless Pen had brought the flowers. He wondered how often she came. Prior to tonight, and other than the day of the funeral, he'd come here only once before. He had thought it might help. It hadn't.

Now here he was again.

Why?

To seek forgiveness would be the obvious assumption.

But that wasn't the reason. No. He wanted to tell his brother he understood. That was all. He stared down at the bare earth. 'We're all capable of doing what you did,' he said, his voice low. 'No one's beyond temptation, of doing the unthinkable.'

He stood for a while to see if he would begin to feel ashamed at what he'd done. If it didn't happen here, where would it?

Minutes passed. The moon came and went intermittently

behind scudding clouds. But nothing. He felt no shame. None whatsoever.

He drove on. Then once again he slowed his speed. He turned into The Meadows. Here he did need to ask for forgiveness.

When Pen opened the front door to Stirling, she let out a small cry. 'Oh, thank goodness you're all right. I've been so worried about you.'

'I'm sorry,' he said, stepping inside and closing the door behind him. 'I couldn't face being around people today. I just had to be somewhere else, anywhere but here.'

'Stirling, you don't have to explain yourself to me. Not ever. But please, another time, promise me you'll let me know you're all right. That's all I ask. After what happened to Neil, I couldn't bear ...' Her voice wobbled and she broke off. She covered her mouth with a hand and shuddered.

'Oh, Pen,' he said, giving her a hug, 'nothing's going to happen to me. Come on,' he soothed, 'no tears over me. I'm not worth it.' He guided her through the hallway to the kitchen. 'Let me make you a drink. You look exhausted. Have you eaten?'

'Yes. Pam and Sue stayed on again this evening while Lloyd took Katie and her friends into Henley. They've gone now, back to London and Brighton.'

'And Katie and Lloyd, where are they?'

'In the garden. I was just going upstairs for a bath.'

'Would you rather I left you in peace so you could do that?'

'No, stay and have a drink with me. There's something I want to discuss with you.'

'Do you ever swim in the river here?'

'Of course. Why? Fancy a skinny-dip now?'

Katie laughed. 'Another time.'

Lloyd nudged his shoulder against hers. 'Chicken.'

'Watch it, mister, or I'll shove you in.'

'I'd like to see you try.'

'Oh, please don't tempt me.'

'I'm twice the size of you.'

'And everyone knows size isn't everything.'

He laughed and put his arm around her. They were sitting on the jetty at the end of the garden, their feet dangling a couple of feet above the water. He had waited all day for this moment. To be alone with Katie. 'So how did I measure up with your friends?' he asked.

'Pretty well. Zac, of course, is wildly in lust with you.'

He laughed again. 'I've not lost my touch, then. And for what it's worth, I liked them. It's going to seem very dull round here when you've gone. Do you have to rush back to Brighton after tomorrow?'

'I can't stay here with your mother indefinitely. And apart from anything, I have to try and find a job.'

'You could always come and stay with me while you do that.'

She turned and looked at him. Just looked at him.

'Sorry,' he said. 'Probably too soon to suggest something like that, isn't it?'

She placed a soft kiss on his mouth. 'Let's not do things too quickly,' she murmured.

'You're right, of course,' he said lightly, hoping she wouldn't pick up on his disappointment.

'I'll come back soon,' she said.

'Define soon?'

She kissed him again, brushing her lips over his. He held her close and deepened the kiss, lingering over every sensation, his eyes closed, his pulse racing.

Stirling was staggered at what Pen had told him, of her suspicions about Lloyd and Katie. People joked that she didn't know what was going on around her, other than what was growing in her garden, but he'd never gone along with that.

When it came to Lloyd, Pen was always on the money.

But he for one hadn't seen it coming. Lloyd and Katie? Potentially it could complicate things. On the other hand, it could create a bridge between Katie and the rest of the family. He feared, however, that it wouldn't. Besides, wasn't it a bit soon for Lloyd to have made a move on her? They hardly knew each other.

He drove home, having decided not to disturb Lloyd and Katie in the garden. He'd asked Pen to say hi to Katie from him and to tell her that he'd catch up with her tomorrow.

He let himself in at Willow Bank, bracing himself for Gina's wrath. He had his lie prepared: he'd spent the day at the office, working his temper off after her ultimatum this morning.

Chapter Thirty-six

Rosco had set aside Bank Holiday Monday as a day entirely for himself. No boring household chores to do, no bills to deal with, and no company work of any kind to pore over. He'd done everything yesterday, including a lengthy session of catching up on emails and checking a list of recent client money transfers made.

After Uncle Neil's stunt, they now had strict procedures in place in the office regarding the double-checking of client portfolios. Bolting horses and stable doors sprang to mind, but never again – not if Rosco had anything to do with it – would Nightingale Ridgeway be involved in such a damaging financial scandal. Never again would it be possible for someone to do what Uncle Neil had done. Rosco's modus operandi now was to suspect everyone of foul play until proven innocent. And if people didn't like that, they could look elsewhere for employment. If it created an atmosphere of unease, good. That was what he wanted. He wanted everyone to be afraid and looking over their shoulder.

Naturally Dad didn't agree. He claimed that trust was the bedrock of Nightingale Ridgeway, that it always had been so and always would be. Yeah, well, tell that to the clients who'd had their money stolen. Tell that to the CPS when the case finally went to court. Worried that Dad wasn't his usual clear-thinking self, Rosco had started working even longer hours and was trying to instil a greater sense of diligence and efficiency in the office. Lead by example was his motto.

So with a weekend of efficient organization behind him,

Rosco had planned that today he would be free to do exactly as he pleased, which was a pleasantly lazy day followed by dinner with a girl he'd recently met at a friend's thirtieth birthday party.

Except his lazy day wasn't turning out that way. His well-earned lie-in had been disturbed by Scarlet ringing him. For twenty minutes he'd been forced to listen to her histrionics about Dad and Katie Lavender. 'How can we be sure she really is who she says she is?' Scarlet was now asking. 'I mean, she's got red hair. *Red*. No one in our family has red hair. Has anyone thought to check her out? She could be someone pretending to be his daughter. What are we going to do about it? Rosco, are you listening to me?'

'Scarlet,' he said, when finally given permission to speak, 'don't be a dope. The red hair is from Granza. Although strictly speaking the colour in question isn't red, it's chestnut.'

'So you're not questioning who she is? I can't believe that. And I can't believe you're quibbling over the colour of her hair. My God, next you'll be saying that you thought she was quite nice. Do you think she's nice?'

'Don't be stupid, of course I don't.'

'Then what are we going to do about her?'

'We're going to ignore her. That's what we're going to do. We've done our duty; we met her just as Dad wanted. We don't have to do anything more.'

'I told Mum to give him an ultimatum, to tell him he has to choose us or her. I told her to tell him that if he has anything more to do with her, he can say goodbye to us.'

'Did you now?' This had been Rosco's Plan A when divorce had been in the air, but he'd been reluctant to go through with it in case it backfired on him. But with the initiative coming from Scarlet, it meant he was removed from the equation; he could be seen as the objective one. He would be there to give Dad his support and to say that as hard as it was, he was doing the right thing. He would tell his father that Katie had managed well enough all these years without him; she could manage the rest of her life equally well. It was as simple as that. Faced with such a convincing bottom line, Dad would see things perfectly clearly.

The only way to get Scarlet off the phone was to play on her pregnancy. 'Now stop worrying about all this, Scarlet,' he said. 'You know it can't be good for the baby. Go and make yourself a cup of coffee and put your feet up and relax.'

She tutted. 'You know I'm not drinking coffee whilst I'm pregnant. Honestly, Rosco, sometimes I don't think you listen to a word I say.'

If only that were possible, he thought when he at last got rid of her.

Now, showered and dressed, and putting the finishing touches to his breakfast of scrambled eggs on a toasted and buttered bagel, he heard the phone ring again. He knew straight away from the tone of his mother's voice that there was no way he could ask if he could ring her back when he'd eaten.

He set his plate down on the breakfast bar, and with the phone placed on speaker, resigned himself to a ruined day. It seemed to him, as his mother went on and on about how awful Dad was making her life, that she had turned into exactly the kind of neurotic and needy woman he couldn't abide. Whilst trying silently to eat a mouthful of bagel and egg, he listened to a repeat version of the ultimatum Dad had been given yesterday, and how he had disappeared for the day, and how everyone at The Meadows had been asking why he wasn't there to help as arranged. 'Where had he been?' Rosco asked when there was a lull in the monologue and a response seemed to be expected of him. 'Off in the boat somewhere?'

'No. He was at the office all day. He said he'd gone there to do some work and to clear his head. He said he needed to be alone. For pity's sake, who does he think he is, saying he needs to be alone?'

Rosco's attention was caught. 'He told you he was at the office all day?'

'That's what I just said.'

Rosco was about to say this wasn't possible when he stopped himself. He knew categorically that there had been only one person in the office yesterday, and that was him – that was where he'd gone to check on the client portfolios. So why had Dad lied? Where had he been that he wanted to keep it from Mum? What reason would he have to hide something like that? Or maybe it wasn't the actual place he was being so secretive about, but a person. Had he been with someone he didn't want Mum to know about? But who?

An awful thought occurred to him. A woman. It was a woman Dad had been with. It was the only explanation.

But how could he? With everything the family was going through, how could he do something so low and shabby? Was it a case of once a cheat, always a cheat? Or maybe he had been having a string of affairs throughout his entire marriage. And that was why he was so sympathetic to what Uncle Neil had been up to. God knew how many more bastard children were going to come out of the woodwork at this rate!

He decided to keep his suspicions to himself. There was no point in winding his mother up yet further. Better for him to tackle Dad on his own. When the time was right.

'Where's Dad today?' he asked.

'Back at The Meadows helping Pen. With that wretched girl again,' she added bitterly.

'And how do things stand regarding the ultimatum you gave him?'

'He says he needs time to think about it. Can you believe that? What is there to think about, Rosco?'

'He'll do the right thing, Mum. Don't worry. He's all over the place right now.'

'Can't you talk to him? Can't you make him see reason?' The tone of her voice had changed; she sounded tired and whiny. 'I don't know, ever since Neil's death, everything's gone wrong.'

'I'll do my best. Leave it with me.'

A few minutes later and he managed to ring off. He took a bite of his half-eaten breakfast and found it was stone cold. Thoroughly out of sorts, he took it over to the bin and threw it away.

Stirling wasn't sure that he had done the right thing. He had texted Simone, feeling in some way that he ought to. He really didn't want her to think badly of him. That he was the kind of man who was in the habit of turning up on a woman's doorstep – a woman he hardly knew – and behaving in the way he had yesterday.

He had sent the message before lunch, and now, at five o'clock, as he was closing the gate – the last of the visitors gone – Simone still hadn't replied to his message. Had she felt insulted by his thanking her for lunch and for asking how she was today? It hadn't felt glib at the time, but with hindsight perhaps it was. He hadn't known what else to say. What could he have said? An apology? Would she have expected that from him? Had it also been too distant and formal to thank her for lunch? The more he thought about it, the worse it became in his mind. He was beginning to think that he should text her again to make sure he hadn't offended her with that first text. But would a second message make things worse? Would she think he was becoming a pest, thereby making a nonsense of his assurance that he wouldn't be a nuisance to her? Would she worry that he was trying to invite himself back for a repeat of yesterday? Which he certainly wasn't. But just thinking of that possibility made his pulse quicken. Shocked, he dragged a hand over his face, and picking up the plastic box of entrance money, walked quickly round to the back of the house. He suddenly needed to be amongst people. He needed the distraction of them.

He spotted Katie and Lloyd inside the pavilion. They were busy stacking dirty crockery on to trays.

Throughout the day they had given no obvious signs that there was anything going on between them, but there

267

were plenty of subtle indications and undercurrents, if you knew what to look for. Stirling had most definitely noticed the occasional look or smile, or Lloyd's lingering hand on Katie's shoulder as he moved to get past her. He'd also caught Katie blushing as Lloyd whispered something in her ear. For whatever reason, they had decided to keep to themselves what they were up to.

He wasn't sure what to make of it, though. To his surprise, deep inside him, some primal instinct was uncoiling itself: Katie was his daughter, and as her father he wanted to keep her safe, which meant no man was to be trusted. He had been the same with Scarlet. How he'd ever survived those nightmarish years and the fast turnaround of unsuitable boys with whom Scarlet had proclaimed herself to be in love, he didn't know. The most memorable duds had been a would-be rock star who hadn't possessed one iota of musical know-how, a long-haired dropout who'd claimed to be a conceptual artist and destined to be the next big thing in the art world, a Greek waiter who had wanted to marry her after only a fortnight of knowing her, and a thug who'd spent time in prison for GBH, a case of mistaken identity apparently. But the very worst of the bunch had been a man fifteen years older than Scarlet who had wanted to take off with her to Thailand with nothing but a couple of backpacks. Oh, and Scarlet's credit cards. After some surreptitious digging, Stirling had discovered that the man was married with two small children. And then along had come Charlie Boy, and whilst he wasn't the sharpest knife in the drawer, in comparison to his predecessors he had been the model boyfriend. Within no time he had achieved the impossible; he had anchored the flighty Scarlet, and for that Stirling would always be grateful. But make no mistake: if he hurt her, there would be hell to pay.

As there would be if Lloyd hurt Katie. Just articulating the thought amazed Stirling. He and Katie had had no real time or opportunity to bond and form what would be called a meaningful relationship, but nonetheless, the instinct to protect her was there. It was why he knew he couldn't do what Gina wanted of him; he couldn't cast Katie aside. However that bond was made, it existed. It was very real.

He stepped into the pavilion and at once Lloyd and Katie fell quiet, their animated conversation abruptly brought to an end. They both smiled at him. A little too eagerly. A little too like he'd interrupted them. That, and the way Lloyd was staring at Stirling, told him that there was definitely something going on between the two of them. In Lloyd's eyes there was the same unmistakable solicitous and circumspect look he'd seen in so many of Scarlet's suitors. Whether he knew he was doing it or not, Lloyd was seeking Stirling's approval.

'Katie,' Stirling said, 'are you doing anything this evening?'

'I don't have anything planned,' she said with a smile.

'In that case, can we spend the evening together? Just the two of us? Only we've hardly had any time alone, and you leave tomorrow.' He glanced at his nephew. 'That's if you don't mind, Lloyd?'

Lloyd pushed his hands into his pockets and took a step back. 'Of course not. Don't worry about me.'

But I do, Stirling thought. I worry about Katie as well. And the whole bloody family and what lies ahead.

Chapter Thirty-seven

'So you'll be heading back to Brighton tomorrow?' Tess said.
   'That's the plan.'
   'You're not tempted to stay on for a bit longer?'
   'No.' Katie tried to put as much conviction as she could into that one simple word. It would be all too easy for her to give in to Lloyd and Pen and Cecily, who kept asking her to stay on for a few more days.
   'Really?' said Tess. 'What have you got to rush back for?'
   'Don't you start. I've had enough of that from everyone here.'
   'What's the hurry, then?'
   'It's difficult to explain, and you'll probably think I'm going all airy-fairy, but this place has a sort of magical and intoxicating pull to it. It's like the rest of the world doesn't exist. I felt it when I first stayed here. I remember looking out of the window at Pen's incredible garden and thinking that if I didn't leave that day, I might never leave.'
   'Isn't that how everyone feels at the end of a really good holiday?'
   'I suppose so. But imagine your best ever holiday experience and times it by a hundred. It's just so beautiful here. And weirdly, I feel so at home.'
   'Sounds like the place has seduced you as much as that cousin of yours.'
   'He's not my cousin.'
   'Sorry, slip of the genealogical tongue. What is he, then?'
   'What do you mean?'

'I'm asking if he's officially your new boyfriend now. Has that been established?'

'I wouldn't go so far as to say anything's official.' Katie glanced at her watch; seeing how late it was, she said, 'Hey, look, I'm going to have to go. Stirling's taking me out this evening and I've got to smarten myself up.'

'Oh, so the absent father's returned, has he? I hope he's taking you somewhere nice. And tell him from me, I'm on his case. He doesn't get my approval until he's been properly vetted.'

Katie laughed. 'He probably knew that and that's why he disappeared yesterday. I'll ring you tomorrow when I'm back in Brighton. Say hi to Ben from me. By the way, what did he think of Lloyd?'

'He thought he was great. And way better than Ian. You really crossed over to the dark side with him.'

'I had no idea you all disliked Ian so much. Why weren't you honest with me?'

'As Zac told you yesterday, you weren't receptive to honesty then. And perhaps we were scared to give it to you.'

'And now you're not?'

'Now we've seen the error of our ways. Total truthfulness from now on.'

Katie ended the call and got off the bed, where she'd been lying whilst chatting to her friend. She went and stood at the window, looking out at the area of the garden where she had first met Pen, after she had stepped through that small arched doorway with the sign reading 'Open Me' on it, and which would forever be her favourite part of this enchanting world. She watched Pen wandering the trampled lawns, inspecting the damage inflicted by so many visitors. The poor woman looked a tired and forlorn figure.

Katie had been amazed at the nerve of some of the visitors to the garden. As if they had a God-given right to do so, they had taken cuttings and helped themselves to sprigs of herbs; one man had even snapped off a rose to make a buttonhole for himself and had brazenly strolled around the garden with it openly on show on his jacket lapel. Lloyd had told her of far worse things that had gone on in previous years, such as a woman who he had discovered actually digging up a particularly rare species of plant. When he had asked her what she was doing, she had become quite shirty and told him to mind his own business. This, Lloyd had explained, was why help was always required on the open days, not only to answer queries visitors might have about the plants, but to keep an eye on the more light-fingered punters.

Seeing Pen take out a ball of green twine and a penknife from her pocket, Katie watched her carefully negotiate her way to the back of one of the borders and get to work on supporting the slender stalk of a hollyhock that was almost nine feet tall and drooping with the weight of so many showy, saucer-sized pink flowers. She then turned her attention to a neighbouring delphinium and cut off another length of twine. Watching her, Katie wondered what she would do in the coming days and weeks, now that the open weekend was over, now that she would have nothing into which she could pour all her energy and thoughts, when finally she would be alone with only her grief to face. Katie knew that feeling all too well. To avoid it after Mum's death, she had thrown herself headlong into her relationship with Ian.

Moving away from the window, she finished getting dressed for her evening out with Stirling. It would be the first time they spent any time alone together, and she was part looking forward to it and part dreading it. What if they ran out of things to talk about? What if she suddenly decided she didn't like him? Or if he didn't like her?

There was a knock at the door, followed by: 'Katie?'

It was Lloyd.

She went to open it. 'How do I look?' she asked him. 'Smart enough for an evening with Stirling?'

He stood in the doorway, rested a shoulder against the

frame and scrutinized her from head to toe. 'Honest opinion?' he said.

She nodded, suddenly doubting her choice of dress. In Brighton and London, she wouldn't think twice about her black and white polka-dot miniskirt and lacy black top with its puff sleeves, but maybe here in Henley, especially if Stirling was taking her somewhere chi-chi and upmarket, her outfit might not pass muster. She waited for Lloyd's verdict.

'You've got legs,' he said.

'Well *durr*, so have you.'

He smiled. 'Not like yours I haven't. How come I haven't seen them before?'

'Never mind my legs, what about the rest of me?'

He pushed himself away from the door frame and stepped into the room. 'The rest of you looks amazing. I like what you've done to your hair.'

He'd never commented on her appearance before, and out of the blue she felt inexplicably shy. 'Zac taught me how to do it,' she said, putting a hand self-consciously to her walnut-whip hairdo, as she called it.

'You smell nice, too.'

'Thank you.'

'If I promise not to muss up your hair and make-up, can I kiss you?'.

She smiled and nodded.

He deftly closed the door behind him with his foot and dipping his head, he grazed his lips against hers with a feather-light caress, no other part of him touching her.

'I can redo the lip gloss,' she said, putting the palms of her hands against his chest and wanting more. He stared back at her, and losing herself in the mesmerising soft blue of his eyes, she decided to take Tess's advice and stop overanalysing the situation. Surely all that mattered was what they felt for each other? If it didn't work out, they'd just have to find a way to deal with it.

'I wouldn't want to put you to any trouble,' he said.

'It's no trouble.'

'Well, if you're sure.'

Their arms wrapped around each other, they kissed long and hard.

'I wish it was me taking you out this evening,' he said a little breathlessly when they pulled apart. 'Which unfortunately reminds me, I was sent up to tell you that Stirling's here, and he has a surprise for you.'

'This was a lovely idea of yours,' Katie said after they'd waved goodbye to Lloyd and Pen on the jetty and they were on their way.

'I thought you might like to see the river from a different vantage point,' Stirling replied. 'Being on the water often helps me to get things into perspective.'

'In what way?'

'I'm reminded that nature always has the upper hand and the last word, and that whatever seems vitally important today probably won't matter a jot tomorrow.'

'That's what I feel when I'm at home and I look at the sea.'

'Would you like a go at steering the boat?'

Sitting alongside him in a comfortable Lloyd Loom chair, she shook her head. 'Later perhaps. For now I'm happy to enjoy the ride.'

'In that case, we'll push on a little further and then we'll stop for something to eat. I've brought a picnic. Is that all right with you?'

'More than fine.'

'And if you get cold, you can have my sweater. Just say the word. I want the evening to be perfect for you.'

She smiled happily. 'It already is.'

He smiled back at her. 'Excellent. Now if you lift the lid on that box to your left, you'll find a bottle of wine and two glasses. There's a bottle opener in there too. Would it be less than chivalrous to ask if you could do the honours?'

'It would be an insult not to ask me.'

'I thought as much.'

'I happen to be an expert at pulling corks, as a result of working in a bar whilst I was at university.'

'Where did you study?'

'At Warwick. I did media studies.'

'And did you enjoy it?'

'I loved it, and don't laugh, but naively I believed I was going to become an award-winning documentary-maker and change the world.'

'Nothing to laugh at in that. We all dream of making an impact on the world at that age. So what happened when you graduated?'

She eased the cork out of the bottle on her lap and gave him a brief run-down on her working career so far, culminating in her stagnating at Stella Media. Cringing, she told him about some of the programmes she'd been associated with. She laughed when he apologized for not having watched any of them. 'You have absolutely nothing to apologize for,' she said.

His expression changed and he gave her a deeply troubled look. 'But I do, don't I? I have so much to be sorry for. I should have tried harder to persuade your mother to allow me to know you when you were growing up.'

Katie shook her head. 'I've given the matter a lot of thought this weekend, and I don't think you could, or should, have done anything differently. The way things were, it meant that Dad could be a real father to me. If you'd been a part of our lives, he might not have been able to be what he wanted to be to me. I've decided that Mum must have known that, which was why she was so firm with you. She knew what was important to Dad.' Katie passed Stirling a glass of wine. 'But what I don't understand is why Mum had the affair with you in the first place. Was she unhappy when you two met? And if so, *why* was she unhappy?'

'Oh no, she wasn't unhappy. Quite the reverse. It was her

happy, carefree nature that attracted me to her. She was like the sun bursting through the clouds.' He smiled as if recalling the memory. 'She always made me feel better about life. I think it was her joyful spontaneity that I loved most about her. She could make me laugh over the slightest thing. She was so different to Gina. Gina has always taken life very seriously. I don't mean that as a criticism, it's just the way she is.'

'But I still don't understand why she had the affair with you. If she was happy with Dad, why look elsewhere?'

Steering the boat with one hand, Stirling stared ahead. It was a few moments before he spoke. 'I think what it comes down to is that she loved your father, but wasn't *in* love with him. There's a wealth of difference between the two things, Katie.'

'I know. What about you and Gina?'

He sighed. 'It was the same. I loved her but I never felt for her what I experienced with Fay.'

'Do you think it would have lasted between you and Mum if things had been different?'

'If we'd met each other before meeting Desmond and Gina?'

'Yes.'

He swallowed, and once again his expression turned serious. 'I think we could have been extraordinarily happy together.'

Seeing how sad he looked, and wanting to lighten the mood, Katie said, 'Mum would have driven you crazy with her untidiness.'

He smiled faintly. 'And you know what, I'd have forgiven her for it. That's what happens when you really love a person: forgiveness comes easily. Perhaps that's why Desmond was able to put the affair behind them.'

'And what about you and Gina? Does she love you enough to forgive you for me?'

'That,' he said with great feeling, 'is the million-dollar question. But I fear not.'

A much larger boat came into view in front of them, and

after it had passed by – causing the *Lady Cecily* to bob in its wake – Stirling turned and faced Katie. He raised his glass of wine and said, 'May I suggest a toast? To happier times ahead for us both, and to getting to know each other a lot better. If that doesn't sound too presumptuous.'

She tapped her glass lightly against his. 'Why presumptuous?'

'You might not want to get to know me any better. You might think you've seen enough.'

'And why would I think that?'

'Because you probably thought your own life was complicated enough as it was without getting involved with us Nightingales. You're not seeing us at our best.'

'I'd rather get to know the real you, the honest you. I'm not interested in a Sunday-best version.'

He laughed. 'I'm not sure I have a best version of me.'

'Well, I like the version I'm seeing now; relaxed and candid.'

'Maybe it's being round you. Perhaps you have this effect on people. How else do you explain why Pen can't speak highly enough of you and my mother adores you? And if I'm not overstepping the mark, I'd say that Lloyd is more than a little taken with you.'

She turned her head slightly so he couldn't see the colour rising to her cheeks. 'Really?' she said, looking intently at the large and fabulously impressive house they were passing. 'What makes you think that?'

'Oh, you know, little things. That and the fact that Pen is convinced there's something going on between the two of you. And trust me, Pen never gets anything wrong when it comes to Lloyd.'

She returned her gaze to Stirling's face. 'Does she disapprove? Is it the cousin situation? Even though we're not blood cousins?'

'Not at all. But I have to confess to feeling a bit confused myself. And I know I have no real right to feel this way, but I

277

have this strong need to protect you, just as I did with Scarlet. I feel compelled to ward off any unsuitable suitors. It's called being a father.'

'Does that mean you class Lloyd as unsuitable?'

'No. He's eminently suitable. I've known him all his life and I'd go so far as to say you couldn't find anyone better than my nephew.'

'And yet you still feel the need to protect me from him? That's silly.'

'Now that I've said it aloud, I agree. In my head, it didn't sound so stupid.' He put his wine glass down on a small shelf in front of him, seeming suddenly to apply all his concentration – lips pursed, his brow creased with a frown – to the task of navigating the curve in the river. She watched him for a few minutes out of the corner of her eye, then, sensing he needed a moment to think, she sipped her wine and gave her attention to the beautiful houses they were passing. With their trim lawns coming right to the water's edge, the graceful willow trees turned golden by the evening sun, Katie was awed by the loveliness of it all. It was so tangibly peaceful, so calming. There was a feeling of space, yet at the same time a comfortable sense of containment. Just as tangible, however, was the abundant air of wealth and privilege these palatial riverside homes were giving off.

It was all very different to how she had grown up. Whilst her parents had managed to make a relatively good and steady living out of the antiquarian bookshop they'd run, they had lived modestly. They had been a one-car family, and holidays had been limited to one a year, though that had had more to do with Dad not wanting to close the shop for more than a couple of weeks. What holidays they did take had usually been carefully planned driving tours through France, either staying in reasonably priced hotels or on campsites. Being an only child, Katie had always preferred the campsites, because there were other children to make friends with.

They passed an elderly man walking a black Labrador along

the towpath, and he raised his stick at them. 'Nice evening,' he called out.

'It certainly is,' replied Stirling pleasantly.

When the man and his dog were distant figures behind them, Stirling said, 'Maybe I'm jealous. Maybe the truth is I don't want Lloyd to take you away from me before I've had a chance to get to know you properly.'

Touched that he should feel this way and be so open with her, Katie put a hand on his arm. 'That won't happen. I promise you. But in return for that promise,' she said, seizing the opportunity, 'I want you to do something for me.'

'Go on.'

'I want you to take back the money that's in that trust fund. I can't possibly accept it.'

He shook his head. 'No, Katie. It's yours.'

'Sorry,' she said. 'My mind is made up. I don't want it.'

Chapter Thirty-eight

Cecily was furious with Gina. She couldn't believe the intransigence of the silly woman. Couldn't she see the harm she was causing the family?

It had only been by chance that she had learnt of the ultimatum Gina had given Stirling. Katie had come to say goodbye to her before returning to Brighton after the Bank Holiday weekend and had mentioned something about Stirling having gone missing on the Sunday and not knowing why. She'd said that she had asked him what had happened to him, but he'd been evasive and changed the subject. Knowing that Stirling never let people down, not without good reason, Cecily had felt uneasy and so had phoned him at work and asked him to come and see her that evening. The moment he'd arrived, she had known by the strain in his face that she had done the right thing, and without preamble she had asked him what was going on, and told him that he wasn't to think of fobbing her off with some half-baked lie. He'd then told her what Gina had said, that he had to choose between his family and Katie; he couldn't have both. Cecily's heart had gone out to him.

Now, a week later, she had invited Gina to join her for tea in the hope of making her see sense, or at least find a way to smooth the waters. But all she was getting from her daughter-in-law as she sat stiff-backed and bristling with reproach was pig-headed intolerance.

'I wouldn't expect anything else from you,' Gina was now saying. 'Of course you'd take Stirling's side in all this.'

'I like to think I'm taking the side of reason,' Cecily replied, trying to keep the tone of her voice affable.

Gina laughed bitterly. 'Again, that's entirely what I'd expect of you. You really think it's reasonable for me to have to accept your son's unfaithfulness as though it's nothing but a trivial misunderstanding? Not only that, I'm expected to welcome the product of his tawdry deceitfulness with open arms.'

'I don't think anything of the kind. As I've tried explaining, all I'm asking you to do is let Stirling know his daughter. Is that so very difficult for you?'

'He *has* a daughter. Her name is Scarlet.'

Cecily put her cup and saucer down with a bang. 'Gina, please don't try my patience. Having Katie in his life is not going to push Scarlet out of it.'

'It's already doing that. Scarlet can hardly bring herself to speak to her father.'

'And who's responsible for making that happen?'

'Oh, so this mess is my doing, is it?' Gina's voice had risen and her face was flushed. 'You'll be saying next that it was my fault Stirling had an affair.'

'Fault is not the issue here.' Cecily sighed. 'What's important is that if you want to keep your husband and not cause untold damage to your family, you have to forgive him. He made a mistake, for which he's apologized. He can't undo that mistake.'

'And as I've told you before, I'll forgive him if he cuts all ties with that girl. I don't want her in our lives.'

'But why? Why do you feel so threatened by Katie?'

Gina looked at Cecily with undisguised contempt. 'I don't feel threatened by her. What a preposterous suggestion. And frankly, I don't see that there's any point in our continuing this conversation if you're going to keep insulting me like this. I came here today in good faith, with the smallest of hopes that, woman to woman, you might see things my way and that maybe I could convince you to make Stirling do the right thing. I can see that I've had a wasted journey.' She rose exaggeratedly from her seat.

'Oh, sit down, Gina, and stop being so tiresomely melo-dramatic. I'm not insulting you. But carry on acting in this childish way and I may well start doing so. Really, you can be so thoroughly infuriating at times!'

Still on her feet, Gina's eyes narrowed and her expression hardened. 'Ever thought just how thoroughly infuriating *you* can be at times? Not to say meddlesome and patronizing, manipulative and domineering. No, I suppose not. You're too busy perfecting your role as the high-and-mighty matriarch of this bloody family and taking sides. Always the side of your precious favourites. It's Pen this and Lloyd that. How I've stood it all these years I'll never know. But I did it for Stirling's sake. And what a slap in the face that has turned out to be. What has Stirling ever done for my sake? Apart from humiliate me?'

'He stayed married to you, for a start. He's always put you and the children first. You can't deny that.'

'You make it sound like a terrible sacrifice, as though I should be grateful. But it's no more than any good husband and father should do. It's what I want him to do now, to prove that he really does love me. Why can't you see that? Just once, why can't you see things from my point of view?'

'What poppycock! Insisting that he cuts Katie out of his life is your petty way of punishing Stirling. It's pure spite on your part. You should be ashamed of yourself.'

Gina snatched up her handbag from the sofa. 'I think we've said all that needs to be said on the matter. I'm going.'

Cecily rose stiffly to her feet. 'Yes, perhaps you should, and before either of us says something that we'll regret. But Gina, whatever happens from here on is entirely of your own making. I hope you can live with the consequences of your actions. Because they won't affect only you; it will be Rosco and Scarlet and your grandchild who will be caught in the crossfire of your fight with Stirling. You're going to make everyone very unhappy if you pursue your need for vengeance.'

'And there you go again. It's my actions, never Stirling's.'

'I freely admit he made a mistake; I've never once suggested otherwise. But the mistake you're intent on making is one that could so easily be avoided.'

'And screwing his secretary couldn't have been avoided?'

'That's not what I'm saying.'

'Then exactly what are you going on about?'

'For whatever reason Stirling was unfaithful to you, it wasn't to punish you. That's the difference.'

'In *your* opinion.'

In my opinion, my son married the wrong woman, Cecily thought as she showed Gina to the door.

When she was alone, she went back to the sitting room and sat down. She was exhausted. She was too old for this. Her wits were not as sharp as they once were. And her patience was certainly not as pliable or accommodating. She had probably gone too far with Gina, had pushed her into saying things that shouldn't have been said. Yet she had done it because she so badly wanted to make Gina understand what she was in danger of doing.

Cecily knew Stirling; he didn't like his hand to be forced. Everyone had a flashpoint, and if backed into a corner not to his liking, Stirling was liable to behave very much out of character. Just as he had the day of Neil's funeral, when Rosco had made him so angry.

Many, many years ago, there had been a memorable occasion when Stirling had got into a fight at school and had been caned and suspended for a fortnight – the reason for his punishment was that with one perfectly aimed fist, he'd broken the nose of a particularly vicious bully who'd been making fun of Neil for being adopted. Bullying wasn't taken as seriously then as it is today; in those days one was expected to assume a stiff upper lip and accept that it was part and parcel of growing up. Stirling hadn't agreed with that, and had taken matters into his own hands.

Cecily didn't think for one moment that Stirling would resort to violence in this instance, but if Gina didn't relent, he was likely to do the one thing she didn't want him to do. And as difficult as she found her daughter-in-law at times, she didn't wish her ill. Nor did she want to see Rosco and Scarlet estranged from their father.

She closed her eyes and wished that she'd gone next door to watch *Countdown* with Marjorie and stayed out of things. Meddlesome, Gina had called her. Amongst other things. Perhaps she was right.

She felt herself drifting off to sleep. She tried to fight it, but with the afternoon sun flooding in through the window, she soon gave in to the inviting drowsiness, letting her thoughts meander back to the past. To Stirling and Neil as mischievous small boys. To them playing one of their favourite games, that of shrieking their heads off in the garden and chasing each other with a hose, and then turning it on to their father when he went outside to tell them to keep the noise down while pretending he was cross. William never was cross with them, and the boys knew that. They knew he loved them with a fierce devotion, knew also that he could not have been prouder of his sons, their achievements had been as significant and rewarding to him as his own.

William had been a rock-solid source of encouragement and support when the boys had been growing up. His death had hit them hard. He had left such a vast hole in their lives, hers included. And whilst she had long since learnt to live without him, she still experienced occasional moments when she missed her husband with an intensity that could stop her in her tracks. Whenever that ache of sadness made itself known, she imagined him telling her to pull herself together. 'Come on, Cissy,' he'd say, 'you know the rules, no sloppy blubbing. I'm not worth it.' He was the only person she had ever allowed to call her by her pet name from when she'd been a child.

He'd always tell her he didn't deserve her, that she could have married someone so much better than him. 'Shut up, you silly man,' she'd say, 'or I might start having second thoughts.' When he'd been in hospital and it was clear he was near the end of a six-month battle with stomach cancer, he'd still managed to keep the joke up. 'Cissy, this is your chance to find that better man,' he'd said. She had gripped his hand hard and told him for the last time to stop being such a bloody idiot. 'You are that better man,' she'd said. He had died the next day.

They had had the happiest of marriages, and it saddened her that neither of their sons had found true happiness in their own marriages.

Oh, but how weary she was, and how she missed William right now. What she wouldn't give to have him by her side as she fought to keep the family from tearing itself apart. Or for her not to be here any more, to slip quietly away to be with William instead.

Gina arrived home in a foul mood. She slammed the front door behind her, and glad that Mrs Perry, her cleaner, had already left, she marched through to the kitchen and flung her handbag and keys on to the table: the keys skittered off and landed on the oak floor with a crash. How dare that interfering busybody woman speak to her the way she had! Just who did she think she was? The sooner the domineering old bat died, the better!

She picked up the keys and immediately regretted the thought. Not that it wasn't the first time she had considered how much easier life would be if Cecily was no longer around, but still, to think it with such vehemence was not healthy. So often a wish granted was a wish regretted. And they certainly had enough on their plates right now without Cecily kicking the bucket and making things worse. It would be just their luck if Cecily did die and put herself centre stage, just as she always was. That was why she couldn't resist poking her damned self-important nose into their affairs under the guise of helping; it was her way of saying that she was indispensable. Gina had news for her! They would manage jolly well when she was gone. What was more, with no one stirring the family pot, they would probably get on a lot better. She was convinced that if Stirling didn't have his wretched mother taking his side and poisoning him against her, he would realize it wasn't unreasonable for a wife to feel the way she did.

Thank goodness she had Rosco and Scarlet backing her. Between them they had decided to give Stirling another week to make his decision. In the circumstances, she thought she was being astonishingly generous and patient with him. It was taking its toll, though. She wasn't sleeping well and she had lost weight. She simply couldn't understand why he was finding it so difficult to do as she'd asked, if not for her sake, for his children's. Didn't that mean anything to him? Didn't he love her at all?

The answer to that question frightened her. She had always thought of herself as a strong-minded and independent woman, but she was beginning to doubt she was as independent as she'd believed. The reality was, she didn't want to live without her husband; being married to Stirling was the only life she had known.

But it was too late now for her to turn back. She could not, and would not, climb down. She had to hold firm, and for the coming days she had to carry on as if everything was normal.

To this end, she took a deep breath and opened the fridge. Right, what to cook for supper this evening? Something that Stirling would really enjoy. Something that would make him appreciate what he had.

In the middle of a meeting, Stirling's mobile pinged and lit up with a text message. He tried not to look at it, to keep his focus on the client. Normally during a client meeting he put his phone away in a drawer as an act of courtesy, but he'd forgotten this time and had left it out on his desk.

'Go ahead,' John Holmes said, glancing up from the papers he was reading, 'I don't mind.'

'I'm sure it can wait,' Stirling responded.

John smiled. 'How do you know without looking to see who it is? It could be important. Go on. I don't mind.'

Stirling returned the smile and reached for the mobile. When he saw who'd texted him, he kept his expression perfectly neutral. 'As I thought,' he said without bothering to read the message and putting the phone into his top drawer, 'it can wait. Now then, where were we?'

As soon as the meeting was over and he'd seen John Holmes out, he closed his office door and opened his desk drawer. He sat down and read the message Simone had sent him.

Ever since his first text to her, which she had eventually replied to twenty-four hours later, they had got into the habit of messaging each other several times a day. She had explained that initially she had been wary of replying to him, uncertain that it would do either of them any good. He was glad she had changed her mind. He now looked forward to hearing from her. Perhaps he looked forward a little too much to her texts. He knew too, as he began keying in his reply, that he was playing with fire: *Can I come and see you again?* He hit send. Then sat back in his chair. He swivelled it round to look out of the window. The mobile still in his hand, he tapped it against his chin. He was tempted to close his eyes and relive being in bed with Simone. But he didn't. He wouldn't allow himself to do that.

His mobile pinged in his hand, making him start. *When do you want to come?* Simone had texted.

Now, he thought. Now, so that for a few hours I can lose myself in you, so I can forget about the impossible situation Gina has put me in.

Whenever he tried to discuss Katie with Gina, she refused to listen. 'There's nothing to discuss,' she would say. Her mind was as closed as her heart was cold. Was that of his making? He couldn't deny that there had always been an air of indifference to Gina, but he would never have called her heartless. Until now. Was he to blame for that?

He thought of the evening ahead. Of either sitting in silence or trying to make pointless small talk. A feeling of dread came over him. He couldn't do it. He would go mad if he had to sit through another soul-destroying evening of watching his every word in the hope that she would concede.

Are you free tonight? he replied to Simone's question.

If she said yes, he would ring Gina to say he wouldn't be home until late. He would tell her he was having dinner with a client. There would be no reason for her to think he was lying.

As he waited for Simone to reply, he thought of the cause of Gina's ire: Katie. He had enjoyed their evening together on the boat last week – an evening that Gina believed he had spent alone on the *Lady Cecily*. During those brief hours with Katie he had felt at last as though he was getting to know her properly and to be genuinely relaxed in her company. At times – particularly when she smiled or laughed – she reminded him of Fay, and then at other times, when she was considering an answer to one of his questions, he could see himself in her. Or was that merely wishful thinking, a built-in desire to see his genes successfully passed down to his progeny?

It seemed wholly inadequate to say he liked Katie – those words didn't cover the half of it – but he did. He enjoyed her company, her quickness, her intelligence and her thoughtfulness. Most of all, he admired her incredible strength of character. The last few years must have been a great strain on her, but she seemed to have come through it remarkably unscathed. Whatever happiness lay ahead for her, she deserved it. And if it was within his means to add to that happiness, he would.

Since the Bank Holiday weekend they had been regularly in touch by email, but only when he was at work, so as not to antagonize Gina at home. An email from Katie was now the first thing he looked for in his inbox when he switched his computer on in the morning. She had sent him photographs of her house in Brighton, and a few of her as a young child. The Lost Years, as he now thought of her childhood that he'd missed out on.

The issue of the trust fund had yet to be resolved, but as far as he was concerned, it was hers. He had no intention of letting her walk away from it. He'd tried pointing out to her that if nothing else, it would give her some breathing space to reconsider what she wanted to do next with her life. It was obvious to him, from everything she'd told him, that she was ready for a change of direction when it came to her career. With this in mind, the next opportunity Stirling got, he planned to enlist Lloyd's help to persuade her that she not only deserved the money, but it could be life-changing for her.

It still wasn't common knowledge within the family that Lloyd and Katie – to use the popular vernacular – were an item. Apparently, and wisely in Stirling's opinion, they wanted to keep it that way for some time yet.

It was the complication of their being an item that had scuppered a line of thought Stirling had had, a plausible way to solve his problem with Gina. In truth, it had only ever been a half-hearted solution: he had begun to imagine that he could lie to his family, that he could tell them that he'd made his choice and wouldn't have any further contact with Katie, but secretly he would go on getting to know her and become more of a father to her. However, that wouldn't be possible if Lloyd continued seeing her. Either Katie would have to lie to Lloyd, or Stirling would have to ask Lloyd to be a party to the deception. And what would Pen and Cecily have to say on the matter? Would they have to be party to the lies also? No, it was hopeless. He couldn't do that to them all. More importantly, what message did it give Katie? That he didn't care enough about her to have an honest father-and-daughter relationship with her?

Once more his mobile pinged.

An hour later and he was in his car.

Chapter Thirty-nine

'But it's so unfair! She can't do that to Stirling.'

Lloyd's heart sank. He'd made a terrible mistake. He should never have mentioned the conversation he'd had with his grandmother about the ultimatum Gina had given Stirling, and how intransigent she was being. But stupidly he'd assumed that Katie knew, that Stirling would have shared this with her. Now it seemed blindingly clear to him that his uncle hadn't wanted her to know; he would have tried to protect her from the unreasonable position Gina had put him in, knowing full well how it would make her feel. Nice going, he mentally rebuked himself.

Their meal finished and the bill paid, he folded his napkin in half, then in half again, smoothing it out so the edges lined up perfectly. 'I'm sorry,' he said. 'I shouldn't have said anything.'

'No, you were right to tell me. It's important. I genuinely had no idea what was going on. Stirling hasn't so much as hinted at it.' She sighed. 'I feel awful. Really awful. I should never have tracked him down. I should have stayed away, let sleeping dogs lie, blah, blah.'

Lloyd tossed the napkin away from him. 'Firstly, it's not your fault. Secondly, it's absolutely not your fault. So get all that self-recrimination nonsense out of your head. OK?'

She raised an eyebrow. 'Wow, is that your stern voice?'

'Not even close.'

'But seriously, Lloyd, if I'd stayed away, Stirling wouldn't be in the mess he is now. He was perfectly happy before I showed up.'

'Who knows if that's really true? Look at my own parents: I thought Dad was happy enough, but I couldn't have been more wrong. I'm beginning to realize that it's not possible to truly know another person.'

'I agree,' she said solemnly. 'I thought I knew all there was to know about my parents, but all the time they were hiding a colossal secret, not just from me but from everyone.'

'Don't think too badly of them,' he said gently, wanting to ease the tension he'd created so clumsily. 'Everybody hides something about themselves. We all reveal just what we want to reveal.'

Looking thoughtful and placing her elbows on the table, she rested her chin in the palms of her hands. She stared at him hard. 'So what are *you* concealing from me? What are you hiding?'

A moment passed. Then, seizing on a way to lift the mood of their conversation, he said, 'You really don't want to know.'

'Yes I do.'

'No you don't. You'd be shocked.'

'Trust me, I'm unshockable.'

'OK, but you have to come nearer; I don't want the entire restaurant hearing.'

She did as he asked, leaning over so he could whisper in her ear. It didn't take him long. She sat back in her chair, her hands flat on the table. 'Well,' she said, giving him a studied look of enquiry, 'if that's what's been on your mind all during lunch, I'm surprised you managed to eat anything.'

'I was building up my strength, just in case.' He reached across and took one of her hands in his.

'How much strength do you think you need?' she asked.

'That all depends, but I wouldn't like to disappoint you. I suspect you're a girl with extremely high standards.' He smiled, lifted her hand and entwined his fingers through hers.

'Have you disappointed many girls in your time?'

'Um ... I hate to break this to you, but I've never been given the opportunity before.'

She laughed.

He feigned hurt pride. 'You don't believe me?'

'Not a word.'

He stroked her slender wrist and felt a tremor run through her. Knowing that his touch had that effect on her stirred something deep inside him. He stared into her eyes. God, she had amazing eyes. He could look at them all day. He swallowed. There was so much he suddenly wanted to say, but he didn't have a clue how to go about it. He'd never been more sure of a thing, but because he'd never felt this way before, he'd never been more scared. They'd known one another for so little time, yet, and as cheesily unoriginal as it sounded, he felt he'd known her for ever. It felt so right being with her. So natural. Some things you just knew. This was one of them.

They'd spoken every day since she'd left The Meadows almost two weeks ago, usually twice a day, in the morning before he went to work and then again in the evening. They chatted online with Skype, just as he did with his friends in New Zealand, except he didn't chat with them from his bed on his laptop. They talked about anything and everything – his family, her family, friends, and a lot about his father. Sometimes he felt better for talking about Dad, and sometimes he didn't. Sometimes an enormous debilitating swell of anger rose up within him when he thought about the utter selfishness of his father's actions. Mostly, though, it was a profound weight of sadness he felt, and being able to share that with Katie helped more than he could put into words.

Mindful that she wasn't without her own problems, he tried not to offload on to her too much. He knew that her lack of employment really bothered her, and in her search for a job she was sending her CV out on a daily basis. But the replies were all the same – numbers had been cut back everywhere; nobody new was being taken on. She frequently talked about a change of career, of doing something completely different, she just didn't know what yet. He'd been through the same process himself, opting out of what was expected of him

– a high-flying City career of some sort following on from Cambridge – but not really knowing what he wanted to do. Since making his decision, he'd never looked back.

She had invited him to come down to Brighton, and today – Saturday – had been the first opportunity he'd had to get away. Work had been crazy, especially with Neville, his right-hand man, being off sick. He'd left Henley early and was knocking on Katie's door at just gone nine. 'I was hoping to catch you in your pyjamas,' he'd said when she let him in and they kissed. 'Having seen them so often on the computer, I wanted to see them for real.'

'I could change if you like,' she'd responded with a smile.

'No,' he'd said, taking in her black leggings, close-fitting black top, short red miniskirt and flat red shoes. 'You look great.'

'That's good, because I spent ages trying to decide what to wear.'

He'd liked her honesty, that she was prepared to admit that she'd wanted to look nice for him. Girls he'd gone out with previously all claimed to have thrown on the first thing to hand whenever he'd complimented them on their appearance.

She had made him a cup of coffee and then pulled on a denim jacket and said they were going to Bill's for brunch. Disappointed at the prospect of having to share her with someone else – he'd wanted her to himself for the day – he'd then been happily surprised when she'd taken him to a large café that was buzzing with punters. She had explained that it was one of her favourite places to eat in Brighton, and had recommended the eggs Benedict with smoked salmon. Her advice had been bang on the money.

'What do you think, then?' he asked now, still stroking her wrist and still, much to his satisfaction, making her quiver. 'What's the plan? Some sightseeing, or ... or something else' – he glanced outside – 'since it looks like it's about to rain?'

She leant in close and kissed him lightly on the mouth. '*Something else* sounds like it might be interesting.'

On a mission now, he peered under the table. 'Can you run in those shoes?'

'You'll have a job keeping up with me. Come on, let's go.'

No sooner had she closed the door behind them than Lloyd caught her in his arms, turned her around and kissed her deeply. They took the stairs slowly, one step at a time, kissing all the way. At the top, Katie pushed open the door to her bedroom. 'You can see the sea from here if you stand on a chair at the window,' she said, helping him out of his leather jacket.

'You sound like you're trying to sell me the house,' he said, easing her own jacket off and kissing first one side of her neck, then the other.

'Just making conversation.' She started to lift up his T-shirt.

'Allow me.' He pulled it up roughly over his head and flung it to the floor. Her mouth dry, she stared at his chest, for once no ready quip to hand. It was no ordinary chest. It was a fully fledged chestathon of tanned and honed muscle. It was the kind of chest she wanted to lie against and never move from again. He placed a hand on the nape of her neck and kissed her, his hands then moving further down her body, sending a million tingles of electricity through her, just as when he'd stroked her wrist earlier. How did he do that?

In a perfect world, her clothes should have either come off in a frantic whirl of high-octane passion or in a seductively slow tease, but true to form, Katie's world wasn't perfect. She'd managed to lose her skirt and top – Lloyd was effort-lessly down to his Calvin Klein boxers – but in her haste to rip off her leggings, she was making an embarrassing fool of herself, failing miserably to balance on her left foot with her right leg half in, half out of the unhelpful cotton and Lycra mix. She could not have wobbled more had she been on a tightrope with a howling gale at her back. Coming to her rescue, Lloyd placed his hands firmly around her waist, and blushing furiously she said, 'I've never mastered the art of seductive undressing. I'd make a lousy stripper. God, I must be the unsexiest girl on the planet!'

He smiled. 'Not from where I'm standing.' Then he wasn't standing any more, he was on his knees and sliding the offending leggings down to her ankles and she was stepping out of them and all the while his hands were working their magic and doing that tingle thing again. Then they were slowly making the return journey up the backs of her legs, passing her knees and up to her thighs, and just as his fingers slowly, oh, so slowly, slid to a critical point and she tensed with heart-thudding anticipation, he stopped. No! she wanted to cry. Don't stop! He stood up and kissed her hard, as if diverting her attention from what he was doing at the back of her. Her bra dropped to the floor and he stared at her breasts. Just stared. Then in one ridiculously easy movement, he lifted her up in his strong arms and set her down on the bed.

'Nobody's ever done that to me before,' she said with a small laugh.

'Having just seen how unsteady you are on your feet, I didn't want to risk you falling over,' he said huskily.

'It's you,' she said, gazing into his face and breathing hard as she recalled his whispered words back at Bill's when he'd said he wanted to make love to her. 'You make me dizzy.'

He looked almost grave, his steady blue eyes locking with hers, his hand tracing the curve of her body. 'That's nothing to what you do to me.'

'You must have super powers,' she said afterwards when she was lying with her head on his chest and listening to the steady reassuring beat of his heart. 'Because that was indescribably wonderful.'

His arm around her, he said, 'I didn't disappoint, then?'

'Well, there was that moment when you ...' She felt him raise his head from the pillow and she looked up at him. 'I'm joking,' she said.

He put both of his arms around her and kissed her forehead tenderly. 'It's raining,' he murmured.

'You're right,' she said, glancing at the window. 'Just as well we came back when we did.'

'I once read that if you make love with someone for the first time when it's raining, it means that relationship is going to last.'

'Do you believe that?' she asked, listening to the rain pattering softly against the glass.

He held her closely. 'I do now.'

Chapter Forty

Pen had got into the habit of visiting St Oswald's every Monday afternoon. People probably wouldn't understand, but it lifted her spirits to go and tend Neil's grave. She had a fixed routine – broken only by the Bank Holiday two weeks ago – and she found that the hour spent in the churchyard was something she actually looked forward to. She always hoped to find it empty. She preferred to be entirely alone with Neil.

Today she wasn't alone. Cecily was with her. Cecily freely admitted that she felt no real comfort in visiting the churchyard, but today she had asked if she could join Pen. She seemed in a distant and faraway mood this afternoon, spending just a few short minutes inspecting the gravestone that had recently been erected for Neil and then wandering off to look at her husband's grave, something she admitted she hadn't done in a long while, other than the day of Neil's funeral, when not surprisingly, she'd said the two deaths had felt inextricably bound together.

The few weeds that had dared to spring up dealt with and the dead flowers replaced with fresh ones which she'd brought from the garden – Achillea 'Moonshine', Crocosmia, Campanula lactiflora and pink astilbe – Pen sat on the wooden bench a few yards away from Neil. Late in the afternoon, there was a hint of autumn in the cool air. With the evenings drawing in, it wouldn't be long before the leaves, already on the cusp of changing colour, would start to fall from the trees and the air would be rich with the earthy scent of decay. For the last two mornings she had woken to the sight of the river cloaked in a diaphanous layer of mist, a sure sign that summer was nearing its end. But whatever the season, Pen couldn't imagine a time when she wouldn't come here. Rain, wind or snow, she would always want to be with Neil.

She was constantly being told that she was still in the early stages of bereavement and that she should expect to experience a whole range of emotions. Suicide, she had been told, didn't conform to the usual laws when it came to grief. As if she needed telling that. Once or twice, when people in the village had been exaggeratedly solicitous with her, she had been overcome with the urge to wage war and throw every foul-mouthed obscenity she knew at them. Scared she might do exactly that, she would hurriedly back away and dash home, where she could defuse her anger in the garden. Never had it benefited from so much ferocious digging! She had to be careful not to reach for the pruning shears when she was having one of those days. But no matter how near to the edge she felt she was being drawn, she refused to give in to it. As battered and as weakened as it was, her stubborn will kept her from the abyss of her grief.

There was a new grave alongside Neil's. It had appeared last week and at first Pen had been appalled by its appearance, resenting the infringement of what had become her right of ownership over the grassy space – it was where she knelt to tend Neil's plot. But then she had learnt that the grave was for a four-year-old boy from the village who had died of leukaemia, and her resentment was instantly replaced with sadness.

There were signs that the small grave had been visited since last week; some toys had been placed amongst the heart-shaped wreaths, which were now sadly past their best. There was a plastic cowboy that she recognized from those *Toy Story* films, a blue and white penguin, also made of plastic, and a donkey made of furry grey fabric, the floppy ears and mournful face picked out with white. Had they been the little boy's favourite toys? But why had they been left on top of the grave? Why hadn't they been tucked safely inside the coffin before the funeral? How would the family feel if someone stole them? It worried Pen. It worried her immensely. It would be too awful for the family to visit the grave and find the toys gone. They would be heartbroken that someone could act with such malicious intent. It was enough to make her cry just to think of it.

Slow footsteps behind her had her glancing away from the child's grave. It was Cecily, who, following a stumble last week, was now reluctantly using a walking stick. 'Are you all right?' Pen asked her. 'You look tired.'

Cecily tutted. 'Don't fuss. I'm fine.'

None the less, Pen stood up and offered her hand as support for the old lady. 'Come and sit down for a while.'

Cecily didn't argue. She settled herself on the bench and let out a sigh. Adjusting the silk scarf at her throat, she said, 'Pen, you won't become obsessed with this place, will you?'

'Is that what you think I'm doing?'

'I think it gives you great succour for now, but Neil isn't only here. He's everywhere, but most importantly, he's where he always was, in your heart.'

'I know that. But it helps being here.'

'And how are you nursing your wrath?'

Pen looked at her in surprise. 'My wrath?' she repeated.

Cecily fixed her with a firm gaze. 'You've done extraordinarily well not giving into it, I take my hat off to you, but it stands to reason that you'd be angry. Not just with Neil for committing suicide, but for the fraud and for having an affair and planning to leave you. It would be nothing short of a miracle if you weren't furious with him.'

'I'm coping,' Pen said in a carefully measured tone.

'I've never told anyone this before,' Cecily went on, 'not even Stirling or Neil, but when William died, I was livid with him. I was angry with him for not realizing sooner that he was so ill. "Typical doctor!" I fumed. "Too busy saving other lives to save his own!"'

'Are you angry now? With Neil?' Pen asked hesitantly.

'Goodness me, yes. I think of the waste. The utter waste of such a good life and all the years ahead of him. I also think of what this has done to you and Lloyd.'

'What do you do with your anger?'

'You mean, how do I deal with it?'

'Yes.'

'I shout at Neil inside my head. I tell him how selfish he was. And I swear at him. I don't mean a genteel curse, I swear like a good old-fashioned trooper. You wouldn't recognize me.'

Pen smiled. 'I feel like that at times. But my anger isn't directed at Neil. I feel it for the people who try to be nice to me, who think a dutiful word or two of sympathy will suddenly make everything right again. I can see it in their eyes: they're desperately willing me to snap out of my grief and get back to normal.'

'It's understandable. They want the old Pen back. The Pen you are now makes them uncomfortable.'

'Maybe I'll always be this way from now on.'

'Maybe you will. Maybe you won't. What have you done about Neil's clothes?'

Taken aback by the question, Pen said, 'I'm afraid I haven't done anything. I can't bring myself to start the job of sorting through his things. I'm putting it off, I know.'

Cecily nodded her head. 'For years I kept one of William's pullovers; I couldn't bear to part with it. It smelt so redolently of him. I had to throw it away in the end; the moths had done their worst to it. I cried like a baby when I put it in the bin.'

Pen tucked her arm affectionately through Cecily's. She was so very fond of her. Throughout all the years of her marriage, the old lady had been much more of a mother to her than her own.

'I've always been honest with you, Pen,' Cecily said. 'So please don't be upset with me when I say that I'm worried about you. You mustn't care about what others think of you.'

'But I don't.'

'Yes you do. You know only too well how people perceive you and you're frightened of appearing differently. What's more, because you're so nice, there are those who want to cushion you from the blows. But some blows are inevitable and you have to face up to them. They're the ones you never see coming.'

Pen frowned. 'Well I certainly didn't see this conversation coming.'

'And now that it has, are you going to confront what I've said?'

Pen shook her head. 'No. Not today.'

Cecily patted her hand. 'Very well. Now tell me about Lloyd and Katie. I have great hopes for them.'

Thankful for the change of subject, Pen said, 'I only spoke very briefly with Lloyd late last night when he was driving back from Brighton, so I can't tell you much. Only that he had a good time.'

Cecily chuckled. 'He spent the whole of the weekend with Katie, did he? Better and better.'

'You old romantic, you.'

'But you must agree with me, they make a fine couple.'

'I do agree with you, but I have a bad feeling. I think there's trouble ahead.'

'There's always trouble ahead, even in the most perfectly ordered life. They'll manage. I have every confidence in them. Now, Pen, I want you to promise me something. When I'm no longer around, will you keep an eye on Stirling for me? I'm concerned about him.'

'Don't be so maudlin. You're not going anywhere any time soon.'

'You've never insulted me by being disingenuous before; please don't start now. Just promise that you'll look out for Stirling for me.'

'Why are you so worried about him?'

'I'm getting the same feeling that I had with Neil shortly before he took his life.'

'Oh my God! You don't think Stirling would do the same, do you?'

Cecily shook her head. 'No, but something's very wrong with him at the moment.'

'He's got a lot on his mind right now, what with Neil and the ongoing police investigation and Katie and Gina.'

'I know all that,' Cecily said impatiently, 'but there's something else. I feel it every time I look at him. You'd know if there was something wrong with Lloyd, wouldn't you?'

'Yes,' Pen said quietly. 'Yes, I would.'

'Then you'll do as I ask? You'll keep an eye out for Stirling for me?'

'Of course. Come on, we ought to go. I can feel a chill in the air; autumn is definitely on its way. Do you want to come back with me for some supper? It won't be anything fancy; I haven't been to the supermarket. It'll be soup or scrambled eggs.'

'Do you want the company, or are you fussing over me?'

Pen helped Cecily to her feet and smiled. 'A bit of both.'

Cecily smiled too. 'In that case, yes.'

They had finished eating and were checking to see if there was anything of interest on the television when the telephone rang.

'Hello, Gina,' Pen said, alerting Cecily to who it was. 'Oh my goodness ... But it's too soon, isn't it? ... I'm sorry, of course you know that ... I'm sorry, I'm thinking aloud ... No, I don't have a clue where he is ... No, he's not with Cecily, she's here with me ... And he's definitely not at the office? ... Sorry, yes, of course you would have tried there first ... Sorry, Gina, I'm not thinking straight ... Is there anything I can do? ... Please call me if there is. Goodbye. And try not to worry too much.'

She ended the call and looked at Cecily 'It's Scarlet,' she

said. 'Charlie's had to take her to the hospital and Gina can't get hold of Stirling. Nobody can. Nobody knows where he is. He's disappeared again.'

Chapter Forty-one

Not once had Simone stood at the door and waved Stirling off. And not just because she knew that the ever-vigilant hawk-eyed Miss Tinstell would be observing the comings and goings from her window across the road. You only had to leave your wheelie bin or recycling boxes out for longer than was considered acceptable for the wretched woman to knock on the door and protest that the street was being brought into disrepute. She had complained once that Neil had woken her with the noise of his car; it had been nine thirty in the evening.

But the real reason she closed the door the moment Stirling stepped on to the pavement was because it was beyond her capabilities to stand there with a smile on her face whilst waving him goodbye, as though it was perfectly normal what they were doing. It would be too great a lie, too great an act of painful dishonesty. Better to close the door and tell herself that it wouldn't happen again. That this would be the last time.

Now was the third time she had told herself this lie, and just as before, she was consumed with guilt and self-loathing. But just as before, she knew that it would soon pass and she would be waiting for Stirling to contact her. This time it had been she who had initiated his visit, texting him first thing that morning. He had arrived shortly after she had got back from work, and whilst she had poured them both a glass of wine, he had removed his jacket and tie and placed them tidily on the back of a chair. She had asked him about his day and then without another word spoken they had gone up to her bedroom.

Listening now to the throaty sound of Stirling's car starting, she closed her eyes until she could hear it no longer. Then she went upstairs. She turned on the shower, stripped off her clothes and stepped into the cubicle. Stirling had showered earlier, and as on previous visits, he hadn't moved any of her toiletries. He was a very considerate lover.

Lover.

Was that what he was? If not, what was he? Other than a means to vanquish the loneliness and her growing sense of isolation. Colleagues at work had given up trying to talk to her, to jolly her along. They left her alone now, not knowing what to say. Perhaps they were scared to say the wrong thing. She didn't blame them. They had no comprehension of the depth of her grief; she had only been able to tell them that a close friend of hers had died. She could hardly share the truth with them, that her married lover had killed himself. Thank God the press hadn't discovered that she was the 'other woman' in Neil's life. She knew, though, that once the inquest took place her anonymity would come to an end. For now, on she went, blindly stumbling from one day to another, never knowing what emotion was in store for her. Some days loneliness and tearful regret at what she had lost would overwhelm her, and then another day she could almost believe that she was successfully moving on. Worst were the times when she wanted to punish Neil for abandoning her, for wilfully throwing away what they had, and what they would have had in the future. Together. They had planned to be *together*. Why had he thrown their dream away? Why hadn't he shared his deepest worries with her? Why had he shut her out? Why hadn't he been honest with her? It wouldn't have mattered what he'd done, she would have stood by him. She would have done anything for him.

When these thoughts crowded her head, she couldn't help but wonder if he had ever really loved her. What exactly had she meant to him? Clearly not enough. If he'd really loved her, he wouldn't have left her. She would never have done that to him. *Never.*

She squeezed shower gel into the palm of her hand, and as she began rubbing it vigorously over her body, she thought of Stirling's hands touching her. His touch was very different to Neil's. But then she hadn't wanted it to be the same. She didn't want Stirling to be gentle or tender with her. She wanted to feel consumed by him. She wanted to feel that she was in a vacuum, that nothing else existed beyond the physical bonding of their flesh. It wasn't love she was looking for. It wasn't even an emotional connection. She wasn't capable of that.

This evening in bed with Stirling she had felt something new; she had suddenly wanted to forget she had ever met Neil. More than that, and just as Stirling had climaxed inside her, she had felt a great need to punish Neil for hurting her so badly.

Scrubbing at her body, the shower washing away the tears that had sprung from her eyes, she wondered if that was what she had been doing all along, taking Stirling to her bed to punish Neil. Nothing else could have hurt him more. Just as he had done his worst to her, she was repaying him in kind. She turned her face up to the water and cried harder still.

Stirling felt euphoric. He had felt the same way the last time he had left Simone. He couldn't be sure quite what she got out of the arrangement, but for himself, the physical release he experienced with her was like a powerful drug that liberated and re-energized him.

Being with her this evening had helped him to see things with unexpected clarity and had brought him to a decision. There would be no more sitting on the fence. No more pleading with Gina to see sense, to have compassion on him, to look at things from a different perspective.

No. His mind was made up. As soon as he got home, he was going to tell her exactly how things stood. He would not give up Katie. And if she couldn't accept that, she could do her worst, no matter how bad that was. If Gina divorced him, so be it. At least his conscience would be clear when it came to Katie. He would be able to look himself in the eye and say he had done the right thing. Would Gina be able to do the same? What was more, he was convinced that Rosco and Scarlet would come round to his point of view in the end. It would take time, that was all. They just needed to get over the shock of suddenly discovering they had a half-sister. Time *would* heal the hurt they were currently feeling. And he was to blame for that hurt, he knew that. He should never have told them about Katie the way he did. He'd thrown it in their faces the day of Neil's funeral, when his temper and his need to protect Neil's memory had got the better of him. It had been a catastrophic mistake on his part.

He was a few miles from Sandiford when he remembered he hadn't switched his mobile back on – he had made it a rule to turn it off when he visited Simone. No matter. He'd be home in five minutes.

The first thing he noticed when he approached the house was that it was in darkness; there wasn't a single light on. He couldn't remember Gina saying she was going out, but then they were hardly communicating these days, so why should she bother to inform him of her day-to-day activities? After all, he hadn't said he was going to be late home himself, had he?

He let himself in, flicking lights on as he went. Propped against the fruit bowl on the island unit in the middle of the kitchen was a note. Expecting it to be some kind of angrily written message about his supper being in the bin, he put on his reading glasses.

He tried ringing Gina's mobile from his car, but there was no answer. Hospital rules meant she probably had it switched off.

Not knowing how bad the situation was, only that Scarlet

had been rushed to hospital, that something was wrong, he drove like the wind, all the while imploring some higher being to keep her and the baby safe. He pictured Scarlet as a baby herself. He recalled the day she was born. She'd been such a beautiful baby. He had held her in his arms and felt an instant and extraordinary weight of love. He had looked into her face and known, truly known, that he would do anything within his power to keep her safe and happy. Holding her with great care, he had bent down with her so that Rosco could get a closer look. 'There,' he'd said. 'What do you think of your baby sister?'

Rosco had inspected her with an expression of disappointment. 'She's not very big, is she? You said I'd be able to play with her.'

'You won't be able to play with her right away,' Stirling had said with a laugh, 'but when she's grown a little, you will. For now we have to look after her really well so that she'll grow big and strong, just like you.'

'Can't Mummy do that?'

'We need to help Mummy do it. It's very tiring having a baby. Do you think you can do that, help me to help Mummy?'

He'd nodded solemnly and then asked if he could hold Scarlet.

One of Stirling's favourite photographs was a picture he'd taken of Scarlet when she was a week old being carefully cradled by her brother. Earlier this year, when Scarlet and Charlie had shared the news that they were expecting a child, he had had the photograph copied and framed and had given it to Scarlet as a present. He remembered how delighted she'd been. As a small girl she had loved her brother, had idolized him to the point of driving him crazy at times. But with her legendary tantrums and her scatterbrain nature during her teens – as she hopped and skipped from one heartfelt crusade or hopeless enterprise to another – she had driven them all crazy over the years. It was the way she was, and they had long since understood that that was how things were. It would have been wrong ever to think about trying to change her, like trying to force a square peg into a round hole. It would have snuffed out the very essence of her.

With a tightness forming in his chest and hot tears pricking at the backs of his eyes, Stirling contemplated the unthinkable – what if something happened to Scarlet?

Whatever it takes, he thought, whatever it takes to keep her safe. Even if it meant she lost the baby.

He drove on, realizing with shame how lately he'd lost sight of what his children meant to him.

With Charlie at Scarlet's side whilst an emergency Caesarean was carried out, Rosco had taken charge. He'd calmed his mother down and had just managed to get hold of Charlie's parents, who were holidaying in Tuscany. Everything was under control. Everything except Dad.

A doctor had explained that Scarlet's blood pressure had gone sky high and she was suffering from something called pre-eclampsia; that meant the baby had to be delivered a month early, which was not without risk. According to Charlie, Scarlet had woken that morning with a headache and swollen ankles, but had gone out for the day as arranged to meet up with friends. When she arrived home with an even worse headache and started being sick, he had called the doctor, who had instructed him to take her straight to hospital. Thank God, Rosco thought now as he carried two cups of vending-machine coffee back to his mother, that Charlie had done the sensible thing just once in his life and made that call.

'Where on earth can your father be?' Gina said when he handed her one of the plastic cups. He'd lost count of how often she'd asked him this – another time, another place, and he might have been tempted to tell her the truth.

Oh yes, he knew the truth all right. Ever since Dad had disappeared that day and claimed to be in the office, he'd made it his business to keep an eye on him. By checking his father's computer when he was out of the office, he'd found the series of emails he'd exchanged with Katie. That wasn't so bad in itself, other than the secrecy of the correspondence, but what he'd discovered today had been the last straw. Expecting to find further evidence that perhaps he was secretly meeting Katie, Rosco had taken the opportunity to check his father's mobile this morning. They'd been in his office – just the two of them – when Dad had gone to make a copy of a document, leaving his phone on Rosco's desk. Whilst he had suspected Dad might be seeing a woman, the last thing he'd expected was for that woman to be Simone Montrose. Like an idiot, Dad hadn't deleted the SMS history on his phone, and so the evidence of their sordid affair was there for anyone to read. According to the latest text exchange, they were meeting again this evening.

The discovery so shocked Rosco – the bitch had had an affair with one man and destroyed him; now she was trying to do the same with Dad! – he hadn't trusted himself to confront his father. Instead, when Dad had returned with the copied document, he had carried on as if everything was perfectly normal.

Now that he'd had time to think, he knew what he had to do. The knowledge he had was his trump card to hold the family together. This, he now realized, was all that mattered. His father was in the middle of some kind of emotional crisis. Which wasn't surprising, given what Uncle Neil had done and then his own dubious past catching up with him in the form of Katie Lavender. If pushed one step further, who knew what could happen; a full-blown breakdown would help no one. So it was down to Rosco to take charge and keep everything held firmly together.

He took a sip of his coffee, stared out of the window and thought of his sister. As much as she irritated the hell out of him at times, he couldn't imagine the world without her. He refused to let his thoughts go down that route. Nothing bad was going to happen to Scarlet.

Hearing hurried footsteps, he turned and saw his father. Gina saw him at the same time and leapt to her feet. 'Where've you been?' she demanded, her shrill voice ringing loudly in the waiting room, which luckily they had to themselves.

'I'm sorry,' he said breathlessly. 'I was with a client.'

'Why didn't you have your mobile switched on?'

Resisting the urge to yell *Liar!* in his father's face, Rosco intervened. 'That's not important now, Mum.' He stepped between his parents and filled his father in on what was happening.

'But she'll be OK, won't she?' Dad said, raking his hand through his hair. 'The doctors have said she'll be fine, right?'

'No!' Gina snapped. 'They've said no such thing, and if you'd been here with us, you wouldn't be asking such a stupid question.' She started to cry.

'Come on, love,' Dad said. He put his arm around her. At first she tried to shrug him off, but as her tears took hold, she relaxed against him. 'I'm sorry I wasn't here,' he said. 'But I'm here now and everything's going to be all right. You'll see.'

Rosco caught his eye but had to look away. He couldn't believe the duplicity of his father. He was about to toss his empty coffee cup into the bin when he saw Charlie coming towards them. A nurse was with him. For some reason Charlie had something white stuck to the side of his head. 'Mum, Dad,' Rosco said. They both turned.

'What's the news?' Stirling asked as they surged towards Charlie. It was then that Rosco realized that the white thing on his brother-in-law's head was a dressing. The guy looked completely dazed. 'I'm a dad,' he said, his face suddenly cracking into a huge grin. 'I'm a father! I have a daughter!'

They all spoke at once, but it was Stirling's voice that cut through the cacophony of voices. 'And Scarlet? How is she?'

The nurse spoke. 'Scarlet is fine. We had to carry out a C-section, but it was quite straightforward. She's resting for now and will be a bit sore for a while, but she'll be as right as rain before too long.'

'And what happened to you, Charlie?' Rosco asked.

'I ... um ... I fainted and hit my head.'

The nurse smiled. 'It all got too much for you, didn't it, Charlie?'

He grimaced. 'Not my proudest moment, I'll admit.'

They all laughed.

'Can we see the baby?' Gina asked.

Ten minutes later they were pressed against a window looking at an incubator that contained Louisa-May Benton-Norris. The nurse explained that born four weeks earlier than expected, she had been placed in the special-care baby unit because she required help with breathing.

'But she'll be all right, won't she?' Stirling asked. 'Coming so early, there won't be any serious problems or complications, will there?'

'She needs help with regulating her temperature and with feeding, and is a little jaundiced,' the nurse answered, 'but all the signs are good. She weighs a respectable five pounds and six ounces, so she's far from being one of our tiniest babies in SCBU.' The nurse then left them alone.

Stirling stared and stared at his granddaughter. She looked so helpless. So vulnerable, with that ghastly tube attached to her nose. Her skin seemed painfully thin, almost translucent. He could see her tiny heart beating in her miniature chest. Her hands were impossibly small. She was altogether too fragile. He didn't imagine he would ever be able to hold her. He said her name inside his head: Louisa-May. It was a surprise to him. At no stage during her pregnancy had Scarlet or Charlie mentioned it as a possibility. Wherever it had come from, he liked it. *Welcome to the family, Louisa-May*, he said silently.

To his left, Rosco was congratulating Charlie with a high five. Poor Charlie, he looked like a stunned survivor from a war zone. To Stirling's right, Gina stood motionless, staring through the glass. She looked worn out. Ready to drop. He should have been with her when she'd got the call from

Charlie. He should have been with her to share the strain. Without a word, he slipped his hand into hers. She turned her head and looked at him. Her lips trembled and her eyes filled. 'She's so beautiful, isn't she?'

He nodded but couldn't speak.

'She looks just like Scarlet did when she was born. Just smaller.'

Again he couldn't speak, could only manage a nod. A couple of hours ago he had truly believed that he'd come to the right decision about how to resolve things. God help him, but now everything had changed. Louisa-May had seen to that.

Chapter Forty-two

It was nearly midnight when they left the hospital. They'd been allowed to see Scarlet for a short while. Not surprisingly, she was tired and emotional. The poor girl was in despair that she couldn't have the baby with her. 'She won't know me,' she'd said tearfully. 'She's all alone. She'll think I don't love her. What if she gets muddled up with another baby?' It had been Rosco who had calmed her down and even made her smile. 'Scarlet, there's no danger of my niece getting muddled up with anyone else's baby; she's easily the most beautiful baby here. I'd know her anywhere.' It was such a lovely thing for him to say; Gina had been so proud of him.

Back at home now, and alone with Stirling, Gina felt tired and emotional herself. Relief and exhaustion had combined to assuage the worst of the anger she had felt earlier when she couldn't get hold of him, but she knew it wouldn't take much for her anger to resurface and for her to lash out at him. Her anger had been based entirely on fear, the fear that something awful could happen to Scarlet and that she would have to face that nightmare alone, without Stirling. It had thoroughly panicked her.

'Shall I make us a drink?' Stirling asked as they stood in the hallway.

At the bottom of the stairs, her hand on the newel post, she shook her head. 'No thank you. I'm too tired. I need to go to bed.'

'Have you eaten this evening?'

His question took her unawares. 'Concern, Stirling?' she said. 'What's brought this on?'

He frowned. 'Why wouldn't I be concerned?'

She stared at him impassively. 'You tell me.'

'Please, Gina, let's not argue. Not tonight of all nights.'

'Tomorrow then? Would that suit you better? Will it be business as usual in the morning? You not talking to me. You disappearing at the drop of a hat and not telling anyone where you are?'

'I'm sorry.'

'So you said.'

'I mean it.'

'And I meant it when I said I'm tired.'

'But I want to talk.'

'Well I don't want to talk.' She started moving up the stairs.

'Gina, please.'

'Good night,' she said. 'I'd appreciate it if you slept in the spare room tonight.'

As late as it was, Rosco wasn't ready to go to bed yet. A bottle of beer in hand, he slid the patio door back and went outside. It was a chilly, starry, clear-skied night. He went and stood at the edge of the decking, rested a hand on the wooden rail and looked down on to the water. Having grown up on the river, he couldn't imagine living anywhere else. After leaving Cambridge, the bulk of his friends had headed straight for London. They were still there. One by one they were getting married. Soon there would be children arriving. A few of them teased him that he was getting left behind. In turn, he teased them that they were under the cosh, ruled by the tyranny of married life.

He took a long, satisfying swallow of his beer and thought of Scarlet. His little sister, a mother. Unbelievable.

He recalled the relief he'd felt when they'd known that Scarlet and the baby were OK. Until then, he hadn't realized just how scared he'd been. With a smile, he pictured poor old Charlie keeling over in the delivery room. He'd never live it down. And rightly so. It was a worthy anecdote for the family annals. Nobody would ever tire of hearing it.

Rosco drank some more of his beer and thought of the enormity of what lay ahead for Scarlet and Charlie. No one in their right mind would think of them as being ideal parent material, but witnessing his sister's instinctive need to protect her newborn baby, and seeing how proud Charlie was of both Scarlet and Louisa-May, Rosco had experienced a flash of envy. And respect. Marriage and fatherhood had never been something he had craved. He hadn't exactly ruled it out; it had just never featured too highly in his plans. Certainly not his immediate plans. But seeing his niece for the first time, seeing her so tiny and so helpless, had moved him greatly. She was his niece. He was her uncle. They were family. They would forever be tied.

In the car on the way home, he had checked his mobile and found that Laura had texted him to ask how his sister was. Since Bank Holiday Monday, he and Laura had enjoyed several evenings together, and he'd been looking forward to seeing her again tonight. He'd been on his way to pick her up to go out for dinner when he'd got the frantic call from his mother asking him to meet her at the hospital. Laura had been fine about him cancelling dinner at the last minute, urging him not too worry too much and to drive carefully.

He was tempted now to ring her, to share the good news with her. But it was much too late. He would speak to her tomorrow. All the same, it was nice that she'd been thinking of him. Perhaps he'd send her some flowers by way of apology for messing up their evening. He wondered if it was too soon to ask if she'd like to go away for a weekend. Rome would be nice at this time of year. Definitely not Paris. The last girl he went there with, it ended in disaster. They'd had a blazing row – not only had she wanted to spend the whole of Saturday shopping, but she had expected him to pick up the tab. When he'd made it clear that wasn't going to happen, she'd packed her case and got the Eurostar home a day earlier than arranged. Two days later, she'd phoned him as if the row had never happened and asked what they were doing the following weekend. He'd said he didn't know about her, but he was going to Twickenham to watch the rugby. He didn't hear from her again.

As a commercial litigation lawyer for a growing law firm in Reading, Laura didn't strike him as being the kind of girl who would behave like that. He didn't think she was the kind of girl who would want to spend all day shopping, either. In the meantime, flowers would definitely be a good idea. And while he was about it, he'd organize some for Scarlet as well.

His thoughts switched back to the evening spent at the hospital, and his parents. In particular his father and his breathtaking hypocrisy – being with that woman and then comforting Mum for all the world like he was a loving husband.

Tomorrow he would tackle Dad and tell him that he knew exactly what was going on. It wasn't that he wanted to deliberately shame his father into doing the right thing, but if that was what it took, then so be it. It was a means to an end.

The cold night air had seeped through his clothes, and with his beer finished, he went back inside the house to get ready for bed. Before he turned out the light, he remembered his mobile needed recharging. He then remembered the photos he'd taken with it at the hospital. Looking at the images as he lay in bed, there was no getting away from it: Louisa-May was every inch her mother's daughter. Rosco wouldn't have thought it possible, but even at so young an age, the family resemblance was unmistakable. She was a true Nightingale.

In the bedroom furthest away from Gina, Stirling was wide awake. He couldn't sleep.

When he'd left Oxford earlier that evening, he'd believed he had everything sorted. Now he saw that he'd been woefully deluded. He'd been mad to think he could choose Katie over his family. His family needed him. Gina needed him.

Tonight, at the hospital and downstairs when he'd tried to talk to her, to explain how sorry he really was, he had seen for the first time just how much he'd hurt her. He'd been so sorry, he'd wanted to hold her tight and beg her forgiveness. People spoke glibly about wanting to wipe the slate clean, but he truly did. And it was all down to Louisa-May. Her birth had brought him crashing to his senses.

Right from the start of Scarlet's pregnancy, he'd been delighted at the prospect of being a grandfather. He'd joked with Neil about it. In turn, Neil had given him a bag of Werther's toffees. 'Here you go, Grandpappy,' he had said, tossing the bag at him.

Remembering how they'd drunk a toast to the next genera-tion of Nightingales, an awful thought crossed Stirling's mind. Had his excitement been divisive or pejorative? Had he clum-sily laboured the point about the family line continuing and inadvertently made Neil feel that he wasn't a part of that line? If so, had Scarlet's pregnancy held a different significance for Neil? Had it marginalized him in some way? Stirling sincerely hoped not.

He rolled over on to his other side, pulling his shoulder as he did so. He winced with both pain and shame. It served him right. What else should he expect after indulging in energetic sex with a much younger woman?

To ease the pain, he rolled on to his back. But sleep was never going to come to him. He was too restless. His brain was a maelstrom of activity and he felt breathless with the effort of trying to keep his anxiety under control. He was like a man spinning too many plates, madly running between them, backwards and forwards, trying to keep them from slowing and toppling to the ground.

He recalled how he'd felt the first time he'd driven to Oxford to see Simone, how he had wanted to be reckless, to be utterly out of control, and how he had speculated that maybe that was how Neil had felt. Now he feared that he was experiencing something akin to what his brother must have been going through, when everything had been spinning out of control for him.

To his utmost regret, Stirling had wilfully turned an already difficult situation into an even worse mess, and as far as he could see, the only way he could attempt to regain some kind of control of his life was to cut off all contact with Simone. There would be no more text messages. And absolutely no more sex. He hoped she would accept that things couldn't go on as they were. He would try to explain to her what he had felt when he had looked at his granddaughter this evening, how he had seen the purity in her, and that it had made him want to cleanse himself of all that was grubby and reprehensible in him. The realization that he didn't feel worthy to be Louisa-May's grandfather had shocked him to his core. She deserved better. And better was what he wanted to be. What he *needed* to be.

But what if Simone wouldn't accept that it had to end between them? What if her need of him was greater than his of her and she threatened to expose him to his family unless he agreed to carry on seeing her? He shuddered at the shame he would feel if anyone did find out about his visits to Oxford. How would he ever justify what he'd done?

Yet even if he dealt with the Simone situation, there was still the far greater problem of Katie to resolve. How was he ever going to do that?

It was a disgraceful and cowardly thought, but he now wished whole-heartedly that Katie had never wanted to meet him. If only she had stayed away. If only Fay had never written that letter.

He pulled the bed covers up over his head as though trying to hide from the world, wishing it would go away. But there was no place to hide. Not from himself anyway.

Chapter Forty-three

It was Thursday evening – four days since he had seen Katie – and in the last twenty-four hours Lloyd had notched up an unnatural number of hours cleaning and tidying his small house. It had been far from a state of rat-infested squalor, but with Katie coming to stay, and knowing what a neat-freak she was, he wanted to give a good impression.

Which was why he'd finished work earlier than usual, stopping off at the supermarket on the way home and stocking up. At home, and glad he'd got the heavy-duty cleaning done late last night, he'd changed the sheets on his bed, scrubbed the bathroom, emptied the kitchen bin and then given himself a good clean in the shower. At the workshop, Jim and Neville had teased him before he'd left, joking that the only reason they could think of for his leaving work early – a rare occurrence in itself, and compounded by his refusal to say why – was that he had to be going on a hot date. 'Don't forget to get the sawdust out of your ears!' had been Jim's parting shot.

The only people who knew that he and Katie were officially seeing each other were his mother and Cecily, and Stirling, although Stirling probably didn't realize the extent of their involvement. Whatever his uncle knew or didn't know, Lloyd reckoned it was safe to assume that it was unlikely he would have talked about it to the rest of his family. Besides, for now, they were all caught up in Scarlet and her baby.

Lloyd had visited Scarlet in hospital last night with his mother; they'd deliberately held back, waiting for the advance party of friends and family to launch the initial strike. The private room that Scarlet had been moved to was chock-a-block with flowers, balloons, cuddly toys and bottles of champagne. Scarlet, it had to be said, was looking amazingly well, and at the centre of all the attention, in an incubator, was the smallest baby Lloyd had ever seen, not that he was any kind of an expert. Two days old and healthy enough to be out of the special-care baby unit, Louisa-May was now allowed to be with her mother.

They hadn't been alone with Scarlet – Stirling and Gina had been there, along with Charlie. For most of their visit, Louisa-May had slept soundly, but at one point, whilst everyone else had been talking about when she might be allowed home, Lloyd had taken a close look at this latest addition to the family through the lens of his camera – in line with Scarlet's instructions, the pictures he'd taken had all been without flash so as not to harm her daughter's eyes. He had been slightly unnerved when, and as if sensing his scrutiny, his niece had opened her eyes and stared steadfastly back at him. He'd snapped her picture and then, lowering the camera, he'd smiled at her. He was sure he'd read something about new-born babies not being able to see beyond a few inches, but the smile had been an instinctive response; she was, as Cecily had described her the day before, as cute as a button. Her dark bluey-grey eyes had held his steadily, and then she'd opened her mouth, wiggled her lips a little, blinked twice, relaxed her tiny fists and flexed her fingers, and then returned her efforts to the strenuous job of sleeping. 'I think she's just said hello to me,' he'd joked with Scarlet. 'Either that or goodbye.'

Shortly before he and his mother left, Rosco turned up. And not on his own; he had an attractive girl with him. Her name was Laura. Lloyd had met only a few of Rosco's girlfriends over the years, but this one definitely seemed a cut above the usual selection, in as much as she didn't appear to be the fluff-headed bit of arm candy he generally went in for, the type of girl to whom he could feel superior. For once it looked as if Rosco had found himself a decent girlfriend.

Lloyd gave the two cushions on the sofa a final positioning thump for good measure, checked his watch, then went to make a start on the preparations for the Jamie Oliver piri-piri chicken with which he was endeavouring to wow Katie.

Depending on traffic, she was due any minute. He poured himself a glass of wine and tried not to feel nervous. Stupid really to feel jittery, but there it was, he *was* jittery. Anticipation did that to him. The more he wanted something, the more anxious he became. Katie was staying for a few days, so there was plenty of time and opportunity for things to go wrong, for her to realize that she'd made a terrible mistake when it came to being with him.

She had given him no real cause to think this was on the cards – their weekend together in Brighton had gone well, and all their subsequent conversations this week had been positive and fun – but he'd always been suspicious of anything that came too easily or felt too good to be true.

But as Dad often used to say, if it isn't to be, then it isn't to be. Better to have tried a thing and realized it wasn't right than never to have been brave enough to take the step and spend the rest of your life wondering and regretting. It was why, and with his father's help and encouragement, he'd started up his own business. Not once had he regretted the decision. But the advice now had a painfully disconcerting ring to it. His father should never have taken the steps he had in the last year or so.

In the car coming home from the hospital last night, Mum had asked him if he felt angry at all. She'd said that Cecily had asked her the same question earlier in the week when they'd been at Dad's grave. 'At times, yes,' he'd said simply. 'How about you?'

Without answering him, she'd said quietly, 'I just wanted to check how you were feeling. That's all.'

Sensing she was holding back, but not wanting to push her, he said, 'Don't worry about me. I'm fine. But you must promise me something. If at any time you want to talk about

Dad, if there's something really upsetting you, you must tell me. Don't keep it to yourself. It doesn't matter what time of day or night it is, you pick up the phone and talk to me. Do you promise?'

She'd smiled sadly. 'That's the second time this week I've been asked to make a promise.'

'Oh?'

'Cecily made me promise to look out for Stirling when she's no longer with us.'

What Lloyd found most alarming in what his mother had told him was that Granza was talking about not being around. He couldn't think of a time when she'd spoken in such terms. He supposed that losing one of her sons, the natural order of things therefore defied, had made her morbidly consider her own demise. Maybe even wish it to come sooner rather than later.

But why was Granza so concerned about Stirling? Was it simply that Katie's showing up out of the blue had thrown a spanner in the works of his marriage? Was that what she was so worried about? He'd seemed right enough last night at the hospital. But mothers, as his own often said, always had the heads-up on their children's well-being. Pen had admitted last night that she had known very early on that there was something between him and Katie. 'I probably knew it before either of you two did,' she'd said with a small laugh. More seriously, she'd added, 'Take care, though. It's not going to be easy for you to make things work, bearing in mind the situation. There are going to be people who won't be overjoyed at Katie being a fixture in your life.'

'Katie and I both know that,' he'd assured her, 'which is why we're being as discreet as we are. And who says anything about Katie being a fixture? She'll soon see through my carefully polished act to the real me, and that will be that.'

'Don't be silly; she'll see the real you and love you even more. Now, are you coming in for something to eat?' He'd pulled into the drive and had parked in front of the house.

'No thanks. Too much to do. I have a stack of VAT paper-work to wade through, and then I need to muck out the house ready for Katie tomorrow night.'

Kissing his cheek, she'd said, 'It'll be fine. Don't worry. Just enjoy the time together. Give her my best wishes and tell her to come and see me. Cecily as well. Or there'll be hell to pay.'

Lloyd was just about to pour himself a second glass of wine when he heard a car outside. His heart bounced against his ribcage. OK, nice and calm. Nice and easy. This is no different to last weekend. That had gone perfectly well, hadn't it? He smiled, thinking of Katie in bed with him in Brighton. Without any clothes. Just that lovely sexy body of hers lying next to his. He wondered if he would be considered a very poor host if he whisked his guest straight up to bed without offering her a welcome drink.

He quickly checked his reflection in the mirror by the front door – freshly shaved, hair still damp from the shower, best hole-free jeans and decent shirt on. Oh, and no sawdust in his ears. Definitely no sawdust.

He opened the door.

Oh hell!

Not Katie, but the last person on earth he expected to see.

'Rosco. What brings you here?' He couldn't remember the last time his cousin had paid him a visit.

'You left this at the hospital last night,' Rosco replied. He held out Lloyd's digital camera.

'Thanks. I hadn't even missed it. Thanks,' he repeated.

A moment passed. A very awkward moment.

'Aren't you going to invite me in, then?'

'Er ... yes, of course. Sorry. I just assumed you'd be on your way somewhere.'

'I am, but not until later. I'm meeting Laura.'

'Oh, Laura. Right. She seems nice. Have you known her long?'

'A few weeks. It's a relatively new thing.'

They were now in the sitting room, and Lloyd watched anxiously as his cousin looked about him, taking in the lighted candles in the empty grate, the matching pair of coasters on the coffee table, and the bowls of olives and pistachio nuts. His gaze then returned to Lloyd, an eyebrow cocked. 'Expecting company?'

Lloyd shoved his hands into the pockets of his jeans. 'I might be.'

'Anyone I know?'

'Not really,' he said.

'*Not really?*' Rosco echoed with a mocking tone. 'That suggests there's a possibility I might. Come on, Lloyd, who's the lucky girl? Who are you hiding from me?'

'I'm not hiding anyone,' he said defensively. *Please, Katie,* he thought, *don't turn up now. Be stuck in traffic. Be anywhere but here.*

'So why the secrecy?' Rosco asked. 'Why the huge deal?'

'It's not me who's making a huge deal out of it.'

Rosco laughed. 'You should take a look at yourself in the mirror; your body language is giving you away big time. What have you done, phoned up Dial-a-Tart for the evening?'

'What, and make do with your leftovers?'

'Hey, I'm joking! Come on, why are so uptight?'

Same old Rosco, thought Lloyd. He never could leave well alone. It was a wonder he hadn't won the Nobel Prize for Persistence. On and on he'd goad, prodding and poking until he'd got what he wanted. Usually a rise from his victim. Usually a feeling of having got the better of someone. Well, in this case, he might get more than he bargained for.

Rosco had goaded him. Check.

Rosco had riled him. Check.

But he hadn't got the better of him. Not this time, because however cross Lloyd felt, it was nothing as to how Rosco was about to feel. Because as much as he wished it wasn't going to happen, it was happening. From outside he could hear the unmistakable sound of a car coming to a stop, and unless his guess was way off the mark, he was damned sure that Katie was about to answer Rosco's question for herself. He just hoped she was going to be able to handle what was likely to be a difficult situation.

'That's my guest,' Lloyd said, playing it cool and tipping his head towards the hall. 'I'll go and let her in and you can meet her properly. I don't believe you've had that pleasure yet. Oh, but wait, you have already, haven't you, at Mum's?'

Katie knew that Lloyd had someone with him because of the Range Rover parked outside his house, and so she took the precaution of dispensing with the X-rated entrance she'd been fantasizing over in the car all the way from Brighton.

'Sorry,' Lloyd whispered in her ear when he opened the door to her, 'but Rosco's sprung a surprise visit on me.'

Her heart sank. Putting a brave smile on her face, she prepared to play along and act as normally as she could. 'Hi,' she said, all breezy lightness and as if he hadn't spoken. 'Sorry I'm a bit late.'

'That's OK,' he said with the same artificial level of breeziness. Any breezier and the Met Office would be reporting strange localized winds blowing in the area. 'Come on through, Rosco's here.'

'Oh, really?' she said. She swallowed and stepped into the lion's den. 'Hi, Rosco,' she greeted him. 'It's good to see you again. I hear you're an uncle now. Congratulations.'

Rosco's face said it all. His mouth opened, his eyes widened and he looked first at his cousin's arm around her shoulders – clearly Lloyd wasn't bothering with any kind of pretence – and then at her overnight bag, which Lloyd had taken from her. 'I see,' he said. He breathed in, then exhaled slowly. Katie had to stifle a sudden urge to laugh as she pictured him pawing the ground like a bull making ready to charge. 'It seems as if the entire family is currently obsessed with secrets,' he said.

'It's no secret that Katie and I have been seeing each other,'

Lloyd said. 'My mother and Granza know about us. As does your father.'

Rosco's expression hardened. 'How long? How long has this been going on for? And doesn't the whole cousin issue make a relationship between the two of you altogether in-appropriate?'

'Nice try, Rosco, but I would have thought you'd be the first to raise the spectre and stigma of me being adopted. As for our seeing each other, and to quote you earlier, it's a relatively new thing.'

Make it end, thought Katie. She thrashed around inside her head trying to conjure up something helpful to say, something to defuse the situation. 'How's Scarlet?' she asked. 'Are she and the baby out of hospital yet?'

Rosco switched his gaze to her. 'What's it got to do with you?'

Lloyd dropped Katie's bag and stepped forward. 'Don't you dare speak to Katie like that. Apologize and then go.'

'I'll go. But I shan't apologize. In any case, it was a fair enough question. What has any of our business got to do with her?'

'She's a member of our family.' Lloyd's voice was low and controlled, but Katie could hear the depth of anger to it as surely as if he'd hurled a ton of raging abuse at his cousin. A muscle was ticking ominously in his tightly clenched jaw. He looked like he wanted to punch Rosco into next week.

Rosco shook his head. 'She's no more a member of the family than you are. The same was true of Uncle Neil, that so-called loser father of yours.'

Katie put a hand out to Lloyd, convinced that things were about to escalate to the point of a brawl. But she was wrong. Lloyd calmly took a step backwards and indicated the door and the hallway beyond. 'Thank you for dropping by with my camera. Have a nice evening with Laura. I hope she has a thick skin; she's going to need it to stay the course with you.'

Rosco opened his mouth to say something but seemed to

think better of it. Instead he swept past them. Seconds later the front door slammed shut.

'I'm sorry you had to witness that,' Lloyd said tightly, his hands pushed into his pockets, his shoulders hunched. Katie could feel the tension vibrating off him.

'I think I'm developing a serious case of hero worship,' she said. 'You were fierce.'

His expression grim, he said, 'I wasn't. I should have hit him.'

'Not on my account. But maybe for your father's. He crossed a line there. Another time and *I'll* hit him.'

Lloyd's face softened and a smile flickered across his handsome face. 'I like you, you know. In fact, I like you a lot.'

She moved closer to him and linked her hands at the back of his neck and kissed him lightly on the mouth. 'That's good, because I like you. A lot. Was that a typical exchange between you and your cousin?'

'It can be.'

She kissed him again. 'I think I've heard quite enough about Rosco. Why don't we start the evening all over again?'

'Good idea.'

'I'm full of them. Here's another: why don't you give me a guided tour, starting with upstairs?'

He smiled, and she felt him fully relax in her arms. 'I like your thinking, Miss Lavender.'

Chapter Forty-four

With no sign of Mum's car on the drive, Rosco ground his finger against the doorbell, keeping it there for a full twenty seconds. He wanted his father to be in no doubt how he felt. He pressed the doorbell again. And again.

Upstairs, having just changed out of his work suit, Stirling was on the phone. 'I'm sorry but I'm going to have to go, there's somebody at the door. I'll speak to you tomorrow ... No, I told you, I can't see you again this week ... It's just not possible. And please, Simone, don't ring me at home again. Look, I really must go; whoever's at the door is about to break it down by the sound of it.' He ended the call hurriedly, wishing he'd had the courage to finish things there and then. But Simone ringing him whilst he was at home had thrown him off stride. Tomorrow, he promised himself. Tomorrow he would ring her and make things clear.

Alarmed by the insistent ringing at the door, he rushed downstairs to answer it, thanking God that Gina wasn't at home, that she was visiting Scarlet. It didn't bear thinking how she would have reacted to overhearing that conversation with Simone. Knowing he was going to be home late – he'd had a genuine meeting with a client lined up this evening – he'd suggested to her that she should go to the hospital without him. She hadn't believed him. He'd seen it in her eyes. Suspicion. Suspicion that he didn't have a client to meet, that he was having an affair. But he wasn't. He hadn't. Whatever had been going on between him and Simone – and he really wouldn't call it an affair – it was over. The madness was over. Now if he could just sort things out with Gina, life would feel like it used to. Or something close to it.

'I'm coming!' he shouted when he'd reached the bottom step and the bell started being pumped again. He wrenched the door open. 'Rosco! What the hell's got into you?'

Rosco pushed past him. 'I could ask the same of you, Dad. In fact, that's exactly what I am going to do. I take it Mum's not here?'

'She's visiting Scarlet.' His alarm turning to fear, Stirling closed the door. 'You look and sound like you need to calm down. Do you want something to drink?'

'Don't treat me like a child. I haven't come here for a drink or to be patronized. I've come for the truth. Though I suspect you've lost all notion of what that means.'

Stirling's fear multiplied. 'If I had half an idea what's bothering you,' he said calmly, 'I might be able to help you. Let's go into the kitchen. Have you eaten yet? I was about to throw something together ready for when Mum gets back from the hospital.'

Rosco gripped his car keys, the knuckles of his hand white. 'Are you being deliberately obtuse, Dad? Deliberately trying to make out you don't have a clue what I'm angry about?'

'You've always been the hot-headed member of the family, Rosco.' Somehow Stirling managed to produce a light-hearted chuckle. 'You're angry quite often. It's one of your less than endearing qualities. So what's on your mind? A problem at work?'

They were standing in the middle of the kitchen now, and Rosco was looking at him in a way he'd never seen before. His mouth dry with dread, Stirling tried once more to lighten his son's mood. 'Are you sure I can't tempt you to a beer? There's some in the fridge. I think I'll have one.'

Rosco shook his head. 'Tell me about Simone Montrose,' he said. 'Tell me why you've been exchanging text messages, and why you've been visiting her in Oxford.'

The fear and dread increased and a rushing sound filled his ears. He played for time. He went over to the fridge and helped himself to a beer. He took the bottle over to the drawer where they kept the opener. He levered the top off. He went over to the other side of the kitchen, opened the cupboard under the sink and dropped the metal cap into the bin. At last he forced himself to turn and face his son. He leant back against the worktop, put the bottle to his mouth and took a long, calculating swallow, hoping the liquid would quell the queasy knot of panic in the pit of his stomach. 'Have you been checking my mobile phone?' he asked, doing his best to keep his voice steady and controlled, at the same time trying to remember the exact words he and Simone had exchanged. God, what a fool he'd been to keep the messages. He'd enjoyed rereading them. He'd been like a lovesick teenager, relishing the illicit excitement of their communication. But the texts hadn't been explicit. He was sure of that.

'Any reason why I shouldn't?' Rosco asked, switching his car keys from one hand to the other, then back again.

'Lots of reasons. All to do with respecting another person's privacy. I would never, under any circumstances, do something like that to you.'

'You haven't answered my question.'

'I don't think I have to.'

'I'm not going to leave here until you do.'

Stirling shrugged. 'Suit yourself.' He took another long swallow of the beer. Outwardly he knew he was doing a reasonable job of appearing composed, just as an innocent man would, but internally he was a mess. His heart was beating fast and he could feel pools of sweat forming between his shoulder blades.

'I'm serious, Dad. I know you've been seeing that woman. I want to know why. Why are you having an affair with a woman who your own brother had an affair with? Who's next to have a go at her? Me? Is it my turn next? What is she, the family shag?'

Stirling fought hard to keep his anger in check. 'How dare you,' he said.

'I dare because I don't trust you any more. That stopped the day Katie Lavender popped up into our lives.'

'You leave Katie out of this.'

'The hell I will! Just how many affairs have you had over the years? How many other brothers and sisters do I have out there? Do you even know?'

'Katie is the only child I've fathered outside of my marriage to your mother. It happened at a time in our lives when things weren't going so well for us. I admit it was a mistake, but I can't undo that. And I refuse to keep on justifying myself.'

'And what about Simone Montrose? How do you explain her? Don't even try to deny you've been to Oxford to see her. I know that you lied to us that Bank Holiday weekend when you disappeared for the day, when you said you were in the office. How do I know? Because *I* was in the office that day.'

Shaken at how simply he'd been caught out, Stirling said, 'Why didn't you say something at the time?'

'I was curious. I wanted to know why you'd lied so blatantly and what it was you were hiding from us. I suspected a woman was at the bottom of it. I just never dreamt that you'd sink so low.'

'So you decided to keep tabs on me, did you? What a devoted son you are.'

'At least I'm honest. Unlike you.'

'Except you've jumped entirely to the wrong conclusion. That's the problem with being so hotheaded.'

'What do you mean?'

'You assumed that I was in contact with Simone because I was having an affair with her. Whereas in fact I've been helping her.'

'Helping her? How? And why?'

'She's fallen apart since Neil's death. She loved him and has no one else to turn to. All I'm being is a shoulder for her to cry on. I felt I owed it to Neil. Whatever you think of him, he was my brother and I'll always stand by him.' Pressing his point home, Stirling thought he saw a flicker of doubt pass across his son's face.

'Why didn't you tell us about her?' Rosco asked.

'I didn't think it would go down well with you or your mother. And anyway, it wasn't anyone else's business. Are you sure you wouldn't like that beer now?' The internal shaking had lessened and his heart rate was slowing. Unbelievably, it looked as if he might get away with it. Thank God he'd always been able to improvise and think on his feet.

'No,' Rosco said. His tone was less aggressive, but there was still an edge to it. 'There's something else you've been hiding from us. Katie. You've been in touch with her all this time. Secretly emailing her, haven't you?'

Stirling sighed. 'Discreetly, Rosco. Not *secretly*. I could hardly talk openly about writing to her, could I? Not without starting yet another fight with your mother.'

'If you really cared about Mum, you'd do as she wants and wouldn't have anything more to do with that girl.'

'How would you feel if you were in Katie's shoes and I turned my back on you?'

Without hesitating, Rosco said, 'I'd be angry and I'd resent you. I'd hate you.'

Stirling frowned. 'And you think that's a healthy state to be in?'

'What the hell do I care how she feels? She means nothing to me. Do you know where she is right now, this very minute?'

'No.'

'She's staying with Lloyd. And I don't suppose for one moment she'll be sleeping in the spare room. But then you know all about them, don't you? Probably given them your blessing. No better way to ensure she gets her feet well and truly under the table.'

'I knew she and Lloyd had hit it off, but I didn't know she was here.' Absurdly, given the circumstances, he felt slighted that Katie hadn't let him know she was coming.

'You've clearly figured out,' Rosco went on, 'that if they get serious about each other, we'll be stuck with her in the family. But you know what, I don't believe a word of what you said about being a shoulder to cry on for Simone Montrose. No man in your position would do that. Not unless he was getting sex into the bargain.'

Stirling felt his heart pick up speed again. 'Don't judge others by your own standards,' he said.

'I think my standards are pretty high, Dad, compared to yours. I'm not the one with a bastard child and a woman in Oxford who I'm screwing on a regular basis. A woman who just happens to be my dead brother's mistress. It's about as sordid as it gets, I'd say.'

'Enough!' Stirling shouted, banging his bottle of beer down on the work surface. 'Enough. If you can't be civil, get out. Just leave me alone.'

'Touched a nerve, have I?'

'I said *enough*.'

'I'm not a child. You can't tell me when to speak and when not to. You disgust me. You disgust me almost as much as your precious brother did. Well, I tell you this. You can have Katie in your life. She can take my place in the family, because as far as I'm concerned, I don't want anything to do with it. And I don't think Mum will either when I tell her about your trips to Oxford.'

'It'll be your word against mine.'

'That's right. And whose word do you think she'll be more inclined to believe?'

Stirling shook his head in disbelief. 'Why would you do that? Why would you be so malicious? Why would you deliberately hurt your own mother so cruelly?'

'To protect her. To keep her from being hurt by you any more.'

'Please, Rosco. Don't. Don't do it. I'm begging you, please.' His voice cracked. It was all too much. He couldn't keep the act up any longer. He didn't have the strength. He took a deep breath and realized as his son stared back at him that he had wedged himself into a corner of the kitchen cupboards. Physically and mentally he felt trapped. 'All I want is for things to be how they were,' he said. 'I want to put all the bad stuff behind us. I ... I admit I've been a fool with Simone, but please believe me when I say it's over and I want to make it up to your mother. I just don't know how at the moment.'

Rosco continued to stare at him. 'I'll help you, Dad. All you have to do is get rid of Katie from our lives and your dirty secret stays strictly between us. But don't you dare ever hurt Mum again. Do you understand?'

Unable to move, Stirling felt as if a heavy weight was crushing him, making it difficult for him to breathe. He began to panic, gulped for air. But still he couldn't breathe. Shaking, a black terror ripped through him. It was in his stomach, his chest, his head, his hands. He was paralysed by it. The kitchen began to spin, and suddenly everything was slipping away from him and he was letting out a gut-wrenching cry. It was the cry of an animal howling in pain. And he *was* in pain. Huge convulsions of it racked his body as, dry-eyed, he sank slowly to his knees and wept.

Chapter Forty-five

Gina was driving home from the hospital. Every now and then she had to wipe her eyes with a tissue. Heaven only knew what she looked like. Her mascara would be shot. For the first time since Louisa-May had been born, she had been allowed to hold her. Gently cradling her grandchild had been poignantly evocative of Rosco's birth and then Scarlet's, and had reduced her to inexplicable tears.

If she was honest, she had approached grandparenthood with trepidation. Even reluctance. She had been happy for Scarlet when she had announced she was pregnant – happy because Scarlet was so ecstatic – but not happy at the prospect of becoming a grandmother. She had never been one of those women who went all gooey-eyed over babies and who, when they hit the menopause, started applying pressure to their off-spring to repeat the process of procreation just so they could get their hands on a baby.

Not so long ago she had read a piece in a magazine written by a journalist about the same age as her, who'd said she was dragging her heels reluctantly towards becoming a grand-mother because she was terrified she would suddenly wake up one morning 'old and undesirable' and have to swap her trademark high heels for sensible flat Ecco sandals. *I won't be so much a style icon as a 'Landslide Ahead' warning sign,* the woman had written, summing up exactly how Gina had felt. Which was why each time she visited Scarlet in hospital, she made sure she wore her most stylish and flattering outfits, did her hair and applied full make-up. This evening she was wearing her favourite black Armani trouser suit with a silvery-grey silk blouse and pearls. One of the nurses had asked her if she'd just been somewhere special or was on her way out for dinner. In comparison, Charlie's mother – Caroline and John were now back from Tuscany – had been wearing a mud-coloured corduroy skirt with the hem coming down at the back and a misshapen turtleneck sweater that was badly felted. Her thatch of coarse greying hair looked like she had tried cutting it herself, which she probably had, and with a pair of dog-hair trimmers.

Being as reluctant as she was to embrace this new phase in her life and, horror of horrors, turn into a version of Charlie's mother, Gina hadn't been prepared to feel such love for her grandchild. Holding Louisa-May this evening had been one of the most emotional experiences of her life. She had wanted to hug the child close, to wrap her in love, to pour every ounce of her love and protection into that small vulnerable body. Or had she, she wondered now, wanted to absorb the essence of what a newborn represented – a new beginning?

It was what she and Stirling needed: a fresh start. If only Stirling would see things from her point of view, that it was expecting too much of her to have a reminder near her that rubbed salt so excruciatingly into the raw wound of his betrayal. Why couldn't he see that? She would forgive him for what he'd done if he would just get rid of that wretched girl from their lives. The only way she could move on was to pretend that Katie Lavender had never existed. Was that so very awful?

Home now, she brought the car to a stop and switched off the engine, surprised and pleased to see Rosco's car parked alongside Stirling's.

Her key poised to let herself in, the door flew open and she was nearly knocked off her feet by Rosco bursting out of the house. 'You're in a hurry,' she remarked good-humouredly. 'Where's the fire?' As soon as she'd uttered the words, she realized something was wrong. 'What is it?' she asked.

'You'd better ask Dad.' And then he was off, marching towards his car.

'Rosco,' she called after him. 'Come back!'

'Just ask Dad.'

She watched him get into his Range Rover. Drive carefully, she wanted to say as his headlamps lit up the driveway and he revved the powerful engine and took off much too fast.

The red tail-lights gone, she closed the door and went to look for Stirling. What on earth had been going on here?

She found him in the kitchen. On the floor, his knees drawn up to his chest, his head in his hands, he was emitting an ugly groaning sound. It was guttural. Like nothing she had ever heard before. Her first thought was that he and Rosco had had a fight and that Stirling was hurt. She threw down her handbag and keys and crossed the kitchen. She knelt on the floor in front of him. 'Stirling, what is it? What's wrong?'

His hands batted her away. 'No,' he said hoarsely, not looking at her. 'Leave me alone. Just go.'

'Don't be ridiculous. I'm not going anywhere.' She grabbed his hands, held them firmly. 'Talk to me. Did you and Rosco have a fight?'

He shook his head, tried to snatch his hands from hers. She held on tight.

'Stirling. This is absurd. How can I help you if you won't tell me what's wrong? Are you hurt? Do I need to call for a doctor?'

He shrank away from her. 'You can't help me. Nobody can.'

'Why? What have you done?'

'I've ruined everything.' He groaned and started to rock, backwards and forwards, backwards and forwards. He still hadn't looked at her. He was crying now.

Oh God, what had he done? What could he possibly have done to reduce himself to this awful state? Frightened, Gina could only think that he was having some kind of breakdown. 'I'm going to call for a doctor,' she said firmly.

He stopped rocking. 'No!' he cried.

'But you're ill.'

'No! Please. No doctors.'

'But I'm scared, Stirling. I don't know what to do to help you.' She put her arms around him. He started rocking again. She moved with him, gentling him as if he was a baby. She rubbed his back, trying to soothe him. Confused and frightened, she began to cry as well. How had they reached this awful point? How had they gone from heaven to hell in one such easy step? She felt Stirling's head raise and then it came to rest on her shoulder. He slipped his arms around her. 'I'm so sorry,' he moaned, 'so very sorry. Forgive me, please.'

Rosco hadn't heard his mobile ringing when he'd been in the car – he'd hiked up the volume on the CD player to block out any thoughts of his father – but now, at home, a second large glass of Jack Daniel's in his hand, he saw that he'd missed three calls, all of them from Laura. Oh shit! They were supposed to be having dinner, weren't they? He'd forgotten all about it. He pictured her patiently waiting for him at the restaurant he'd booked, then giving up, mad as hell. He didn't dare check his voicemail.

He threw himself down into the nearest chair and drained his glass in one long mouthful. Now he definitely couldn't drive to the restaurant to put in a late and apologetic appearance. In all probability he'd just thrown away any chance of seeing Laura again.

He leant back into the chair. In his mind's eye, he saw his father shuddering and bawling like a child. Repulsed by the sight of him, he'd been unable to do anything but walk away. He just couldn't stand to see his own father reduced to such a pitiful state. That wasn't the father he'd known.

But then nothing about Dad now bore any resemblance to the father he'd known. That man on the kitchen floor was a stranger to Rosco. He would never be able to respect or admire him in the way he once had.

Always he would think of that pathetic creature begging him to keep quiet about his affair with Simone Montrose.

Always he would think of him sneaking around behind their backs, keeping secrets. Not just his sordid affair, but the relationship that he was encouraging between Katie and Lloyd. Encouraging it because then, if they were serious about each other, the family would never be rid of the girl.

On the coffee table in front of him, his mobile pinged. This time it was a text. He picked it up and read the message. It was from Laura: *Have gone home. Hope all is OK with you. Speak soon. Goodnight. X*

He read it again, searching it for any sign of thinly disguised subtext, such as *Sod off! Don't ever think of getting in touch with me again!* He found none. To all intents and purposes, she didn't sound angry with him. Perhaps he hadn't blown it with her after all. He'd give himself a few more minutes to fully calm down and then he would ring her back and apologize. He would explain that he'd had a family crisis to deal with and that he would make it up to her.

Chapter Forty-six

'We should get up.'

'Really? Says who?'

'Says I, the one and only Katie Lavender!'

Lloyd laughed. 'Sorry, you're overruled by a massive majority. As I told you before, I'm bigger than you, so therefore my say out-says your say.'

'Say there, you're making the rules up as you go along.'

'Is there any other way?'

'Hmm ... remind me not to play Monopoly with you.'

'I can think of plenty of other games we could play instead.'

She pushed his hands away, laughing. 'Oh no you don't.'

'But you know you like it.'

'I've been pretending. I'm a world-class faker.'

'In that case, I need to up my game. I'd hate for you to miss out on one of life's greatest pleasures.' He kissed her and rolled her on to her back.

'Well,' she said later, when she lay exhausted and content with her head resting on Lloyd's chest while he traced languid circles on her back with his hand, 'ten out of ten for effort; you did indeed up your game.'

'But you still faked it, right?'

She sighed. 'I'm afraid so. I really can't see what all the fuss is about with this sex lark.'

'I know what you mean; I'm beginning to go off it too. If

we're going to continue seeing each other, we'll have to find something else to amuse ourselves with.'

'Just not Monopoly.'

'How about Scrabble?'

'How about we scrabble out of bed?'

'Hey, what's the hurry? It's Saturday.'

'Oh, you know, things to do, people to see.'

'I thought you'd come to see me.'

She wriggled out of his arms and pushed back the duvet. 'I've seen lots of you, Lloyd. Lots and *lots* of you.' She widened her eyes and smiled suggestively.

'I feel so used,' he said, in a mock-trembling voice.

She laughed. 'You better get used to it. OK if I have a shower?'

'Be my guest, but only if I can share it with you.'

Showered and dressed and watching Lloyd cook breakfast – a man-sized fry-up of bacon and eggs, tomatoes and sausages – Katie set the table that was against the wall in his small kitchen. Above the table were four pine shelves that were home to a couple of cookery books – Jamie Oliver and Nigel Slater – but were mostly packed with paperbacks and CDs. Happily his musical taste coincided with hers. Right now they were listening to Arcade Fire's *Funeral*. When he'd stayed with her last weekend, and in view of previous occasions when she'd pretended to like something for the sake of the relationship, she'd told him outright that she didn't like U2 and if that was a deal-breaker, so be it. There would be no pretending with Lloyd, she'd promised herself. Smiling, he'd said that since he wasn't a fan either, it wouldn't be a problem. Just so long as she didn't expect him to listen to Mariah Carey or Justin Bieber. 'You're safe on both counts,' she'd told him.

The table set, she poured out two mugs of tea and passed one to Lloyd. 'You don't mind me going to see Stirling, do you?' she asked.

'Of course I don't. I was only teasing you upstairs. It would be wrong for you not to see him. Whilst you're out, I thought I'd go to the workshop and check on a delivery of timber that came in yesterday. I'm not convinced the order is correct.'

She sat down at the table and watched him cook, a tea towel draped over his shoulder. Unshaven, and dressed in old jeans and a white T-shirt, he looked as sexy and divine as he always did. She had never seen him wear anything other than jeans and a shirt, and she wondered if he even possessed a suit.

Sipping her tea, her thoughts turned to Stirling, and how surprised she'd been yesterday when, and while Lloyd was at work, he hadn't replied to any of her attempts to contact him. Deciding he was simply too busy, she had tried not to dwell on it or admit to herself how disappointed she was. It was her own fault, she further concluded; she should have got in touch with him sooner to let him know she was coming, but somehow in all the excitement of seeing Lloyd again, she had forgotten. However, late in the afternoon, while she was visiting Cecily, the old lady had asked when she was planning to see Stirling, and her response to Katie's reply that she didn't know was to say, 'We can't have that. Why don't we give him a little tinkle now and see what he's up to?' This time Stirling had answered his mobile almost immediately.

Twenty seconds into Cecily's robust interrogation of him, it became evident that he wasn't at work but was at home not feeling well. Cecily had then handed the phone over to Katie, and straight away she could hear he didn't sound right. He was muted and distant, as if all the energy had been sucked out of him. Thinking that perhaps he wasn't alone, that maybe his wife was with him, she had told him not to worry about meeting. 'There'll be plenty of other opportunities,' she'd said, 'I'm sorry for bothering you.'

'No,' he'd replied hurriedly, 'it's better that we do, there's something I want to discuss with you.' He'd suggested they meet in the car park at the Riverside this afternoon, and that they go for a walk along the river and then afterwards have a bite to eat or a drink, whatever suited them best.

Now, as the time drew nearer, Katie felt anxious about seeing him. What was it that he wanted to discuss with her? She hoped it wasn't anything to do with the trust fund. Her mind was made up, so he needn't waste his breath. She had told Lloyd about the fund and he, to his credit, had agreed that if he was in her shoes, he would feel awkward about accepting the money.

'You're looking very serious all of a sudden,' Lloyd said as, with a pair of oven gloves, he put her breakfast plate in front of her. 'Don't touch, it's hot.'

She immediately did what he'd told her not to. 'Ouch,' she said.

'I did warn you.' He tossed the oven gloves over to the work surface and sat opposite her. 'So why the solemn face?'

'I was thinking of Stirling. I have this niggling feeling about him.'

'You said yourself that he's not well at the moment.'

'I know, but it's more than that. I can't put my finger on it, but there was something in his voice on the phone yesterday. Something jarred. But what do I know? I hardly know the man.'

Lloyd looked at her thoughtfully. 'I wasn't going to say anything, but I know for a fact that Cecily's concerned about him. Perhaps you could draw it out of him. He might talk to you in a way that he doesn't feel able to do with the rest of us.'

'Why, because I'm an outsider?'

'No,' he said firmly, 'because you're his daughter. And where the hell did that come from, you being an outsider? You're new to the family, like Louisa-May; you're not an outsider.'

'But unlike Louisa-May, I'll never be accepted by everyone, will I?'

He continued to frown at her. 'The people who matter have accepted you. Isn't that enough?'

Annoyed with herself for having single-handedly destroyed her good mood so thoroughly, she said, 'It's not nice knowing there are people who wish I didn't exist.'

'Three people you're talking about: Gina, Rosco and Scarlet. Forget about them. Otherwise you'll drive yourself crazy. Now eat your breakfast.'

'Yes, boss.'

He smiled. 'That'll be the day.'

One look at Stirling as he got out of his Aston Martin and Katie could see he wasn't at all well. He looked agitated and nervy, almost feverish. His hair, usually stylishly pushed back from his forehead, was messy and sticking up in places, as if he had been continuously pushing a hand through it. His sickly pallor emphasized how red-rimmed and bloodshot his eyes were. He looked like he should have been at home resting in bed.

'Should you be out?' she asked.

'I'm fine,' he said.

She didn't believe him. 'Would you rather we just had a drink and forgot about the walk?'

He shook his head. 'No, a walk might help.'

Help what? she wondered.

He seemed reticent to talk as they walked along the towpath, and Katie found herself gabbing for England, asking about Scarlet and the baby, and how he felt about being a grandfather. His responses were clipped and lacking any real enthusiasm, as if she was tiring him. Or worse, boring him.

'What's wrong?' she finally asked.

'There's ... there's something I have to tell you,' he said.

They both stopped walking at the same time. Both looked at the other. Both quickly looked away. It was as if they were mirroring each other. And from the troubled look on Stirling's face, it was obvious he had something awful to say. Better to let him get it off his chest, Katie thought. 'Go on,' she said.

A cyclist came into view ahead of them with a small panting

dog running alongside, and after they'd stepped back to let them pass, Stirling started walking again, his pace faster now. Katie fell in step. They passed a pair of swans on the water, and he said, 'The thing is, Katie, everything's got out of hand. I've made a spectacular mess of things. I've done something so stupid I can hardly believe I did it. But I did. And please don't ask me what it is, I'm too ashamed.' He took a breath. Then continued. 'The only way I can make amends and to keep everything from falling apart is to do something I don't want to do. But I can't see any other way round it. If I do what I want to do, I'll destroy my family. And you must believe me, I've hurt Gina enough as it is.' He took another breath. And another.

Katie looked at him closely. There was an expression of real anguish in his face. He seemed to have aged since she'd last seen him.

'I don't want to hurt you,' he said quietly. 'Truly I don't. I don't want to hurt anyone. But I can't see a way out of the mess without hurting someone.'

Suddenly Katie knew what the problem was. Or rather *who* the problem was. It was her. She was what was making Stirling so ill. Before she'd come to Sandiford, his life had been happy and trouble-free. OK, she had nothing to do with his brother killing himself and the ensuing difficulties the family was facing, but she was the main cause of distress for him now. She had known that his wife had wanted him to make a choice – Katie or her – but naively she hadn't thought the woman would force him to choose. She realized now that she had seriously underestimated Gina and what she was going through. She had dismissed the poor woman's reaction as nothing more than a hissy fit, something she could easily get over.

But if Katie was in Gina's place, would she really be able to behave any differently? The answer was no. Which made everything crystal clear. She knew exactly what had to be done. She had started this; she had to be the one to end it.

She slowed her step, put a hand on Stirling's arm and stopped him. 'Stirling,' she said, 'are you talking about me?

His gaze rested on hers and he nodded. 'I know it's unfair, but I ...' His voice broke, and he faltered. He turned his head to look at the river. But not before Katie saw his eyes mist over.

'This isn't right,' she said. 'You shouldn't be feeling this way because of me.'

He didn't speak.

'I'm the cause of making you so unhappy, so it seems only fair that I should be the one to resolve the problem.'

He turned to face her again.

'It's simple,' she said. 'I disappear. I go back to Brighton and you forget all about me. You tell Gina and Rosco and Scarlet that I no longer exist.'

'But you do exist. I can't un-know you.'

'I've always existed in your head, and always will, but as for knowing me, that's only been for a few months. And you haven't got to know the real me, have you? There hasn't been time.'

'I want to, though.'

'You can't. To do that you have to make too great a sacrifice. And I won't let you do that.'

'But—'

'No,' she said, cutting him off. 'I can't bear to see you like this. So unhappy. It's making you ill. I won't be responsible for that.'

He blinked. 'I don't want it to be like this.'

'Nor do I, but I should never have come. It was wrong. I was angry, though. Angry at Mum and Dad for keeping something like this from me. I was angry with you as well – the unknown man who hadn't cared enough to come and find me. Somebody very clever once said that whatever begins in anger ends in shame. And I started all this because I was angry.'

'You must never think that I didn't care. I did. And I care now.'

'I believe you do, but the thing is, it's not going to work, is it? I know that and you know that. It's why you wanted to meet me here today. You needed to tell me you couldn't see me again, didn't you? For the sake of your family and your grandchild, you have to be rid of me.'

He swallowed and pushed his hand through his hair. 'Don't say that.'

'Even though it's the truth?'

He lowered his head. 'I didn't think I could feel any more ashamed, but I was wrong. I feel utterly ashamed and unworthy of you. At least now you know you're better off without me.'

Katie didn't want to hear any self-pity from him. Her tone brisk, she said, 'I'm glad we met, but now it's time for us to resume our lives as they once were. Don't worry, you won't hear from me again. You must assure your family of that.' She cleared her throat. 'This is supposed to be a time of happiness, the birth of your first grandchild, and I can see that I'm spoiling it for you.'

He looked genuinely pained 'What about Lloyd?'

'What do you mean?'

'I mean, you and Lloyd.'

She hesitated. But then forced herself to go on. 'As from now, there is no me and Lloyd.'

'You can't just end it with him.'

'Yes I can.'

'But Katie, that's not—'

She cut him off again. 'That's none of your concern. Now please, let's just get this over with. Let's say goodbye. And before I change my mind.'

'I ... I can't.'

She opened her arms. 'A last hug. Come on.'

'I can't do this.'

'Yes you can.'

He did as she said and hugged her tightly. On the verge of

crying, she released herself from his hold. 'Thank you,' she said.

'But what do I tell Cecily and Pen?'

'Tell them whatever you want. I can't do everything for you. Goodbye.'

There were tears in his eyes.

She walked away.

And kept on walking.

She didn't look back.

Chapter Forty-seven

Long after Katie had left him, Stirling stood looking at the river. He stared at the same spot with the intensity of a man hoping it held the answers to all of life's mysteries. He stared and stared. Not seeing. Not really thinking. Just staring.

Eventually, when the surface of the water was disturbed and the silence shattered by a cruiser chugging by, he shook himself out of his trance-like state. When the boat had gone, he put his hand into his pocket and took out his mobile. He held it for a moment and then raised his arm and threw it into the river. Now Simone wouldn't be able to text or ring him.

Retracing his footsteps to where he'd left his car, he waited for a sense of relief to settle on him. After what he'd done, wasn't that his due? He had kept his bargain with Rosco and done what his family wanted. He had eradicated Katie from their lives. They could go back to how things used to be. Just as they wanted. Just as *he* wanted. Because deep down he wanted it too. He wanted the simplicity of his old life back.

Maybe it would take a day or two before he felt any relief, he pondered morosely as he unlocked his car and got in. Settled behind the wheel, he thought back to Thursday, to that dreadful night when it had all become too much for him.

Too much for him. What a colossal understatement that was! It had been like an earthquake inside him when he'd broken down. As though the very ground beneath him had rumbled and shaken and then ripped apart, dragging him down into a hellish place of dark pain. At the blurry faraway

351

edge of his consciousness, he'd been aware of Gina holding him, of her wanting to help him.

The depth of her compassion since that night had touched him. Yesterday she had fussed around him constantly, insisting he stayed in bed and rested. She had wanted to call a doctor, but he had put a stop to that. Instead he had let her call the office to say he wouldn't be going in to work, and screen his phone calls. She had put his mobile and laptop out of reach. The only call she had allowed him to take was the one from Cecily. Which was when – and when Gina had left him alone – he had spoken to Katie.

This morning at breakfast – having refused to stay in bed any longer – he had told Gina that he was meeting Katie later that day. She had cried when he had explained the reason why. Her only comment was to suggest that he speak to Katie on the phone, that he might find it less painful. 'No,' he'd said, 'it's the least I can do. I have to do it face to face. I owe her that much.'

But when he'd been face to face with Katie, he'd been a coward. He'd stood back and allowed her to decide things. What kind of a father did that? What kind of a man had he turned into? He was cowed by his shame, sickened at what he'd done and by what he hadn't done.

Whatever begins in anger ends in shame, Katie had quoted to him earlier. Benjamin Franklin had said it. The man was right. Anger had brought Stirling to this point. Anger had made him use Katie as a weapon against his family the day of Neil's funeral. And anger had propelled him to Oxford and Simone's bed.

But none of this was about his feelings. It was about the feelings of his family – Gina and Rosco and Scarlet. And little Louisa-May. He had to stay focused on that. He had promised Rosco he would do the right thing. The thing that he'd known all along in his heart he had to do, to make up for betraying Gina, not just with Fay thirty years ago, but with Simone.

How was he ever going to justify his actions to Cecily?

Gina was on the telephone in the kitchen when he arrived home. 'It's Charlie,' she mouthed at him.

He went out to the garden, taking the key to the boathouse with him. Brian, their gardener, waved to him from the other side of the garden, where he was raking the grass. From an age ago, Stirling recalled him mentioning something about the need to tackle the moss situation. When he thought about it, it was only last week that they'd had the conversation. He had a vague recollection of Brian being quite insistent on the matter, as though their lives depended upon it. Maybe in Brian's world moss wasn't the insignificant thing it was to Stirling. Especially now.

He'd got as far as putting the key in the lock of the boathouse door when he heard Gina calling to him. He turned and watched her hurrying across the lawn towards him. From a distance she looked as young as the day they'd first met. Simply but elegantly dressed in straight-legged jeans and a white blouse with the sleeves rolled up to her elbows, a pale pink cardigan draped over her shoulders and a string of pearls around her neck, the sight of her caught in his throat. She was still a very beautiful woman. Better than he deserved. The thought reverberated in his head, crashed against the very same thing he'd said to Katie about her. It was what he'd thought about his baby granddaughter as well. He didn't deserve any of them.

'How did it go?' Gina asked breathlessly. There was none of the combative hard edge to her voice that he had grown accustomed to hearing of late.

'It's done,' he said flatly. 'You don't need to worry about Katie any more.'

'It's for the best,' she said. 'You know that, don't you? Look how ill it was making you. You couldn't go on as you were.'

'Yes,' he said. He had allowed her to think his breakdown was due to losing his brother and Katie showing up and disrupting the balance of their lives. In a nutshell it was true. 'You're right. I couldn't go on as I was.' He swallowed. 'I'm sorry I've been such a poor husband to you.'

'I know of far worse husbands.' Her voice was soft, almost tender. There was a sadness in her eyes, and new lines of strain and tiredness around them.

'I'll try and make it up to you,' he said.

'You have already. By doing what you've done. That's enough for me.' She put a hand to her necklace and played her well-manicured fingers lightly over the pearls. 'I know it wasn't easy for you, but now we can put it behind us and move on. Can't we?'

'Yes,' he said. 'That's what I want to do. I want to put it all behind us.'

She smiled. 'Do you think you're up to a little family get-together? With Scarlet and the baby leaving hospital and going home today – that's what Charlie was telling me on the phone just now – it would be nice to have them over for lunch tomorrow. Charlie's parents as well. And Rosco, of course. I just think we should celebrate our granddaughter's arrival, especially now that she's well enough to leave hospital. How do you feel about the idea? I'll keep it low-key. You won't have to do anything.' She was treating him as if he was an invalid.

'It feels symbolic,' he said.

'Perhaps that's what we need. What we *all* need.'

A party to jolly us all along, he thought. Never before had he felt less like being jollied along. 'I think it's a great idea,' he lied. 'Just what's required.'

Her smile widened. It pained him to see how keen she was for his approval and how easy it was to please her now. 'Excellent,' she said, shifting the cardigan around her shoulders. 'I'll make some calls and go to the supermarket and then get cracking with the preparations.' She turned to go, but hesitated. 'By the way, did you have something to eat whilst you were out?'

He shook his head.

'Do you want me to make you a sandwich?'

'I'm not hungry.' He turned the key in the lock of the boat-house door and pushed it open.

'If you change your mind, there's plenty of bread and some of that applewood Cheddar you like in the fridge,' she said. But again she hesitated. 'What are you going to do? You're not taking the boat out, are you?'

'I thought I might. Or is there something else you'd rather I did?'

'No. I just want you to rest. I don't want you tiring your-self.'

Her consideration and the gentleness in her voice sliced through him. 'I won't,' he said.

It wasn't until she was safely inside the house that Gina lowered her guard and dropped her act of calm composure. Exhausted, she leant with her shoulders against the wall between the conservatory and the kitchen, and tipped her head back. Her heart was beating too fast and her whole body felt jittery. She was light-headed too. She had expected to feel relieved – maybe even a little triumphant – at the news that Stirling had finally done what she'd wanted. But she didn't. It was a hollow victory. There was nothing victorious in seeing Stirling in the state he was now.

But he would get better. She would help him to recover. They would work as a team. Just as they always had. He may have been the financial brains of their marriage, the one with the business acumen, but she had been there every step of the way with him. She had given him her absolute loyalty and unswerving support at all times. There was no reason why it couldn't be like that between them again.

Feeling stronger and more in control, she stepped away from the wall. Tea. A nice cup of Assam tea to settle her jittery nerves. That was what she needed. She filled the kettle and put it on the Aga, careful – as she'd been ever since Thursday night – to avoid looking at the spot where she'd found Stirling on the floor. It was akin to trying not to look at the scene of a road accident.

She didn't think she would ever forget how frightened she'd been that night. She never wanted to go through an experience like that ever again. That wreck of a man hadn't been her husband. That man, who she'd helped upstairs and put to bed – in their bed – had been a stranger. Even now, he wasn't his normal self. He was the shell of the man he'd once been. Worse, it was as if he was trying with excruciating effort to go through the motions of pretending to be Stirling Nightingale. In turn, she was playing her part, pretending to be calm and sure and strong, but all the while terrified that she would find Stirling huddled on the floor again howling like a wounded animal.

She had got no sense out of him that night, other than him apologizing over and over for everything he'd put her through, and she'd lain awake in bed beside him wondering what on earth had taken place between him and Rosco.

The next morning, and while Stirling was still sleeping, she had phoned Rosco. He'd been on his way to meet a client in Worcester and when pressed he had admitted that he had argued with Stirling and that it was a private matter. 'A private matter?' she had repeated. 'Is that a euphemism for a fight? What kind of a private matter would reduce your father to the state I found him in? And how could you leave him like that?' She had been so cross with her son.

'How is he now?' Rosco had asked.

'He's asleep. But it's good to know that you are at least concerned.'

'Of course I'm concerned,' he'd said.

'Then tell me what happened.'

And Rosco had, explaining that he had gone to Lloyd's the evening before and found that Katie was staying with him, that apparently they'd been seeing each other for some time now, and not as cousins. He had gone on to say that Lloyd had said that Stirling had known about the relationship all along. 'It was the fact that he was keeping it from us, Mum, that made me so mad,' Rosco said. 'I'm sorry, but I was so furious I went to have it out with him. I guess it was the straw that broke the camel's back,' he added. 'But Mum, I confronted him about it because I was angry, not only for me, but for you and Scarlet. I couldn't just stand back. I hope you can understand that. By the way, has he said anything about what he's going to do with regard to Katie?'

'No. But frankly he wasn't in any condition to talk coherently last night. I thought I was going to have to call for a doctor.'

Before she'd rung off, she'd made Rosco promise that he wouldn't breathe a word of Stirling's breakdown to Scarlet. 'Your sister's got enough on her plate without worrying about your father,' she had said.

Then at breakfast this morning, Stirling had announced that he was meeting Katie to sort things out today. He'd said that he saw things very clearly now, that it was seeing his granddaughter for the first time that had helped him to come to the decision he had. That the only way to put the lie right – a lie that he'd lived with all these years, and indirectly forced her to live with – was to nail his colours to the mast and prove to those he held most dear just what they meant to him.

His words had moved her to tears. And because he had proved his love to her so unequivocally, she would do whatever she had to to make him well again. She would continue to be strong and capable and would take care of him for as long as it took. Anything rather than see him as broken as he'd been on Thursday night.

In the kitchen, she shrugged off her cardigan and got on with making a list. A list of things to do for tomorrow's lunch. A list to stabilize her. A list to stabilize the family. She would do it. She would drag the family back to the way they'd been before Neil killed himself.

Chapter Forty-eight

In his small cramped, extremely untidy office at the workshop on the outskirts of Marlow, Lloyd had gone through the paperwork for the timber order he'd been concerned about, and found that everything was as it should be. Better safe than sorry, he told himself as he filed the delivery docket.

But that was him all over: cautious and suspicious to the last. He'd always been like it; it was in his nature to take things slowly. Just as it was to commit one hundred per cent to something once he was convinced it was the right thing to do.

And he supposed that was where he was with Katie: he felt committed to her and their relationship. Something he hadn't ever felt before.

From the moment he'd set eyes on Katie he'd been drawn to her, and under normal circumstances that would have given him cause to hesitate. He would have been suspicious that it was merely a superficial attraction that wouldn't stay the course and therefore wouldn't be worth the bother. He'd grown tired of jumping through the relationship hoops of getting to know someone, only for it to end with recriminations and bad feeling.

Looking back on it, there had been none of that carefully-finding-one's-way with Katie. He realized now that from the off, it had felt as if he knew her already. They fitted together well. He was tempted to say they fitted together perfectly, but he was reluctant to go that far. It was tempting fate to slap him down for getting above himself.

Better to err on the side of caution and say there was always room for improvement, especially on his part. Doubtless any number of past girlfriends would rush to agree with that sentiment. He'd been criticised for many things over the years during break-ups, often unjustly in his opinion, but then he would say that, wouldn't he? But was he really expected to justify himself for condemning the Black Eyed Peas as being as cerebral as a bag of dolly mixtures? Not likely. One girlfriend had been annoyed with him because he walked too fast. Another had accused him of being on a par with Jack the Ripper because he wouldn't convert to vegetarianism. And the last one had claimed he was laddish and immature. His crime? He'd been resistant to taking their relationship to the next level, which amounted to her moving in with him. They had only been seeing each other for a month when she had started leaving her things in his bedroom and bathroom after staying the night. 'Easier to have them here instead of dragging them backwards and forwards,' she'd said when he had mistakenly used her shower gel instead of his own. He'd spent the rest of the day smelling like a sickly banana milkshake and working up the courage to tell her he didn't want to see her any more. For weeks afterwards he couldn't eat a banana without thinking of her.

But with Katie it was different. For the last two mornings he had liked seeing her things neatly placed on the windowsill in his bathroom, along with her red-spotted (complete with black furry ears on the hood) Minnie Mouse dressing gown hanging on the back of the door. 'Minnie Mouse?' he'd asked, amused.

'Don't ask,' she'd said.

'But I just did.'

'A silly present from Zac. All his presents are silly.'

Recalling Katie wearing her comical dressing gown as she brushed her teeth that morning, Lloyd couldn't help but think that when it was the right person leaving their shower gel in your bathroom, it didn't matter.

As he switched off the computer and tidied away some files, he wondered how Katie would react if he suggested she left some of her things with him, just so that she wouldn't have to carry them backwards and forwards from Brighton. Would she think he was jumping the gun?

Out in the workshop area, he went over to his bench, where yesterday he'd laid out the drawings of a new range of garden furniture he was planning to make. Harking back to the smooth, sensual lines of the art deco period, he was putting together a new range of luxurious daybeds, tables, chairs and swing seats. It was an ambitious project, but one that excited him. Everything would be made of reclaimed oak, which he was sourcing from a supplier in France who was salvaging it from old agricultural buildings.

He thought of Katie's courtyard garden and Cecily's suggestion that he should make something for her. He already had something in mind from this new range and planned to surprise her with it as a Christmas present. Again, was that jumping the gun? Thinking ahead to Christmas when it was only September?

It was four o'clock when he arrived home. He was disappointed to see there was no sign of Katie's car. He let himself in and wondered about ringing her, just to find out an approximate time when she thought she would be back. He decided not to. He didn't want to look like he was pestering her. This was her day to see Stirling.

He checked the answering machine for messages. Nothing of any importance. He then made himself a ham sandwich, realizing that he hadn't eaten since their late breakfast that morning. Sandwich in hand, he flipped open his laptop at the kitchen table and dealt with a string of emails.

That done, he then slipped into the frustrating limbo land of trying to decide what to do with himself while he waited for Katie to return. His arms folded behind his head, he leant back in the chair and thought how eerily quiet the house was.

And how empty. Katie had only been here two days, hardly any time at all, but the place suddenly felt incomplete without her. If she were here, he would know exactly what to do. After all, he'd been thinking of little else in the car driving home. The thought made him smile. And at once aroused in him the by now familiar desire for her. He sighed deeply. Only one thing for it, he'd go for a run. He hadn't been running in ages. There just didn't seem enough hours in the day or enough days in the week to spare the time.

He went upstairs to change. It was when he was sitting on the end of the bed and about to kick off his shoes that he noticed Katie's overnight bag wasn't where she'd left it this morning. He glanced round the room. He then noticed that the bedside table on her side of the bed was bare – her make-up bag was gone, as was her hairbrush and small pot of lip salve. He crossed the landing to the bathroom. Her Minnie Mouse dressing gown was gone. So were all her other things. There wasn't a sign of her having been here.

He rushed downstairs to the hall and snatched up his mobile from where he'd left it on the bookcase with his keys. There were no missed messages from her. No texts either. Despite having checked earlier, he rechecked the answerphone. Nothing.

He rang her mobile. It went straight to voicemail.

He rang Stirling's mobile. Nothing. Not even voicemail.

His heart thudded in his chest. It had done the same thing just minutes ago when he'd thought of Katie, but now it was a different type of thud. Now it was a hollow, aching thud.

He sat at the bottom of the stairs and stared at the front door, as if willing her to come through it. He replayed their conversation at breakfast and when her mood had changed so abruptly. He hunted through the minutiae of what had been said, hoping to find a clue, some kind of hint that would make sense of her disappearing without so much as a word. All he could think of was the moment when she had described herself as an outsider. He had dismissed the description out of hand, but had he been too flippant in his response? Had he been insensitive? But even if he had, why had she gone?

Not just gone.

She had *left* him. He knew it with every ounce of his being.

She must have seen Stirling and then come back here, let herself in with the key he'd given her and packed her things. Had she known she was going to do that when she'd said goodbye to him?

The key, he suddenly thought. Where was the key he'd given her? If it wasn't here, did that mean she still had it and meant to return with it?

Clutching at straws, he told himself.

Even so, he went over to the front door and looked down at the mat to see if she had pushed it through the letter box. Nothing, of course. Anyway, he would have spotted it straight away when he let himself in. And the door had definitely been locked. He hadn't imagined that.

But then he saw a glint of metal sticking out from beneath the bookcase to the left of the door. He got down on his hands and knees and fished the key out. It must have bounced off the mat and skittered a few inches across the tiled floor to the bookcase.

He stood up. He may have solved the mystery of the key, but it didn't explain Katie's disappearance.

And why hadn't she left a note, some kind of explanation? Something for him to make sense of.

First Dad not leaving a note.

Now Katie.

Chapter Forty-nine

Sunday morning and thirty minutes into the journey, and it had begun to rain.

The wipers on Lloyd's car were doing little more than smearing the windscreen with dried-on dead flies and whatever else was stuck to the glass. Even the weather was conspiring to make him think of Katie, reminding him of the first time they made love. He remembered what he'd said to her about the rain, and felt a curdling mixture of foolish anger and sadness. Mostly sadness.

I'm a world-class faker, she'd said in bed yesterday morning. Had she been pretending? Could she be that devious, or that clever an actress? He didn't think so. It *had* been real between them. He just knew it.

He'd left numerous messages on her mobile and landline last night, but she hadn't replied. *Just let me know you're all right*, he'd texted her at midnight. Still nothing. He felt hurt. And worried. What if something had happened to her?

He had to know.

Which was why he was driving to Brighton at six thirty in the morning.

Gina was up early. She had lots to do. She wanted everything to be perfect. She wanted to look back on this day and remember it as being the day everything began to feel right again. She wanted Stirling especially to remember it. She wanted him to sit proudly at the head of the table during lunch and think, *This is what counts. This is what I so very nearly lost.* She wanted him to be proud of his family. And of her.

She'd had a few moments of awkward dilemma over the guest list, but all was in hand now. Which was more than could be said for the weather: it had turned unseasonably chilly and was raining.

The weather aside, she had everything else under control. As she'd promised Stirling, it would be a small family get-together – Charlie and Scarlet and little Louisa-May, John and Caroline, and Rosco, who had asked if he could bring his new girlfriend with him. Gina was particularly pleased by this; it suggested Rosco had met someone he was serious about. Previous girls had come and gone with increasing rapidity and often without Gina ever meeting them. 'You wouldn't have approved of her, Mum,' Rosco would say when she asked how things were going with his latest girlfriend only to learn that she was history. She had long since accepted that she was on a need-to-know basis when it came to her son's love life.

Her dilemma had been whether or not to invite Cecily. The trouble was, if she invited Cecily, it would look bad not to invite Pen and Lloyd. But she didn't want Pen and Lloyd here, not when she considered them as Katie Lavender allies. Cecily was one too, of course, but being Stirling's mother, Gina felt she didn't have much choice about including her in the luncheon party. She had no such qualms about Pen and Lloyd. Quite the reverse, given that Lloyd and Katie were carrying on together. Rosco had been right when he'd foreseen the danger of that liaison continuing; it could only ever be divisive and result in creating a massive schism in the family. But frankly, she didn't care. What did it matter to her if she never had to speak to Pen and Lloyd again? And as brutal as it was, how much longer would Cecily be with them? Gina still hadn't forgiven the appallingly high-handed way the imperious old woman had spoken to her.

Having decided she had no choice but to invite Cecily, she had called her last night only to be told by her mother-in-law that she had come down with a cold and had declared herself to be in quarantine for the sake of her great-granddaughter. Much relieved, Gina had said with considerable magnanimity that if there was anything Cecily needed or if she was feeling particularly poorly, she mustn't hesitate to ring. In her customary off-hand manner, Cecily had told her not to fuss, that she had nothing more life-threatening than a light head cold. Gina had said goodbye, relieved also that the brief conversation had revealed that Cecily knew nothing about Stirling and Katie's meeting yesterday, or the outcome. Doubtless that particular storm was yet to arrive. For now, Gina was happy to put it to one side. They would deal with it when Stirling was feeling more like his old self and was strong enough to explain matters fairly and squarely. She would support him in that whole-heartedly. She didn't care how the old woman reacted, but she would not allow Cecily to bully Stirling into changing his mind.

Lloyd deliberately parked a few houses down from Katie's, suspecting that if she saw his car and knew it was him, she might not answer the door.

The rain pelting down on him, he walked the short distance and rang the bell.

There was no answer.

He rang the bell again.

And again.

He hated the idea that she was inside the house hiding from him. And she had to be here; her car was right there on the road behind him in the deserted street. The sight of her Mini Cooper lessened his anxiety. It meant she was all right; she hadn't had an accident in it.

He bent down and pushed open the letter box, half hoping, half fearing that he might see her sitting at the bottom of the stairs looking back at him.

There was no sign of her.

'Katie,' he called out, straining to make himself heard, but not wanting to arouse attention from the neighbours. 'Katie, it's me, Lloyd. Please let me in.' He risked raising his voice. 'I just want to talk. I want to know what I did wrong.'

Nothing.

'I'll tell you what you're doing wrong, mate,' said a voice to his right.

He stood up straight and saw an elderly man in his pyjamas and dressing gown leaning out from the doorway of the adjoining house. 'You're disturbing the peace, that's what you're doing.'

'I'm sorry,' Lloyd said, wiping the rain from his face. 'I'm worried about Katie.'

The man looked suspiciously at him. 'Why's that, then?'

'I can't get hold of her.'

'Maybe she doesn't want you to.'

'Do you know if she's OK?'

'She looked right enough last night when I saw her.'

'Did you speak to her?'

'What's it to you?'

'I'm her boyfriend.'

'Doesn't sound much like you are. If you were, you'd know how she was.'

'Something happened yesterday,' Lloyd said patiently, wishing he could take the old man by his scrawny neck and wring whatever truth out of him he was trying to withhold. 'She was staying with me and then suddenly disappeared. All I want to know is that she's OK. I'm worried.'

The old man tugged on the belt of his dressing gown. 'Like I said, she looked fine to me last night when I saw her passing my window.'

'Did she come back?'

'Look, I'm not one of those nosy neighbours always peering out of my window. I've got better things to do with my time. I didn't see her come back, but that's not to say she didn't. She did have a bag with her. I remember that.'

'An overnight bag?'

'Could've been. Mind you, could've been an ordinary

handbag for all I know; some of the handbags girls lug round with them these days are the size of coal sacks. God knows what they find to put in them.'

'Thank you for your help,' Lloyd said, keen to cut the old man off. 'I'm sorry to have disturbed you.'

He set off quickly down the street to where he'd left his car. If Katie had gone somewhere with her overnight bag, there was a strong chance it was either to London to see Tess or to Zac here in Brighton.

But the old man wasn't finished with him. 'If I hear she's come to any harm, fella,' he called out, 'I'll remember your phizog. I'll be able to give the police a full description. Just you remember that!'

Lloyd put his hand in the air and gave him a cheery no-problem-with-that wave.

When he reached his car, he did a quick rethink and put his keys back in his pocket. Katie had shown him Zac's salon when they'd gone out for lunch during his stay with her. All he had to do was remember the way. It shouldn't be too difficult; it was in the North Laines, the trendy boho part of town. If he got lost, he could ask for directions. His hopes raised, he followed his nose, on foot, looking out for familiar landmarks.

Within no time, he saw the salon. It was closed. It would be, it was Sunday. Lloyd wasn't deterred. Katie had said that Zac lived above the salon; she'd talked about how he'd converted the office space above into an amazing apartment.

The rain still pouring down, Lloyd stared at the windows above the salon, then looked to the left of the shopfront, where there was a door. A firmly shut door. There were three bells, each with a nameplate and an intercom. His hopes raised yet further, he pressed the buzzer alongside Zac's name. He didn't really think Katie would be here – why stay the night with Zac, when her own place was within walking distance? But Zac, he was sure, would help. He would find a way to get Katie to talk to him.

'You won't get any joy there, he's not in. He's gone out for some milk.'

Startled, Lloyd spun round. 'Zac!'

From beneath a large black and white leopardprint umbrella, Zac grinned. 'I thought it was you. I'd know those strapping shoulders anywhere. What brings you here? Katie not with you?'

Upstairs, and while he towelled himself dry, Lloyd told Zac everything. What little there was to tell.

'And you swear that's what really happened?' Zac asked when he'd finished. 'You didn't have a big bust-up argument? You didn't hurt Katie in any way?'

'Why would I do that, Zac? I'm crazy about her.'

'Yes, but crazy can lead to all sorts of things. Sugar in your coffee?'

'Just milk. And I swear, I'm not keeping anything from you. She went out to see Stirling. I went to my workshop, and when I came back she, and all her things, was gone. There was no note. Nothing. And she hasn't replied to any of my calls or messages. She's ignoring me.'

Zac frowned. 'So something must have happened between her and her biological father.'

'That's the conclusion I've reached.'

'What does he say? I presume you've spoken to him?'

'No. I can't get a response from his mobile. And for all sorts of reasons, I don't want to ring the house.'

Zac handed him a cup of coffee, which he'd made with a state-of-the-art machine that would not have looked out of place in a Starbucks. But then everything in Zac's loft-style apartment looked state-of-the-art, from the Alessi kitchen gadgets to the stunning black-and-white photographs on the whitewashed walls.

'Waffle?'

'Sorry?'

Zac smiled. 'I was going to make waffles for my breakfast. Do you want one?'

'I'm not really hungry.'

'You will be once you smell them cooking.' He began opening cupboards and drawers – a bowl, a whisk, flour, milk, sugar, baking powder and eggs. 'So,' he said, 'odds on Katie got back from yours yesterday and went to Tess, either for comfort or to hide from you. Or a combination of both, perhaps.'

'It certainly looks that way.'

'Then stop worrying. We'll have breakfast and then we'll give the girls a call and have this settled in no time.'

'Couldn't we call them now?'

'Goodness me, no! It's much too early. If I know my sister, she will have got out the hard liquor last night and they'll be sleeping off a stinker of a hangover.'

Normally if Cecily was ill, even with a cold, Stirling would go and see her to make sure it was nothing serious. But in this instance, Gina had persuaded him that visiting her would put Louisa-May at risk and that it was better to keep away for today. So instead, he had phoned her. 'You don't sound right,' his mother said to him now.

'I've been a bit under the weather myself,' he admitted.

'A cold?'

'No. I think everything's caught up with me.'

'Neil's death, you mean?'

'That and other things.'

'What things?'

'Katie.'

'Why should Katie make you ill?'

He stared out of the window at the rain. The lawn was sodden. 'Don't be disingenuous, Mum,' he said. 'Her showing up the way she did has had a big effect on everyone.'

'You're talking specifically about Gina, I take it?'

'And Rosco and Scarlet.'

'They'll come round in the end.'

He fought to suppress a flash of irritation. 'So you keep saying,' he said stiffly.

'Stirling?'

He closed his eyes, then opened them. 'Nothing, Mum,' he said tiredly. 'Forget I said anything.'

'Stirling, I do appreciate the strain you're under – I've been concerned about you for a while – but she's your daughter. Please don't forget that.'

He heard the warning tone in his mother's voice and backed off. He had hoped to tell her about yesterday, to come clean, but he couldn't. He just couldn't face it. 'I won't,' he said, utterly defeated.

'Good. Don't lose sight of that. Oh dear, I'm going to have to go. That'll be Marjorie at the door. She said she'd call round with some Vicks VapoRub for me. She's feeling very guilty, as she's the one who's given me this wretched cold. Give my love to everyone, especially Scarlet and the baby.'

Oh, to feel guilty about something as insignificant as passing on a cold, thought Stirling when he'd hung up.

Not until they had eaten and tidied everything away did Zac put Lloyd out of his misery and say it was at last time to ring Tess.

The telephone in London rang and rang and was eventually answered. Zac had his phone on speaker so that Lloyd could hear both sides of the conversation.

'Hi, little sis,' Zac said. 'How's things?'

'Keep your voice down, will you?'

'You sound like you've been gargling with Cillit Bang. Heavy night?' Zac gave Lloyd a told-you-so look.

'You could say that.'

'I've told you before, your body is a temple, you should respect it more.'

'I think Ben does enough worshipping of my body for the two of us.'

'Ooh, hark at you with your boasting. Not all of us are so fortunate to have such an attentive lover.'

'Voice and lower, please, Zac. But look, there's some serious mad shit going on. I've got Katie here. She turned up last night in floods of tears. She's dumped Lloyd.'

'*No!* Why's she done that? I mean, the boy is seriously gorgeous. He's *sooo* the one for her.' Zac was looking straight at Lloyd as he said this. Lloyd felt his face redden. And then redden some more.

'I agree with you,' Tess went on. 'And I think she knows that. I haven't seen her this upset in ages, not since her mum died. To be honest with you, I reckon she's crying more over this than she did with her mother. I'm not saying she didn't care about her mum, but you and I both thought the same, she didn't really get all her grief out then. It was the same with her dad, she thought she had to hold it all in to help her mother.'

'So what's going on? Why has she dumped poor Lloyd without telling him? Why did she just run off? That's so unlike her.'

There was a pause. And then Tess said, 'How do you know she didn't tell Lloyd what she was doing?'

Zac glanced at Lloyd. Lloyd nodded.

'Because he's here with me. And he's not a happy bunny. Far from it.'

'You haven't got your phone on speaker, have you?'

Zac squeezed his eyes shut and crossed his fingers. 'No.'

'Good. The thing is, Katie says she's done it because of her biological father.'

Lloyd froze.

'Why? What's it got to do with him?' Zac asked.

'He was being made to choose between her and his wife and other children. Apparently he couldn't have both. From what Katie says, it was making him ill. She says she hated knowing that she'd done that to him. She could see he didn't want to make the choice, so she did it for him.'

'But what the hell has that got to do with Lloyd?'

Good bloody question, thought Lloyd.

'Use your head, Zac. She can't walk out of Stirling's life but be seriously involved with Lloyd. If she ends it with Stirling, she has to end it with Lloyd, it's as simple as that.'

'I don't think Lloyd is going to think it's as simple as that. In fact, I know so.'

Lloyd couldn't keep silent any longer. He gestured to speak to Tess for himself. Zac gave him the go-ahead.

'Tess, it's Lloyd.'

'Oh,' she said. Then: 'Zac, you were lying, weren't you? You've had this conversation on speaker the whole time, haven't you?'

'Don't be cross with him,' Lloyd said. 'Can I speak to Katie?'

'She's still asleep.'

'When she wakes up, then?'

'I don't know whether she'll want to. She made me promise I wouldn't get in touch with you. She knows I think she's made a mistake, but I have to respect her wishes.'

'Please, couldn't I come and see her?'

'Oh Lloyd, don't put me in an impossible situation. Katie's my best friend; please don't force me to break a promise. You see, she must have known that you'd try and change her mind, so she made me swear I wouldn't let you talk me into seeing her. All I can suggest is that you wait. Let her calm down and maybe, given time, she'll realize she's done the wrong thing.'

It's not Katie who's done the wrong thing, thought Lloyd grimly when he was driving back to Henley.

Chapter Fifty

Pen had woken up that morning with the unexpected urge to go to church. By no stretch of the imagination could she be called a regular attendee of St Oswald's, but over the years she had gone often enough to feel comfortable there. Though not since Neil's funeral.

Today, however, she'd had a sudden longing to enjoy a sense of peaceful communion in the familiarity of the age-old liturgy. But it was not to be. The Reverend Roger Batley was away on a fortnight's holiday and the service, extraordinarily long and drawn out, and led by the lay readers and team ministry, hadn't provided the quiet solemnity she had hoped for. It had been a scrupulously modern affair, a family service that had covered everything but touched nothing. The hymns were all modern and naively simplistic and tediously repetitive. There had been too much clapping, too many squeaky recorders and far too many rattling bean-filled shakers in the hands of far too many uncontrollable children. A play had been acted out by the older members of the Sunday school, put together, one presumed, to bring to the complacent middle-class attention of the congregation the plight of the homeless, along with prostitution, drug addiction and gang warfare. It had gone on for an eternity – or, more accurately, purgatory – and had laboured its point of hard-hitting edginess to the nth degree. Pen hadn't been the only one to wonder if it wasn't just a touch too near the knuckle. What next for Sunday school: incest and paedophilia? During coffee and biscuits, which she was roped into helping with, there was much tutting and murmuring of just-wait-till-the-vicar-hears-about-this amongst the more traditionally minded.

A wasted morning, Pen thought now as she tactfully withdrew, having also been roped into helping in the kitchen afterwards to wash up. It was very nearly one o'clock, and she felt cross and snappy for being cheated out of what she'd come here for. During the long reaches of the interminable service, her irritation had grown and her patience had been tested. Every time the children had rattled their shakers or hit a piercing note on their recorders, another layer of angry disappointment had compounded her frustration. It's not the children's fault, she had told herself. Then whose fault is it? she had wanted to know, her hands itching to take those wretched instruments of musical torture and smash them to smithereens.

To the sound of Andy Wilson – the organist, who exerted more zeal than actual skill – thumping out something she didn't recognize on the organ, Pen shook open her umbrella in the porch and braved the rain. There was only one way to salvage the time lost and maybe sooth her jagged mood, and that was to go and talk to Neil for a few minutes. The thought that he would have felt the same about the service as she did comforted her.

Just as Cecily had remarked, Pen knew very well that Neil wasn't there in the churchyard. Not the real Neil. He was no more present amongst the tombstones than God had been inside St Oswald's that morning. No, if God had any sense, he was on holiday in Normandy with Roger Batley, drinking Calvados and eating delicious crêpes. But talking to Neil was a euphemism for remembering the Neil she had known, certainly not the Neil she hadn't known. She didn't want to know anything about the man he had been when he was with Simone Montrose. Simone was welcome to that man. She just wanted to remember the Neil who had been her husband and best friend. The man she still missed with all her heart.

The rain coming down even harder, she hurried through

the churchyard. As the sound of the organ grew fainter, not only with distance, but drowned out by the pitter-patter of rain against the taut fabric of her umbrella, she caught the sound of boisterous voices. And laughing. It was an ugly, jeering kind of laughter. And quite out of place.

When she came upon the source of the noise, she stood stock-still. She couldn't believe what she was seeing. It went beyond any form of decency that she knew. And she would not stand for it. She absolutely would not let these young louts get away with desecrating a grave. She opened her mouth and screamed at them. She screamed and screamed. Unleashing God knew what, she rent the air with all her might. They just stood there, slack-jawed and eyes popping, staring at her as if she were quite mad. Then they took to their heels and were gone.

And in that moment, with the rain hammering down on her – for some strange reason for which she couldn't account, her umbrella was no longer in her hand – Pen knew that she *was* mad.

She was mad with grief.

She was mad with anger.

She was mad with an indescribable fury that these mindless savages could so wantonly defile a child's grave. It was more than she could take.

Simone had promised herself she wouldn't do it. She had sworn she would stay away.

But she had broken that promise.

It was Stirling's fault. He was entirely to blame. He shouldn't have fobbed her off with a lie about ringing. She had waited and waited and he hadn't called. She had tried ringing him, but he must have switched off his mobile. He was avoiding her. Ignoring her. And it was unfair and wrong of him to do that. She had expected better of him. If he'd wanted to end things, why not simply say so? Why be so needlessly cruel?

Because he was a coward! That was why. He'd had his fun,

he'd used her and now he wanted nothing more to do with her. But he had to know that he couldn't get away with that. She deserved to be treated with respect.

Her plan had been to come here and speak to him face to face. It was a plan that was fast disintegrating. She had found Sandiford without any difficulty, having been here for Neil's funeral, but it was beginning to dawn on her that driving round in the pouring rain looking for a house for which she didn't have an address was the behaviour of a very foolish woman, who, if she wasn't careful, ran the risk of tipping over into the realms of insanity. What had she imagined? That his house would be helpfully signposted with the words *Stirling the Adulterous Coward Lives Here*?

And what precisely had she planned to do when she did find his house? Make an embarrassing spectacle of herself?

When it came down to it, all she'd wanted, and still wanted, was an explanation and an apology. She could accept it was over, that whatever it was they had experienced wasn't sustainable; it wasn't ever meant to go on indefinitely. She knew that. But he couldn't just shrug her off as if she counted for nothing. That was what hurt, knowing that he cared so little about her feelings. She had thought he understood, that they'd shared something that had mattered, that they were helping each other. When all along he'd only been helping himself. 'You're not half the man Neil was!' she wanted to yell at him. 'Neil wouldn't have treated me so shabbily! Neil would have had had the guts to end it properly.'

Realizing what she'd just said, and that she'd said it aloud, she brought the car to a stop.

Neil hadn't had the guts to end it properly, had he? He had abandoned her, just as Stirling had done. No word of explanation. No apology.

The windscreen wipers swished slowly and rhythmically from side to side in a now-you-see-it-now-you-don't fashion. The truth, she now saw, was that unable to take out her feelings on Neil, she had come here today to do so with Stirling. Retribution by proxy.

She laid her head back against the headrest and closed her eyes. How had she got into this mess? She was an intelligent woman. She had a satisfying and successful career, was even respected for the work she did. She had a lovely home. She had money in the bank. What was the matter with her that she attracted the wrong man every time? Her husband had been an alcoholic and a gambler. Her lover had committed fraud and killed himself. Now her substitute lover – how else could she describe Stirling? – had dumped her.

She banged her fists on the steering wheel and cried out, 'Why do I attract these men? What's wrong with me?'

She forced herself not to cry. The degrading self-pity had to stop. Be glad that you did nothing silly, she thought, as she pulled back out on to the road and drove on. Be glad that you can go home and face yourself in the mirror.

Ahead of her was a T-junction and a church. It was, she remembered, the church where Neil's funeral had taken place: St Oswald's.

Another moment of clarity struck her. It would be a final goodbye. A way for her to start living again.

She parked on the verge opposite the church, found an umbrella in the boot and crossed the road. She hadn't been back since the day of the funeral. How could she come back? How could she do that when there was the risk of bumping into Neil's wife?

But now it felt right. And on such an awful day, who else would be mad enough to be in the churchyard?

She pushed open the lychgate and walked up the path, her shoes grinding the gravel underfoot, the rain drumming on her umbrella overhead. She turned right, just as she remembered doing before, and followed the path round to the side and almost to the back of the church. She could hear the sound of an organ playing.

Her heart began to beat faster at the thought of seeing

Neil's grave. A great weight of sadness and remorse surged through her. Oh Neil, forgive me for what I've done since you died. Forgive me, please. Forgive me for everything I ... She broke off. What was that noise? She slowed her step, suddenly unsure whether to go any further.

Don't be a coward, she told herself. Somebody's hurt. They need help. She walked on, but stopped abruptly.

An opened umbrella lay discarded on the ground, and sitting in a crumpled heap between two graves was Pen Nightingale. She was sobbing, her shoulders heaving, and on her lap was a collection of broken toys. Strangest of all, she was cradling a small furry donkey that looked like someone had tried to rip off its tail and legs; white stuffing oozed from the broken seams. Simone thought it was the saddest sight she had ever seen, and nothing in the world would have allowed her to leave Pen in this dreadful state.

Knowing that she was oblivious to her presence, Simone approached with care. She didn't want to alarm the poor woman – no more than her appearance was bound to anyway. 'Pen,' she said softly. It sounded wrong to call her by her Christian name, but what other term of address could she use? The formality of 'Mrs Nightingale' seemed even more inappropriate. 'Pen,' she repeated, crouching on the sodden ground next to her and holding her umbrella over their heads. It was then that she noticed that the grave the other side of Pen was Neil's. She swallowed. Help me, Neil, she implored. Help me to help your wife.

She put a hand out to the other woman. Pen started and looked up, rain dripping off her face, her hair plastered to her scalp. She clutched the bedraggled donkey to her chest as though frightened Simone would snatch it away from her. Recognition slowly flickered through her expression. 'You,' she murmured.

Simone nodded. 'Yes, it's me.'

The bleak wretchedness with which Pen stared back at her made Simone's own sadness shrivel to insignificance. She was ashamed of her own petty feelings; Pen's anguish was so much greater. Guilt and regret shivered through her.

Pen finally glanced away, her gaze coming to rest on the other grave. Not Neil's, but the one on her left. 'The children,' she murmured. 'They were ... I found them destroying these toys ... The family left them there for their little boy ... He died of leukaemia ... How could they be so wicked?'

Simone's heart cleaved. She had no answer. All she could do was put her umbrella to one side and offer physical comfort to this shattered woman. She put her arms around her and held her in the same way that Pen was cradling the mangled and sopping-wet donkey.

Chapter Fifty-one

With everyone gathered around the table and with Laura at his side, Rosco felt more cheerful and positive than he had in a long while. He took a long, appreciative sip of his wine – a particularly excellent Amarone that was big and bold and full of complex character – and allowed himself a metaphorical pat on the back, for in some small measure he was partly responsible for making today happen. If he hadn't stepped in when he had, Dad may well have continued down the path he'd been on and made the worst decision of his life, a decision that would have made today – and future days like it – impossible.

He turned to glance at Laura and found that she was looking at him. She was, he'd decided, a vast improvement on any of his previous girlfriends. She was intelligent, easy-going and fun, and he liked being around her. Dark-eyed and dark-haired, and with a great body, she also just happened to be one of the most beautiful girls he'd dated. Scarlet had commented on this earlier, whispering to him, 'She's gorgeous, Rosco. Bet you any money you like you can't hang on to her.'

Not prepared to put a price on Laura, he had whispered back to his sister, 'I bet I can.'

'Ooh,' she'd said with a laugh. 'That must be because you really like her.'

It was true, he did. And after their somewhat shaky start, with him cancelling one dinner and forgetting all about another, he wanted her to see him – and his family – in a good light.

'You OK?' he asked her, his voice low. Beneath the table, he linked hands with her and laced his fingers through hers.

She smiled. 'I'm fine.'

'Not too awful being thrown in at the deep end with my family, then?'

'Not at all. I'm really enjoying myself. Your family's great, your mum and dad are lovely.'

He looked down at the other end of the table, where his father had got to his feet and was going round refilling wine glasses. Mum had told him in the kitchen before lunch that she was still worried about Dad, and Rosco thought she was right to be concerned. Dad didn't look himself at all. He hadn't looked this bad since the days following Uncle Neil's suicide.

Whilst Rosco was glad that his intervention the other night had brought Dad to his senses, he hated to think back to what he had reduced him to. That had never been his intention. He was ashamed now of his reaction to his father's breakdown; he should never have walked away as he had. He had tried to reason with himself that no son wanted to see his father fall apart; that he had acted out of a combination of anger, vengeance and confusion, but he couldn't really justify his behaviour that night. What if he'd pushed Dad too far and he'd had a heart attack?

But as brutal as the exchange had been, it had brought about today. It had made Dad get his priorities in order. As of yesterday, Katie Lavender had been dispatched to where she belonged, which was outside the walls of the Nightingale family. How could Dad have thought it could be any other way? He had to see from this gathering today to celebrate Louisa-May's arrival that Katie could have no place in it. Apart from anything else, it simply wasn't fair to Mum.

'More wine, Rosco?'

Dad had worked his way round the table and now stood at Rosco's shoulder. He let go of Laura's hand under the table and shifted his glass to an easier spot for his father to reach. When the glass was full, he looked directly up into his father's face. 'Thanks, Dad,' he said. His father stared back at him, and noticing that Laura's attention had been diverted by something Gina was saying to her, Rosco lowered his voice and added, 'Perhaps we could talk later, just the two of us?'

His father blinked. 'Of course.' He then moved on to Charlie's mother's wine glass.

It was the nearest they'd got to a private conversation since that dreadful night, which meant it was the nearest they'd got to referring to the deal Rosco had struck with him – get rid of Katie and he wouldn't tell Mum about Simone Montrose. Hopefully, later in the afternoon, when everyone was once again focusing their attention on Louisa-May, he would be able to have a quiet word with his father, to reassure him that he would uphold his end of the bargain, that he wouldn't breathe a word of his affair. Providing it was well and truly over and that it really had been a moment's madness as his father had claimed.

Until now, Rosco hadn't realized just how much he wanted that to be true. He wanted his parents to be happy. He wanted to see them the way they used to be around each other, relaxed and natural. Laura might think his parents were great and didn't have a care in the world, but to his eye they were a shadow of their real selves. He could see the strain on both their faces. It stood to reason, though: what they'd been through couldn't be rectified overnight, it would take time. But today was a step in the right direction. He was sure of it.

Stirling was watching his family as if through the lens of a camera. Or perhaps more accurately through a telescope but the wrong way round. He felt horribly distanced from everyone.

'He was so disappointed in himself. He'd woken up this morning determined to enjoy himself today. Possibly that had been his mistake. But for everyone's sake, he was throwing what little energy he had into the role of genial host. Despite his efforts, he was convinced it wasn't working, that people could see through the pretence. Surely they knew he was hitting a false note with almost everything he said?

The only place where he felt he could lower his guard and be himself was in the kitchen. He kept making up excuses for being there – taking out the dirty crockery, fetching more wine and soft drinks, or simply checking on his granddaughter.

He was doing that now. Scarlet had placed the car seat containing Louisa-May safely in the middle of the central island unit directly opposite the Aga. She was sound asleep and looked as snug as a bug. Her tiny head was covered with a pink cotton hat that was tied loosely under her chin, and her skin was smooth and creamy-pale and thankfully devoid of all trace of the jaundice she'd had. Her eyelashes were incredible. So astonishingly long. As were her fingers. The rest of her tiny body was swaddled in clothes and a white fleece blanket. Unable to resist the opportunity, and while supposedly stacking the dishwasher with dirty plates, he had taken heaven only knew how many photos of her. He planned to get one of those albums put together online and present it to Scarlet and Charlie when their daughter was a month old – on the date she had been officially due to arrive. One day, when she was older, Stirling would sit down with his granddaughter and go through the album with her. He would tell her how beautiful she had been and how she was the absolute apple of everyone's eye. Little girls loved being told things like that. He'd done the same thing with Scarlet when she'd been small. 'Again!' she would say, her hands eagerly flicking through the pages back to the start of the photo album. 'Tell me again how pretty I was in this picture. Tell me again how much you loved me.'

Filled with a sudden wave of sadness, he bent down closer to Louisa-May. 'Tell me that I've done the right thing,' he whispered, breathing in the sweet milky smell of her. 'Tell me that Katie won't hate me from now on.'

'Hello, Dad. You're not trying to wake her, are you?'

Stirling started. He straightened up and smiled at Scarlet. She looked radiant; motherhood clearly suited her. 'No,' he said, 'just telling her that she has the most beautiful mother in the world.'

Smiling, Scarlet came and joined him. He put his arm around her. 'She's quite perfect, isn't she?' he said.

'I still can't believe she's here. Or that she's mine. Or more amazingly, that anyone thinks I'm to be trusted with her.'

'From what I've seen, you're doing just fine. I'm so proud of you.'

'Thanks, Dad. You know, and this might sound a bit wacky, but I feel as though I've found what I've always been searching for. I've never known what I really wanted to do with my life, and now I do. I want to be the best mother I can. I know some people will think that it's a cop-out, that I'm using motherhood as a reason not to pursue a proper career, but this *is* a career, isn't it? Mum was always happy doing it, so why shouldn't I be?'

'I don't think that sounds at all wacky. I think it's wonderful. But how are you feeling? You seem to have bounced back so fast. You're not overdoing it, are you?'

'I get tired pretty quickly, and I'm a bit sore, but on the whole I'm OK. And it's just so lovely to be out of hospital and at home with Charlie.' She laughed. 'He's completely dotty about his daughter. He talks to her all the time, calls her his little Lulu-May. Do you know what he said to me this morning?'

'Go on, tell me.'

'He said that he's glad I'm normal again. According to him, I turned into the Pregnant Mother From Hell, and was driving everyone crazy. Did I?'

Stirling smiled affectionately at her. 'You were a little zealous maybe, but with good reason.'

She smiled too and nestled in closer to him, tucking herself in under his shoulder, something she had always done, but hadn't in ages. 'I've missed you, Dad,' she said, her voice suddenly sad. 'Ever since Uncle Neil ... and ... and Katie turned up, you haven't been my dad. You've been someone else.'

He swallowed. 'I don't think any of us have quite been ourselves since Uncle Neil's death.'

She turned her face to gaze up to his and gave him a long, searching look. 'Mum told me what you did yesterday. Was it very awful?'

He suddenly couldn't speak. He swallowed again and watched his sleeping granddaughter stretch out the delicate fingers of one of her hands, and then do the same with the other. They'd all seen her do this many times over and it had already become the family joke that she was destined to grow up to be a virtuoso pianist. Funny how no parent ever wanted their child to be an average pianist or an average footballer. Always the expectation was for it to be the absolute best, to reach the pinnacle of high achievement. Was that wrong of parents? Probably it was. It was too easy to categorize children and not see beyond the label. He and Gina had done it themselves with Rosco and Scarlet – Rosco had been labelled the brains of the family ever since he could recite his times tables at the age of five, and Scarlet, well, Scarlet with her fondness for melodrama had been the drama queen. Had they done their children a disservice? Could they have been different people had they not been labelled and treated as such?

'It's all right, Dad,' Scarlet said. 'If you don't want to talk about it, you don't have to.' She looked at her sleeping child and lightly touched Louisa-May's delicate cheek. 'It's just that ... well, having a baby of my own has ... it's made me think differently about all sorts of things, and I really want you to know that I can appreciate now how hard it must have been for you to do what you did yesterday. I don't think I would be strong enough to do it. But don't tell Mum I said that. She'd have a fit.'

His throat constricted, and knowing that his emotions were too raw and too near the surface to carry on with this conversation, he kissed the top of Scarlet's head and said, 'Come on, we'd better get back to the others before we're missed.'

'You go ahead; I need the loo.'

With a heavy heart he reluctantly left the warmth and safety of the kitchen and returned to the dining room, where once again he would have to face his son.

How was he going to repair the damage he'd done to his relationship with Rosco? Could things ever be the same again between them?

Chapter Fifty-two

The drive back to Henley might have had the effect of taking the heat out of another person's anger, but Lloyd was not that other person, and by the time he entered the village of Sandiford, he was fully pumped up and ready to lay waste to the individual responsible for putting him in this mood.

He swung through the gates of Willow Bank and tore up the long drive. He saw and recognized the collection of cars parked in front of the garage block and pulled in behind the Benton-Norrises' Land Rover. So what if Stirling and Gina had company? So much the better! Let them know what Stirling had done. Let them know what a miserable coward he was.

The rain coming down, he rang the doorbell long and hard. Not once. Not twice. But three times.

He could hear voices from the other side of the door. Light-hearted voices debating who the devil it could be and a single voice saying that he would go and see. The voice belonged to Rosco.

The door opened, and Rosco looked at Lloyd with an expression of puzzled bemusement. 'What's with all the hammering on the bell?' he asked. 'It's not like we didn't hear you the first time.'

Lloyd had no intention of humouring his cousin with an answer. Instead he pushed him aside and marched through to the hallway. He stood in the middle of the wide-open space and shouted, 'Uncle Stirling, I want a word with you.'

'Hang on! Just what the hell do you think you're up to?'

Rosco demanded. 'What gives you the right to burst in—'

Lloyd turned on him, a hand raised, his forefinger in Rosco's face. 'Save the self-important act for someone who gives a shit. I'm not interested. Now close the door and get your father's sorry arse here, right now. I'm not leaving until I've—'

'Lloyd, whatever is the matter?'

Lloyd spun round. It was Stirling.

'As if you don't know!' he shouted. 'I'm here about Katie. Your *daughter*. The daughter you're prepared to turn your back on and pretend doesn't exist. The daughter who is a better person than you will ever be. The daughter who has more morality and backbone than you'll ever have.'

The colour drained from Stirling's face. 'Right,' he said. 'I can see you're upset, Lloyd. Now why don't we go into my study and discuss this?'

'Dad, let me throw him out.'

Stirling shook his head. 'No, Rosco. Lloyd's perfectly entitled to an explanation.'

'It's not an explanation I want,' Lloyd said, his voice still raised. 'There's nothing you could say that could make me think you did the right thing.'

'What *do* you want, then?'

'Everything all right here?'

It was Charlie, along with his father and Scarlet, her baby draped over her shoulder. 'What's going on, Dad?' she asked.

'Go back and join everyone else,' Stirling said. 'Rosco, take them back to the dining room, please.'

It was too late. Gina and Rosco's new girlfriend and Charlie's mother had now joined them in the hall. They all stared in puzzled astonishment at Lloyd. All except for Stirling. Because Stirling knew. He knew what this was about. Lloyd looked at his uncle in disgust, daring him to refute the truth in front of everyone.

Then something happened which he hadn't bargained on.

He suddenly felt sorry for Stirling. He could see the pain of regret deeply etched in his face. And seeing that, the fight went out of Lloyd. He had wanted so much to hurt Stirling, but he couldn't go through with it. How could he when there was Gina, stricken to the core, her customary expression of cool politeness congealing on her tired face; Scarlet anxiously clutching her newborn baby; Charlie and his parents just their usual absurdly affable what-in-the-world-is-going-on? selves; Laura glancing nervously at Rosco, and Rosco looking like he might take a swing at Lloyd. But most of all, it was the expression on Stirling's ashen face that held him in check. His uncle was a beaten man and he knew it. And whatever else Lloyd might be, he could not kick a man when he was down.

Moreover, he could not put a slur on his parents' integrity, dead or alive. His mother was the gentlest and most kind-hearted woman he knew, with not a malicious bone in her body. What would she think of him coming here like this? And Katie. She had walked away with her dignity and integrity intact, able to know that in years to come she had behaved with impeccable strength.

But even so, Lloyd had to make his position clear; he had to do that much. 'I just want you to know that because of you, Uncle Stirling, I'll never see Katie again. She's not only left you in peace, just as you wanted, she's left me as well. I don't think I'll ever forgive you for that. And now I'll leave you to get back to your lunch. I'm sorry to have disturbed you.'

'Who the dickens is Katie?' asked Charlie's father in the stunned silence.

'She's no one,' Rosco said bitterly.

The barbed dismissal was too much for Lloyd. He might not be able to bring himself to thump Stirling, but Rosco was a different matter altogether.

The punch landed squarely on Rosco's jaw and before he even saw it coming, causing him to lose his balance and tumble backwards, landing ungainly on his backside, his hand catching against a vase of cut flowers on a console table and knocking it flying.

'She's your half-sister,' Lloyd said, looking down at his cousin on the floor, amidst gasps of shock. 'And don't you ever forget it.'

Rosco got to his feet, making a great play of picking off several stems of roses from his clothes. He squared himself up to Lloyd, as if ready to take him on.

'Stop it!' cried Scarlet tearfully. 'Daddy, make them stop.'

Stirling put himself between the two of them. 'Enough,' he said quietly. 'This has gone too far.'

'Not for me it hasn't,' snarled Rosco.

'Careful,' warned Lloyd. 'You don't want your new girl-friend to see the real you, do you?'

'I said *enough*!' Stirling then turned to face everyone. He focused in particular on Charlie's parents. 'Katie is my daughter from an affair I had thirty years ago. It was a mistake on my part, but I can never describe Katie as a mistake.' He looked at his wife, then at Rosco and Scarlet. 'I'm sorry,' he said, 'but Lloyd is right. I've behaved badly in bowing to your wishes to cut Katie out of our family. I thought I could do it, but I just can't go through with disowning her.' He hesitated.

Could he go on? Yes, he told himself, he had to. Witnessing Lloyd's own act of stoicism, of stepping back from the brink of what he'd obviously come here to do – spoiling for a showdown for the sake of the girl he cared about – was the final nail of shame in the coffin. If Lloyd could behave with such strength of character, then he had to try and match that strength. Or at least come close to it. And it was now or never. He might never find the courage again; he needed this heat-of-the-moment opportunity to make a clean breast of things. If he didn't, he could see no future for himself. Just as his beloved brother hadn't been able to.

He took a deep breath. 'There's more I have to tell you,' he said to the group. 'Gina, this is going to hurt you far more than Katie's appearance in our lives, and it would be easier and perhaps kinder to you if I kept quiet about it, but I can't. Selfishly, I'm putting my feelings before anyone else's, because if I don't, the alternative is too awful to contemplate. The thing is, I—'

'Dad, don't! You don't have to do this.'

Stirling looked at his son. 'Oh, but Rosco, I do. I know we had a deal, but the price is too high. To see it through would take what scrap of respect I still have for myself and crush it completely.'

He went over to his wife and put a hand on her arm. 'I'm sorry, Gina, but I made the same mistake again recently that I did thirty years ago. I stupidly slept with another woman. And not just any woman; it was Simone Montrose.'

'Who the devil is—'

'She was my brother's mistress,' Stirling said with weary patience to Charlie's father.

'Why?' whispered Gina. 'How ... how could you?'

He shook his head slowly. 'I don't know. I really don't know. When you gave me your ultimatum about Katie, I drove around on my own then went to see Simone, and ... it just happened. I never intended it to happen. But it did. And not just once. It's over now. Now I have nothing left to hide from you.'

Her lips trembling and her face deathly white and wreathed with yet more pain and shock, Gina said, 'And you knew, Rosco? You knew and kept it from me.'

'I didn't want you to be hurt, Mum.'

'So you made a trade-off?' Lloyd said quietly. 'Katie in exchange for your silence on your father's affair with Simone?'

'I wanted to keep the family together,' Rosco said. 'And if you hadn't got involved with that bloody girl, it would have worked.' He glanced at Laura, who was staring hard at him. 'I did nothing wrong,' he said. 'Nothing. It was for the good of the family.'

Stirling heard the lack of conviction in his son's voice and felt a pang of sympathy for him. 'I don't blame you for what you did, Rosco,' he murmured, 'but the truth is, I think we've all said and done something wrong. Lloyd,' he went on, 'please tell Katie that whenever she wants to, she can get in touch with me. That's if she still wants to. And ... and you did the right thing in coming here. Don't ever think otherwise, no matter what transpires. Your father would have been proud of you.'

Lloyd got in his car and drove to the end of the drive. The engine idling, he hesitated there. Home, or go and see his mother. With all this rain, she was probably at a loose end and might appreciate some company.

Yes, he would go and see her and tell her first-hand everything that had happened, rather than her hear it from somebody else.

Your father would have been proud of you.

Would he?

Lloyd wasn't so sure. If he hadn't gone to Willow Bank, would Stirling have made that confession?

And just what would his father have thought of Stirling sleeping with Simone?

Stupid question. It would never have happened if his father hadn't died. But hypothetically, what would he have thought? Would he have gone looking for a punch-up with Stirling?

No matter what transpires.

He couldn't begin to think what the fallout would be. Could Gina put a second bombshell behind her?

More important than anything, could he convince Katie that she should continue seeing him? Would she want anything to do with the family? Not if she had any sense, he thought gloomily.

He turned left for The Meadows.

There was no sign of his mother's car, but there was a red two-seater Mazda in front of the garage, which he didn't recognize.

He went round to the back of the house, and as he always

did, he knocked on the door. He had his own key but he refused to use it. He'd told his parents it didn't feel right letting himself in once he'd left home. It was a respect thing.

The door opened, and as if he hadn't had enough shocks that day, he found himself staring into the face of Simone Montrose.

Chapter Fifty-three

'Don't look so worried, Lloyd.'

'Worried doesn't come close, Mum. Are you sure you're all right?'

'I'll survive,' Pen said. 'Now sit down and tell me what you know.'

He did as she said. 'All I know is that Simone found you in the churchyard in a terrible state and brought you back here and put you to bed.'

'Yes, she's been very kind. And I suppose you think that's a ridiculous thing for me to say, because by rights I should hate her. But I don't.'

He gave her one of his soft smiles. 'You're not the hating kind, Mum.'

'Don't you believe it. I came close to it in the churchyard.' She told him about going to church that morning, and then about the little lad's grave and what the teenage boys, who only earlier had been acting out that awful play, had done to it. She could feel her eyes filling and her throat tightening as she remembered how she'd reacted. 'It was terrible, Lloyd. I went berserk at them. I felt such a surge of uncontrollable violence. What really frightens me is that if they hadn't run off, I might have hurt them. I was so angry. I mean *really* angry. I've never experienced such a fury before. It makes me shake to think about it. Look.' She held out her wavering hands.

Lloyd wrapped his own around them. 'It's all part of grieving for Dad. The way he died was a massive shock. It's going to take time for you, for us both, to get over it fully. If we ever do.' He inclined his head towards the door. 'And what about Simone? What was she doing at St Oswald's?'

'What do you think? She'd gone to see Neil's grave. You're giving me that look again.'

'What look?'

'The how-can-I-be-so-reasonable look.'

'No I wasn't. But since you mention it, you are being extra-ordinarily reasonable. I don't think many widows would be as generous as you.'

Pen let go of his hands and shrugged. 'I feel sorry for her. I believe she's lonely. I certainly don't think she deserves our animosity. Forget about all the rights and wrongs of it, the truth is, she loved your father and doesn't know how to go on without him. I can empathize with that. You're giving me another of your looks.'

'Which one is it this time?'

'The there's-something-I-need-to-know look.'

'You're incredible.'

She shook her head. 'No I'm not, I just know you too well. What's wrong? What are you hiding from me?'

'It can wait. For now, I'm more concerned about you resting. You look tired.'

'Tell me, Lloyd. Or I'll only worry. And then I won't be able to rest. By the way, where's Katie? Is she downstairs?'

He turned his head, towards the window, where the afternoon light was fading fast. 'She's gone,' he said.

'Gone where? Back to Brighton?'

He returned his gaze to hers. 'Gone for good.'

'Now I *am* worried. What's been going on? Have you argued?'

'I'm not sure where to begin. One way or another, it's been a hell of a weekend.'

'For heaven's sake, Katie, you really don't expect me to agree with you, do you?'

'But it's true, I'm a malign force when it comes to that

family. That's why I have to stay away.'

'Now you're exaggerating. I'll stand for most things, but not hyperbole.'

'Well bully for you!'

'Don't go taking it out on me.'

'I don't see anyone else round here who's winding me up, so hey, I guess it must be you who's been touched by the Big Mouth Genie.'

'Jog on, girlfriend!'

Katie could count on one hand how many times she and Tess had argued over the years, and the few times it had happened had always been over something trivial, such as her cream leather jacket, which Tess had managed to ruin by spilling red wine over it, or Tess's favourite Ugg boots, that Katie had left out in the rain. But this was different. This really mattered. And Katie couldn't find it within her to climb down, for no other reason than she was right and Tess was wrong.

In the continuing silence – broken only by the sound of Ben hiding in the sitting room watching the telly – Tess suddenly grinned. 'Is this when we have fierce make-up sex?' she said.

In spite of everything, Katie smiled as well. 'Only if you admit that I've done the right thing.'

'Not gonna happen. And I'm not going to apologize for talking to Lloyd.'

'But you and Zac have ruined everything by talking to him.'

'We've been over this I don't know how many times already. Talking to Lloyd was inevitable. And you'll never convince me that it was fair of you to walk away from him without any kind of an explanation. Yes, I'm all too aware that you knew you wouldn't be able to go through with it if you'd had to look him in the eye, but it still doesn't make it right. And so what if he has gone haring off to Henley at top speed to have it out with Stirling? Another inevitability. You can't control other people's behaviour. And I hate to break it to you, you're not in charge of the universe. Not yet, at any rate.'

'Speech over?'

'For now. But start whingeing and I'll come right back at you with some more.'

Katie gaped. 'Whingeing? You think I'm whingeing?'

'Yeah. Lots. Big-time.'

'That's so unfair.'

'So is what you did to Lloyd.'

'Wow! When did Lloyd get to replace me in your affections? When did you switch allegiance?'

'Don't be an idiot. I just feel for the poor guy. And what does it tell you about him that he went looking for you in Brighton at crazy-o'clock this morning?'

Katie crossed her arms defensively. 'It doesn't matter what he feels for me; I'm looking long-term. It won't ever work between us. Me being with him will ostracize him, it'll divide his family and I won't be responsible for people taking sides. Too many would get caught in the crossfire.'

'Romeo and Juliet but without the tights and swordfights, eh?'

'Don't joke about it.'

'I'm sorry. I just think you're not the one to solve the problem. That wretched family has to do that. They need to grow up and sort themselves out.'

'Ever thought that maybe I don't want to be a part of that wretched family, as you so aptly describe it? Why put myself through the bother? They're never going to accept me, so why give them the chance to keep ramming it down my throat?'

'You didn't think it was such a bad thing when you were all loved-up and getting ready to stay with Lloyd. I distinctly recall you on the phone sounding like you were on cloud nine.'

'I wasn't thinking it through. I'd got caught up in the madness. It's been a summer of high emotion, what with finding out Dad wasn't really my father and meeting Stirling and then Lloyd. And don't forget my doubts about getting involved with Lloyd in the first place.'

'The cousin thing?'

'No. That whilst he was still grieving for his father, a relationship wasn't a good idea. I don't want him to do to me what I did to Ian.'

'Again, you're second-guessing him.'

Tired of justifying herself, Katie turned away and looked out of the window at the heavy rain. It was a horribly dismal day. The view from Tess and Ben's second-floor flat – where she used to live – was never good, even on a sunny day, but today it had never looked more depressing. Down on the rubbish-strewn street, cars swished by, their headlights on, although it was only the middle of the afternoon.

She suddenly wanted to be home in Brighton, to hear the gulls screeching, to go for a walk on the beach, to trudge over the shingle and feel the wind snatching at her hair.

Still looking out of the window, she said, 'Summer's over, it's time to get back to reality. I have to chalk Lloyd up as nothing more than a holiday fling.'

She turned round and faced her friend. 'And that's my final and absolutely definitive word on the subject. From now on, I'm going to put all my energy into carving out a new career for myself.'

After everything that Lloyd had told her – about Katie, his going to Brighton and then what had happened at Willow Bank – Pen couldn't remain in bed in a self-absorbed state of inertia a moment longer, despite Lloyd making her promise she would stay put and rest.

Instead, she got dressed and went downstairs. She was surprised to find Simone standing at the Rayburn; she had expected her to leave once Lloyd got here. 'Where's Lloyd?' Pen asked.

'He's gone to fetch your car from St Oswald's, I offered to drive him so he wouldn't get wet, but he insisted the walk would do him good.'

'Did he indeed?'

'I thought you might be hungry,' Simone said, looking at the pan she was stirring, 'I found some carrot and lentil soup in the cupboard.'

'That's very kind of you. Now what's all this I hear about you and Stirling?'

The other woman's jaw dropped. She stopped stirring the soup. 'Oh my God, how do you know about that?'

'I'm afraid everyone knows about it. Well, that's not entirely true, but Stirling's wife and children know. Lloyd has just told me.'

'But how? How do they know?'

'Stirling made a big announcement of it today.'

'Why? Why would he do that? Oh my God, he's not thinking of leaving his wife, is he?'

'Is that what you want?'

'No!'

Pen went over to the cooker. She took the spoon out of Simone's hand. 'I think I'd better take over now, don't you?' She gave the pan a stir, could feel where the soup had just started to stick to the bottom of it. To see better, she switched on the overhead alcove light, and that was when she noticed the donkey. He looked a lot better than when she had last seen him – his legs and tail were properly attached, and he was cleaner.

Simone said, 'Lloyd found your sewing box for me and I had a go at mending the donkey. I gave him a wash, too. I thought the Rayburn was the best place for him to dry out.'

Pen had to take a moment to compose herself. So silly that a toy should upset her. 'Thank you,' she said at last. 'That was a very thoughtful thing to do. I'll take him back to St Oswald's later. When it's stopped raining. Hopefully he won't have been missed.'

'I'm afraid the rest of the toys are beyond repair. Perhaps we could find some replacements.'

Pen stirred the soup. 'I knew it was a mistake for the family to put them there.' She glanced at the donkey; he seemed to be watching her, his head tilted with intense concentration. 'He's got such a sad expression on his face, hasn't he?' she said. 'But then donkeys do. Can you honestly say you've ever seen a cheerful-looking donkey?'

'I can't say I have. Where do you keep the bowls?'

'Over there, the cupboard to the right of the dishwasher. Cutlery in the drawer above.' Pen watched Simone open the cupboard door and locate the bowls, and then some soup spoons. When she had everything and was setting the table, Pen said, 'Why did you really come here today to Sandiford? Was it to see Stirling?'

'You mean did I come here to cause trouble for him?'

'Yes.'

'I'm ashamed to say that in some ways I did. I wanted to tell him exactly what I thought of him.'

'And did you?'

'No, my anger fizzled out. Plus I didn't know where he lived, only that it was this village. As missions of retribution go, it was poorly executed.'

'Why did you want retribution?'

'Call it a cliché, but it was unfinished business. I felt he'd used me and then tossed me aside when he no longer needed me. It wasn't that I was looking for a real relationship with him, but I did expect him at least to behave as a gentleman and let me know when it was over; to have the decency to say the words. But he simply refused to speak to me. He made me feel as if I was desperate and was hounding him.'

Pen lifted the bubbling pan of soup off the hotplate and lowered the lid. 'To be fair, it looks like you did become desperate.'

'Well yes, but only because he wouldn't speak to me.'

'I heard he hasn't been feeling too well; maybe that's why he didn't return your calls.'

'Maybe,' Simone repeated doubtfully.

'And the "using" part of your relationship,' Pen continued. 'You're talking about sex, I presume?'

'It was a release and a relief for us both. I'm not proud of that. And I would imagine neither is Stirling.' She frowned. 'Why do you want to know so much about it?'

'I want to try and understand you. In particular, how you could sleep with my husband and then his brother. For some strange reason I want to think well of you, but I'm having trouble doing so.'

Simone's expression dropped and her shoulders sagged. 'Join the club. Nobody could think less of me than I do myself. I'm not the woman I've become, if that makes any sense. Truly I'm not. Despite all the evidence to the contrary, I don't go around having affairs at the drop of a hat with married men. I tried not to fall in love with your husband, but I did. And I still love him. With Stirling, it was ... it was a means of escape, a way to feel whole again and to stop feeling so alone and isolated. I think also there was a part of me that was angry that Neil had abandoned me, and sleeping with his brother was a way to say, "This is how much you've hurt me by what you've done!"' She closed her eyes briefly. Then: 'If I could turn back time, I would erase what happened with Stirling, but I'm afraid I wouldn't with Neil. If I met Neil all over again, I'd still fall in love with him. Do you hate me for saying that?'

Pen carefully filled the soup bowls. 'No,' she said, 'I don't hate you. I think it was wrong what you did with Stirling, but I think I now understand why. I also admire you for your honesty. Now then, if that's enough soup for you, I'll leave the rest for Lloyd for when he gets back.'

When they were both sitting at the table, Simone said, 'I don't think your son likes me very much. Not that I blame him.'

'Lloyd has problems of his own at the moment. Come on, eat your soup whilst it's hot.'

Simone smiled faintly. 'Somewhere along the line things have become skewed. I was meant to be looking after you.'

'I'm fine now. Maybe I needed that loss of control in the

churchyard. That final cry of anguish. I meant what I said earlier: it was very kind of you to look after me. And to mend the donkey. I think that says all I need to know about you to know that we could be friends.'

Simone looked up from her soup. 'Really? You want to be friends with me?'

'Would you rather we were enemies?'

A cautious smile appeared on her face. 'Friends would be better. Friends would be good.'

'Excellent. So that's that settled. Next I have to find out what's going on at Willow Bank. And then I want to speak to Katie.'

'Katie?'

'Lloyd's girlfriend. Or she was until yesterday afternoon. It's a long story. And one that I'm determined should have a happy ending. His father would have wanted it too. He so loved a happy ending.'

They shot each other a look. They didn't speak, not until they heard Lloyd knocking at the back door.

Chapter Fifty-four

'I knew there was something you were hiding from me,' Cecily said, with a weary shake of her head.

Stirling hated to see his mother look so troubled. In the last forty-eight hours he seemed to have upset everyone he cared about.

'I'm sorry,' he said. 'I've made everything a hundred times worse. But I couldn't keep the lie to myself any longer.'

'I understand that, but it might have been better if you had.'

'Mum, I tried. You must believe me. I wanted to bury it so deep I would never think of it again, but it was tearing me apart.'

'I know, I saw the change in you. I wish you'd told me before now.'

'I couldn't, I was too ashamed. Are you very disappointed in me?'

Cecily looked at him sharply. 'Is that what you're worried about, my being disappointed in you?'

'Aren't you?'

'Don't be so ridiculous! Do you really think I would be capable of condemning you for what you've done when I've lost a son because he dug himself into a hole from which he believed there was no climbing out? My love for you and Neil has never been conditional, and that's not about to change because you've done something stupid.'

'Having an affair with Simone Montrose rates as being a little more than merely stupid.'

'Oh, do stop feeling sorry for yourself! That isn't going to help anyone. Now tell me what you're going to do next; that's far more important than raking over the rights and wrongs of what you did. Have you broken it off with Simone? Or is the relationship ongoing?'

Stirling shook his head. 'It's not ongoing. I've spoken with her and everything has ...' His words trailed off. How to describe his conversation with Simone late last night? Extraordinary was the nearest he could get. Awkward at the thought of speaking to her, but knowing he had to, he had rung her to explain the point he had reached, that things couldn't go on as they were between them. They had spoken for a good half an hour, she saying how upset she had been with him, and he explaining how he'd hit rock bottom and realized the enormity of what he'd done. 'Everything has been resolved between us,' he said eventually to his mother. 'Did you know that she was with Pen yesterday?'

'Yes, Lloyd told me.'

Stirling suddenly couldn't look at his mother. He knew how fond she was of Lloyd and how she felt about Katie. He went and stood at the window and looked down on to the communal gardens of South Lodge. Yesterday's rain had given way to a blue sky patched with ragged white clouds; a blustery wind was blowing. A gardener was hoeing one of the circular rose beds – or he would have been had he not had a mobile pressed to his ear.

'What are you going to do about Lloyd and Katie?'

He turned back to answer his mother's question. 'I've tried ringing Katie but she's not answering her phone. Not for calls or texts. I think she might have put a block on my number.'

'That wasn't what I asked.'

Stirling tried to hold his ground. 'I've told Lloyd to tell her how things now stand.'

'And from what Lloyd says, she's not responding to his calls or texts either. Honestly, Stirling, what were you thinking, letting her walk away? She's your daughter. What's more, she's my granddaughter.'

'You don't need to tell me I behaved badly,' he said tiredly. 'I have to live with the knowledge that I looked Katie in the eye and said goodbye. That I was prepared to go through with what Gina had asked me to do. But I honestly thought it was for the best.'

'The best for you, certainly.'

'For the family. Not just for me.'

Cecily looked at him sternly. 'I can forgive you for sleeping with Simone, but casting Katie aside, that's altogether a different matter.'

'But I didn't in the end, did I?'

'If Lloyd hadn't challenged you, would you have changed your mind?'

He nodded. 'Yes. It might have taken a few days or even weeks for me to admit I'd made a terrible mistake, but I would have done so eventually.' He kept to himself that he also now believed that Scarlet's views regarding Katie had softened, and that if he had her support, he might be able to win over Rosco. He said none of this for fear his mother would think he wasn't brave enough to do the right thing by himself.

'So back to my question. What are you going to do to put things right?'

'I have to go and see Katie.'

'And Lloyd?'

'How receptive do you think he is to talking to me right now?'

'I think the urge to black both of your eyes has passed, but you need to speak to him. As far as I can see, he's serious about Katie and doesn't want to lose her. If he does, goodness only knows if you'll ever be able to make things right between you. Don't look so surprised; you knew perfectly well that you'd have to find a way to placate Lloyd, and that it wouldn't be easy. And yes, you might well think I'm being overly harsh, but I'm just being honest with you. I've never lied to you before and I'm not about to start now.' She paused for breath. 'You look like you could do with a drink. Shall I make us some tea?'

'I'll do it.'

Out in the kitchen, Stirling busied himself with the task of boiling the kettle and placing cups and saucers on a tray. All the time he thought how true to form his mother was behaving. Fiercely honest, but fair. That had always been her modus operandi. If she behaved any differently, Stirling would have cause to worry.

Back in the sitting room, he sat opposite Cecily and suspected that he was in for Round Two. He wasn't wrong.

'Now then, what's the state of play with Gina?'

Where to begin? thought Stirling. The one intractable truth in what yesterday had revealed to him was that when he had been craving for his life to return to how it had been, he had been wishing for the wrong thing. Only now did he have the courage to admit that something had changed in him since Neil's death and Katie's appearance – that it wasn't the security of the past he wanted; it was the unknown: the future. More precisely, he wanted a different future to the one the past had assigned him.

'I love Gina but I'm not in love with her,' he said carefully. 'You may think that that is beside the point at my age, but actually I can't think of anything more *to* the point at my age.'

His mother lowered her cup and stared hard at him. 'Why would you think I wouldn't understand the distinction and the importance of it?'

'Because most people would say I should be thankful for what I have, and that love becomes irrelevant after so many years of marriage.'

'So now you disregard me as being "most people". Really, Stirling, I despair of you. Why on earth would you think that I would expect you to stay married to someone for the sake of merely retaining the status quo? All I want is for you to be happy. I can't say that I've ever been Gina's greatest fan, but until now I've held my tongue because I thought she made you happy. Perhaps I should have spoken my mind sooner.'

Stirling shook his head. 'Sooner wouldn't have been the right time. I'm beginning to think that I needed to be taken to the brink before things became clear to me. I've told Gina I'll make it as painless as I can for her when it comes to the divorce. None of this is her fault. I don't want the good years we've shared to be destroyed by what's happening now.'

'Presumably she doesn't see it quite that way. Has she insisted you move out again?'

'No, she's being remarkably good about it all. I think she's beyond fighting now. She's had enough.'

'And you really think you're doing the right thing in parting? There's nothing that could be done to salvage the marriage?'

'For the first time I feel that I'm doing absolutely the right thing. I keep coming back to the same crucial point: that if I loved Gina as I should, I would never have gone to bed with Simone.'

Cecily tutted. 'There are no shoulds or should nots in a situation like this. You were upset over Neil and behaved entirely out of character.'

'Was it out of character, Mum? Who knows, maybe that was the real me.'

Driving away from South Lodge, Stirling felt better than when he'd turned in at the gate two hours ago, full of dread at what he had to tell his mother.

But now that was behind him. Another hurdle cleared. And even though he knew there were many more ahead of him, he felt more in control and better able to cope. No longer did he feel as if his life was slipping through his hands like quicksilver.

In the last twenty-four hours his brother had been a constant presence in his thoughts, and always those thoughts bounced back and forth between wishing that Neil had found the courage to own up to what he had done, and wondering how he had hidden his state of mind from everyone. Because to all intents and purposes his brother had appeared entirely the same person; there had been no clue as to the desperate point he'd reached. Only Cecily, with her highly tuned mother's intuition, had been aware of a difference in Neil's behaviour. Just as she had noticed there was something wrong with Stirling. Ninety years of age, and still nothing got past her.

He hated knowing that he had put his elderly mother through yet more family turmoil. Only one thing could make amends, and that was to do the right thing for Katie. And to do that, Stirling needed help. He hoped he would find it at The Meadows. But before he asked Pen for help, he needed to explain himself to her with regard to Simone, and more importantly about Lloyd and Katie.

Rosco decided to finish work early. He'd had enough. He unlocked his car and got inside.

It had been a long and tiring day. People were anxious. They had every reason. Rumours were circulating. Not just within the office, but amongst clients. With Stirling absent from the office yet again, everyone wanted to know if he was all right. Rosco had done his best to cover for his father, but it hadn't been easy. Bottom line was, he didn't know if Dad *was* all right.

He pulled out of the car park and rubbed his jaw where Lloyd had punched him yesterday. The sting of his humiliation outweighed any actual physical pain – being hit by his cousin in front of his new girlfriend wasn't the outcome to the day he'd been expecting, but then nor was witnessing his father confessing to his affair with Simone Montrose. Something else he hadn't expected was to feel responsible for that confession. If he hadn't pushed Dad the way he had, maybe it would have stayed buried and forgotten. Wouldn't that have been better than what was going on now?

It had shaken him when both his mother and Scarlet had criticized him for knowing about Dad's affair and using that knowledge to reduce him to breaking point. 'What if you'd driven him to what Uncle Neil did?' his sister had said. He wished whole-heartedly that he hadn't gone looking for trouble by checking on his father's movements. It had been a big mistake. He should have stayed well out of it.

On the up side, Laura hadn't kicked him into touch as he'd assumed she would. She had left Willow Bank minutes after Lloyd had gone, along with Charlie's parents, who had politely excused themselves on the pretext that the family needed to be alone at such a difficult time. Rosco had been sure he'd seen the last of Laura as she drove away.

But not so. She'd texted this morning to invite him to join her for dinner this evening; a simple home-cooked meal, she'd further texted when he'd responded. He was on his way there now. An evening in her company was a hundred per cent preferable to an evening of his own morose company. He had to admit, though, that he was slightly uncomfortable about seeing Laura again. He felt she knew just a little too much about his family. And him. He didn't feel proud of himself right now.

Whilst he hadn't been to her place before, he knew where it was in Henley, and knew that the view overlooking the river was particularly good; he had even contemplated buying one of the apartments in the development himself two years ago. Laura had explained to him that she would never have been able to afford it without her father's help. He didn't know much about her family, other than that her mother and father were divorced, but one thing he was confident of: they had to be a lot more straightforward than his own was proving to be.

Armed with a conciliatory bottle of wine and a bunch of flowers, he took the lift up to the third floor of the modern building and rang Laura's bell. The door opened almost immediately. She looked genuinely pleased to see him. He stepped inside and kissed her on the cheek. 'For you,' he said, 'by way of apology for yesterday. It must have been horribly embarrassing for you. A regular freak show.'

'I think it was more embarrassing for you than me. How's your face?'

He automatically rubbed his jaw. 'It's OK. Worst thing is, I can't joke about how bad the other fella looks.'

She smiled and took him through to the sitting room, which had a large picture window looking on to the river and a sliding glass door leading to a balcony. 'I'm afraid it's too cold to sit outside,' she said when he went over to look at the river.

'That's all right,' he said. 'I can admire the view from here.'

'Well, you do that while I put these lovely flowers in some water. They look very extravagant; I hope you're not expecting me to be some kind of master chef. I did say it would only be a very simple supper. I hope you like shepherd's pie.'

'It's my favourite dish.'

'And you lie so easily,' she said with a smile. 'What would you like to drink? A glass of wine, or maybe a beer?'

'A beer would be great.'

Minutes later she reappeared with their drinks and suggested they sit down. 'It's a lovely apartment,' he said, having had a discreet prowl in her absence.

'I like it, and as I told you, I couldn't have bought it without my father's help with the deposit. Cheers.'

They chinked glasses. 'Tell me about your parents,' he said.

'What do you want to know? How they shape up compared to yours?'

He should have known she would see through an attempted fishing exercise. 'Yes,' he said, 'I suppose I do.'

'In that case, take a good long sip of your beer and brace yourself. Your family has nothing on mine. My father once took a swing at a vicar over a sermon about adultery and nearly got himself arrested for it. You see, Dad considers himself to be something of an expert on the subject, and with good reason. He's been married four times, and the first three all ended in divorce because he couldn't stay faithful. So far so good with wife number four. But maybe that's because he's slowing down.'

'He sounds ... erm ... interesting.'

'Wait till you hear about my eight brothers and sisters.'

'Eight!'

'Oh yes. And there's another on the way.'

'My God! When does your father find the time? Or the energy? How old is he?'

She laughed. 'Old enough to know better! He's seventy this year. And a grandfather five times over. We're having a big party for him in November. All those wives and their new partners and children will be there; it'll be a riot.'

'Do the ex-wives get on with each other, and with the new wife?'

'Amazingly well. But that's largely down to Dad doing his best to look after everyone. He's very generous. Not just with his money, but with his help and support. Just because he falls in and out of love at the drop of a hat, it doesn't make him a bad man. He is what he is. He's human. And just a bit bonkers. But we all love him. We accept him, and each other, for what we all are.' She shrugged. 'Why wouldn't we? Besides, life's so much simpler that way.'

She got up and went over to an occasional table, where there was a framed A4-sized photograph. She brought it back to the sofa. 'There's my family. That's Dad in the middle, and the girl who looks young enough to be his daughter is Natalie, wife number four.'

Rosco studied the photograph. 'She looks the same age as you.'

'She's actually five years older.'

He frowned. 'And you really don't mind?'

'Not a bit. Natalie doesn't alter the relationship I have with Dad. I'm not jealous, if that's what you mean. I've never felt that I'm in competition with anyone for my father's attention, or my mother's for that matter. She's also remarried. Look, that's her there, and that's her new husband.'

When he didn't say anything, she said, 'After what I witnessed yesterday, I gather you're not entirely happy about the idea of a half-sister.'

Rosco rubbed a hand over his chin, then winced. 'It's a long story.'

She put the photograph down on the coffee table in front of them and smiled. 'We have all evening.'

'But I don't want to spoil it by boring you with my family troubles. Especially as I don't think I'll come out of it well. In fact, you may well think I'm a bit of a shit.'

She touched his bruised jaw gently with her hand and then kissed him equally lightly on the mouth. 'I promise you I won't be bored. And as for you being a bit of a shit; who hasn't been one at some stage in their life? But you know what you need right now?'

'What?'

'You need loosening up. And I'm just the person to do that.' She removed his beer glass from his hand and then took hold of his tie. 'This can go, for a start.'

He allowed her to undo his tie and the top button of his shirt.

'Laura?' he said, when later they were lying in her bed.

'Yes?'

'When you said I needed loosening up, did you mean that in a good way?'

'I meant it in all sorts of ways. Mostly I think – and this is based on the little I've so far seen of you, and throwing in a handful of speculation – that you're like one of my stepbrothers: you've spent the greater part of your life in competition with those around you, yourself included, and you need to learn how to channel that energy in a different direction. I also think you take life far too seriously.'

'Bloody hell! What are you, some kind of smart-arse psychologist?'

'No, I'm your smart-arse girlfriend who knows best.'

He smiled. 'And why would you want to be my girlfriend? Why take me on when you see so much room for improvement?'

'Because I'm a sucker for a challenge.'

'What if you've taken on more than you can handle?'

'What if you stop asking so many stupid questions and kiss me?'

He laughed. God, he was glad she'd invited him here tonight. He placed his hands either side of her face and kissed her very deeply; he felt as if a great weight was being lifted from his shoulders. Perhaps she was right: maybe he did take life too seriously. 'What are you doing next weekend?' he asked.

'Nothing in the diary as yet.'

'Good. Let's go to Rome.'

She held his gaze and he could see he had surprised her. Which gave him a nice feeling. 'I bet you take all your girlfriends to Rome,' she said with a raised eyebrow. 'To impress them.'

'Only the really beautiful ones.'

She punched him playfully on the shoulder. 'I'm starving; let's have something to eat. And then you can tell me about your family troubles.'

'Only if you agree to come to Rome with me.'

She sat up and wagged a finger at him. 'Bad negotiating, Rosco.'

'How do you work that out?'

'Because in your head you've already booked the flight tickets and pictured the hotel room where we'll spend hours and hours having amazing sex. It's going to happen whether I agree to your terms or not.'

He smiled and kissed her again. She was right, of course. And about the sex. It would be amazing. Because, as he was beginning to realize, everything about her was amazing.

Chapter Fifty-five

Since leaving London that morning, Katie had spent most of the day working in the garden. Making good the damage of her neglect over these last weeks had given her something to think about other than the events of the weekend. It had also helped her to see her future more clearly.

Now out of the shower and wearing her pyjamas and Minnie Mouse dressing gown, she was curled up on the sofa taking comfort in a mug of hot cocoa and a bag of marshmallows. On the sofa next to her were two photograph albums that contained countless happy memories of her and her parents from a pre-digital era. On her laptop on the coffee table were more recent pictures; most poignant of all, a series of photos taken several weeks before Mum died. They'd been for a walk on the Downs, a place that both Mum and Dad had loved. It was where their ashes had been strewn. They had both said that that was what they wanted when the time came.

Just as she had neglected her mother's garden lately, Katie felt she had neglected the memory of her parents. She had become so caught up in the lives of the Nightingales, she hadn't had Mum and Dad at the forefront of her thoughts. But now, sitting here on her own, she missed them more than she had in a long time.

She took another marshmallow out of the bag and, just as she'd done as a child, dunked it into the mug of cocoa. She knew perfectly well what she was doing, that she was retreating to her childhood, to that happier time when the worst she'd had to worry about was if her mother was going to cook broccoli for tea and make her eat it, a regular tea-table battle of wills. It had been Dad who, in the end, had found a compromise – if Katie ate the floret part of the vegetable, she didn't have to eat the stalk, which was the bit she hated most. Dad had always been good at finding a compromise. Presumably that was why he had been able to bear the weight of Fay's affair with Stirling and accept Katie as his own child. What incredible and unconditional love that must have taken, and how easily his love could have turned to hatred. Knowing that she could not have had a better father, and that she would forever be grateful for his selfless act of love, Katie was determined to follow his example and let the Nightingales get on with living their lives without her as a constant thorn in their sides. If that was what it took for Stirling to be happy again, then so be it.

She reached for another marshmallow and thought how much she would have liked her parents to meet Lloyd. Dad had never been one of those overbearing fathers who had routinely, as a point of principle, disapproved of any boyfriends she had brought home. 'I'm prepared to give the lad the benefit of the doubt,' he would say, 'until proved otherwise.' Mum, on the other hand, had been only too ready to voice her opinion and condemn an unsuitable boyfriend on any number of grounds, such as that his eyes were too close together, his clothes were too scruffy, his clothes were suspiciously too smart, he had too many piercings, he was too quiet, or he was too full of himself. Katie just knew that Lloyd would have met with Mum's total approval.

Leaning forward, she stared at the screen of her laptop. After scrolling through various files of photographs, she stopped at one of her mother. Katie had taken the picture herself, and it showed Mum – her hair messily scooped up on top of her head, the sleeves of her chunky cardigan dangling well past her hands – with a look of intense concentration on her face as she set about redesigning the small garden here. Katie could remember how her mother had been so lost in the moment, she had been oblivious to Katie taking any pictures of her.

She smiled sadly at the memory. She wished her mother was here now to share in the plans she had for herself. Mum would have been full of encouragement and enthusiasm. Dad, too.

This morning in London, and as if the idea had come to her in her sleep, Katie had woken up knowing exactly what she was going to do next. With Ben and Tess rushing around getting ready for work – crashing about in the kitchen and bathroom before coming to a stop in the hall to kiss her goodbye with pieces of toast in their hands – there had been no time to share her news with them. She hadn't minded; her news could keep. She had waved them off, and an hour later she had been on the train for Brighton.

She had needed to be back at home. For all sorts of reasons. One of them was that she wanted to feel closer to her parents. Her father had never lived in this house, but his presence was all around her in the framed photographs she had of him, along with his books and CDs that Mum had kept. And which, in turn, Katie had kept.

There was no question in Katie's mind that Mum had loved Dad, but what she wasn't so sure about was whether she had ever been tempted to tell her about Stirling after Dad had died. In those awful days when they'd been reeling with shock from the suddenness of his death, had Mum ever come close to blurting out the truth? Katie didn't think she would be able to keep such an enormous secret, but Mum, she supposed, had done it because she loved Dad. Perhaps a promise made out of love was far easier to keep than one made out of duty. Wasn't that what Stirling had said he'd done when he'd given in to Fay's terms: he'd agreed to let her go because he'd loved her?

What Katie had done for Stirling on Saturday could not be described as a true act of love, as such, but it came close. She had only known him for a short time, yet she had begun to feel close to him. Seeing him so distressed, and knowing she was the cause of it, had upset her deeply. What else could she do but make the problem go away for him? That he had struggled to make the decision himself was good enough for her; it showed that he did care. It meant that she didn't feel entirely rejected. Disappointed, yes. But not rejected.

Poor Mum. She had written that letter in the hope that Katie would meet her biological father and not feel alone in the world. 'It didn't work, Mum,' she murmured. 'I feel even more alone now.' And it wasn't just because she knew she would never see Stirling again; it was also because of Lloyd. She missed him already. So quickly she had got used to sharing things with him – a joke, a thought or even a whinge. It was the sign of a good relationship, Mum had always said, wanting to share the trivial as much as the important stuff.

She chewed on another marshmallow, then another, and reluctantly pushed Lloyd from her thoughts. It was no use dwelling on him; she would only start crying again if she did. She had to look to the future. And that future lay in a career change. She was going to go back to school to study. What was more, she would use a small part of Stirling's trust fund to finance herself through the course. She had appeased her conscience by coming to the conclusion that to refuse to touch the money would be tantamount to throwing it back in Stirling's face, and that seemed unnecessarily unkind to him. Coincidentally, a letter had arrived in the post today from Howard Clifford, asking her to get in touch about activating the fund. She had rung him immediately and arranged an appointment for later in the week. Next, she had sent off for a selection of brochures and application forms.

She was moving in the right direction, she had told herself when she went out to the garden to do battle with the weeds that had taken over in her absence. It was a shame she would never have the chance to thank the person who had inspired her to go down this route. But again, there was no point in dwelling on that.

She reached for another marshmallow and found that there was just one left; she'd eaten a whole bag. By rights she should be buzzing with sugar overload, but she wasn't. She was bone-weary tired. She drank the last of her cocoa and put the empty mug next to her laptop on the table in front of her. She ran her finger over the mouse pad and the screen sprang to life. No new emails. And no chance that one from Lloyd or Stirling would pop up and take her by surprise – she had put a block on them both. A terrible thing to do, but it was for the best. She had done the same with her mobile, and had deliberately not switched on the answering machine. Hearing Lloyd's voice would be too upsetting. Especially if he was angry with her. Which he had every right to be. She hoped he wasn't angry with Stirling; that he could appreciate the impossible situation his uncle had been in.

She yawned. She should really go upstairs to bed, but she didn't have the energy. She wriggled down on the sofa to get more comfortable and closed her eyes. Just five minutes, she told herself.

'She might not let us in,' Lloyd said, and not for the first time.

Stirling looked at him in the rear-view mirror. 'As I said before, then we'll have the conversation on the doorstep.'

'She might not even open the door to us.'

'She will. What's more, we'll stay there until she does.'

Lloyd thought of the grumpy neighbour he'd encountered early yesterday morning and had visions of the police being called. He also thought how this expedition in Stirling's Aston Marton DB9 had all the makings of a very peculiar road trip.

Squashed in the back with Pen, whilst Cecily rode up front with Stirling, Lloyd kept hoping that Katie really was back in Brighton. At lunchtime today he'd got a call from Tess to say that she had gone home. 'You mustn't tell her I told you, though,' Tess had said.

'But how did you get my number?' he'd asked.

'I sneaked a look at her mobile when she was in the bath last night.'

'I owe you,' he'd said.

'Yeah, you do. Just be sure to keep me out of things. Or at least until you've got it sorted with Katie. Then I'll be happy to take the credit.'

That had been his first surprise of the day. Later, when he'd been locking up the workshop to go home, Stirling had appeared. 'I know you won't want to talk to me, Lloyd,' his uncle had said, 'but hear me out. Please.'

He had. Moreover, he'd agreed to Stirling's plan, that of turning up in Brighton unannounced with both Pen and Cecily. The logic being that Pen and Cecily would be sure to convince Katie that she should listen to Stirling, along with anything Lloyd might want to say. Two grown men using two women, one of whom was ninety years old, to hide behind? Oh, Lloyd was more than happy to do it. The alternative had been for either Pen or his grandmother to ring Katie – assuming that Katie hadn't put a block on every member of the Nightingale family – but Stirling wouldn't listen; he'd said that this way, appearing en masse, would have far more impact and would convince Katie they meant business.

'You OK, Granza?' he said, worried that this might all be a bit much for her.

'I'm as right as rain, Lloyd. Don't you worry about me. In fact I'm rather enjoying myself. I can't wait to see Katie's face. Just make sure you have a winning speech up your sleeve when the time comes.'

Despite the mounting apprehension that was churning away at his stomach, Lloyd smiled. 'I'm not going to give a winning speech with an audience, you know.'

Next to him, his mother put a hand on his knee. 'Stop worrying, it's all going to work out just fine.'

As Stirling followed the directions on the satnav and pulled into Katie's street, Lloyd wished he had his mother's certainty.

The plan was for Pen and Cecily to knock on the door while Stirling and Lloyd stood to one side unseen, and only when Katie had recovered from the shock and invited the women in would he and his uncle reveal themselves.

Helping his grandmother out of the car, Lloyd gave her her walking stick and then rested a hand under her elbow as they walked the short distance to Katie's house in the light cast from the street lamps. It was almost ten thirty, much too late to be making unexpected house calls. What if Katie had already gone to bed and was fast asleep? What then? Would they keep knocking on the door until she woke up?

When they were level with the grumpy neighbour's house, Pen took over from him, and together the two women took the remaining steps. Noting the light glowing faintly through the closed curtains, Lloyd's hopes rose. At least it looked like Katie was at home.

Pen rang the doorbell, and the four of them waited.

Chapter Fifty-six

Gina was thankful for one very important thing: that she had wrested control of this day. Had it been left to Charlie's parents, heaven only knew what hellishness they'd have been in for. Actually, she knew perfectly well what they'd have been subjected to – an afternoon of shivering with cold and avoiding food as edible as old leather boots, only less flavoursome.

Whilst she may have managed to ensure that her granddaughter's christening party wasn't held at Wilton Park, there was no avoiding lunch there on Boxing Day in three weeks' time. Already she was dreading it and planning how many layers of clothing she would have to wear to survive the icy draughts. But she would do it for Scarlet. And for her granddaughter. She would even put a smile on her face.

She scanned the sitting room, checking that everyone had something to eat and drink, that the waitresses from Elite Caterers were doing their job. Over on the other side of the room, next to the Christmas tree, she spotted Rosco and Laura talking to Cecily. Laura had won the old lady's approval – the first of Rosco's girlfriends to do so. More to the point, she was the first to gain Gina's approval. She seemed to be good for Rosco. She appeared to challenge him, yet at the same time anchor him. Gina wouldn't be at all surprised if the relationship became permanent. She had yet to meet Laura's parents, but would do so over New Year at a drinks party in Pangbourne. Laura had described her family as being conventionally unconventional. A short while ago Gina might have raised an eyebrow at such a remark, but now she didn't.

She continued to observe Rosco as he chatted with his grand-mother. Gina couldn't remember the last time she had seen her son look so relaxed. Or so happy. Which troubled her. It meant that he hadn't really been happy before. Something had changed in him since he'd met Laura. But then they'd all changed since June. Since Neil's death, nothing was the same. Even Cecily, who had always been the defining rock-solid constant within the family, had altered. She had aged more in the last few months than at any other time – she had far less energy and moved with increasing frailty. Gina might not have always seen eye to eye with the old lady, but she could accept that the family would be the poorer without her; she would be missed.

'You okay, Mum?'

It was Scarlet.

Gina gave herself an exaggerated little shake. 'I was miles away,' she said. She absently picked off a white thread from the sleeve of Scarlet's dress. 'I was just thinking how happy Rosco looks.'

Scarlet smiled. 'You mean he behaves like he's almost human now. Laura's done wonders with him. Plus he's got what he's always wanted.'

Gina frowned. 'You don't think it's going to prove too much for him?'

'Lord, no. He'll love every minute of it.'

'You're probably right. Where's the guest of honour?'

'Still asleep upstairs; I've just been to check on her.'

'A shame she's missing her own party.'

'She was exhausted. All that crying in church wore her out.' Looking over to the Christmas tree, Scarlet said, 'Thanks again for putting up the decorations. I know how you hate to do it too early. You've always had a thing about that.'

'I think my first grandchild's christening is a worthy exception to the rule, don't you?'

Scarlet laughed. 'Well, I'm going to grab myself something to eat before Lulu-May wakes up. Have you eaten? Knowing you, you haven't, have you? Shall I put a plate together for you?'

'I'll get something in a moment.'

And there's someone else who's changed, thought Gina as she watched her daughter go. As unlikely as it was, Scarlet had at last grown up. Being a mother had been the making of her; it was as if finally she was the person she was always meant to be. During Scarlet's pregnancy, there had been times when Gina had feared that her daughter would grow away from her after giving birth, but the reverse had happened: they had grown closer, as if bonded by motherhood.

Just as instantly and naturally as Scarlet had come to being a mother, so too had Gina taken to being a grandmother. The joy of having Louisa-May in her life – or Lulu-May, as Scarlet and Charlie now called her – could not have surprised Gina more. It was extraordinary how much she enjoyed bathing and dressing her granddaughter, rocking her to sleep, or simply trundling her round the garden in her peculiarly shaped pram. Unbelievably, she had turned into something she would never have imagined possible: a doting grandmother. She had goodness knows how many photographs of Louisa-May stored on her mobile phone, including a few short videos. She also had one of those small granny-boasting albums, which she carried around with her in her handbag, never missing an opportunity to show off her granddaughter.

She was also fiercely protective of Louisa-May, and couldn't bear to see the slipshod and cavalier way Charlie's mother treated her, as if she was nothing more than a puppy. There were times when Gina had to fight the urge to snatch Louisa-May out of Caroline's coarse and careless hands. She never held the baby correctly, and as for hygiene, well, she didn't have a clue. The woman saw nothing wrong in stroking her revolting slobbering dogs and then touching Louisa-May without washing her hands. And as for the ghastly nickname she had given her, Gina despaired. Really, how could anyone call such a beautiful and precious child Spud?

As if knowing Gina was thinking about her, Caroline chose that moment to approach. She was dressed in a horror of a tartan frock that was probably a size too small and made her stout body look stouter still. 'Lovely do,' she bellowed, her face flushed, the plate in her hand piled high. 'Super nosh. But then you always serve up a first-rate feed. Where's Spud?'

Gina recoiled within the silk and cashmere mix of her Karen Millen suit and fixed a smile on her face. 'She's upstairs having a nap. Do excuse me, Caroline, I must see about getting myself something to eat, I'm simply starving.' As rude as it was, she hurried away.

Pen watched Gina move elegantly across the sitting room before coming to a stop to speak to one of the young waitresses. Funny to think that Katie had passed herself off here as a waitress for Cecily's ninetieth birthday party. How things had changed since that appalling night. And how she still missed Neil, especially on a day like today. Well of course she did! What an absurd thought, as if she would ever stop missing him.

All these months on and she could still be taken unawares and reminded that Neil was never walking through the front door again; never again would he call out to her, or ask how her day had gone. It was the silliest of things that could stop her in her tracks and reduce her to tears. Yesterday a holiday brochure in his name had dropped through the letter box. The stark realization that he would never again look forward to a sailing holiday had left her feeling hollow for the rest of the day. He would always be there in her thoughts; she would remember him for the good things he'd achieved, for the happy years they'd had bringing up Lloyd together. For that she would always be grateful. She refused to think of him in any other way. Some would say she was denying the truth of what he'd done, but she didn't see it that way. She knew exactly what he'd done – he'd lied and cheated clients out of their money and slept with another woman – but that didn't diminish the love she continued to feel for him. If people couldn't understand how she felt, that her love was unconditional, that was their problem, not hers. She just wished he'd come to her and explained that he'd met someone else and wanted a divorce. She would have been heartbroken, but at least he wouldn't have got into the mess he had, and more importantly, he'd still be alive.

It didn't happen too often, but if she ever started to feel sorry for herself, she thought of the family whose little boy was buried next to Neil. She couldn't begin to imagine how she would have coped if Lloyd had died at that young age.

The day after she'd broken down in the churchyard, she had spoken to the churchwarden and found out the boy's name and where the family lived. She could so easily have just returned the mended donkey to his grave, but she had wanted to meet the family. Perhaps it was interfering on her part, but she had wanted them to keep the donkey safe, not to leave it at risk of being damaged again.

Eddie and Ros Tate lived on the outskirts of the village, and had been tearfully relieved to be reunited with the donkey – they had been to the churchyard only that morning and had been beside themselves when they'd found that the toys had disappeared. It turned out that the donkey belonged to the boy's sister; she had wanted it to keep Ryan, her brother, company. They were a nice family, but a devastated one. To compound their misery, Eddie Tate had recently lost his job as a builder. Pen's heart had gone out to them. But one thing she had always believed in was that sentiment, no matter how genuine, wasn't enough; practical help was of far more use. What Eddie needed was not her sympathy, but a job, even a temporary one.

And that was when Stirling had come up with his proposition. Of course, it had always been there at the back of her mind, but hearing him actually say the words out loud made everything seem possible and real, and very exciting. From there their ideas just kept on growing, and as Lloyd had

425

said, it was a win-win situation for everyone concerned. She couldn't wait to get going with it all.

In the meantime, they had something looming on the horizon that the whole family was dreading. A date had been set for the inquest: the third week of January. Pen was going to have to stand in front of a jury in court and be subjected to the most awful and intimate questions. She would have to discuss the state of Neil's mind prior to his suicide, their marriage, his affair with Simone, and whether or not she had been a party to the fraud.

Their barristers had warned them that the case could drag on, and that it would be horribly unpleasant. Everything would have to be laid bare; Pen's feelings, or anyone else's for that matter, would not be spared. Stirling would come under intense scrutiny as well. As would Rosco. Other employees of Nightingale Ridgeway would also be called to answer questions. No stone would be unturned. As his mistress, Simone would attract a particularly vile level of prurient interest.

The people Pen felt most sorry for were Lloyd and Cecily. It wasn't fair that they should have to go through this. 'It's not fair for anyone to go through it,' Cecily had said, 'but we'll do it, and we'll provide a strong, united front.'

Looking about her here today, surrounded by the family – Charlie's family too – and friends, Pen could feel the strength of that united front as palpably as the warmth coming from the fireplace where she was standing with Stirling. He looked very much his old self as he added more logs to the grate. He'd told her that for a short while, at his lowest point, he'd lost all respect for himself and had come close to what he'd described as unravelling. For peace of mind, he'd known that he had to come clean about Simone; he couldn't lie to Gina about that. Pen admired him for his honesty. But then she had always admired honesty. Perhaps that was why she had forgiven Simone, and why they had become such unlikely friends. She had made it very clear to the family that when the inquest got under way, Simone was not to be isolated or ostracized. Regardless of what outsiders would think, she was to be part of the united front; they would all stand together.

A flurry of movement had Pen turning to the double doors that led out to the hall. She smiled. Louisa-May, the guest of honour, had finally made her entrance. She was being carried by her proud mother, with her godfather on her right and her godfather's girlfriend on her left. Everyone noticed the group at the same time, and led by Charlie's mother, a cheer went up, followed by a round of applause. As Charlie joined the small group and kissed Scarlet on the cheek, Pen tried not to think how much Neil would have enjoyed this moment.

Lloyd had been astounded when Scarlet had asked him to be Louisa-May's godfather. 'I don't want any animosity,' she had said. 'I want Lulu-May to be part of a happy family, not one at war with itself. I know I behaved badly about your father and about Katie, but I really want to put that behind us. So, I was wondering if you'd like to be Lulu-May's godfather. What do you think?'

'I think I'd be honoured.'

'Really? You're not angry with me any more?'

'As you say, let's put all that behind us.'

She'd given him a small hug and then said, 'I'm genuinely sorry how Rosco and I behaved about Katie before. It was very wrong of us. If she'll accept my apology, I'd like to get to know her. After all, she is my half-sister. And that makes her at least a half-aunt to Lulu-May.'

This conversation had taken place a week after Lloyd had gone down to Brighton with Stirling, Cecily and his mother. When Katie had opened the door, Lloyd had heard her intake of breath, and only when Cecily had said why they were there had he and Stirling shown themselves. The look of astonishment on Katie's face had been a picture. A mental picture he still liked to replay in his head. With the four of them working to persuade her that they weren't leaving until they'd got everything sorted, she hadn't stood a chance. She had put up a valiant show of resistance, but Stirling was having none of it. He was adamant that his mind was made up and that he knew exactly what he was doing, and that now he knew what he wanted, he felt infinitely better.

In the end, when they'd worn her down, Katie had taken Lloyd outside to the garden so they could talk in private. She was dressed in her pyjamas and dressing gown, and he'd tucked her in close to him. He had planned to say so much, but when it came to it he'd got sidetracked by kissing her. And then he'd just blurted out how he felt.

In the early hours of the morning, the journey back to Sandiford had been a lot less tense than the drive to Brighton. Both Cecily and Pen slept for most of the way home, but Lloyd and his uncle had talked, their voices low. They had spoken mainly about Dad, the good stuff, the bad stuff. Not once did Stirling mention Gina and what lay ahead for the two of them. And Lloyd didn't ask.

The first he knew of a family thaw regarding Katie was when Scarlet rang and asked if they could meet up, as she had something important she wanted to discuss with him. It seemed obvious yet overly simplistic to say that motherhood had changed Scarlet, but how else to explain the transformation in her? According to Cecily, it was Scarlet who had talked her mother and Rosco round, asking them to reconsider and accept that it would be wrong for Stirling not to be able to treat Katie as a proper daughter. Apparently she had even said that the three of them were responsible for pushing Stirling to breaking point, and that she personally felt guilty about that.

It was supposition on Lloyd's part, but he had the feeling that Stirling's affair with Simone, as brief and as inconceivable as it was, had overshadowed the whole business with Katie. As Katie had said herself, perhaps she was the lesser of the two evils for them to cope with.

Whatever the truth was, Lloyd felt sorry for Gina; she'd had a hell of a lot to contend with lately. Having everything under control was her default mode, so the last few months must have been a nightmare for her. Looking at her today, though, you'd never guess at what she'd been through, or was continuing to go through. She hid her emotions well. Better than he ever could. But then he wasn't sure he wanted to be that kind of person. He preferred being honest with himself and with others. Which was why he'd laid his cards on the table with Katie; he wanted her to know how much he cared for her, and to hell with any of her doubts about him using her as a crutch whilst getting over his father's death. He knew he wasn't doing that. He knew what he felt, that it was real; it wasn't a passing phase.

Just as he knew that the love and respect he'd always had for his father had not been diminished in any way. Nor would it when it came to the inquest in January. He would stand by his father no matter what. As he hoped Dad would have done for him.

Six months on since his father's death, and rarely did a day go by when Lloyd didn't think of picking up the phone to ring him to get his advice on something, or to chat about nothing in particular, just as they always had. Katie said she regularly had the same reflex with her parents. He liked knowing that she understood; he felt he could share anything with her.

Now that they were alone – Scarlet and Charlie were posing with the baby, whilst Rosco took some photographs of them – Lloyd turned to Katie and slipped his hand through hers. 'Let's get a glass of champagne and go and talk to Granza,' he said.

Stirling looked fondly at his mother. With Lloyd on one side of her and Katie on the other, it was a perfect tableau of a loving grandmother with her grandchildren. Always at the heart of this family, always rock-sure in her love, never blinkered by sentimentality, never afraid to stand up for what was right, Cecily was an exceptional woman. He was glad that Katie was having the opportunity to get to know her. Was it this that Fay had had in mind for her daughter? A sense of belonging?

He had come close to letting Fay down, but thank God he'd done the right thing in the end. The cost had been high, but he didn't regret it. He was beyond regret. Or perhaps not entirely; he regretted hurting Gina. That she had forgiven him to the extent she had showed that she was also an exceptional woman.

'You look very thoughtful.'

He turned to see Gina at his side. She held out a glass of champagne for him. He took it and smiled. 'I was just thinking that this family would be nothing without one very important element.'

'What's that then?'

'Its extraordinary women. Without you, Cecily, Pen and Scarlet, we'd be nothing.'

'It's good to be appreciated.'

'I always did appreciate you, Gina, just not to the extent I now do.'

'I hope you're not going to say that you have to lose something to know its worth; that would be too trite.'

'It's true, though.'

Her expression softened. She held her glass up to his. 'Well, here's to being appreciated. As friends.'

'*Good* friends,' he added.

She nodded. 'As good friends,' she repeated.

They each took a sip of their champagne, and then Gina said, 'Won't you miss the office when you step down?'

He shook his head. 'Not really. Working reduced hours as I have been these last few weeks, I feel even readier to leave. It's time for me to go. Better for Rosco as well.'

'You're sure he's ready to take over? These are difficult times.'

'It doesn't matter what I think. It's what Rosco thinks that counts. But I have evry confidence in him meeting the challenges ahead.'

'He'll still feel the need to prove himself to you, you realize that, don't you?'

'Of course, and to do that he'll want to make the firm bigger and better. I've decided that just as soon as the court case is over, I'll resign. I won't hang around. I'm looking forward to getting stuck in with the plans Pen and Katie have come up with for The Meadows. It's a long time since I felt so excited about something. How about you? Do you have any plans?'

She laughed. 'I'm enjoying being a full-time grandmother too much to think about doing anything else. But I have decided not to sell this house, once we're divorced.'

'I thought you were set on doing that?'

'Thanks to Scarlet, I've had a rethink. Odds on there'll be more grandchildren to come, and Willow Bank is ideal for having children to stay. And for hosting occasions like this.'

'I'm glad you've changed your mind. I hated the thought of you leaving here. The house is yours; you made it what it is.'

She suddenly looked serious. 'Perhaps I should have put as much effort into our marriage.'

He laid a hand on her arm. 'Don't say that.'

'What if it's true? I've talked about this with Pen. She's adamant that she let things slide with Neil, that she kidded herself he was happy with the way things were because that's what she wanted to believe. All along I thought that she was being weak and pathetic, but I can see that I underestimated her, that I always have. It took courage for her to admit her part in Neil having an affair. She could so easily have played the victim card, but she didn't. Something I'm guilty of doing.'

'No,' he said firmly. 'You mustn't think that. Our situation was different to Pen and Neil's. I acted badly. There's no excuse for what I did.'

'Do you really believe that, or are you trying to make me feel better? I've noticed you doing a lot of that lately. There's no need, you know. I'm strong enough to face up to the truth. I just wish I'd done it sooner; it might have saved us both a lot of misery.' Without giving him a chance to respond, she said, 'Well then, I'd better circulate and make sure everyone is having a good time.' Her tone was brisk and businesslike.

Stirling watched her walk away, her movements as fluid and distinct as ever. In recent weeks, every so often he would catch a glimpse of a woman he didn't really know – a refreshingly honest and vulnerable Gina – and then, just as she had now, the old Gina surfaced and took over, her hand firmly on the tiller of her emotions once more.

As he'd explained to his mother, he still loved Gina, he just wasn't in love with her. He'd never set out to hurt her, but he had, and that was why he was trying to make everything as easy as he could for their divorce. To his surprise and relief, she was making things easy for him too. She had told him that so long as he played it straight, she didn't want to fight him. 'What's the point?' she had said. 'I don't want us to end up hating each other. But I do know I can't stay married to you. Not now. Not after Simone. I still don't understand how you did that, and doubt I ever will. What I do understand, and accept, is that for you to do that, I had already lost you.'

At Pen's suggestion, Stirling had recently met up with Simone at The Meadows. 'You both need to talk face to face about what happened,' she had said. 'Unfinished business is what they call it, I believe.' What an extraordinary woman Pen was. Some would say she was too forgiving for her own good, but he disagreed; the world needed more people like her. She had been right, of course. Talking to Simone over a cup of coffee in Pen's kitchen had given them both the chance to explain what they'd done and the reasons why. They had gone to the churchyard at St Oswald's afterwards and apologized to Neil; neither of them believed for a single second that he was there, but it felt symbolic. And apposite.

For the last two months Stirling had been renting a two-bedroom apartment in the same building as Rosco's girlfriend. He had settled in well to his new pared-back lifestyle and had been invited several times now to join Rosco and Laura for dinner at Laura's. She reminded him a little of Katie, in that she was practical and cut straight to the chase. 'Laura's doing a fine job of smoothing away Rosco's rough edges,' Cecily had said to Stirling in church earlier that morning. 'Let's hope he has the sense to realize that she's a keeper.' Stirling hoped so too. He wanted Rosco to be happy. But then he wanted everyone to be happy.

Across the room he heard John, Charlie's father, say, 'Come on, everyone, nice and close. That's it. Move in a bit there, Rosco. That's it. Perfect.' At the centre of a group photograph was Cecily with her great-granddaughter in her arms. Gathered around her were Scarlet and Charlie, Rosco and Laura and Lloyd and Katie. 'Smile!' John instructed them.

And everyone did. Stirling might have been imagining it, but even Louisa-May, her tiny hands flexing in the air, seemed to manage a perky little grin.

Chapter Fifty-seven

'It feels almost cold enough to snow,' Katie said when they left the party and got into Lloyd's car.

'Snow would be good. Mind you, a white-out blizzard would be even better. It would mean you definitely wouldn't be able to leave tomorrow morning.'

Katie looked at Lloyd but she didn't say anything. Neither of them liked it when she had to go back to Brighton. She used to leave on a Sunday evening, but then they slipped into the routine of her staying the extra night and getting up early the next morning so she could arrive in time for her ten o'clock lecture.

'What?' he said. 'You don't fancy the idea of being snowed in with me?'

She smiled. 'I like the idea too much.'

He smiled back at her. 'Me too.'

'Eyes on the road, mister, or we'll end up in a hedge.'

'Yes, ma'am.'

They'd only driven a short distance when his face turned serious and he said, 'Do you mind if we stop off somewhere before going home?'

She liked it when he used the word *home*. 'Of course not,' she replied.

He parked the car and took her hand as they crossed the road to St Oswald's. With the moon hidden by a cloud-filled sky, the churchyard was in total darkness and they had to pick their way carefully along the gravel path.

They stood beside Lloyd's father's grave; fresh flowers had been carefully arranged in a pot in front of the headstone. Katie knew that Pen came every week. She knew also that Lloyd didn't. She had wondered this morning when Louisa-May's christening had finished if he would want to visit the grave before going on to Willow Bank, but he hadn't. He'd told her once before that he didn't like it here, that he didn't feel any real connection. But he was here now. With her. His grip on her hand tightened and she saw that his eyes were closed.

When he opened his eyes, he turned to face her; he took hold of the ends of her scarf and gently pulled her towards him. His arms around her, they stood very still. It wasn't the time for words. Resting her cheek against the expensive soft wool of his coat – his father's coat that Lloyd had kept, along with Neil's treasured Patek Philippe watch – she reflected how dramatically their lives had changed in the last six months. Lloyd could never have predicted the way in which his father would die, and she certainly would never have foreseen the consequences of coming here to Sandiford.

She thought of the night in Brighton when she had been woken by the ringing of the doorbell, and how, when she had cautiously opened the door, she had found Cecily and Pen on the step. And then Stirling had appeared, followed by Lloyd. One look at Lloyd's anxious face and his hands pushed deep into his pockets, his shoulders hunched, and her heart had all but bounced out of her ribcage. They had swarmed into her house like a SWAT team, leaving her in no doubt as to why they'd come, and that they wouldn't leave until she had seen sense. 'It's not fair to do this to me when I'm half asleep and in my pyjamas,' she had pleaded in vain, at the same time wanting to giggle at the absurdity of it all.

'This is a take-no-hostages situation,' Stirling had said. 'I want you in my life as a daughter, a real daughter and properly recognized as such, and Lloyd wants you—'

'I can speak for myself,' Lloyd had interrupted, his blue

eyes fixed on hers with that frank and questioning stare of his. But he didn't speak, not until they were out in the garden, just the two of them. He had kissed her for the longest time, and when they'd finally parted, he'd said that he loved her. He'd looked as surprised to say the words as she was to hear them. Her chest had suddenly felt so tight she had struggled to breathe. 'You're not saying anything,' he'd added.

'I'm too shocked.'

'That sounds bad.'

'No, it's good. Very good.'

'That's a relief. I thought I might have just messed up.'

Now, as the icy cold seeped through her coat, she pressed in closer to him.

'I wish you'd had the chance to meet my father,' he said quietly. 'The man he really was.'

'I wish I had as well, and that you'd met my parents.'

Another moment of silence passed, and then Lloyd tugged on her scarf. 'Come on,' he said. 'Let's go home.'

That word again: *home*.

Changed out of their grown-up clothes – as Lloyd had referred to his seldom-worn suit and her dress – and lying on the sofa in front of the log fire, Katie lifted her head from Lloyd's chest. He opened his eyes. 'I thought you were asleep,' she said.

He stroked her hair away from her face. 'I was pretending. I was waiting for you to nod off, and then I was going to sneak outside and disable your car.'

'Now why would you do a mean thing like that?'

'Because I don't want you to leave in the morning.'

'But I have to go.'

'Doesn't mean I have to like it.' He shifted her off him and stood up. 'I'm hungry. Party food never satisfies. How does a chicken tikka masala sound to you.'

'It sounds delicious. I'll come and help you.'

'I think I can manage to ring for a takeaway on my own.'

She affected a look of disappointment. 'And there was me thinking my man was going to cook for me.'

'And there was *your* man thinking he was going to strip you naked and make love to you in front of the fire whilst we waited for the food to arrive.'

'Ooh, I like that idea.'

He shrugged. 'Like I say, I was only thinking about it.'

'We'll see about that.'

An hour later, when the delivery man knocked on the door, Lloyd hurriedly pulled on his jeans and went out to the hall. Katie stayed where she was on the rug in front of the fire and covered her body with the throw from the sofa. How tempting it was to stay here for ever, just as Lloyd wanted, but she couldn't. Not yet. She had to complete the garden design course she had started in Brighton; then in the summer, next year, when she had sat her exams, everything would change. She couldn't wait.

The Meadows was being turned into a fully fledged business concern with Stirling and Pen at the helm, and she would be a part of it. In the spring, and for six months of the year, the garden would be open to the public every Friday and weekend. Planning permission had been granted and Eddie Tate was in the process of converting and extending the outhouses into a café. At Stirling's suggestion, and with Pen's full approval, Katie would be in charge of running a small on-site nursery so that visitors could buy plants just like the ones growing in the garden. Katie had had no idea, but the land adjoining The Meadows, to the left of the house, had always belonged to Lloyd's family; they just had never had a use for it before. Now it would be where the nursery would be created, along with space for cars to park. As well as being in charge of the nursery, Katie would offer her services as a garden designer. She doubted she would earn as much as she had at Stella Media, but the happiness she felt at being a part of something new and exciting far outweighed the drop in salary. And who knew how things would progress?

Learning all that she could from Pen, she was soaking up in-depth horticultural knowledge fast. Any free time she had, she would spend poring over the books Pen had lent her. Tess and Ben and Zac kept saying they couldn't recall seeing her so happy. 'One part intellectually fulfilled and two parts carnally satisfied,' Zac teased her. 'It's the perfect combo and makes for a very happy Katie.'

Out in the kitchen, Katie could hear Lloyd humming to himself as he put the delivered food into the oven to make sure that it would be hot. He detested lukewarm food; it was one of his pet hates.

Her thoughts returned to The Meadows, and in particular to Stirling, who had carried out hours of online research as to how other gardens that were open to the public operated. He was coming up with all sorts of ideas, such as offering guest-lecturer days and specially guided tours. He also wanted to use the garden to better promote Lloyd's outdoor furniture.

Lloyd had always had a few pieces of his furniture on view at The Meadows – it was what his mother used on a daily basis – but Stirling wanted to give his new range more prominence, to showcase it properly. Lloyd wasn't so enthusiastic. He said that a dramatic increase in orders would mean that he would be too stretched and he'd have to employ a third person in his workshop. He said he wasn't convinced he wanted to do that; he was happy as things were. Katie liked that in him; that he was not only so content, but that he was fully at ease with what he had and who he was. In that respect, he reminded her of her father. Her *real* father. She didn't mean that unkindly to Stirling, but Dad would always be Dad to her, and Stirling would always be Stirling. There was no ambiguity.

Which couldn't be said of her relationship with Scarlet and Rosco. There was no hostility between them these days, but having been an only child all her life, it felt weird trying to think of them as her brother and sister. Genetically linked as she was to them, she had yet to detect anything of herself in either of them. Of the two, she found Scarlet the easier to get on with, but maybe that was because she knew it was Scarlet who had been the first to support Stirling and accept Katie as her half-sister.

'Hey, who do you think you are, lying there on the floor in a wanton state of erotic undress when there's food to be eaten?'

She turned to look at Lloyd as he stood in the doorway in only his jeans. Her heart lurched. The sight of his strong, beautifully defined body never failed to have an impact on her. There were moments, such as now, when she could look at him and be so overwhelmed by her feelings, she felt tearfully euphoric.

In the heat of the moment, back in June after she had read her mother's letter, she had set out to find her biological father to discover who she really was. It hadn't crossed her mind that she would end up falling in love as a result. But she had. And not just any old falling in love. This was the real thing. With absolute conviction she knew that she belonged with Lloyd. With his family, too. *Her* family, as he frequently reminded her.

She sat up. 'I don't know,' she said, as he came towards her. 'You tell me who you think I am.'

His blue eyes intense, he knelt on the rug in front of her. 'That's easy,' he said with great solemnity and letting his warm lips touch hers lightly. 'You're the girl I love.'

She slipped her arms around his neck and kissed him.

Six months ago, she had questioned who she was. Yet the answer had been staring her in the face all along: she was the same Katie Lavender she had always been.

Just infinitely happier now.

Marianne Fredriksson
Simon

Marianne Fredriksson

SIMON
Roman

Aus dem Schwedischen von
Senta Kapoun

Wolfgang Krüger Verlag

2. Auflage August 1998
Die Originalausgabe erschien 1985 unter dem Titel
»Simon och ekarna«
im Verlag Wahlström & Widstrand, Stockholm
© 1985 by Marianne Fredriksson. Published by agreement with
Bengt Nordin Agency, Sweden
Deutsche Ausgabe:
© 1998 Wolfgang Krüger Verlag GmbH, Frankfurt am Main
Satz: Wagner GmbH, Nördlingen
Druck und Einband: Clausen & Bosse, Leck
Printed in Germany 1998
ISBN 3-8105-0635-4

Für Ann

I

Eine von oben bis unten gewöhnliche Eiche«, sagte der Junge zu dem Baum. »Knapp fünfzehn Meter hoch, was zum Angeben nicht gerade viel ist.«

»Und hunderttausend Jahre bist du auch nicht alt. Vielleicht so ungefähr hundert«, schätzte er und dachte an seine Großmutter, die fast neunzig und auch nichts weiter als eine ganz gewöhnliche unzufriedene alte Frau war.

Benannt, vermessen und verglichen verlor der Baum an Großartigkeit für den Jungen.

Aber dennoch konnte er in der mächtigen Krone ein wehmütiges und vorwurfsvolles Rauschen hören. Da blieb ihm nur Gewalt, und er schlug den großen Stein, den er schon lange in seiner Hosentasche mit sich herumtrug, fest in den Stamm.

»Das hast du davon, und jetzt schweig«, brummte er.

In diesem Augenblick wurde der große Baum still und der Junge, der wußte, daß etwas Wesentliches geschehen war, schluckte den Kloß im Hals herunter und achtete nicht auf seine Trauer.

Es war der Tag, an dem er Abschied von seiner Kindheit nahm. Er tat es zu einer bestimmten Stunde und an einem bestimmten Ort, und deshalb würde er sich immer daran erinnern. Und viele Jahre lang würde er darüber nachgrübeln, was es gewesen war, worauf er an diesem Tag in dieser sehr fernen Kindheit verzichtet hatte. Mit zwanzig sollte er eine Ahnung davon bekommen, und von da an würde er sein Leben lang versuchen, das Verlorene wiederzufinden.

Doch jetzt stand der Junge auf dem Felsen hinter Äppelgrens Garten und sah aufs Meer hinaus, wo sich der Nebel zwischen den kleinen Inseln verdichtete, um sich dann langsam auf die Küste zuzuwälzen. Im Land seiner Kindheit hatte der Nebel viele Stimmen, von Vinga bis Älvsborg sangen an einem Tag wie diesem die Nebelhörner.

Hinter sich hatte er den Berg und die Wiese mit dem Land, das es eigentlich nicht gibt. Am Ende der Wiese, wo der Boden tiefer wurde, lag der Eichenwald, dessen Bäume all die Jahre zu ihm gesprochen hatten.

In ihrem Schatten war er dem kleinen Mann mit dem seltsamen runden Hut begegnet. Nein, dachte er, so war es nicht. Er hatte den Mann immer gekannt, aber im Schatten der Laubbäume hatte er ihn auch gesehen.

Das konnte ihm jetzt gleichgültig sein.

»War alles nur Quatsch«, sagte der Junge laut und kroch unter dem Stacheldraht von Äppelgrens Zaun hindurch.

Er entging der Frau, Edit Äppelgren, die an einem Vorfrühlingstag wie diesem aus schnurgeraden Beeten Unkraut zu reißen pflegte. Die Nebelhörner hatten sie ins Haus getrieben, sie vertrug keinen Nebel. Der Junge verstand das. Der Nebel war die Trauer des Meeres und ebenso unendlich wie das Meer. Eigentlich unerträglich …

»Quatsch«, sagte er dann, denn er wußte es ja besser, hatte er doch soeben beschlossen, die Welt so zu sehen, wie andere Leute sie sahen. Der Nebel war die Wärme des Golfstroms, die in den Himmel stieg, wenn die Luft sich abkühlte.

Das war alles.

Aber so ganz konnte er die Traurigkeit, die im langgezogenen Heulen der Nebelhörner an der Hafeneinfahrt lag, nicht abstreiten, als er Äppelgrens Rasen überquerte und zu Hause in die Küche schlüpfte. Dort bekam er heiße Schokolade.

Er hieß Simon Larsson, war elf Jahre alt, klein von Wuchs, mager und von etwas dunklerer Hautfarbe als andere. Seine Haare waren borstig, braun, fast schwarz, und die Augen so dunkel, daß es manchmal schwierig sein konnte, die Pupillen zu erkennen.

Das Andersartige an seinem Aussehen war ihm bisher nie aufgefallen, denn bis zu diesem Tag waren ihm Vergleiche kein Anliegen gewesen, und er war dadurch vielen Qualen entgangen. Er dachte an Edit Äppelgren und ihre Schwierigkeiten mit dem Nebel. Aber vor allem dachte er an Aron, ihren Mann. Simon hatte Aron immer gern gemocht.

Als Junge war Simon ein kleiner Ausreißer gewesen, eines von diesen Kindern, die wie übermütige junge Hunde den Lockungen der Landstraße erliegen. Es konnte mit einem grellbunten Bonbonpapier im Straßengraben vor dem Zaun beginnen, mit einer leeren Zigarettenpackung weitergehen, und dann lag irgendwo eine Flasche und dann noch eine, und dort blühte eine rote Blume und weiter weg lag ein weißer Stein und dann tauchte vielleicht schattenhaft irgendwo eine Katze auf.

So kam es, daß er sich weiter und weiter von daheim entfernte, und er erinnerte sich sehr deutlich daran, wie ihm bewußt wurde, daß er verloren war. Das war, als er die Straßenbahn erblickte, groß und blau auf rumpelnder Fahrt aus der Stadt heraus. Er war fast von Sinnen vor Schreck, aber genau in dem Augenblick wo er den Mund öffnete um zu schreien, stand Aron vor ihm.

Und Aron beugte sich mit seiner langen Gestalt über den Jungen und seine Stimme kam wie aus dem Himmel als er sagte:»Guter Gott, Junge, willst du schon wieder ausreißen.«

Dann hievte er Simon auf den Gepäckträger seines schwarzen Fahrrads und begann heimwärts zu gehen. Er sprach von den Vögeln, von dem dicken Buchfinken und den geschäftigen Kohlmeisen und von den Spatzen, die im Staub der Landstraße ganz in ihrer Nähe herumhüpften. Für sie hatte er nur Verachtung übrig, fliegende Ratten, sagte er.

Im Frühling gingen sie zusammen über die Weiden und der Junge lernte das Lied der Lerchen erkennen. Danach sang Aron mit dröhnender Stimme ein Lied, das die Hänge bergab rollte und als Echo von den Klippen zurückkam:»Wenn der Früüühling in den Bergen ...«

Am schönsten war es, wenn Aron pfiff. Er konnte jeden Vogelruf nachmachen, und der Junge platzte fast vor Spannung, wenn Aron das Amselweibchen zum Antworten brachte, sehnsüchtig und willig. Dann grinste Aron sein breites, gütiges Grinsen.

Nun war es aber so, daß das Vogellied, das alle anderen zwischen den Felsen dort an der Flußmündung übertraf, das Schreien der Möwen war. Aron konnte auch sie nachmachen, und es kam vor, daß er sie bis zum Irrsinn reizte und sie sich wütend auf den Mann und den Jungen herabstürzten.

Da mußte Simon so sehr lachen, daß er fast in die Hose gemacht hätte. Auch die Nachbarn, die auf dem Weg geschäftig vorbei eilten, blieben stehen und verzogen den Mund über den großen Mann, der ebensoviel Spaß hatte wie der kleine Junge. »Aron wird nie erwachsen«, sagten sie.

Aber das hörte Simon nicht. Bis zu diesem Tag war Aron in seiner Welt König gewesen.

Jetzt saß der Junge am Küchentisch vor seinem mehr als süßen Kakao und sah Aron so, wie andere Leute ihn sahen. Begriff vor allem, daß die seltsame Fähigkeit des Mannes, ihn, Simon, zu retten, wenn er sich als kleiner Junge verlaufen hatte, mit Arons Arbeitszeiten zusammenhing. Simon war nach dem Frühstück ausgerissen, Aron hatte zumeist erst in den Morgenstunden Arbeitsschluß und war gerade aus der Straßenbahn gestiegen, als der Junge an der Haltestelle ankam und feststellen mußte, daß er sich verlaufen hatte. Aron hatte dort sein Fahrrad stehen und, wie es eben so war, stand manchmal auch dieses merkwürdige Kind dort, das sich so oft verirrte.

Plötzlich sah Simon die Verachtung, das schiefe Grinsen und die abgehackten Worte, die Aron seit jeher von sich gegeben hatte. Er war Rausschmeißer in einer schlecht beleumundeten Hafenkneipe und hatte einen Spitznamen, den Simon nicht verstand, der aber so gemein war, daß seine Mutter, wenn sie ihn hörte, vor Ärger rot anlief.

Simon mußte wiederum an Tante Äppelgren denken, die dauernd saubermachte und eine so feine Küche hatte, daß er dort nie hineingehen durfte. Er glaubte zu verstehen, daß man Küche und Gartenbeete so adrett halten mußte, wenn man einen Mann mit einem widerwärtigen Spitznamen hatte, der die Frauen erröten ließ.

Als Simon das letzte Stück Hefebrot gekaut und die Kakaotasse mit dem Löffel ausgekratzt hatte, dachte er, daß Aron den Schritt nie getan hatte, den er heute vollzog. Aron Äppelgren hatte nie auf einem Felsen gestanden und Abschied von seiner Kindheit genommen.

Die Küchenbank diente dem Jungen als Bett. Das ließ ihn zum Sozialisten werden.

Es war eine geräumige Küche, sonnig, mit großen Sprossenfenstern nach Westen und Süden, mit weißen Gardinen, Topfpflanzen drinnen und alten Apfelbäumen draußen. Unter dem Südfenster befand sich das eingelassene Zinkbecken mit dem Kaltwasserhahn, in der Ecke gegenüber stand der eiserne Herd und daneben die Holzkiste mit dem zweiflammigen Spirituskocher darauf. An der langen Wand unter dem anderen Fenster nahm die Küchenbank ihren Platz ein, blau gestrichen wie die Stühle, und davor stand der große Küchentisch mit dem Wachstuch am Werktag und einer bestickten Baumwolldecke an den Sonntagen.

Kochfleisch, häufig Suppe. Kaffee. Selbstgebackenes, gute Düfte am Mittwoch, wenn das weiße Hefebrot aus dem Ofen kam. Nachbarschaftsklatsch. Man konnte jedes Wort von der Holzkiste aus in sich aufsaugen, wenn man sich klein und unsichtbar machte, die endlosen Gespräche über all das, was um ein Haar hätte passieren können, oder wer ein Kind erwartete und wer einem leid tun mußte.

Es konnten einem viele leid tun, eigentlich sogar alle. Der Junge lernte Mitleid zu haben anstatt Abneigung zu empfinden. Dadurch kam ihm der Zorn so frühzeitig abhanden, daß er eigentlich nie damit umgehen lernte. Es gab ihn, manchmal versuchte er in seinem Leben einen Aufschrei, aber immer zu spät und immer an der falschen Stelle.

Er wurde ein lieber Junge.

Er selbst hatte es gut, das brachte man ihm früh und so gründlich bei, daß er im Verlauf der Jahre nie auf die Idee gekommen wäre, sich selbst leid zu tun.

Da gab es diesen Hansson, der arbeitslos war und aus diesem

Grund seine Frau jeden Samstag schlug, wenn er seine Schnapsration zugeteilt bekommen hatte. Da war Hilma, die zwei Töchter im Sanatorium hatte, und deren Jüngste bereits an der Schwindsucht gestorben war. Und dann war da Anderssons schöne Tochter, die immer neue Kleider trug und in der Stadt auf den Straßen herumging.

Aber als die Nachbarn dahinterkamen, was sie auf den Straßen machte, warfen sie den jungen Mann, der bei ihnen wohnte, hinaus. Die Frauen hatten Angst vor unehelichen Kindern.

Die Männer waren anders. Das war das Schöne am Schlafen auf der Küchenbank. Am Abend saßen die Männer in der Küche, Bier statt Kaffee, Politik statt Gerede über allzu Menschliches, und dann dieses verdammte Auto, das wieder seine Mucken hatte.

Anderssons hatten ein Fuhrunternehmen, aber das hieß nur, daß sie ein Lastauto besaßen. Es beförderte tagsüber Holz zu den Baustellen im Umfeld der wachsenden Stadt. Und Lebensmittel für die Haushalte. Nachts wurde es repariert, denn die Lager holperten, und die Ventile mußten immer wieder nachgeschliffen werden, und das Getriebe war auch schon fast hinüber.

Sachkundig waren sie beide, der Vater und der Onkel. Sie wechselten aus, schmiedeten und fertigten neu. Die Freude war groß, als sie eines Tages einen sechszylindrigen Motor als Ersatz für den alten ausgeleierten vierzylindrigen ergatterten. Aber der Tausch zwang sie dazu, die Kardanwelle zu verlängern, wofür sie ein zusätzliches Kreuzgelenk brauchten. Da sie hartnäckig an der bewährten Zahnradübersetzung festhielten, hatten sie bald ein Auto, das die steilsten aller steilen Straßen der Stadt hinauftuckern konnte. Und das sogar bei Glatteis.

Das Auto war mit der Zeit fast bis ins kleinste Detail von Hand gefertigt. Zwar stand Dodge auf der Kühlerhaube, aber man konnte sich fragen, ob wesentlich mehr als die prächtige rote Karosserie noch aus Detroit stammte.

Sie machten jeden Abend um zehn Uhr mit einer Flasche Bier und den Spätnachrichten im Radio, das auf einem Schemel am Fußende des Küchensofas stand, eine Pause. Am Kopfende lag Simon unter einem rosafarbenen Zelt, einem Stück rotweißkariertem Stoff, das zwischen der Klappe und der Rückwand des Sofas gespannt und an den vorderen Füßen eingehakt wurde, wenn der Junge sich hingelegt hatte und man davon ausging, daß er schlief.

Auf diese Weise erfuhr er von dem Schreckgespenst, das aus dem Herzen Europas herankroch und Hitler hieß. Manchmal hörte man diesen Hitler persönlich im Radio brüllen, und die Deutschen schrien ihr Heil, und danach sagte der Vater, daß früher oder später alles beim Teufel sein werde und bald alles nur noch ein Scherbenhaufen, was die Arbeiter und Per Albin aufgebaut hatten.

Einmal kam ein Mann mit einer Sonderanfertigung handgeschmiedeter Muttern, er habe sie aus reiner Herzensgüte angefertigt, sagte die Mutter, nachdem der Vater ihn hinausgeworfen hatte.

»Herzensgüte!« schrie der Vater. »Ein Judenhasser, ein Nazi in meiner Küche! Bist du nicht gescheit, Frau!«

»Du wirst mit deinem Geschrei noch den Jungen wecken«, mahnte sie.

»Dem können schlimmere Dinge passieren als das«, sagte der Vater, doch da begann die Mutter zu weinen und der Streit verebbte bald in beruhigenden Worten.

Unter dem Zelt auf dem Sofa lag der Junge und fürchtete sich und versuchte zu begreifen. Jude. Das Wort hatte man ihm in der Schule nachgeschrien. Sein Vater war blaß geworden, als Simon es erzählt hatte, und an einem unglaublichen aber wunderbaren Abend hatte er dem Jungen gezeigt, wie man seine Fäuste gebraucht. Stunde um Stunde hatten sie im Keller geübt, gerade Rechte, schneller linker Haken und dann ein Uppercut, wenn die Lage es erforderte.

Am nächsten Tag hatte der Junge sein Können in der Schule ausprobiert, und seither hatte er das Wort nicht mehr gehört.

Erst heute abend wieder.

2

Simon hatte eine gute Mutter.

Das durfte nicht vergessen werden, denn ihre Güte war irgendwie immer vorhanden. Sie gestaltete die Welt, in der der Junge aufwuchs. Die Mutter war auch schön, war hochgewachsen und blond, hatte einen großen empfindsamen Mund und überraschenderweise braune Augen.

Ihre Güte war nicht von dieser aufdringlichen Art, sie besaß eigene Kräfte und war nicht bedroht von fremden Einflüssen. Karin war vielleicht einer jener seltenen Menschen, die wissen, daß Liebe nicht auf künstlichem Nährboden herangezüchtet werden kann.

Weil Liebe nichts anderes ist als ein Nichtvorhandensein von Angst.

Sie hatte auch begriffen, daß gegen die Angst, die das Leben der Menschen durchzittert, nur selten etwas unternommen werden kann, daß kein Mensch einem anderen innerlich helfen kann. Und daß dies der Grund ist, warum Trost so unendlich notwendig ist.

Also war sie diejenige, bei der alle Schutz suchten. Es gab nicht eine geplagte Frau, nicht einen Mann, die in ihrer Küche nicht Kaffee und Zuspruch bekamen. Ganz zu schweigen von all den Kindern, denen etwas zugestoßen war, und die sich hier ausweinen und Kakao trinken konnten.

Sie trocknete keine Tränen und dachte sich keine Lösungen aus. Aber sie konnte zuhören.

Sie war nicht auf Dank aus, ihre Geduld und ihr großes Herz schenkten ihr wenig Freude. Es war im Gegenteil eher so, daß das ganze Elend des Lebens, dem in ihrer Küche Trost zuteil wurde, ihre

14

Trauer noch vermehrte. Aber sie bekäme dadurch, wie sie sagte, neuen Auftrieb für ihre sozialistische Überzeugung, weil nämlich Menschen einander wie Tiere behandeln, wenn sie selbst wie Tiere behandelt werden. Wie alle guten Menschen glaubte Karin nicht an das Böse. Es war zwar vorhanden, aber nicht als das Böse an sich, es war nur ein Irrtum, der in Ungerechtigkeit und Unglück wurzelte.

Der Junge wurde gerecht behandelt und war glücklich. So konnte er der Flut düsteren Schmerzes und roter Traditionen standhalten. Er wollte es nicht wahrhaben, aber manch alte Schuld gab dem Schmerz Nahrung.

Die Ågrensche hatte acht Kinder und haßte sie alle. Simon war vermutlich der einzige Mensch im Dorf, der sich zu ihr hingezogen fühlte. Das ging sogar so weit, daß er sich mit einem ihrer Söhne anfreundete. Es war keine einfache Freundschaft. Wie alle Ågren-kinder war der Junge hinterhältig und mißtrauisch.

Aber die Freundschaft verschaffte Simon Zutritt zu Ågrens Küche, und da er das Talent hatte, sich unsichtbar zu machen, konnte er den Haß beobachten und belauschen. Dieser Haß war so voller Kraft, daß er dauernd überkochte und jeden erfaßte.

»Verdammte Kuh!« schrie die Ågren ihre älteste Tochter an, die sich vor dem Küchenspiegel kämmte. »Was nützt dir das schon, du siehst aus wie eine elende Kuh und bist so dürr, daß du nicht mal das Geld für den Schlachter wert bist. Glaub bloß nicht, daß einer Lust kriegt, dich zu decken.«

Gegen ihre Töchter war sie besonders gemein, die Söhne bekamen ihr Fett eher beiläufig ab.

»Euch hab ich für meine Sünden gekriegt«, schrie sie. »Raus aus meiner Küche, damit ich euch aus den Augen hab.«

Eines Tages erblickte sie Simon, und plötzlich stand er im Brenn-punkt ihres Hasses: »Du Satansbraten«, sagte sie langsam, leise, gedehnt. »Zur Hölle mit dir und nimm deine verdammte schein-heilige Mutter gleich mit. Aber vergiß sie ja nicht vorher zu fragen, wo sie dich her hat.«

Simon holte tief Luft als er merkte, wie sein Zorn sich an ihrem entzündete. Aber er fand keine Worte, sondern stürzte ins Freie und lief zum Strand und den Felsen am Badeplatz. Es war Herbst, die See war grau und böse und half ihm, Worte zu finden. »Du Aas«, sagte er. »Du verdammtes Aas.«

Aber das war nicht genug, er mußte schnell handeln. Er schnitt ihr die Brüste ab, schlug ihr die Augen ein. Dann trampelte er sie tot. Danach fühlte er sich merkwürdig erleichtert.

Die Ågrensche war nicht alt. Aber sie hatte in dreizehn Jahren vier Fehlgeburten gehabt und acht Kinder geboren, und sie hatte jedes einzelne schon in ihrem Leib gehaßt. Die verdammten Gören fraßen sie auf, verschlangen ihr Leben, zerhackten ihre Nächte und erfüllten ihre Tage mit gallebitterem Verdruß. Sie nahmen ihr jegliche Selbstachtung und jegliche Freude. Nur der Zorn hielt sie aufrecht, ermöglichte gekochtes Essen und saubere Kleider für Mann und Kinder.

»Sie ist wie eine samende, überreife Gurke«, sagte Karin. »Das ist ihr Unglück.«

Selbst schob die Frau alles auf Ågren, den liederlichen Teufel. Aber immerhin brachte er jeden Freitag eine volle Lohntüte nach Hause, und so wagte sie nicht wirklich, sich gegen ihn aufzulehnen.

Sie hatte sich schon sehr jung mit einem netten Mann in geordneten Verhältnissen verheiratet, einem Mann im Dienste der Krone, einem Zöllner. Viele hatten das für ein großes Glück gehalten, und sie selbst hatte irgendwann vielleicht von einem guten Leben in dem neuen Haus am Meer geträumt.

Dann, an einem Frühlingstag ging die älteste Tochter ins Wasser. Sie war sechzehn Jahre alt, doch als die Polizei den Leichnam fand, stellte sich heraus, daß sie schwanger war. Beim Krämer sagte die Ågrensche, sie sei froh, daß das Mädel Verstand genug gehabt hatte, sich umzubringen, sonst hätte sie, die Mutter, die verdammte Hure eigenhändig erwürgen müssen.

Danach ging sie heim und hatte eine Fehlgeburt.

Zum Winter hin wurde ihr Bauch wieder dick, aber dieses Mal war

es kein Kind. Die Ågrensche starb im siebenunddreißigsten Lebens-
jahr an einem Krebs, der ebenso verheerend war wie ihr Haß.

Simon trauerte um sie. Und als Ågren sich ziemlich bald mit einer
ganz gewöhnlichen Frau wiederverheiratete, einer Frau, die unter-
tänig war, alles sauber hielt und Plätzchen buk, hörte der Junge mit
seinen Besuchen in diesem Haus auf.

Jetzt aber war der Abend des Tages gekommen, an dem Simon sich
entschlossen hatte, erwachsen zu werden. Gegen den Nachmittag hin
hatte sich der Nebel gelichtet. Der helle Maihimmel vor dem Küchenfenster färbte sich durch den rotweißkarierten Stoff über dem
Küchensofa rosa, während er dort lag und an seinen Entschluß
dachte.

Er hatte es für seine Mutter getan, soviel war sicher. Aber er hatte
die Worte nicht gefunden, die es ihr hätten erklären sollen, und so
mußte er auf die Belohnung verzichten, die darin bestanden hätte,
daß die Trauer in ihren braunen Augen verschwunden wäre.

Diese Traurigkeit war das einzig wirklich Gefährliche im Leben des
Jungen, das einzig Unerträgliche. Er sollte es erst viel später verstehen, dann, wenn er erwachsen und sie bereits tot war, daß ihre Trauer
kaum etwas mit ihm zu tun gehabt hatte.

Er konnte sie fröhlich machen. Er hatte sich im Laufe der Jahre
viele Tricks ausgedacht, die den Glanz eines Lachens in ihren braunen
Augen hervorriefen. Trotzdem glaubte er immer, daß er es war, der sie
traurig machte.

Einige Tage zuvor hatten sie erfahren, daß Simon in die Oberschule
aufgenommen worden war. Er war der erste in der Familie, der
studieren sollte. Obwohl er erst elf war, hatte er selbst die Antrags-
formulare ausgefüllt und war allein den weiten Weg zur von den
Eltern sogenannten Hochmutschule geradelt, als die Zeit für die
Aufnahmeprüfung gekommen war.

Der Junge hatte den Freudenschimmer in den Augen der Mutter
gesehen, als er mit der Nachricht, daß er aufgenommen worden war,
nach Hause kam.

Dieser Schimmer erlosch aber sofort, als der Vater sagte: »So, aus dir soll also etwas werden. Und ich soll's natürlich bezahlen. Bist du sicher, daß wir uns das leisten können?«

»Das mit dem Geld wird schon in Ordnung gehen«, antwortete die Mutter. »Aber der Rest ist deine Sache. Schließlich war es auch dein Einfall.«

Einige Jahre später, in den Jahren der Reife, sollte Simon sie beide für die Worte hassen, die an diesem Abend in der Küche gefallen waren. Und auch wegen der Einsamkeit, die folgte. Doch später im Leben begann er seine Eltern zu verstehen. Ihre zwiespältige Einstellung zur bürgerlichen Schule, die die begabten Kinder verschlang und damit die Arbeiterklasse von innen heraus aushöhlte. Zu dieser Zeit begann er auch ihre Gefühle zu erahnen, wenn sie zusammen beim Essen saßen und vage begriffen, daß nun ihr Junge sie überholen würde.

Aber man wollte ja, daß die Kinder es besser hätten.

Als Karin damals den Tisch abgeräumt und das Wachstuch saubergewischt hatte, nahm Erik sich das Wirtschaftsbuch vor und setzte sich mit den terminbedingten Ausgaben auseinander. Dann berechnete er die Ausgaben für Schulbücher und Straßenbahn und machte ein bekümmertes Gesicht. Aber das war wie bei vielen Dingen eher ein Ritual, sie hatten eigentlich nicht zu wenig Geld.

Nur diese ewige Angst vor der Armut.

Die Mutter dachte wohl kaum an das Geld. Aber ihr war nicht wohl zumute, und ihre Augen wurden schwarz vom Gewicht ihrer Worte, als sie sagte: »Dann muß eben Schluß sein mit den Träumen.«

Vielleicht galt ihre Sorge etwas ganz anderem als dem, daß Simon die Schule nicht schaffen könnte, vielleicht dachte sie vielmehr daran, daß ihr Junge jetzt einer von der Sorte Mensch werden würde, die weder das eine noch das andere waren, Menschen, die aus eigener Kraft entweder etwas werden oder untergehen mußten.

Doch Simon hörte nur die Worte, und jetzt lag er dort auf der Küchenbank und dachte darüber nach, wie sehr Karin sich freuen würde, wenn er ihr nur in irgendeiner Weise sagen könnte, daß er ein Kind wie alle anderen sein wollte, nur eben noch ein bißchen mehr und ein bißchen besser. Denn er hatte ja gemerkt, daß sie stolz auf die guten Zensuren war und auf die Worte der Lehrerin beim Schulabschluß im vergangenen Jahr.

»Simon ist sehr begabt«, hatte sie gesagt.

Der Vater hatte gegrunzt, er wehrte sich gegen das Wort. Und dann genierte er sich auch für die Lehrerin. So etwas zu sagen, wenn der Junge zuhörte, das war wohl mehr als dumm.

»Der Junge kann doch eitel werden«, sagte er, als sie gemächlich heimgingen. Es war die Zeit, als die Baumblüte gerade begonnen hatte. »Begabt«, sagte er, ließ das Wort über die Zunge gleiten, spuckte es aus.

»Er ist tüchtig«, betonte Karin.

»Klar ist er tüchtig«, sagte Erik. »Schließlich gerät er uns nach.«

»Und du redest von Eitelkeit«, lachte die Mutter, aber ihr Lachen klang glücklich.

Der Junge war immer ein Bücherwurm gewesen, wie man so sagt. Das war eine Eigenart, die so hingenommen wurde wie auch sein kleiner Wuchs und seine schwarzen Haare. Aber sie durfte nicht in Übertreibung ausarten.

Simon hatte schon in den ersten Sommerferien alle Bücher im Haus verschlungen.

Er erinnerte sich an eine Frau, die ihn mit ›Gösta Berling‹ im guten Zimmer auf dem Sofa entdeckt hatte: »Liest der Junge doch Lagerlöf...« Die Stimme hatte vorwurfsvoll geklungen.

»Man kann ihn nicht davon abhalten«, sagte Karin.

»Aber er kann ein solches Buch doch nicht verstehen.«

»Etwas muß er wohl verstehen, sonst würde er ja nicht weiterlesen.«

Mamas Stimme bat nicht etwa um Entschuldigung, aber die andere Frau hatte trotzdem das letzte Wort. »Glaub mir, das kann auf keinen Fall gut für ihn sein.«

War bei Karin ein Anflug von Unruhe zu bemerken gewesen? Vielleicht, denn sie mußte es dem Vater erzählt haben, der zu Simon sagte: »Glaube nur nicht, daß die Welt aus Herrenhoffräuleins und verrückten Pfarrern besteht. Lies lieber Jack London.«

Und Simon las Jack Londons gesammelte Werke, marmorierte braune Bände mit rotem Leinenrücken. Aus dieser Zeit waren ihm noch einige Figuren in Erinnerung geblieben, Wolf-Larsen, ein Geistlicher, der Menschenfleisch aß, ein wahnsinniger Geigenspieler. Und einige Bilder, der lange See von Löven und die Slums in East End.

Der Rest versank im Unterbewußtsein und trug dort reiche Frucht.

Jetzt, mit elf, hatte er den Weg zur Volksbücherei in Majorna gefunden, sein Verlangen war nun weniger brennend, wie das eben so ist bei einem, der weiß, daß er nicht mehr entbehren muß. Er war jetzt auch vorsichtiger geworden, hatte die Angst in Mutters Gesicht auflodern sehen, wenn sie sich fragte, ob ihr Junge allen Ernstes anders als die anderen sein könnte.

»Lauf raus und beweg dich, bevor das Blut in dir fault,« konnte sie sagen. Es war ein Scherz, aber darin verbarg sich auch Besorgnis.

Einmal fand sie ihn auf dem Dachboden, vertieft in Joan Grants Buch über die Königin von Ägypten, seine Augen starrten Karin von pharaonischen Höhen herab an und er hörte nicht, was sie sagte. Erst als sie ihn durch die Jahrhunderte zurück rüttelte, konnte er sehen, daß sie Angst um ihn hatte.

»Du darfst das Leben nicht einfach so aus den Augen verlieren«, sagte sie.

Es tat noch immer weh, obwohl er versuchte, es zu vergessen.

An diesem Abend machte er sich auf der Küchenbank ihre Frage zu seiner: War vielleicht irgend etwas wirklich bei ihm verkehrt?

Er hatte den Schritt hinüber in die Welt der Vergleiche getan.

Aber am nächsten Tag hatte er fast alles wieder völlig vergessen. Er begleitete seinen Cousin im Kanu hinaus zur Flußmündung, lag dort mit dem Paddel in Bereitschaft und wartete auf die Fähre aus Dänemark. Sie kam so pünktlich, daß man die Uhr danach stellen konnte, und war längst nicht das größte Schiff auf dem Weg in den großen Hafen. Aber im Unterschied zu den Amerikadampfern und den weißen Schiffen aus dem Fernen Osten durfte die Fähre die Mündung in voller Fahrt passieren.

Sie pflügte durch die hohe See, und die Jungen waren inzwischen sehr geschickt in der Kunst, das Kanu in die erste Welle zu lenken und auf ihr bis an den Strand zu reiten.

Da kam sie, schnell und schön. Simon hörte den Cousin vor Spannung aufschreien, als sie sich auf den Wellenkamm zubalancierten. Aber sie näherten sich in einem zu schrägen Winkel, so daß das Kanu zu schwanken begann und die Jungen hinausschleuderte, die mit der Welle in die Tiefe glitten.

Für einen Augenblick war Simon von Furcht gepackt, doch er war wie sein Cousin ein guter Schwimmer. Er wußte, was er zu tun hatte, um nicht in den Sog der nächsten Welle zu geraten und ließ sich mittreiben, widerstandslos, auch von der nächsten und übernächsten.

Als die See sich geglättet hatte, schwammen die Jungen zu ihrem Kanu und bugsierten es an Land. Dort stand die Clique, erschrocken zwar, aber höhnisch.

Doch der Cousin tat sich groß mit der riesigen Woge, die höher gewesen war als jede andere jemals zuvor – das wurde anerkannt und die Ehre war gerettet.

Simon hatte anderes im Sinn: das Bild des Mannes, dem er auf seinem Weg in die Tiefe des Meeres begegnet war. Der Kleine war dort gewesen, dem er am Vortag für immer Lebewohl gesagt hatte.

Zu Hause bekam er Schelte und trockene Kleider. Dann kletterte er den Felsen hinauf, lief über die Wiese zum Eichenwald. Er fand seine Bäume, zwischen zehn und fünfzehn Meter hoch, schweigend, genau wie sie es sollten. Die Abmachung wurde eingehalten, das war gut, und nur das hatte er wissen wollen.

Aber in der Nacht, im Schlaf, begegnete ihm sein Mann wieder, saß auf dem Grund des Meeres und führte lange Gespräche mit ihm. Und als er am nächsten Morgen erwachte, fühlte er sich merkwürdig gestärkt.

Erst viel später am Tag, als er in der Schule bereits die Rechenarbeit abgegeben und noch eine Weile Zeit hatte, fiel ihm ein, daß er vergessen hatte den Mann zu fragen, wer er sei, und merkte, daß er sich an kein Wort von dem erinnerte, was gesprochen worden war.

Es war ein ungewöhnlich warmer Sommer, voller Unruhe. In der Küche verfolgten die Erwachsenen jede Nachrichtensendung im Radio.

»Es sieht düster aus«, sagte der Vater.

»Wir brauchen Regen«, sagte die Mutter. »Die Kartoffeln vertrocknen und der Brunnen gibt kaum noch Wasser.«

Aber der Regen kam nicht, und schließlich mußten sie Wasser kaufen und den Brunnen mit dem Tankwagen auffüllen lassen.

Im Herbst begann Simon die Schule genau an dem Tag, an dem Ribbentrop nach Moskau fuhr.

Simon war der kleinste in der Klasse und der einzige, der aus einer Arbeiterfamilie kam. Er konnte sich den Manieren schlecht anpassen, stand nicht auf, wenn der Lehrer mit ihm sprach, sagte ja ohne bitte und danke, und ebenso nein.

»Danke-danke, danke-danke«, spotteten die Mitschüler, und Simon fand es albern. Sah aber ein, daß er lernen mußte, es lernen mußte für die Schule und lernen mußte, streng zu trennen. Zu Hause wäre er ausgelacht worden.

Dort war man dankbar, man dankte nicht.

Er war der einzige, der einen Antrag auf Schulgeldermäßigung einreichte. Aber wie alle anderen bekam er ein Deutschlesebuch und eine deutsche Grammatik.

Der Heimweg auf dem Fahrrad war mehr als fünf Kilometer lang. Simon war den Großstadtverkehr, die schweren Lastwagen und großen Straßenbahnen nicht gewöhnt. Er kam nach Hause und brauchte Trost.

Aber Karin war mit Erik beschäftigt, der in der Küche mit einem zerbrochenen Weltbild vor dem Radio saß. Sein politischer Scharfsinn hatte die Sowjetunion immer außen vor gelassen. Der Pakt mit Moskau war ein Verrat an den Arbeitern der Welt.

Simon begriff erst, wie ernst es war, als Karin den Schnaps aus der Speisekammer brachte, obwohl es nur ein ganz gewöhnlicher Wochentag war.

Gegen Abend hatten der Branntwein und Karins tröstende Worte das ihre bewirkt. Erik hatte den Boden unter seinen Füßen notdürftig ausgebessert und war zu dem Schluß gekommen, daß die Russen unterschrieben haben mußten, um Zeit zu gewinnen für die Aufrüstung zur großen und entscheidenden Schlacht gegen die Nazis. Karin konnte aufatmen, ihren Jungen ansehen und fragen: »Na, wie war's in der neuen Schule?«

»Gut«, sagte der Junge, und mehr wurde während der vielen Jahre Realschule, Gymnasium und Universität eigentlich nie geäußert.

Er zog an diesem Abend die Deutschbücher nicht aus dem Rucksack.

Schon in der ersten Pause am nächsten Tag kam es: »Du kleiner Judendreck«, sagte der Längste und Blondeste in der Klasse, ein Junge mit einem so vornehmen Namen, daß beim ersten Aufrufen ein Raunen durch die Klasse gegangen war.

Simon schlug zu, der Arm schnellte seine rechte Gerade direkt aus der Schulter, rasant und überraschend wie er es gelernt hatte, und der Lange fiel mit heftig blutender Nase um.

Zu mehr kam es nicht, weil es zur nächsten Stunde klingelte. Und es kam auch nie zu Schlimmerem, denn Simon hatte sich Respekt verschafft. Aber er wußte, daß nun die große Einsamkeit für ihn begann, genau wie in der Volksschule.

Doch da irrte er sich.

Als die Jungen die Treppe zum Physiksaal hinaufliefen, legte sich ihm ein Arm um die Schultern und er schaute in zwei braune, traurige Augen.

»Ich heiße Isak«, sagte der Junge. »Und ich bin Jude.«

Sie setzten sich im Physiksaal nebeneinander, so wie sie von da an alle Schuljahre hindurch nebeneinander sitzen würden. Simon hatte einen Freund gefunden.

Aber das sofort zu begreifen war nicht einfach, sein Erstaunen war viel größer als seine Freude. Ein richtiger Jude! Simon schaute Isak während der Schulstunde immer wieder an und konnte es nicht fassen. Der Junge war groß, schlank, hatte braune Haare, sah nett aus.

Wie ein ganz normaler Mensch.

In der Mittagspause nahm Isak Simon mit nach Hause, und sie aßen belegte Brote. Es gab dort ein Dienstmädchen, das ganz wie Tante Äppelgren war, und das dicke Scheiben Leberpastete auf die Brote legte und ihnen dazu Tomaten reichte.

Simon hatte noch nie ein Dienstmädchen gesehen und kaum je Tomaten gegessen, aber das war es nicht, was ihn beeindruckte. Nein, es waren die großen düsteren ineinanderführenden Zimmer, der schwere Samt an den Fenstern, die roten Plüschsofas, die endlosen Reihen von Bücherregalen – und der Geruch, der feine Duft von Bohnerwachs, Parfüm und Reichtum.

Simon sog alles in sich auf und dachte, als er am Nachmittag heimwärts radelte, daß er jetzt erfahren hatte, wie Glück aussah. Er hatte Isaks Cousine kennengelernt, die so elegant war wie eine Prinzessin und lange, lackierte Fingernägel hatte. Simon fragte sich, ob sie überhaupt jemals auf die Toilette gehen mußte.

Dann fiel ihm ein, daß Karin fragen würde, ob er seine Schulbrote aufgegessen hatte, machte also einen Umweg über den Eichenwald, setzte sich dort hin und aß sie auf.

Die Bäume schwiegen.

Als er bergab an Äppelgrens Garten vorbeifuhr, begegnete er einem seiner Cousins. Es war der Zurückgebliebene, und Simon schämte sich für ihn, weil er so dreckig und sein anbiederndes Grinsen absolut unerträglich war.

Ich hasse ihn, dachte Simon. Ich habe ihn immer gehaßt. Und dann schämte er sich noch mehr.

Sie waren gleich alt, waren gleichzeitig in die Schule gekommen. Aber der Cousin war bald in der Hilfsklasse gelandet, und jetzt hatte die Schule ihn ganz aufgegeben. Er war meistens im Stall bei Dahls, die hier in dem wachsenden Vorort zwischen den Eigenheimen noch eine kleine Landwirtschaft betrieben. Sie hatten einen Knecht, der schwachsinnig war, aber gutartig und kräftig genug für die schwere Arbeit auf dem Bauernhof.

Zu Hause hatte Karin ein Gästebett vom Dachboden geholt und zeigte Simon jetzt, wie er es allabendlich im guten Zimmer auseinanderklappen und für sich zum Schlafen zurechtmachen sollte. Für das Bettzeug hatte sie im Eichenbüfett ein Fach ausgeräumt. Dann hatte sie die Decke von dem großen Tisch am Fenster genommen und für seine Bücher eine Schublade freigemacht. Er sollte aus der Küche ins gute Zimmer übersiedeln. Das war eine Anerkennung für seine Ernsthaftigkeit an der neuen Schule.

So neigte sich die lange erste Woche ihrem Ende zu und der Sonntag kam, ein Sonntag, den die Welt nie vergessen sollte. Hitlers Truppen marschierten in Polen ein, Warschau wurde bombardiert. Und England erklärte den Krieg und das alles bewirkte so etwas wie ein Gefühl der Erleichterung.

Am meisten merkte man es Erik an, der sich straffte, wenn er sein ›endlich‹ sagte, und man hörte es auch an den Stimmen der Menschen, wenn sie sich in der Küche um das Radio versammelten. Nur Karin war noch trauriger als gewöhnlich. An diesem Abend half sie Simon das Bett zu machen und sagte: »Wenn ich einen Gott hätte, würde ich ihm auf Knien dafür danken, daß du erst elf Jahre alt bist.«

Simon verstand es nicht. Er hatte nur wie immer, wenn seine Mutter betrübter war als sonst, Schuldgefühle.

Auch in der Schule war am nächsten Tag etwas verändert, die Luft war irgendwie reiner und alles schien einfacher geworden zu sein. Sie lebten hier im größten Hafen an der Westküste ihres Landes, dem Meer und England zugewandt. Nazis gab es nur wenige.

In der ersten Schulstunde hatten sie Geschichte, aber es dauerte, bis sie ihre Bücher aufschlugen. Der Lehrer war jung und verzweifelt und betrachtete es als seine Aufgabe, den Jungen das Geschehene zumindest annähernd zu erklären. Sie kamen fast alle aus Elternhäusern, wo man die Kinder vor der Wirklichkeit zu schützen versuchte.

Für Simon war das meiste eine Wiederholung: Faschismus, Nationalsozialismus, Rassismus, Judenverfolgungen, Spanien, Tschechoslowakei, Österreich, München. Plötzlich zeigte die Küchenbank ihren Nutzen, er war derjenige, der Bescheid wußte, der dem Lehrer entgegenkam, so daß sich bald ein Dialog entspann.

»Es ist gut zu wissen, daß wir hier in der Klasse einen Schüler haben, der weiß, worum es geht«, sagte der Lehrer abschließend. Hinter diesen Worten stand ein Aufruf an die anderen, an die Bürgerkinder, in deren Weltbild sich an diesem Morgen die ersten realistischen Konturen abzeichneten.

Isak äußerte sich kaum, aber die Augen des Lehrers ruhten manchmal auf ihm, als wüßte er, daß dieser Schüler schwieg, weil er ein noch weit größeres Wissen hatte.

Simon saß in seiner Bank und dachte, daß es Brücken zwischen seinen beiden Welten gab und daß vieles von dem, wofür Erik und Karin einstanden, auch hier in der Hochmutsschule von Wert war. Daß nicht alles abzulehnen war, und daß man sich nicht dafür schämen mußte.

Das schlimmste an all dem Neuen war für Simon, daß er sich seiner Familie schämte. An diesem Nachmittag brachte er es fertig, Isak zu fragen, ob er an einem Tag mit ihm nach Hause kommen wollte.

Wie es aber dazu kam, daß Isak zu Karin fand und damit zu zwei Armen und einer Begründung, in ihrer Küche heimisch zu werden, ist eine spätere Geschichte. Denn in diesem Augenblick sagte der Lehrer: »Was auch immer geschieht in der Welt, es muß jeder einzelne das Seine dazu beitragen. Wir schlagen unsere Bücher auf. Wie ihr wißt, begann die Geschichte mit den Sumerern.«

Damit war Simon dort und nicht mehr im Klassenzimmer. Nie hätte er sich etwas so Phantastisches ausdenken können.

Sie lasen Grimberg: »Ein Land des Todes und der großen Stille ist Mesopotamien in unseren Tagen. Schwer ruht die rächende Hand des Herrn seit Jahrtausenden auf dem unglücklichen Land. Die Worte des Propheten Jesaia: ›Ach, du bist vom Himmel gefallen, du Vernichter der Völker‹, klingt wie eine Totenklage zwischen den zerfallenden Mauern . . .«

Simon verstand nicht alles, ließ sich aber von der Wortgewalt gefangennehmen. Danach ging Grimberg zu den Sumerern über, den Breitschädeligen, Untersetzten, die an Mongolen erinnerten.

»Sie erfanden die Schriftzeichen«, sagte der Lehrer und berichtete von den unzähligen Keilschrifttafeln in den großen Tempeln. Die gewaltigen Zikkuraten entstanden zum ersten Mal vor den Augen des Jungen und er folgte dem Lehrer hinab in die Grabkammern von Ur und zu den Toten.

Erst viele Jahre später glaubte Simon zu erkennen, daß sein Interesse für Frühgeschichte in dieser Stunde geboren wurde und eine immerwährende Kraft aus dem Erfolg schöpfte, den er gleich zu Beginn dieses Unterrichts gehabt hatte.

Oder weil ihn das alles so stark beeindruckt hatte, weil es ein so überaus gewaltiger Tag gewesen war: der erste des großen Krieges.

Schon der Elfjährige erkannte die Bedeutung, die sich hinter den Worten verbarg, daß die Welt, die sich ihm jetzt eröffnete, verwandt war mit der Wiese daheim.

Er wog das schwere Messer in der Hand und die blauen Steine aus Lapislazuli sprachen in ihrer geheimnisvollen Sprache zu ihm, gaben seiner Hand Kraft. Sein Blick haftete an der langen goldenen Klinge.

Das Werkzeug war gut.

Aber es würde ihm nicht helfen, wenn er nicht in dem sich nähernden Augenblick verweilen, ihn zeitlos machen konnte. Er näherte sich dem großen Tempelsaal, sah nicht, sondern ahnte eher die nach oben gewandten Gesichter der vielen tausend Menschen, die im Gebet vereint waren.

Der Stier war gewaltig, im Augenblick der Entscheidung hatte die Zeit ihn eingeholt. Und damit auch die Verbündete der Zeit, die große Angst. Als der Stier auf ihn zurannte, wußte er, daß er sterben würde, und er schrie ...

Er schrie so laut, daß er Karin weckte, die sofort bei ihm war, ihn wachrüttelte und sagte: »Du hast schlecht geträumt, steh auf und trink einen Schluck Wasser. Man muß immer zusehen, daß man richtig wach wird, wenn der Alb einen reitet.«

Bevor Isak in Karins Küche landete, hatte Simon schon zusammen mit dessen Eltern und der Cousine mit den lackierten Fingernägeln an Isaks Mittagstisch gesessen. Simon hatte Schwierigkeiten mit dem vielen Besteck, lernte aber durch Beobachtung rasch und wagte zu glauben, daß niemand seine Unsicherheit bemerkte.

Er war zum Essen eingeladen worden. Zu Hause bei Simon wurde nie zum Essen eingeladen, wenn jemand gerade zur richtigen Zeit kam, aß er einfach mit. Wenn eingeladen wurde, dann feierte man ein Fest.

Isaks Vater war einer jener seltenen Menschen, die immer intensiv anwesend sind. Ihm war eine gewisse körperliche Geschmeidigkeit zu eigen, und das fein geschnittene Gesicht war lebhaft, voller Abwechslung. Er hatte ein rasches Lächeln, hell, freundlich. Die Augen waren braun und lebendig. In ihnen lag außer Neugier noch etwas anderes. Angst? Simon erkannte es, wollte es aber nicht sehen und wies den Gedanken als ungehörig zurück.

Dieser Ruben Lentov hatte sich eine Existenz in Schweden geschaffen und auf Bücher gesetzt. Seine Buchhandlung mitten im Zentrum war die größte der Stadt und hatte Filialen in Majorna, Redbergslid und Örgryte. Sie war in der ganzen Welt bekannt, und er hatte Kontakte zu London, Berlin, Paris und New York.

In seiner Jugend war Ruben Lentov ein Suchender gewesen, war von Strindberg und Swedenborg nach Schweden gelockt worden, hatte gefroren und verzichtet, ehe sein Unternehmen sicheres Wachstum versprach.

Sein Aufbruch war auch ein Aufbegehren gewesen gegen allzugroße Mutterliebe und eine allzu starke Vaterbindung. Aber die Familie daheim in Berlin hatte das so nie sehen wollen. Sie hatten ihn zum ersten, der Weitsichtigkeit bewiesen hatte, gemacht, zu einem, der lange vor 1933 begriffen hatte, was geschehen würde. Sie hatten ihn mit Geld und Bankverbindungen versorgt und sich um seine Frau und seinen kleinen Sohn gekümmert.

Mitte der dreißiger Jahre war Rubens Frau nachgekommen, als er schon gut etabliert war. Sie war jedoch völlig verängstigt. In den ersten

Jahren erlangte er nie Klarheit darüber, was er von der Neigung seiner Frau zu bösen Vorahnungen halten sollte und davon, daß sie immer alles zum Schlimmsten auslegte.

Aber in den letzten Jahren glaubte er verstanden zu haben. Die Ärzte, die sie in dem neuen Land aufsuchte, sprachen von Verfolgungswahn. Das war ein Wort, das tagsüber brauchbar war. Aber nie im Dunkeln, denn dort gab es ein Jahrtausende altes Gespenst.

Jetzt saß Simon an Rubens Mittagstisch, er, der schwedische Junge, der der Freund des Sohnes war. Ruben war dankbar für jede Verbindung, die in dem neuen Land geknüpft werden konnte, und er hatte sehr aufmerksam zugehört, als Isak von der Geschichtsstunde und dem Jungen erzählt hatte, der politisch so klarsichtig war und der die Nazis haßte.

Doch er war enttäuscht und schämte sich dafür. Diesen kleinen dunkelhäutigen Jungen hatte er nicht erwartet, mit einem langen blonden Schweden wäre er besser zurechtgekommen.

Die Enttäuschung legte sich im Lauf des Gesprächs als Simon loslegte und Ruben sehr bald erkannte, daß dieser Junge der schwedischen Arbeiterklasse entstammte, daß er die Stimme eines Kindes hatte, die Quelle jedoch die wachsende, mächtige Sozialdemokratie war. Sie stritten sich wegen der Kommunisten und Simon verlor für einen Moment den Boden unter den Füßen, als Ruben sich darüber ereiferte, daß die Sowjetunion ein Sklavenstaat von gleichem Schrot und Korn sei wie Hitler-Deutschland. Dann mäßigte sich Ruben, sah ein, daß er kein Recht hatte herabzusetzen und zu verletzen.

Er schämte sich und bot eine zweite Portion Eis an.

Simon sollte den Abend nie vergessen. Weniger wegen der Dinge, die er gehört hatte, als vielmehr wegen der Unruhe und des Unglücks, das er hier inmitten in all dem Reichtum gesehen hatte. Und weil er sich so sehr vor Isaks Mutter gefürchtet hatte.

Simon war bisher noch nie etwas so Widersprüchlichem begegnet. Ihr Mund und ihr Duft lockten, ihre Augen und ihre Töne erschreckten ihn. Sie klirrte mit Armbändern und scheppernden Halsketten und ihr Blick brannte vor Traurigkeit, sie zog ihn an und stieß ihn ab. Sie umarmte und küßte ihn, schob ihn weg, beobachtete ihn und sagte rätselhaft: »Larsson? Das ist doch unmöglich.«

Dann vergaß sie ihn, sah ihn nicht mehr, sie trank Wein und Simon merkte, daß sie auch Isak aus dem Augenblick und ihrem Bewußtsein verdrängte, und er verstand die Trauer in den Augen des Freundes, die ihm schon am ersten Tag aufgefallen war.

Am Samstag des nächsten Wochenendes wagte er den Versuch eines Brückenschlags zwischen seiner alten Welt und der neuen, und erzählte zu Hause am Küchentisch von der vornehmen Familie, die ihn zum Essen eingeladen hatte.

»Sie waren so ... so nervös«, sagte er und suchte nach Worten, die die Besorgnis dort in der großen Stadtwohnung hätten erklären können.

Und Karin fand sie.

»Die leben in Angst«, sagte sie. »Sie sind Juden, und wenn die Deutschen kommen ...«

Aber der Herbst verging und die Deutschen kamen nicht. Etwas anderes passierte, etwas, das aus Eriks Sicht fast noch schlimmer war. Am dreißigsten November bombardierten die Sowjets Helsingfors.

Winterkrieg.

Herrgott, wie kalt war doch dieser Winter, in dem die Erde fast an der Bosheit der Menschen zugrunde ging. Es kamen Tage, an denen die Kinder zu Hause bleiben mußten, wenn das Radio meldete, daß die Schulen geschlossen blieben. Simon saß im guten Zimmer, wo Karin im eisernen Ofen Feuer gemacht hatte und die Kohle ihren trockenen Geruch verströmte und Erik mit rotgefrorenen Ohren heimkam und sagte, wenn das so weitergeht, können wir bald mit dem Auto übers Wasser bis hinüber nach Vinga fahren.

Am nächsten Sonntag machten sie es auch, und es war ein Abenteuer, das sich nie mehr wiederholen sollte. Das allzeit lebendige, allzeit gegenwärtige, unbesiegte und gewaltige Meer ließ sich von dem bösen Wind aus Osten in Ketten legen, dem Wind, der mit zwanzig

Metern in der Sekunde seine dreißig Minusgrade über den Inseln verbreitete.

Russen und Finnen starben wie die Fliegen an Eis und Feuer. Der Tod holte sich etwa 225 000 Menschenleben, wie man später feststellte, als die Verhältnisse wieder derart waren, daß man auch wieder einen Sinn für Zahlen hatte.

In Simons Heimatstadt machten die großen Werften Überstunden und die Arbeiter schenkten ihren Verdienst den finnischen Nachbarn. In Luleå wurde das Haus der Vereinigung Nordlichtflamme in die Luft gesprengt, und fünf beherzte Kommunisten mußten dafür ihr Leben lassen.

Im Februar war alles vorbei und Karelien hatte sein Heimatrecht im Norden verloren. Etwa zu dieser Zeit sagte Karin, sie müßten zum Frühjahr hin versuchen, einen Acker von Dahls zu pachten und mehr Kartoffeln setzen. Und Gemüse pflanzen.

Lebensmittel begannen knapp zu werden.

4

Viele Jahre danach würde Simon sich mit der Frage beschäftigen, ob er an diesem Morgen etwas Besonderes empfunden hatte. Er war in der Dämmerung aufgewacht und hatte seine Mutter im Schlaf weinen hören.

Karin hatte Vorahnungen.

Er selbst fühlte sich wohl wie immer, als er zur Schule losradelte. Die Stadt war zu einem Tag erwacht, der ein gewöhnlicher zu werden versprach. Von der Bergkuppe an der Stadtgrenze konnte er alle Hebekräne des Hafens sich wie tanzende langbeinige Spinnen bewegen sehen. Wie gewöhnlich überholte er die Straßenbahn, die die bessergestellten Kameraden in die Schule brachte, und wie gewöhnlich empfand er dabei eine gewisse Genugtuung. Majorna lag in der Sonne und ein Hauch von Wärme belebte die Karl-Johansgata.

Wie üblich machte Simon seine Deutschaufgaben während der Morgenandacht in der Aula. Er hatte sich noch immer nicht überwinden können, die Deutschbücher zu Hause aufzuschlagen, und in den Stunden fühlte er sich schlecht.

Wie gewöhnlich hatten sie am Dienstagmorgen Chemie und wie gewöhnlich war Simon kaum daran interessiert.

Aber in der dritten Stunde, mitten im Geschichtsunterricht, ging der Schulwart von Klasse zu Klasse und sagte knapp und mit verschlossenem Gesicht, daß Schüler und Lehrer sich in der Aula einzufinden hätten.

Woran er sich hinterher am besten erinnern konnte, war nicht, was der Direktor gesagt hatte, sondern es war die durch ihn vermittelte Angst, als die Jungen nach Hause geschickt wurden. Alle sollten sofort zu ihren Eltern gehen, die Schule könne an diesem Tag keine Verantwortung für sie übernehmen, sagte er.

Es war der 9. April 1940, Ottos Namenstag, und Simons Beine bewegten sich wie Motorkolben, als er heim zu Karin radelte. Sie stand weinend am Küchenfenster. Als sie den Jungen aber hochhob, ihn auf die Küchenbank stellte und in die Arme nahm, fühlte er mit der Gewißheit eines Kindes, daß nichts Schlimmes geschehen konnte, solange Karin bei ihm war.

Aus dem Radio knatterte eine aufgeregte Stimme, daß die Norweger das deutsche Schlachtschiff *Blücher* beim Einlaufen in den Hafen von Oslo versenkt hatten. Karin sagte, es wäre besser gewesen, wenn die Norweger es wie die Dänen gemacht und sich gleich ergeben hätten.

Erik kam mit dem Auto nach Hause. Schweden hielt den Atem an. Der Ministerpräsident sprach im Radio, sagte, daß die schwedische Wehrfähigkeit gut sei, und vielen Familien schenkten seine feste Stimme und die skånische Mundart so etwas wie Zuversicht.

Nicht so jedoch in Larssons Küche, denn dort sagte Erik es geradeheraus, wie es tatsächlich war: »Der lügt, der muß ja lügen.«

Wenige Tage später war Erik an einen unbekannten Ort verschwunden, einberufen. Karin und Simon hackten den Ackerboden auf, den sie gepachtet hatten, und setzten Kartoffeln.

In Simons Träumen stürzten sich wilde Bergvölker mit gezückten Säbeln von hohen Bergen hinunter und fielen wie die Heuschrecken in weite, fruchtbare Ebenen ein, brandschatzten, erschlugen die Menschen und warfen ihre toten Körper in Kanäle und Flüsse.

Die nächtlichen Bilder hatten wenig zu tun mit dem Krieg, der rundherum in Simons Welt wütete, denn wie dieser aussah, wußte er aus Zeitungsberichten und Kino-Wochenschauen. Bei Tag bestand das Entsetzen aus Hakenkreuzen, Stiefeln und schwarzen SS-Uniformen, bei Nacht nahm es die Gestalt beleibter, farbenprächtiger Wahnsinniger an, die ihm mit orientalischer Wollust die Kehle durchschnitten und ihn in den Fluß warfen. Dort schwamm er mit tausend anderen Toten herum und das Wasser färbte sich rot, und er sah Karin mit zerschmettertem Kopf neben sich schwimmen. Und sie war es, obwohl sie sich gar nicht ähnlich sah.

Als Erwachsener würde er noch oft darüber nachdenken, was der Krieg mit den Kindern machte, und wie die tiefe Angst sie prägte. Woran er sich am besten erinnerte, das war die Sehnsucht an jedem einzelnen Morgen, daß der Tag enden möge ohne daß etwas passiert war, dieser Tag und der nächste und der übernächste, ein immer gegenwärtiger schmerzlicher Wunsch.

Fünf Jahre sind eine Ewigkeit, wenn man Kind ist.

Seine Generation wurde zu einer Generation der Ungeduldigen, Menschen, die nicht im Heute verweilen konnten, sondern nur für den morgigen Tag lebten.

Trotz allem gab es immer noch einen Alltag. Die Schule war wieder geöffnet. Viele der Jungen hatten wie Simon keinen Vater mehr zu Hause. Nur für Isak war es anders, bei ihm war es die Mutter, die verschwunden war. In der Nacht zum zehnten April hatte sie versucht, die Kinder zu vergiften und in der schönen Wohnung an der Kvartsgata Feuer zu legen. Isak und seine Cousine waren in eine Klinik gebracht worden, wo man ihnen den Magen ausgepumpt hatte. Als sie wieder nach Hause kamen, war die Mutter nicht mehr da, man hatte sie ans andere Flußufer in ein Krankenhaus für Geistesgestörte gebracht.

Dort gab es Spritzen, die ihr Schlaf schenkten, und die sie nach und nach abhängig machten. Isak bekam seine Mutter nie mehr zurück.

Ruben Lentov lief auf dicken echten Teppichen durch die große stille Wohnung, wanderte in den Nächten zwischen den Bücherregalen in der Bibliothek und der Diele umher, immer vor und zurück. Er war sein Leben lang ein Mann der Tat gewesen, jetzt war er ein Mann umgeben von Ohnmacht. Ein Tier im Käfig. Noch gab es eine Tür, durch die man flüchten konnte. Jüdische Freunde hielten den Luftweg nach London und von dort weiter nach Amerika offen, er konnte seine Läden verkaufen, Kind und Geld nehmen und von hier verschwinden.

Er dachte an seinen Bruder in Dänemark, der zu lange gezögert hatte.

Aber am häufigsten dachte er an Olga, die im Psychiatrischen Krankenhaus eingesperrt war, nur noch ein Wrack, vollgepumpt mit Drogen, ohne jeglichen Kontakt, und doch seine Frau und Isaks Mutter.

Die Käfigtür war ins Schloß gefallen und er wußte es.

Dennoch ging er Nacht für Nacht umher, als müsse er einen Entschluß fassen und brauche die langen Stunden, um Klarheit zu finden.

Für Simon hatte die Angst Namen, und so konnte er sie einigermaßen beherrschen: Bomben, Gestapo, Möllergatan 19. Isak kannte die Wörter auch, aber er konnte sie nicht ordnen und auf Abstand halten. Sein Entsetzen war von einer anderen Art, allumfassend und wortlos wie die Angst nun einmal ist, wenn sie uns sehr früh ergriffen hat und wir uns nicht an das Wann erinnern können oder einfach nicht die Kraft dazu haben.

Karin verstand das, erkannte es schon, als sie den Jungen zum ersten Mal sah.

Einmal war es ihr möglich gewesen, mit Isak über Ängste zu sprechen: »Wir können ja nicht mehr als sterben, keiner von uns.«

Es war eine einfache Wahrheit, doch sie half dem Jungen.

Für ihn wurden Karin, ihre Küche und ihre Mahlzeiten, ihr Schmerz und ihr Zorn zu etwas, womit er leben konnte. Karin schuf Ordnung, sie machte das Leben faßbar.

Den ganzen Sommer über hatte Isak in ihrer Küche gehockt, während seine Mutter zu Hause immer verwirrter und erschreckender wurde. An jenem Sonntag im Mai, als die Norweger ihren Widerstand aufgaben und der König samt seiner Regierung Norwegen verließ, kam Isak zu ihnen hinaus und half Karin und Simon beim Unkrautjäten.

Er kam von seiner Mutter, die er im Krankenhaus besucht und die ihn nicht erkannt hatte.

Am Tag darauf zog Karin sich schön an, wählte den hellblauen

Mantel, den sie selbst genäht hatte, und den großen weißen mit blauen Rosen verzierten Hut und fuhr mit der Straßenbahn zu Ruben Lentovs Büro.

Sie sahen einander lange schweigend an und Ruben dachte, wenn sie den Blick nicht bald abwendet, besteht die Gefahr, daß ich anfange zu weinen. Da sah sie weg und gab ihm Zeit, übers Wetter zu reden, ehe sie ihr Anliegen vorbrachte: »Ich habe mir gedacht, Isak könnte für eine Weile bei uns wohnen, bei Simon und mir.«

Und Ruben Lentov ließ den Gedanken endlich zu, den er jetzt seit Monaten zurückgewiesen hatte, daß nämlich die Angst in Isaks Augen Olgas Angst glich, und daß es für den Jungen schlecht ausgehen konnte, wenn nichts unternommen wurde. Er sagte: »Ich bin so dankbar.«

Viel mehr wurde kaum gesprochen. Als er sie durch das ganze Büro bis zur Haustür geleitete, hatte er das Gefühl, nie eine schönere Frau gesehen zu haben. Erst am Nachmittag fiel ihm ein, daß er für den Jungen bezahlen mußte, Larssons waren Arbeiter und hatten es wohl nicht allzu üppig.

Aber er hatte an Karin Larsson keine Spur von Proletariat wahrgenommen, und als er sie am Nachmittag anrief, um wegen des Geldes zu fragen, fand er keine Worte.

Später war er froh darüber, als ihm bewußt wurde, daß das, was Karin anbot, unbezahlbar war.

So fand er einen anderen Weg und fuhr einmal in der Woche mit Kaffee und Konserven, Büchern für Simon und Geschenken für Karin hinaus in das kleine Haus an der Flußmündung nahe der ausgehöhlten Felsen, in denen die Streitmacht Öl lagerte. Er wurde wie jeder andere in der großen Küche willkommen geheißen, bekam eine warme Mahlzeit, und wenn er sehr betrübt aussah, auch einen Schnaps.

Ruben mochte zwar keinen Branntwein, mußte Karin aber recht geben, daß er gegen die Schwermut half.

Bald zeigte sich, daß Isak für sich selbst geradestehen konnte. Ihm gefiel die körperliche Arbeit, er war praktisch, geduldig, hatte ein gutes Verhältnis zu Äxten, Spaten, Schraubenschlüsseln und zu schwerer Plackerei und übernahm so in vielen Belangen Eriks Aufgaben. Das war in dieser Familie viel wert, weitaus mehr als Simons Bücherwissen.

»Es ist, als hätten wir unsere Kinder ausgetauscht«, sagte Karin zu Ruben Lentov, als er eines Sonntags kam, um Erik zu besuchen, der Heimaturlaub hatte.

Erik war schlanker als früher, aber ebenso wortreich und bis in die Tiefe seiner schwedischblauen Seele empört über den schlechten Zustand der Streitkräfte.

»Wir haben Autos und kein Benzin«, sagte er. »Aber andererseits haben wir Munition und keine Waffen.«

Dann gebot Karins Blick ihm Einhalt, und er sah auch selbst, wie die Unruhe in Rubens Augen wuchs.

An diesem Abend erzählte Ruben, was er aus geheimen Quellen über das Schicksal der Juden in Deutschland wußte. Simon hatte es nie vergessen. Die Jungen wurden zwar aus der Küche geschickt, aber es war der Ausdruck in Eriks Augen, als er sich einmal in die Küche stahl, um etwas Wasser zu trinken.

Sein Vater hatte Angst.

Und weil Karin so blaß war, als sie den beiden Jungen an diesem Abend die Betten im guten Zimmer machte. Aber vor allem war es, weil er ein Telefongespräch mit angehört hatte.

Es war Erik, der irgendwo anrief, er war in Eile, weil er mit der Eisenbahn zu seinem Einsatzort fahren mußte. Aber es war nicht die Eile, die seiner Stimme diese Schärfe und den Klang von etwas unerhört Wichtigem verlieh.

»Du mußt den Brief verbrennen ...«

...

»Ja, ich weiß, daß ich es versprochen habe. Aber da konnte ich ja nicht ahnen ...«

...

»Du mußt doch begreifen, daß sein Leben in Gefahr ist, wenn die Deutschen kommen.«

Simon horchte, saß aufrecht im Bett, um besser hören zu können. Aber eigentlich brauchte er sich nicht anzustrengen, das Telefon hing im Flur an der Wand zum guten Zimmer, jede Silbe drang deutlich zu ihm durch.

Die Fragen schwirrten ihm durch den Kopf. Mit wem sprach Erik, was war das für ein Brief, wessen Leben war in Gefahr?

Dann krampfte sich sein Magen zusammen, denn er wußte, daß er die Antwort auf die letzte Frage bereits kannte.

Es ging um ihn.

Isak schlief in einem eigenen Bett neben ihm, das war gut, denn er durfte nicht beunruhigt werden.

Aber Simon war sehr einsam, als er so dasaß und zu begreifen versuchte, ohne zu irgendeinem Schluß zu kommen.

Er hörte, wie Erik sich von Karin verabschiedete, seinen Rucksack nahm: »Auf Wiedersehen, Karin, gib gut auf dich und die Jungen acht.«

»Auf Wiedersehen Erik, paß auf dich auf.«

Er konnte die beiden vor sich sehen, wie sie sich ein wenig unbeholfen die Hand gaben.

Und kurz bevor die Tür ins Schloß fiel: »Hat sie verstanden?«

»Ich glaube, ja.«

Simon wurde jetzt böse, wie Kinder es werden, wenn sie nicht wissen, worum es geht. Die Wut brachte ihm gespenstische Träume, er begegnete der Ågrenschen, die im Tod noch unheimlicher war als zu Lebzeiten, und die ihm am Strand nachlief und schrie: »Geh heim und frag deine Mutter!«

Aber er hatte die Frage vergessen, hatte sie einfach verloren, konnte sich nicht erinnern, suchte verzweifelt, als hinge sein Leben davon ab.

Er wachte auf, weinte und verharrte im Reich der Dämmerung zwischen Schlafen und Wachen. Er ging auf die Bäume zu, die Eichen, und es gelang ihm schließlich, das Land zu finden, das es eigentlich nicht gibt, und traf seinen Mann, den Kleinen mit dem komischen Hut und dem rätselhaften Lächeln. Sie saßen eine Weile beisammen und sprachen miteinander, wie sie es die Jahre über immer getan hatten, wortlos und jenseits der Zeit.

Am Morgen stand er lange vor dem Spiegel, der über dem Kaltwasserhahn der Spüle an der Wand in der Küche hing, und schaute in die fremden Augen, die wohl die seinen aber doch anders als die aller anderen Menschen waren, dunkler als Karins, dunkler sogar als die von Ruben.

Aber er stellte dem Bild keine Fragen.

Auch Karin fragte er nicht.

Der Alltag um ihn herum behauptete sich. Bei der Hetze vom Haferbrei zu den Broten, die noch geschmiert werden mußten, und den Schulbüchern, die er zusammensuchen mußte, und den Strümpfen, die unauffindbar waren, verblaßte der gestrige Abend, das Telefongespräch verlor seine Konturen, bekam einen Anflug von Unwirklichkeit und Traum.

An diesem Tag bekam Simon ein Ungenügend für seine Deutscharbeit. Isak war bekümmert: »Meinst du, Karin wird traurig sein?«

Simon schaute erstaunt, die Schule lag in seiner Verantwortung, Karin würde nicht einmal fragen.

»Nein«, sagte er. »Die Schule ist ihr egal.«

Isak nickte erleichtert, ihm fiel ein, daß er gehört hatte, wie sie Ruben gegenüber gesagt hatte, als er sich nach Isaks Schulaufgaben erkundigte, man müsse Vertrauen zu seinen Kindern haben.

Dann sagte Isak: »Ich kann ja mit dir Deutsch büffeln, es ist schließlich meine Muttersprache.«

Simon war so verblüfft, daß er sich fast an seinem Rahmbonbon verschluckt hätte, das er sich zum Trost gekauft hatte.

Isak nahm am Deutschunterricht nicht teil, irgendwie hatte Simon es für selbstverständlich erachtet, daß er davon in gleicher Weise befreit war wie vom Religionsunterricht, eben weil er Jude war. Erst jetzt verstand er, daß Isak nicht deutsch zu lernen brauchte, weil er diese erschreckende Sprache mit den vielen harten Kommandowörtern schon beherrschte: Achtung, Heil, halt, verboten ...

So kam es, daß die Küche, die jahrelang Hitler hatte brüllen hören, nun einem ganz anderen Deutsch lauschen durfte, einem weichen und runden Berlinerisch.

Das war komisch, selbst Karin war erstaunt darüber, wie angenehm die Sprache der Nazis klingen konnte. Simon lernte schnell, machte sich mit der Sprache vertraut. Er schaffte die nächste Schularbeit gut, und das Halbjahreszeugnis, das sie an dem Tag bekamen, an dem die Deutschen in Paris einmarschierten, war in Ordnung.

Eine Welle von Hirnhautentzündungen hatte die Gegend erfaßt. In der Nacht, in der die Engländer weit über 300 000 Männer in kleinen Booten von Dünkirchen herüberholten, starb eine von Simons Spielgefährtinnen, ein Mädchen, mit dem er immer seine Schwierigkeiten gehabt hatte.

Dieser kleine Tod bedeutete mehr an Wirklichkeit als alle Toten des großen Krieges zusammengenommen. Simon bekam Schuldgefühle.

Er hatte das Mädchen erst vor vierzehn Tagen bei einem gehässigen und unnötigen Streit Fuchsarsch genannt. Sie war rothaarig gewesen und hatte, wie er auch, ein loses Mundwerk gehabt, war die Mittlere in einer kinderreichen Maurerfamilie gewesen, wo der Vater trank und die Mutter viele Tränen vergoß.

»Sie hatte es schwer. Sie wollte wahrscheinlich einfach nicht mehr«, vermutete Karin.

Aber in den nächsten Tagen beobachtete sie die Jungen sehr genau und war eines Abends sehr beunruhigt, als sie glaubte, Isak habe Fieber.

Noch ein Ereignis blieb Simon aus diesem Frühling deutlich im Gedächtnis. Karin erwachte eines Morgens mit der Erinnerung an einen lebhaften Traum und erzählte den Jungen, wie sie in einem Schutzraum gesessen und den Gekreuzigten an der Wand hängen gesehen hatte. Als Bomben fielen, wurde er lebendig, hob seinen Arm und zeigte mit einem Palmzweig an die Decke, die sich öffnete. Und Karin konnte sehen, daß der Himmel über den winzigen Flugzeugen blau und unendlich war.

»Die Flugzeuge und auch die Bomben sahen aus wie Spiel-zeug«, sagte sie und fügte hinzu, daß der Traum ihr Trost gespendet habe.

Auch die Jungen fühlten sich gestärkt, besonders nachdem Edit Äppelgren in die Küche gekommen war, um eine Schere abzuholen, die Karin sich geliehen hatte, und so auch zu einer Tasse Kaffee und ihrer Vorstellung von Karins Traum gekommen war. Sie war eine Christin und wußte zu erzählen, daß das Pfingstfest, welches sie soeben mit blühenden Narzissen auf dem Frühstückstisch gefeiert hatten, zum Gedenken an den Heiligen Geist stattfand, der sich über die Menschen dieser Welt ergossen hatte.

Sie hatten gerade ihre Kaffeetassen geleert, als sie die Fliegerabwehr auf dem Käringberg feuern hörten, ins Freie stürzten und noch für einen kurzen Moment die deutsche Maschine mit dem Hakenkreuz und dem deutschen Piloten zu sehen bekamen, der in der Luft wie ein Stück Holz brannte, ehe er samt seinem Flugzeug in der Kühle des unendlichen Meeres verschwand.

Simon weinte, aber Isak war erregt, seltsam freudig.

Es wurde trotz allem ein richtiger Sommer, draußen auf den Wiesen zwischen den Felsen – dort, wo der große Fluß ins Meer mündete. Weiße Sommernächte, Zelte am Badestrand, Mädchen, die man ärgern, Jungen mit denen man sich prügeln konnte, Kanus, Segeljollen.

Erik kam nach Hause und berichtete, wie sie in aller Heimlichkeit norwegischen Juden über die Grenze halfen.

Eines Sonntags nahm er das Auto, um Inga, eine seiner Cousinen, zu besuchen. Sie hatte in einiger Entfernung nördlich der Stadt einen kleinen Bauernhof.

Ob Simon mitfahren wolle?

Nein, er mochte Inga nicht besonders gern, sie war dick und faul, roch nach Stall und wagte nie, ihn richtig anzusehen.

Aber Isak sagte, die Sache müsse doch wichtig sein, wenn Erik trotz rationiertem Benzin fahre, und da bekam Simon ein schlechtes Gewissen.

Danach vergaß er alles. Er stand mit Isak auf dem Gerüst und strich das Haus mit weißer Farbe an, die Ruben besorgt hatte. Es war ein Geschenk für Erik, und Isak sang bei der Arbeit: Der Wind weht kalt her, kaltes Wetter vom Meer.

Simon verabscheute Isaks Gesang, aber er mußte zugeben, der Sommer 1940 kam nie so richtig in Schwung.

Vom Fenster der Kammer aus konnte man den See im Herbst zumindest erahnen, dann nämlich, wenn das Laub von den Bäumen gefallen war. Und natürlich auch im Frühling, wenn man hören konnte, wie er sich schwappend vom Eis befreite. Das Haus, das eigentlich nur eine Hütte war, lag in herrlicher Südlage an einem Hang, hatte die Berge im Rücken, was jetzt allerdings weniger herrlich war als zu jener Zeit, zu der es genug arbeitsfähige Männer gegeben hatte, die das Weidengestrüpp entfernt und die Aussicht zum See hin frei gehalten hatten.

Ein paar Wiesen, ein paar Felder, Kartoffeln, kein Getreide mehr. Aber vier Kühe im Stall, zwei Schweine, an die zwanzig Hühner und dann – in der Hütte – zwei sehr alte verwirrte und hinfällige Menschen. Die Verwandten in der fernen Großstadt schoben alle außer Karin den Gedanken daran, wie einsam Inga eigentlich war, beiseite.

Wie alle andern war Inga in jungen Jahren in die Stadt gegangen, hatte bei einer Familie eine Anstellung gefunden und später in einem Laden gearbeitet. Es waren unbeschwerte Jahre gewesen, voller Begegnungen mit Menschen, Eindrücken und Ereignissen. Sie war hübsch anzusehen gewesen, hellhäutig und rundlich in einer zarten, ansprechenden Weise.

Sie hätte wohl auch, wie ihre Schwestern, einen Mann finden können. Aber sie war die Älteste von sieben Geschwistern gewesen und hatte genug von der Liebe gesehen und davon, was sie aus einer Frau machen konnte.

Sie war auf der Hut.

Und so kam es wie es kommen mußte, als die Alten sich selbst und den Hof nicht mehr versorgen konnten. Sie war diejenige, die zurückkommen, die der Angst der Eltern vor dem Armenhaus nachgeben mußte, das jetzt zwar Altersheim hieß aber immer noch schlimmer war als der Tod.

Sie widersprach nicht ein einziges Mal, beugte sich frühzeitig der Schuldigkeit, ergab sich der Pflicht des vierten Gebots.

Alles wäre leichter gewesen, wenn es wenigstens Zuneigung gegeben hätte, die Möglichkeit eines Gesprächs zwischen ihr und der Mutter. Aber nicht einmal die hatte ihr das Leben zum Geschenk gemacht, sie war von Geburt an noch ungeliebter gewesen als die Schwester, die ihre Eltern zur Heirat gezwungen hatten. Sie kam zu früh, nur etwa einen Monat nach der Trauung, und diese Schande blieb die ganze Jugend über an ihr haften.

In den ersten langen Wintermonaten seit sie als Erwachsene zurückgekehrt war, stellte sie sich oft vor, wie es wäre, den Alten Gift zu geben und den Hof anzuzünden. Sie wußte, wo das Bilsenkraut wuchs, erinnerte sich, wie Ida, die Dorfhexe ihrer Kindheit, das Gift aus den Kapseln gezupft hatte.

Dann begriff sie, daß sie drauf und dran war, verrückt zu werden und daß die Ursache dafür ihre vielen Gedanken waren. Sie hatte erkannt, daß man vom Denken wahnsinnig werden konnte, daß es die Grübler waren, die ins Irrenhaus nach Hisingen gebracht wurden.

Also beschloß sie, mit dem Denken aufzuhören, und nach einigen Jahren war ihr das recht gut gelungen.

Als der Vater erblindete, wurde die Zeitung abbestellt. Die Verwandtschaft war nicht bewandert im Schreiben, es kamen nur Ansichtskarten zu den Feiertagen.

Und obwohl die zwanziger Jahre schon dem Ende entgegen gingen, hatte der elektrische Strom noch nicht über den Berg zur Hütte gefunden, also war an ein Radio auch nicht zu denken.

Die Geschwister schickten Geld, aber es verging viel Zeit zwischen den Besuchen, und das war auch gut so. Denn wenn sie kamen, und vor allem die Brüder, wurde die Mutter unruhiger als gewöhnlich, und diese Unruhe hielt danach noch viele Tage an.

Am häufigsten kam Erik, der Cousin mit dem Lastwagen. Und seine Frau Karin, die Inga damals die Stelle in dem Laden in der Markthalle gleich in der Innenstadt verschafft hatte und die so besonders lieb war. Lieb und stark in einem, das hatte Inga immer bewundert.

Sie kamen, weil Karin Mitleid mit ihr hatte, das wußte Inga. Karin hatte zu den Alten einmal geradeheraus gesagt, daß Inga ein Recht auf ein eigenes Leben habe und daß alte Leute heutzutage im Altersheim in der Kreisstadt gut aufgehoben seien. Da bekam die Mutter aber sofort Herzschmerzen und Erik mußte mit dem Auto den Doktor holen, der zwar keinen Herzfehler feststellen konnte, aber doch sagte, man müsse mit so alten Menschen sehr behutsam umgehen.

Dann wurde über diese Sache nie wieder gesprochen, aber Inga sah immerhin, daß Erik zornig war, und sie merkte, daß Karin Vorwürfe gemacht bekommen würde für das, was sie angerichtet hatte.

Dann kam der Frühling, in dem der Spielmann am Bach saß.

Das kann nicht wahr sein, dachte Inga hinterher, er mußte ihren Träumen entsprungen sein. Aber an diesem Abend war er ganz und gar wirklich, und auch am nächsten und übernächsten bis hin zu den weißen Mittsommernächten, wo er schließlich verschwand.

Es war ein recht unansehnlicher Bach, der einen weiten und mühsamen Weg durch die Wälder wandern mußte, um zwischen den Bergen hindurch zum See zu gelangen. Am Ende schließlich wußte er sich keinen anderen Rat, als sich von dem Steilhang über die letzten Klippen hinunterzustürzen, um das Ufer endlich zu erreichen.

Es war kein kleiner Wasserfall, den dieser Bach zustande brachte. Besonders im Frühling war er voller Kraft und Heiterkeit.

Für Inga war der Wasserfall eine Freude. Und eine Befreiung.

Sie versorgte die Alten, sie mühte sich mit den Kartoffeln ab, und sie melkte das Vieh und hielt es gut bei Kräften und Laune. Aber es lag ihr nicht, mit den Tieren zu sprechen, die Persönlichkeit eines jeden zu erkennen, so daß ihr der Umgang kaum Freude bereitete.

Nein, sie ging von den stummen Tieren zu den stummen Menschen. Der Vater hatte schon seit vielen Jahren kein Wort mehr gesprochen, und die Mutter brach von Zeit zu Zeit in immer unverständlichere Tiraden aus.

Sie war boshaft, das war sie schon immer gewesen, dachte Inga.

Aber vor allem dachte sie an den Sturzbach, zu dem sie, wenn die Alten eingeschlafen und die Tiere im Stall versorgt waren, gehen wollte, um sich gründlich zu waschen. Bis weit in den Herbst hinein ging sie jeden Abend dorthin, zog sich aus und stand unter dem Wasserfall, wurde rein und von Kummer frei.

Dann, eines Abends im Frühling, war der Geigenspieler dort, saß einfach da und schaute sie an, als wäre sie ein Wesen aus einer heidnischen Sage.

Sie hatte keine Angst, dafür war alles einfach zu unwirklich. Sie ging geradenwegs auf ihn zu, legte, nackt wie sie war, ihren Kopf in seinen Schoß, und er legte seine Geige ans Kinn und spielte für sie, und das eine war nicht wundersamer als das andere.

Die Musik war wild und schön, genau wie sie sein sollte.

Man kann sagen, es wäre besser für Inga gewesen, wenn es der Milchmann gewesen wäre, der jeden zweiten Tag mit dem Molkereiauto kam, um die Milch abzuholen. Aber der war häßlich und mürrisch und außerdem verheiratet.

Der Spielmann hatte vielleicht auch eine Frau, aber das erfuhr Inga nicht, denn sie konnten nie miteinander sprechen. Er war ein Ausländer. Später brachte Erik in Erfahrung, daß er Jude und Musiklehrer an der Volkshochschule auf der anderen Seite des Sees war. Als das Semester beendet war, kehrte er nach Deutschland zurück, er hatte dort einen Namen, eine Adresse in Berlin.

Aber es hatte ihm nie jemand geschrieben, und Inga wußte ja, daß er nie richtig von dieser Welt gewesen war und bestand deshalb auf ihrem »Vater unbekannt«.

Das alles geschah viel später, tief im Winter, als Inga endlich zugeben mußte, daß sie schwanger war und daß der Mann am Bach aus Fleisch und Blut gewesen war.

47

Sie liebten sich, halbe Nächte lang liebten sie sich in diesem Frühling und Inga begriff endlich, warum Leute alles aufgeben konnten, Würde und Wohlstand, nur um der Liebe willen. Sie hatte nie geahnt, was der Körper alles erleben konnte, wenn er auf diese Weise von erfahrenen Händen gestreichelt wurde, hatte auch nie gewußt, wie schön ein Mann sein konnte. Er war schlank, zart gebaut, aber sein Glied war kräftig und groß, und sie konnte nie genug davon bekommen. Auch nicht von den Augen, die schwarz waren wie der Waldsee.

Er sprach und seine Stimme war voller Zärtlichkeit. Da sie jedoch die Worte nicht verstand, mußte er sein Gefühl für das Wunder und für sie mit der Geige ausdrücken, und er spielte ihr jeden Abend fast wie irr vor Begierde vor.

Später konnte sie sich erinnern, daß er am letzten Abend sehr traurig und daß sein Geigenspiel voll Schmerz gewesen war. Sie wunderte sich also nicht, als er am nächsten Abend nicht kam.

Sie war nur unendlich traurig.

Aber sie sagte sich auch, daß sie die ganze Zeit über gewußt hatte, daß es so kommen werde, daß es ein Traum gewesen war und daß Frauen wie sie früher oder später aufwachen und ihr Los ertragen mußten.

Als sie im Herbst die Kartoffeln aus der Erde zog, war sie plump und schwerfällig, dachte aber trotzdem nicht daran, daß ein Kind in ihr war. Erik und Karin kamen gleichzeitig mit dem ersten Schnee und halfen ihr die Kartoffelsäcke in den Keller zu schleppen, und Karin sah sofort, wie es um sie stand.

»Inga«, sagte sie. »Du wirst ein Kind bekommen.«

»Was, zum Teufel, hast du nur getrieben«, wetterte Erik und seine Stimme war so schrill, daß es Inga wie ein Peitschenhieb traf.

Aber Karin unterbrach ihn schnell und schroff: »Jetzt hältst du ausnahmsweise einmal dein großes Maul, Erik Larsson.«

Dann ging sie mit Inga in die Bodenkammer hinauf und langsam und zögernd begann Inga sich zu erinnern und konnte alles erzählen.

Wäre der dicke Bauch nicht gewesen, hätte Karin wohl geglaubt, Inga wäre da draußen in der Einsamkeit übergeschnappt, was Karin auch nicht weiter verwundert hätte. So wie es jetzt aussah, mußte sie der Geschichte von dem schwarzäugigen Geigenspieler am Bach wohl Glauben schenken.

»Das bringt Mama ins Grab«, weinte Inga, und Karin verschwieg, was sie dachte, daß das nämlich das beste wäre, was passieren könnte.

Sie waren praktische Menschen, auch Inga, die trotz allem ansprechbar blieb und immerhin sosehr Bauerntochter war, daß sie sehr schnell zum Wichtigsten kam, daß nämlich niemand von ihrer Schande erfahren durfte. Keiner im Dorf, nicht die Geschwister, und auf keinen Fall jemals die Eltern.

Erik sprach mit den Alten, sagte, wie es nicht war, daß Inga eine schwere Krankheit im Bauch habe und, wie es war, daß sie ins Krankenhaus in der Stadt müsse. Er konnte nicht beurteilen, wieviel sie wirklich verstanden.

Wer aber alles mitbekam und verstand, war ihre mittlere Schwester, als Inga in ihrer Küche im Amtmannbau in der Stadt auftauchte. Sie sagte, ihre Kinder seien jetzt groß genug, um allein zurechtzukommen, und daß sie, Märta, nach Hause fahren und sich während Ingas Operation um die Eltern kümmern solle.

Märta widersprach zuerst, gab aber dann nach, man hatte sich Erik zu beugen. Und sie glaubte ihm, als er behauptete, Inga könne sterben, wenn sie nicht in Pflege käme. Sie packte und fuhr heim zu den Alten.

Dann hielt sie es dort in der Hütte und in der Einsamkeit aber nur wenige Wochen aus, also kamen zu Beginn des Spätwinters die Eltern doch ins Altenheim, wo alles so verlief, wie sie es immer vorausgesagt hatten. Sie starben beide innerhalb eines Monats.

Zu dieser Zeit war das Kind geboren und von Karin und Erik bereits adoptiert.

Inga kehrte auf den Hof zurück, obwohl sie das jetzt gar nicht mehr mußte und Karin sich angeboten hatte, ihr noch einmal eine Stelle in der Markthalle zu verschaffen.

»Sie ist menschenscheu geworden«, sagte Erik. »Sie hat nicht mehr den Mut, in ein normales Leben zurückzukehren.«

Karin nickte, dachte aber, so einfach sei es nun auch wieder nicht.

Als Karin mit dem Neugeborenen in den Armen dastand und die Krankenschwester sagen hörte, die Mutter habe den Jungen nicht einmal sehen wollen, spürte sie in der Tiefe ihres Herzens, daß sie kein Anrecht auf das Kind hatte. Sie hatte es nicht in Seligkeit und Pein getragen und es nicht in Schmerzen geboren.

Sie sah lange in die Augen des Jungen und erkannte in ihnen die Wehmut der langen dämmrigen Stunden am See. Aber noch etwas anderes sah sie, eine große Einsamkeit, ein Nicht-Sein.

Das kommt, weil Inga ihn verleugnet hat, dachte Karin, es kommt von neun Monaten nicht anerkannten Daseins. Und Karin dachte an Ingas Worte in der Bodenkammer, daß sie geglaubt hatte, der Mann mit der Geige sei der Nöck, der Wassergeist, den es eigentlich nicht gab.

Aber es hatte diesen Mann gegeben, dachte Karin und es beunruhigte sie, daß dieses Kind sehr jüdisch aussah. Das Kind eines fremden Mannes, das ihres werden sollte.

Nicht etwa daß sie an die Schwierigkeiten wegen des Andersseins dachte. Sie liebte den Jungen. Und da sie ein praktischer Mensch war, wußte sie trotz aller Bedenken, daß ihre Liebe Berge versetzen und die Festungen des Himmels überwinden würde, wenn es für die Sicherheit des Kindes notwendig sein sollte.

Er sollte ein guter Mensch mit einer glücklichen Kindheit werden.

Zu Beginn des Frühlings, als sie in den Nächten aufstand, um ihm ein zusätzliches Fläschchen zu geben, war sie über die Frage hinweg, wer ein Anrecht auf das Kind hatte.

Sie hatte starke und wunderliche Gedanken.

Die Kinder gehören der Erde, dachte sie, haben die uralte Geschichte der Erde in ihren Zellen und die ganze Weisheit der Natur in ihrem Blut.

Sie sah doch, daß dieser Junge die Wahrheit in sich trug.

Alle Kinder tun das, dachte sie. Für kurze Zeit sind die Kinder die Weisen. Vielleicht ist jedes neue Kind ein Versuch der Erde, dem Ausdruck zu verleihen, was nicht verstanden werden kann.

Es war Inga, die den Namen bestimmte. Nach dem Begräbnis der Eltern ging sie direkt auf Erik zu und sagte: »Er soll Simon heißen.«

Karin verstand, daß sie sich dem zu beugen hatten. Sie stand mit dem Kind auf dem Arm da und dachte: Er hatte ja trotz allem einen Namen, Nöck.

Karin war ein Nachkömmling gewesen, die Jüngste von sechs Kindern. Alle anderen waren Jungen, und der jüngste von ihnen ging schon in die Schule, als feststand, daß noch ein Kind in Schneidermeister Lundströms Häuschen gegenüber der Eisenbahn in der värmländischen Bergwerksgemeinde dazukommen werde.

Die Mutter weinte und verwünschte das Schicksal und das Kind, das in ihr wuchs. Sie war etwas über vierzig und hatte sich frei geglaubt. Es war ein drei Tage langer harter Kampf, das Kind aus dem Leib zu pressen, fast wäre sie dabei gestorben, aber als sie mit dem Neugeborenen an der Brust dalag, hatte sie doch noch Tränen übrig.

Jetzt weinte sie, weil das Kind ein Mädchen war, eines jener armen Wesen, die zu Sklaverei und schmerzerfüllten Geburten verdammt waren.

Als Kind bekam Karin immer wieder zu hören, wie unerwünscht sie gewesen war und wie sie ihre Mutter fast das Leben gekostet hatte. Es war eine oft gehörte Geschichte, die sie als gegeben hinnahm, und sie verstand ihre Mutter.

Hingegen verstand sie nie den Schmerz, der tief in ihrem Herzen wurzelte, und der mit solcher Macht wuchs und sich verzweigte, daß sie ihn nie würde ausreißen können.

Eigentlich hätte Karin schon frühzeitig aufgeben müssen so wie die anderen unerwünschten Kinder, die in der Gegend von der Tuberkulose dahingerafft wurden. Aber sie überlebte, wurde groß und kräftig, denn sie hatte einen Vater.

Petter Lundström war schon sechzig Jahre alt, als seine Tochter geboren wurde. Er war zweimal verheiratet gewesen und hatte auch Kinder aus erster Ehe. Die Älteren waren Söhne, schon seit langem erwachsen. Aber es hatte auch eine Tochter gegeben, ein kleines Mädchen, das mit sieben Jahren an der Schwindsucht gestorben war.

Und es war ganz eigenartig, dieses tote kleine Mädchen war Petters Verbindung zum Leben, zu dem, was in ihm selbst lebendig war. Er hatte dieses Kind geliebt. Die Söhne, auch die aus der zweiten Ehe, hatten viele Geschichten darüber gehört, wie seltsam zart das kleine Mädchen gewesen war und wie innig er es geliebt hatte.

Daß ihm nun gegen Ende seines Lebens eine neue Tochter geboren wurde, war für Petter eine große Freude. Gott allein weiß, ob er sich nicht sogar einbildete, daß sein kleiner Liebling als Trost und neues Licht in einem immer grauer werdenden Leben zu ihm zurückgekommen war.

Er hatte seine Werkstatt zu Hause, und schon vom ersten Tag an war das Kind seins. Es durfte in einer Kiste auf dem großen Schneidertisch liegen, und er gluckste mit ihm, lächelte es an, sang ihm vor.

Die Leute kamen und gingen in der Werkstatt aus und ein, und mitten in diesem Strom saß Petter mit dem Karinkind, dem Engelskind, der Süße seines Lebens, dem Augenstern. Gewiß lachte der eine oder andere über ihn und seine grenzenlose Liebe, aber hier in Värmland war genug Raum für jegliche Eigenart. Es war im großen und ganzen also ein gutmütiges Lachen. Und das Kind war niedlich und keinem eine Last, und es war auch nicht im Weg, wenn man etwas anprobieren mußte.

Er kannte hundert Lieder, tausend Märchen und noch mehr verrückte lustige Geschichten. All das schenkte er ihr, er führte sie auf einem Weg von Wärme und pfiffiger Weisheit. Sie lernte schon früh fast alles über die Torheit und die Klugheit der Menschen und auch darüber, daß die meisten das Gute wollen aber im Bösen enden.

Petter war immer ordentlich gewesen. Jetzt wurde es so sauber in der Werkstatt, daß die Leute sagten, hier könne man direkt vom Fußboden essen. Er ließ sich ein Buch aus Karlstad kommen, aus dem er alles lernen konnte, was die kleinen Kinder zu jener Zeit brauchten.

Da stand viel von Reinlichkeit, Ernährung und frischer Luft. Über Zärtlichkeit und Liebe stand da nichts, und was Petter Lundström betraf, war das sowieso alles dasselbe.

Auf diese Weise kam Karin zu ihrer inneren Stärke und ihrer Einsicht darüber, wie unbegreiflich das Leben eingerichtet war und wie es trotz allem begreiflich werden konnte.

Als sie dann in die Schule ging, konnte sie längst lesen und schreiben und durfte zu Petters unermeßlichem Stolz eine Klasse überspringen.

Die Mutter? Doch, die gab es, sie ging in der Werkstatt aus und ein, tief gebeugt durch ihr Bild von sich selbst als einem geduldigen Lasttier, und sie war von den vielen Geburten und all der Mühsal des Kochens und Putzens frühzeitig gealtert. Sie war die Schuld in Petters Leben, er konnte sich nie davon freimachen, daß er es gewesen war, der ihr die vielen Kinder gemacht hatte, und davon, wie sie so oft sagte, daß er seine erste Frau in ein zu frühes Grab gelegt hatte.

Sie war im Wochenbett gestorben.

Er hatte das ständige Jammern und die dauernde Müdigkeit seiner Frau zu ertragen. Was ihm jetzt, wo Karin geboren war, nur recht war. Die Mutter konnte das Kind ja nicht zurückverlangen, mußte zugeben, daß er tat, was er konnte, um ihr diese letzte schwere Bürde abzunehmen.

Er rührte sie im Bett nie wieder an und dunkel ahnte sie, daß es da einen Zusammenhang gab, daß sein Bedürfnis nach Nähe befriedigt war, solange er sich um das Kind kümmern durfte.

Die Reibereien mehrten sich, als das Mädchen größer wurde und die Mutter meinte, daß Karin im Haushalt helfen solle. Petter konnte das nicht verweigern und gab das Mädchen her. Aber immer nur für kurze Zeit. Sie wurde nicht häuslich, war oft ungeschickt am Herd. Einmal schlug die Mutter ihr mit dem Feuerhaken auf den Rücken.

Es war ein Ereignis, das niemand in der Schneiderstube je vergessen würde, denn der gutmütige Petter ging mit eben diesem Feuerhaken auf seine Frau los, und auch er schlug zu.

»Damit du weißt, wie sich das anfühlt«, sagte er und war weiß im Gesicht vor Zorn.

Die Mutter vergaß es wie gesagt nie, nicht nur die Demütigung, auch der Schmerz setzte sich tief in ihr fest, was für das Mädchen nicht gut war. Mit der Zeit war sie es ja doch, die diese Rechnung begleichen mußte.

Als Karin neun Jahre alt war, starb der Vater, saß am Schneidertisch und fiel einfach wie ein ausgeleiertes Klappmesser vornüber.

Das Kind begriff es nicht, so etwas konnte doch nicht sein. Sie lief hinaus in den großen Wald, blieb über Nacht dort, wachte am Morgen unter einer Fichte auf und erinnerte sich. Es ging tiefer in den Wald, kam zu einer Lichtung. Dort floß ein Bach, langsam wurde dem kleinen Mädchen bewußt, was geschehen war und es erkannte, daß der Bach zu klein war, um sich darin zu ertränken.

In der Morgendämmerung machte ein Schwarm Seidenschwänze auf der weiten Reise vom Gebirge im Norden zu den warmen Flüssen im Süden am Bach Rast. Sie ließen sich um das Kind herum nieder, das diese sonderbar schimmernden Vögel noch nie gesehen und ihren Gesang, der zwischen Jubel und Trauer lag, nie gehört hatte.

Das Mädchen blieb ganz ruhig sitzen und wußte, daß der Vater ihr diesen Gruß geschickt hatte, daß er noch immer bei ihr war und immer da bleiben würde.

So kam es, daß sie beschloß, ihr Leben durchzustehen.

Die Mutter verkaufte die Schneiderei und zog mit den Kindern, die noch zu Hause waren, zwei fast erwachsenen Söhnen und dem kleinen Mädchen, das sie kaum kannte, nach Göteborg. Dort fand sie in der Fabrik, die sie auslaugte, aber doch Geld für die Einzimmerwohnung in Majorna und das Essen für sie und die Kinder einbrachte, eine neue Verwendung für das Bild, das sie von sich selbst hatte als dem geschundenen Arbeitstier.

Bald kam der Erste Weltkrieg, das Essen wurde knapp und die Menschen mit schwindendem Lebenswillen starben wie die Fliegen an der Spanischen Grippe.

Karin überlebte dank der Seidenschwänze. Und auch dank des einen oder anderen Lehrers, der das ungewöhnliche und begabte Mädchen gern mochte. Als Karin zum Konfirmationsunterricht ging, suchte der Pfarrer die Mutter auf um ihr zu sagen, daß das Mädchen eine höhere Schule besuchen sollte.

Das war der reine Hohn, er sah das selbst, als er dort in der Küche bei der schwergebeugten Witwe stand.

»Flausen«, sagte sie, als der Pfarrer gegangen war. »Dein verrückter Vater hat dafür gesorgt, daß du dir einbildest, etwas Besseres zu sein.«

Als die Söhne nach Hause kamen, erzählte sie von dem verrückten Pfarrer, und sie lachten alle gewaltig und lange. Für ein Mädchen ein Studium zu bezahlen, etwas so Dummes hatten sie wirklich noch nie gehört. Aber der Schweigsamste von ihnen sagte später, wenn der Vater noch lebte, dann ...

Bei dieser Gelegenheit kam ihr zu Bewußtsein, warum die Brüder sie haßten.

Mit dreizehn ging sie als Dienstmädchen zu einer Familie, mit fünfzehn ging sie in ein Nähatelier, mit sechzehn in ein Geschäft in der großen Markthalle. Überallhin folgten ihr die Seidenschwänze, und als sie achtzehn war, lernte sie Erik kennen, sah daß er Petter ähnlich war, wurde Sozialistin und anerkannt, wagte sogar zu glauben, was er zu ihr sagte, nämlich daß sie sehr schön sei.

Erik war der einzige Sohn in der Einzimmerwohnung im städtischen Sozialbau am Stigberg. Er war die Hoffnung seiner Mutter und die Stütze seiner jüngeren Schwester.

Die Schwester war schwächlich, eine von denen, die mit einer punktierten Lunge leben mußten, nachdem die Tuberkulose sie mit sechs Jahren befallen hatte. Ihr waren sowohl eine eigene Persönlichkeit als auch ein eigenes Leben versagt und sie wuchs langsam und krumm im Schatten der Mutter heran.

Die Mutter war ein starker Mensch, schön und verbittert und sehr religiös. Sie hatte spät geheiratet und die Liebe mit solcher Wut gehaßt, daß sie ihren schattenhaften Mann, kaum waren ihre Kinder geboren, aus dem ehelichen Bett vertrieben hatte.

Ein Ventil für ihre Lust verschaffte sie sich, indem sie den Jungen mit dem Teppichklopfer auf den nackten roten Hintern schlug. Es war keine einfache Kindheit, aber es gab doch so etwas wie Respekt vor Erik, vor seinem Geschlecht, dem Mann im Jungen, der die Intelligenz und die Kraft der Mutter geerbt hatte und der ihre Träume wahr machen sollte.

Diese Achtung die er spürte, verlieh ihm soviel Stärke, daß er sich mit der Zeit gegen seine Mutter auflehnen konnte, zumindest gegen ihre Ansichten und ihr düsteres Christentum. Schlimmer war all das, was er so früh erfahren hatte, daß es unsichtbar blieb.

Die körperliche Liebe empfand er sein Leben lang als Sünde, und nie half ihm jemand dabei, den merkwürdigen Zusammenhang zwischen Lust und Grausamkeit zu verstehen, den es in seinen Phantasien gab und für den er sich entsetzlich schämte.

Als die Mutter ihm nicht mehr mit dem Teppichklopfer beikommen konnte, erzwang sie seinen Gehorsam durch ihre ständigen Androhungen eines Herzschlags.

Ihr Herz wurde zu eben jener Zeit krank, als er in die Pubertät kam.

Auch er hätte studieren sollen, war einer der vielen seiner Generation, die es weit hätten bringen können, wie man so sagte. Aber vielleicht war es am besten so wie es war.

Als fünfzehnjähriger Lehrling in den Götawerken trat er der Gewerkschaft bei und pilgerte jeden Abend nach dem Zehnstundenarbeitstag zu den Studienkreisen und den Büchern. Hier fand er das Handwerkszeug, mit dessen Hilfe er endlich die grausame Welt begreifen lernte, in der er aufgewachsen war, und er lernte auch, wie Unterdrückung funktioniert – immer nach unten, immer gegen die noch Schwächeren.

Manchmal konnte er seine Mutter verstehen.

Und er verstand jetzt auch, woher das fürchterliche Gefühl der Demütigung kam, das an den Schuhen haftete, die er als Heranwachsender jedes Jahr zu Weihnachten vom Gemeindepfarrer entgegennehmen mußte, der sie wiederum von einer wohltätigen Organisation bekommen hatte, die sich Älvsborger Weihnachtsmänner nannte.

Mit sechzehn teilte er seiner Mutter mit, daß es Gott nicht gäbe und daß ihre Kirche kaum besser wäre als der Schnaps, wenn es darum ging, das arbeitende Volk zu unterdrücken.

Sie faßte sich ans Herz und drohte mit dem Tod, doch das verfehlte seine Wirkung, denn der Junge war schon auf dem Weg zur nächsten Versammlung.

Weitaus machtloser war er, wenn es um die Liebe ging. Die Mädchen, in die er sich verliebte, trieb ihm die Mutter schnell wieder aus, zu Tode erschrocken bei dem Gedanken, der Sohn könne sie verlassen.

Als er Karin kennenlernte, war er fast dreißig und wußte, schon als er das erste Mal in ihre sanften braunen Augen geblickt hatte, daß es jetzt ernst war, und sein Verlangen war so groß und seine Angst so gewaltig, daß er jetzt eine himmlische Macht gebraucht hätte, zu der er hätte beten können: Guter Gott, hilf mir mit meiner Mutter.

Aber er hatte sich in der Samtäugigkeit geirrt, mußte bald einsehen, daß hinter Karins Sanftmut eine Kraft stand, die sich durchaus mit der seiner Mutter messen konnte. Schon beim ersten Besuch bei ihm zu Hause sagte sie es geradeheraus: »Erik und ich werden heiraten.«

»Das ist mein Tod«, verkündete die alte Frau und wurde blaß, als wolle sie die Drohung hier am Küchentisch unmittelbar wahr machen. Aber Karin besaß die Frechheit, ihr ins Gesicht zu lachen und zu sagen, daß das ja der Sinn des Lebens sei, und die Alten wegsterben mußten, um den Jungen hier auf Erden Platz zu machen.

Dann nahm sie Erik einfach mit. Die Mutter überlebte und war viele Jahre lang eine schwere Last für Erik und Karin.

Erik wurde nie bewußt, vor welchem Schicksal Karin ihn bewahrt hatte. Aber er verstand an diesem Abend, daß seine Frau ebenso stark war wie seine Mutter, und er erschrak bei dem Gedanken, daß er von einer Frauenfalle in die andere getappt war. Und er dachte, daß es wichtig war, seine Männlichkeit zu behaupten, um nicht auch zu einem Schatten zu werden wie sein Vater.

Sie heirateten im Frühling. Beide Mutter weinten, Karins Mutter allerdings, weil die Tochter jetzt das Frauenschicksal mit den ständigen Schwangerschaften und schrecklichen Geburten erleiden mußte.

Dann richteten sie sich ein. Er tischlerte die Möbel selbst, Stühle, Büfett, Eßtisch, Leinenschrank. Sie nähte.

Es wurde ein Heim ganz unüblicher Art, aber schön.

Das junge Paar blieb zur Freude der Schwiegermütter kinderlos.

Bei einem Geburtstagskaffee verspottete seine Mutter Karin unverblümt, und ausnahmsweise brach Eriks grenzenloser Zorn über die Alte heraus als er sagte, die Kinderlosigkeit sei seine Schuld. Er habe eine peinliche Krankheit gehabt, eine die man sich zuzieht, wenn einem die Möglichkeit verwehrt wird, ein eigenes Mädchen zu haben und deshalb gezwungen ist zu den Huren zu gehen. Also mußte sie, die Mutter, einsehen, daß es im Grunde ihre Schuld war.

Als sie an diesem Abend nach Hause fuhren, nahm Karin Eriks Hand und sagte, daß seine Mutter, nachdem sie an diesem Abend nicht auf der Stelle tot umgefallen war, sicher hundert Jahre alt werden würde.

Sie wurde sechsundneunzig.

Karin wagte nie zu fragen, ob sich die Wahrheit hinter der Geschichte verbarg, die Erik erzählt hatte. Er hatte sie schützen wollen. Das sah ihm ähnlich, er war ein Mann, auf den man sich verlassen konnte. Nicht so wie auf Petter, das hatte sie erkannt, er war leichter zu verunsichern aber streitlustig und verletzlich.

Doch auch das war gut so, denn Petter lebte in ihrem Herzen weiter und niemand würde ihn dort gefährden.

Dann bekamen sie ihren Sohn, und was spielte es für eine Rolle, daß dieses lange ersehnte Kind nicht von ihrem Blut war.

Erik war stolz wie ein König, hob die Ersparnisse ab und kaufte draußen an der Flußmündung ein Grundstück, wo das Kind frische Luft und freien Auslauf haben würde.

Dann baute er eigenhändig ein Haus. Es wurde ein lustiges Haus, dessen Maße von den Hölzern bestimmt wurden, die er billig bekommen konnte, wenn er mit dem Lastwagen durch die Stadt fuhr. Er kannte alle Leute vom Bau und wußte von vielen Häusern, die abgerissen wurden. Er kam zu seinem Bauplatz mit Sprossenfenstern und voller Freude am Zimmern, mit stattlichen Kachelöfen aus den Patrizierhäusern in der Allee, die modernisiert wurden, und Türen mit schönem Profil aus einem alten Gutshof in Landvetter, der umgebaut wurde.

Sie sahen es natürlich nicht so, aber es wurde ein Haus von großer Behaglichkeit, voller Überraschungen und Wärme. Und nie waren sie glücklicher als in diesem Sommer, in dem sie dort draußen durch den Lehm stapften und in den warmen Nächten im Wagenaufbau schliefen, den Erik im Hafen ergattert hatte, und der wesentlich wetterfester war als ein Zelt.

Die Schwiegermütter, die nicht wußten, woher das Kind gekommen war, tuschelten von bösem Blut und bösem Erbe. Aber Erik befahl ihnen zu schweigen, und durch Karin fand er in seinem sozialistischen Glauben zu der Gewißheit, daß das Umfeld von großer Bedeutung für die Entwicklung eines Menschen war.

Es konnte vorkommen, daß es Erik durchzuckte, wenn er in die schwarzen Augen des Säuglings blickte. Aber er wies den Schmerz zurück und machte den Jungen zu seinem Sohn, er war wie er. Bald sah er weder die Schwärze der Augen noch die borstigen Haare, Simon war sein und damit gut, erstklassig in jeder Beziehung.

Erik hatte eine kräftige und helle Singstimme, geübt schon in jungen Jahren im Kirchenchor und später dann in der Arbeiterbewegung. Da er es nicht über sich brachte, sich mit dem Kind in einer Babysprache zu unterhalten, wie Karin das dauernd tat, sang er die Internationale, daß es zwischen den Bergen nur so hallte, und platzte fast vor Stolz, wenn der Junge vor Entzücken gurgelte. Wenn Erik die Kampflieder ausgingen, ging er zu den alten Chorälen über, ohne Worte natürlich, aber voller Frieden und Kraft.

Simons Freude am Gesang war nicht anzuzweifeln, auch Karin sah es und staunte.

Karin hatte das Kind fast immer im Arm, doch im Frühjahr, als der

Garten zu grünen begann und sie anpflanzen mußte, baute Erik eine Wiege und hängte sie an den großen Birnbaum, der schon lange bevor sie hierher gekommen waren, auf dem Grundstück gestanden hatte. Dort schlief der Junge und dort wachte er beim Summen der Hummeln und dem Rauschen der Blätter auf, während die weißen Blüten wie Schneeflocken auf sein kleines Bett fielen.

Das Meer war aus Simons Kindheit nicht wegzudenken. Es würzte die Luft mit seinem Salz und erfüllte den Raum mit einem Lied aus Tiefe und Weite. Und es färbte jegliches Licht zwischen den Häusern und Bergen.

Graue Tage wurden undurchdringlich grau. Blaue Tage wurden blauer als alles andere auf Erden, an Tagen an denen das Meer zum Spiegel für den großen Himmel wurde, vervielfachte es das Licht und warf es auf das Land zurück.

Dieses schimmernde Licht nahmen die Kinder fürs ganze Leben mit, es drang durch die Haut, durch Mark und Bein und bis hinein in die Seele, wo die Sehnsucht geboren wird.

Eine blaue Sehnsucht nach Freiheit und Grenzenlosigkeit.

Und als sich diese Sehnsucht einen Fixpunkt in der Wirklichkeit suchte, zog es die Kinder zu den großen Schiffen hin, deren Weg am Oljeberg vorbei zum großen Hafenbecken führte. Fast alle Freunde Simons aus Kindertagen gingen zur See, viele lernten trotz des Krieges die weite Welt kennen, und das noch ehe Simon selbst die Prüfung zur Mittleren Reife hinter sich gebracht hatte.

Sie heuerten auf den Geleitschiffen mit den auf die Bordwände gemalten blaugelben schwedischen Flaggen an. Manche der Jungen kamen nie zurück, sie gingen mit ihrem neutralen Schiff und ihrem Freiheitsdrang unter.

Andere kamen zwar nach Hause zurück, hatten aber etwas im Blick, das sich schwer deuten ließ, und die Mütter sprachen in Karins Küche von einem Alb, der ihre Söhne bei Nacht befiel.

Auch Simon und Isak fühlten sich zu den Schiffen im großen

Hafen hingezogen, wo der Betrieb aus wirtschaftlichen Gründen inzwischen so gut wie still stand. Schweden war abgeschnitten von der übrigen Welt.

Genau wie die Kaianlagen, die jetzt von der Polizei bewacht wurden.

Trotzdem hatten in diesem Hafen noch nie so viele Schiffe gelegen wie jetzt, so viele an Bojen und Anker gekettete Riesen, verurteilt zum Schweigen und Nichtstun. Trotz der gesperrten Kaianlagen konnten sie nicht unsichtbar gemacht werden, und die Jungen erkannten bald, daß man sich den Schiffen am einfachsten nähern konnte, wenn man mit einer der Fähren den Fluß überquerte.

Sie fuhren ab Senkwerk hin und wieder zurück. Dann gingen sie zum Fischereihafen und bestiegen die Fähre zum Sannegården, standen an Deck und sahen die gigantischen Schiffsseiten wie gespenstische Felsen aufragen.

Viele der Schiffe gehörten zur norwegischen Handelsflotte, einige von ihnen waren nagelneu. Sie waren direkt von den schwedischen Werften zum Anlegeplatz gebracht worden, ohne je für die ihnen zugedachte Aufgabe eingesetzt worden zu sein.

Andere hatten alle Häfen der Erde besucht und sich in dem Frühjahr, in dem die Nazis Norwegen überfielen, dem Heimatland müde und erschöpft genähert. Verzweifelt hatten die Schiffe den Kurs geändert und das Nachbarland angelaufen, das noch seine Freiheit besaß. Dort blieben sie liegen, schweigend, arbeitslos, beschlagnahmt.

Doch Anfang des Frühjahrs verbreiteten sich Gerüchte in der Stadt, daß die norwegischen Schiffe, mit Kugellagern und Waffen beladen, Anstalten machten, in See zu stechen, und daß man an Bord Sprengladungen angebracht hatte, damit die Schiffe sich, wenn notwendig, selbst in die Luft jagen konnten.

In der Nacht zum 31. März hielt die Stadt am Strom den Atem an, während zehn norwegische Schiffe sich an der Festung vorbei hinaus zum Rivöfjord schoben. Es herrschte Nebel, aber er sollte ihnen nicht helfen. An Bord befanden sich hunderte von Menschen, die die Morgendämmerung niemals sehen würden, denn in der Höhe von Måseskär wartete bereits die deutsche Kriegsflotte auf sie.

Drei der Schiffe wurden gemäß dem Selbstmordplan von der eigenen Mannschaft versenkt, drei gingen nach der Torpedierung durch die Deutschen unter, zweien gelang es umzukehren und nach Schweden zurückzukommen.

Nur zwei Schiffe durchbrachen die feindlichen Linien und erreichten England. Es waren ein kleiner Tanker und das Schnellboot B. P. Newton, ein Sechzehntonner, der am dritten April, unter dem Geleitschutz des Kriegsschiffes seiner britischen Majestät, Valorous, in einen schottischen Hafen einlief.

Es war ein schwerer Tag für die der See zugetane Stadtbevölkerung, und einer der schwärzesten Tage des Krieges.

Es wurde von Verrat gemunkelt.

Simon saß während der Schulstunden in der Klasse, ohne – genau wie die Mitschüler – ein Wort mitzukriegen. Die Lehrer waren ebenso verzweifelt, aber keiner sprach von dem, was geschehen war. Die Stunden krochen dahin und man folgte, so gut es ging, dem Ritual: Wir schlagen im Lehrbuch Seite 56 auf.

Am Ende des Tages machte sich Simons Anspannung Luft, er warf sich über sein Pult und weinte. Das war während der Schwedischstunde, und auch die Lehrerin gab nach, weinte am Katheder still vor sich hin.

Keiner sprach ein Wort.

Dann läutete die Schulglocke und langsam erhoben sich die Jungen, und langsam und schweigend verließen sie mit feuchten Augen und verrotzten Nasen die Klasse.

Erst als sie im Korridor ihre Jacken anzogen, sah Simon, daß Isak nicht geweint hatte und daß in seinen Augen ein unverständlicher Ausdruck lag.

Sie hatten eigentlich in die Bibliothek gehen wollen, aber Simon war sich bewußt, daß es jetzt wichtiger war, so schnell wie möglich

nach Hause zu kommen, zu Karin in die Küche. Die beiden über-
querten auf dem Weg zu den Fahrradständern den Schulhof. Isak
ging wie eine aufgezogene Puppe, und Simon wußte sofort, daß sie
heute mit der Straßenbahn heimfahren mußten.

Isak folgte ihm wie ein Hund, aber während der ganzen Fahrt
trafen sich ihre Blicke nicht ein einziges Mal, es war, als erkenne Isak
den Freund gar nicht. Als sie ausstiegen, fand er den wohlbekannten
Weg nicht, und Simon bekam solche Angst, daß sein Magen sich
zusammenkrampfte. Er wäre am liebsten geflohen, hakte sich aber bei
Isak unter, und sie gingen zusammen bergauf und bergab den Weg,
den Aron Äppelgren Simon lieben gelehrt hatte.

Und sie kamen heim und Karin war da und sie sah sofort, was los
war, und der Krampf in Simons Magen ließ nach, obwohl er bemerkte, daß Karins Stimme unsicher war, und auch sah, daß in ihren
braunen Augen eine flackernde Schwärze stand, als sie sagte: »Geh
du hinaus.«

Er stürmte durch die Tür hinaus zu den Eichen und zu dem Land,
wo alles einfach ist.

Sanft und vorsichtig, als liefe er Gefahr zu verbluten, zog Karin Isak
Jacke und Schuhe aus. Dann setzte sie sich mit dem großen Jungen
auf dem Schoß in den Schaukelstuhl, wiegte ihn leicht hin und her,
strich ihm über die Haare, gurrte.

Er erwärmte sich ein wenig. Aber die Steifheit blieb und es war
ganz offenbar, daß er Karin nicht erkannte.

Sie sang ein altes Kinderlied: Isak, kleiner Isak ... und vielleicht
war er jetzt etwas weniger steif, doch als sie versuchte, seinen Blick
einzufangen, stand einwandfrei fest: Isak Lentov wußte nicht mehr,
wer er war.

Ich sollte Ruben anrufen, dachte Karin, aber jeder Versuch, sich zu
erheben und die Arme des Jungen zu lösen, steigerten die Angst in
seinem Körper. Sie mußte also warten bis Helen mit der Milch kam
und Karin ihr die Telefonnummer geben und ihr zuflüstern konnte,
sie möge sich um Gottes willen beeilen.

Ruben Lentov erwischte ein Taxi, aber seine Ankunft veränderte nichts. Isak erkannte auch seinen eigenen Vater nicht.

Er war vier Jahre alt und seine Mutter liebte ihn, wie man etwas liebt, das einem angsterfüllten Leben Sinn und Würde verleiht. Diese Liebe zwang das Kind, sich immer den Bedürfnissen der Mutter anzupassen, und hinderte es daran, seinen eigenen Gefühlen nachzuspüren, die es gebraucht hätte, um das eigene Leben einschätzen und begreifen zu lernen.

Er wurde zu einem braven und stillen Kind.

Aber ihn konnten manchmal unbeschreibliche Wutausbrüche überkommen. Dann rannte er schreiend durch die große Berliner Wohnung.

Sein Vater sei in einem fernen Land, das waren die Worte der Mutter, und sie sprach diese mit einer Sehnsucht aus, die sein Bild von Schweden ein Leben lang prägen sollte. Doch er hatte einen Großvater, und der war Gott selber, soviel hatte der Junge begriffen, denn der Großvater hatte eine Stimme, die dröhnte wie die Stimme des Herrn, und an den Samstagen, wenn er mit dem kleinen Enkelsohn an der Hand zur Synagoge schritt, war er majestätisch und würdevoll gekleidet. Genau wie der Herr des Hiob.

Und er strafte wie Gott und sein Zorn traf Gerechte und Ungerechte schwer, und der Junge versuchte nie, das auch nur verstehen zu wollen, denn er hatte in der Synagoge gelernt, unbegreiflich sind die Ratschläge des Herrn.

Außerdem erinnerte sich der Junge später nie an die Stunden, in denen er schreiend durch die Wohnung gerannt war und seiner Mutter Qualen bereitet hatte, und sie den Herrn anrief, der schweren Herzens und mit harter Hand das Kind bestrafen mußte.

Aber genau an diesem Nachmittag, als er zwischen vier und fünf Jahre alt war und in Berlin die Frühlingssonne schien und er seiner Mutter mit seinem Schreien wieder wehgetan hatte und unter dem Speisezimmertisch mit der dicken in Rot und Gold gestickten Decke saß und es schwach nach Bohnerwachs und saurem Wein roch und er die Mutter in ihrem Zimmer weinen hörte und er auf den Herrn wartete, der kommen und ihn schlagen würde – genau an diesem Tag wurde ihm ein neues Gefühl zuteil.

In diesem Gefühl gab es auch eine Wut von gleicher Art wie die, mit der er kurz zuvor schreiend herumgerannt war. Aber jetzt war er sich des Zornes bewußt und das gab Hoffnung, er konnte denken und er dachte, er werde ausreißen und zu seinem Vater in das ferne Land gehen. Er wollte sich durchfragen, er kannte die Adresse.

Er zog die Schuhe aus, um nicht gehört zu werden, und schlich in die Diele. Da stand er eine Weile und sah sich an der Garderobe um und dachte, er werde auf der langen Wanderung in das neue Land, in dem es angeblich so kalt war, wohl seinen Mantel brauchen.

Aber er reichte nicht hinauf.

Es gelang ihm, die Tür lautlos zu öffnen und sie hinter sich wieder zuzuziehen. Und er ging die Treppe hinunter und hinaus auf die Straße, wo die Sonne schien und die Gesichter der Menschen dank der Militärmusik und dem zackigen Marschieren der Hitlerjugend lebhafter wirkten.

Er konnte sich nie daran erinnern, wie sie ihn aufgegriffen hatten, die langen Kerls in Braunhemden mit Hakenkreuzbinden an den Ärmeln. Aber er erinnerte sich daran, wie ihre Nasenflügel vor Begeisterung bebten und wie sie lachten, als sie ihn in der nächsten Kneipe auf den Tresen hoben und ihm die Hose auszogen, um nachzusehen, ob sein Pimmel beschnitten war, ob er ein kleines Judenschwein war, das ihnen die Vorsehung an diesem sonnigen und großherzigen Tag, der so voll Hoffnung für all jene war, die die Geburt des Dritten Reiches miterlebt hatten, über den Weg hatte laufen lassen.

Sie zogen an seinem kleinen Glied bis es blau war, doch im Verlauf dieser Folterung verfiel der Junge dem Dunkel der Bewußtlosigkeit, was das Vergnügen minderte. Trotzdem hörten sie erst auf, als Blut aus dem Glied spritzte und die Kellnerin sich einmischte, das Kind nahm und es in das Zimmer hinter dem Tresen brachte.

Sie war groß und blond gewesen wie Karin.

Und am Abend, als das stramme Marschieren auf den Straßen aufgehört hatte, trug sie ihn heim in die Lentovsche Wohnung.

Sie kannte das Kind.

Als der Junge sich wieder gefaßt hatte, war er zur Einsicht gelangt, daß der Großvater nicht Gott war, und er weinte aus Angst und Verzweiflung. Ein Arzt kam, es gab einen Verband und Medikamente, und bleibende Folgen werde die Sache für den Jungen nicht haben, versprach der Arzt, der selbst Jude war und so verängstigt, daß die Beruhigungsspritze in seiner Hand bebte.

Während der Junge den Schlaf des schweren Giftes schlief, saßen der Vater des Vaters und die Mutter des Kindes an seinem Bett und hatten in ihrem gegenseitigen Haß nur das Bestreben, einander die Schuld zuzuweisen.

Du verdammte dumme Gans mit deinen Tränen und deinen Auftritten, nur du hast mich dazu gebracht, ihn zu schlagen.

Durch dich, alter Satan, war er vor Angst ganz außer sich. Aber sie sprachen kein Wort, und die alte Großmutter mit ihrem Wein und ihrem Trost, den sie aus dem vierten Gebot schöpfen konnte, strich um sie herum. »Kinder vergessen ja so leicht«, sagte sie.

Und nach und nach durchliefen die Erwachsenen alle Phasen von Schock und Haß und wurden in stiller Übereinkunft zu Verbündeten. Ruben Lentov sollte nie erfahren, was seinem Sohn zugestoßen war.

Allerdings waren sie, als sie sich schließlich trennten, um ein wenig zu schlafen, doch in Sorge, daß das Kind etwas verraten könnte. Aber die Besorgnis hätten sie sich sparen können, denn als der Junge aufwachte, war er stumm.

Er sprach nicht und er weinte nicht, nur wenn der Arzt kam, um die Wunden frisch zu verbinden, konnte es vorkommen, daß er ein wenig wimmerte.

»Er steht unter Schock«, erklärte der Arzt.

Und so verhielt es sich auch noch nach einem Monat, als Ruben Lentov zu Besuch kam und wütend und verzweifelt zu wissen verlangte, was geschehen war. Die beiden Verbündeten hielten ihre Abmachung: Ruben Lentov durfte nie zu Ohren kommen, was seinem Sohn widerfahren war. Aber sie hatten nicht mit dem Arzt gerechnet, der, immer besorgter über den Zustand des Jungen, weiterhin im Haus ein und aus ging.

Noch viele Jahre danach mußte Ruben Lentov sich Mühe geben, diese Nacht, das Gespräch mit dem Arzt, sein Entsetzen und die Schuldgefühle zu vergessen. Nie aber kam er auf die Idee zu fragen, warum der Junge versucht hatte auszureißen.

In diesem Drama gab es für ihn nur einen Schuldigen, ihn selbst.

Als der Tag graute, nahm er mit der Kraft der Verzweiflung in Angriff, was er schon längst hätte tun sollen, lief straßauf, straßab durch Berlin, strapazierte Wartezimmerstühle, wurde beschimpft und gedemütigt, konnte aber doch auf seine schwedischen Papiere bauen.

Dann stand er eines Tages mit allen gestempelten Dokumenten im Zimmer des Jungen, hob das Kind hoch und rief: »Du wirst mit mir in das neue Land kommen.«

Und die Stärke in der Stimme des Vaters und die Wärme in seinen Armen hatten die Kraft, die Versteinerung zu durchdringen, Isak wurde lebendig und konnte denken. In ihm nahm der Gedanke Form an, daß es ihm doch gelungen war, und sein Ausreißen zum Ziel geführt hatte.

Er weinte den ganzen Tag still vor sich hin und weigerte sich, Ruben loszulassen.

Am Abend begann er zu sprechen, aber nur sein Vater durfte es hören. Aber als die Mutter in seinem Zimmer auftauchte, schrie er die Düsternis in seinem Inneren dennoch sofort laut hinaus. Ruben verstand und dachte, daß es künftig seine schwerwiegende Pflicht sein würde, das Kind vor der Mutter zu schützen.

Als sie am letzten Morgen in der alten Wohnung in Berlin mit dem Reisegepäck in der Diele standen, sagte Ruben zu seinen Eltern, er hoffe, daß sie bald nachkommen würden. Aber er empfand große und mit Schuld durchsetzte Erleichterung, als sein Vater sagte, sie würden in Deutschland bleiben, in dem Land, das sie liebten, und daß die Sache mit den Nazis bald vorbei sein werde.

Der Junge sah seinen Großvater nicht an, er hatte ihn schon ausradiert.

Lentovs zweiter Sohn ging nach Dänemark, und die einzige Tochter fuhr mit Mann und Kindern nach Amerika. Die Alten blieben zurück, wie sie es beschlossen hatten, und vielleicht gingen sie in eben dem Frühjahr, in dem die von Schweden zurückgehaltenen norwegischen Schiffe bei Måseskär versenkt wurden und Isak erkrankte, ihrem Tod in einem der großen Lager im Osten entgegen.

Jetzt saß Ruben in der Eisenbahn, hörte das Holpern der Räder auf den Schienennähten, sah seine Frau an und wagte zu denken, welche Erleichterung es bedeutet hätte, wenn sie in Berlin geblieben wäre. Neben seiner Frau saß deren Cousine, ein elfjähriges Mädchen, für das zu sorgen sie versprochen hatte, und das in all seiner Selbstsucht doch gut für den kleinen Jungen war.

Sie hatten Glück mit dem Wetter, das Land, das sich, nachdem sie in Helsingborg umgestiegen waren, vor den Augen des Jungen ausbreitete, war licht und von frühsommerlicher Pracht.

In der neuen Wohnung blühte vor dem Fenster des Kinderzimmers ein Ahorn, und der Junge konnte dort stundenlang fast in der Krone des Baumes stehen und dem Summen der Hummeln zuhören und den Honigduft der abertausend lichtgrünen Blüten atmen.

Das ferne Land roch gut.

Aber das beste von allem war, daß es eine andere Sprache hatte.

In der Buchhandlung arbeitete eine große junge Frau. Diese Ulla hatte eine höhere Mädchenschule besucht und konnte Deutsch, war sich jedoch zu fein, um Kindermädchen zu werden. Ruben erkannte aber, wie gern sie den Jungen hatte, erhöhte ihren Lohn und nannte sie Gouvernante.

Sie war eine von den Menschen, die Lieder, Gedichte und Märchen liebten. Drei Jahre lang widmete sie sich dem Jungen, der bald die Lieder von Bellman und auch die von Evert Taube sang. Er liebte die neue Sprache so leidenschaftlich, daß er sie in kürzester Zeit zu seiner

eigenen machen wollte. Schon nach wenigen Monaten war er wort-
gewandter und beredter als er auf Deutsch jemals gewesen war.

Ruben war erstaunt und erfreut. Der Junge war doch nicht minder-
bemittelt, wie seine Mutter und der Großvater es befürchtet hatten.
Er sah, daß es für seinen Sohn um mehr ging als um Worte, daß Isak
mit der neuen Sprache den Weg zu den eigenen Gefühlen fand und
Geschichte und Zusammenhänge erkannte.

Mit seiner Mutter sprach der Junge nie schwedisch.

Schließlich schlief Isak dann doch in Karins Armen im Schaukelstuhl ein. Simon und Ruben zogen zu zweit das Unterbett aus der Couch und legten Isak in Eriks Bett.

Ruben schlief in der Küche auf Simons altem Küchensofa so gut es eben ging. Aber es war wohl nicht die Unbequemlichkeit, die ihn die Nacht über wach hielt.

Karin lag neben Isak mit seiner Hand in ihrer. Er schlief so tief und fest, daß er nicht aufwachte, als Simon am nächsten Morgen in die Schule ging und Ruben in die Stadt fuhr, um in seinem Büro die notwendigsten Arbeiten zu erledigen.

Er wollte mittags zurück sein, und Karin flüsterte mit ihm von Lebensmitteln und anderen praktischen Dingen, die er besorgen sollte, und er nickte ihr von der Küchentür aus zu, schloß sie hinter sich, kam aber noch einmal zurück und sagte, sollte er dort bei Olga landen ...

Da vergaß Karin zu flüstern und meinte, Isak werde nie in eine Irrenanstalt kommen, solange sie, Karin, im Besitz ihrer Kräfte sei.

»Ich bin stark, Ruben«, sagte sie. »Gehen Sie jetzt.«

Aber tief im Herzen war sie weit ängstlicher, als sie zugeben wollte.

Dann, völlig undramatisch, wachte Isak auf, sah Karin an und erkannte sie. Aber er hatte Angst, ließ seinen Blick heimlich durchs Zimmer schweifen, als erwarte er, daß noch jemand anderes da sei.

»Wen suchst du denn, Isak?«

»Großvater«, sagte Isak und war ebenso erstaunt wie sie, verzog fast ein wenig den Mund über seine Dummheit.

»Warum fürchtest du dich vor deinem Großvater?«

»Er hat mich immer geschlagen, wenn ich so wie jetzt fort war und mich an nichts erinnern konnte.«

Brüchig, allzu brüchig war das Eis, über das Karin gehen mußte, nur ja nicht ängstlich sein, nicht zu lange zögern, nicht zuviel denken. Nur ruhig den nächsten Schritt tun. Vertrauen haben.

»Was ist denn gestern passiert?«

»Wir sind in der Pause mit dem Rad zum Bahnhof Olskroken gefahren, weißt du, und haben sie uns angesehen.«

Jetzt weiteten sich seine Augen, die Angst packte ihn. Karins Gehirn arbeitete schnell und klar, sie wußte, was die Jungen gesehen hatten. Die deutschen Züge rollten durch Schweden, im Bahnhof Olskroken machten die Hakenkreuzträger Rast und streckten die Beine.

»Es tut so weh!« schrie Isak und griff sich in den Schritt.

»Wahrscheinlich mußt du aufs Klo«, sagte Karin und wußte im selben Moment, daß sie einen Schritt in die falsche Richtung gemacht hatte und umkehren mußte.

Aber Isak nahm den Ausweg dankbar an und verschwand in Richtung Klohäuschen im Hof hinter dem Haus. Als er zurückkam, hatte Karin Kakao gekocht und Honigbrote geschmiert, denn sie wußte, daß er das mochte, aber sein Blick flackerte jetzt wieder und sie fühlte verzweifelt, daß er drauf und dran war, ihr zu entgleiten.

»Und was ist dann passiert, Isak? Nachdem ihr in Olskroken gewesen wart?«

»Ich erinnere mich nicht.«

Das Eis war brüchig, die Stimme aber warm und sicher. »Natürlich erinnerst du dich, Isak.«

»Wir kamen zur Schule und dort haben wir erfahren ...«

»Was erfahren? Isak!«

»Ich erinnere mich nicht, zum Teufel, ich erinnere mich nicht.«

»Doch, Isak. Dort habt ihr von den ausgelaufenen norwegischen Schiffen erfahren.«

»Ja!« schrie er. »Schweig jetzt, verdammt noch mal, schweig!«

Aber Karin ließ nicht locker, das Eis war jetzt sicherer, es trug.

»Von den Schiffen, die auszubrechen versuchten und von den Deutschen, die auf sie warteten.«

Da warf er sich rücklings auf das Sofa, hielt die Hände in den Schritt und schrie: »Es tut so weh, hilf mir, Karin, hilf mir.«

»Du hast Schmerzen in deinem Glied«, sagte Karin.

»Ja, ja!«

»Was ist dir passiert, Isak?«

»Ich weiß es nicht mehr.«

»Aber du kannst es vor dir sehen, Isak. Mach deine Augen auf, schau.«

In diesem Augenblick verstand der Junge, daß er sich dem Ganzen stellen mußte, er mußte es noch einmal sehen und erleben. Er klammerte sich an Karin fest, er wechselte die Sprache, schrie es deutsch, die Worte schossen aus ihm heraus und ebenso die Tränen und das Entsetzen.

Es war gut, daß Karin nicht alles verstand, denn hätte sie den Vorfall, der an diesem Morgen in ihrer Küche noch einmal erlebt wurde, in seinem vollen Ausmaß begreifen können, wäre ihr fürchterlicher Zorn vielleicht mit ihr und mit dem Jungen durchgegangen. Wie es jetzt aber war, verstand sie das Wesentliche und konnte ihre Ruhe bewahren und ebenso das Gefühl für gut überlegte Schritte auf dünnem Eis und auch ihren klaren, nüchternen Verstand.

Als Ruben zurückkam, war das Schlimmste vorüber, Isak und Karin saßen auf der Küchenbank, hielten einander bei den Händen und weinten alle beide verzweifelte aber erfrischende Tränen.

Ohne Abstriche berichtete Karin Isaks Geschichte, fragte nach, wo sie nicht verstanden hatte, und Ruben, der rot vor Scham war, wenn er nicht vor Schuldgefühlen erbleichte, mußte ergänzen. Isaks Blick ging vom einen zum anderen, und für alles gab es Worte und alles konnte erzählt werden.

Es war eine große Erleichterung, nicht zuletzt als Karin sagte, daß die Nazis ganz sicher Schweine waren, daß sie aber sowohl Isaks Mutter als auch seinen Großvater auch für verdammte Bestien hielt.

Isak ging das ganze Sommerhalbjahr nicht zur Schule sondern blieb zu Hause, denn Karin wollte es so. Aber schon am selben Abend ging er mit Simon zu den Eichen, und Simon erzählte ihm, wie die Bäume, als er klein gewesen war, mit ihm gesprochen hatten.

Isak glaubte ihn zu verstehen, fand es aber schade, daß Simon diese Eichen später gezwungen hatte, zu schweigen.

»Ach was«, sagte Simon. »Bäume können doch nicht reden. So was bildet man sich als Kind doch nur ein.«

Doch Isak erwiderte, er wisse, daß Bäume reden können und daß der Ahorn vor seinem Fenster ihm in dem Frühling, in dem er nach Schweden gekommen war, viel zu sagen gehabt hatte.

»Was denn?« fragte Simon, und seine Stimme klang neugierig.

»Er wollte wohl darauf hinaus, daß nichts wirklich gefährlich ist«, antwortete Isak, und Simon wußte, daß hier etwas Wesentliches in Worte gekleidet worden war.

Karin, die spürte, daß sie frische Luft brauchte, begleitete Ruben zur Straßenbahn. Sie sah wohl, daß auch er Trost brauchte, aber es war, als hätte sie dazu keine Kraft mehr.

»Haben Sie gewußt, daß der Großvater ihn schlug?«

»Ich hätte es wissen müssen.«

»Was mich am allermeisten ärgert, ist aber doch das Verhalten Ihrer Frau«, sagte Karin. »Was ist das für eine Mutter, die ihr eigenes Kind verrät und dann auch noch zusieht, wie es mißhandelt wird.«

»Ich hatte selbst eine solche Mutter«, sagte Ruben.

Da schämte sich Karin, aber er bemerkte es nicht, denn plötzlich sah er in der Dämmerung auf der Straße seine eigene Mutter mit Karins Augen, und er fühlte, daß er sie haßte.

Dann dachte er an die Vernichtungslager.

Es wurde ein langer und schwieriger Frühling für Isak. Am allerliebsten wollte er schlafen, und jedesmal wenn Karin ihn zum Aufwachen zwang, weinte er.

Manchmal dachte er, daß die Trauer in ihm nie ein Ende haben würde.

Er hatte keine Freude mehr am Leben und keine Kraft, irgend etwas zu tun.

Eigentlich änderte sich das erst, als Erik wieder heimkam und mit Isak ein Boot zu bauen begann.

9

Sie bauten ein Schiff hoch im Norden ...

Isak sang und unter der Persenning dehnte sich das Spant über einem Skelett aus kräftigem Abbruchholz.

Es sollte eine Karavelle werden mit Bordwänden aus Mahagoni, der eleganteste Küstensegler an der Strommündung. Wie Erik 1942, dem Jahr der Isolierung Schwedens, zu dem Mahagoni kam, wußten nur er und der liebe Gott. Aber eines Tages wurde es im Hinterhof zwischen Haus und Berg abgeladen und liebevoll und sorgsam zugedeckt.

Erik war vom Bereitschaftsdienst nach Hause zurückgekommen und wie so viele andere Männer arbeitslos. Der Lastwagen war in Betrieb, fuhr jetzt mit Holzgas und brachte gerade mal das Geld ein, das die Familie des Schwagers zum Leben brauchte. Trotzdem war Erik guter Dinge.

»Ihr werdet sehen, wir schaffen es«, sagte er. »Diese Teufel haben jetzt alle Hände voll zu tun, und das alte Schweden hat sich als harte Nuß erwiesen.«

Er war ein schwedischer Tiger, er durfte nicht viel sagen, aber aus seinen Worten ging hervor, daß es jetzt an den Grenzen Ordnung, Soldaten, Waffen und einen verdammt sturen Kampfgeist gab.

In dieser Frühsommernacht feierte man in Larssons Garten ein Fest, Nachbarn und Freunde hoben das Glas und tranken auf Hitlers Tod, den Mut der Russen und die fliegenden Festungen der Amerikaner.

Ruben Lentov trank ermutigt und getröstet sein Glas in einem Zug leer. Schon im vergangenen Jahr hatte er erkennen müssen, daß Erik ein politisch kluger Kopf war. Damals war er nur über die Mittsommertage auf Heimaturlaub gewesen, hatte aber eines Abends an Rubens Wohnungstür geklingelt, in der Diele gestanden und gesagt: »Ich bin nur raufgekommen, um dich wissen zu lassen, daß jetzt die Wende kommt, der ganze verdammte Krieg wird jetzt die Richtung ändern.«

Ruben hatte sich mehr über den Besuch als über die Botschaft gefreut, hatte eine seit langem aufbewahrte Flasche französischen Kognak hervorgeholt und versucht, mit möglichst fester Stimme zu fragen: »Was in Gottes Namen läßt Sie das glauben?«

Damals hatte es nicht viele Hoffnungsschimmer gegeben, außer daß die englischen Flieger Hitler in der Schlacht um Großbritannien standhielten.

»England hat noch nie einen Krieg verloren«, sagte Erik. »Und nur der Teufel weiß, ob nicht bald im Osten etwas passiert.«

Ruben konnte sich nicht erinnern, wieviel von dem Kognak sie schon getrunken hatten, als sie die Radionachrichten anschalteten. Aber er erinnerte sich daran, daß sie ein wenig schwankten, als sie mitten in seiner Bibliothek stehend die aufgeregte Stimme des Sprechers die Nachricht von der Operation Barbarossa herausbellen hörten. Hitlers Truppen im Blitzangriff auf Rußland. Er würde nie vergessen, wie Erik vor Freude aufschrie und Ruben in einer Umarmung fast die Luft abdrückte. Und als er ihn losließ, sagte: »Du, der du einen alten grausamen und gerechten Gott hast, bete! Bete jetzt, Ruben Lentov, um einen höllischen Winter mit Schneestürmen und vierzig saftigen Minusgraden.«

Dann lachten sie wie die Verrückten, tranken die Kognakflasche leer und sprachen über Napoleon und den Schwedenkönig Karl den Zwölften.

Als das Eis sich in diesem Winter an den Küsten türmte und die beiden Männer sich irgendwann trafen, machten sie darüber Scherze. Und als Erik in der Zeitung las, daß die Eisbrecher in der Ostsee bis in den Juni hinein zu tun hatten, sagte er zu Ruben: »Verdammter Kerl, du bist erhört worden!«

Beim Bauen des Bootes hatte es zeitweise gewisse Schwierigkeiten gegeben. Ruben hatte ein Boot bestellt, das dem Sohn neuen Mut geben sollte. Er bereitete einen Vertrag vor, der alles einschloß, auch einen ordentlichen Arbeitslohn für Erik. Doch als er mit seinen Papieren kam, ging ein Engel durch Larssons Küche. Oder vielleicht war es ein Weihnachtsmann, einer von den Älvsborger Weihnachtsmännern, wie die Gesellschaft sich nannte, die Erik während seiner Kinderjahre in ihrer unergründlichen Güte im Gemeindesaal jedes Jahr ein Paar Schuhe geschenkt hatten.

»Nimm dein Geld und fahr zur Hölle«, sagte Erik, und Ruben senkte das Haupt unter diesem Hieb, wie sein Volk es seit Jahrtausenden getan hatte. Dann aber schlug seine Verbitterung in Zorn um und er sagte, er habe sein Geld ehrlich verdient und es stinke nicht, auch wenn es durch die Taschen eines Juden gegangen sei.

»Verdammt, du bist doch verrückt«, wetterte Erik. »Das hier hat doch wirklich nichts mit Juden zu tun.«

Aber er schämte sich wie ein Hund und sagte, weil er fürchtete daß Karin dazukommen könnte, daß sie jetzt angeln gehen sollten.

Sie nahmen die Jolle, setzten das Sprietsegel und ankerten in der Rinne vor Rivö, wo sie mit der Handleine Makrelen angelten und aus einer Viertelflasche sogenannten Volkskognak tranken. Hier bekam Ruben die Geschichte von den Älvsborger Weihnachtsmännern zu hören und erfuhr von Eriks Traum von einer Werft. Er wollte Boote bauen.

»Nach dem Krieg könnte eine gute Zeit dafür sein«, vermutete Erik.

In der darauffolgenden Woche gründeten sie bei Ruben Lentovs Anwalt eine Gesellschaft, und damit war der Grundstein gelegt für die Tätigkeit, die Erik nach und nach zu einem wohlhabenden Arbeitgeber machte, was für einen Mann wie ihn, mit all seinen Widersprüchlichkeiten, schwierig war.

Aber in diesem Sommer wurde das erste Boot auf Kiel gelegt. Simon fühlte sich ausgegrenzt, saß lieber über seinen Büchern, als daß er an der Arbeit am Boot mithalf. Er haßte Isak wegen seiner guten

Zusammenarbeit mit Erik, und er haßte sich selbst, weil er ihn haßte, denn Isak mußte einem doch wirklich leid tun, und alle mußten sich doch über sein Interesse am Bootsbau und seine Freundschaft mit Erik freuen.

So drückte Karin es jedenfalls aus.

Auch sie zeigte in diesem Sommer kein größeres Interesse an Simon, er war nichts weiter als ihr wohlbehüteter Sohn, der es immer nur gut gehabt hatte. Ihre Gedanken kreisten um Isak, ständig auf der Jagd nach Anzeichen, ob er doch noch einmal ins Niemandsland abgleiten könnte. Und Isak, der von seiner eigenen Mutter nie beachtet worden war, genoß Karins Besorgnis.

Sie sah Simon ab und zu etwas zerstreut an, wenn sie feststellen mußte, daß er in die Höhe schoß und aus den Kleidern herauswuchs. Sie änderte Isaks alte Hosen ab und nahm nicht einmal den Zorn in Simons Augen wahr, wenn sie ihn zu einer Anprobe zwang.

Er lief zu den Eichen, saß dort und weinte wie ein Kind, doch dann ging er zum Meer und brachte Isak um. Aber auch das gelang ihm nicht besonders, es verschaffte ihm keine Erleichterung, und der kleine Mann seiner Kindheit war verschwunden. Lange überlegte er, ob er nicht weglaufen sollte, der Gedanke, wie traurig Karin sein und wie die Reue sie packen und wie sie verzweifelt die Hände ringen und schreien würde, daß sie ihren Sohn in den Tod getrieben habe, gab ihm eine gewisse Genugtuung.

Denn sie würden ihn finden, getötet von eigener Hand.

Der Plan hatte nur einen Haken, Simon wollte nicht sterben. Als er das erkannte, schämte er sich, denn Isak mußte einem doch leid tun und Karin war ein Engel, das hatte Ruben gesagt, und Simon hatte es immer gewußt. Er kam zerknirscht nach Hause und war froh, daß Karin nicht mehr wach war, denn wenn sie seine finsteren Gedanken bemerkt hätte, wäre er gestorben.

Dessen war er sicher.

In dieser Nacht träumte er einen Traum vom Wald und einem weitgestreckten See. Er erkannte alles wieder, wußte, daß er schon einmal dort gewesen war und daß die Wehmut in diesen Bildern sich zu wilder Angst steigern würde. Er war vorhanden, aber keiner sah ihn, er schrie, weinte, trat um sich, alles in der Notwendigkeit, daß jemand ihn sähe, und da war eine Grotte, und in wütendem Entschluß fand er den Ausgang, schmal war er, und es schmerzte am ganzen Körper, als er sich hindurchzwängte, aber die, die ihn sehen mußte, damit er leben durfte, gab es dort nicht, und die Raserei ebbte ab zu einer großen Müdigkeit, und er starb, und dann war jemand da, der ihn sah, und das war Karin, und ihre Augen waren braun wie die Treue und voller Liebe, aber seine Verzweiflung über die, die nicht gesehen hatte, war weiterhin vorhanden und würde ihm sein Leben lang folgen.

Dann war es Morgen und niemand sah, daß Simon seltsam blaß war, als sie alle – wie gewöhnlich mit Zeichenpapier und Stiften zwischen den beiseite geschobenen Kaffeetassen und den Tellern mit Haferbrei – um den Frühstückstisch saßen und erneut skizzierten, wie sie das eine oder andere Detail der Kombüseneinrichtung lösen könnten. Karin machte sich, wie in dieser Zeit üblich, Sorgen um das Mittagessen. Sie hatte keine Fleischmarken mehr, die alten Kartoffeln waren ausgewachsen und ihre Phantasie am Ende.

Aber ihr fiel trotzdem auf, daß Simon ohne Appetit aß.

»Iß deine Haferflocken, Junge«, sagte sie. »Du brauchst das jetzt, wo du so schnell wächst.«

Da sah Simon seine Mutter an und fühlte, daß er sie haßte.

Dann wurde er von den Cousins gerettet, die an Larssons Küche vorbeigekommen waren, um Simon zu fragen, ob er mit zum Fischen kommen wolle. Es war ein trüber Tag mit tiefhängenden, regenschweren Wolken, so daß Karin ihm Ölzeug, eine Kapuze und Stiefel aufnötigte. Doch dann war er frei, war sie und die Bootsbauer mit ihrem dauernden Gemecker, daß er wenigstens Handlangerdienste leisten könnte, los.

Der Wind kam ausnahmsweise von Land, sie hielten kurz auf Danska Liljan zu, kamen hinter Böttö in Lee und setzten den Anker. Normalerweise hatte Simon keinen Spaß am Fischen, aber heute paßte ihm das lange Warten an der Handleine.

Er war erschrocken über den Gedanken, der ihm während des Frühstücks gekommen war, nämlich daß er Karin haßte, und so sagte er sich, während er auf die aus dem Wasser ragende Sandbank starrte, daß er eigentlich gar nicht sie gemeint hatte. Gemeint hatte er die Ågrensche und ebenso Isaks verdammte Mutter oder auch Tante Jönsson aus dem Lebensmittelgeschäft, die ihn erwischt hatte, als er einmal ein Rahmbonbon mopsen wollte, und dann Tante Äppelgren, die nicht ganz bei Trost war und immer nur saubermachte und ihn einmal beschuldigt hatte, in ihrem Garten Äpfel geklaut zu haben.

Verdammte Spinatwachtel, dachte er und erinnerte sich, wie die Äpfel geschmeckt hatten, süß und verboten.

Dann dachte er an Tante Inga und fühlte, daß er sie am allermeisten haßte, obwohl sie ihm nie etwas getan hatte. Er sah ihr feistes Gesicht vor sich und ihren Blick, der immer auswich.

Sie ist eine Sau, murmelte er und war darüber erstaunt, wie groß sein Abscheu war, als er an sie dort in der dreckigen Hütte dachte. Doch dann sah er den langen See und hörte das Rauschen des Waldes, und im nächsten Moment hatte er Herzklopfen und wußte, daß er etwas sehr Gefährlichem nahegekommen war.

Da biß ein Fisch an, der Ruck war so kräftig, daß Simon fast von der Ruderbank gerutscht wäre, aber er zog die Leine an, wie es die Lage erforderte, und hatte einen Riesen von einem Dorsch erwischt, einen Kerl von sicher fünf Kilo. Es war ein Glück, daß die Angelschnur hielt, und die Jungen zogen den Fang über die Reling und schlugen den Fisch unter Jubelgeschrei tot.

Die Sonne brach durch die Wolken, als sie auf dem Heimweg waren, ein freundlicher Wind kam auf und trocknete die Segel, er kam von der richtigen Seite, vom Meer. Sie konnten den ganzen Weg raumschot segeln, es ging schnell, und Simon sah den Dorsch dankbar an, der ihn gerettet hatte und ihm einen guten Tag bereiten würde. Karin würde sich freuen, sie würde ihn willkommen heißen wie einen Mann, der in schlechten Zeiten Nahrung nach Hause brachte.

Es war, wie er es sich vorgestellt hatte, Karin drückte sowohl den Dorsch als auch den Jungen an sich, überwand ihr schlechtes Gewissen und ging hinaus, um junge Kartoffeln auszugraben. Aber das war wirklich eine Sünde und eine Schande, denn die Kartoffeln waren noch sehr klein und hätten gut doppelt so groß werden können, wenn Karin einen Monat oder sogar länger gewartet hätte.

Dann riefen sie Ruben an und sagten ihm, es sei Simon zu verdanken, daß sie in der Küche ein Fest feiern könnten, und ob er kommen wolle und vielleicht ein Stückchen Butter übrig habe, die sie bräunen könnten? Und er kam und brachte nicht nur ein Stück Butter, sondern auch eine Flasche Wein mit.

Und eine Nachricht für Isak. Schon ab der nächsten Woche sollte er Privatunterricht bekommen, um nachzuholen, was er während seiner Krankheit in der Schule versäumt hatte. Ruben hatte schon mit dem Lehrer gesprochen, drei Stunden täglich mußte Isak zum Unterricht gehen.

Erik machte ein erstauntes Gesicht, sagte aber nichts. Auch Karin schwieg, obwohl sie die Sache für unnötig hielt, denn jetzt war Freude für Isak das Wichtigste.

Isak selbst wurde rot vor Zorn, wagte aber nicht zu widersprechen. Nur Simon freute sich von Herzen.

Dann aber sagte Erik, nun müsse eben Simon in den Stunden, die Isak abwesend war, beim Bootsbau mithelfen, und Simon wußte genau, wie das ausgehen würde, weil er ja mit zwei linken Händen geboren war, wie Erik zu sagen pflegte.

Ruben Lentov besuchte gern Konzerte. Irgendwann hatte er versucht, die Larssons mitzunehmen, aber Erik hatte ein verlegenes Gesicht gemacht und Karin hatte gemeint, das ist wohl nichts für uns.

»Für mich ist es eine der Möglichkeiten zu überleben«, sagte Ruben.

»Ja, jeder von uns hat wohl eine solche Möglichkeit«, sagte Karin, doch Ruben wagte nicht zu fragen, welche sie für sich habe. Aber er kannte sie inzwischen so gut, daß er ihre Traurigkeit sah, diese Trauer, die sie immer umgab.

An einem Samstagabend, als er sich von Larssons und dem Bootsbau frühzeitig verabschieden mußte, weil die *Symphonie Fantastique* von Berlioz gespielt wurde, nahm er Simon mit. Niemand machte sich Gedanken darüber, wie es zugegangen war. Vielleicht hatte Ruben Simons Einsamkeit erahnt und wollte ihm etwas Trost spenden, und vielleicht hatte Simon zugesagt, um Karin zu ärgern. Oder weil er sich geschmeichelt fühlte. Vielleicht war es auch nur ein Zufall.

Oder das große Schicksal zog im Spiel um Simon Larssons Leben einen entscheidenden Stein auf dem Brett.

Zunächst empfand Simon es als äußerst unbehaglich. Der große Konzerthaussaal, die elegant gekleideten Menschen mit den feierlichen Gesichtern und die ernsten Männer auf dem Podium, die ihre Instrumente stimmten und wie Elstern aussahen – das alles flößte ihm ein so befremdendes Gefühl ein, daß er am liebsten geflohen wäre. Wenn er sich getraut hätte.

Dann aber hob einer der schwarzweißen Männer einen Stab.

Und Simon hörte die Gräser in einem anderen Land und in einer anderen Zeit singen, als die Welt noch jung und voll Hoffnung war. Der Himmel wurde von wildem Vogelrufen durchdrungen, er war, wie das Gras, ohne Ende, und jeder Vogel in diesem Blau besaß Persönlichkeit wie die Gräser am Boden.

Der Wind, der sich frei über die Ebene bewegte und alles berührte, bisweilen herausfordernd heftig, sanft und zärtlich im nächsten Moment, hauchte allem Leben ein. Aber es gab da auch einen Schmerz und eine blaue Sehnsucht, eine Ungeduld und einen Traum. Und einen Mann, der all dies in sich trug. Er saß an dem großen Strom und er war zugleich das Wasser des Stroms, immer dasselbe und immer wieder neu. Und er suchte die Ufer auf, als könne er nie genug bekommen von deren Schönheit und den sanften Hängen.

Andere kamen, Menschen, die sich in ständig wachsender Erwartung in dem Strom spiegelten, und er nahm ihre Bilder in sich auf und wußte, daß es sein Schicksal war, ihren Träumen Gestalt zu geben.

Da wuchs der Wind zum Sturm an und trieb ihn der Entscheidung entgegen, und seine Pein steigerte sich fast bis zum Wahnsinn, denn sein Gemüt war sanft wie das des Stromes und er wollte keine Gewalt.

Aber der Sturm hatte den Säbel gezogen, er kam aus den Bergen im Osten und war vom Tode berauscht, von der Freude am Töten, und das Blut spülte über die Felder.

Als der Sturm über die Ebene weitergezogen war, scharten die Überlebenden sich um ihn und legten alle ihre Erwartungen in seine Hände. Und er sprach zu ihnen von dem Gott, dessen Tempel zerstört worden war und dessen Name nicht mehr genannt werden durfte. Aber das Bemerkenswerteste war doch die Sprache die er benutzte, die uralte Sprache, die jahrhundertelang geschlafen hatte.

Sprache und Tempel, seine Aufgabe war es, sie beide wieder auferstehen zu lassen. Die gewichtige Sprache, die die Heimat dieser Menschen während tausenden von Jahren gewesen, die jedoch niedergemacht und verboten worden war. Und den alten Gott, der aus seiner Heimat im Herzen des Volkes vertrieben worden war.

Als er dort am Strand stand, fühlte er, daß die alte Sprache auch die Sprache des Stromes und der Gräser, der Bauern und des Friedens war, schwer von Erde und harter Arbeit. Er sah über die Ebene hin, sah die Kanäle, die die Landschaft mit ihren Silbersträngen durchzogen und das Wasser des Stromes über die Äcker ausgossen. Nicht anders als die Sprache stand es nun unter fremder Herrschaft.

Obwohl es verboten war, sang er den Leuten die alten Hymnen vor, die Lieder von der Heiligkeit der Erde und der Liebe des Wassers, vom Fluß, der der Erde, unserer großen Mutter, Leben spendete.

Die alten Männer und Frauen, die dabeistanden, kannten die Worte noch und fielen in den Gesang ein. Die Jungen, denen es verwehrt blieb sich in der Muttersprache heimisch zu fühlen, vernahmen dennoch, daß die Sprache die Macht besaß, am Kopf vorbei das Herz zu berühren.

Die Freude stieg in den Himmel, zeitweise klang es wie Tanz, wie Spiel aus einer entschwundenen Zeit, als alles noch einfach war und die Herzen der Menschen weit offen für das Grundlegende. Es waren Klänge, die aus der Erde hervorgegangen waren, die Farbe und Kraft aus dem endlosen Grasmeer geholt hatten und aus der gelben Wärme des sanften Flusses.

Seit langem vergessene Bilder ließ der Mann wieder auferstehen, der dort am Fluß sprach und sang und dessen Worte die Trauer weckten, die so groß war, daß sie hunderte von Jahren hatte verleugnet werden müssen. Unter der Trauer schlummerte der Zorn, die besinnungslose Wut. Jetzt erwachte sie und die Menschen schrien: »Tod dem Akkad!«

Da wanderte er einsam fort und seine Angst war groß. Aber noch größer war die Trauer, denn er kannte den Preis für sein Handeln. Und er betete zu dem verbotenen Gott dort oben im blauen Himmel um Entbindung von diesem Auftrag, und der Gott antwortete ihm mit Vogelgesang, der erfüllt war von Freiheit. Und der Mann erkannte, daß er die große Tat nicht vollbringen mußte und ein kleines Leben in Zwang und Ruhe leben konnte.

Als die Dämmerung hereinbrach, war er noch immer am Fluß, ruhte unter dem großen Baum aus, in dessen Krone sich die Vögel das Nachtlager bereiteten. Und er sprach mit den Vögeln von seinem großen Zweifel. Aber der Gesang der Vögel hatte nur eines zu sagen, daß das Leben schön war so wie es war, und die Taten der Menschen Torheiten. Der Baum sprach zu ihm von den wortlosen Schöpfungen jenseits von Gut und Böse. Dieses Sprechen gab Kraft, er verstand es so, daß er die Grenze überschreiten mußte, die von der Schuld und der Schande bewacht wurde.

Aber der Fluß sang in der Nacht von der Veränderung, der Bewegung, die unabhängig vom Menschen ist.

Du bist nur zu Gast in der Wirklichkeit, weil du sie nicht siehst. Du siehst nur die mit Namen versehenen Teile, nie die Zusammenhänge, aus denen die Ganzheit besteht.

Das war die Botschaft des Flusses und der Mann war völlig zwiegespalten. Doch als die Morgendämmerung mit dem ersten Sonnenflimmern im Fluß und dem ersten Vogelruf in der Luft kam, hatte er seinen Entschluß gefaßt. Im Trotz erwiderte er ihnen allen, dem Baum, dem Fluß und den Vögeln, daß er ein Mensch sei und den Weg eines Menschen gehen müsse, der ein Weg der Tat und des Gedankens ist.

Und der neue Krieg wurde grausam wie der erste und das Wasser des Flusses färbte sich rot vom Blut der vielen, die seinetwegen ihr Leben verloren, seiner großen Idee wegen, die ihm gehörte und wiedergeboren werden wollte, jedoch Haß säte und Tod erntete.

Am Tag des Sieges legte er den Grundstein zum Tempel, während die müden Soldaten nach Hause zurückkehrten. Ihre Schritte waren schwer wie die des Todes, und das Gras welkte unter ihren Füßen.

Er sah es, strich den Anblick jedoch aus dem Gedächtnis. Er hatte die Zwangsjacke des Mitgefühls abgelegt und war allein mit dem Gott, dessen Ehre er wiederhergestellt hatte und dessen Tempel der größte der Welt werden sollte. In schwindelerregender Schönheit ragte er bis in die Wolken, enthielt fünfzig kleinere Tempel, einen für jeden Sohn, jede Tochter des Gottes. Saal auf Saal wurde mit dem

Gold ausgekleidet, das den Hymnen und der alten Sprache Glanz verleihen sollte. So groß war sein Sieg, so gewaltig, daß alles Leise und Behutsame vernichtet wurde. Die Mauern des Tempels waren so massiv, daß der Wind an den Steinen zerschellte, und sie waren so gut verfugt, daß kein Vogel sich dort niederlassen konnte.

Die Trommelschläge dröhnten am Abend in wuchtigen Rhythmen über die Stadt hin. Sie sollten die Botschaft vom Frieden zum Volk tragen, das endlich seine eigene Sprache sprach, das aber wegen der vielen Toten, wegen seiner Zerrissenheit und den Brudermorden, wegen der Verräterei und Falschheit im Herzen als Folge des Freiheitskrieges keine Ruhe finden konnte.

Das Volk kannte die Kunst nicht, Erinnerung von sich zu weisen. In jedem Haus der Stadt stampfte die Scham auf der Schwelle und die Schuld stand nachts an den Betten Wache. Die Tage waren nicht wesentlich leichter zu ertragen, denn da weinte die Trauer im Wind und alle konnten sie hören außer dem Mann in dem riesigen Tempel, dem Mann, der seine Erinnerungen abgetötet hatte.

In der Stadt wurde geflüstert, daß der Gottkönig nicht schlafen könne, daß er ihre Schuld in endlosen Wanderungen um die Mauern des neuen Tempels trage. Und die Wahrheit war, daß er Nacht für Nacht im ständigen Zweikampf mit der Frage unterwegs war, was zwischen ihm und dem Gott stand, dessen Herrschaft er auf der Erde wiedererrichtet hatte.

Er bekam keine Antwort und er bebte vor dem unerhörten Gedanken, daß Gott tot war.

Doch seine Sterndeuter waren voller Hoffnung für das neue Reich, und es wurden Lieder zu seiner Ehre gedichtet. Und die Trauer des Volkes wurde gedämpft durch die großen Zeremonien, Schauspiele von nie geahnter Pracht.

Er hatte zwei Mütter, Ke Ba, die die Priesterin der Göttin Gatumdus war und die ihn im geheimen geboren hatte. Sie war noch immer schön und ihr Ansehen im Volk war groß.

Doch Lia, die ihn großgezogen hatte, kannte er nicht, sie war im Volk untergetaucht, in der grauen, gesichtslosen Menge. Sie liebten ihn beide, wie Mütter das tun, und vielleicht war es so, daß es ihre Liebe war, von der er lebte.

In schweren Stunden erwog er, zurück zum Fluß zu gehen, zum Baum und den Vögeln, aber er war jetzt so weit von der Wahrheit entfernt, daß er glaubte, Fluß, Baum und Vögel würden nicht mehr auf ihn hören.

Und das konnte er nicht ertragen.

So kam es abschließend zu seinem letzten Opfer in der Frühlingsnacht, in der er dem langgehörnten Stier begegnen sollte, um ihm das goldene Messer ins Herz zu stoßen. Er wußte, daß die Tat nur gelingen konnte, wenn er frei war von Furcht und daß sie von jedem Gedanken rein sein mußte.

Er hatte lange dafür geübt, er hatte es Jahr für Jahr zu der Zeit getan, zu der der Gesang der Vögel sich wieder über den wiedergeborenen Gräsern und über den Feldern erhob, zu der schon die erste Saat in der roten Erde keimte.

Doch in dieser seiner letzten Stunde auf der Erde trat die Schuld in der Erinnerung hervor und sprengte die Tür, die er mit vielfachen Schlössern verriegelt hatte. Und die Hörner des Stieres spalteten seinen Brustkorb, das Herz fiel heraus und zersprang.

Da sah das ganze Volk, daß nur das Äußere des Herzens aus Stein gewesen war und daß dieser Stein so dünn war wie eine Eierschale. Und daß das Innere die schwarze Trauer war, so überschäumend groß, daß sie irgendwann doch die zerbrechliche Schale gesprengt hätte.

Ruben hatte Simon während des Konzerts beobachtet, anfangs mit Freude, dann mit Erstaunen und schließlich mit Beunruhigung. Der Junge war im Gesicht weiß wie eine Leinwand und schien irgendwann gegen Ende nur schwer atmen zu können.

Sie sollten die Nacht gemeinsam in der Stadt in Lentovs Wohnung verbringen, so war es beschlossen worden. Keiner von beiden sagte ein Wort, während die Straßenbahn hinaus nach Majorna ratterte. Auf dem Eßzimmertisch stand, mit einem weißen Tuch abgedeckt, ein Teller mit Broten, doch Simon schüttelte den Kopf, ging sofort in Isaks Zimmer und ließ sich ins Bett fallen. Ruben hatte noch nie einen Menschen so augenblicklich einschlafen sehen. Der Junge hatte mit Mühe und Not gerade noch die Kleider ablegen können.

Aber er lächelte Ruben dabei an und er lächelte im Schlaf, und als Ruben einige Zeit später die Eindrücke des Abends mit einem Kognak verdaut hatte, konnte er Simon im Schlaf lachen hören.

Beim Frühstück fragte Simon: »Warum mußte er sterben?«

»Wer?« fragte Ruben, der ins Handelsblatt vertieft war.

»Der in der Musik, König oder Priester oder wie immer er genannt wurde.«

»Simon«, sagte Ruben, »ich habe keinen Priester gesehen. Die Musik handelt nicht von etwas Bestimmtem, jeder Mensch hat dabei andere Erlebnisse.«

Simon war grenzenlos erstaunt. »Und der, wie hat er noch geheißen, der sich das ausgedacht hat ...«

»Berlioz ...«

»Ja, Berlioz, der, der hat den Priester nie gesehen?«

»Nein.« Ruben spürte den Ernst, der über dem Frühstückstisch lag, faltete die Zeitung umständlich zusammen und versuchte zu antworten, unsicher, ob er die richtigen Worte fände. »Das, was wir Kunst nennen, Simon, entsteht in den Menschen, die zuhören oder lesen oder ein Gemälde betrachten. Da wird etwas geweckt, Gefühle, für die es keine Worte gibt.«

Simon strengte sich an, und wie immer, wenn er intensiv daran arbeitete, etwas zu verstehen, blinzelte er, und Ruben dachte wie schon mehrmals zuvor, daß in diesem Jungen ein Feuer brannte.

»Es ist also nicht wirklich?«

»Das hängt davon ab, was man unter Wirklichkeit versteht. Du liest sehr viel und mußt daher verstanden haben, daß die Menschen in den Büchern nicht auf die gleiche Art wirklich sind wie du und ich, und daß das, was ihnen passiert, nicht dort passiert, wo du Wirklichkeit erlebst.«

Simon hatte darüber noch nie nachgedacht, er hatte es für gegeben erachtet, daß die Welten, in die er sich begab, und die Menschen, denen er in den Büchern begegnete, genau so waren und aussahen wie er sie vor sich sah.

Er hatte das Gefühl, daß in seinem Kopf etwas in Bewegung geraten war, und er zog die Stirn in Falten und biß sich in dem Bemühen, Ordnung in seine Gedanken zu bringen, auf die Unterlippe.

Da sagte Ruben: »Gebrauche nicht den Kopf, Simon. Gebrauche dein Herz.«

Simons Gesicht glättete sich und die Augen wurden weit, als sich sein Blick fern im Ungreifbaren verlor und er sich an die Bäume erinnerte, die in seiner Kindheit so deutlich zu ihm gesprochen hatten, ohne daß er es sich später hatte in die Erinnerung zurückrufen können. Er dachte an den Mann und die Gespräche unter den Eichen, daran, wieviel Kraft ihm zuteilgeworden war, ohne daß er sich je an Worte hätte erinnern können.

Ruben, der die Veränderung sah, traute sich zu fragen: »Kannst du davon erzählen?«

91

Da wagte Simon das Unerhörte und sagte rasch: »Ich habe in der Musik den Mann wiedererkannt, einen Priester oder König. Er war bei mir, als ich klein war.«

Ruben nickte und lächelte: »Ich verstehe dich, Simon, es hat ihn für dich einmal gegeben und die Musik hat dich daran erinnert.«

»Aber es hat ihn wirklich gegeben.«

»Ja, ich glaube dir. Er war einmal ein Teil deiner Wirklichkeit, deiner inneren Welt. Es ist normal, daß Kinder sich in ihrer Einsamkeit zum Trost Phantasiefiguren schaffen.«

Simon fühlte sich erleichtert und doch hintergangen, denn er spürte, daß an dem, was Ruben sagte, etwas nicht richtig war.

Dann kam das Dienstmädchen und räumte den Tisch ab und Ruben mußte zu Olga ins Irrenhaus von Hisingen fahren. Es war einer der zu dieser Zeit seltenen Warmwassertage im Haus, und Ruben ermunterte Simon, ein Bad zu nehmen, ehe er mit der Straßenbahn zu Erik und Karin nach Hause fuhr. Simon nickte, wusch sich dann aber doch nur so notdürftig wie immer.

Als Ruben das Haus verlassen hatte, ging der Junge durch die Wohnung, um sich alles anzusehen. Es gab ein paar große Gemälde, über die Erik sich gern lustig machte, Schmieralien, die nichts darstellten. Simon stand lange davor, sah sie sich an und dachte, es werde sich vielleicht in seinem Herzen etwas regen – aber nichts dergleichen geschah.

Dann fuhr er nach Hause und dort war alles wie immer, alles drehte sich nur um das Boot und niemand hatte Zeit für ihn und niemand fragte, wie ihm das Konzert gefallen hatte. Für letzteres war er allerdings sehr dankbar.

Doch Ruben ließ der Gedanke an den Jungen nicht los, der in der Musik versunken war, und am Sonntagabend rief er Karin an und sagte, er habe Grund zu der Annahme, daß Simon musikalisch sei und daß er gerne wolle, daß der Junge sein Talent entwickeln könne, wenn es tatsächlich vorhanden sei. Er, Ruben, habe einen Freund, einen Musiklehrer, und Simon könne es immerhin einmal versuchen.

»Ich kann mich irren«, sagte er. »Aber es würde mich nicht wundern, wenn da noch etwas in Simon steckte, ja, vielleicht, ein Geigen-spieler.«

Es war gut für Ruben Lentov, daß er Karins Gesichtsausdruck nicht sehen konnte. Jetzt hörte er nur, daß ihre Stimme unsicher war, als sie sagte, Simon müsse das selbst entscheiden, daß sie sich aber keine Musikstunden leisten könnten.

Doch Ruben war seit der Sache mit den Älvsborger Weihnachts-männern selbstsicherer geworden und sagte mit Nachdruck, falls seine Vermutung sich bestätigen sollte, mache er es zur Bedingung, Simons Stunden bezahlen zu dürfen.

Der Junge lag wie üblich, die Nase in einem Buch, oben in der Dachkammer. Aber obwohl Lord Jim in Joseph Conrads Roman gerade seinen schicksalsschwangeren Sprung vom rostigen Deck des Dampfers *Patnas* hinter sich hatte, war Simon nicht dort, war nicht voll dabei in der Einfahrtrinne zum Persischen Golf. Seine Gedanken waren auf einem Streifzug durch das Land, in dem die Gräser sangen und der Fluß in seiner milden Weisheit mit den Menschen sprach.

Der Priesterkönig hatte davon gesprochen, eine Sprache wieder wachzurufen, die verboten und vergessen worden war.

Simon gab sich alle Mühe, das zu verstehen. Dann fiel ihm ein, was Ruben vom Erinnern mit dem Herzen gesagt hatte, und da konnte er den Fluß hören und auch die Stimmen der Menschen.

Dann aber trug der Kopf den Sieg davon, was hatten sie gerufen? Welches Geheimnis steckte hinter dem Vergessen der Sprache?

Karin kam die knarrende Holztreppe herauf und sagte: »Onkel Ruben bildet sich ein, daß du musikalisch bist und will, daß du Geige spielen lernst.«

Ausnahmsweise hörte er den besorgten Vorwurf nicht, der ihm sonst immer durch Mark und Bein ging. So überwältigt war er von Freude, als der Gedanke in seinem Kopf explodierte: Wenn er ein Instrument spielen konnte, würde er das Wunder selbst neu erschaf-fen.

Die Jungen schliefen wie immer im Sommer auf dem Dachboden, Isak tief und körperlich müde. Daher wachte nur Simon von der Auseinandersetzung unten in der Küche auf und hörte, wie Erik Karin anschrie, daß sie, Himmel, Arsch und Zwirn, nicht gescheit sei und daß er, Erik, in seinem Leben von mysteriösen Geigenspielern schon lange mehr als genug habe.

Wie immer wenn die beiden stritten, steigerte sich Simons Schuldgefühl, und dieses Mal war er ganz sicher, daß die Schuld bei ihm lag. Er setzte sich im Bett auf und ihm wurde übel, und als die Stimmen lauter wurden und die Schimpfworte schlimmer und das Weinen kam und alles noch unerträglicher wurde, kletterte er die Bodentreppe hinunter und öffnete die Küchentür und stand dort und weinte und sagte, daß er nicht in eine Geigenschule gehen wolle.

Karin empfand es, als habe der Junge sie mitten ins Herz getroffen, und Erik schämte sich so sehr, daß er weiterschreien mußte: »Du sollst doch schlafen, du verdammter Unglücksrabe.«

Aber das hörte Simon nicht, denn er lag in Karins Armen und war vier Jahre alt und das Leben war wieder heil und sie sorgte sich nur um ihn, als sie Tränen trocknete und tröstete und versicherte, daß sie und auch Erik im Leben nichts anderes wollten, als ihn froh und glücklich zu sehen.

»Aber ihr kümmert euch doch immer nur um Isak«, sagte Simon und im nächsten Augenblick war er eingeschlafen.

Es war ein schwerer aber heilsamer Augenblick für Erik, der in den Keller hinunter ging und dachte, er werde das Bootbauen eine Woche auf sich beruhen lassen und mit Simon fischen gehen. Und es war auch wegen Karin, die den Jungen in ihr Bett gelegt hatte und die auf den Frühling und den Sommer zurückblickte und auf all das, was sich ereignet hatte, seit Isak krank geworden war.

Nach dieser Nacht war Simon im Haus an der Flußmündung wieder sichtbar.

Am nächsten Vormittag, als Simon zu seiner Musikprüfung und Isak zu seinem Förderunterricht gegangen waren, konnten Erik und Karin wieder miteinander sprechen. Nicht über den bösen Streit und ihre Angst, verletzt zu haben, und nicht über die gemeinsame Schuld gegenüber dem Jungen, der sich verlassen gefühlt hatte. Und am allerwenigsten darüber, was sie an Rubens Vorschlag so in Aufregung versetzt haben mochte.

All das berührte Gefühle, und für Gefühle gab es nur dann Worte, wenn in ihrer Küche oder in ihrer Ehe gestritten wurde. Wo es aber um Tatsachen ging, konnten sie sich über das Merkwürdige an Rubens Idee austauschen.

»Simon hat Musik doch nie leiden mögen«, sagte Karin und erinnerte daran, wie sie damals gelacht hatten, als Simon aus dem Kindergarten nach Hause gekommen war und gesagt hatte, er hält das nicht aus mit *Die helle Sonn' leucht' jetzt herfür*, das jeden Morgen gesungen werden mußte.

»Erinnerst du dich, wie er gesagt hat, ihm wird bei der Abschlußfeier schlecht, wenn die Kinder singen *Der Mai ist gekommen*, und die Lehrerin begleitet das auf dem Harmonium?«

»Doch«, nickte Erik. Aber er erinnerte sich auch daran, wie die Lehrerin gespielt und wie die Kinder geklungen hatten, und daß Simon schon als er noch ganz klein war, vor Unbehagen richtig in sich zusammengesackt war, wenn Karin ihm etwas vorgesungen hatte.

Karin besaß überhaupt kein musikalisches Gehör.

»Er mochte auch das Koffergrammophon nie«, sagte Karin, und Erik dachte an die schwankenden Platten mit *Wenn ich groß bin, liebe Mutter*, und wie er selbst Schwierigkeiten gehabt hatte, Olof Sandberg anzuhören wenn er noch mehr winselte als sonst, nur weil Karin vergessen hatte, das Grammophon aufzuziehen.

Und dann dachte er daran, wie er dem Jungen, der damals höchstens drei Jahre alt gewesen war, aus Holz ein Lastauto gebaut und der Kleine auf der Hobelbank gesessen und Erik beim Tischlern die Torero-Arie aus Carmen gepfiffen hatte. Plötzlich hatte der Junge, so klein er war, die Melodie nachempfunden und mitgesungen.

Glockenrein.

Das hatte Erik schon damals bedrückt, er hatte an das Erbe gedacht.

Den Scheitel mit Wasser gezogen, mit frisch gebügeltem Hemd und Geld für die Straßenbahn in der Tasche, ging Simon den gewohnten Weg zur Haltestelle. Ihm war leicht ums Herz wie damals, als er auf Onkel Arons Gepäckträger gesessen hatte und gerade vor dem Verloren- und Verlassensein gerettet worden war.

Er stieg am Järntorg um und kam nach und nach dorthin, wo er hin sollte, zu einer großen und merkwürdigen Wohnung am Viktoriapark, wo ein aufgeregter und ungeduldiger Mann ihn erwartete.

Aber Simon war an diesem Tag nicht leicht zu erschrecken.

Dennoch war der Besuch eine Enttäuschung, der Aufgeregte, der lange Haare hatte und in gebrochenem Schwedisch herumschrie, klimperte nur auf seinem Klavier herum und wollte, daß Simon die Töne nachmachte. Eine Geige war nirgends zu sehen, aber der Langhaarige war zum Schluß recht nett und brummelte etwas von interessant.

»Sehr interessant«, sagte er.

»Nicht besonders«, sagte Simon, als er nach Hause kam und Karin ihn fragte, wie es gewesen sei.

»Du hast also kein Interesse?«

Jetzt öffnete Simon sich ganz ihrer Besorgnis und antwortete, nein, das habe er wohl nicht.

Aber etwa eine Stunde später rief Ruben an und berichtete, daß der ungeduldige Mann am Viktoriapark gesagt habe, Simon besitze etwas, das man absolutes Gehör nennt und das sei sehr selten.

»Aber er will keine Stunden nehmen«, sagte Karin und jetzt hörte Ruben, daß sie erleichtert war.

»Das ist nicht möglich«, sagte Ruben. »Ich komme raus und rede mit dem Jungen.«

Dann saßen sie abends im guten Zimmer, allein, Ruben und Simon.

»Du wirst eine neue Sprache lernen«, sagte Ruben.

Simon dachte an Englisch, das ihm Freude machte, und an Deutsch, das schwierig war, und konnte nicht verstehen, warum er noch eine weitere Sprache lernen sollte.

»Was soll ich damit?«

Ruben wirkte traurig, als er sagte: »Ich habe mir eingebildet, du hättest diese Sprache als Veranlagung mitbekommen und könntest viel von dem damit ausdrücken, was du in dir trägst ...«

Der Junge verschwand so blitzschnell, daß Ruben nie dazu kam, das Erstaunen und den Schmerz in den schwarzen Augen zu sehen.

Er wurde nie ein Geigenspieler.

Etwa zu dieser Zeit fing Simon an zu lügen. Es ging leicht, als schlummere auch dafür ein Talent in ihm.

Es war wie laufen, wie damals, als er auf dem Sportplatz der Neuen Werft die sechzig Meter schneller als jeder andere gelaufen war und einen Preis bekam und plötzlich im Mittelpunkt stand.

Bald war er zum Meister geworden. Die Lügen quollen ihm nur so über die Lippen, die erste ergab die zweite, die zweite gebar die dritte, der wiederum die nächste und übernächste entschlüpfte.

Er konnte kein Ende finden.

Die Lügen sicherten ihm einen Platz an der Sonne, in der Schule, unter den Freunden zu Hause, in Karins Interesse und Eriks Wertschätzung. Er wurde einsamer denn je.

Im Haus am Meer war das Dasein einfach, denn dort gab es klare Grenzen zwischen Schwarz und Weiß. Lüge war schwarz, mildernde Worte über Phantasien gab es nicht.

Simon log, und sobald er allein war, schlug ihm die Schuld ihre Krallen ins Fleisch. Und die Angst. Er glaubte, wenn Karin ihn ein einziges Mal ertappte, würde ihre Liebe, von der er lebte, aufhören. In wachsender Angst trainierte er sein Gedächtnis, um sich an das zu erinnern, was er gesagt hatte um sich nie zu widersprechen. Die Anstrengung setzte sich im Magen fest, der sich verkrampfte und schmerzte.

Es begann mit Dolly, dem Mädchen im zweiten Stock des Nachbarhauses, das er geliebt hatte, seit er denken konnte. Sie hatte Augen wie Vergißmeinnicht und eine Wolke aus blonden Locken, vom Vater, der Friseur war, wöchentlich sorgsam gelegt.

Dolly war ein Einzelkind und wie Mama und Papa fein bis zum Äußersten. Als die Familie in die Wohnung bei Gustafssons einzog, waren die Wände mit kleinblumigen Tapeten verkleidet, die Fußböden mit bunten orientalischen Teppichen ausgelegt, Stilmöbel schnurgerade aneinandergereiht worden, und an den Zimmerdecken klirrten Kristallkronen.

Dolly hatte ein eigenes Zimmer, schon allein das war hier in der Stadt etwas so Besonderes, daß es ihr Glanz verlieh.

Ihr Papa war mit seiner Tochter an der Hand durch die Gegend gegangen und hatte ihr die Häuser gezeigt, wo sie die Kinder kennen und in der Küche spielen durfte. Nicht bei Olivia, denn dort wohnten Zigeuner, nicht bei Helene, denn dort hatte man die Schwindsucht gehabt.

Die Häuser hatten Frauennamen wie die Boote.

Larssons gehörten zu den Anerkannten, und das war ein Glück für Dolly, denn damit hatte sie Zugang zu Karins Küche, zu Wirklichkeit und Hausmannskost.

Zehn Jahre später war Dolly zur elegantesten Nutte der Gegend geworden, aber davon ahnte man noch nichts, als sie und Simon vierzehn Jahre alt waren und einander liebten.

Nun ist allerdings nicht erwiesen, ob Dolly ihn liebte, aber Simon war etwas Besseres, er ging auf die höhere Schule und die Bootswerft seines Vaters entwickelte Macht und Herrlichkeit. Außerdem war Simon groß und hübsch geworden, die Schwärze, die seine Andersartigkeit offenbart hatte als er klein war, machte ihn jetzt interessant.

Vom halbrunden Fenster auf Larssons Dachboden konnte man direkt in Dollys Jungmädchenzimmer sehen. Keiner von beiden sagte je etwas zu jemand darüber, aber Dolly entkleidete sich jeden Abend – bei brennender Deckenlampe und ohne die Rollos herunterzuziehen – langsam und wollüstig.

Und Simon stand am Dachbodenfenster, die Hand in festem Griff um sein Glied, und der Genuß war groß und die Koordination gelang schnell. Wenn Dolly das Unterhöschen endlich abgestreift hatte, stellte sie einen Fuß auf das Fensterbrett, fuhr sich mit der Hand zwischen ihre Beine und schob Hinterteil und Geschlecht in immer schnellerer Folge vor und zurück.

Da ging es los bei Simon, die Lust, die in ihm schwoll, explodierte in einer schwindelerregenden Sekunde, seine Hand füllte sich mit warmem Samen und sein Herz mit Dankbarkeit gegenüber dem Mädchen, das sich ihm so freizügig anbot.

Wenn sie einander begegneten, begegneten sich nie ihre Blicke. Und nicht ein Wort wurde gesprochen, denn Simon verschlug es die Sprache. Doch eines Sonntags sagte er den Jungen der Umgebung, daß er Dolly im winterverlassenen Kiosk neben dem Bad gebumst habe.

Er hatte nicht ganz begriffen, wieso das Interesse an der Geschichte so groß war, alle wollten mehr wissen und er erzählte ihnen mehr. Lüge erzeugte Lüge, er malte erregende Bilder in Weiß, Rosa und Rot.

Ja, sie hatte Haare zwischen den Beinen. Und ein Muttermal auf der Pobacke, wo sie reingebissen werden wollte. Nein, sie hatte nicht besonders geblutet, das mit der Jungfräulichkeit war nicht so schwierig. Ja, man durfte an ihrer Brust lutschen.

Simon war selbst so verblüfft über das, was er sagte, daß er gar nicht bemerkte, wie die Luft um ihn herum vibrierte. Und bald genoß er die Bewunderung in vollen Zügen, die aus den aufgerissenen Augen der ihn umringenden Jungen strahlte.

Also probierte er am Montag alles mit demselben Resultat noch einmal in der Schule aus. Sogar Isak war stumm vor Staunen und stolz auf den Freund.

In der großen Pause strichen sie, wie es jetzt Brauch geworden war, frierend am hohen schmiedeeisernen Zaun der Mädchenschule entlang und schauten sich die Trauben kirchernder Mädchen dahinter an und haßten sie alle, weil sie alles hatten, was Jungen brauchen, all diese weichen, feuchten, geheimnisvollen Löcher, um die sich alle Träume rankten.

»Man stelle sich vor, selbst so ein Loch zu haben, mit dem man tun kann, was man will«, sagte Isak, und Simon war erschrocken und erregt, sie hatten das bisher nie in Worte gekleidet. Jetzt nach der Erzählung über Dolly war alles möglich, das verstand Simon.

»Bist du mit deinem Schwanz richtig in sie rein?«, fragte Isak.

»Nein«, sagte Simon. »Ich habe mich mit dem Finger begnügt.«

In diesem Augenblick verfluchte er sich selbst, spürte die Mauer, die sich zwischen ihn und den Freund schob und hätte sie gern kurz und klein geschlagen. Aber es gab kein Zurück.

Die Lügen quollen weiterhin aus ihm heraus und wurden mit der Zeit immer brauchbarer.

An einem Spätwintermorgen mit Sturm über der Hafeneinfahrt machte er einen Umweg zum Meer, zum Strand, setzte sich dort auf die Klippen und versuchte sich einzureden, der Sturm blase ihn von aller Verlogenheit rein. Dann kam er zu spät zur ersten Stunde, mußte an die Tür klopfen und um Entschuldigung bitten. Das war ihm schon früher passiert, er gab nie einen Grund an und steckte ohne Protest einen Tadel ein. Den Karin ohne Vorwürfe zu unterschreiben pflegte.

Dieses Mal sagte er: »Ich war bei einem Unfall dabei.«

Dann schilderte er den Lastwagen mit den quietschenden Bremsen und die Frau, die überfahren worden war, und wie auf der Karl-Johans-Gata das Blut in den Rinnstein geflossen war und wie er mit knapper Not sein Fahrrad hatte anhalten können und wie er als Zeuge von der Polizei verhört worden war.

Sie hatten Rubbe in Mathe, einen grobschlächtigen Mann um die Fünfzig, seit Jahrzehnten darin geübt, Jungen zu durchschauen. Er beachtete also das aufgeregte Tuscheln in der Klasse nicht, sondern sagte zu Simon nur, er solle sich setzen und seine Wurzeln ziehen. Es lag Mißtrauen in den kalten Augen des Lehrers und Simon fühlte, wie sein Magen sich zusammenzog. Diese Geschichte konnte überprüft werden und Rubbe sah aus, als hätte er das auch vor.

Aber Simon sollte erfahren, daß sein eigenes Böses Verbündete hatte, hilfreiche Kräfte auf Gebieten, wo die meisten Menschen schon an ein Eingreifen des Zufalls glaubten. Am nächsten Tag stand in der Handelszeitung von einem Unglück in der Karl-Johans-Gata und Rubbe griff die Sache erneut auf: »Larsson hat sich geirrt«, sagte er. »Es war keine Frau, die überfahren wurde, sondern ein älterer Mann.«

Dann hielt er ein Referat über Zeugenpsychologie und darüber, wie die Aufregung, wenn man einem Unfall beiwohnt, die Sichtweise verdreht.

»Zeugen irren sich häufig und man kann sich nur selten auf sie verlassen«, sagte er.

Zunächst fühlte Simon nur Erleichterung, fast so etwas wie Triumph. Dann aber kam die Angst wieder angekrochen, setzte sich diesmal im Zwerchfell fest und nicht im Magen.

Der Teufel beschützt die Seinen, war einer von Eriks Sprüchen.

Jetzt wußte Simon, daß das stimmte. Der Teufel half ihm immer wieder. Erik gegenüber behauptete er der einzige in der Klasse zu sein, der am Seil bis an die Decke zu klettern wage, und der Turnlehrer sei ganz verblüfft gewesen und habe gesagt: Teufel noch mal.

Erik strahlte vor Glück.

Am nächsten Tag kletterte Simon, der an sich Höhenangst hatte und eher zaghaft war, bis an die Decke, und der Turnlehrer, ein alter Rittmeister mit lächerlichen O-Beinen, sagte: Teufel noch mal.

Simon erzählte Karin, er habe die Großmutter besucht, und Karin freute sich. Am nächsten Tag wurde ihm bewußt, daß er die alte Frau besuchen mußte. Er nahm Blumen mit, für die er sich das Geld von Isak lieh, dem er sagte, er habe eine Wette verloren, die er während der Religionsstunde mit Abrahamsson eingegangen war. Diese Geschichte brauchte er nicht so genau zu nehmen, denn Isak nahm am Religionsunterricht nicht teil und kam mit Abrahamsson nie zusammen. Aber Simon erntete großes Lob für die Blumen, die das Herz seiner Mutter rührten.

Als er einmal nachmittags von der Straßenbahnhaltestelle heimwärts ging, hatte jemand mit Kreide an die Wand der Bäckerei geschrieben, Simon liebt Dolly, und das Ganze mit Herz und Pfeil und so. Simon spürte, wie sein Nacken vor Anstrengung steif wurde, weil er den Kopf so halten wollte, daß er das Gekrakel unmöglich hätte lesen können.

Als er die Straße entlang auf Larssons Garage zuschlenderte, sah er sie dort an der Biegung unter der Hecke sitzen: Dolly. Rote Wangen, glänzende Augen.

»Hast du's gelesen«, sagte sie.

Er nickte.

»Ist das wahr«, sagte sie und er wollte sterben oder zumindest im Erdboden versinken, und er dachte an den Weg von Nordenskiöld und Vega durch die Nordostpassage und an die großen Eisfelder dort oben in der Polarnacht und fühlte, wie trocken sein Mund war und wagte es nicht, in die Vergißmeinnichtaugen zu schauen.

Aber sie war hartnäckig, sagte lauter: »Ist das wahr?«

Und Simon, der fürchtete, Karin könnte es hören, nickte und sagte kaum hörbar: »Wird wohl so sein.«

Er dachte vorsichtshalber, daß man Mädchen nicht schlagen durfte, sollten sie ihn anspringen und kratzen. Doch sie sah äußerst zufrieden aus und sagte, wenn sie sich nach dem Essen unten bei den Badeklippen träfen, wo niemand sie sehen könnte, dann dürfe er sie küssen.

Er hatte keine Lust, zu dem Rendezvous zu gehen, wagte aber nicht wegzubleiben. So kam es, daß der erste Kuß, den er einem Mädchen gab, nur nach schwarzer Lüge und gelber Angst schmeckte. All seine Liebe hatte mit diesem Kuß ein Ende, er verabscheute dieses Mädchen, von dem er in all den Jahren seiner Kindheit geträumt hatte.

Und als er erkannte, daß sie bald von ihm fordern würde, all das zu tun, was er schon getan zu haben behauptet hatte, geriet er beinahe in Panik.

Da kam die Lüge aus dem Mund gesprungen, als Rettung und Hilfe wie immer. Schwermütig blickend zog er die Stirn kraus und sagte: »Ich werde bald sterben. Weißt du, ich habe Tuberkulose, aber bisher hat es noch niemand erfahren. Aber ich huste die ganze Nacht Blut.«

Dolly war auf und davon.

Stärker als die Eroberungslust, stärker als die Geilheit, stärker sogar als die Eitelkeit war die Angst vor der Schwindsucht.

Als an diesem Abend in der Küche die Zehnuhrnachrichten angeschaltet wurden, ging Simon wie immer auf den Dachboden, um Dolly beim Auskleiden zuzusehen. Aber diesmal hatte sie die Rollos heruntergezogen.

Simon war erleichtert.

Eine Woche später sagte Karin: »Tante Jenny war hier und hat behauptet, daß du so stark hustest. Ich habe zwar nichts bemerkt, aber sie hat so ängstlich ausgesehen, daß ich fast beunruhigt war.«

»Ach was«, sagte Simon. »Ich war irgendwann ein bißchen erkältet und habe zufällig als Dolly auch in der Straßenbahn war gehustet.«

Karin verzog den Mund, dann seufzte sie in Gedanken an die feinen Nachbarn in den hübschen Zimmern, bei denen die Bazillenangst die Wände entlangkroch.

Dann kam der Frühling mit heftigen Stürmen aus dem Westen. Sie bliesen zwischen den Bergen alles rein und die Gräser ganz grün, und die Stimmen der Menschen klangen hoffnungsvoll und heller als seit vielen Jahren. Als die Apfelbäume blühten, wurde Isaks Boot vom Stapel gelassen, und es war, genau wie Erik sich das vorgestellt hatte, das prächtigste Kielboot in der Flußmündung. Es wurde an Boje und Anker unterhalb des Oljebergs festgemacht, bekam als Ersatz für das Blei, das für Geld nicht zu haben war, Feldsteine als Ballast. Der Segelmacher verzögerte die Sache, aber an einem Tag Ende Mai konnten sie auf Probefahrt gehen.

Das Boot flog, durchschnitt das Meer wie im Tanz und Isak vergaß die Träume von Mädchen mit feuchten Löchern über dem Glück, sein Boot in den Wind zu stellen. Es zeigte sich, daß es teuflisch gut am Wind lag, und es wurde nach Karin und dem Westwind auf Kajsa getauft.

An jenem Tag, als die große Invasion ihren Brückenkopf in der Normandie aufschlug, legten Isak und Simon die Prüfung zur Mittleren Reife mit gutem Erfolg ab. Simon bekam das Prämium in Schwedisch, den literarischen Anerkennungspreis der Schule, wie es hieß.

Er hatte einen Aufsatz über den Bauern geschrieben, der die Äcker unter dem Oljeberg bearbeitete und ein mürrischer alter Mann war, vor dem Simon sein Leben lang Angst gehabt hatte. Aber im Aufsatz verwandelte er den Alten in einen Mann von großer Begabung, in einen Runenmeister, der um die Kraft der alten Zeichen wußte, Umgang mit den Mächten hatte und die Leute mit dem bösen Blick bedenken, jedoch auch von schweren und seltenen Krankheiten heilen konnte.

Die Studienrätin Kerstin Larberg las der Klasse den Aufsatz vor und sagte, das sei eine wunderbare Geschichte. »Gibt es eine Spur Wahrheit darin? Oder steckt in Larsson ein Dichter?«

Die Worte zuckten wie ein Blitz durch Simons Kopf, und in einem einzigen befreienden Atemzug sagte er: »Ich habe es mir ausgedacht.«

Eine Weile trug er den Spitznamen Dichter, aber das kümmerte ihn wenig. Er dachte viel an Onkel Ruben und an das, was dieser nach dem Konzert von einer Wirklichkeit gesagt hatte, die aus Lügen aufgebaut ist, aber Wahrheit enthält.

Bevor er einschlief, faßte er einen Entschluß: Er wollte sich aus den Lügen freischreiben. Den ganzen Sommer über würde er Geschichten von Frauen und Brüsten und Löchern und von Polarforschern und dem Tod in Europa schreiben. Er wollte von Karin als einer Norne, einer Schicksalsgöttin dichten, die in ihrer Küche am Spinnrocken saß und die Schicksale der Menschen zu einem Faden drehte, und von dem kleinen Mann aus den Träumen, der einen so merkwürdigen Hut aufgehabt hatte und im fernen Reich der hohen Gräser Krieg führte und starb, als er einen Stier im Tempel opfern wollte. Und über Dolly wollte er schreiben, diese treulose Schlampe, die den Mann betrügt, der sie liebt, und über Tante Inga in der einsamen Hütte am blauen See. Dieses letzte erstaunte ihn, was, zum Teufel, konnte man von Inga erzählen.

Aber er zerbrach sich darüber jetzt nicht den Kopf. Morgen würde er Onkel Ruben um Schreibhefte bitten, einen ganzen Stapel.

Dann entließen die Sommerferien die beiden Jungen in ihre fröhliche Freiheit. Sie waren jetzt nicht mehr so unzertrennlich.

Isak segelte, Simon schrieb.

Und Karin arbeitete in der Gartenerde, Erik sang und legte den Kiel für den dritten Einmaster, und die Amerikaner und Engländer befreiten Paris.

Als der Sommer rundum am schönsten war, versiegten die Lügen in Simon Larssons Mund. Vielleicht hatte das Schreiben ihm geholfen, obwohl es nicht so viel war wie er sich vorgestellt hatte. Er hatte bald herausgefunden, daß zu dichten viel schwieriger war als zu lügen. Da geschah inmitten aller Wirklichkeit etwas, das so verblüffend war, daß es alle Phantasien Simons bei weitem übertraf.

Es ist unmöglich zu erzählen, denn niemand würde es glauben.

Sie hieß Maj-Britt und war eine von den Frauen, die wie zum Gehen angesetzter Hefeteig überquellen, wenn man mit Mehl gegeizt und mit Hefe gewuchert hat. Üppig, milchig weiß, überschäumend.

Sie war neunzehn Jahre alt und Tochter eines Witwers und Sprengmeisters, der sein Haus an der Stadtgrenze am höchsten Punkt gebaut hatte, und sie litt an gebrochenem Herzen, denn sie hatte einen von den Seeleuten geliebt, die der Tod im stählernen Rumpf der *Ulven* ereilt hatte. Maj-Britt hatte aus tiefstem Herzen getrauert, die Tränen hatten sie vollends aufgeschwemmt.

Zu ihr wurden Isak und Simon an einem warmen Nachmittag zum Haareschneiden geschickt. Sie war beim Friseur angestellt, schnitt und tat schön und hatte nicht Worte genug über den schönen Fall von Isaks Haaren, und darüber, mit welcher Qualität, welcher Pferdemähne, die Natur Simon bedacht hatte. Die Jungen waren rot wie die Geranien, die an diesem heißen Nachmittag voll Bienengesumm vor dem Fenster prangten, einen Ständer hatten sie beide, das Mädchen sah es, und ihr überschwengliches Lachen hallte durch den Frisiersalon hinaus in den Garten, wo selbst die Hummeln in den überreifen Blütenkelchen erstaunt verstummten.

»Kommt heute abend zu mir nach Hause. So um sechs. Ins Haus des Sprengmeisters. Durch den Kellereingang«, sagte sie, als sie sich vom Lachen erholt hatte. Sie befanden sich allein im Salon, der Friseur war mit seiner Frau und Dolly in Urlaub gefahren.

Zu Hause sagte Karin, das sei aber kein guter Haarschnitt, das Mädel hätte Vernunft genug haben müssen, mehr zu kürzen, wenn sie schon dafür bezahlt wurde. So wie die Jungen jetzt aussahen, hätte Karin das selbst besser fertiggebracht.

Sie aßen zeitig, Gott sei Dank, und kurz vor sechs flitzten die Jungen auf ihren Rädern der Stadtgrenze und dem Berg mit der schwindelerregenden Aussicht über Meer und Stadt entgegen. Es war so steil, daß sie im Stehen treten mußten. Aber ihre Herzen klopften wohl nicht nur vor Anstrengung, und auch der Schweiß floß nicht nur aus diesem Grund, als sie am Haus des Sprengmeisters entlang zur Rückseite und zur Kellertür fanden.

Maj-Britt erwartete die beiden, sie hatte im Keller ein Zimmer mit einem großen Bett, das der Matrose von der *Ulven* auf einer Auktion billig gekauft und bis hier herauf geschleppt hatte. Und sie lachte ebenso überschwenglich wie sie es im Frisiersalon getan hatte und auch so hemmungslos, daß die Jungen bald mitlachen mußten.

Es war wie ein Traum, ein verrückter und wunderbarer Traum, als sie das Kleid auszog und darunter keinen Faden am Leib hatte und sich mit ausgestreckten Armen und Beinen aufs Bett legte. »Kommt jetzt, ihr Knirpse«, sagte sie. »Laßt uns genießen. Ich will es euch lehren.«

Und das tat sie, bald lagen sie dort, einer auf jedem Frauenarm, und sie führte ihre Hände an alle heimlichen Stellen und übte mit ihnen die richtigen Handgriffe, abwechselnd fest und sanft. Sie lutschten jeder an einer großen Brust und bissen hinein, und Maj-Britt stöhnte und jauchzte vor Lust und Freude, als Simon als erster sein Glied in ihr Loch schob.

Dann kam auch sie, und sie schrie, daß die Kellerdecke sich wölbte.

Aber nach einer Weile hatte sie sich wieder erholt und Isak durfte lernen, wie man zu der glatten Erbse in ihrer tropfnassen Spalte findet, und sie stöhnte: »Mehhhhr, das ist das Beste.«

Dann sprengte die Lust sie wieder und sie sank zusammen und lachte ihr gewaltiges Lachen und machte es Isak, der immer noch einen Ständer hatte, mit dem Mund.

Das kann nicht wahr sein, dachte Simon, aber das war es, und mittendrin schaute Maj-Britt auf die Uhr und schrie: »Lieber Himmel, gleich kommt der Sprengmeister. Ab durch die Mitte, ihr Hurenböcke.«

Und ihr Lachen folgte ihnen, als sie den Berg hinuntersausten, und sie fühlten sich wie die Götter, kamen zum Badeplatz und warfen sich ins Meer und durchpflügten das Wasser in kräftigen Zügen.

Sie hatten gar nicht gewußt, daß sie so schnell schwimmen konnten. Als sie bei Isaks Boot ankamen, waren sie immer noch erhitzt und erregt, sahen aber, daß an der Zugleine klebrige Quallen hingen und wußten, daß sie so schnell wie möglich an Bord gehen mußten. Simon hatte sich verbrannt, aber es gab Süßwasser im Boot und sie spülten Salz und Quallenfäden ab, ehe Isak den Schiffsboden anhob und Bier aus dem Kielschwein holte, geheimes Bier, bei Ruben geklaut.

Und sie tranken. Versuchten sich zu beruhigen.

»Hast du gehört, was sie gesagt hat, als wir abhauen mußten?«

Jaja, Simon hatte es gehört. Kommt morgen um dieselbe Zeit wieder, hatte sie gesagt.

An jedem Abend in diesem heißen Sommer, in dem 30 000 Balten in kleinen Booten über die Ostsee flüchteten, kamen sie zum Haus des Sprengmeisters und ergötzten sich, wie Maj-Britt das nannte, und lernten alles über die richtigen Handgriffe beim Lieben, alles, was Jungs so brauchen. Sie würden es beide im Leben gut mit den Mädchen haben und sie würden dieser sagenhaften Maj-Britt vom Berg oft dankbar gedenken.

Eines Abends, als sie wie gewöhnlich beim Sprengmeister um die Hausecke schlichen und an der Kellertür klopften, öffnete ihnen ein Matrose in weiten Hosen aber ohne Hemd. Er war breit wie eine Ladeluke und lang wie ein Fahnenmast.

»Was in aller Welt wollen diese Zwerge?« erkundigte er sich bei Maj-Britt, die drinnen in der Kühle des Kellers im Bett lag. Simon, der nicht alles vergessen hatte, was er im vergangenen Winter gelernt hatte, reagierte schnell: »Wir kommen für die Älvsborger Weihnachtsmänner sammeln«, sagte er.

»Mitten im Sommer«, wunderte sich der Matrose, verfolgte diesen Gedanken aber wegen Maj-Britts Lachen, das aus dem Bett herüber schallte, nicht weiter.

Auf dem Heimweg versuchten die beiden Jungen, Haß auf den Mann zu entwickeln, aber es gelang ihnen nicht besonders gut. Sie waren dankbar für das, was sie geradezu im Überfluß bekommen hatten, denn sie hatten ja die ganze Zeit gewußt, daß dieses Unglaubliche nicht ewig andauern konnte.

Dann war er da, der längste Frühling aller Zeiten. Noch nie war die Zeit so langsam vergangen. Die Tage krochen den Abenden entgegen, an denen sich aber auch nichts ereignete.

Raoul Wallenberg verschwand in Budapest.

In Deutschland wurden nun auch schon die Vierzehnjährigen zum Kriegsdienst verpflichtet.

Bedeutende Männer trafen sich in Jalta, um die Welt unter sich aufzuteilen. Dann starb Roosevelt, und Karin sagte in aufladerndem Zorn, das sei ungerecht.

Irgendwann stand die Zeit still, das war, als Hitler sich in seinem Bunker in Berlin erschossen hatte und trotzdem der Friede nicht kam. Das Radio lief in seiner Ecke im Leerlauf, der Zeiger der alten Küchenuhr rührte sich nicht vom Fleck, und Karin ertappte sich dabei, wie sie an der Uhr herumschüttelte. Aber das alte Ding war nicht kaputt, die Zeit selbst war stehen geblieben und machte die wartenden Menschen verrückt.

Schließlich kam der Tag doch, es war der siebte Mai, und die Knospen an den Bäumen begannen auszuschlagen. Die Gärten duften nach feuchter Erde, und die Vögel hätten sich eigentlich in die Herzen der Menschen singen müssen. Aber die Menschen hatten keine Kraft mehr, sich diesem Gesang zu öffnen. Sie versammelten sich wie üblich um das Radio in Larssons Küche und hörten den Jubel in Oslo, London und Stockholm, aber bei ihnen selbst konnte keine rechte Freude aufkommen.

Wallin saß auf der Küchenbank und besah sich trotzig seine Arbeiterhände, die bleiern und tatenlos in seinem Schoß lagen, als könnten sie nie wieder zum Leben erweckt werden, Ågren hatte Fieberrosen auf den Wangen und stieß Flüche aus. Himmel, Arsch und Zwirn.

Erik schwieg ausnahmsweise. Äppelgren stolzierte wie ein knikkebeiniger Kranich durch die Küche, verhedderte sich im Läufer und weinte ungehemmt wie ein Kind.

Auch Karin weinte, still und tonlos.

Simon und Isak saßen wie üblich eng aneinandergedrängt auf der Holzkiste, und Simon konnte nur denken, daß heute nacht dort unten in Europa kein Mensch einen anderen totschlagen werde. Er hätte auch gerne geweint, aber dazu war er inzwischen wirklich zu groß. Seine Aufregung machte sich Luft, indem er mit Beinen und Füßen wie mit Trommelschlegeln an die Holzkiste schlug, bis Karin um Rücksicht bat: Um Gottes willen, Simon, sei ruhig!

Isak saß neben ihm, ebenso seltsam tatenlos wie Wallin. Sein Herz brannte, aber sein Kopf war kalt und leer und sein Körper so steif, als wäre er zu Eis gefroren. Erst als Johansson, der Briefträger, der als Fischer geboren und groß wie ein Haus war, sagte, jetzt müsse man alle Naziteufel in heißem Öl sieden und sie so lange wie möglich zappeln lassen, ließ die Spannung in Isaks Körper nach.

Er holte tief Luft und erkannte, daß das, was seinem Körper Krämpfe verursacht hatte, Haß, und das, was in seinem Herzen brannte, die Einsicht war, daß Rache möglich und süß sein konnte.

Irgendwann kam Helen mit der Milch. Sie strahlte eine gewisse Feierlichkeit aus, sah all die Herumsitzenden herausfordernd an und wagte zu sagen: »Ich finde, ihr solltet heute abend alle in die Kapelle kommen und Gott für den Frieden danken.«

Da endlich wurde Erik lebhaft, er sprang auf und schrie: »Und wem, zum Teufel, sollen wir für den Krieg und all die Toten danken?«

»Der Krieg ist Menschenwerk«, sagte Helen, die keinen Funken von ihrer Feierlichkeit einbüßte.

»Du bist nicht gescheit«, sagte Ågren, aber Karin fiel ihm ins Wort und sagte, daß zumindest in ihrer Küche jeder den Ansichten des anderen Respekt entgegenzubringen habe.

Von den Worten her war es Karin, aber ihrer Stimme fehlte die übliche Kraft.

Gegen Abend kam Ruben mit einem schwer zu deutenden Ausdruck in den Augen, einer großen Erleichterung gemischt mit einem solchen Schmerz, daß es nicht auszuhalten war. Als Karin seinem Blick begegnete, holte sie die Branntweinflasche und die Schnapsgläser, goß jedem einen ordentlichen Schluck ein und sagte mit einer hauchdünnen Stimme: »Dann stoßen wir also an – auf den Frieden.«

Und die Männer tranken und Karin trank. Sie schluckte dieses schreckliche Zeug in einem Zug, und wäre es nicht eine so große und geschichtsträchtige Stunde gewesen, hätten die andern es sicher bemerkt, und sie wären erstaunt gewesen, erschrocken.

Jetzt aber war jeder mit sich selbst beschäftigt.

Karin ging hinaus auf den alten Abort hinterm Haus und übergab sich. Dann lehnte sie bleich und in kalten Schweiß gebadet an der gekalkten Wand und ließ die Wellen der Übelkeit über sich ergehen.

Aber viel schlimmer war, daß es in der Brust so schmerzte.

Sie war erstaunt über sich selbst. Und wütend. Warum, zum Teufel, tat es jetzt weh, wo alles vorbei war und die Erde und die Menschen aufatmen konnten.

Der Schmerz bohrte und stach, als wäre da drinnen einer mit dem Messer am Werk. Sie versuchte an ihren Vater Petter und an die Seidenschwänze zu denken, aber es gelang ihr nicht. An Petters Stelle trat in diesem Moment die Mutter mit den verbitterten Augen und der boshaften Zunge. Etwas schien in Karins Herzen ins Wanken zu geraten, die alte, beständige Trauer kam in Bewegung, riß an ihren Wurzeln.

Karin dachte, der große Krieg werde auch die Seidenschwänze das Leben gekostet haben.

Sie stand an der Hauswand bis es zu dämmern begann, erkannte, daß die Zeit wieder ihren normalen Gang ging, daß sie ins Haus gehen, die Männer aus der Küche schicken und zu kochen anfangen mußte. Also preßte sie ihre geballte Faust an die linke Brust und nahm ihren Alltag in Angriff.

Im Winter davor hatten sie das Haus umgebaut, im oberen Stockwerk waren Wände eingezogen worden, den Dachboden gab es nicht mehr, Simon hatte ein eigenes Zimmer bekommen, in dem auch für Isak reichlich Platz war. Ein Gästezimmer mit Aussicht aufs Meer hatten sie für Ruben vorgesehen, der, weil er die vielen Flüchtlinge nicht mehr ertrug, die mit der Familie seines Bruders Aufnahme in der großen Wohnung in Majorna gefunden hatten, immer öfter hier draußen bei ihnen blieb.

Larssons hatten ein Badezimmer bekommen und eine Innentoilette.

Es war großartig und Karin und Erik hatten sich den ganzen Winter gemeinsam daran erfreut.

Sie hatten die Spüle in der Küche in der Höhe versetzt und das Zink gegen rostfreien Stahl ausgetauscht, sie hatten jetzt Zentralheizung und Kalt- und Warmwasser. Karin wagte es kaum zu glauben, daß jetzt Schluß war mit dem Schleppen von Holz und Kohle und mit den qualmenden Kachelöfen, oder daß sie nur an einem Hahn zu drehen brauchte, damit heißes Wasser hervorsprudelte, in dem man die Hände waschen oder anwärmen konnte. Wo früher die Waschgelegenheit für die Familienangehörigen in der Küche gestanden hatte, befand sich jetzt ein großer Kühlschrank.

Für Karin gab es vieles, worüber sie sich freuen konnte. Sie ließ sich das alles durch den Kopf gehen, als sie spät an diesem Abend wieder unter sich waren und das Essen auf dem Tisch stand. Als sie sich ein Stück Kartoffel in den Mund steckte, konnte sie endlich zugeben, wie sehr sie Kartoffeln verabscheute – ob gekocht, gebraten, gerieben, gratiniert, in der Schale –, es blieben gekochte Kartoffeln. Damit war jetzt Schluß, dachte sie, die Sorge ums Essen würde bald nur noch Erinnerung sein, genau wie die Kohle und das kalte Örtchen im Hinterhof.

Die Rationierungen würden aufhören, es würde wieder Obst geben. Bananen, dachte Karin und erinnerte sich daran, wie gern Simon Bananen gegessen hatte, als er klein gewesen war. Inzwischen hatte er vermutlich vergessen, wie sie schmeckten.

Sie schaute Erik an, dessen Brust vor Stolz nur so geschwellt war. Es ging ihm und seinem Bootsbau gut, die Liste mit Bestellungen war lang, vier Mann hatte er angestellt. Sie versorgten vier Familien, wie Karin das gern ausdrückte.

Auch das Geld gefiel ihr, dieses Geld, das jetzt immer vorhanden war, wenn es gebraucht wurde.

Wie immer, wenn Karin sich an den Vorsatz hielt, alles aufzulisten wofür sie dankbar zu sein hatte, ließ sie Ruben aus und hob sich Simon bis zum Schluß auf.

Dieser Junge, der ihr so viel Freude geschenkt hatte.

Er ist bald erwachsen, dachte sie. Und er hat sich richtig gemacht, sieht blendend aus. Wie ein fremder Vogel, der sich durch einen wunderbaren Zufall in ihrer Küche niedergelassen hatte.

Es waren Gedanken voller Unruhe, und wieder stach es ihr in der Brust. Simon, der jede ihrer Regungen immer gleich bemerkte, sah den Schmerz, der über ihr Gesicht zuckte, und sagte: »Du bist müde, Mama. Geh ins Bett, ich werde abwaschen.«

Sie nickte, wußte aber, als sie seinem besorgten Blick begegnete, daß alle dankbaren Gedanken ihr an diesem Abend nicht geholfen hatten. Ihre Reichtümer halfen nicht, um all das zu besänftigen, was in ihrer Brust brannte und stach.

Was ist nur mit mir los?

Erik machte noch eine Runde durch die Werft. Karin hatte das Schlafzimmer für sich allein, und so stand sie vor den Rosen der neuen Tapete und besah sich im Spiegel. Sie war mit ihrem Aussehen immer zufrieden gewesen, das energische und schön geschnittene Gesicht mit dem großen Mund und der geraden Nase hatte ihr gefallen.

Jetzt betrachtete sie ihre Züge lange und gründlich, als verrieten sie ihr etwas Neues. Als gäben sie Antwort. Und sie sah sehr wohl, daß die braunen Augen, die bei ihrem blonden Haar jeden erstaunt hatten, jetzt von neuer Tiefe waren.

Was mochte sich wohl im Hintergrund verbergen?

Furcht?

Nein, das wollte Karin nicht. Ich habe mehr Falten bekommen, dachte sie, die Haare sind fahl wie Stroh. Dick bin ich noch nicht aber schwerer geworden, massiger.

Morgen ist das vorbei, sagte sie sich. Ich muß nur schlafen.

Und am nächsten Morgen, als sie alle Verdunkelungsrollos herunterrissen und in der Frühlingswärme die Fenster putzten, war sie fast fröhlich.

Doch dann kam der Abend, an dem Ruben die ersten englischen Zeitungen mit Augenzeugenberichten aus den geöffneten Vernichtungslagern in Polen und Deutschland mitbrachte. Er saß am Küchentisch und las, Isaks Stimme schlug bis an die Decke, als er übersetzte, Erik war weiß im Gesicht, und das Blau seiner Augen wurde schwarz. Simon suchte Karins Blick, wie immer, wenn er sich fürchtete.

Im nächsten Augenblick riß er Ruben die Zeitung aus den Händen und schrie, jetzt sei aber genug damit, und Ruben schaute durch seine große Müdigkeit hindurch von dem Jungen zu Karin und sah, daß sie einer Ohnmacht nahe war.

Er schämte sich, dann bekam er Angst.

Doch sie sagte, wie es war, daß, wenn seine Verwandten das hatten durchstehen können, sie wohl aushalten müßten, daß darüber gesprochen werde.

Trotzdem war es von diesem Abend an auch für die anderen ganz offensichtlich, daß mit Karin etwas nicht stimmte. Man versuchte sie zu schonen, Erik nahm das Radio mit in die Werkstatt und Simon schmuggelte morgens die Zeitung *Ny Tid* an ihr vorbei. Aber Karin fühlte sich zu all dem Entsetzlichen irgendwie hingezogen, sie fuhr in die Stadt und kaufte Zeitschriften mit Bildern von Leichen, die zu Haufen übereinandergestapelt auf der Erde lagen.

Dann kamen die weißen Busse des Roten Kreuzes nach Malmö herüber, und Karin ging selbst die Morgenzeitung mit den Fotos von Menschen kaufen, die das Böse erlebt hatten, und die besser hätten tot sein sollen, statt den Betrachter so aus erloschenen Augen anzustarren.

Nun wußte Karin, daß auch sie sterben würde. Und ihr war dieser Gedanke willkommen.

Einige Tage danach sagte Ruben zu Erik, so könne das mit Karin nicht weitergehen, und sie brachten sie zu einem Herzspezialisten, den Ruben kannte. Der horchte lange und bekümmert das ungesunde Rasseln in ihrer Brust ab und sagte dann, sie müsse all ihre Arbeit anderen überlassen, wenn das nicht ganz böse enden sollte.

Karin war so erschöpft, daß sie nicht einmal protestieren konnte, und wurde in die Privatklinik des Arztes aufgenommen. Dort bekam sie Medikamente und damit auch Schlaf. Im Schlaf begegnete sie ihrer Mutter und ließ endlich den Gedanken zu, daß ihre Mutter sie vom Tag ihrer Geburt an gehaßt hatte.

So wie sie auch Petter gehaßt hatte.

Wie eine riesige schwarze Krähe ging die Mutter in den Träumen in der vornehmen Klinik auf Karin los. Sie krächzte und schrie, und die Hakenkreuze blitzten rundum auf, und sie flog zwischen den Kreuzen hin und her, die plötzlich daheim in der Hütte in der Schneiderwerkstatt standen, und Karin sah, daß Petter unter den Kreuzen kauerte und daß er den Menschen merkwürdig ähnlich sah, die aus den weißen Bussen in Malmö quollen, und die tot hätten sein sollen, und daß das schreckliche Krächzen ihn mitten ins Herz traf und so weh tat, daß das Herz zum Schluß kaputtging, und er auf seinem Schneidertisch tot zusammenbrach.

Die Träume kamen und gingen und Karin ließ es geschehen, ließ die Bilder ihre deutliche Sprache sprechen, ohne sich zu widersetzen oder Erklärungen zu suchen. Es war, als sollten ihre Gedanken reingewaschen werden ehe sie starb, es tat weh, war aber gut. Es war irgendwie notwendig.

In wachen Momenten führte sie Gespräche mit ihrer Mutter: »Warum bist du so geworden?«

Doch die Mutter krächzte nur ihr Mit-leid, Mit-leid, und Karin wandte sich angeekelt ab und erkannte, daß sie das Böse immer hatte leugnen müssen, gerade weil sie in seinem Schatten aufgewachsen war.

Dann, im Halbschlaf, hörte sie sich selbst über Simon krächzen: Mit-leid, Mit-leid, und sie sah seine ängstlichen Blicke, die ihr immer folgten.

Da schrie sie laut auf und der Arzt kam und sagte, daß sie auf keinen Fall trübe Gedanken haben dürfe, und sie bekam neue Medikamente, um diese Gedanken zu vertreiben.

In der nächsten Nacht kam Petter zu ihr, und der Schlaf war tief und friedvoll, und sie glaubte, nun wäre es vorbei und sie dürfe ihm folgen und brauche nicht mehr zu einem neuen Tag aufzuwachen.

Er war die ganze Nacht bei ihr, wiegte sie in seinen Armen, sang ihr vor, und es gab das Böse nicht und Karin fühlte sich so geborgen wie ein kleines Kind.

Sie wußte, daß er ihr etwas sagen wollte, aber sie war zu müde, um zuzuhören.

Dann kam die Morgendämmerung, und als Karin das Sonnenlicht wahrnahm, das unerbittlich durch den Schlitz zwischen Rollo und Fenstersims drang, wußte sie, daß nichts vorbei war. Sie war noch hier, allein. Während sie gewaschen und mit Brei gefüttert wurde, dachte sie darüber nach, was Petter ihr wohl hatte sagen wollen. Aber nicht lange, sie konnte ihre Gedanken nicht zusammenhalten.

Dann, plötzlich, war Simon da und es war wieder Nacht und er war schwer zu verstehen, doch Simon war ganz wirklich und hielt ihre Hand so fest, daß es fast weh tat und sie hörte den Zorn in seiner Stimme, als er sagte: »Du darfst mich nicht verlassen, Mama.«

Als Karin das nächste Mal aufwachte, war es wieder hell und er saß neben dem Bett und sie sah ein, daß er recht hatte. Sie durfte nicht gehen, noch nicht.

»Simon«, flüsterte sie. »Ich verspreche dir, daß ich wieder gesund werde.« Seine Freude war so groß, daß sie sofort auf Karin übersprang, sie wärmte und ihr neues Leben spendete.

Als er gegangen war, weinte Karin lange tonlos vor sich hin. Sie hatte nie geahnt, daß sie so viele Tränen in sich barg. Woher die Tränen kamen, konnte sie nicht begreifen, aber sie fühlte, wohin sie gingen, geradenwegs in ihr Herz, warm und erlösend.

Simon radelte wie ein Verrückter durch die Stadt, sah, wie die schrägen Sonnenstrahlen dieses Morgens glitzernde Lichter auf Hafen und Meer warfen, er strampelte, keuchte bis hinaus zur Werft und zu Erik. »Papa, sie überlebt, sie hat es mir versprochen!«

Normalerweise hätte Erik für eine solche Botschaft nicht viel übrig gehabt. Doch jetzt war er so voller Angst und hatte ein so großes Bedürfnis nach Trost, daß er Simons Worte ohne weiteres als unumstößliche Wahrheit annahm.

Erik und Simon waren jetzt fast gleich groß, und sie standen jeder auf einer Seite des Einmasters und weinten beide die gleiche Art von heilsamen Tränen wie Karin.

Dann ging Erik ins Haus, wusch die Sägespäne von Hals und Händen, rasierte sich und zog seinen besten Anzug an, der dunkelblau und eigentlich für den Winter war. Es gab kein gebügeltes Hemd, dafür pflückte Simon im Garten einen riesigen Strauß frisch erblühter Tulpen.

Erik kam sich ein wenig albern vor, als er mit seinen vielen Blumen im Arm im Korridor der vornehmen Klinik stand. Karin sah es, sah seine Unsicherheit, die Angst des Arbeiters und den ungebügelten Hemdkragen, und ihre Zärtlichkeit war groß, und sie verstand, daß sie auch um dieses zerbrechlichen Menschen willen bleiben mußte.

14

Die Tage der Erholung waren von Ruhe erfüllt.

Ruben kam mit Rosen. Mit ihm konnte sie darüber sprechen: »Ich hatte mich zum Gehen entschlossen.«

Er sagte nur: »Ich sehe schon lange, daß du eine tiefe Traurigkeit mit dir herumträgst.«

Karin war erstaunt, so hatte sie es selbst nie verstanden. Aber sie war von dieser Wahrheit betroffen, und sie erzählte von ihrem Vater Petter und den Seidenschwänzen. Und von der Mutter und dem Bösen, das sie immer hatte abwehren müssen.

Ruben äußerte dazu nicht viel, eigentlich nur: »Nichts ist einfach.«

Lange danach dachte Karin über diese Worte nach.

Sie wollte ihn wegen Gott fragen, dem zu begegnen er jeden Samstag in die Synagoge ging, und der ihm immer wieder die Kraft geben mußte, bei allem Unglück weiterzuleben.

Aber sie fand keine Worte.

Dann, als er ging, schon in der Tür stand, sagte er – und sie sah, daß es ihm schwerfiel: »Du mußt zu leben versuchen, Karin. Auch meinetwegen, damit ich durchhalte.«

Dann war er weg und Karin lag lange da und sah, wie die Sonne ihr Licht durch die dunkle Tanne vor dem Fenster siebte. Eine Straßenbahn rumpelte um die Kurve vor dem Krankenhaus, und als die Schwester mit dem Essen kam, sah Karin, daß sie leuchtend blaue Augen hatte.

Das eingemachte Kalbfleisch in Dillsauce duftete kräftig und lekker, und das Apfelmus zum Nachtisch erfrischte den Mund.

Es schien, die Welt war neu und wieder greifbar geworden.

Am Nachmittag versuchte Karin sich eine Weile zu schämen, weil sie Ruben mit ihren Sorgen belastet hatte, der doch selbst schon seinen Teil zu tragen hatte. Aber es gelang ihr nicht, dem Gefühl fehlte alle Kraft.

Vielleicht ist mir das Gewissen abhanden gekommen, dachte sie.

Doch als Simon gegen Abend kam und Karin sah, wie blaß er war und wie mager, wurde ihr bewußt, daß ihr Gewissen sie keineswegs verlassen hatte.

»Ihr eßt doch wohl ordentlich«, sagte sie, und die Schuld hackte auf die alte wohlbekannte Art nach ihr.

Als Simon ging, fragte sie ihn mit einer Stimme in der das ganze Gewicht der alten Verantwortung lag: »Wo hast du Isak gelassen? Sage ihm Grüße und er soll mich doch morgen besuchen kommen.«

Simon nickte, aber sie hatte den Eindruck, er mache ein eigenartiges Gesicht, und sie erkannte, daß sie etwas Wesentliches vernachlässigt hatte.

Simon radelte durch die Stadt, von dem Gedanken gestärkt, daß Karin sich gleich geblieben war, daß sie so stark und anspruchsvoll war, wie es sein sollte. Aber gleichzeitig war er beunruhigt. Und wütend.

Verdammter Isak, dachte er.

Simon wußte genau, wo er ihn finden würde, im Hafen draußen bei Långedrag, wo Ruben einen Liegeplatz gemietet hatte, und Isak im Abglanz seines prächtigen Bootes König war. Simon konnte schon von weitem das Gejohle aus der kleinen Kajüte hören, und sein Zorn stieg bis zum Siedepunkt, als er die Bierflaschen im Wasser um das Boot tanzen sah.

Sie rauchten, die Luft schlug ihm dick entgegen, als Simon die Luke zur Kajüte aufriß und es aus ihm herausbrach: »Schert euch alle zum Teufel! Ich will mit Isak allein sprechen.«

Sie verschwanden nicht auf der Stelle und es folgten etliche Flüche, doch nach einer Viertelstunde waren Simon und Isak allein. Simon nahm den Kescher, befestigte ihn am Bootshaken und fischte die leeren Flaschen aus dem Wasser, die noch nicht gesunken waren, entleerte Aschenbecher, spritzte Sitzraum und Deck sauber und sagte zu Isak, der zusammengesunken auf einer Pritsche in der Kajüte saß: »Morgen wirst du Karin besuchen.«

»Das trau ich mich nicht.«

»Sie ist jetzt gesund. Es geht ihr gut. Kapiert?«

»Kommt vom Bier«, sagte Isak.

»Verdammt noch mal, sie trinkt doch gar kein Bier«, erwiderte Simon erstaunt. »Spinnst du? Oder bist du besoffen?«

Dann standen sie aufrecht in der Kajüte und starrten einander an, und tief in Isaks Augen war eine Leere, die Simon vom Krieg her kannte, von dem Tag, an dem die Embargoschiffe vor Måseskär in der Tiefe versanken, und der Zorn in Simons Herz verflüchtigte sich, und er bekam furchtbare Angst, und er dachte, diesmal gibt es keine Karin, die das Unbegreifliche in die Hand nehmen kann, er mußte es alleine schaffen, und er schlang die Arme um Isak und sagte ohne im geringsten zu ahnen, woher die Worte kamen: »Isak, zum Teufel, du hast doch nichts mit Karins Krankheit zu tun.«

Er merkte, daß es die richtigen Worte waren, denn Isak entspannte sich, und als ihre Blicke sich trafen, war die erschreckende Leere verschwunden.

Am nächsten Tag saß Isak im Krankenhaus und sah mit eigenen Augen, daß Karin fast wie früher war. Er konnte ganz wie immer mit ihr sprechen: »Ich wollte sie in Öl sieden und ihnen den Schwanz abdrehen, weißt du. Ich wollte in den Oslofjord segeln, denn in der Zeitung steht, daß sich viele Deutsche noch dort verstecken und ich wollte sie finden und ...«

»Und ...?«

»Ja, und dann bist du krank geworden.«

Mit wenigen Worten brachte sie ihn zur Einsicht, daß die Trauer um all das Geschehene und um das, was im Frieden zutage getreten war, sie krank gemacht hatte, und daß seine bösen Gedanken nur ein Windhauch waren in dieser Welt der bösen Taten. »Diese Rachephantasien waren vielleicht gut für dich, Isak«, sagte sie.

Da erzählte er vom Bier, von den Jungs im Boot auf Långedrag und davon, daß sie das Bier mit Kognak verstärkt hatten, den Isak aus Rubens Schrank geklaut hatte. Und da war Schluß mit ihrer Nachsicht. Karin setzte sich im Bett auf, schaute den Jungen fest an: »Das läßt du sofort bleiben, Isak Lentov. Das wirst du mir hier schwören und zwar sofort ...«

Isak war rot vor Scham und duckte sich unter ihrem Zorn.

»Du mußt lernen, zwischen Phantasie und Wirklichkeit zu unterscheiden, Isak. Vielleicht brauchst du die schlimmen Rachegedanken, aber solltest du einen verängstigten deutschen Jungen, der nach Norwegen ausgerissen ist, erwischen, würdest du vor Mitleid weinen. Rache ist nur in der Phantasie süß, das mußt du begreifen.«

Isak schwieg. Er glaubte ihr nicht.

»Alkohol stehlen und andere ins Verderben locken, das ist Wirklichkeit. Und damit mußt du aufhören.«

Isak legte ein feierliches Versprechen ab und verließ sie beschämt und glücklich.

Und Karin lag in ihrem Bett und dachte darüber nach, wie dumm sie gewesen war, wie selbstsüchtig. Es war doch offensichtlich, daß sie leben und den Menschen das Leben begreiflich machen mußte, für die sie die Verantwortung trug.

Der Gedanke machte sie so zufrieden, daß sie sofort einschlummerte und die ganze Nacht ohne Tabletten fest schlief.

Seltsamerweise dachte sie kaum an Erik, der es doch von allen am schwersten hatte.

Er war eines Tages gekommen, um mit dem leitenden Arzt zu sprechen, es fielen gewichtige Worte. Karin mußte geschont werden. Heftige Gefühle müßten vermieden werden, sagte der Doktor.

Erik allein trug die Verantwortung dafür, daß Ruhe in ihr Leben einkehrte.

»Wenn sie Angst bekommt oder zornig wird, kann das schlimme Folgen haben«, sagte der Herzspezialist.

Erik hatte Gewissensbisse, er fühlte, wie der Hemdknopf seine

Gurgel beengte, empfand so etwas wie Klassenhaß und dachte, da ist es nun wieder, das alte Gefühl der Unterlegenheit.

Verdammt noch mal.

Als er sich schließlich verabschieden und zu Karin ins Zimmer gehen konnte, war er zerstreut und irgendwie abwesend. Er hatte ihr von dem Wagen erzählen wollen, den er gekauft hatte, war schon auf ihren erregten Protest, ihre Worte von Verschwendung gespannt gewesen und auf ihre Freude, wenn er abschließend sagen würde: Aber ich habe ihn doch gekauft, damit du in die Welt hinaus kommen und dich umsehen kannst.

Daraus wurde nichts.

Auch er empfand keine Freude über den wendigen Fiat Balilla, als er durch die Allee und entlang der Kais heimwärts fuhr, wo die Hebekräne wieder tanzten wie in früheren Zeiten. Er fuhr bei Majnabbe hinauf zur Karl-Johans-Gata, ging in die dortige Niederlassung des Alkoholmonopols und kaufte eine ganze Flasche Klaren.

In der Werft war er am Nachmittag kurz angebunden und rastlos und sah sehr wohl, daß ihm die Leute das übelnahmen.

Zu Hause in der Küche sah es furchtbar aus, es roch nach Abfällen und ungespültem Geschirr. Simon kam kurz und ging sofort wieder, er wollte mit Isak hinaus aufs Meer.

»Hau du nur ab«, sagte Erik, es war freundlicher gemeint als es klang, und er hielt das für genau richtig. Weshalb richtig, das wurde ihm erst klar, als er die Tür zuschloß und den Schnaps auspackte.

Beim dritten Glas dachte er an seine Mutter, wie sie ihn die ganzen Jahre mit ihrem Herzen in Angst und Schrecken versetzt hatte. Jetzt war er wieder dort angelangt, aber diesmal war es Wirklichkeit, die Falle war zugeschnappt und es gab kein Entrinnen.

Eine ganze Weile haßte er Karin wegen ihres Herzens. Dann schämte er sich. Karin war anders als seine Mutter. Sie hatte nie gedroht.

Aber dann packte ihn auch deswegen die Wut und er dachte, Karin sei hinterhältiger als seine Mutter gewesen, sie hatte nicht beunruhigt, nicht gewarnt, sie hatte einfach zugeschlagen.

Keine Auseinandersetzungen, hatte der Chefarzt gesagt, nichts was Aufregung verursacht. Mitgehen, beistehen.

Du lieber Himmel.

Was hatte ihn die Auflehnung seinerzeit gekostet, als er aus der Kirche aus- und der Gewerkschaft beigetreten war. Aber die Mutter war entgegen seiner Befürchtung nicht gestorben, sie lebte noch heute bei bester Gesundheit. Karin, die konnte jeden Augenblick sterben.

Dafür gab es ärztliche Befunde.

Und Erik kamen sonderbare Gedanken, als er so allein bei seinem Schnaps saß, der die Grenzen für ihn verwischte. Ein alter Fluch ging seiner Vollendung entgegen, eine alte Sünde sollte gerächt werden.

Dann versuchte er sich zusammenzunehmen, wärmte den Kaffee auf, und es dämmerte ihm, daß alles wieder so werden würde wie in seiner Kindheit, als er immer gewußt hatte, daß das zerbrechliche Herz in der Brust seiner Mutter sein Werk war, und daß er sich immer so verhalten mußte, daß es schlug und nicht zu schlagen aufhörte.

Herrgott!

Am nächsten Tag sprach er mit Anton, dem Innenausstattungstischler seiner Werft, über dessen Frau Lisa. Erik hielt es selbst für eine Demütigung, war sich bewußt, daß er reichlicheren Lohn anbot als es üblich war, aber Anton freute sich und versprach, mit Lisa zu sprechen. Das Geld konnten sie gut brauchen, und Lisa hatte jetzt, wo die Kinder schon fast aus dem Haus waren, daheim nicht mehr so viel zu tun. Sie war unübertrefflich im Putzen und Aufräumen, und auch nicht gerade schlecht im Kochen.

Erik baute Barrikaden gegen das Düstere, lief ins Krankenhaus und war so liebenswürdig, daß ihm ganz übel davon wurde, während Lisa inzwischen das weiße Haus bis in den entferntesten und geheimsten Winkel aufräumte und auf Hochglanz brachte. Aber nichts von alldem half Erik seinen Zorn, diese mächtige Wut, die in seiner Brust brannte, und die er nur dann begriff, wenn er Schnaps trank, zu bezwingen.

124

Bald würde auch damit Schluß sein, Karin sollte aus der Klinik entlassen werden, und er wußte, wie ihre Augen aussahen, wenn er trank.

Pfui Teufel.

Es war eine Falle, und er rannte in ihr im Kreis herum wie eine tobsüchtige Ratte.

15

Sie kam am Mittsommerwochenende nach Hause und Erik bezahlte eine Rechnung, die der Hälfte des Gewinns an einem Einmastschoner entsprach. Er tat es mit einer verbissenen Befriedigung, so als hätte er sich freigekauft.

Sie gaben ein Festessen mit Räucherlachs und jungen Kartoffeln, Ruben brachte Wein mit und Nachbarn und Freunde kamen mit Blumen. Karin freute sich und war zutiefst und auf eine stille Art glücklich.

Sie freute sich auch über das Auto, in dem Erik sie abgeholt hatte.

Und natürlich über das blitzblank geputzte Haus.

Als dann aber der Alltag Einzug hielt, war da die Sache mit Lisa, die immer so fein tat, und mit der Karin seit jeher ihre Schwierigkeiten gehabt hatte. Trotzdem mußte sie anerkennen, daß ihr Haus nie so schmuck ausgesehen hatte wie jetzt, und daß aufgeräumte Schränke und schön gestapeltes Leinen auch glücklich machen konnten. Ganz zu schweigen von den gebügelten Herrenhemden, den spiegelnden Fensterscheiben und den prächtig gedeihenden Topfpflanzen.

Karin war in ihrem Leben selbst einmal Dienstmädchen gewesen. Dabei hatte sie gelernt, wie man als Frau des Hauses nicht sein durfte. Nicht gelernt hatte sie jedoch, wie man zu sein hatte.

Also war sie letztlich die Unterlegene.

Und wenn schon, sie mußte ja zugeben, daß sie müde war und den Haushalt einfach nicht schaffte. Und daß es lieb von Erik gewesen war, Lisa aufzunehmen. Bald erkannte sie auch, daß es unwiderruflich war. Das war zu dem Zeitpunkt als sie sah, daß Anton und Lisa, die immer fast an der Armutsgrenze gelebt hatten, sich und ihre Träume schon in einem anderen Licht sahen und daß ihnen das Lisas neue Entlohnung ermöglichte.

Karin mußte sich zufriedengeben.

Als sie kräftiger wurde, fand sie eine Lösung und sagte zu Lisa, Hilfe genüge jetzt wohl stundenweise. Also einigte man sich darauf, daß Lisa vormittags um elf kam und nachdem sie aufgeräumt, abgewaschen und die abendliche Mahlzeit vorbereitet hatte, täglich um drei Uhr wieder heim ging. Auf diese Weise hatte Karin sich die eigenen Morgenstunden in der Küche mit der Kaffeekanne in Reichweite und Nachbarsfrauen zu Besuch zurückerobert, so wie es früher immer gewesen war.

Auch die Nachmittage gehörten ihr, sie schlief ein Stündchen, erledigte kleine Näharbeiten, las viel.

Abends konnte es vorkommen, daß sie sich ein bißchen über sich als einer Dame des gehobenen Standes lustig machte.

Aber der größte Gewinn dieser neuen Lebensweise waren ihre Streifzüge. Wenn Lisa um elf Uhr kam und Karin die Verantwortung fürs Haus abnahm, begann sie ihre Wanderungen. Sie ging am Flußufer entlang hinaus zu den schäbigen Bootsstegen, die versteckt im Schilf lagen, sie blieb stehen, hörte dem Wasser zu und betrachtete lange die lustigen grauen Glöckchen der Strandgräser.

Hinter den Felsen ging sie dann durch den wild wuchernden Naturgarten bis hinaus ans Meer, das alles so großartig und zugleich einfach scheinen ließ.

Auf dem Heimweg durchstreifte sie die Hügel, saß auf warmen Felsen und sprach mit dem Wind und den Glockenblumen. Einmal fand sie den Weg zu Simons alten Eichen. Von da an stattete sie ihnen täglich einen Besuch ab, und zwischen ihr und den großen Bäumen entstand eine Art Freundschaft.

Zum ersten Mal in ihrem Leben hatte Karin Zeit und Raum für viele Gedanken, auch für die schweren, die sich durch Beschäftigung nicht vertreiben ließen.

Die meisten Gedanken drehten sich um ihre Mutter. Sie sprach mit den Eichen viel über die alte Frau und ihre eigene Kindheit. Und die

Eichen lauschten mit großem Ernst und lehrten sie, daß sie alles gar nicht immer verstehen mußte.

Daß es nicht notwendig war.

Daß es das Unglück des Menschen war, alles erklären zu wollen und dadurch alles nur mißzuverstehen.

Sie sagten wie Ruben: Es ist nicht so einfach.

Das Schlehendickicht war tückischer, seine Dornen stachen gerne und ohne Grund zu, erinnerten unsanft an Bosheiten in der bitteren Kindheit.

Da ging Karin dann ans Meer, saß dort, schaute in die Endlosigkeit hinaus und lauschte der Botschaft, daß das Leben um so vieles großartiger war als das Schlehengestrüpp, und daß es weit über das Bittere hinaus eine große Geschmacksvielfalt besaß.

Auf Anderssons Wiese war das Heu zum Trocknen gehäufelt, und der kräftige Geruch rief einen Kitzel in ihren Brustwarzen und in ihrem Schoß hervor. Karin errötete wie eine Siebzehnjährige, denn Lust zu empfinden war sie nicht gewöhnt.

Doch sie pflückte einen Strauß Sommerblumen, Margeriten und Kornblumen und hauchzarten, duftigen Kerbel, stellte ihn im Schlafzimmer in eine Vase und lockte Erik ins Bett, als der Abend kam.

Es war ein schönes Beisammensein, aber es entging Karin nicht, daß ihr Mann ängstlich war. Hinterher versuchten sie darüber zu sprechen. Er sagte: »Du weißt, der Arzt hat gewarnt ...«

Da lachte Karin ihr altes, kräftiges Lachen und sagte: »Dann pfeifen wir halt auf den Doktor.«

Auch Erik lachte und wagte zu glauben, daß es doch auch Ausnahmen geben konnte. Und er schlief ein wie ein getröstetes Kind, die Hand auf Karins Herzen, das gleichmäßig schlug.

Eines Tages nahm Karin all ihren Mut zusammen, zog sich städtisch und hübsch an, und fuhr mit der Straßenbahn zu ihrer Mutter auf Besuch. Die ungewohnte Kleidung, weißer Sommermantel, Handschuhe und großer Hut mit blauen Rosen, machte ihr Spaß und sie stand lange vor dem Spiegel und dachte, daß sie gut aussah, so mager wie sie jetzt war. Sie nahm sogar einen Lippenstift zur Hand und malte sich den Mund rot an.

Dann ging sie zur Werft, um Erik zu sagen, daß sie in die Stadt fuhr. Aber er kletterte vom Mast des Bootes, mit dem er beschäftigt war, herunter und sagte: »Zu ihr gehst du nicht allein. Warte einen Moment, ich zieh mich um und bringe dich mit dem Auto hin.«

Karin blieb auf der Bank neben der Treppe sitzen und überlegte verblüfft, daß Erik wohl eine ganze Menge mehr begriffen hatte, als sie geglaubt hatte.

Bei der Mutter ging es leichter als erwartet, sie freute sich aufrichtig, Karin wiederzusehen. Und erschrocken darüber, daß Karin jetzt so mager war, sagte sie: »Herrdujemineh, du siehst aber elend aus!«

Karin hörte die Besorgnis in ihrer Stimme und schluckte die widerlich fetten Speckbrote, die die Mutter auftischte. Damit Karin wieder ein bißchen zulegen würde.

Das värmländische »herrdujemineh« rührte sie sogar ein bißchen. Erik war gesprächiger als sonst, und Karin sah die Freude der Mutter und erinnerte sich daran, daß ihre Mutter den Schwiegersohn immer besonders gerne gehabt hatte. Er sprach von den Altenwohnungen, die in Masthugget gebaut werden sollten und konnte das Interesse der alten Frau dafür wecken. Plötzlich begriff Karin, daß aus dem Alptraum nichts werden würde, sie würde nicht gezwungen sein, der Mutter einen Platz in ihrem Haus einzuräumen, wenn die alte Frau nicht mehr allein zurechtkäme.

Der älteste Bruder tauchte auf, und Karin fühlte, daß sie ihn mochte. Auch das war neu für sie, denn ihre Brüder waren ihr schon vor Jahren fremd geworden.

Sie brachen gemeinsam auf, der Bruder wollte Eriks Auto ansehen.

Auf der Treppe sagte Karin: »Heute war unsere Mutter ja richtig nett.«

»Du wirst gemerkt haben, daß sie sich um dich Sorgen macht«, sagte der Bruder.

Aber Karin ging das zu schnell: »Ich habe bisher nie gemerkt, daß sie sich für mich interessiert.«

Der Bruder wurde verlegen, wie Männer das tun, wenn Frauen gefühlvoll werden. Und er sagte nicht ohne Bosheit: »Du hast nicht nur ihr, sondern auch uns, den Mann und Vater weggenommen. Also ist wohl nicht alles nur ihre Schuld.«

Karin blieb mitten auf der Treppe stehen, hatte Herzklopfen, und Erik, der das sah, unterbrach: »Jetzt hältst du die Klappe. Karin darf sich nicht aufregen.«

Die Männer gingen voraus, aber Karin hörte die Worte des Bruders an der Haustür trotzdem: »Du wirst es auch nicht gerade leicht haben.«

Im Auto legte Karin Erik die Hand auf die Schulter, ihr gingen Rubens Worte durch den Kopf: Was ist schon einfach.

16

Am sechsten August fiel die Bombe.

Hiroshima, das ist ein schöner Name, es muß eine schöne Stadt gewesen sein, dachte Karin.

Die Rede war von 300 000 Toten.

Die Zahl war zu groß, um sie fassen zu können, der Kopf konnte sie nicht aufnehmen, und das Herz, ihr Herz, hatte inzwischen genug.

Erik las aus der Zeitung vor, daß nach dieser Bombe die Welt nie mehr wie vorher sein werde. Jetzt wußte der Mensch, daß er sich selbst und alles, was auf der Erde wuchs, ausrotten konnte.

Karin konnte es nicht fassen, ihre Welt war bereits zu sehr verändert. Aber die Jungen, die mit in der Küche saßen und Erik vorlesen hörten, überlief mitten in der Sommerwärme ein kalter Schauer. Isak dachte an Hitler und daran, daß man sich jetzt rechtzeitig vor den Irren dieser Welt in acht nehmen mußte. Und Simon dachte, daß sich seine Welt schon in der Nacht im Krankenhaus, als er bei Karin gewacht und geglaubt hatte, sie werde sterben, vom Vertrauen hin zur Unberechenbarkeit verändert hatte.

Die Schule fing wieder an. Dritte Klasse Gymnasium. Alles war wie früher, weder Kriege noch Atombomben konnten diese Welt verändern.

Hier herrschte die Unlust.

Sie klebte in dicken Schichten an den Wänden, sie tropfte in die Ecken, wo sie sich sammelte, um sich unerbittlich in den Bankreihen breitzumachen. Sie roch nach Kreide und Schweiß, wurde im Mund des Lateinciceronen wiedergekäut und knirschte zwischen den Zähnen des Mathepaukers. Diese Unlust durchdrang alles. Sie war im Deutschunterricht anwesend und im Unterricht der schwedischen Muttersprache, die sofort den Geist aufgab, wenn man ihr die Versfüße beschnitt.

Es gab Augenblicke, da bekam Simon Angst und dachte, gleich werde er ebenso leblos sein wie die Lehrer am Pult. Die Unlust werde seine Lungen füllen, sein Blut vergiften und den Körper erstarren lassen.

Das ist eine Krankheit, dachte Simon, und das Schlimmste an ihr ist, daß man daran stirbt, ohne es zu merken. Man macht weiter wie bisher, die Beine bewegen sich, der Mund leiert unregelmäßige französische Verben herunter.

Manche von den Leblosen waren in der Hölle gelandet und Teufel geworden, deren einziges Vergnügen aus Bosheit bestand.

»Es wäre gut, wenn Svensson etwas im Kopf hätte, woran er die Verben aufhängen könnte. Zum jetzigen Zeitpunkt wirbeln sie nur im leeren Raum herum.« Svensson, Dalberg und Axelsson gehören eher nach Stretered, sagte der Mathelehrer. Das war die städtische Anstalt für geistig Behinderte.

Larsson gehörte dort nicht hin, ihm fiel alles leicht. Zu leicht, er brauchte das Wissen, das sich in Heu verwandelt hatte, um die Schüler zu Wiederkäuern zu machen, nicht wiederzukauen. Kauen, schlucken, aufstoßen und nochmals kauen, schlucken, aufstoßen.

Aus dem Klassenzimmer kroch die Unlust hinaus in den Korridor, in die Physik- und Chemiesäle. An der Tür zur Bibliothek mußte sie anhalten, aber sie kroch weiter in Richtung Aula.

Das war ein schöner Raum, aber die Unlust überschritt die Schwellen und fand reichliche Nahrung in all den erbaulichen Reden vom Frieden und von Gott, dem besonders dafür zu danken war, daß er das Vaterland verschont hatte. Am besten ging es der Unlust mit dem Pfarrer, der einmal in der Woche zur gemeinsamen Morgenandacht kam und ganz erstaunlichen Blödsinn von sich gab, während vierhundert Schüler von schmuddeligen Zetteln Vokabeln büffelten, die sie in ihre Gesangbücher geschmuggelt hatten.

132

Vielleicht wäre Simon schließlich doch an der Unlust zerbrochen, hätte er nicht das Glück gehabt, in der Dickinsonschen Bibliothek ein bestimmtes Buch zu finden. Es ging darin um Yoga und man konnte daraus lernen, wie man das Bewußtsein dazu bringen konnte, den Körper zu verlassen.

Man mußte sich auf einen Punkt in der rechten Gehirnhälfte konzentrieren, und zwar auf den angenommenen Schnittpunkt einer vom rechten Auge ausgehenden Geraden mit einer vom rechten Ohr ausgehenden Linie. Mit etwas Übung war es nicht allzu schwierig, diesen Punkt zu finden. Nun blieb man zwei Minuten regungslos sitzen und konzentrierte sein Bewußtsein auf diesen Punkt.

Der nächste Schritt war schon schwieriger, denn jetzt ging es darum, das Bewußtsein mit Energie aufzuladen. Aber Simon lernte auch das, und bald konnte er seinen Verstand vorsichtig durch die Naht zwischen dem Schläfenknochen und dem Stirnbein lotsen.

Und das Bewußtsein wanderte in die Welt hinaus, es flog über den Atlantik und traf auf die Wolkenkratzer von New York, wo es lange und erstaunt um das Empire State Building kreiste. Dann flog es westwärts in die Prärie, machte aber an der Küste des Stillen Ozeans abrupt kehrt und nahm seinen Weg zurück nach Europa. Über dem Mittelmeer machte es einen Abstecher nach Istanbul zum Harem des Sultans und Simon erkannte mit Entzücken, daß er auch unabhängig von der Zeit durch den Raum schweben konnte. Denn jetzt befand er sich im siebzehnten Jahrhundert, und der Harem war wunderbar anzusehen. Er verliebte sich in eine Bauchtänzerin, die sich wie eine Schlange in goldenen Schleiern wand. Bei diesem Anblick mußte er das Schulbuch herunter auf seinen Schoß ziehen, damit niemand bemerken konnte, daß sein Glied steif geworden war.

Auf den Klippen des Badeplatzes zu Hause saß Karin und beobachtete, wie der breite Strom auf das Meer traf. Sie dachte darüber nach, ob der Strom um sein Wasser trauerte, das sich nun im Grenzenlosen verlor. Aber sie glaubte es eigentlich nicht, dachte eher, daß es ein Gefühl der Vollendung und Befreiung sein mußte.

Und das Wasser, das sich hier mit dem Meer vereinte, wußte bestimmt, daß es das Seine getan hatte. Es war in rasender Wucht durch die Fälle bei Trollhättan getost, war im Strombett vorbei an Lilla Edet gewirbelt, hatte den Turbinen aus Menschenhand und dem ruhigen Grün der Ufer etwas von seiner Kraft geschenkt. Es brachte die Süße der langen Wanderung durch den Vänersee, entlang der Steilufer des Klarälv und der Gletscher der norwegischen Berge mit. Bis ganz hinaus nach Rivö Huvud würde diese Süße zu riechen und zu schmecken sein, ehe sie sich im Salzmeer verlor.

Sie dachte an den Frühling, in dem auch sie nahe daran gewesen war, sich mit dem Grenzenlosen zu vereinen und daran, wie sie sich in jener Nacht, in der Simon an ihrem Bett saß, selbst Einhalt geboten hatte.

Sie war nicht wie das Wasser des großen Stroms, sie hatte das ihre noch nicht vollendet.

Er hatte ein Recht, es zu wissen, dachte sie.

Und sie dachte es immer und immer wieder, wie sie es schon den ganzen Sommer über gedacht hatte, und es war so offenbar und so drohend, daß es wie eine Felswand vor ihr stand. Steil, ohne Halt für Hand und Fuß.

Simon mußte es erfahren.

Die Schuld hieb nach ihr, er hätte es schon vor langer Zeit wissen müssen.

Aber sie wehrte den Stoß ab. Es hatte Gründe gegeben.

Von Anfang an hatten sie es ihm eigentlich sagen wollen, sobald er groß genug wäre, es zu verstehen. Aber dann, in den dreißiger Jahren, hatte sich der Judenhaß im Dorf breitgemacht, hatte hier und dort Wurzeln geschlagen, hatte die Luft vergiftet und sie und Erik so erschreckt, daß sie schwiegen.

Sie erinnerte sich an einen Hausierer, einen von den vielen Landstreichern und Wanderhändlern, die im Lauf der Jahre in ihrer Küche zu Kaffee und Butterbrot gekommen waren. Der Hausierer war etwas Besseres gewesen als alle andern, denn er hatte eine Nichte beim Film gehabt.

Karin hatte ihm ein Nadelbriefchen abgekauft und erst gemerkt, daß der Mann verrückt war, als Simon rotwangig und schwarzäugig in die Küche gestürmt war, um Wasser zu trinken. Er war als Kind immer durstig gewesen, als würde er innerlich brennen und Kühlung brauchen.

Sie konnte es wie ein Theaterstück vor sich sehen, Szene um Szene. Der Junge, der stehen geblieben war, einen Diener gemacht und höflich gegrüßt hatte. Und der Mann, dessen Gesicht verzerrt war vor Haß.

»Ein Judenschwein«, hatte er gesagt. »Beim Herrn Christus! Sie hat ein Judenbalg in ihrer Küche.«

Dann verwischte sich die Szene, sie erinnerte sich nicht, wie sie den Mann aus dem Haus bekommen hatte, wußte nur noch, daß sie ihm das Nadelbriefchen nachgeschmissen und mit der Polizei gedroht hatte, falls er noch einmal käme. Aber das Bild des bleichen Jungengesichts mit den vielen Fragen darin war noch ganz deutlich. Genau wie die Erinnerung daran, daß sie mit dem Jungen auf dem Schoß am Küchentisch gesessen und versucht hatte zu erklären, was nicht zu erklären war.

Und sie erinnerte sich an den Abend, als Erik den Lastwagen in die Garage gebracht hatte und sie nicht rechtzeitig eingreifen konnte, als Simon fragte: »Papa, was ist ein Judenschwein?«

Erik war zuerst wie erstarrt, fing sich, antwortete: »Die gibt es nicht.«

Doch Karin wußte, daß Simon den Schrecken in Eriks Augen gesehen hatte.

An diesem Abend hatten sie ihren Entschluß gefaßt. Es war besser für den Jungen, nichts zu wissen.

Im Dorf wurde getuschelt, Karin erinnerte sich an ihre Sorge wegen der Ågrenschen Giftzunge und wie Simon eines Tages nach Hause gekommen war und gesagt hatte, Tante Ågren will wissen, wo du mich aufgegabelt hast.

Dann kam der Krieg und das Frühjahr 1940, als das Finstere sich von bodenloser Boshaftigkeit zur unmittelbaren Bedrohung wandelte. Oh, diese Frühlingsnächte im April, als die Deutschen Norwegen besetzten und Karin dachte, sie könnten jeden Augenblick auf ihrer Schwelle stehen und auf den Jungen zeigen.

Damals hatte ich auch Herzschmerzen, dachte Karin, erstaunt darüber, daß sie sich daran bisher gar nicht erinnert hatte.

Wie sie Rubens Angst verstanden hatte. Und Olga, die Mutter, die sie nie gesehen hatte, die Frau, die sich für den Wahnsinn hinter den Mauern von Lillhagen entschieden hatte.

Ich hätte mit Ruben sprechen sollen, dachte sie.

Jetzt wurde das Meer hinter der rosafarbenen Festung grau, es würde noch vor dem Abend Regen geben, und so stand Karin auf, wußte, die Uhr hatte längst dreimal geschlagen und Lisa war nach Hause gegangen und Helen mit der Milch gekommen. Ihr selbst blieb noch Zeit für ein kurzes Schläfchen, ehe Simon aus der Schule heimkommen würde.

Aber es wurde nichts aus Karins Schlaf, denn als sie sich auf dem Bett ausgestreckt und sich in die Decke gewickelt hatte, stand die Felswand vor ihr.

Er mußte es erfahren.

Ihre Gedanken wanderten wieder zurück in die Kriegsjahre, zu dem Abend, als Erik und sie sich wieder an den Brief erinnert hatten. Inga hatte einen Brief von dem Spielmann bekommen, einen langen Brief in deutscher Sprache, den keiner von ihnen lesen konnte. Und sie hatten beschlossen, Inga solle ihn aufbewahren, bis sie ihn Simon irgendwann geben könnten.

Sie erinnerte sich an das Telefongespräch, Eriks Stimme, die Inga gezwungen hatte, den Brief zu verbrennen. Danach hatte die Angst vor den Kirchenbüchern Karin verfolgt, was stand dort, wen hatte Inga als Vater angegeben?

Sie hatte gehofft, Erik werde sie beruhigen, wenn er das nächste Mal auf Heimaturlaub kam, werde ihr sagen, sie solle den Teufel nicht an die Wand malen. Aber ihre Angst war auf ihn übergesprungen und er opferte kostbare Benzinmarken, um zu der Landkirche weiter im Norden zu fahren, wo Inga eingeschrieben war.

Es schmerzte nur noch mehr. Erik hatte dem Pfarrer die ganze Geschichte erzählt, einem Mann mittleren Alters, der sich die Lippen geleckt hatte.

»Der verdammte Pfarrer ist ein Nazi«, sagte Erik beim Nachhausekommen. »Aber das habe ich erst begriffen, als er davon zu faseln anfing, wie wichtig es sei, die arische Rasse reinzuerhalten.«

Sie hatten Streit bekommen.

»Ich hätte ihn umbringen können«, sagte Erik.

Im Kirchenbuch stand: Vater unbekannt.

Karin öffnete die Augen, aus dem Mittagsschlaf konnte nichts werden. Ihr Blick fiel auf den Schaukelstuhl neben dem Kachelofen, in dem sie mit Isak gesessen hatte, zu der Zeit, als die Embargo-Schiffe verschwanden und Isak nicht nur sich selbst, sondern auch seinen Verstand verlor.

Alles zusammen hatte dazu beigetragen, ihre Angst lebendig zu erhalten. Aber die Erinnerung an Isak in jenen Tagen gab dennoch Kraft.

Ich habe ihn durchgebracht, dachte sie.

Dann hielt Simon seinen Einzug, schmiß die Schulbücher auf die Treppe und stand nun dort, konzentriert und voller Leben.

»He, Mama! Wie geht's dir heute? Was gibt's zu essen?«

»Falschen Hasen«, sagte sie. »Hast du's eilig?«

»Ja, ich muß nach Långedrag zum Tanzen.«

Karin sah den hübschen Jungen an und dachte, wie gerne sie jetzt jung wäre, um mit ihm tanzen zu gehen.

Es ist gut für ihn gewesen, daß er nichts weiß, dachte sie, als sie das Bett verließ, um mit dem Kochen anzufangen.

»Geht Isak auch mit tanzen?«

»Ja, Ruben bringt ihn her und läßt bestellen, daß er gerne eine Tasse Kaffee hätte.«

Das trifft sich gut, dachte Karin, und nach dem Essen, als Simon in sein Zimmer rannte, um sich umzuziehen, sagte sie zu Erik: »Er muß es erfahren, er ist siebzehn Jahre alt und hat ein Recht, es zu wissen.«

Erik sah mit einem Mal zehn Jahre älter aus, aber er nickte: »Ja, ich habe mir das auch schon gedacht.«

»Es ist schwierig«, sagte Karin. »Ich möchte, daß wir uns vorher mit Ruben beraten.«

Sie sah, daß Erik das nicht wollte.

»Alle, die uns nahestehen, müssen es irgendwann erfahren«, betonte Karin.

»Ja, du hast recht.«

Als Ruben kam, war der Kaffeetisch im guten Zimmer gedeckt, und schon daran erkannte er, daß es kein gewöhnlicher Abend werden würde.

Sie sprachen, schleppend und unsicher im Anfang, dann immer lebhafter, Karin und Erik nahmen einander dabei fast das Wort aus dem Mund. Karin hatte immer gewußt, daß Ruben ein Zuhörer war, aber sie hatte nicht geahnt, daß es ein so gutes Gefühl sein würde, ihm die ganze lange Geschichte darlegen zu dürfen. Dichtes Oktoberdunkel herrschte vor den Fenstern, sie konnten einander nicht sehen. Als Erik schließlich aufstand, um Licht zu machen, sahen sie, daß Ruben feuchtglänzende Augen hatte.

Er sagte einfach nur: »Dann war es also kein Zufall, daß ihr Isak helfen konntet.«

»Wir saßen ja im selben verdammten Boot«, erklärte Erik.

Es herrschte langes Schweigen bis Ruben sagte: »Ich habe mir anfangs so meine Gedanken gemacht, er sah nicht gerade besonders schwedisch aus.«

Und er erinnerte sich daran, wie Olga gesagt hatte: Larsson? Das ist doch nicht möglich.

Aber das erzählte er nicht, sagte, im Lauf der Jahre habe er oft gefunden, daß Simon seinen Eltern gleiche.

»Vom Gemüt her ist er dir sehr ähnlich, Karin, die gleiche Redlichkeit, wenn ihr versteht, was ich meine. Und er ist auch in vielem wie Erik, aufgeschlossen und engagiert.«

Das tröstete.

Aber wie schätzte Ruben Simons Reaktion ein?

Ruben seufzte: »Das wird nicht leicht. Aber ich glaube nicht an eine echte Gefahr. Er hat ein starkes Fundament.«

Dann meinte Ruben, sie müßten sich ganz natürlich verhalten, Simon die Wahrheit nicht einfach ins Gesicht schleudern, sondern den richtigen Augenblick abwarten.

»Und wann ist der?« fragte Karin erschrocken.

»Das werdet ihr wissen, wenn es soweit ist«, sagte Ruben mit solcher Sicherheit, daß sie ihm glauben mußten.

Als die Jungen vom Tanzen zurückkamen, saßen alle wie üblich mit einem Bier und einem belegten Brot in der Küche. Ruben umarmte Simon, klopfte ihm auf den Rücken und sagte: »Herrgott, Junge, wenn du wüßtest, was für ein Weihnachtsgeschenk ich für dich in Amerika bestellt habe!«

Am nächsten Morgen lag der Nebel wie Watte zwischen den Häusern. Simon erwachte wie so manchen Morgen vom Heulen der Nebelhörner vor der Hafeneinfahrt und meinte, diesmal klängen sie unheilkündender als gewöhnlich. Karin wirkte bleiern wie der Nebel als sie das Frühstück auf den Tisch stellte und sagte, sie müsse hinüber zu Edit Äppelgren gehen, bevor die wegen des Nebels völlig durchdrehe. Simon solle das Fahrrad stehen lassen und mit der Straßenbahn fahren.

»Man sieht ja kaum die Hand vor den Augen«, meinte Karin.

Er mußte das letzte Stück bis zur Haltestelle rennen, um die blaue Straßenbahn zu erwischen, die wie ein Phantom aus dem Nebel auftauchte, ihn dann aber mit freundlich blinkenden Glühbirnen in ihrem warmen Inneren aufnahm.

Am Rednerpult in der Aula stand der Pfarrherr persönlich. Er war der Dümmste von allen Pfarrern, die das Gymnasium mit Morgengebeten segneten, und Simon beschlich Unbehagen.

Schon beim Einleitungssermon zum Vaterunser gelang es ihm, in Gedanken auszusteigen, doch merkte er zu seiner Enttäuschung, daß sein Bewußtsein dieses Mal auf kürzestem Weg nach Hause gegangen war.

Er fand die Küche leer, Karin war schon drüben bei der Äppelgren. Simons Gedanken schweiften weiter zur Werft, aber dort konnte er sie einigermaßen zügeln. Erik und seine Leute hatten Pause, und Simon konnte Erik über der Kaffeetasse das große Wort führen hören. Er sprach von der Bombe und der veränderten Welt und alle hörten andächtig zu.

Jetzt fühlt er sich, dachte Simon. Jetzt ist er der Schrecklichste und Beste und Größte.

Simon spürte, daß er seinen Vater haßte, ihn verachtete.

Wie der Vater Simon verachtete, den Jungen mit den zwei linken Händen und dem Kopf voller Flausen, die zu überhaupt nichts Nützlichem zu gebrauchen waren.

Der nie ein ehrlicher Arbeiter werden würde.

Gott, wie satt hatte Simon dieses Haus.

Und die Werft. Und die Angeberei mit den Booten. Und die Politik. Und alles Handfeste.

Simons Gedanken machten auf dem Gartenweg plötzlich kehrt und trafen dort im Nebel auf Karin, er sah sie auf sich zu kommen und sah sie mit neuen Augen, als Außenstehender. Sie war nicht gerade schön, und der Zug von Selbstzufriedenheit um den Mund war verabscheuungswürdig. Sie, der Engel, hatte die gute Tat des Tages vollbracht.

Er haßte auch sie, dachte, daß nie ein vernünftiges Gespräch mit ihr möglich war, daß sie ungebildet und dumm war und daß sie ihn nie verstanden hatte.

Dann brach es los: »Danke, Herr, für Deine Gaben ...«

Und Simons Gedanken mußten die Schwelle am Schläfenknochen wieder passieren und ihm wurde wie immer schlecht, wenn in seiner Nähe laut und falsch gesungen wurde.

Selbst sang er nie einen Ton.

Dann bekam er Bauchschmerzen wegen der schlimmen Gedanken, und im Physiksaal, wo Alm sich auf irgendein idiotisches Experiment versteifte und ihm genügend Zeit zum Nachdenken blieb, erinnerte er sich an den gestrigen Abend und daß in der Küche eine eigenartige

Atmosphäre geherrscht hatte, als er und Isak vom Tanzen nach Hause gekommen waren.

Etwas Eigenartiges. Erik hatte müde ausgesehen.

Aber die Erinnerung an Erik fachte den Zorn nur noch an, Simon fühlte wieder seinen Abscheu Erik gegenüber – Erik mit seinen groben Händen und seinen simplen Wahrheiten.

Auch Karin dachte an Erik. Der Nebel hob sich im Lauf des Tages und sie begab sich wie üblich auf einen ihrer Streifzüge.

Erik hatte gestern keinen leichten Abend gehabt. Der Beschluß, den sie während des Krieges gefaßt hatten, nämlich Simons Herkunft zu verschweigen, hatte dazu geführt, daß sie alles verdrängten. Von nichts wußten.

Von nichts zu wissen, das lag Erik.

Er war immer empfindlicher gewesen als sie selbst, wenn es um Simons Herkunft ging. Jedenfalls hatte er immer stärker reagiert, wenn sie irgendwie daran erinnert wurden. Wie etwa damals, als Ruben sich einbildete, Simon solle Geige spielen lernen.

Erik war vor Zorn fast durchgedreht.

Er ist ein Mensch, der sich seine eigene Wirklichkeit schafft, dachte Karin. Er baute sie selbst auf, Stein für Stein, ohne jemandem etwas schuldig zu bleiben. Alles, was in dieses Gebäude nicht hineinpaßte, wurde verworfen oder abgestritten. Andere Menschen mußten die Güte haben, sich so zu ändern, daß sie sich einbauen ließen.

Simon paßte immer schlechter hinein.

Es lag Streit in der Luft, das wußte Karin, obwohl Simon und auch Erik die Worte ihretwegen zurückhielten, um sie nicht aufzuregen. Es ging nicht nur darum, daß Simon ungeschickt war, nein, es ging um viel mehr. Eriks Überlegenheit war Voraussetzung dafür, daß seine Wirklichkeit stimmte, er mußte als der einzige Sohn seiner groß- artigen Mutter mehr sein als andere. Und wenn nicht?

»Ja, da würde er wohl sterben«, sagte Karin, zornig wie immer, wenn sie das Erbe ihrer Schwiegermutter aufdeckte, laut vor sich hin.

Inzwischen hatte Simon ihn auf vielerlei Art überholt, an Scharfsinn, an Kenntnissen, an Wendigkeit. Erik war gefährdet, wurde höhnisch.

»Faß mal mit an, Junge, vorausgesetzt du hast keine Angst, dir die Finger dreckig zu machen.«

Simon war ein Intellektueller, und dafür mußte er bezahlen. Schuld daran war natürlich die Schule, aber auch einiges mehr. Er wurde schon als Intellektueller geboren, dachte Karin, und im nächsten Augenblick: Aber das ist ja lächerlich.

Konnten die Gründe dafür in seiner Herkunft liegen, hatte Simons Wesen mit diesem Jüdischen zu tun?

Nein. Isak war nicht nur Jude, er gehörte außerdem der Oberschicht an, und bei ihm fand sich alles, was Erik forderte, Schläue und die nötige Fingerfertigkeit im Umgang mit Nägeln und Schrauben. Und dann natürlich das wichtigste von allem, eine große Bewunderung für Erik, sowie die selbstverständliche Anerkennung seiner Autorität.

Jetzt brach die Sonne durch, das Licht war silberweiß vom Nebel, und Karin ging zu den Eichen.

Dort unter der breitesten Krone, die üppig und golden war vom beginnenden Herbst, erkannte sie, daß sie mit all diesen Gedanken um Erik nur sich selbst schützen wollte. Sie wagte es nicht, ihre eigene Angst ans Tageslicht kommen zu lassen.

Er war drauf und dran zu zerreißen, diese Nabelschnur, die auch ihrem eigenen Leben Nahrung gegeben hatte.

Wenn Simon es erfährt, ist er frei, dachte Karin. Sie war nicht seine Mutter, und darum konnte er sie abwählen. Sie wußte sehr wohl, daß es Augenblicke gab, wo er sich ihrer schämte.

Sie hatte jetzt Schmerzen in der Brust, und es kamen keine Tränen, sie zu lindern.

Zu Hause sah sie im Spiegel, daß ihre Lippen blau waren. Sie nahm Herztabletten und schlief daraufhin ein. Sie träumte, daß sie unter großen Schmerzen einen Sohn gebar, und es war Simon, der aus ihrem Leib kam, und sie wickelte ihn in Windeln und ging mit dem Kind zu seinem Vater.

Es war ein weiter Weg zu dem Mann, der sie oben auf dem Hügel erwartete, aber sie ging mit großer Würde, trug das Kind zu ihm hin. Und er nahm es in seine Arme, und erst da sah sie ihn an, sah empor in sein Gesicht und erkannte Ruben.

Direktor Ruben Lentov?«

»Ja, das bin ich.«

»Mein Name ist Kerstin Andersson. Ich bin Kuratorin am Sanatorium Söråsen.«

Der Name einer Stadt wurde genannt, Ruben konnte sie einigermaßen im småländischen Hügelland lokalisieren.

»Ja«, sagte er. »Guten Tag.«

Die Stimme am Telefon tat alles, um einigermaßen sicher zu wirken, doch gelang es ihr nicht.

»Könnte es stimmen, daß Ihre Gattin eigentlich Leonhardt heißt, ich meine, bevor sie verheiratet war.«

»Ja.« Jetzt fühlte Ruben Bedrohung.

»Olga Leonhardt?«

»Ja, wieso?« Sein Ton war jetzt so formell, daß die Stimme am anderen Ende ihr Selbstvertrauen völlig einbüßte und sagte: »Ist sie vielleicht telefonisch zu erreichen?«

»Nein«, sagte Ruben. »Meine Frau ist geisteskrank.«

»Oh, tut mir leid.«

Um was, zum Teufel, geht es hier, dachte Ruben, wußte aber bereits, daß das Unentrinnbare ihn schon eingeholt hatte. Die Stimme sprach weiter, als hätte sie seine Gedanken vernommen.

»Wir haben hier ein Mädchen, eine von den Geretteten aus Bergen-Belsen. Sie heißt Isa von Schentz und behauptet, eine Nichte Ihrer Gattin zu sein.«

Die Wände in dem geräumigen Kontor zogen sich enger um Ruben, der Raum verkleinerte sich, die Bilder jagten durch seinen

Kopf. Iza, eine lebhafte Fünfjährige, die einst in einer anderen Welt Blumenstreukind bei seiner Hochzeit gewesen war. O Gott, dachte er, Gott Israels, hilf mir, und er legte den Hörer auf den Schreibtisch und es gelang ihm, das Fenster zur Norra Hamngatan zu öffnen, atmete tief durch und sah, daß die See bis hinauf zum Hafenkanal weiß von Schaumkronen war. Es herrschte Sturm über Göteborg.

Dann hörte er, weit weg von seinem Schreibtisch, wie aus einem anderen Universum die Stimme aus dem Telefon: »Hallo, hallo! Sind Sie noch da, Direktor Lentov?«

Er mußte sich zusammennehmen, er griff zum Hörer, um viele Fragen zu stellen, aber er konnte die Fragen nicht finden.

»Iza«, sagte er. »Die kleine Iza.«

Kerstin Anderssons Stimme hatte ihre Kraft wiedergewonnen, als sie sagte: »Ich verstehe, daß Sie Zeit zum Denken brauchen. Vielleicht können Sie später zurückrufen.« Er bekam eine Telefonnummer, seine Hand notierte, und als er den Hörer aufgelegt hatte, merkte er, daß er fror.

Doch als er aufstand, um das Fenster zu schließen und draußen im Büro Bescheid zu geben, daß er nicht gestört werden wolle, hatte der Raum wieder seine normale Größe. Dann legte er sich mit dem Handelsblatt überm Gesicht auf das schwarze Ledersofa.

Er versuchte sich an das Kind zu erinnern, sich das Gesicht vorzustellen. Er konnte es nicht.

Eine von Millionen Toten war zurückgekehrt, aber sie hatte kein Gesicht. Glich sie ihrer Mutter? Ruben erinnerte sich plötzlich, was es ihn gekostet hatte, nicht an Rebecca zu denken, während all dieser Jahre in Schweden nicht an das Mädchen zu denken, das er in Berlin einmal geliebt hatte.

Rebecca Leonhardt. Sie war wunderbar.

Sie hatte einen deutschen Offizier geheiratet, Ruben hatte auch kein Bild dieses von Schentz vor Augen, aber er erinnerte sich sehr deutlich an ein Gespräch in einem Café in Paris, wo Rebecca versucht hatte, ihm die Verlobung mit dem Deutschen zu erklären.

Er ist ein guter Mensch, dieser von Schentz, hatte sie gesagt. Mit seiner Hilfe würde sie dem Judentum entkommen, das sie einengte und ankettete. »Ich kriege keine Luft auf der Frauenempore in der Synagoge.« Er, Ruben, hatte seine Verzweiflung nicht erkennen lassen, hatte sich großzügig gezeigt, verständnisvoll.

Die Ehe hatte ihr also nicht geholfen, dachte er und stand auf, er brauchte Wasser, fand eine Flasche Mineralwasser, öffnete sie, trank.

Sie war Schriftstellerin geworden. Bis zum Ende der dreißiger Jahre hatte sie Olga Briefe und Bücher mit Widmung geschickt.

Ruben hatte es nie über sich gebracht, ihre Romane zu lesen, aber er wußte, daß sie anerkannt war.

Ich habe Olga geheiratet, um Rebecca nahe sein zu können, dachte er.

Nein.

Doch.

Die beiden Töchter des reichen Doktor Leonhardt, deren eine alles mitbekommen hatte, Begabung, Schönheit und einen weit offenen Sinn. Während die andere ...

Ruben empfand jetzt für Olga eine fast wilde Zärtlichkeit, die kleine Schwester, die in der großen Irrenanstalt mit Puppen spielte.

Das Bild von seiner Frau und ihren Puppen brachte Ruben Lentov zurück in die Wirklichkeit, nach Göteborg im Spätherbst 1945, zu Handlungsfähigkeit und Verantwortung.

Ich habe nicht einmal nachgefragt, wie es dem Mädchen geht, dachte er, setzte sich an den Schreibtisch, wollte anrufen. Aber seine Hand wählte Karins Nummer, und als er ihre Stimme hörte, erkannte er, was er immer gewußt aber nie zu erkennen gewagt hatte, daß Karin in ihrer ganzen Wesensart Rebecca glich.

»Aber Ruben!«, sagte Karin. »Wie wunderbar. Wir müssen zusehen, daß sie gesund wird und sich hier in Schweden wohlfühlt.«

Das war richtig. Es war das, was er hören wollte.

»Du mußt dich zu allererst erkundigen, wie geschädigt sie ist. Möglicherweise hat sie Tuberkulose, wenn sie jetzt in einem Sanatorium ist. Du mußt mit den Ärzten reden, du mußt hinfahren.«

»Ja.«

»Und du mußt nach ihren Angehörigen fragen. Ihrer Mutter.«

»Ja.«

»Du mußt die Kuratorin fragen, nicht das Mädchen. Du lieber Gott, Ruben, es ist wie ein Wunder!«

Er hörte, daß Karin aufgeregt war, dachte an ihr Herz und wollte etwas Beruhigendes sagen, aber er hatte nur Raum für die Erkenntnis, daß er Rebecca schon beim ersten Mal in Karin wiedererkannt hatte, als sie in sein Büro gekommen war.

»Ruben.«

»Ja?«

»Wir werden ihr wieder Lebensfreude schenken.«

Beide sollten sich dieser Worte erinnern, als sie nach und nach erkannten, daß Iza ein Mensch von rücksichtsloser und brennender Lust am Leben war.

»Wie alt ist sie, Ruben?«

Er dachte nach, er hatte 1927 geheiratet, sie mußte 1923 geboren sein.

»Sie ist zweiundzwanzig.«

»Wie schön«, sagte Karin. »Ich glaube, junge Leute werden leichter wieder gesund.«

Er spürte von Karins Trost noch einiges in sich, als er das Ferngespräch mit Kerstin Andersson anmeldete.

»Einige Schatten auf der Lunge, gut ausgeheilt«, gab sie Auskunft. »Iza gehört zu denen, die überleben werden. Sie hat hier bei uns die Schule besucht, hat die Sprache leicht erlernt, war unerhört neugierig auf das Leben in dem neuen Land.«

»Aber die Sache mit Ihnen wird schwierig werden«, fuhr die Kuratorin fort.

»Inwiefern?«

Kerstin Andersson berichtete, daß ihre Patienten Schwierigkeiten damit hatten, freudige Überraschungen zu verkraften. Er erfuhr von einer Frau, die die besten Voraussetzungen hatte, die aber starb, als sie einen Brief von ihrer Schwester erhielt, die auch überlebt hatte und jetzt in Palästina wohnte.

Ruben versuchte zu verstehen. »Ist das der Grund, warum Sie nicht früher Kontakt mit mir aufgenommen haben?«

»Nein«, sagte die Kuratorin. »Iza hat den ganzen Sommer von einer Tante in Norwegen erzählt, konnte sich aber an deren jetzigen Familiennamen nicht erinnern, darum haben wir das wohl nicht ganz ernst genommen.«

Das Mädchen wußte nicht, wie ich heiße, dachte Ruben. Rebecca hat mich ausgelöscht wie ich sie ausgelöscht habe.

»Eines Tages hat sie dann in der Zeitung eine Anzeige Ihrer Buchhandlung gesehen.«

Ruben erinnerte sich an die Annonce, angekündigt wurden die amerikanischen und englischen Neuerscheinungen dieses Herbstes, Bücher, die durch seine Filialen zu beziehen waren.

»Sie erkannte den Namen wieder und war wie verrückt, bekam erneut Fieber und erschreckte damit die Ärzte. Selbst habe ich nicht unbedingt an die Geschichte geglaubt, aber der Chefarzt meinte, ich solle der Sache nachgehen. Vor allem, um Iza zu beruhigen, müssen Sie verstehen. Darum habe ich Sie jetzt angerufen.«

»Weiß sie davon?«

»Nein, ich muß heute mit ihr darüber zu sprechen versuchen.«

»Ich würde sie am Wochenende gerne besuchen.«

»Aber warten Sie ab, bis ich mich wieder melde.«

»Ja. Gibt es etwas, das Iza vielleicht gern haben möchte, Fräulein?«

Jetzt kam Lachen aus dem Telefonhörer: »Sie will alles haben. Kleider, Schuhe, Schminke, Süßigkeiten, Bücher, Handtaschen, Strümpfe. Sie wollen alle alles haben.«

Ruben konnte nicht lachen, er konzentrierte sich auf die schwierigste Frage: »Weiß man etwas von ihrer Mutter?«

Die Stimme am anderen Ende war jetzt von solchem Ernst, daß der Telefonhörer in Rubens Hand bleischwer wurde: »Ja, sie ist in Auschwitz vergast worden, beide Kinder haben gesehen, wie die Mutter zum Ofen gebracht wurde. Der Bruder starb in Bergen-Belsen eine Woche nach der Befreiung.«

»Oh nein!«

»Ja, das war schwer für Iza. Und gerade an dieser Schwelle haben viele aufgegeben. Es hat ja auch etliches an Krankheiten gegeben. Unter anderem Fleckfieber.«

Kerstin Anderssons Stimme klang müde, und es war eine Weile still ehe sie wieder zu hören war: »Ihre Frau? Ist sie sehr krank?«

»Sie hat keinen Kontakt mit der Welt mehr, ist im psychiatrischen Krankenhaus. Aber Sie können unbesorgt sein, ich habe einen Sohn, habe Freunde, ich werde mich gut um Iza kümmern.«

»Das war nicht der Grund, warum ich gefragt habe, ich wollte nur wissen, was ich dem Mädchen mitteilen kann.«

Es gelang Ruben, abschließend etwas Freundliches zu sagen, ihm war bewußt, daß er mit einem Menschen sprach, der es nicht leicht hatte.

Bald darauf rief Erik an und sagte, er werde Ruben am Samstag gerne in dieses Krankenhaus bringen. Im småländischen Hügelland waren die Zugverbindungen schlecht, und er kannte Rubens Abneigung gegen lange Autofahrten über Land.

»Ich finde gut hin«, sagte Erik. »Ich war in meiner Jugend selbst einmal Patient dort.«

Ruben nahm dankend an, es war in jeder Beziehung eine Erleichterung für ihn. Aber er war doch auch erstaunt: »Bist du lungenkrank gewesen?«

»Ja, eine leichte Erkrankung nach Herzenskummer in jungen Jahren.«

Herzenskummer klang aus Eriks Mund recht ungewohnt, aber er fand wohl kein anderes Wort. Und Ruben mußte denken, wie gut sie einander doch kannten und wie wenig sie voneinander wußten.

Kerstin Andersson hatte den Hörer mit Nachdruck aufgelegt und war sitzen geblieben. Sie wußte, der ganze Frauenpavillon war vor Aufregung schon auf dem Siedepunkt, weil Iza möglicherweise Verwandte in Schweden hatte, märchenhaft reiche Verwandte. Die Hoffnung aller Frauen hatte sich an Izas Hoffnung entzündet.

Sie ist so zerbrechlich, dachte Kerstin. Aber sie wird sicher nicht sterben, es sind ja trotz allem keine persönlichen Bande. Iza konnte sich an diesen Onkel nicht erinnern.

Aber familiäre Bande waren immerhin ein Zeichen dafür, daß man dazugehörte, ja, mehr als das, sie waren ein Verbindungsglied in der Kette, die mit der Welt verband. Kerstin erhob sich, ging zum Regal und nahm das Journal mit den Aufzeichnungen über die Gespräche heraus, die sie mit Iza geführt hatte. Ja, sie erinnerte sich jetzt, der Vater war deutscher Offizier gewesen und hatte sich mit seiner Dienstpistole erschossen, als die Gestapo Frau und Kinder abholen kam.

Sie erinnerte sich an Izas Verwunderung: »Weißt du, er ist direkt vor unsern Augen gestorben.«

Es war, als hätte das Mädchen es vergessen gehabt und sich plötzlich daran erinnert, an diesen ersten Tod von tausend Toden, die sie gesehen hatte.

Es hatte auch eine kleine Schwester gegeben, sie war schon auf dem Transport gestorben.

»Das war für sie das beste«, hatte Iza gesagt. »Aber unsere Mama hat das nicht begriffen, wir mußten ihr das Kind wegnehmen.«

Dann die üblichen Vorgänge, aber es war Iza und ihrem Bruder gelungen, durch die Hölle hindurch zusammenzuhalten. Als er während der Befreiung starb, war Iza krank geworden, hatte zwischen Leben und Tod geschwebt.

Kerstin seufzte, schob die Mappe an ihren Platz zurück, dachte wie viele Male zuvor, daß diese Arbeit über ihre Kräfte ging. Iza lebte in einem starken Spannungsfeld, sie war etwas Besseres. Im Sanatorium hielten sich vor allem Polinnen auf, die in den Ghettos von Lodz und Warschau aufgewachsen waren, und Iza provozierte sie mit ihrem guten Deutsch, ihrem scheißvornehmen Namen und ihren Manieren.

Und ihrer Rücksichtslosigkeit, dachte Kerstin widerwillig.

Aber sie sah aus wie die andern, entsetzlich.

Ich muß Lentov darauf vorbereiten, auf die Fettsucht und den Haarausfall, dachte Kerstin.

Dann ging sie hinaus, um Iza zu suchen und fand sie mit einem

Buch im Schulsaal. Einem schwedischen Roman. Vilhelm Mobergs »Reit heute nacht!«.

»Ist das nicht etwas schwierig für dich?«

»Nein, es ist unheimlich spannend.«

Und Kerstin dachte an den eigentümlichen Eifer, mit dem das Mädchen sich in die Sprache hineinwühlte, in alles, was schwedisch war. Sie erinnerte sich daran, wie Iza Zeitung gelesen hatte, wie sie auf der ersten Seite begann und alles las, Annoncen, Todesanzeigen, Radioprogramme, Anzeigen über entlaufene Hunde, verlorene Brieftaschen und Inserate von jüngeren und älteren Menschen, die Kontakt suchten: Ehe n. ausgeschl. Alles erstaunte sie, entzückte sie, sie fragte wegen eines jeden Wortes, das sie nicht verstand, sie zwang Krankenschwestern, Pflegepersonal, Kerstin, ja selbst den Arzt, es ihr zu erklären.

Es war vorgekommen, daß die Befragten über die Eigentümlichkeiten des schwedischen Lebens ebenso erstaunt waren wie Iza.

›Ich bin ein hübsches Mädchen von 22 Lenzen, das auf Kleiegrütze ebenso versessen ist wie auf Spaziergänge. Wo ist der Mann, der mich zähmen kann. Antwort unter *Wildkatze*.‹

»Das ist ja total verrückt«, sagte Iza mit glänzenden Augen. Und damit hatte sie durchaus recht.

Jetzt bat Kerstin Iza, mit in ihr Büro zu kommen, bot ihr einen Stuhl an, blieb aber selbst stehen, als sie kurz und bündig von Ruben Lentov berichtete, daß er sich an Iza und auch an deren Mutter erinnerte und daß er sich gerne um sie kümmern wollte.

Izas Triumph war grenzenlos.

»Ich habe es gewußt!« schrie sie »Ich habe es gewußt, aber du hast es mir nicht glauben wollen.« Dann hielt sie nichts mehr, sie rannte durch den Korridor, von Krankenzimmer zu Krankenzimmer tobte ihr Geschrei.

»Ich habe einen Onkel in Schweden, einen reichen Onkel, der sich um mich kümmern wird.«

Und die Aufregung setzte sich überall fort, und die Träume blühten auf. Man vergaß, daß Iza stinkvornehm war, ein Wunder hatte sie

ereilt, also konnte jeder von den anderen auch ein Wunder widerfahren.

Jetzt kriege ich wieder geschimpft, dachte Kerstin Andersson und
sah die Stationsschwester kommen, feierlich wie immer, aber strenger
als sonst: »Habe ich nicht gesagt, die Patienten dürfen sich nicht
aufregen? Heute abend werden sie wieder alle Fieber haben, und
daran sind nur Sie schuld, Fräulein.«

Kerstin rannte Iza nach.

»Jetzt kommst du mit mir. Zieh deinen Mantel und die Stiefel an,
und dann gehen wir in den Park.«

»Deine Tante ist krank. Geisteskrank.«

»Wieso das?« Iza blieb unvermittelt stehen.

»Wie soll ich das verstehen? Sowas kann man doch nicht wissen.«

»Das ist lächerlich«, erwiderte Iza. »Hier, mitten im Frieden satt zu
essen und noch dazu einen reichen Mann zu haben und dann verrückt
werden.«

Sie war wütend. Und ängstlich, denn ihr war bewußt, daß das ihre
Position veränderte. Ruben Lentov war kein Blutsverwandter, sie war
die Nichte seiner Frau.

»Du sagst, er will sich um mich kümmern?«

»Ja. Er ist bestimmt ein Mann, auf den man sich verlassen kann.«

Iza beruhigte sich, ihre Stimme war weniger hart: »Ist es wahr, daß
er reich ist?«

Kerstin dachte an ihre ärmlichen Studienjahre am Sozialinstitut in
Göteborg, und wie sie und ihre Kollegen sich dort in der eleganten
Buchhandlung mit den weichen Teppichen und dem Geruch von
schönen Büchern herumgedrückt hatten.

»Ich glaube schon«, sagte sie.

Sie fuhren am frühen Samstagmorgen in Rubens altem Chevrolet weg,
der während des Krieges aufgebockt gewesen war und jetzt, schnur-
rend wie eine zufriedene Katze, die Kurven der engen Borås-Straße
nahm, bergauf vor Freude brummte und es genoß, in die Welt hinaus
zu kommen und sich bewegen zu dürfen.

»Was für ein Wagen«, sagte Erik. »Sowas wird heute gar nicht mehr gebaut.«

Aber das Auto fraß Benzin, und in Borås fing es noch dazu an zu schneien. Erik tankte, hörte, daß das Wetter sich im Raum Ulricehamn verschlechtern werde, und kaufte vorsichtshalber Schneeketten.

Auf dem Rücksitz saßen Simon und Isak, die nach einem gewissen Zögern beschlossen hatten mitzufahren und sich die Kusine anzusehen, die aus dem Totenreich zurückgekehrt war.

Im Gepäckraum lag Olgas Pelzmantel, eine neue Handtasche aus feinstem Lackleder, ein Beutel mit Kosmetikartikeln, die Karin besorgt hatte, Schokoladetafeln und ein Berg Bücher.

»Sie liest alles, was ihr in die Finger kommt«, hatte die Kuratorin gesagt.

Sie schlängelten sich aus Borås hinaus und begannen ihre Kletterpartie durch das småländische Hügelland und hinein in das Reich des Schnees. Hohe, blaue Berge, meilenweit Wälder, weiß verschneite Fichten.

»Hier ist es schön«, sagte Ruben, der immer wieder darüber staunte, wie großartig Schweden war, wenn er, wie so selten, die Stadt hinter sich ließ.

Aber Erik meckerte über die abgefahrenen Reifen, kroch im zweiten Gang dahin, war dann schließlich auch noch zum Anhalten gezwungen, um die Schneeketten anzulegen. Isak half ihm, Ruben und Simon gingen ein paar Schritte in den Wald, um zu pinkeln. Dann stand Ruben eine Weile stampfend im Schnee, um sich warm zu halten, und sah Erik zu, der routiniert und ohne Zögern an allen vier Rädern die Ketten festzurrte.

In dieser Situation fiel Ruben ein, wie Otto von Schentz ausgesehen hatte.

Beim Weiterfahren dachte er an den Deutschen, den Vater von Iza. Er konnte immer noch am Leben sein, irgendwo in einem russischen Gefangenenlager auftauchen.

Nun ja.

Es war still im Auto, sie hatten inzwischen alle vier schlechte Laune. Sie dachten an Berichte, die sie gelesen und Bilder, die sie gesehen hatten, und erkannten, daß nichts von alldem für sie Wirklichkeit geworden war.

Nicht – bis heute.

Dann waren sie am Ziel, fuhren in den Hof ein, der Schnee funkelte in der Sonne und der Wagen war umschwärmt von ganz wirklichen Menschen, dick, belustigt, neugierig. Und lebhafter als normalerweise die Menschen in Schweden waren, kindlicher, aufgeschlossener.

Ob sie etwas zu essen bei sich hätten? Brot?

Nein. Hatten sie Hunger? Bekamen sie nicht genügend zu essen?

Erik fühlte Zorn in sich aufsteigen, aber dann war die Kuratorin da, eine große, grauäugige junge Frau, die kurz darüber aufklärte, daß hier alle die doppelte Ration bekämen, daß sie aber wie Fässer ohne Boden seien.

»Sie sehen doch, wie sie sich dick essen.«

Simon fand die Frau schrecklich, aber ihre Patienten lachten und sagten, es sei furchtbar, daß sie vom Essen nie genug kriegen könnten. Sie sprachen in einer Mischung aus Deutsch und Schwedisch.

Erik konnte sie einigermaßen leicht verstehen, und bald saß er mit einem Hefekranz und einer Kanne Kaffee zwischen zehn dicken Frauen und fühlte sich unwirklich. Aber fröhlich, gut gelaunt.

Iza wartete im Zimmer der Kuratorin auf Ruben. Die letzten Tage hatten sie verändert. Sie war ruhiger geworden, hatte versucht weniger zu essen, hatte sich die Haare gewaschen und verzweifelt geweint, als diese büschelweise ausfielen. Im Schulsaal allein, hatte sie stundenlang versucht sich zu erinnern, wie man aufzutreten hatte, wie man in den Salons gebildeter Menschen sprach, wie man sich dort verhielt. Sie hatte sich von einer Pflegerin Nagellack geliehen, das gab ihr Selbstvertrauen, denn sie hatte schöne Hände.

Aber in dem hohen Spiegel des Turnsaals wagte sie sich nicht anzusehen.

Am Morgen dieses Tages hatte das Fieberthermometer fast 38°

angezeigt, die Schwester war verärgert, aber Iza freute sich, denn sie konnte in ihrem Taschenspiegel sehen, daß das Fieber ihre Wangen rosig färbte und den Augen Glanz verlieh.

Sie war Olga ähnlich. Nicht Rebecca, sondern Olga. Die gleiche nervöse Lüsternheit um den Mund, die gleiche leicht gebogene Nase und die schmale, hohe Stirn. Sogar das feine andeutungsweise blaue Netz der Adern an den Schläfen war vorhanden. Und der gleiche rastlose Eifer, der gleiche Hunger, für den es keine Sättigung gab.

»Iza, meine Kleine«, begrüßte Ruben sie.

Und Iza sah auf den ersten Blick, daß sie sich nicht anzustrengen brauchte, daß sein Schuldgefühl so groß war, daß er sie hinnehmen würde, so wie sie war.

»Ich will hier weg«, begann sie. »Jetzt, sofort.«

»Ich kann das verstehen«, antwortete Ruben. »Aber das letzte Wort hat der Chefarzt.«

»Ich hasse ihn«, sagte Iza und Ruben erschrak vor der Intensität ihrer Stimme und vor ihrem Haß. »Er ist ein Nazi, ein Satan, genau wie die Deutschen im Lager.«

Sie kann recht haben, dachte Ruben bestürzt.

Aber er wechselte lieber das Thema.

»Die Kuratorin hat mir von Rebecca erzählt«, sagte er.

»Ich will mich nicht daran erinnern.«

»Das verstehe ich.«

Die Antwort kam blitzschnell: »Nein, verstehen kannst du überhaupt nichts.«

Und Ruben neigte den Kopf. »Weißt du etwas von deinem Vater?«

Die Frage kam zögernd, aber er mußte doch alles wissen. Iza sprach sofort darauf an, sie wirkte jetzt offen, echt und erstaunt wie ein Kind. »Er hat sich erschossen«, sagte sie. »Direkt vor unseren Augen. Wir standen da, und er hat sich einfach erschossen.«

Ihr Blick schweifte zurück zu dem Augenblick, in dem das Unbegreifliche begann.

»Warum? Wann?« Ruben konnte es nur flüstern.

»Als die Gestapo kam, um uns abzuholen, Mama und uns Kinder.«
Jetzt kehrte der Blick in den Raum und zu Ruben zurück, und sie
lachte auf: »Kannst du dir so einen feigen Kerl vorstellen?«

Ruben wagte sie nicht anzusehen.

Nach einer Weile öffnete er die Tür, rief nach Isak und bat die
Jungen, die Geschenke zu holen. Iza sah ihren Vetter kaum an und
Simon überhaupt nicht, sie hatte nur Augen für die Geschenke.

»Gott, was für ein wundervoller Pelzmantel.«

Sie riß ihn aus der Hülle, versuchte sich hineinzuzwängen.

Es ging einigermaßen, aber zuknöpfen ließ sich der Mantel nicht.

»Ich werde wieder schlank werden«, sagte sie. »Ich will, ich will.«

Als Simon ihr aus dem Mantel half, sah er die Nummer, die plump
eintätowierten Ziffern auf ihrem Arm.

Es war ein Augenblick jenseits der Zeit, eine Sekunde, die alles
enthielt, was man jemals zu wissen brauchte. Er las die große Zahl und
sah die vielen Toten, wußte, daß sie die Lebenden nicht zur Verantwortung ziehen würden.

Daß sie aufgehört hatten, im Wind zu flüstern.

Aber auch, daß es die Toten waren, die die Stille auf der Erde
schufen und alles, was keiner verstand.

Als sein Blick vom Arm der jungen Frau zu ihren Augen wanderte,
sah er, daß sie boshaft war, und er wußte, daß ihre Bosheit Wirklichkeit in sein Leben bringen würde und daß er alles würde ertragen
müssen.

Isak hatte die Ziffern auch gesehen, bemerkte aber nur: »Warum
gehst du mitten im Winter ärmellos?«

Doch sie hörte es nicht, denn sie war vertieft in die wunderbare
Lacktasche, den Lippenstift, das Parfüm.

Jetzt kam die Kuratorin mit dem Bescheid, daß der Chefarzt Ruben
zu sprechen wünsche. Der Nazi, dachte Ruben, als er der großen
jungen Frau mißmutig durch den Korridor folgte, an eine Tür klopfte
und einem alten jüdischen Freund gegenüberstand.

Olof Hirtz!

Sie waren einer wie der andere gleich verblüfft.

»Ich hatte nur von einem reichen Onkel gehört.«

»Und ich bekam etwas von einem nazistischen Chefarzt zu hören.«

Sie fielen einander in die Arme.

Hirtz war ein bedeutender Forscher, auf Tuberkulose spezialisiert. Er war mit einer Psychiaterin verheiratet und Ruben erinnerte sich, daß Olof immer an der Psychologie der Tuberkulose interessiert gewesen war, am Zusammenhang zwischen Tbc, Trauer und schwachem Lebenswillen.

Trotzdem mußte Ruben fragen: »Was tust du hier?«

»Ich habe mich vom Sahlgrenschen Krankenhaus freistellen lassen«, antwortete Olof. »Du weißt selbst, man will irgend etwas beitragen. Außerdem habe ich hier interessantes Studienmaterial.«

Das Wort war beabsichtigt zynisch, er unterstrich es noch mit einer Grimasse.

»Aber diese Fälle hier können doch keineswegs als repräsentativ angesehen werden, ich will damit sagen, diese Menschen haben die Krankheit ja unter außergewöhnlichen Umständen bekommen.«

Ruben fand nur zögernd Worte.

»So habe ich am Anfang auch gedacht«, sagte Olof Hirtz. »Aber ich fange an, mir selbst Fragen zu stellen.«

Er steigerte sich langsam hinein. »Diese Menschen hier waren doch einmal normale Leute, sie sind großgezogen, geliebt, gehaßt worden, hatten gute oder schlechte Mütter, frostige Elternhäuser, Elternhäuser voll Wärme, Geschwister, arme Eltern, reiche.«

»Nun, das ist klar, aber ... Aber dann ...«

»Ja, sie kamen in die Hölle, wurden bis zum Äußersten gedemütigt, mißhandelt, und reagierten, je nach Herkunft, ganz verschieden, abhängig von der Kraft, die sie in ihrer Kindheit empfangen haben.«

»Sie sind gar nicht so anders als wir, meinst du?«

»Nun, sie sind deutlicher erkennbar. Der Unterschied besteht darin, daß sie Geprüfte sind. Sie wissen – nicht selten ganz unbewußt –, was Bestand hat, und was nur Schein ist. Wir normal Sterblichen erfahren das nur äußerst selten.«

»Das ist wahr«, nickte Ruben.

»Wir dürfen es vielleicht erfahren, wenn wir an der äußersten Grenze angelangt sind, kurz vor dem Sterben, meine ich. Wenn wir dann nicht schon so sehr von Medikamenten betäubt sind, daß wir nichts mehr merken.«

Olof klang zornig, also hielt Ruben zurück, was er auf der Zunge hatte, nämlich daß es dann ja sowieso egal sei. Er erinnerte sich jetzt, daß Olof Hirtz tief religiös war, und Ruben wollte keine Diskussion über die letzten Dinge herausfordern.

»Iza!« begann er. »Ich bin ja hergekommen, um mit dir über Iza zu reden ...«

»Die wird es schaffen«, sagte Olof. »Eigentlich wundert es mich, daß sie überhaupt Tuberkulose bekommen hat, denn sie gehört zu den Lebenshungrigen, die aus purem Lebenswillen überlebt haben. Vielleicht ist es typisch, daß die Krankheit erst spät ausbrach, sie war noch ganz frisch, als man sie während der Quarantäne in Malmö feststellte.«

»Ich verstehe nicht ganz?«

»Solange sie kämpfen mußte, hatte sie Kraft. Als der Kampf vorüber war, konnte sie sich ihrer Erschöpfung hingeben. Dann starb ihr Bruder, und von da an konnte sie ihre kindheitsbedingten Gefühle des Verlassenseins nicht mehr verdrängen.«

»Wie meinst du das?«

»Iza hat es als Kind nicht leicht gehabt.«

Ruben fühlte sich bis ins Mark getroffen.

»Ihre Mutter war ein wunderbarer Mensch.«

»Das ist möglich. Aber Iza war in hohem Grad die Tochter ihres Vaters, und er ...«

»Und er?«

»Nun, er war preußischer Offizier ...«

Alle Worte hingen jetzt im Raum, Ruben ahnte, daß Olof mehr wußte, als er erzählen wollte.

»Jedenfalls muß sie über den Winter hierbleiben«, fuhr Olof fort. »Wir werden im Frühjahr eine neue Diagnose stellen, es besteht die

Gefahr, daß wir operieren müssen. Du weißt vielleicht, daß sie einen Pneumothorax hat, ein Lungenflügel ist mit Gas ...«

Nein, Ruben wußte nichts über die Behandlung von Tuberkulose, aber er reagierte sofort auf das Wort Gas!

»Du kannst uns voll vertrauen, bessere Pflege als hier bekommt sie nirgends.«

»Ja, davon bin ich überzeugt.«

Die Worte stellten die alte Vertrautheit zwischen den beiden Männern wieder her. Sie sprachen eine Weile über gemeinsame Freunde, über Bücher, die Olof gern haben wollte und die Ruben zu beschaffen versprach.

Als Ruben schon an der Tür stand, sagte Olof: »Du kannst Iza am besten helfen, wenn du dich traust nein zu sagen und Bedingungen stellst. Hüte dich vor deiner alten Feierlichkeit.«

»Was meinst du damit?«

»Daß du einen Anflug von christlicher Hochachtung vor dem Leiden hast, und das ist keine Hilfe für die Überlebenden der Konzentrationslager.«

Ruben hatte eine Szene erwartet, als er dem Mädchen sagen mußte, daß sie noch lange im Krankenhaus zu bleiben hatte.

Sie aber zuckte nur mit den Schultern, vermutlich hatte sie es gewußt.

Ruben versuchte es mit fester Stimme zu sagen: »Der Chefarzt ist ein alter Freund von mir, ein bekannter Wissenschaftler und Humanist. Er ist kein Nazi, er ist Jude.«

»Ich weiß wahrscheinlich mehr über Nazis als du«, sagte Iza. »Und die Juden verachte ich.«

»Wie es die Nazis taten«, warf Isak ein, und seine Stimme war einem Peitschenhieb gleich. Iza erschrak, sagte, sie habe es nicht ganz so gemeint, sei sehr müde, das viele Sprechen habe sie sehr angestrengt und sie habe Fieber.

Im Auto wurde auch auf der Heimfahrt nicht viel gesprochen. Eigentlich ließ sich nur Erik gleich zu Anfang kurz darüber aus, wie stark der Überlebenswille des Menschen sei und wie sehr er über die Freude dieser Kranken gestaunt hatte.

»Sie glauben wirklich an die Zukunft«, sagte er.

Ruben nickte, dachte aber, daß ein nur auf das Überleben ausgerichtetes Leben seine Kraft wohl aus einer großen Einfachheit bezog.

Simon saß auf dem Rücksitz und schämte sich wegen Erik. Isak hörte nicht zu.

Sie fuhren bis zum Haus am Strom, wo Karin mit dem Essen auf sie wartete, Kalbfleisch mit eingelegten Gurken und Erdbeerkompott.

»Wie war sie?«

»Sie war voller Leben«, erklärte Erik. »Und Zorn.«

»Kaputt«, ergänzte Ruben. »Hektisch und kaputt.«

»Sie war verdammt affig«, fand Isak und ließ seine Gabel auf den Boden fallen.

Karin schaute von einem zum andern und dachte an die Gespenster aus den weißen Bussen und an ihre Gefühle, dachte, daß diese Gestalten eigentlich ebenso tot sein müßten, wie sie selbst längst tot sein sollte, und daß sie sich genau wie Iza zum Überleben entschlossen hatte. Aber sie sprach es nicht aus, denn Erik brüllte: »Du hast es dir einfach gemacht, Isak.«

Ruben dachte an die Ähnlichkeit des Mädchens mit Olga und schwieg.

Später, als Karin mit Simon allein war, griff sie die Frage noch einmal auf.

»Und wie ist sie wirklich, Simon?«

Simon sah Karin lange an und dachte, das würdest du nie begreifen.

Aber er versuchte eine Antwort: »Lebhaft«, erwiderte er, suchte nach Worten, fand zwei. Ein anständiges: »Unnatürlich«, meinte er. Und dann nach einer Weile ein Göteborgisches: »Åpen. Süchtig nach allem ist sie, heißhungrig. Und manchmal hat sie so einen Blick, du weißt schon, Augen wie Isak sie damals hatte.«

Karin nickte.

Ausdruckslos, dachte sie. Vielleicht müssen sich Augen, die zu viel gesehen haben, leeren.

Zwei Tage vor dem Heiligen Abend kam völlig überraschend und mitten am Vormittag Ruben in einem gemieteten Lastwagen hinaus zum Haus an der Strommündung.

Er strahlte förmlich vor guter Laune.

»Was in aller Welt ...«, konnte Karin nur stammeln, und offenbar waren das die richtigen Worte, sie hörte es seinem Lachen an.

Der Fahrer half beim Abladen einer großen, schweren Holzkiste mit amerikanischer Aufschrift: Handle with care. Ruben hatte den Morgen auf dem Zollamt verbracht, und jetzt war es hier, sein Weihnachtsgeschenk für Simon.

Als der Lastwagen weggefahren war, ging Ruben zur Werft, denn er brauchte Eriks Hilfe.

»Was, um Gottes willen, ist das?« fragte der.

»Ich bin so aufgeregt, daß ich Kaffee kochen muß«, erklärte Karin, aber Lisa hatte das Wasser schon aufgesetzt.

Sie tranken also Kaffee, während Ruben weiterhin vor Überraschungsfreude strahlte und bald zu kommandieren anfing: »Auf, auf, ihr Frauen, jetzt wird in Simons Zimmer Ordnung geschaffen.«

»Dort ist tadellos aufgeräumt«, bemerkte Lisa.

»Aber so doch nicht«, beschwichtigte Ruben. »Alles von der Längswand gegenüber dem Bett muß weg.«

Jetzt lachte Karin, angesteckt von seiner Freude, laut auf.

»Es wird alles geschehen, wie du es möchtest, Ruben«, sagte sie, und dann ging sie mit Lisa die Treppe hinauf, um die Einrichtung umzukrempeln.

»Das kriegen wir nie die Treppe hoch«, meinte Erik, aber dann nahm er Maß, berechnete die Winkel und kam zu dem Ergebnis, doch, doch, es werde schon gehen.

»Hast du einen Elektriker auf der Werft?«

»Nein, so was schaffe ich selbst«, behauptete Erik und seine Augen funkelten vor Neugier.

»Ist es eine Maschine?«

»Ja, so könnte man es vielleicht nennen.«

Es kostete sie viel Schweiß und eine gute halbe Stunde, die Kiste die Treppe hinauf zu bugsieren, und das war gut, denn Lisa und Karin brauchten ihre Zeit, um das Bücherregal erst einmal auszuräumen, an die schmale Wand zu schieben, und dann wieder einzuräumen.

Die Männer bekamen jeder ein Bier, während sie in der oberen Diele verschnauften, und ehe sie sich über den Inhalt der Kiste hermachen konnten, war der Deckel noch mit einem Messer zu lockern. »Vorsicht!« mahnte Ruben.

Aus der Kiste quollen Holzwolle und Papier, und Lisa dachte, wenn sie das gewußt hätte, hätte sie mit dem Saubermachen gewartet. Schließlich war sie dann ausgepackt, die schreckliche Musiktruhe aus hochglanzpoliertem Nußholz mit protzigen Leisten aus gelbem Metall und silberglänzendem Stoff vor den Lautsprechern.

»Die ist alles andere als schön«, kritisierte Ruben.

»Mir gefällt's«, sagte Karin. »Einfach prachtvoll. Aber wozu braucht man das?«

Erik lachte von einem Ohr zum andern, als er den Stecker montierte, und er fragte, ob Ruben dafür wirklich einen Elektriker gebraucht hätte.

»Moment!« sagte Ruben, drückte auf einen Knopf und betätigte einen Hebel. Durch den Raum dröhnte das Radiosymphonieorchester, als stünden die Musiker alle Mann im Frack hier im Zimmer.

Das Haus hielt den Atem an, noch nie hatte man hier etwas Ähnliches gehört. Aber daran würden sie sich jetzt gewöhnen müssen. Eriks Gesichtszüge zerflossen, Karin saß auf Simons Bett und stöhnte vor Staunen, und Lisa hätte um ein Haar den Staubsauger fallen lassen, mit dem sie gerade die Treppe heraufkam.

»Das, was ihr hier jetzt hört«, erklärte Ruben, »ist nicht die Hauptsache. Wo, du lieber Himmel, ist der Plattenteller?«

Nur hörte bei dieser Musik keiner, was er sagte.

Da stellte Ruben den Ton leiser und sah befriedigt in die verblüfften Gesichter: »Hör zu, Erik Larsson, du bist doch ein technisches Genie. Sei so gut, suche den Plattenteller und schließe ihn an.«

Erik nickte, er hatte verstanden.

»Der muß doch irgendwo zu finden sein«, murmelte er und tastete mit der Hand das Möbel ab, das *Victorola* hieß, denn dieser Name war darauf in kleinen goldnen Lettern angebracht.

»Schalte das Ding ab!« schrie Karin. »Es kann doch explodieren!« Aus dieser Bemerkung wurde eine Geschichte, über die in diesem Haus noch lange und viel gelacht werden sollte.

»Frau, nimm dich zusammen!« forderte Erik, und Ruben mußte sich mit aufs Bett setzen, weil er vor Lachen nicht mehr konnte. Solchen Spaß hatte er lange nicht mehr gehabt.

Nun verhielt es sich mit Erik so, daß er mit allen Dingen schnell vertraut war, egal wie neu und unbekannt sie auch waren. Es dauerte also nicht lange, bis er den Knopf gefunden hatte, durch den sich die eine Hälfte der Abdeckhaube wie ein Deckel hob. Der Plattenteller, schwer und solide, war an seinem Platz. Der Tonabnehmer aber lag säuberlich verpackt samt Montageanweisungen in einem eigenen Karton.

Ruben übersetzte langsam, doch Erik riß ihm ungeduldig das Blatt aus der Hand, warf einen Blick auf die Zeichnungen, setzte den Tonabnehmer zusammen und montierte ihn dort, wo er hingehörte.

»Also los!« kommandierte Ruben, der eine Schallplatte in der Hand hielt. »Die hier ist für euch, die beiden andern gehören Simon.«

Aus den häßlichen Lautsprecherboxen ertönte ein Lied, gesungen von Jussi Björling, das von Schweden handelte, und das im Raum eine feierliche Stimmung verbreitete.

»Donnerwetter ist das schön!« rief Erik aus, und Ruben sah, daß er feuchtglänzende Augen hatte, und wieder einmal dachte er, wie wenig man doch voneinander weiß.

Danach gingen sie hinunter in die Küche und Ruben meinte, nun sollten sie auf die Jungen warten, und sobald sie die Auffahrt heraufkämen, wollte er, Ruben, nach oben laufen und Berlioz auflegen.

»Was ist das denn?« fragte Karin.

Da mußten wieder alle über sie lachen, sie lachte selbst und meinte, es sei nur gut, daß sie sich nicht so leicht auf den Schlips getreten fühle.

»Ich hatte doch geräucherten Lachs und Wein dabei«, überlegte Ruben. »Wo sind die Sachen geblieben?«

»Vermutlich im Lastwagen«, kicherte Karin, und dann mußten sie wieder alle lachen.

»Müssen wir eben nochmal einkaufen gehen«, meinte Ruben. »Denn ein Fest feiern wollen wir.«

Während Karin den Tisch deckte, erzählte er, daß er über die Weihnachtsfeiertage mit Isak nach Kopenhagen zu seinem dort ansässigen Bruder fahren wolle. Sie wollten am 24. morgens zusammen mit Iza, die vom Sanatorium die Erlaubnis für diese Reise bekommen hatte, von Torslanda aus hinüber nach Dänemark fliegen.

»Wir haben während des Krieges, als sie alle bei mir wohnten, oft davon gesprochen«, sagte Ruben. »Davon, den Frieden in Kopenhagen zu feiern. Es war der Traum meines Bruders.«

Karin nickte, sie verstand, daß es über Rubens Kräfte ging, sich allein um das Mädchen zu kümmern, daß er die Unterstützung der Verwandten brauchte, um Iza zu einer gemeinsamen jüdischen Familienangelegenheit zu machen.

Das wird nicht einfach werden, dachte sie und erinnerte sich an Rubens überängstliche Schwägerin.

»Isak hat sich nicht gerade darüber gefreut«, bemerkte Ruben. »Er hat so seine Schwierigkeiten mit der dänischen Verwandtschaft. Von Iza ganz zu schweigen. Aber er hat sich überreden lassen, und das vermutlich vor allem, weil er so gern einmal fliegen möchte.«

Ein Engel ging durch die Küche während Karin an Iza dachte. Sie hatten sich inzwischen kennengelernt, Karin hatte selbst in die unnatürlich großen Augen geblickt und dabei gedacht, daß Simon sich irrte. Izas Blick war nicht leer, er war angefüllt mit all dem, was sie gesehen hatte, der Erniedrigung, dem Grauen. Und in der Tiefe brannten diese Augen, ganz unten auf dem Grund existierte ein Hunger, den niemand und nichts würde stillen können, der aber jeden verzehren konnte, der ihren Weg kreuzte.

Sie begreift es selbst nicht, hatte Karin gedacht, sie glaubt, sie kann alles nachholen, was ihr vorenthalten worden ist.

»Und du, was hast du während des Krieges gemacht?« hatte sie Karin gefragt. »Hast Kartoffeln gepflanzt und dich ums Mittagessen gesorgt?«

»Ja. Und was hättest du an meiner Stelle getan?«

Die Worte hatten Karin weder zornig noch traurig gemacht. Aber sie hatte gespürt, wie das Mädchen Zwietracht säte, und als Karin Simon angesehen hatte, erkannte wie bezaubert er war, hatte Angst sie befallen.

Doch Ruben schlug die Gedanken an Iza in den Wind, heute war ein Tag der Freude. Und im Moment als er das dachte, fuhr der Lastwagen wieder in den Hof und der Chauffeur klopfte an die Tür. Lachs und Wein waren gerettet.

»Das hatten Sie wohl bei mir vergessen«, schmunzelte der Fahrer.

Etwa eine Stunde später hörten sie die Fahrräder der Jungen die Einfahrt herauf scheppern und Ruben rannte wie von der Tarantel gestochen die Treppe hinauf, legte die Schallplatte auf und stellte den Ton so laut wie nur möglich.

Den Jungen wird der Schlag treffen, dachte Karin, doch im nächsten Augenblick war er schon in der Diele und hörte die Musik die Treppe herunterfließen, wurde ganz still und so glücklich, daß er wie lichtumflutet da stand. Langsam ging er hinauf in sein Zimmer, legte sich noch in der Jacke aufs Bett.

Sie sprachen in der Küche nicht viel, während die Musik das Haus erfüllte. Es war, als hätten sie verstanden, daß Simon sich jetzt in einer anderen Welt befand, in einem Land das seines war, und nach dem er sich immer gesehnt hatte.

Ruben hat es begriffen, dachte Erik und schämte sich, als er sich an das Gespräch vor vielen Jahren erinnerte, wo Ruben versucht hatte, Simon zu ermöglichen, Geige spielen zu lernen.

Ich habe es doch auch gewußt, dachte er verdrossen und war von der Musik beunruhigt, die eigenartig und fremd weiter durchs Haus strömte.

Schließlich war es still und Simon kam die Treppe herunter, stand in der Küchentür, sah Ruben an, sagte dann: »Du bist verrückt, Onkel Ruben.«

Darin lag mehr als nur Dankbarkeit für das Geschenk, und Ruben empfand es, als hätte er eine Auszeichnung bekommen, und wie schon viele Male zuvor streifte ihn der verbotene Gedanke: Wenn das mein Junge wäre.

Erst spät am Abend, nachdem Erik Ruben und Isak nach Hause gefahren hatte, und sie in der Küche die Musik aus der oberen Etage noch einmal hörten, konnten sie sich der Frage widmen, die sie sich insgeheim schon den ganzen Tag gestellt hatten: Was mochte dieses Grammophon gekostet haben?

»Allein die Fracht von Amerika bis hierher«, überlegte Erik. »Bedenke nur die Fracht und den Zoll ...«

»Aber er ist ja reich«, tröstete ihn Karin, und Erik dachte, daß allein das Kapital, das Ruben in die Werft investiert hatte, ihm guten Ertrag brachte.

So äußerte er sich auch Karin gegenüber, und auf diese Weise kamen sie über die beunruhigende Frage hinweg, was die Musikmaschine Ruben wohl gekostet haben mochte.

Sie sahen in diesen Weihnachtsfeiertagen nicht viel von Simon. Er machte kurze Ausflüge in ihre Welt, um etwas zu essen und Karin mit ein paar Handgriffen in der Küche zu helfen, er war am Heiligen Abend körperlich anwesend und öffnete die Pakete der beiden Groß-mütter, die handgestrickte Socken und andere Sachen enthielten, die er nicht haben wollte, aber er mochte die beiden Alten dann doch ein klein wenig mehr als sonst.

Am Morgen des Weihnachtstages, der nicht glitzerte, sondern das Haus mit dickem grauem Nebel umgab, wusch er ab, während Erik den Nachbarn die Musiktruhe vorführte und alle sagten, das sei ja gerade so, als ob Jussi Björling persönlich mitten im Zimmer stehen würde.

Simon nahm Erik diese Angeberei nicht übel und haßte auch nicht die Berge von Tellern mit den eingetrockneten Resten der traditionellen schwedischen Weihnachtsspeisen, Stockfisch und Reisbrei. Alles war, wie es sein sollte, und als Erik mit den Nachbarn fertig und die Küche tadellos aufgeräumt war, kehrte Simon zur *Symphonie Fantastique* von Berlioz zurück.

Die ersten Male war er beim Abspielen seiner Platte wieder im Reich der hohen Gräser, er sah den Mann, der die verbotene Sprache sprach, Krieg, Tempelbau, den Tod auf den Hörnern des großen Stiers.

Doch nach und nach verblaßten die Bilder und Simon konnte die unerhörte Trauer in den langen Tönen des Anfangs empfinden und die schmerzhafte Schönheit, wenn der erste Satz in voller Pracht erblühte. Mitten in dem befreienden Sturm wurden ihm die Schrecken der Finsternis im Hintergrund bewußt, der Ernst, der der Welt Ordnung schenkte. Und, erschreckend und herrlich, die Macht. Er empfand das All und die Himmel, die gewaltigen Himmel, ohne sie zu benennen oder zu sehen, ebenso wie das Licht, das von links einströmte, weiß und befreiend. Dann folgte das Spiel von Sonne und Wind im Grasmeer, und wieder waren die Bilder da, gefärbt von zerbrechlicher Freude.

Danach erfüllte ihn wortlose Wehmut.

Er spielte den ersten Satz wieder und wieder und machte eine eigenartige Entdeckung. Wenn er seinen Gedanken freien Lauf ließ, sie schweifen ließ wohin sie wollten, und dabei gleichzeitig seinen

Empfindungen nachspürte ohne sie zu benennen, fand eine Verschmelzung statt. Gedanken und Empfindungen nahmen ein Ende, lösten sich gegenseitig auf.

Die Ewigkeit, dachte er. Das Himmelreich. Doch sobald er zu denken anfing, ging alles verloren.

Er spielte den ersten Satz noch einmal, versank. Kehrte zurück zum Fußboden auf dem er lag, wußte, daß er etwas wiedererkannt hatte, erinnerte sich an die Eichen, an das Land, das ist, das es aber nicht gibt.

Er mußte an seinen Philosophielehrer denken, einen der wenigen an der Schule, dem es gelang, die Unlust zu vertreiben. Er hatte über den Gedanken gesprochen. Ist er unbegrenzt? hatte er gefragt. Oder ist er es, der uns Grenzen setzt?

Simon hatte das dumm gefunden, es war doch ganz selbstverständlich, daß man mit dem Gedanken das Universum erobern konnte.

Der Lehrer hatte von Einstein und von Niels Bohr gesprochen, von der Theorie des Unbegreiflichen. Er hatte etwas Komisches gesagt, etwas worüber die Schüler hatten lachen müssen, was? Simon begann in seinen Aufzeichnungen zu blättern, er wußte, daß er es aufgeschrieben hatte, weil es so widersprüchlich war.

Er fand das Heft, es waren mehrere Zitate, aber Simon hatte, weil seiner Meinung nach unnötig, nicht dazugeschrieben, wer das gesagt hatte: »Jeder Versuch, das Unbegreifliche zu verstehen, führt zum Selbstbetrug. Du denkst daran, im nächsten Augenblick hast du eine Idee daraus gemacht und damit hast du es verloren.«

Etwas weiter unten stand, schlampig, fast unleserlich: »Der Gedanke kann alle Fragen über den Sinn des Lebens stellen, aber er kann nicht eine einzige beantworten, denn die Antworten liegen jenseits des Gedankens.«

Das stimmt ja, murmelte Simon laut und verwundert.

Dann spielte er den ersten Satz noch einmal ab.

Er brauchte fast die ganzen Weihnachtsferien dazu, sich die Symphonie zu erschließen, sie zu einem bekannten Weg zu den eigenen Quellen zu machen.

Bevor er abends einschlief, dachte er in heimlicher Freude an die andere Schallplatte, die er bisher noch nicht abgespielt hatte. Die Erste Symphonie von Mahler, sie ist einfacher, irdischer, ich glaube, du wirst sie mögen, hatte Ruben gesagt.

Am Abend vor Dreikönig wollte er sich Mahler anhören, denn Karin und Erik waren zum Essen eingeladen.

Irgendwann an diesem Abend schien ihm, diese Musik werde ihn vor Freude um den Verstand bringen, in ihr lag Humor, Junges und Unbezwungenes, Freiheit, die durch die großen Wälder stürmte. Es ging dieses Mal leichter, die Bilder loszulassen, er tat es fast mit Wehmut, denn sie waren voll Heiterkeit.

Als er am Dreikönigstag im Lauf des Nachmittags auch bei Mahlers Musik hinter die Bedeutung kam, fühlte er sich mächtig und siegessicher wie ein König.

Aber auch böse, von Zorn erfüllt. Ohne Schuld, ohne Furcht.

Genau zu diesem Zeitpunkt hatte Erik genug. Er tat, als sähe er das Flehen in Karins Augen nicht, und schrie die Treppe hinauf: »Kann man denn keinen Augenblick Ruhe vor dieser verdammten Musik haben!«

Simon schaltete das Grammophon ab, sprungbereit ging er die Treppe hinunter.

Jetzt, dachte er. Jetzt!

Er stand in der Küchentür und sah die beiden an, groß und schlank war er, und seine Augen loderten, sie schienen von der Musik noch dunkler geworden zu sein. Doch als er sich Karin zuwandte, lag in seiner Stimme mehr Trauer als Zorn: »Was, verdammt noch mal, habt ihr gegen meine Musik? Wovor fürchtet ihr euch nur?«

Und Tränen traten ihm in die Augen, als er sich daran erinnerte, wie sie ihn einst daran gehindert hatten, Geige spielen zu lernen, und er sagte: »Um was ist es bei eurem Streit damals eigentlich gegangen, als Ruben wollte, daß ich ein Instrument spielen lerne? Was war da denn Furchtbares dran?«

Schnee fiel draußen in der Dämmerung, Flocken groß wie Kinder-hände, und wie immer bettete der frischgefallene Schnee das Haus in eine große Stille ein.

Sie lauschten ihr alle drei, und Karin wußte, jetzt waren sie bei dem Augenblick angelangt, von dem Ruben gesprochen hatte. Sie sah es Erik an, daß auch er es wußte, es aber nicht wahrhaben wollte, daß er sich in Kürze erheben und sich zur Werft aufmachen würde, wenn sie ihn nicht in der Küche halten konnte, und so sagte sie: »Wir werden jetzt darüber sprechen, Simon. Wir trinken unsern Nachmittagskaffee im schönen Zimmer.«

Da wußte Simon, daß etwas Unerhörtes auf ihn zukam, ihn befiel solche Angst, daß ihm übel wurde, und auch er versuchte zu entkommen, sagte zu Erik: »Können wir nicht mit dem Auto einen Ausflug machen?«

Aber sie gingen alle zwei ins schöne Zimmer, saßen dort auf den unbequemen Stühlen und hörten Karin mit dem Kaffeegeschirr klappern. Erik wich Simons Blick aus, und als Karin mit dem Kaffee kam, sagte er zu ihr: »Nimm lieber eine Herztablette bevor wir anfangen.«

Der Augenblick war so groß, daß darin kein Platz war für kleine und umständliche Worte.

Nun, es war so, daß Erik und sie keine Kinder bekommen konnten, begann Karin. Es war ihnen nie möglich gewesen. Simon war adoptiert worden, er war zu ihnen gekommen, als er drei Tage alt war.

Simons Blick wanderte von Karin weg zum Fenster. Der Schnee fiel, es dämmerte. Alles, was jetzt geschah, war jenseits der Wirklichkeit.

Ich habe es immer gewußt, dachte er, irgendwie habe ich es immer gewußt. Ich habe nie hierher gehört. Es war ein alter Gedanke, er gehörte zur Unwirklichkeit, zu den Phantasien.

»Wer bin ich denn?«

Karin nahm einen Mundvoll Kaffee, schluckte geräuschvoll, und Simon fühlte, daß er die beiden schon lange verabscheute, Erik mit seiner Angeberei und Karin mit ihrer Schlichtheit. Aber auch dieses Gefühl gehörte der Phantasie an, der heimlichen Welt, die er schuf, wenn er zornig oder traurig war.

Karin begann von dem Spielmann zu erzählen, dem jüdischen Spielmann, von dem sie so wenig wußten.

Die Mutter spielt in meinen Tagträumen mit, dachte er. Das ist verrückt, irgendwie sogar schändlich.

»Inga hat ihn für den Wassermann gehalten«, sagte Karin.

»Inga«, wiederholte er.

Das stimmte nicht, das paßte nicht in seine Träume, er wurde eiskalt und sah sich im schönen Zimmer um und erkannte, daß das Unglaubliche sich trotz allem in der Wirklichkeit abspielte.

Nein.

»Sie war damals jung und schön«, sagte Erik.

»Sie haben sich im Wald am Wasserfall ineinander verliebt«, ergänzte Karin. »Aber sie konnten nicht zusammen sprechen.«

Die unwahrscheinliche Geschichte beruhigte Simon, sie konnte gar nicht wahr sein. Sein Blick suchte den von Karin, aber dann hörte er sich fragen: »Weiß Inga, wie er hieß?«

»Nein«, sagte Erik.

»Er hieß wohl Simon«, vermutete Karin. »Er war Musiklehrer an der Volkshochschule gegenüber am andern Seeufer, aber er kam aus Berlin und war Jude.«

»Ein Judenschwein«, sagte Simon, und dann war alles wieder wahr, denn dieses Wort war wie eine Bestätigung.

Der Schnee fiel, es lag Schweigen zwischen den Menschen, bis Simon sagte: »Aber ich bin Inga ja überhaupt nicht ähnlich?«

»Nein, du bist deinem Vater nachgeraten. Zumindest wenn man Inga glauben darf.«

»Also sind wir jedenfalls verwandt, du und ich?«

»Ja«, bestätigte Erik. »Um zwei Ecken.«

»Papa«, sagte Simon, und jetzt wollte er eine Unterbrechung, wollte die beiden sagen hören, jetzt spucken wir drauf, jetzt kehren wir zurück in die Wirklichkeit, damit alles wieder wird wie es sein soll. Aber er wollte es wissen: »Warum habt ihr nie was gesagt?«

Sie sprachen beide gleichzeitig, der unterschwellige Judenhaß, der Nazismus, die Deutschen die in Norwegen saßen und Halb- und Vierteljuden aufstöberten.

Da endlich wußte Simon, daß alles seine Richtigkeit hatte: »Ich erinnere mich an ein Telefongespräch im Frühjahr 1940. Ich habe dich zu jemand sagen hören, ein Brief müsse verbrannt werden.«

O Gott, dachte er. Ich habe schon damals gewußt, daß es um mich ging.

»Wir hatten solche Angst.« Karin sprach, aber Simon hatte kein Mitleid mit ihr.

»Es gab einen Brief?«

»Ja.« Das war wieder Erik. »Inga bekam einen Brief aus Berlin, aber keiner von uns konnte ihn lesen. Wir beschlossen ihn aufzuheben und ihn dir zu geben, wenn du größer wärst.«

»Jemand hätte ihn doch wohl übersetzen können!« Simon schrie es fast heraus.

»Schon, aber das war da draußen auf dem Land eine solche Schande, und wir hatten Inga versprochen, daß niemand es erfährt.«

Da stimmte etwas nicht, Karin erkannte das selbst, aber Simon fuhr fort: »Der Brief wurde verbrannt?«

»Soviel wir wissen, ja.«

Erik erzählte die Geschichte von den Kirchenbüchern, von dem nazistischen Pfarrer. Doch Simon hörte nur das Wort Kirchenbuch und sagte: »Was stand da drin?«

»Vater unbekannt«, sagte Erik, und die alte Bitterkeit schwappte über ihn hinweg.

»Du mußt verstehen, ich habe dich diesem Nazischwein von einem Pfarrer ausgeliefert.«

Der Schnee verbreitete unendliche Stille, Simon fror, er fror so sehr, daß er zitterte. Aber er sah die beiden an, sah von einem zum anderen: »Ich muß also dankbar sein, noch dankbarer?«

Karin fand keine Worte, hatte einen Mund, rauh wie Sandpapier.

»Für uns warst du ein Gottesgeschenk.«

Das war Erik, und Simon war so erstaunt, daß der Schock ihn für einen Moment lähmte. Wegen des Wortes, das so ungewohnt aus Eriks Mund kam und wegen der großen Wahrheit, die dieses Wort enthielt. Er wußte es ja, es gelang ihm zu sagen: »Verzeih mir, Papa.«

Karin trank wieder einen Schluck Kaffee und wollte von den Nächten mit dem kleinen Kind erzählen, von den starken und seltsamen Gedanken, die sie gehabt hatte, daß alle Kinder Kinder dieser Welt waren. Aber sie sagte nur: »Du warst erst drei Tage alt.«

»Das hast du schon gesagt.«

Wieder langes Schweigen, dann Simon: »Weiß es jemand?«

»Ja, Ruben. Wir haben mit ihm darüber gesprochen.«

»Was hat er gesagt?«

Karins Papierstimme hörte zu flattern auf, als sie sich erinnerte: »Er hat gesagt, Kinder gehören zu denen, die sie lieben und beschützen.«

»Und er hat noch etwas gesagt, nämlich daß du Karin ähnlich bist, das gleiche Gemüt hast wie sie«, fügte Erik hinzu.

Simon fror so sehr, daß er mit den Zähnen klapperte, und Karin ging ihm die warme Jacke holen. Als sie sie ihm um die Schultern legen wollte, zuckte er bei der Berührung zusammen, sie mußte das Kleidungsstück über die Stuhllehne hängen. Er schlüpfte hinein, sah Erik an: »Dann brauche ich gar nicht so tüchtig zu sein wie du?«

»Mein Gott, Simon, du bist doch viel tüchtiger.«

Simon sah, daß das Erstaunen echt war.

Zum Schluß schien nichts mehr übrig geblieben zu sein was noch zu sagen war. Simon wirkte gefaßt, zitterte aber immer noch vor Kälte. Daran ist dieses verdammte feine Zimmer schuld, dachte Erik.

In der Küche trank der Junge Wasser, ein Glas nach dem anderen. Dann stand er in der Tür, schaute die beiden an und sagte: »Irgendwie habe ich es immer gewußt.«

Bald darauf hörten sie oben das Grammophon wieder spielen. Die unbegreifliche Musik erfüllte das Haus. Aber bald klang sie aus, und als Karin leise die Treppe hinaufging, um nach Simon zu sehen, schlief er wie ein Bär.

Das ist fast enttäuschend, dachte Karin.

Und Erik sagte: »Ist ja alles gut gegangen.«

Und sie waren beide auch so müde, daß sie ohne Abendessen ins Bett fielen.

Am nächsten Tag war Schule, und in der Küche herrschte beim Frühstück die übliche Hast. Das Halbjahreszeugnis! Simon holte es, Karin unterschrieb: »Zur Kenntnis genommen.«

Aber das stimmte eigentlich nicht, sie überprüfte Simons Zeugnisse nie. »Alles in Ordnung?«

»Klar, Mama. Nur keine Sorge.«

Aber schon nach wenigen Stunden kam er mit hohem Fieber nach Hause zurück.

Daran war nichts Merkwürdiges, die halbe Stadt hatte Grippe. Karin brachte ihn zu Bett, kochte Honigwasser und maß die Temperatur. Fast 40°, sie erschrak: »Du hast keine Genickschmerzen?« Es gelang ihm, den Kopf zu schütteln und sie anzulächeln. Dann schlief er.

Mit allen Müttern jener Zeit teilte Karin die Angst vor Kinderlähmung, sie lag wie eine eisige Bedrohung über allen, die hohes Fieber oder Nackensteife bekamen. Karin rief also den alten Kreisarzt an, der ihr sagte, das klinge alles nach Grippe, und sie möge am nächsten Tag wieder anrufen, falls das Fieber nicht zurückginge.

Es lief ein Mädchen im Reich der hohen Gräser neben ihm her, die Vögel bauten Nester in ihrem Haar und sie sagte: Hübsch, was?

Und er begehrte sie und er bekam sie, durfte alles mit ihr tun, wenn er nur achtsam mit dem Vogelnest umging. Er entkleidete sie, saugte an ihren Brustwarzen, küßte alles, was sie war, und seine Begierde war wild wie der Frühling, und er konnte nicht genug von ihr kriegen, und er sah, daß sie schöner war als jede irdische Frau. Die Gräser spielten den zweiten Satz aus Mahlers Erster Symphonie, die Wogen des Rhythmus schlugen mit ihrem zusammen, und als er dem Unbekannten entgegentrat, dröhnten die Trommeln wie besessen und er wurde vernichtet und er trat über die Grenze des Landes, in dem nichts eine Form hat und alles faßbar und vollendet ist.

Sie war bei ihm und fragte ohne Worte, ob er das verstand, was er immer gewußt hatte.

Da sah er, daß ein Ei in ihrem Vogelnest lag, daß es schimmernd weiß war und wie von selbst leuchtete, und er wußte, daß das Ei Leben bedeutete, und daß das Junge die Schale bald sprengen würde und seine Form annehmen würde, und er liebte das Ei, es war kostbar wie das Leben selbst.

Dann war Karin mit Fleischbrühe da und sie sagte, Flüssigkeit sei wichtig, und falls es ihm nicht bald besser ginge, müßten sie den Arzt herbitten. Er schluckte gehorsam, hörte die Worte von der gesunden

Suppe und zwang sich, dachte es wäre gut für das Ei, für das Junge, das bald schlüpfen sollte.

Aber er wollte zurückkehren zu den Gräsern, zu dem unendlichen Gräsermeer und dem Mädchen mit dem Vogelnest im Haar. Doch er fand sie nicht und seine Angst war ebenso gewaltig wie die Gräsermeere, durch die er lief und ihren Namen rief. Aber sie hatte keinen Namen, er wußte es, und trotzdem konnte er ihn über die Ebenen hallen und in den weit entlegenen Bergen ein Echo hervorrufen hören.

Er wurde fast irr vor Erschrecken, begriff sie denn nicht, daß er zurück zu ihr und dem Ei mußte, sollte nicht alles zunichte werden und das Leben, seine eigene Möglichkeit zu leben, verloren sein.

Aber sie war verschwunden.

Jetzt stand er am Fuß einer Klippe und sah, daß dort hoch oben unter dem Himmel ein großer Vogel sich niedergelassen hatte, und er wußte, das war der Vogel der Weisheit, und er glaubte, daß dieser Kenntnis davon hatte, wo das Mädchen mit dem Ei sich befand. Er sammelte seine letzten Kräfte und kletterte den Berg hinauf und betete: Guter Gott, laß mich den Vogel nicht erschrecken. Und der Vogel blieb, es war, als hätte er auf ihn gewartet, und als er näher kam, sah er, daß der Vogel brütete, und er verstand, daß das Ei, das der Vogel mit seiner Wärme am Leben erhielt, sein Ei war, sein Leben.

Im nächsten Augenblick hörte er eine Geige, die eine wundersame Melodie voller Wehmut spielte, und als er den Blick dem Berghang zuwandte, sah er das Mädchen, sah, daß sie jetzt ein Mann war, ein junger Spielmann, der mit seiner Geige davonzog und daß die Einsamkeit, die ihn umgab, groß war.

Der große Vogel betrachtete Simon mit Karins Augen und er erkannte, daß es der Vogel der Trauer und nicht der Weisheit war, und daß er sich um sein Ei keine Sorgen zu machen brauchte und auch nicht um das Leben, das sich in der zerbrechlichen Schale mit den zarten Häuten befand.

Der Vogel der Trauer war treu und liebevoll. Und stark, nichts Böses würde dem Jungen widerfahren.

Jetzt rief der Vogel:

»Aber Simon, so beruhige dich doch!«

Und der Vogel gab ihm Tabletten, und das Fieber klang mit einem gewaltigen Schweißausbruch ab, und der Vogel zog ihm kühle Kleider an und trocknete ihm Körper und Stirn.

Karin war außer sich und holte den Arzt, obwohl es schon zehn Uhr abends war. Der tastete und drückte und leuchtete mit der Taschenlampe und horchte und beruhigte.

Es war nur eine ungewöhnlich hektische Grippe.

»Ist ihm irgend etwas zugestoßen?« fragte der Arzt beim Abschied. »Es gibt gewisse Anzeichen eines Schocks.«

Und Karin faßte sich an die Stirn und zweifelte ihren Verstand an, weil sie nicht zwei und zwei zusammengezählt und alles begriffen hatte.

Erik trug das alte Gästebett in Simons Zimmer, und Karin legte sich für die Nacht neben den Jungen. Aber er schlief die ganze Nacht durch, wachte jedoch vor ihr auf, lag im Bett und betrachtete den Vogel der Trauer, der über sein Leben gewacht hatte.

Dann mußte er wieder eingeschlafen sein, denn als er das nächste Mal aufwachte, stand Erik mit Tee und Broten bei ihm, und Simon aß mit gutem Appetit, und Karin und Erik seufzten erleichtert auf. Simon sah Erik an und dachte, wie gut, daß du bist wie du bist, irdisch und rücksichtslos.

Begrenzt, ein kleines Stück Boden begrenzend, den du zu deinem gemacht hast.

Simon konnte auf seinen eigenen zittrigen Beinen ins Badezimmer gehen, und als er zurückkam, hatte Karin das Bett frisch überzogen.

»Zum wievielten Mal weiß ich selbst nicht«, sagte sie und dachte dankbar an Lisa, die nun bald kommen und sich des Hauses und der Wäsche annehmen würde.

Sie holte einen Überwurf für das Gästebett und eine Decke, legte sich darauf, als hätte sie gewußt, daß Simon und sie jetzt würden reden können. Und die Worte waren vorhanden, bildeten ganz natürliche Sätze.

178

Sie erzählte von dem Winter, in dem sie nachts aufgestanden war, um ihm zusätzliche Mahlzeiten zu geben, wie sie mit dem Säugling im Arm in der Küche gesessen und starke, seltsame Gedanken gehegt hatte. »Ich war wohl sehr übermütig«, sagte sie. »Ich war so sicher, dir alles geben zu können was du brauchtest, um ein starker und glücklicher Mensch zu werden.«

Da konnte Simon erwidern: »Aber du hattest doch recht.«

Und da mußte Karin ein bißchen weinen. Sie fand auch Worte für all die Freude, die er ihnen geschenkt hatte, wie er ihnen die Kraft gegeben hatte, sich aus der Umklammerung und dem Armeleutegetue der Schwiegermütter zu lösen, Grund und Boden zu erwerben und ein Haus zu bauen.

»Sie empfanden uns als völlig übergeschnappt und hochmütig und meinten, das alles werde schlecht enden«, sagte sie. »Aber wir wußten beide, daß wir für dich ein Haus am Meer brauchten.«

Ein Nest am Meer, dachte Simon.

Sie erzählte von dem Hausierer, dem Judenhasser mit den Nadelbriefchen, wie er Simon angesehen und dreckiges Judenkind gezischt hatte.

»Mich hat vor Schreck fast der Schlag getroffen«, sagte Karin. »Weißt du das noch?«

»Nein.«

Simon fielen die Landstreicher wieder ein, die von Haus zu Haus gegangen waren und erinnerte sich nur, daß ihnen etwas Merkwürdiges angehaftet hatte, etwas Erschreckendes.

Er hatte die Schulzeit nicht vergessen, in der Schimpfwörter gefallen waren. Judenschwein. Und wie Erik weiß im Gesicht geworden war und ihn kämpfen gelehrt hatte.

»Ja, ich war damals eigentlich dagegen«, erinnerte sich Karin. »Aber es hat dir immerhin geholfen. Es war auch für mich eine nützliche Lehre, denn ich mußte ja begreifen lernen, daß ich dich nicht ununterbrochen beschützen konnte, daß du stark werden mußtest, um allein zurechtzukommen.«

Tagelang redeten sie, riefen Simons Kindheit zurück.

Am Morgen des sechsten Tages schien die Sonne auf den Schnee und Simon tauchte wie üblich in seiner Musik unter, während Karin einen Spaziergang am Fluß entlang und hinaus zum Meer machte.

Lange stand sie dort und sah Vinga wie eine Fata Morgana durch die glasklare Winterluft schimmern.

»Ich habe meinen Teil getan«, sagte sie zum Meer.

Als sie wieder heim ging, war sie müde, aber nicht auf die alte hoffnungslose Art müde. Ihr Herz schlug ruhig und gleichmäßig.

Kräftig.

Es heilt, dachte Karin, jetzt endlich hat es Ruhe zu heilen.

Ein paar Tage später kam Ruben zu Besuch. Isak ging auf die Werft, so daß Karin erzählen konnte, daß sie sich ausgesprochen hatten, niemand war daran gestorben, aber Simon hatte eine Grippe mit Fieberphantasien hinter sich bringen müssen.

»Es wäre sicher gut, wenn du auch mit ihm sprichst«, sagte sie. Ruben nickte und ging die Treppe hinauf in Simons Zimmer.

Beim Essen konnten sie alle fünf über Simons Herkunft reden, das lange Verheimlichte, sorgfältig Versteckte und unerhört Gefährliche war sichtbar geworden.

Es war eine echte Erleichterung.

Doch Erik, der nicht nur alles verdrängt, sondern es auch zu vergessen versucht hatte, biß die Zähne zusammen, als Karin sagte: »Ich habe mir gedacht, wir sollten vielleicht nachforschen, ob Simons Vater noch am Leben ist.«

»Er war Musiker«, sagte Ruben schnell. »Viele Künstler haben Deutschland verlassen, bevor es zu spät war.«

Er dachte an die jüdischen Organisationen, die jetzt bemüht daran arbeiteten, getrennte Familien wieder zusammenzuführen.

Doch Simon sah den jungen Rücken des Spielmanns vor sich, der mit seiner Geige den Berg hinunter wanderte, und er sah, daß dessen Weg zu den Öfen führte, deren Schornsteine am Horizont aufragten.

»Er ist tot«, sagte er. »Er ist eine von den Ziffern auf Izas Arm.«

Simon sagte es so bestimmt, daß niemand einen Einwand wagte, und nur Isak dachte: Wie zum Teufel kann er das wissen.

Es war Karin, die das Gespräch wieder aufnahm: »Er war bestimmt ein guter Mensch.«

Gut! Simon mußte über sie lachen. Laut sagte er: »Er war einsam und traurig.«

Da konnte Isak sich nicht mehr zurückhalten: »Wie willst du das wissen? Vielleicht war er wild und fröhlich.«

Simon lachte: »Das auch, möglicherweise.«

»Ich dachte an das Erbe«, sagte Karin, und da sprach Ruben lange über alles, was man jetzt über die Bedeutung der Umwelteinflüsse in der Kindererziehung wußte.

»Wir erben bestimmte körperliche Merkmale und das eine oder andere Talent, wie zum Beispiel Simon seine Musikalität«, sagte er. »Güte ist nicht in den Genen verankert, Karin, die ist abhängig von der Sicherheit, die dem Kind zuteil wird.«

Simon hörte nicht so genau zu, er dachte vor allem an das, was Ruben oben im Zimmer gesagt hatte, daß alle Jugendlichen herumphantasieren, vermuten daß sie uneheliche Kinder sind und daß jeder junge Mensch irgendwann inneren Aufruhr und Abscheu erlebt und auch seine Eltern verachtet.

»Ich habe oft genug darüber nachgegrübelt, warum ich nicht ebenso praktisch veranlagt bin wie Erik«, gestand Simon. »Aber ich konnte seine Fähigkeiten ja gar nicht geerbt haben.«

Da lachte Ruben: »Und was ist mit Inga, deiner leiblichen Mutter? Ich habe immer wieder gehört, daß sie Hof und Vieh wie ein ganzer Mann bewirtschaftet.«

Simon gefiel das Gespräch nicht, aber er mußte genau wie die andern wenigstens den Mund zu einem leichten Grinsen verziehen.

»Du hast nie darüber nachgedacht, warum Isak nicht genauso belesen und an Büchern interessiert ist wie ich?«

»Nein«, sagte Simon.

»Vielleicht ist es so, daß jeder Sohn seinen Vater besiegen muß«, überlegte Ruben. »Da liegt es auf der Hand, ein Gebiet zu wählen, in dem der Vater nicht überlegen ist, und wo der Sohn seinen Papa haushoch schlagen kann.«

Während des langen Spätwinters kam es dazu, daß Simon schmerzhaft von einer Angst befallen wurde, die sich vom Bauch bis zum Hals bemerkbar und das Atmen schwer machte.

Er dachte an Inga, wies aber den Gedanken von sich, sie besuchen zu fahren. Er dachte an Wurzeln, daran, daß er keine hatte, kam aber nicht ganz damit zurecht.

Und dann dachte er an das Mädchen, das im Sanatorium auf ihn wartete wie die Spinne auf die Fliege. Ruhig und gelassen in der Gewißheit, daß er sich fangen lassen werde, daß es nur eine Frage der Zeit war.

Dann kamen die letzten Sommerferien. Die würden sie in Erinnerung behalten: Simon, weil er hintergangen worden, und Isak, weil er der Liebe begegnet war.

Iza war im Frühjahr aus dem Sanatorium entlassen worden, sie zog zu Ruben und fand die Wohnung beengend und die Stadt langweilig. Sie fand Ruben selbst ebenso hoffnungslos wie seinen Freundeskreis von literaturbeflissenen Männern mittleren Alters. Mit ihm hinaus zu Karin und Erik zu fahren, weigerte sie sich.

»Karin ist genauso eine Kuh, wie meine Mutter eine war«, sagte sie und übersah Rubens Reaktion.

Er versuchte sie mit jüdischen Familien der Stadt bekannt zu machen, wandte sich an Mütter mit Töchtern. Aber trotz guter Vorsätze hielt niemand es mit ihr aus, und Izas Angst wuchs, wenn sie in den Geschäften der Avenue und der Kungsgata versuchte, sich Erleichterung zu erkaufen. Isak hatte solche Angst vor ihr, daß er sich schon vor Schulschluß hinaus zu Larssons und der Werft verzog.

Karin suchte Hilfe bei Ruben: »Wir müssen ihn verstehen, das Mädchen erinnert ihn an das, was passiert ist.«

Sie erinnert auch an etwas anderes, dachte Ruben. An Olga. Er empfand es ja selbst so, dieses rastlose Laufen auf hohen Absätzen durch die Wohnung, das Klirren von Hals- und Armbändern, überall der Geruch von schweren Parfums, aber vor allem die Unruhe, die durch die Räume vibrierte.

Eigentlich gab es nur eines, was Iza interessierte, und das war Simon.

»Er hat etwas Rätselhaftes an sich«, sagte sie, und Ruben versuchte abzuwehren: »Er ist doch nur ein Junge, der noch nicht einmal die Schule hinter sich hat.«

»Ich habe nichts gegen kleine Jungen«, sagte Iza.

Sie war schlank und hübsch geworden, wie sie es sich vorgenommen hatte, und sie sprach mit Simon über das Vernichtungslager und seine Schrecken.

»Sie muß sich aussprechen können«, sagte Simon zu Ruben, als dieser sie unterbrach.

»Nein«, widersprach Ruben. »Sie schwelgt darin und weiß, daß sie dich dadurch fesselt. Paß um Gottes willen auf, Simon, paß auf!«

Es war an einem Spätnachmittag nach der Schule. Ruben hatte Simon in Izas Zimmer vorgefunden und ihn so gut wie hinausgeworfen und war ihm dann bis auf die Straße gefolgt.

Simon hing über seinem Fahrrad, schaute den Mann an, den er mehr als jeden anderen bewunderte, und war so verzweifelt, daß seine Augen schwarz wurden.

»Ich entkomme ihr nicht, Onkel Ruben.«

Aber schon als er heimwärts radelte, hatte er nicht nur die eigene, sondern auch Rubens Angst vergessen, fühlte nur das Verlangen nach ihr, den roten Lippen und dem verführerischen Körper mit all seinen unglaublichen Erinnerungen.

Eine Woche später, kurz vor Schulschluß, war Iza zur Erholung in einen Schweizer Kurort geschickt worden. Olof Hirtz, ihr Arzt und Rubens Freund, leitete alles in die Wege und verschaffte ihr auch einen Psychoanalytiker in Zürich. Iza war zufrieden, sie wollte in die Welt hinaus. Simon konnte warten, dachte sie, denn trotz allem waren Simons Worte nicht spurlos an ihr vorbeigegangen.

»War das notwendig?« fragte Karin, als sie es erfuhr.

»Du weißt ebenso gut wie ich, daß es verdammt notwendig war«, antwortete Ruben.

Simon fühlte sich hintergangen, aber in die Enttäuschung mischte sich auch Erleichterung. Er konnte wieder befreiter atmen, seit das Mädchen abgereist war.

Nach Mittsommer gingen Simon und Isak segeln, sie befanden sich fast einen Monat lang auf See. Die Küste von Bohuslän hinauf, hinein in den Oslofjord. Sie kamen in die Stadt, durch die die Nazis in ihren Stiefeln marschiert waren.

»Ich meine, ich kann sie noch hören«, sagte Isak, und Simon blieb stehen und lauschte dem taktfesten Dröhnen der Stiefel auf dem Straßenpflaster.

»Hauen wir ab, Isak.«

Sie sahen also nicht viel von der Stadt, schauten sich nicht einmal das Osebergschiff an, von dem Isak geträumt hatte, und auch nicht das Nansen-Museum, das Simon hatte besuchen wollen.

Sie kamen braun wie die Indianer, verdreckt, ausgelaugt von Wind und Salzwasser, und stolz auf ihre schütteren Bärte nach Hause zurück. Karin lachte laut auf vor Freude, schickte sie sofort in die Badewanne und legte Rasierapparate bereit.

»Wenn ihr einen Bart wollt, müßt ihr warten bis er gleichmäßiger wächst,« meinte sie, und die Jungen gaben ihr recht, nachdem sie sich gründlich im Spiegel betrachtet hatten.

Sie bockten das Boot auf, entfernten Muscheln und Tang und machten Ordnung an Bord, denn nun wollten Erik und Ruben auf große Fahrt gehen. Sie wollten Karin mitnehmen, die jedoch verzichtete. Ruben dachte, daß sie Angst um ihr Herz hätte, Erik, daß sie die Jungen nicht unbeaufsichtigt lassen wolle.

Aber der wahre Grund war, Karin wollte nicht so lange in Rubens Nähe sein.

An einem Hochsommerabend machten sich die Jungen zu einem Tanzfest auf einem Bootssteg bei Särö auf.

Isak lernte Mona kennen.

Und Isak erkannte augenblicklich, daß sie eines jener seltenen Wesen war, die die Welt begreiflich machen.

Sie war tropfenförmig, hatte alles Gewicht unterhalb der Taille und von oben bis unten gleichmäßig dicke Beine, die sie immer, egal wo sie war, mit der Erde verbanden, mit dem Mittelpunkt der Erde.

Bis Isak es erkannte und es nun der Welt offenbarte, hatte niemand gesehen, wie unendlich schön sie war. Sie schaute ihn mit Karins Augen an, aber seltsamerweise waren diese Augen blau, und sie liebte Isak vom ersten Augenblick an.

In einer alles umfassenden, ruhigen Art.

Sie war für ihre zwei kleinen Geschwister zur Mutter geworden, und das hatte ihr geholfen, die Welt als etwas Handfestes zu betrachten. Sie trug seit dem Tag, an dem ihre Mutter starb, eine tiefe Verletzung in ihrem Inneren, und trotz ihrer vierzehn Jahre war sie schon damals ebenso unerschütterlich, zuverlässig und gradlinig wie ihre Mutter es gewesen war.

Im übrigen hatte sie keine Zeit gehabt, sich krank zu trauern oder über das Schicksal nachzugrübeln, denn die kleinen Kinder mußten täglich und stündlich bekommen, was sie brauchten.

Wäre da nicht eine Tante gewesen, hätte es schiefgehen können, aber diese Tante gab es und sie achtete streng darauf, daß Mona ihr Recht auf ein eigenes Leben wahrte.

So war also trotz allem für die Tochter des Fischhändlers der Besuch der Mädchenschule möglich gewesen, und gerade in diesem Frühjahr hatte sie die siebente Klasse abgeschlossen und peilte zielstrebig vier Jahre Krankenschwesternausbildung an der Sahlgrenschen Klinik an.

Der Welt zeigte sie eine leicht verächtliche Haltung gegenüber Männern, sie hatte nie verstanden, daß diese es wert sein sollten, ernst genommen zu werden. Möglicherweise hatte sie in dem einen oder anderen Wochenblatt etwas über Liebe gelesen. Aber sie hatte kaum an diese geglaubt und nie hatte sie sich vorgestellt, daß sie selbst jemals davon betroffen sein könnte.

Eigentlich war sie deshalb über alle Maßen erstaunt.

Das war Simon ebenfalls. Er war der großen Liebe zwar schon in tausend Büchern begegnet, jener Leidenschaft, die die Menschen mitriß, sie vor Verzweiflung oder Glück um den Verstand brachte. Aber auch er hatte nicht so recht an sie geglaubt und sie im wirklichen Leben noch nie beobachtet.

Jetzt sah er, wie sie sich direkt vor seinen Augen ereignete. Das erfüllte ihn mit Staunen, Eifersucht und noch etwas anderem, das er nach und nach als Neid erkannte.

»Die sind verrückt, Mutter«, sagte er zu Karin. »Die sind wie in Trance und sehen nur noch sich.«

»Ich hoffe, er bringt sie bald mal mit, damit ich mir dieses Wunder ansehen kann«, meinte Karin.

Aber sowohl Karin als auch Simon existierten in Isaks Welt nicht mehr.

Er schlief in der Stadt, in Rubens Wohnung, stand jeden Morgen auf, holte den alten Chevrolet aus der Garage und fuhr ohne Führerschein zu Axelssons Kolonialwarengeschäft an einer Straßenkreuzung in Askim. Dort wartete sie und war noch schöner als am Tag zuvor, und das Auto brachte sie in die Laubwälder weiter südlich, zu den Klippen bei Gottskär, zum Süßwasser in den Delseen und den tiefen Nadelwäldern von Hindås. Sie fanden immer wieder irgendwo weiches Moos, sich darauf auszuruhen, neue Wiesen, um drüberzuwandern, neue Blumen für Sträuße.

Widerstandslos und wie selbstverständlich gab sie sich ihm hin, und er kam ihr sanft und voller Zärtlichkeit entgegen und gedachte, als er mit Mona schlief, dankbar der Sprengmeisterstochter an der Stadtgrenze. Dieses Mädchen war eine Unschuld, aber auch dadurch wurde nichts schwierig oder peinlich. Am Tag danach ging sie ohne Zögern zu einem Arzt, ließ die Tests machen und lernte mit einem Pessar umzugehen.

Erst gegen Ende dieser lichtvollen Woche nach dem Tanz in der Nähe von Särö erinnerte sich Isak, daß es in der Welt noch andere Menschen gab und daß Karin und Simon ein Recht darauf hatten zu erfahren, daß und wofür er lebte.

Ganz zu schweigen von Ruben, der eine Woche später auch wieder zurück sein würde.

Er ließ es Mona gleich wissen, als sie sich trafen: »Wir müssen einen Besuch machen, es ist nicht gerade meine Familie, aber es sind immerhin die Menschen, die mir am nächsten stehen.«

Sie nickte, das mußte ja kommen.

Dann wollte er erklären, wer er war, aber das machte ihn verlegen, in seinem Kopf gab es keine Gedanken mehr und in seinem Mund keine Worte. Sie sagte: »Ich weiß nicht einmal deinen Nachnamen.«

»Lentov«, sagte er. »Isak Lentov.«

Da wurde sie verschlossen, er fühlte es, und Angst durchzitterte ihn.

»Ich bin Jude«, sagte er.

Da lachte sie: »Ich bin schließlich kein Idiot, und ich habe von der Sache mit der Beschneidung gelesen.«

Die Angst ließ nach, er mußte den Wagen anhalten, sie küssen. Aber es gab da eine Art Ablehnung, ein Erstaunen und so etwas wie Verwirrung. »Was stimmt denn dann nicht?«

»Lentov«, sagte sie. »Der reiche Lentov mit den vielen Buchhandlungen?«

»Ja, und was ist daran verkehrt?«

»Nichts«, sagte sie und wurde steif wie ein Brett. Sie mußte sich so verhalten, um den Jubel in ihrem Inneren zu unterdrücken. Wenn Mona in ihrem Leben Träume gehabt hatte, dann hatten sie sich immer um Geld gedreht, um Reichtum und teure, schöne Dinge.

»Das ist einfach unfaßbar«, sagte sie. Und dann mit einer Stimme, die dünn war vor innerer Unruhe: »Was wird dein Vater sagen?«

»Mein Vater wird dich lieben«, sagte Isak.

»Das siehst du jetzt aber sehr einfach. Du mußt doch kapiert haben, daß deinem Vater für dich eine Verbindung mit einem reichen und vornehmen jüdischen Mädchen vorschwebt.«

»Da kennst du Ruben Lentov schlecht«, erwiderte Isak. »Er wird auf unserer Hochzeit vor Freude tanzen.«

Es erstaunte sie nicht, daß von Hochzeit die Rede war, das war vom ersten Augenblick an selbstverständlich gewesen. Aber sie glaubte nicht an den Vater, den Isak ihr da beschrieb.

Im Augenblick ging es aber um Karin und Simon. Eigentlich war es bis zu ihnen mit dem Auto nur eine Viertelstunde, und doch brauchten sie mehrere Stunden. Es gab vorher so viel zu erzählen.

Es war ja nicht so einfach zu erklären, wer Karin war, wenn er sich nicht einmal traute von damals in Berlin zu erzählen, als die Hitlerjugend marschierte.

Mona weinte, wie es ihr als dem feinfühligen Kind, das sie war, zustand, und sie umarmte und tröstete Isak als die gute Mutter, die sie ebenfalls war. Ich werde ihn nie im Stich lassen, dachte sie, nie. Nicht einmal, wenn Ruben Lentov ihn enterbt.

Dann konnte sie von ihrer eigenen Mutter erzählen, vom Tod, der eines Nachts kam und alles Blut aus dem Unterleib der Mutter drückte, konnte von den vielen roten Laken und den seltsamen Gedanken erzählen.

»Man will es nicht glauben«, sagte sie. »Es läuft vor deinen Augen ab, dieses Sterben, und trotzdem glaubst du nicht daran. Ist das nicht seltsam?«

»Nein«, Isak fand das eigentlich nicht.

Nach einer Weile fiel ihm Olga ein und daß das auch besprochen werden mußte. »Meine Mutter ist im Irrenhaus«, sagte er. »Sie ist über Nacht wahnsinnig geworden, damals als die Deutschen Norwegen besetzten.«

»Die Arme.«

»Das ist erblich«, sagte Isak und wußte, daß er das nicht einmal zu denken gewagt hatte, ehe er Mona kennenlernte. Aber er wollte ihr nichts vorenthalten: »Ich habe eine Cousine, die auch irgendwie verrückt zu sein scheint«, sagte er. »Aber die ist in einem Konzentrationslager gewesen.«

Mona weinte jetzt wieder, sagte aber: »Wir werden vier glückliche Kinder haben.«

Schließlich saßen sie dann doch bei Karin auf dem Küchensofa, sprachen nicht viel, erfüllten aber die ganze Küche mit Helligkeit. Sie sind der reinste Sonnenschein, dachte Karin und sah durchs Fenster den Regen wie Bindfäden auf die Erde fallen, während sich in ihrer Küche ein helles Leuchten ausbreitete.

»Ihr bleibt doch hoffentlich zum Essen«, sagte sie.

»Ja, gerne.«

Als der Platzregen vorbei war, gingen sie alle in den Garten, um Erdbeeren für den Nachtisch zu pflücken. Simon kam vom Meer, er war mit dem Kahn fischen gewesen, freute sich, betrachtete die beiden jungen Leute lange und sagte dann: »Ihr zwei seid das Erstaunlichste, was ich je erlebt habe.«

Darüber mußten sie natürlich lachen, alle miteinander.

Karin nahm Simon mit in die Küche, während das Liebespaar weiter Beeren pflückte.

»Kannst du sehen, wie sie von Licht umgeben sind, Simon?«

»Ja, Mutter, ist das normal?«

»Normal?« fragte Karin. »Ich kann dir nur eins sagen. Nicht einmal wenn ich meine ganze Phantasie aufgeboten hätte, um mir für Isak etwas Besonderes auszudenken, hätte ich dieses Mädchen ersinnen können.«

Im Erdbeerbeet sagte Mona zu Isak: »Ich mag sie.«

»Selbstverständlich«, meinte Isak.

»Aber Simon ist eifersüchtig.«

Da lachte Isak Mona an: »Das soll ihm gegönnt sein.«

Dann steckte er ihr eine Erdbeere in den Mund und holte sie sich küssend zurück.

Sie übernachteten im Gästezimmer in Rubens schmalem Bett, und Karin lieh Mona ihr schönstes Nachthemd.

Ich habe eine Tochter bekommen, dachte Karin, als sie im Bett lag und hörte, wie das Mädchen zu Hause anrief und seelenruhig geradeheraus log: »Sagt dem Papa einen schönen Gruß und daß ich über Nacht bei einer Freundin in der Stadt bleibe.«

Bei so einem lieben Mädchen muß das eine liebe Familie sein, sagte sich Karin, ehe sie einschlief.

Es blieben ihnen einige Tage, um sich richtig kennenzulernen, ehe Ruben und Erik heimkommen würden. Es gelang Karin, Isak bestimmte Arbeiten zu übertragen, so daß sie zumindest hin und wieder mit dem Mädchen allein sein konnte.

Schon am ersten Morgen schickte sie ihn mit dem Auto nach Hause: »Du stellst es in die Garage. Aber erst wirst du es waschen. Und kein Wort zu Ruben, daß du ohne Führerschein gefahren bist.«

Er gehorchte und Karin sagte genau wie Monas eigene Mutter immer gesagt hatte: »Männer! Da siehst du's mal wieder.«

Als die Jungen mit dem Wagen wegfuhren, gingen Karin und Mona zum Badeplatz. Karin tauchte wie üblich ein paarmal unter, aber Mona schwamm wie eine Robbe.

Sie war offen, schien nichts zu verbergen zu haben. Erzählte von ihrer Mutter, das war nicht leicht. Von den kleinen Geschwistern, die jetzt alt genug waren, um ohne die große Schwester zurechtzukommen.

Vom Vater, dem Fischhändler.

»Von dem haben wir nicht gerade viel«, erklärte Mona. »Schreit herum, ist gleich eingeschnappt, fühlt sich dauernd auf die Füße getreten. Beschränkt und geizig ist er auch. Aber man muß sich damit abfinden, schließlich ist er mein Vater.«

Karin mußte lachen: »Und wie wird er das mit Isak aufnehmen?«

»Na, das wird natürlich einen Aufstand geben.«

»Weil Isak Jude ist?«

»Ja, das auch, aber vor allem, weil er zu Hause sein Dienstmädchen verliert.«

»Ist er religiös? Freikirchlich? Das sind doch die meisten Schärenbewohner.«

»Na ja, manchmal brüllt er herum von Antichrist und sowas. Aber das Religiöse spielt bei ihm nur eine ganz kleine Rolle.«

Monas Augen glänzten vor Entzücken, als sie weiterdachte: »Er wird schnell einlenken, wenn er das mit dem Geld kapiert hat.«

Nicht einmal eine leibliche Tochter hätte mir so ähnlich sein können, dachte Karin erstaunt und sehr zufrieden. Aber Mona runzelte die Stirn.

»Viel schlimmer ist, was Isaks Papa sagen wird.«

»Nicht doch«, beschwichtigte Karin. »Der wird dich mögen.«

»Wie kannst du das wissen?«

»Na ja«, meinte Karin. »Wie kann ich das wissen.« Sie schwieg eine Weile, dann sagte sie: »Er ist ein Mensch ohne Falsch.«

»Das ist ein komischer Ausdruck«, meinte Mona. »Und hilft mir das?«

»Du wirst ja sehen«, erwiderte Karin lachend.

Am Samstag rief Erik aus Marstrand an. An Bord war alles in Ordnung.

»Wir kommen morgen, wie ausgemacht«, sagte er. »Wir kommen an der Werft an und ich schaffe den Proviant dort an Land. Geht's dir gut?«

»Mir geht es prima«, lachte Karin. »Sag Ruben einen schönen Gruß, und wir haben hier eine große Überraschung für ihn.«

»Für mich nicht?«

»Nein. Leider«, sagte Karin und dachte an Simon und Iza. »Man muß das Leben nehmen, wie es kommt.«

Sie klang ganz normal, so, wie sie immer geklungen hatte. Eine Norne, die in ihrer Küche Lebensschicksale spann, die sich um die Fäden sorgte, damit sie nicht rissen oder sich verhedderten, die aber hinnahm, daß das Lebensgewebe kompliziert war und sich nicht immer entwirren ließ.

»Und dein Herz? Deine Medikamente nimmst du doch?«

»Erik, ich spüre es überhaupt nicht.«

»Darauf achtest du doch gar nicht«, sagte Erik.

Aber es klang froh, er und Ruben hatten über allerlei gesprochen, darüber, daß Karin seit dem Gespräch mit Simon letzten Winter um so vieles gesünder geworden war. Auch der Arzt war beim letzten Besuch zufrieden gewesen.

Als das schöne Schiff mit vollen Segeln das Oljenäs umschiffte, atmete Mona, die sich auf Boote verstand, tief durch vor Bewunderung.

»Das Boot gehört mir«, sagte Isak mit leuchtenden Augen.

Das Großsegel wurde eingeholt, und die Fock schlug beim Ankern an die Reede und flatterte dann beim Wassern des Beiboots im Wind.

Erik blieb an Bord, Ruben ruderte allein zum Steg und rief Karin zu: »Wo hast du die Überraschung?«

»Kommt schon noch«, versprach Karin.

Wie jung er ist, dachte Mona. Und schön, jeder Zentimeter gefiel ihr. Sie hatte Herzklopfen und hielt sich mit feuchten Händen an Isak fest.

Sie konnten nicht hören, was Karin am Bootssteg sprach, doch Isak kannte sie so gut, daß er es sich denken konnte, und er wußte, daß er keine bessere Abgesandte hätte haben können: »Eine große Liebe, Ruben. Und sie ist alles, was Isak braucht.«

Und Ruben war so überrascht, daß er sich auf einen Poller setzen mußte.

Er hatte im Lauf der Jahre gelernt, sich auf Karins Urteil zu verlassen, und war, noch ehe er das Mädchen begrüßt hatte, schon überzeugt. Es war ein verhangener Tag, so daß er den Sonnenschein, der die beiden jungen Menschen umgab, sofort wahrnahm.

Er sah das bodenständige Mädchen an und erfaßte den Kern ihres Wesens mit einem Blick. »Herrgott! Was soll man da sagen?«

Dann umarmte er Mona und lachte: »Du bist mir eine schöne Überraschung.«

Danach sah er Isak lange an, und alle empfanden die Zärtlichkeit in seinem Blick und die Freude, als er sagte: »Mein Junge.«

Mit dem Fischhändler ging es im wesentlichen, wie Mona es vorausgesagt hatte. Er brüllte vor Wut, sie sei zu jung! Ein Jude, war sie total übergeschnappt! Was würden die Leute sagen, und die Glaubensgemeinschaft?

Aber dann, als er den Namen hörte und an das Geld dachte, erhellte ein schwacher Abglanz des Goldes sein Gemüt und beschwichtigte es: »Die Juden sind zweitausend Jahre gestraft worden«, sagte er. »Vielleicht ist die Schuld inzwischen bezahlt.«

Sie verlobten sich am Sonntag vor Schulbeginn feierlich im Restaurant des Gartenvereins.

Am Vormittag vor dem Fest fuhr Mona mit Ruben auf einen Besuch zu Olga. Es war seit vielen Jahren wieder das erste Mal, daß Ruben diese schwierige Fahrt nicht allein machte.

Er war auch dankbar, als er sah, wie natürlich und furchtlos Mona Olga gegenübertrat, wie sie über die Puppen Kontakt mit ihr aufnahm und ein Aufflackern in Olgas Augen bewirkte.

Auf dem Heimweg sagte das Mädchen im Auto: »Sie ist nicht unglücklich. Und das ist ja irgendwie das Wichtigste.«

Ruben nickte, ihm selbst war der Gedanke auch schon gekommen, daß Olga jetzt glücklicher war als in all den gesunden Jahren, in denen sie der Angst gnadenlos ausgeliefert gewesen war.

»Das stimmt«, sagte er. »Aber für mich ist das kaum ein Trost.«

»Ja, das kann ich verstehen«, antwortete Mona.

Als Ruben im Restaurant mit dem Fischhändler anstieß, ehe sie zu Tisch gingen, dachte er, daß das Leben an sich und der Weg des Menschen durch eben dieses Leben rätselhafter waren als jegliche Psychologie jemals erklären konnte.

Wie, um Gottes willen, hatte dieses Mädchen sich im Schatten dieses Mannes so entfalten können?

Erik hielt eine Rede, sagte das Wesentliche: »Du hast eine Karin gefunden. Hüte sie wohl, sie sind selten.«

Das Göteborger Symfoniorchester spielte Gösta Nystroems *Sinfonia del Mare.*

Liebevolle Indianderfrauen wuschen ihre Kinder in der Quelle des großen Flusses, dort wo die Welle geboren wurde, die zum Meer gehen und die Erinnerung an den Geruch der Menschenkinder mitnehmen würde. Auch an die Düfte der Bäume am Fluß, an ihren Geruch nach Schlamm und Moos würde die Welle sich erinnern, die großen Bäume, die mit ihren starken Wurzeln den Lauf aufhalten und das Wasser für eine Weile, für eine Nacht, in den Schlaf singen konnten, ehe es zur neuen Geburt im Meer weitereilen mußte.

Dort in der Mündung traf die Welle auf die Lachse, die, besessen von ihrer Liebe zum Leben, flußaufwärts unterwegs waren.

Dennoch vergaß die Welle die spielenden Fische bald. Es war die Angst, die Furcht des Flußwassers, sich im Grenzenlosen zu verlieren.

Aber die Welle wurde nicht vernichtet, sie gefror zu Eis, war gefangen, und die Kälte kostete sie beinah die Lebenslust.

Dann kam eines Tages der Frühling und die Welle brach sich aus dem Eis frei und wußte, daß sie überlebt hatte, daß sie ein Ganzes war und gleichzeitig teilhatte an allem Meer. Sie begann ihre lange Reise, zog ostwärts, und die großen Schiffe durchfurchten sie, und die großen Winde spielten an ihrer Oberfläche.

Die Welle liebte die Winde, den starken Wind, der seine Kraft zum Sturm ballte und die Welle zum Tanz einlud. Aber sie liebte auch den Sonnenwind, der die Welle in den Schlaf und in die Träume vom

Himmel und den riesigen Wolken wiegte, die am Leben der Welle durch Nebel und Regen Anteil hatten.

An der Südspitze Grönlands traf die Welle auf die Eisberge, überschlug sich vor Staunen, hielt inne, gluckste um das durchsichtige Grün der glatten Steilwände und spürte ein sehnsuchtsvolles Bersten im Innern der Berge, heraus aus dem Frost und dem Reglosen in das Grenzenlose, allen Gemeinsame, zu gelangen.

Als die Welle weiterzog, hatte sie die Farbe des Schmelzwassers angenommen und die Trauer kennengelernt, die in allem ist, das sich als Form festlegen läßt.

Zwischen Island und den Shetland-Inseln war sie schwer geworden vom Salz, hatte Freude am Brausen und dem ständigen Austausch von weißen Kronen und grünem Grund empfinden gelernt. Über den Skagerrak bewegte sie sich in schweren Dünungen, umrundete Lister langsam und mächtig, wissend um ihre Kraft.

Dann eines Tages im Herbst wurde sie an den Küsten von Bohuslän zerfetzt, begegnete ihrem grauen Tod und wußte, daß sie nicht sterben konnte, daß sie dem Meer all ihre Erfahrungen zurückgeben mußte, ehe sie wiedergeboren werden und mit neuen Erinnerungen an tiefe Fjorde und harten Granit mit dem Golfstrom erneut nach Norden gehen konnte, dem Eis und den gewaltigen Stürmen entgegen.

Simon blieb im Konzertsaal sitzen, als das Pulikum hinausströmte. Schließlich legte Ruben ihm die Hand auf die Schulter und sagte: »Wir müssen jetzt wohl auch gehen.«

Olof Hirtz, der das Konzert ebenfalls besucht hatte, kam, um Ruben zu begrüßen. So ergab es sich, daß Simon seiner neuen Erkenntnis vor einem Fremden Ausdruck verlieh: »Die Welle stirbt nicht«, sagte er. »Für sie gibt es keine Vernichtung, denn sie erliegt nie der Versuchung, eigene Wege zu gehen.«

Olof Hirtz freute sich in einem Maß, wie es nur bei wesentlichen Begegnungen möglich ist. »Kommen Sie doch noch mit zu mir nach Hause auf einen späten Imbiß«, sagte er.

Nur wenige Häuserviertel weiter standen sie bald in der geräumigen Küche einer alten Wohnung und trafen dort auf Maria, eine der Indianerfrauen von der Quelle des großen Flusses. Sie hatte eine kräftige Adlernase, einen breiten, fröhlichen Mund, Augen, die schwarz und viel zu groß in dem dreikantigen Gesicht standen, und ihr kurzer Herrenschnitt wirkte wie ein schwarzer Helm.

Das kann nicht wahr sein, dachte Simon, aber er wußte ja, daß es wahr war, und daß Maria Olofs Frau und ebenfalls Ärztin war.

»Psychoanalytikerin«, sagte Ruben bei der Vorstellung, und das war ebenso verblüffend wie ihre lange Hose und die rote Samtjacke, die sie trug, und daß ihr Handschlag fest war und ihr Lächeln breit und voller Neugier.

Während Simon ihr half, Räucherlachs, Käse, Brot, Butter und Bier aus Speisekammer und Kühlschrank zu holen, hörte er, wie Ruben Karin anrief. »Es wird spät werden«, sagte er. »Wartet also nicht auf Simon, möglicherweise übernachtet er bei mir.«

Olof Hirtz hatte seinen Dienst an der Sahlgrenschen Klinik wieder aufgenommen, beschäftigte sich nach dem Jahr im Sanatorium im småländischen Hochland wieder mit Forschung und Lehre. Die Begegnung mit den Folgeerscheinungen all der Leiden in den Konzentrationslagern hatte ihn gezeichnet und nachdenklich gemacht. Er und Ruben trafen sich jetzt oft in Gesprächen über Iza, die Bekanntschaft hatte sich in Freundschaft gewandelt, wie das geschieht, wenn man über heikle und persönliche Probleme sprechen muß.

Ruben hatte von den Larssons erzählt, wie Karin und Erik Isak durch die Jahre hindurch beigestanden hatten, und von Simon, dem Jungen, der inmitten dieser glücklichen Familie so einsam war.

»Er fühlt sich zu Iza hingezogen«, hatte Ruben gesagt.

»Wenn die Mutter so gut ist wie du glaubst, ist es vielleicht nötig, daß er sich die Flügel versengt«, hatte Olof geantwortet und die üblichen gescheiten Worte hinzugefügt, daß jeder junge Mensch seine eigenen bitteren Erfahrungen machen muß.

»Das einzige, was wir ihnen wünschen können, ist die Kraft, ihr Schicksal zu ertragen.«

Jetzt, wo sie in der alten geräumigen Küche am Tisch saßen, empfand Olof das gleiche Bedürfnis wie Ruben, Simon zu schützen, und er sagte: »Nimm dich vor Iza in acht.«

Aber er war so klug, über das Mädchen kein einziges Wort zu verlieren. Statt dessen erzählte er Maria, was Simon im Konzertsaal geäußert hatte, und er sagte, er komme immer mehr zu dem Schluß, daß das Elend des Menschen in dem Bestreben liege, aus sich eine Persönlichkeit zu machen, die ihn von den anderen unterscheidet.

»Aber das ist doch wichtig«, betonte Maria.

»Es macht uns nur noch einsamer.«

»Sind wir denn nicht von Natur aus einsam? Wir werden einsam geboren und sterben einsam, wir sind keine Wellen im Meer.«

Ruben protestierte. »Im übrigen«, sagte er. »Im übrigen liegt eine tiefe Befriedigung darin, Persönlichkeit zu besitzen.«

»Nicht am Grunde der Seele«, widersprach Olof. »Eine Persönlichkeit wird nie den Sinn des Lebens finden und auch den Seelenfrieden nicht.«

Simon sah ihn aus Augen an, die rund waren vor Staunen, aber Ruben gab nicht klein bei: »Es gibt wohl noch andere Dinge, die dem Leben Inhalt verleihen. Kampf. Die Freude, ein Ziel anzustreben und zu erreichen, alles, was eine Persönlichkeit erfordert.«

»Macht und Geld?«

»Das auch«, bestätigte Ruben, und als Olof lachte, fügte er hinzu: »Damit kann man zumindest der Angst entgegentreten. Und es hilft auch ein wenig gegen Schuldgefühle.«

Jetzt wurde auch Olof ernst und sagte, er habe im vergangenen Jahr des öfteren darüber nachgedacht, ob es nicht gerade die eigene Schuld ist, die den Mythos aufrecht erhält, daß wir anders als andere sind. Er erzählte von seinen lungenkranken Patienten aus den Lagern, und wie sehr sie sich wegen alldem, was sie hatten ausstehen müssen, schuldig fühlten.

»Das ist ja verrückt«, sagte Simon.

»Nein, es stärkt vielmehr das Empfinden des eigenen Schicksals und verdeutlicht die Abgrenzung gegenüber dem Henker.«

Ruben wurde rot vor zurückgehaltenem Zorn: »Wenn es Schuld ist, daß ich nichts finde, was ich mit den Nazis in Buchenwald gemeinsam habe, dann bezahle ich den Preis. Teufel nochmal, Olof, wir leben doch immer im Zwiespalt.«

Da lachte Maria, sie hatte eine besondere Art, den Kopf zurückzuwerfen, und ihr Lachen war urwalddunkel. Indianisch, dachte Simon. »Olof«, sagte sie. »Ich weiß, daß du den Gedanken an den Sündenfall nicht magst, aber er hat nun einmal stattgefunden, und der entzweite Mensch ist leider gezwungen, vom Baum der Erkenntnis zu essen. Du weißt ebenso gut wie ich, daß jedes Kind seine Identität braucht, ein Ich, mit dem es sich als Er oder Sie behaupten kann. Sonst geht es schief. Dann erst kann man bedauern, daß Identität oder Persönlichkeit, wie ihr es nennt, so verwundbar ist, und daß Angst und Schuld immer wieder gerechtfertigt werden müssen. Aber das ändert nichts an der Tatsache, daß das Ich-Erlebnis das Schicksal oder die Aufgabe des Menschen ist.«

Jetzt lachte auch Ruben: »Eva«, sagte er. »Immer ist es eine Eva, eine irdische Frau, durch die wir auf dem Boden bleiben.«

Auch Olof amüsierte sich, hielt aber fest: »Ich glaube, daß der Sündenfall ein Irrtum ist und die Persönlichkeit ein Bollwerk gegen Bedrohungen, die es nicht gibt. Die Zwiespältigkeit betrifft ja nur einen kleinen Teil alles dessen, was der Mensch ist, nämlich den Intellekt.«

»Du vergißt den Körper«, bemerkte Maria.

»Wir sind keine Körper«, erwiderte Olof.

»Ich bin allerdings einer«, lächelte Maria etwas frostig.

Wie immer, wenn Simon sich anstrengen mußte, um etwas zu verstehen, wurden seine Augen schmal, und die Gesichtsmuskeln zogen sich zusammen. So viele Worte flogen über seinen Kopf hinweg, die eingefangen und von ihm heruntergeholt werden mußten. In der Furcht, ausgeschlossen zu sein, begann er von der Welle zu erzählen, die bei den Indianerfrauen geboren worden war.

Alle hörten zu, interessiert. Das machte ihm Mut, er begann vom Reich der Gräser zu sprechen.

»Irgendwie habe ich mich immer in diesem Land befunden«, sagte er. »Meine ganze Kindheit hindurch war ich dort, und jetzt gehen meine Träume dorthin.«

Er erzählte von dem Mädchen mit dem Vogelnest, von dem kostbaren Ei und dem Vogel der Trauer.

Maria war tief beeindruckt: »Wann hast du das geträumt?«

»Damals als ich erfahren habe, daß ich ein Adoptivkind bin und krank wurde.«

Maria nickte und sagte, daß er zu den Menschen gehörte, die durchlässige Wände zum Unbewußten hin haben, und daß er darüber froh sein solle. Simon verstand es zwar nicht, fühlte sich aber ermutigt und erzählte von der Berlioz-Symphonie, die ihm die Schicksalsstunde des Grasreiches beschert hatte, und vom Priesterkönig, der ihm seit seiner Kindheit vertraut war.

»Ein kleiner Mann mit einem witzigen runden Hut«, erzählte er.

Er hatte sich so hineingesteigert, daß er es vermied, die anderen anzusehen, er wollte nicht durch ihre Verwunderung abgelenkt werden. Er sprach von dem Grammophon, wie er die einzelnen Sätze der Symphonie wieder und wieder hören konnte, um sich zum Schluß durch die Bilder und deren Inhalt befreit zu fühlen.

»Wo befindest du dich danach?« fragte Olof.

»In der Wirklichkeit«, erklärte Simon und war darüber selbst so erstaunt, daß er Olofs Blick suchen mußte, um den Boden unter den Füßen nicht zu verlieren. Doch Olof nickte nur, als hätte Simon etwas völlig Natürliches ausgesprochen.

»Das ist gut ausgedrückt. Manche nennen es Gott.«

»Näää«, sagte Simon, und die Erwachsenen mußten sich anstrengen, bei diesem Ausruf eines breiten Göteborger Neins nicht zu grinsen.

»Bei mir ist es ähnlich«, sagte Olof, und als er Simons Verwunderung sah, mußte er erklären: »Ich bin keiner von denen, die in Kirchen oder Synagogen gehen«, sagte er. »Ich versuche im Gegenteil so wenig wie möglich an Gott zu denken, aber ich will immer in Ihm sein.«

»Wie die Welle im Meer?«

»Ja, das ist ein gutes Bild. Drum hat es mich so interessiert, als du sagtest, die Welle könne nicht sterben, weil sie es vermeidet, sich vom Meer abzugrenzen. Ich glaube, dieselben Bedingungen gelten für den Menschen, es ist erforderlich, daß er auf ein Ich verzichtet.«

»Aber erst muß er seinen Teil auf der Erde geleistet haben«, bemerkte Maria. »Der Mensch muß Verantwortung für sein Leben und seine Welt übernehmen, seine Verhältnisse in den Griff bekommen, ein liebevoller Elternteil sein und ein anständiger Verwalter.«

Simon hörte ihr nicht zu, er hatte sich Olof zugewandt.

»Wie wird man sein Ich los?« fragte er. »Wie macht man das?«

»Ja«, sagte Olof. »Wie tut man den Willen Gottes? Das ist ein und dieselbe Frage, nicht wahr.«

So sah Simon es nicht, aber er brachte keine Einwände vor.

»Eine Möglichkeit ist, es so zu machen wie du und sich hinter die Bilder zu begeben. Aber das ist nicht so leicht, denn wer ein starkes Ich hat, hat auch viele Bilder. Er muß sich doch ein Bild von all dem schaffen, wovon er sich abgegrenzt hat.«

»Das würde bedeuten, wenn man eine Vorstellung von Gott hat, dann trennt man sich von ihm«, sagte Ruben.

»Ich glaube das. Man kann den Willen Gottes nur tun, wenn Er einem weder als Bild noch als Begriff gegenwärtig ist. Das hast du durch die Musik doch gelernt, Simon, du hast nur andere Worte. Und Worte haben keine Bedeutung.«

Ruben, der sah, wie der Junge innerlich brannte, und wie nahe er daran war, aus seiner Einsamkeit auszubrechen, warf ein: »Die Erfahrung, die du gemacht hast, wurde schon oft beschrieben, Simon. Suchende und Mystiker sind den gleichen Weg gegangen, sie haben sich des Gebetes oder der Meditation bedient, wo du die Musik brauchst.«

Simon war in seinem ganzen Leben noch nie so erstaunt gewesen. Er dachte an die endlosen Religionsstunden, an die Morgenandachten in der Schule und daran, wie er sich immer wieder gefragt hatte, wie man nur so vernagelt sein konnte wie dieser Geistliche da vorn am

Rednerpult. Konnte es möglich sein, daß er, Simon, derjenige gewesen war, der nicht begriffen hatte? Er erzählte von den Pastoren in der Schule, fragte: »Dann bin also ich der Idiot?«

Sie mußten wieder lachen, und Ruben sagte: »Nein, vermutlich bist nicht du der Dumme. Die Religionen schaffen ein System, das verdummt.«

»Jede Antwort trägt zur Verdummung bei«, warf Maria ein.

»Trotzdem muß man Fragen stellen«, betonte Olof. »Und ich meine, daß jeder Mensch, der Antworten auf die Frage über den Sinn des Lebens sucht, religiös ist. Du bist es, Simon.«

Es blieb lange still, als brauche jeder für sich Zeit zum Überlegen, bis Maria irgendwann sagte: »Ich habe im Lauf der Jahre durch meine Patienten gelernt, daß man sich, um einen anderen Menschen zu verstehen, fragen muß, in welcher Richtung dieser seine Antworten sucht, was seine geheime Religion ist.«

»Aber viele kommen ja nicht einmal auf diese Idee«, meinte Simon. Er dachte an Karin und Erik, die ihr Leben als etwas Selbstverständliches hinnahmen.

»Viel mehr Menschen als du denkst«, sagte Ruben.

»Denk doch nur an Mutter, Onkel Ruben, an Karin!«

Da lächelte Ruben so strahlend, daß es ganz hell am Tisch wurde.

»Karin gehört zu den Menschen, die nicht zu fragen brauchen. Sie lebt in der Antwort.«

Auch Maria lächelte.

»Solche Menschen gibt es«, bestätigte sie, »Ganz vereinzelt.«

»Und alle andern, die irgendwie nur von der Hand in den Mund leben?« warf Simon ein.

»Manche werden sich selbst und auch anderen fremd«, sagte Maria. »Wieder andere versuchen das Ziel ihrer Sehnsucht zu erreichen, indem sie regredieren.«

»Was ist damit gemeint?« Simon war so gespannt, daß er es fast herausschrie.

»Nun, sie suchen sich zurück in ihre Kindheit, in die paradiesische Zeit, ehe sie von ihrer Mutter getrennt wurden.«

»Willst du damit sagen, das Kind weiß die Antwort?« Simon merkte, daß er sie duzte und wurde rot, dachte, er sollte vielleicht Tante sagen, fand das aber albern.

»Ja«, sagte Maria. »Kinder haben auf ihre Weise eine Antwort, jenseits des Bewußtseins. Ich glaube das.«

Die Eichen, dachte Simon.

»Und das Regredieren ist kein guter Ausweg?«

»Nein«, sagte sie. »Es wird immer ein Elend.«

»Es gibt wahrscheinlich keinen Weg zurück«, überlegte Olof, und Ruben lachte, als er sagte: »Du weißt vielleicht noch von der Schule, daß das Paradies von einem Engel mit flammendem Schwert bewacht wird?«

Simon, der an den Schöpfungsbericht nie einen Gedanken verschwendet hatte, erinnerte sich an den Stein, den er damals in den Stamm des großen Baumes geschlagen hatte, und dachte, dann war dieser Abschied also notwendig gewesen, den er mit elf Jahren vollzogen hatte.

Später sagte Maria, daß die meisten Menschen tatsächlich vom Traum der Mutterbrust besessen seien, und da fühlte sich Simon ganz miserabel.

Aber Maria kochte Kaffee und fand eine Schachtel Pralinen, und die alltäglichen Handgriffe beruhigten Simon. Sie diskutierten über die Sprache als Werkzeug und Behinderung des Menschen, und daß wir die Dinge nie so lassen können wie sie sind und sie immerzu beschreiben müssen.

»Stell dir vor, wir könnten ein offenes Verhältnis zu unserer Welt haben«, sagte Olof. »Aufgeschlossen und empfindsam sein, ohne zu werten.«

»Nicht messen, nicht abwägen, nicht urteilen«, ergänzte Ruben.

»Genau das.« Olof klang so betrübt, daß Maria über ihn lachen mußte.

»Nimm eine von diesen feinen Pralinen«, schlug sie vor. »Ich weiß doch, wie sehr du sie magst.«

»Simon«, meinte Maria, als sie aufbrachen. »Glaub diesen alten

Männern nicht zu sehr. Es gibt auch befreiende Worte. Und du bist jederzeit hier bei uns willkommen, es war ein angenehmes Kennenlernen, wenn ich ausnahmsweise noch einmal eine Wertung wagen darf.«

Ruben telefonierte nach einem Taxi und wollte Simon mit zu sich nach Hause nehmen. Aber der hatte das Fahrrad vor dem Konzerthaus stehen, und außerdem wollte er allein sein.

Er raste durch die schlafende Stadt, dem Meer entgegen, hinaus bis zur letzten Anlegebrücke bei Långedrag. Dort stand er dann und ließ sich das, was im Lauf des Abends gesprochen worden war, kreuz und quer durch den Kopf gehen, bis er sicher war, alles im Gedächtnis behalten zu haben.

Wind kam auf, er konnte das Meer weit draußen zwischen den Schäreninseln toben hören. Die Sturmwolken jagten an einem erstaunten Mond vorbei, alle Düfte des Wassers schlugen Simon entgegen.

Wonach riecht das Meer?

Als er mit dem Sturm im Rücken heimwärts radelte, nahm er sich vor, heute nacht ein Gedicht über das Meer zu schreiben. Er stahl sich die Treppe hinauf, nahm in seinem Zimmer Papier und Bleistift zur Hand, die Meeressymphonie durchbrauste ihn, und er versuchte die Welle zu beschreiben, die bei den Indianerfrauen an der Quelle des Flusses geboren wird.

Aber die Worte wurden zu Asche, bis er seine Frage unverhohlen zuließ.

Wonach riecht das Meer?
Wend' das Gesicht dem Sturm zu
der draußen bläst und dir die Meeresdüfte bringt,
Fülle dir Nase und Lungen.
Beginne mit faßbaren Wörtern.
Tang. Salz.
Die Antwort ist nicht in den Wörtern.
Wonach riecht das Meer?

Versuche die anderen Wörter, die schwieriger sind:
Kraft, Freiheit, Abenteuer.
Sie fallen zu Boden, begrenzen das Unbegrenzte.
Stelle die Frage noch einmal:
Wonach riecht das Meer?
und sieh endlich ein, die Frage ist ohne Sinn.
Wenn du aufgehört hast zu fragen.
Dann vielleicht
kannst du das Meer erfahren.

Es war schon nach zwei Uhr nachts, aber Simon spürte keine Müdigkeit. Als er ins Badezimmer ging, mußte er Mona und Isak geweckt haben, die im Gästezimmer schliefen, er konnte sie lachen hören, zärtlich und leidenschaftlich, und er blieb in der Diele stehen und lauschte, bis er Monas unterdrückten Vogelschrei hörte.

Da schämte er sich, aber nur einen Augenblick, und als er endlich in sein einsames Bett kroch, spürte er, wie abgrundtief er Isak haßte.

Doch dann erinnerte er sich an sein Gedicht und dachte darüber nach, wie er diesem die Kraft von Musik und Rhythmus der Symphonie verleihen könnte.

Während seines ganzen letzten Schuljahres schrieb Simon an seinem Gedicht vom Meer weiter. Und haßte Isak weiterhin.

Sie machten das Abitur im Frühjahr 1947. Es war kein großer Tag, denn weder Simon noch Isak gehörten der Welt an, in der diese Prüfung ein bedeutendes Ritual war.

Das einzig Wichtige war, daß sie nun frei sein würden.

Frei von Zwängen, dachte Isak.

Frei von Eintönigkeit, dachte Simon.

Es war auch kein spannender Tag, denn keiner von beiden hatte riskiert, durch die Prüfung zu fallen.

Ruben veranstaltete ein Fest in seiner Stadtwohnung, und darüber war Karin sehr froh. Ein echt schwedisches Fest zur Erlangung der Universitätsreife wäre draußen zwischen den Felsen an der Flußmündung eine Herausforderung gewesen. Es reichte schon, daß Simon da draußen in der Vorstadt mit der weißen sogenannten Hochmutsmütze auf dem Kopf durch die Straßen flanierte. Sie schien tagelang auf seinem Kopf festgewachsen, doch bald vergaß er sie wieder.

Isak wollte an der Technischen Hochschule Chalmers weitermachen, das war kein Problem, denn sein Notendurchschnitt reichte dafür bei weitem aus. Simon wollte an der Universität Geschichte studieren.

Erik und Karin waren mit Simons Wahl nicht zufrieden, Geschichte, wozu sollte das gut sein, und was sollte daraus für ein Beruf werden?

Aber Ruben erklärte ihnen das Vorhaben, sprach von Forschung und davon, daß Simon in einigen Jahren Gymnasiallehrer werden konnte.

Das tröstete Karin, aber Erik meinte, Isak habe den besseren Weg gewählt. Diplomingenieur, das hatte er selbst immer gerne werden wollen.

»So, wie ich gern Historiker geworden wäre«, warf Ruben ein, und da mußten sie wieder einmal über den alten Scherz lachen, daß sie die Kinder vertauscht hatten.

Doch erst mußten die Jungen ihre Wehrpflicht ableisten.

Karin war insgeheim froh darüber, das waren für Simon noch einmal neun Monate weit weg von Iza, die wieder zurück war und eine Wohnung in Stockholm bezogen hatte, um dort eine Kunstschule zu besuchen.

Erik machte sich Sorgen um den Militärdienst, mein Gott, sie waren doch fast noch Kinder. »Betrachtet es eher als Spiel. Nehmt es nie zu ernst, leistet Gehorsam und denkt dabei, daß es bald vorüber sein wird.«

Simon nickte, er verstand, was Erik sagen wollte.

Aber Isak betonte mit großem Ernst, für wie wichtig er diesen Dienst hielt und daß er auf jeden Fall lernen wollte, Schweden zu verteidigen. Karin und Mona lachten, Karin nachsichtig, Mona stolz, und keinem fiel am Kaffeetisch in der Gartenlaube auf, daß Erik alles andere als fröhlich war.

Der Augenblick ging vorüber, Isak stimmte ein Soldatenlied an, und wie immer, wenn Isak sang, zog sich in Simon vor Unbehagen alles zusammen. »Daß ich es mit dir all die Jahre über ausgehalten habe, ist ein Wunder«, sagte er und erzählte von den Morgenandachten, wo er aus seinen Träumen geweckt wurde, weil Isak aus voller Kehle sang: »Felsen, der für mich geborsten ...«

Alle mußten lachen, doch dann begann Mona mit dem alten Kirchenlied und sang es schließlich mit Erik zweistimmig.

Simon war ganz einverstanden, so mußte es klingen.

»Ich habe keinen Unterschied herausgehört«, sagte Isak.

Aber Karin mochte aus irgendeinem Grund das »will geborgen sein in Dir« nicht.

Eriks Unbehagen hatte sie angesteckt.

»Vorrrwārrts mmmarrrrsch! Abteilung halt! Links um!«

Das Unbeschreibliche drohte Isak einzuholen, es kroch vom Hals zum Zwerchfell durch seinen Körper, begann dort zu schmerzen, es setzte sich fort in die Arme und bis in die Hände, stach dort mit tausend Nadeln, es erreichte die Beine, die den Gehorsam verweigerten.

»Lentov, Gleichschritt halten, zum Donnerwetter...«

»Annns Gewehhhhr.«

»Robben.« Es folgte eine kurze Instruktion.

»Auf. Nieder. Auf. Nieder.«

Das Unbeschreibliche lag in der Luft, die er atmete, im taktfesten Marschieren, in den schnurgerade ausgerichteten Reihen. Es klebte an ihm, eroberte ihn, und als es den Kopf erreichte, wußte er, daß er sich selbst verleugnen mußte, um nicht kaputtzugehen.

Doch dann war da Simon, dicht neben ihm.

»Isak, um Gottes willen, du gewöhnst dich dran, du kommst bald drüber weg.«

Und vielleicht hätte es eine Möglichkeit gegeben, wenn nicht die Mutter des Vizeleutnants Nilsson gestorben und an dessen Stelle ein Feldwebel getreten wäre. Er hieß Bylund und hatte seinen Beruf nicht zufällig gewählt, denn er hatte seine Freude daran junge Männer zu quälen. Jetzt stand er vor ihnen, dieser Neue, ein langer grobschlächtiger Kerl, der gar nicht übel aussah, dem jedoch ein unvermittelt plötzliches und merkwürdiges Lächeln zu eigen war.

Er grinst wie ein Wolf, dachte Simon, der noch nie einen Wolf gesehen hatte. Dieses Lächeln kam und ging, er war zufrieden, zwei Judenschweine in seinem Zug, das war mehr als Glück.

»Ihr da.«

»Wer, ich?«

»Ja! Und: Herr Feldwebel, zum Teufel.«

»Ja, Herr Feldwebel.«

Und dann hagelte es: Kriechen, auf, nieder, robben, links um, halt. Lentov ist eine Schande für die Streitmacht, aber etwas anderes kann man ja nicht erwarten.

Das trockene, knarrende Lachen.

Bylund amüsierte sich, dieser Sommer würde lustiger verlaufen als er gedacht hatte, in dem Nilssons verdammte Mutter sich zum Sterben bequemt hatte. Hügeliges Gelände, schützende Felsen zwischen ihm und dem Leutnant, der übrigens Juden auch nicht mochte und bestimmt ein Auge zudrücken würde. Bylund lächelte dem Leben sein Wolfslächeln zu.

Er riecht, er müffelt, er hatte eine Ausdünstung von Schwäche, von Leiche, ich kenne ihn, ich erkenne ihn wieder.

Doch Isak wählte nicht die Selbstverleugnung, nicht sofort. Er stand den Tag durch, kroch, robbte, ließ sich demütigen, beschimpfen.

Simon wurde fast verrückt vor Wut und vor Angst, denn als sie beim Abendbrot im Speisesaal saßen, sah er Isak immer automatischer werden.

Nicht erreichbar.

Wie damals auf dem Schulhof.

Er brachte Isak in die Unterkunft, legte ihn zwischen sechs andern ins Bett, die seinem Blick auswichen, und ging zum Leutnant, nahm Haltung an und begann: »Nun, Isak Lentov...«

»Dienstnummer und Name!« der Leutnant brüllte nicht, aber die Stimme war eiskalt.

Simon nannte Nummer und Namen, konnte kurz und präzise melden: »Isak Lentov ist in Berlin als Kind von den Nazis schwer mißhandelt worden. Später wurde er krank, psychisch krank. Er erträgt die Behandlung nicht, der er durch den Feldwebel Bylund ausgesetzt ist.«

Die blauen Augen des Leutnants wurden schmal: »Ist das eine Anzeige?«

»Ich wollte... Bericht erstatten. Es könnte für Lentov eine Gefahr bedeuten.«

Simon war und blieb auf peinliche Art Zivilist.

»Hat der Soldat meine Frage nicht verstanden?«

»Doch...«

»Ja, Herr Leutnant, heißt das.«

»Ja, Herr Leutnant.«

»Es ist also keine Anzeige?«

Da sah Simon den Hohn in den blauen Schlitzen, der amüsierte sich, der verdammte Kerl amüsierte sich. Verzweiflung überflutete Simon, er drehte sich auf dem Absatz um und rannte davon.

Leutnant Fahlén unterdrückte den routinemäßigen Impuls, ihn zurückzurufen um ihm beizubringen, wie man sich von einem Offizier verabschiedet. Die Disziplin konnte bis zum nächstenmal warten.

Eine verdammt ungemütliche Geschichte, dachte er. Bylund war bekannt, seine Methoden unbekannt.

Wozu, zum Teufel, braucht man Juden beim Militär.

Larsson, aber vermutlich trotzdem kein Schwede. Jüdischer im Aussehen als der andere.

Lentov, Sohn dieses reichen Bücherjuden natürlich.

Aber er ließ es auf sich beruhen.

Am nächsten Tag behielt er Bylunds Gruppe in Sichtweite und sorgte dafür, daß der Feldwebel sich der Gegenwart des Leutnants bewußt war. Aber bald vergaß er das alles.

Und Bylund holte Versäumtes bei der Geländeübung nach. Simon nahm es hin, sah aber plötzlich einen Ausweg, stellte sich schwerfällig und ungeschickt an, zog Bylunds Haß auf sich, gab dessen Zorn Nahrung, kroch, robbte, ließ sich demütigen, jeden Augenblick der Tatsache bewußt, daß er von Isak ablenkte. Das erfreute Bylund weit weniger, sein Bauch sagte ihm, daß Larsson nicht zu beugen war. Aber er tröstete sich, der Sommer war lang, er hatte noch genug Zeit für Lentov.

Abends auf der Stube sah Simon, daß die innere Leere jetzt auch bei Isaks Augen angekommen war. Es war vermutlich keine Erleichterung für ihn, Simons Qualen zu sehen. Guter Gott, was soll ich nur tun.

Es gab eine Telefonzelle in der Nähe, er hatte sie beim Kommen gesehen. Ein gewöhnlicher Münzapparat. Aber als Soldat im Grundwehrdienst war er in der Kaserne eingesperrt.

Heimlich abhauen?

Die Wachen schossen scharf, war gesagt worden.

Aber er mußte unbedingt eine Nachricht durchgeben.

Am nächsten Morgen ging Isak wie eine Marionette zum Appell, wurde angeschrien, reagierte aber nicht. Wieder wurde eine Geländeübung angesagt, und plötzlich hatte Simon eine Idee.

Bei der ersten Rast sorgte er dafür, daß er sich mit Isak allein hinter einer Felskuppe befand, Bylund war für einen kurzen Augenblick außer Sichtweite, und Simon nahm einen großen Stein und schlug ihn mit voller Wucht gegen Isaks Unterarm.

»Isak«, sagte er. »Verzeih mir, aber ich sehe keinen anderen Ausweg.«

Und Isak lächelte Simon an, als hätte er begriffen, und als wäre er durch den Schmerz wieder zu sich gekommen.

»Jetzt landest du auf jeden Fall im Revier«, sagte Simon, aber Isak hörte nicht mehr, er war wieder vollkommen abwesend.

Simon rannte zu Bylund: »Herr Feldwebel!«. Haltung, Namen und Nummer, nichts vergaß er: »378, Lentov hat sich den Arm gebrochen.«

»Was, zum Teufel?«

Bylund überkam Unruhe oder vielleicht war es nur Enttäuschung, daß die Maus seinen Krallen entkommen war. Aber er befolgte die Vorschriften: Tragbahre, Transport, Krankenrevier.

Simon begleitete Isak, Bylund schrie: »Larsson bleibt!«

Simon ging weiter neben der Tragbahre her.

»Halt.«

Simon ging.

»Halt oder ich schieße.« Aber Bylund schoß nicht, denn er wußte plötzlich, daß die sechs Übriggebliebenen aus seinem Zug über ihn herfallen würden, wenn er die Pistole zog.

Isak war jetzt bewußtlos. Der Arzt hieß Ivarsson und war Hauptmann. Simon ging bis in den Behandlungsraum mit, und während der Arm untersucht – ja, er war tatsächlich gebrochen – und eingegipst wurde, erzählte Simon völlig unmilitärisch und sehr erwachsen von Bylund, von Isaks Kindheit in Berlin und von der Gefahr einer Psychose.

»Aber warum haben Sie nichts gesagt?« fragte Ivarsson, der mehr Arzt als Hauptmann war und sich furchtbar aufregte.

»Ich habe dem Leutnant Meldung gemacht.«

»Herrgott!« stöhnte der Arzt, und da sah Simon, daß er Angst hatte.

Aber dann setzte der Arzt das Gesicht des Hauptmanns auf und brüllte: »Der Soldat verläßt augenblicklich das Krankenrevier.«

Simon ging hinaus in die Sonne, sah auf dem Kasernenhof sofort, daß man ihn vergessen hatte, erkannte seine Chance und nahm sie wahr.

In seinem Spind hatte er eine Brieftasche liegen, Gott gib, daß kleine Münzen darin sind, sprang über den Zaun und rannte zur Telefonzelle.

Er hatte eine ausreichende Anzahl Zehnöremünzen bei sich.

»Onkel Ruben, ich bin's, Simon.«

Die gellende Stimme drang unmittelbar in Ruben ein.

»Du mußt dafür sorgen, daß Isak hier weg kommt, die bringen ihn um. Ich habe ihm den Arm gebrochen und er ist jetzt im Krankenrevier, aber er ist nicht bei sich, du weißt schon, wie damals im Krieg.«

Ein paar Worte konnte er noch hinzufügen, doch dann waren die Münzen durchgefallen.

»Der Arzt heißt Ivarsson.«

Alle Gefühle schalteten sich bei Ruben aus, das mit Sauerstoff angereicherte Blut schoß ihm in den Kopf, die Hand wählte die Nummer der Sahlgrenschen Klinik.

»Professor Hirtz, es eilt.«

»Einen Augenblick.«

»Olof, ich bin's, Ruben. Du weißt, was Isak in Berlin passiert ist.« Dann erzählte er kurz, was Simon berichtet hatte.

»Die Telefonnummer von dort, hast du die?«

»Ja.« Ruben hatte sie im Taschenkalender.

»Ich rufe an und lasse von mir hören.«

»Danke.«

Kaum eine Minute später kam Olof durch: »Doktor Ivarsson, hier

Professor Hirtz vom Sahlgrenschen. Ich bin ein guter Freund von Ruben Lentov, der soeben beunruhigende Dinge über seinen Sohn durchtelefoniert bekam.«

Ivarsson hatte bei Hirtz Vorlesungen gehört und bewunderte ihn.

»Ein unkomplizierter Armbruch, es besteht keinerlei Gefahr.«

»Ich möchte ein psychiatrisches Gutachten haben.«

»Das wird nicht leicht sein, er ist kaum ansprechbar.«

»Er soll sofort per Krankenwagen hierher gebracht werden. Er braucht fachärztliche Betreuung.«

»Ja, Herr Professor.«

Ivarsson überwachte persönlich Isaks Abtransport mit der Ambulanz und erteilte Simon den Befehl, mitzufahren, obwohl Fahlén, der breitbeinig danebenstand, aussah, als wolle er protestieren.

Als der Wagen den Kasernenhof verließ, sah der Arzt den Leutnant lange an.

Der ist auch ein Faschist, dachte er. Beide spürten die Stille auf dem großen Hof, beide erkannten gleichzeitig, daß jeder von ihnen wußte, was passiert war.

Mit schweren Schritten ging der Arzt zum Regimentskommandanten, der zu ihm sagte: »Lentov. Der ist reich.«

»Und einflußreich.«

Der Regimentskommandant stöhnte, dieser verfluchte Bylund, wieso, zum Teufel, ist der wieder im Dienst?

Ivarsson wußte es nicht, berichtete aber, daß Simon Larsson Anzeige bei Leutnant Fahlén erstattet hatte.

Fahlén wurde hereinbeordert.

»Er hat keine Anzeige erstattet, nicht formell. Er hat etwas von Nazis gestottert und daß der Junge Bylund nicht ertragen könne. Ich habe das nicht so ernst genommen.«

»Leutnant Sixten Fahlén«, sagte der Regimentskommandant äußerst langsam. »Erfolgt hier eine Anklage und es kommt zu einem Skandal, und damit ist fest zu rechnen, dann sind Sie es, Leutnant, der seinen Kopf dafür hinhalten wird. Sie haben dem Regiment Schande bereitet.«

Fahlén schlug die Hacken zusammen und ging auf die Suche nach Bylund. Aber der Feldwebel war verschwunden.

In der Dämmerung kletterte der Krankenwagen die Hänge hinauf, dem großen Krankenhaus entgegen, Simon saß bei Isak und hielt dessen Hand, aber Isak war weit fort.

Der Ambulanzfahrer fragte am Tor nach Professor Hirtz und bekam seine Anweisungen. Ruben war dort, aber Isak erkannte ihn nicht, und die Bahre wurde direkt zur psychiatrischen Abteilung der Klinik geschoben.

Während Olof den Jungen untersuchte, standen Ruben, Simon und der Fahrer draußen im Gang.

»Ich habe getan, was ich konnte«, erklärte Simon, aber die Stimme versagte ihm.

»Ich weiß, Simon.«

»Es war ein Feldwebel«, setzte Simon an.

Er kam aber nicht weiter.

Da übernahm der Ambulanzfahrer das Wort, und Ruben bekam eine ausführliche Schilderung der Ereignisse und erfuhr einiges über Bylund, auch wie Simon versucht hatte, dessen Zorn auf sich zu lenken, und auch von der Anzeige beim Leutnant.

»Bylund, der ist ein Faschist«, sagte der junge Mann, der jetzt vor Aufregung zitterte. »Macht ihm den Garaus, macht allen diesen verdammten Kerlen den Garaus.«

»Es hat nicht viel gefehlt, und er hätte Simon Larsson erschossen«, fuhr er fort. »Die Jungs aus Zimmer achtzehn haben gesagt, daß er fast auf ihn geschossen hätte, nur weil Simon nach dem Unfall Isak begleitet hat.«

»Unfall«, sagte Ruben, begegnete Simons Blick.

»Ja, der Armbruch«, sagte der Ambulanzfahrer, aber in diesem Moment kam Olof Hirtz zurück.

»Schock! Unmöglich, eine Diagnose zu stellen, möglicherweise eine Präpsychose. Er muß hierbleiben.«

»Ruf Mutter an«, sagte Simon. Olof nickte, Ruben dachte an Karin und wie sie einmal gesagt hatte: Isak kommt in kein Irrenhaus, dafür werde ich sorgen.

»Darf sie über Nacht hier bleiben?« fragte er.

»Ja, wir geben ihm ein Einzelzimmer.«

Ruben ging telefonieren, blieb lange mit dem Hörer in der Hand stehen, um sich die richtigen Worte zu überlegen.

»Es ist besser, du fährst gleich mit mir zurück«, sagte der Ambulanzfahrer zu Simon. »Sonst brummen sie dir noch eine Strafe wegen Fernbleiben von der Truppe auf.«

Simon nickte. Als Ruben zurückkam, stand er schon an der Tür.

»Ich weiß nicht, wie ich dir danken soll.«

»Ach was«, sagte Simon und verschwand.

Eine Stunde später war Karin mit Mona da, die zum Glück im Haus gewesen war, als Ruben anrief.

Karin war blaß aber ruhig und gefaßt, als sie sich auf den Stuhl neben dem Bett setzte und ein paar Worte mit Olof Hirtz wechselte.

»Ich rufe an«, sagte sie.

Sie wollte, daß er ging, und sobald er verschwunden war, sagte sie zu Mona, sie solle sich zu Isak ins Bett legen.

Draußen im Gang traf Olof auf Erik, der im Gesicht weiß wie ein Laken war und zu Ruben sagte, das alles sei seine Schuld. »Ich habe doch gewußt, wie es ist, ich hätte das voraussehen müssen.«

»Aber er wollte es doch selbst«, erwiderte Ruben.

Erik ließ sich nicht trösten: »Mir fehlt, was Menschen angeht jegliche verdammte Phantasie«, sagte er. »Was wird jetzt mit ihm?«

»Ich weiß noch nicht«, antwortete Olof. »Warten wir ab, was ist, wenn er aufwacht. Karin ist es ja schon einmal gelungen, ihn zu stabilisieren.«

Erik seufzte: »Soll ich Sie nach Hause fahren, oder bleiben Sie auch über Nacht hier?«

»Danke«, sagte Olof. »Ich glaube, es ist am besten, wenn jeder von uns zu sich nach Hause fährt und zu schlafen versucht. Karin ruft mich an, wenn der Junge aufwacht.«

Im Auto sagte Erik auf dem Nachhauseweg: »Wenn die verdammten Kerle sich nur nicht an Simon rächen.«

Ruben fühlte, wie sein Magen sich zusammenkrampfte und wie müde er war. Und ängstlich.

»Ich rufe Ivarsson morgen früh an«, sagte Olof Hirtz.

Das tat er auch, aber da war es schon zu spät. Um viele Stunden zu spät.

Simon saß in dem Krankenwagen und war so müde, daß sein ganzer Körper schmerzte. Er konnte nicht mehr denken, seine Gedanken waren von dem Moment an, als er Isak an Ruben übergeben hatte, wie ausgelöscht gewesen.

»Leg dich ein bißchen schlafen, Kamerad«, sagte der Fahrer. Und Simon streckte sich auf der Krankenliege aus und schlief augenblicklich ein. Als der Fahrer ihn nach rund einer Stunde weckte, war ihm übel.

Der Kasernenhof war öde und leer, und Simon hatte nur einen Gedanken im Kopf, als er aus dem Wagen sprang: Ins Bett.

Als er aber in dem dunklen Korridor der Unterkunft stand, verflixt, wie finster es hier war, roch er etwas. Jeder Muskel in seinem Körper spannte sich zum Sprung, und er wußte noch ehe er Bylunds Schatten an der Wand gesehen hatte, wo dieser sich befand, und daß es hier um sein Leben ging.

Er selbst war im Licht aus der offenen Tür gut sichtbar, also schloß er sie schnell.

Nur so tun, als ahne er die Gefahr nicht. Einfach drauflosgehen und zuschlagen.

Sein Gehirn arbeitete blitzschnell, Eriks alte Instruktionen saßen. Die gerade Rechte war exakt, schnell und kraftvoll, auch der linke Haken saß, es knirschte, die Knöchel schmerzten, er duckte sich vor dem zu erwartenden Schlag, und als er sich wieder aufrichtete, sagte ihm sein Gehirn: Nur im äußersten Notfall, Simon, trittst du deinem Gegner mit voller Wucht in den Schritt ...

Und er trat zu und war fast beglückt von dem Schrei, und er schlug wieder zu, diesmal in den Magen, gemein aber zielführend. Bylund stand zusammengeklappt vor ihm, Simon schlug wieder zu, an den Kopf, und der Feldwebel fiel.

Mindestens fünfzig Augenpaare starrten ihn in dem hellen Licht, das jetzt plötzlich in den Korridor strömte, an. Aber Simon sah sie nicht, er sah Bylunds Schneidezähne in einer Blutlache am Boden, und er dachte, jetzt ist er tot, und er empfand eine wilde Freude.

Der Ambulanzfahrer, der gesehen hatte, wie die Lichter angingen, übernahm den Befehl.

»Licht aus!« brüllte er.

Sie gehorchten. Dann kam die Stimme aus dem Dunkel: »Zwei Mann bringen Bylund unter die Dusche. Alle andern verschwinden ins Bett, niemand, aber überhaupt niemand hat auch nur irgend etwas gesehen. Verstanden?«

Das nur geflüsterte Ja klang begeistert. Die beiden, die das Duschen übernommen hatten, kamen bald zurück und berichteten, Bylund sei am Leben.

»Ist er der Offizier vom Dienst?«

»Nja, er hat mit Fahlén getauscht.«

»Mein Gott«, sagte der Ambulanzfahrer, der Simon die Uniform ausgezogen und ihm die kaputten Knöchel verpflastert hatte.

»Legt Bylund ins Bett des Offiziers vom Dienst.«

Und er wiederholte: »Niemand hat etwas gesehen oder gehört.«

Dann brachte er Simon ins Bett und sagte: »Du hast dir beim Sprung aus dem Krankenwagen die Hand verletzt, das kann ich bezeugen. Kapiert?«

»Ja.«

Das wird nie durchgehen, dachte Simon, aber ihn beschäftigte viel mehr, daß er Bylund totgeschlagen hatte und daß ihn das so sehr beglückte.

Ich bin auch reif für die Klinik, dachte er. Und er flüsterte: »Ist er tot?«

»Gar nicht dran zu denken. Der Scheißkerl wird weiterleben und noch Generationen von Rekruten schinden.«

Trotz aller Erleichterung war Simon enttäuscht, aber bald fielen die widersprüchlichen Gefühle von ihm ab und er schlief wie ein Bär.

Beim Morgenappell erhielt Simon den Befehl, sich im Krankenrevier einzufinden. Am Eingang stand der Ambulanzfahrer und flüsterte: »Kein Wort!«

Zu der Krankenschwester sagte er: »Hier ist der Soldat, der sich gestern bei einem Sturz aus dem Ambulanzwagen die Hand verletzt hat.« Die Schwester war hübsch, stellte während des Verbindens keine Fragen. Ivarsson kam für einen Augenblick herein.

»Arm in die Schlinge«, sagte er. »Eine Woche Krankenrevier.«

Er schaute Simon nicht in die Augen.

Das ist ja total verrückt, die haben Bylund noch nicht gefunden, dachte Simon.

Der Ambulanzfahrer begleitete ihn in die Krankenstube und flüsterte: »Die haben Bylund heute morgen so gut es ging zusammengeflickt, und dann habe ich ihn ins Lazarett gefahren. Verdacht auf Gehirnerschütterung.«

»Die müssen das doch kapiert haben.«

»Sie haben noch kein Verhör durchgeführt, sieht aus, als sollte es vertuscht werden.«

Im Dienstraum des dritten Stockwerks ging der Regimentskommandant auf und ab und brüllte wie ein gereizter Tiger: »Leutnant, haben Sie die Absicht Bylunds nicht erkannt, als er den Wachdienst übernehmen wollte?«

»Nein, Herr Oberst.«

Der Alte zügelte seinen Zorn, sah den blonden Leutnant lange an und sagte dann: »Er ist kein Idiot, Fahlén. Er ist etwas viel Schlimmeres.«

Fahlén verschwand, der Alte setzte sich an seinen Schreibtisch und wählte die Nummer Ruben Lentovs.

»Ich brauche vielleicht nicht zu betonen, daß es mich sehr betroffen macht, was Ihrem Sohn passiert ist. Wie geht es ihm?«

»Er liegt im Sahlgrenschen auf der Psychiatrie.«

»Bedaure.«

»Haben Sie nur angerufen, um mir das zu sagen?«

»Nein.«

Lange Pause. Simon, dachte Ruben, hier geht es um Simon.

Dann meldete sich die Stimme wieder: »Simon Larsson hat den Feldwebel Bylund heute nacht fast umgebracht.«

Ruben fiel das Atmen schwer, aber seine Stimme war ruhig: »Das muß Notwehr gewesen sein«, stellte er fest.

»Durchaus möglich. Aber selbst hat er nicht einmal eine Schramme abgekriegt, es ist also offensichtlich, daß die Gewaltanwendung größer als erforderlich war. Bylund liegt mit eingeschlagenen Zähnen und einer ordentlichen Gehirnerschütterung im Lazarett.«

Ruben war stumm vor Staunen.

»Herr Direktor, Sie werden vielleicht verstehen, daß das für Larsson Gefängnis bedeutet, und zwar voraussichtlich für einen längeren Zeitraum. Wenn wir das Ganze nicht vertuschen.«

»Was ist der Preis dafür?« fragte Ruben, obwohl er es schon wußte.

Sie vereinbarten also in geschäftsmäßiger Form, auf beiden Seiten Schweigen über das Geschehene zu wahren.

»Ich werde Larsson zum Patrouillendienst in den Küstengewässern einteilen lassen«, sagte der Oberst.

Ruben rief auf der Werft an, verlangte Erik.

»Donnerwetter!« sagte Erik. »Was für ein Junge.«

Sein Stolz war nicht zu überhören. Die beiden Männer einigten sich, gegenüber Karin, Isak und Mona kein Wort darüber zu verlieren.

»Er soll irgendwie Dienst auf einem Boot an den Schäreninseln antreten«, sagte Ruben. »Es wird also ein Weilchen dauern, bis er Urlaub kriegt.«

Im Büro des Obersten saß Kapitän Viktor Sjövall, Kommandeur des Patrouillendienstes vor der Küste, und lauschte dem Bericht des Alten mit wachsendem Unbehagen.

»Pfui Teufel«, sagte er.

»Du nimmst dich des Jungen an?«

»Ja, muß ein feiner Kerl sein.«

»Ein Teufelskerl von einem Kämpfer«, sagte der Oberst voller Bewunderung und legte Simons Papiere auf den Tisch. »Abitur mit Auszeichnung«, fuhr er fort. »Einer der höchsten Werte, der im IQ-Test bei der Musterung je herausgekommen ist. Er sollte Offizier werden.«

Da mußte Sjövall lachen: »Die Lust daran haben wir ihm wohl gründlich ausgetrieben. Falls er sie je gehabt haben sollte.«

Der Alte seufzte.

Simon lag in der Krankenstube und schlief, wurde aber am Nachmittag geweckt, in größter Eile gesundgeschrieben und zu einem Patrouillenboot an der Landungsbrücke geschickt. Irgendwann dachte er: Die wollen mich in aller Stille ersäufen.

In dem Boot wartete ein Mann, der Kapitän war, Simon aber zum Sitzen aufforderte und ihn voll Verständnis und Wärme anblickte.

»Ich heiße Viktor Sjövall, und du wirst den Rest deiner Wehrpflichtzeit mit mir draußen bei den Schären verbringen.«

Simon hatte von diesem Patrouillendienst schon gehört und wußte, daß er heiß begehrt war.

»Ich weiß, was passiert ist, Larsson.«

Der ist ja fast ein Mensch, dachte Simon, aber er war auf der Hut und sagte: »Ja, Herr Kapitän.«

»Das heißt, ich weiß nicht, was mit Bylund heute nacht passiert ist, und es weiß niemand etwas, auch du nicht. Hast du verstanden!«

»Ja, Herr Kapitän«, sagte Simon, doch als er das Zucken in Sjövalls Mundwinkeln sah, fügte er hinzu: »Ich könnte vielleicht in einer finsteren Nacht auf See Näheres berichten.« Da lachte Sjövall, und Simon fühlte, wie sein Körper sich entspannte.

»Wissen Herr Kapitän, wie es Isak Lentov geht?«

»Nein, aber du kannst über Funk zu Hause anrufen, sobald wir auf See sind.«

»Danke«, sagte Simon, aber dann hielt er die Zuvorkommenheit des anderen nicht mehr aus, mußte die Augen zukneifen, um die Tränen zurückzuhalten. Viktor Sjövall sah es und meinte: »Das ist wohl ein bißchen zuviel auf einmal gewesen, Larsson.«

»Für Isak ist es viel schwerer, Kapitän.«

»Ich verstehe.«

»Ich glaube, das kann keiner verstehen«, sagte Simon, und während das Boot sich an den Schäreninseln vorbeimanövrierte, erzählte er von Isak und den Embargoschiffen und den jungen Nazis, die den Vierjährigen an einem Maimorgen in Berlin abgefangen hatten.

Als er alles gesagt hatte, sah er sein Gegenüber an, sah, daß der Mann feuchte Augen hatte und daß er Ähnlichkeit mit Erik besaß.

Eine Stunde später meldete der Telegraphist: »Wir haben deine Mutter in der Leitung, Larsson.«

Karin hatte noch nie über Funk telefoniert, ihr war klar, daß es drahtlos übers Meer kam, und daß man schreien mußte.

»Isak geht es gut. Er kommt morgen nach Hause.«

»Oh, Mutter«, sagte Simon.

»Er kommt zu Maria Hirtz in Behandlung.«

Die Indianerfrau, dachte Simon und schrie zurück: »Das ist prima, Mama.«

Zum ersten Mal seit vielen Tagen fühlte Simon, daß er zurück in der Wirklichkeit war. Doch dann sagte Karin: »Und wie geht's dir?«, und da wurde er wieder unwirklich.

»Sehr gut, ich bin jetzt auf See.«

Doch er dachte, wenn sie wüßte, wenn sie jemals erführe, daß ich fast jemanden totgeschlagen und Freude dabei empfunden habe ...

Sein Leben wurde einfach: eine Anlegebrücke, ein paar Baracken, Patrouillen- und Transportboote, Wachdienst.

Aber die Unruhe nagte an ihm.

Sjövall sah es und sagte: »Wie steht's mit den Nerven, Larsson?«
Da sagte Simon, wie es war: »Ich müßte mit meinem Vater reden.«

Am nächsten Tag wurde Simon von einem Transportboot mitge-
nommen, das in der Neuen Werft etwas zu erledigen hatte. Der
Schiffer wurde beauftragt, Larsson bei Rivö Huvud für zwei Stunden
Urlaub an Land zu setzen.

Simon telefonierte drahtlos mit seinem Vater, vereinbarte Zeit und
Ort. Bring Ruben mit, wenn du willst, aber nicht Karin, hörst du,
Papa, Karin nicht.

»Kapiert«, sagte Erik.

Sie waren frühzeitig dort, legten mit dem Schiff an der Windseite an,
um vom Meer her voll sichtbar zu sein.

Es ging ein frischer Wind, und das Boot riß an der Draggenleine.

»Wir müssen die Augen offenhalten«, betonte Erik.

Dann saß er mit Ruben an Bord und sie starrten Richtung Vinga.
Erwarteten ein Torpedoboot, doch dann kam nur ein Fischkutter,
und es dauerte eine Weile, bis sie erkannten, daß er unter dreieckiger
Flagge fuhr. Der Kutter beschrieb eine Kurve, näherte sich dem
Felsen, und Simon setzte zum Sprung an.

Die beiden Männer sahen es gleichzeitig, er war erwachsen geworden. Alles Jungenhafte war von ihm abgefallen, aus seinen Augen
sprach eine neue, bittere Erkenntnis.

Sie gaben sich die Hand wie Fremde, dann sagte Erik feierlich und
gefühlvoll in genau der Art, die Simon verabscheute: »Ich bin so
verdammt stolz auf dich, Junge.«

Simons Augen verfinsterten sich, es zuckte um seinen Mund, als er
sagte: »Nimm's leicht, Vater. Du weißt das Schlimmste noch nicht, ich
habe nämlich den Feldwebel fast umgebracht.«

»Doch, Simon, wir wissen es.«

Und Simon hörte Ruben von dem Gespräch mit dem Oberst
berichten, erfuhr von den gegenseitigen Drohungen und schließlich
von der Abmachung.

»Verdammt!« sagte er. »Verdammte Scheiße, Onkel Ruben, ich

werde verrückt, wenn ich daran denke, denn wenn du ein ganz gewöhnlicher armer Teufel gewesen wärst, säße Isak jetzt im Irrenhaus und ich im Gefängnis. Ist das zu fassen!«

»Nein«, sagte Ruben. »Das ist nicht zu fassen.«

Sie setzten sich alle drei in den Windschatten.

»Weiß es Mama?«

»Nein, die halten wir da raus, du weißt schon, ihr Herz.«

Das Herz, dachte Simon, sonst nichts ...

Einen Moment später legte er Erik den Kopf in den Schoß und bedeckte seine Augen mit der verletzten Hand.

»Schmerzen?«

»Naja, das heilt schon, aber vom Salzwasser brennt es im Augenblick ganz höllisch.«

Er nahm die Hand vom Gesicht, sah Erik an, braune Blicke bohrten sich in blaue: »Stell dir vor, Vater, alles war ganz präzise, jeder Schlag fiel, wie er sollte.«

Da wagte Erik seine Finger durch die Haare des Jungen gleiten zu lassen, wie er es seinerzeit getan hatte, als Simon noch ein Kind war.

Ruben ging zum Boot: »Ich hole den Kaffee und die Brote.«

Während sie aßen, erzählte Simon, und sie bekamen in allen Einzelheiten zu hören, was im Korridor passiert war, als Bylund Simon dort aufgelauert hatte.

»Zur Erinnerung wird er sein Leben lang ein Gebiß tragen müssen. Und, verflixt und zugenäht, der Gedanke freut mich.«

Er sah die beiden Männer an, als erwarte er Einwände. Aber beide lachten auf dieselbe zufriedene Art wie er selbst auch. Da fuhr er fort: »Später, als der Ambulanzfahrer mich ins Bett gebracht hatte, dachte ich, Bylund ist tot und daß ich ihn umgebracht hatte. Ich war wie im Himmel vor Glück. Und dann dachte ich, ich bin Bylund wahrscheinlich gar nicht so unähnlich.«

Sie mußten wieder lachen, und Erik sagte: »Wir haben wohl alle einen kleinen Feldwebel in uns.«

Es war alles ganz einfach, selbst für Ruben war es einfach, eine Selbstverständlichkeit.

Als der Fischkutter wieder auftauchte, schüttelten sie einander die Hände.

»Auf bald«, verabschiedeten sie sich, und Simon ging an Bord und empfand jetzt selbst, daß er nun erwachsen und den beiden Männern ebenbürtig war.

»Er hat überhaupt nicht nach Isak gefragt«, wunderte sich Erik, als sie die Segel setzten.

»Nein. Danken wir Gott dafür«, sagte Ruben.

Isak war gegen vier Uhr morgens, erwärmt von Monas Körper, in seinem Krankenhausbett aufgewacht. Er hatte ihre Nähe überall gespürt aber nicht daran zu glauben gewagt.

Dann hatte er Karins Stimme gehört: »Es wird Zeit, daß du wieder zu dir kommst, Isak.«

Er hatte die Augen nicht aufgeschlagen, aber gesagt: »Erklär's mir, Karin.«

»Nun, Simon hat dir den Arm gebrochen, um dich von diesem Feldwebel wegzuholen.«

Isak erinnerte sich daran, an den Stein, an Simons Augen. Aber dann kam ihm Bylunds Stimme dazwischen und es entstand wieder Leere.

Karin hörte nicht auf zu sprechen: »Simon hat ein Telefon erwischt und konnte Ruben anrufen.«

»Er ist über den Zaun gesprungen, dieser verdammt mutige Kerl ist einfach abgehauen.«

Karin hatte nicht verstanden, was er meinte, aber von dem Wunsch getrieben, alle Zusammenhänge zu erfassen, hatte sie weitererzählt. Dann hatte sie zu fragen begonnen, hatte versucht, Isak diese ganze elende Geschichte zu entreißen. Stück für Stück. Immer und immer wieder. »Wem hat er ähnlich gesehen?«

»Ich weiß nicht.«

»Isak, du weißt es.«

Aber die Nazis aus der Kindheit verschwammen für Isak, er konnte die Gesichter nicht auseinanderhalten.

»Da war etwas mit seiner Nase, Karin, er schniefte. Und dann sein Lachen. O Gott.«

Isak hatte vor Angst aufgeschrien, geweint, gebettelt und gebeten, daß sie ihn nie wieder dorthin schicken dürften, zurück zum Regiment und zu Bylund.

Sie hatten es ihm versprochen.

Dann war Ruben mit Rudolf Hirtz und Maria gekommen. Isak hatte sie angesehen und an Simon gedacht, daran, daß Simon für Maria schwärmte.

Er mußte eingeschlafen sein, denn als er aufwachte, war nur noch Maria bei ihm. Er weinte nicht mehr, denn die Angst in seiner Brust war zu groß für Tränen.

»Werde ich jetzt verrückt?«

Sie hatte nicht gekichert wie Karin und ihn auch nicht getröstet, sondern nur gesagt: »Die Gefahr besteht, Isak.«

Da hatte er zurück in das Unsagbare gewollt, in die Stille der Auslöschung. Aber Marias Gesicht war nicht wie das von Bylund, sie hatte ihn also nicht über die Grenze jagen können, obwohl sie gesagt hatte: »Du mußt Schluß damit machen, dich der Furcht hinzugeben, Isak. Ich glaube schon, daß ich dir helfen kann, aber du mußt dich deiner Angst stellen.«

»Lieber sterbe ich!« hatte er geschrien.

Aber das war nun schon lange her, viele Wochen. Er war entlassen worden, war zu Karin und Erik gefahren, aber ihre Kraft und die des Hauses hatten keinen Einfluß mehr auf ihn.

Manchmal konnte er für wenige Stunden die Angst vergessen, das war, wenn er auf der Werft gebraucht wurde und seine Hände ihm gehorchten. Doch manchmal wußte er nichts mit ihnen anzufangen, konnte stundenlang sitzen und sie anstarren.

Mona kam und fuhr wieder weg, er sah, daß auch sie immer ängstlicher wurde, und in einem Anflug von Klarsicht dachte er, daß er wenigstens eines tun könnte, sie freigeben.

Er gab ihr den Ring zurück, bat sie, zu gehen. Aber sie ging nicht, und da haßte er sie. Haßte sie, wie er Karin wegen ihrer düsteren Unruhe in den Augen haßte, und der alternde Ruben schrumpfte für ihn von Tag zu Tag mehr.

Maria kam abends heraus, sie saßen in Simons Zimmer, und es kam vor, daß er sich bemühte, einen Faden aus dem Knäuel der Angst zu lösen, das schmerzhaft in seiner Brust steckte. Doch wenn jemand an dem Faden zog, entwirrte sich nichts, das Durcheinander wurde nur schlimmer, wurde noch unerträglicher.

Eines Tages rannte er weg. Er kam zur Halbinsel Onsala und stand einen Nachmittag lang auf den Badeklippen, wo er und Mona sich vor nur einem Jahr geliebt hatten. Er dachte an den Jungen, der das Mädchen geliebt hatte, ohne sich selbst noch zu kennen, und daß damals ein ganz anderer so glücklich und voller Hoffnung gewesen war. Lange dachte er darüber nach, ob er mit sich selbst Schluß machen, ob er von der Klippe ins Wasser springen sollte.

Aber dafür war er ein viel zu guter Schwimmer.

Er erinnerte sich an eine Katze, die er einmal mit Simon ertränkt hatte.

Sie hatten sie in einen mit Steinen beschwerten Sack gesteckt und in den Fluß geschmissen, aber in ihren Träumen hatten sie die Katze noch lange schreien hören.

Obwohl es eine alte verwilderte Katze gewesen war, der man, wie Erik gesagt hatte, als er ihnen den Auftrag gab, nichts Besseres tun konnte, als sie sterben zu lassen.

Träume, Maria redete von Träumen.

Ich habe in meinem ganzen Leben nicht geträumt, dachte Isak.

Wie er wieder auf die Landstraße gekommen war, daran erinnerte er sich nicht, aber als er an einem Lebensmittelgeschäft vorbeikam, ging er hinein und rief Karin an.

»Meine Güte, Isak, Ruben hat gerade die Polizei verständigt.«

»Polizei, warum das?«

»Du bist seit drei Tagen verschwunden.«

Er war erstaunt, aber es berührte ihn nicht.

»Ich komme jetzt nach Hause.«

Ein Autofahrer nahm ihn bis zum Käringberg mit, von dort ging er zu Fuß. Alle saßen wartend in der Küche. Er ertrug ihre Blicke nicht, machte also an der Tür kehrt und ging zur Treppe. Dort überlegte er es sich aber anders, ging wieder zurück und sagte zu Karin: »Vielleicht ist es besser aufzugeben, Karin, und mich ins Irrenhaus zu stecken.«

Aber Karin schaute ihm tief in die Augen: »Maria sagt, es wird sich bessern, je schlechter du dich fühlst, desto sicherer ist eine Besserung.«

»Die spinnt ja selber«, sagte Isak.

Als Maria am nächsten Tag kam, fragte er trotzdem: »Wieviel schlimmer muß es noch werden?«

»Ich weiß es nicht«, antwortete sie. »Aber ich wünschte, du würdest mir vertrauen.«

Da fühlte Isak, daß er das tat, und er konnte es ihr sogar sagen.

Sie zogen wieder an einem Faden, dem Faden der Erinnerung an das Ertränken der Katze. Aber das Knäuel verknotete sich nur, wurde härter, und der Faden riß.

»Ich schaffe es nicht«, sagte er.

Beim Weggehen meinte Maria: »Wir können dich ja wieder in die Klinik einweisen.«

»Warum das?«

Da war sie ganz ehrlich und sagte, damit er nicht ausreißen und sich Schaden zufügen könne. Er fühlte, wie sein Körper sich verkrampfte, und in dieser Nacht hatte er einen Traum. Er steckte Maria in einen Sack und füllte ihn voll Steine, und sie weinte und bettelte um ihr Leben, aber er ertränkte sie und dachte, als der Sack sank, daß er jetzt nie mehr würde an Fäden zu ziehen brauchen.

Es war eine große Erleichterung.

Am Morgen erinnerte er sich an den Traum, wußte aber, daß er nie den Mut haben würde, ihn Maria zu erzählen. Er blieb, während Lisa das Haus aufräumte und Karin ihren Spaziergang machte, im Bett liegen.

Dann kam ihm der Gedanke, wegzugehen und diesmal das Boot zu nehmen. Hinaus aufs Meer, dachte er, und es lag eine Freiheit in dem Gedanken, ein Augenblick des Freiseins von allen Ängsten. Er fand sein Fahrrad nicht, schnappte sich das von Erik aus der Garage, mußte bald anhalten und die Reifen aufpumpen. Aber es dauerte nicht lange, und er war an der Brücke von Långedrag, und dort lag sie! Die *Kaja*, sein Schiff.

Wie idiotisch von ihm, nicht früher an sein Boot gedacht zu haben.

Er kreuzte in westlicher Richtung, vorbei an Vinga, geradenwegs in den Sonnenuntergang hinein. Als die schwedische Sommernacht, die keine Dunkelheit kannte, ihn umschloß, gab es nur noch das Meer und das Boot, Isak konnte kein Land mehr sehen.

Doch dann mußte er am Ruder eingeschlafen sein, denn plötzlich war da ein Fischerboot mit einem alten Mann, der schrie: »Brauchst du Hilfe, Junge?«

Die Segel schlugen wie besessen, er bekam sie nicht in den Wind.

»Das Ruder ist kaputt!« schrie er.

Sie warfen ihm eine Leine zu und nahmen ihn ins Schlepptau, und er dachte, daß er sich also auch nicht totsegeln konnte. Sie schleppten ihn in den Schärengürtel, frühmorgens erreichten sie die Rinne von Korshamn, der Schipper deutete auf die Werft an der Nordseite von Brännö und den dortigen Kran, meinte, dort würden sie ihm das Ruder bestimmt in Ordnung bringen.

Isak machte die Leine los und rief seinen Dank übers Wasser, das jetzt reglos war, als hielte es den Atem an. Er wußte natürlich, daß das Ruder keinen Defekt hatte, aber er schämte sich, es zuzugeben, also ruderte er auf die Werft zu und legte dort für ein, zwei Stunden an.

Keine Menschenseele war um diese Tageszeit dort, und dafür war er dankbar.

Schließlich setzte er die Fock, strich an der Felsenküste entlang, suchte sich eine windstille Bucht, vertäute, kroch in die Kajüte, und schlief. Ich bin sogar zu beschränkt, um mir das Leben zu nehmen.

Es war später Abend, als er vom Regen geweckt wurde, der auf das Deck prasselte, er war mutloser denn je. Hier gab es keinen Lebensmittelladen, also konnte er nicht einmal zu Hause anrufen und seine Leute beruhigen.

Ich muß ins Irrenhaus, das wird für alle eine Erleichterung sein, dachte er, als er die Segel setzte. Er nahm Kurs auf Långedrag, war aber unkonzentriert, kam zu weit nach Norden, und rammte bei Kopparholmen das Bollwerk, das im Jahr 1914 zur Verteidigung Göteborgs errichtet worden war.

Der Aufprall dröhnte im Boot wie ein Kanonenschuß, und dann stand Isak zitternd auf der Befestigungsmauer, als hätte er deren Würde verletzt, doch er ließ seine Angst nun Angst sein und begann zu handeln.

Das Boot hatte keinen großen Schaden erlitten, er bekam es mit dem Bootshaken flott, und steuerte dann mit vollen Segeln die Werft und Erik an.

Es drang Wasser ein.

Kurz dachte er, jetzt kann ich wenden, zurück ins Meer segeln und mit dem Boot versinken. Aber das Boot war wertvoll, unersetzlich, es war damals gebaut worden, als er schwer krank gewesen war, und es war für ihn zu einem Symbol des Lebens geworden.

Also hielt er weiter auf die Flußmündung zu.

Alle saßen wie gewöhnlich in der Küche, um auf ihn zu warten, doch es waren an diesem Abend mehr Leute als sonst, Olof und Maria waren da, und auch Mona, die merkwürdig klein wirkte.

Aber Isak sah nur Erik: »Ich bin bei Kopparholmen aufgelaufen. Das Boot ist untenrum kaputt und leckt vorne an Backbord wie verrückt.«

Da brannte bei Erik die Sicherung durch. »Du verdammter, verwöhnter Nichtsnutz«, schrie er. »Du bist der größte Egoist, der je in einem Paar Schuhen gesteckt hat.«

»Erik«, sagte Karin warnend, aber er hörte sie nicht.

»Für wen hältst du dich eigentlich, du verdammter Prinz auf der Erbse, segelst wie ein Idiot durch den Schärengürtel und denkst an nichts als an deine schwachen Nerven.«

»Schwache Nerven!« schrie er weiter. »Die sind verdammt noch mal bestimmt nicht schwächer als Karins krankes Herz. Du mußt endlich mit deinen Nerven leben lernen, wie sie mit ihrem Herzen lebt.«

Isak hob die Hände, streckte sie Erik entgegen, als bäte er um Schonung. Aber Erik war nicht zu bremsen.

»Wie, denkst du, wird es Karins Herzen gehen, wenn sie sich dauernd um dich Sorgen machen muß. Ganz zu schweigen von Ruben, der schon fast zusammenbricht. Oder Mona.«

Erik war so wütend, daß ihm die Stimme versagte.

»Ich habe mit Mona Schluß gemacht«, flüsterte Isak.

»Schluß!« schrie Erik, daß die Teetassen auf dem Küchentisch klirrten. »Du hältst dich wohl für eine Art Gott, der einfach Schluß machen kann mit einem Menschen. Ihr gehört zusammen, wir gehören alle zusammen, und du bist der einzige, der so verdammt beschränkt ist, daß du das nicht begreifst und deinen Teil der Verantwortung einfach nicht übernimmst.«

Isak dachte, jetzt kommt sie wieder, die Auslöschung, jetzt verschwinde ich. Aber Eriks hellblaue Augen ließen Isaks Blick nicht eine Sekunde los, und die Wut in ihnen zwang Isak zum Stehenbleiben, die Wut und noch etwas anderes.

Verzweiflung.

Isak liebte Erik, bewunderte ihn.

»Lieber«, sagte er.

»Ich bin nicht lieb«, brüllte Erik. »Und ich werde, verdammt, einen Kerl aus dir machen.«

»Erik!« schrie jetzt Ruben, und sein Rufen war so beschwörend, daß Eriks Wut für einen Moment verebbte. Doch jetzt griff Olof ein und sagte: »Mach weiter, Erik, du hast mit jedem einzelnen Wort recht.«

Eriks Stimme war normal, als er sich vorbeugte und zu Isak sagte: »Ich werde dir einen Job bei den Götawerken verschaffen, Junge. Dort, wo das Geld deines Vaters dich aus keiner noch so kniffligen Situation freikaufen kann. Denn jetzt sollst du erwachsen werden, Isak Lentov, dafür werde ich sorgen.«

231

Es war ganz still in der Küche, bis Karin fragte: »Hast du schon was gegessen, Junge?«

»Hier gibt es erst was zu essen, wenn das Boot auf dem Trockenen ist«, warf Erik ein. »Komm mit, Isak, wir holen es raus, ehe es sinkt.«

Fünf Minuten später wurden in der Werft die Scheinwerfer angeschaltet, Erik kam noch einmal in die Küche zurück und sagte: »Wir brauchen Hilfe.«

Ruben ging, Olof ging, Maria hielt Erik noch einen Moment mit den Worten an der Tür auf: »Ist schon gut, Erik. Und beschaffe ihm, um Gottes willen, wirklich diesen Job.«

»Du kannst dich auf mich verlassen«, erwiderte Erik und warf Karin einen langen und zufriedenen Blick zu.

Isak schlief in dieser Nacht nicht viel, er stand am Fenster seines alten Kinderzimmers und hatte genauso viel Angst wie vorher.

Aber er fühlte sich wirklich.

Immer wieder kam er auf das zurück, was Erik gesagt hatte, daß er nämlich mit seinen Nerven ebenso leben mußte wie Karin mit ihrem Herzen.

Und, Teufel noch mal, er würde es schaffen.

Am nächsten Tag rief er Mona an: »Willst du's wagen?«

Schon während des Frühstücks begann Erik mit seiner Planung bezüglich der Götawerke.

»Abitur wird unterschlagen«, sagte er. »Es ist schon schlimm genug, wenn du die Mittlere Reife hast, aber natürlich mußt du irgendwelche Abgangszeugnisse vorlegen.«

»Und wenn sie dann fragen, was ich nach dem Realschulabschluß gemacht habe?«

»Hast du etwa nicht hier bei mir auf der Werft gearbeitet? Klar stelle ich dir ein Zeugnis aus.«

Und es stimmte ja, daß Isak auch während der Jahre auf dem Gymnasium auf der Werft ausgeholfen hatte. Mit Karins Hilfe formulierte Erik noch am selben Abend eine Bestätigung, so daß er, ohne zu lügen, ein ganzes Arbeitsjahr zusammenbrachte.

Isak arbeitete an der Reparatur der *Kaja,* die zum Glück längst nicht so ramponiert war, wie er am Abend zuvor befürchtet hatte. Zwei Borde mußten ausgewechselt werden, aber jetzt gab es ja genügend Mahagoni auf der Werft.

»Du kannst es in Raten abbezahlen«, erklärte Erik. »Jetzt wirst du ja bald Geld verdienen.«

Isak faßte es als Scherz auf, aber Erik sah nicht aus, als hätte er einen Witz gemacht. »Bist du immer noch wütend auf mich?«

»Nööö, den meisten Dampf habe ich wohl schon abgelassen. Was ich hatte sagen wollen, war eigentlich nur, daß man Verantwortung tragen muß, auch wenn es da drinnen noch so mistig aussieht.«

»Du warst noch nie in Gefahr, verrückt zu werden.«

»O doch«, sagte Erik. »Wahrscheinlich haben das die meisten Menschen schon erlebt. Aber, wie gesagt, man muß damit leben.«

»Ich habe verstanden«, sagte Isak.

Ruben rief auf der Werft an. »Wie geht's?«

»Besser, glaube ich.«

»Dann war es also gut, daß du deine Wut rausgelassen hast?«

»Ja, unsere beiden Ärzte haben es so formuliert.«

»Eriksberg sucht Lehrlinge, steht heute in der Zeitung.«

»Das ist mir schnuppe«, sagte Erik. »Der Junge muß zu den Götawerken. Diese Werft ist für ihr gutes Arbeitsklima bekannt.«

»Oh, das wußte ich nicht.«

Zum Glück konnte Erik die Worte zurückhalten, die er auf der Zunge hatte, daß es nämlich eine ganze Menge Dinge gab, von denen er keine Ahnung hat, der Direktor Lentov.

Er sagte statt dessen: »Wir sind an einem Wendepunkt, Ruben, ich fühle, daß wir an einem Wendepunkt sind.«

Zum ersten Mal seit langem hörte er Ruben lachen.

»Das hast du schon einmal zu mir gesagt, Erik, erinnerst du dich?«

»Nein«, sagte Erik. »Habe ich recht behalten?«

»Ja, in höchstem Maße.«

»Na siehst du.«

»Du mußt dir einen Job in den Maschinenhallen geben lassen«, sagte Erik beim Mittagessen. »Die Werft sucht ganz dringend Leute, und mehr als alles andere brauchen sie Revolverdreher.«

Im Personalbüro ging alles wie geschmiert, sie nahmen Isaks Zeugnisse entgegen, nickten, stellten einige Fragen bezüglich Larssons Werft, die bauen schöne bohusläner Segelschiffe, und sagten dann: »Hier bei uns ist alles etwas größer und weniger aus Holz.«

Dann kam die ärztliche Untersuchung, atmen, nie Herzbeschwerden gehabt, Asthma, Tbc? Gut, schöne Blutwerte, der Nächste bitte.

Ein Fragebogen war besonders schwierig, aber Isak füllte ihn aus. Es gab mehrere Alternativen bezüglich der Religion: lutherisch, katholisch, mosaisch, anderes Glaubensbekenntnis?

Er kreuzte ›mosaisch‹ an. Nicht lügen, hatte Karin gesagt.

Abgeleistete Wehrpflicht? Hier gab es nur ja oder nein, aber Isak schrieb ohne Zögern: Freigestellt. Nationalität: Schwedisch. Geburtsort: Berlin.

Nach etwa einer Stunde waren seine Papiere dort angekommen, wo sie hin sollten, waren wieder zurückgekommen, sein Name wurde im Warteraum aufgerufen und der Mann hinter dem Tresen sagte: »Sie fangen Montag um sieben Uhr als Lehrling bei Egon Bergman in Maschinenhalle zwei an.«

Ein Stundenlohn wurde genannt, und als Isak ein erstauntes Gesicht machte, sagte der Mann hinter dem Tresen, daß er schon nach etwa einem Monat im Akkord arbeiten werde.

Isak verschwieg, daß er nie damit gerechnet hatte, bezahlt zu bekommen.

Er hatte Angst als er dort wegging, aber es war eine erfaßbare Angst, die in den Knien und im Magen saß. Auf der Rückfahrt mit der Fähre kroch diese Angst ihm bis in den Hals und er konnte sie in Worte fassen: Wenn ich das jetzt nicht schaffe, ist es aus mit mir.

»Was immer geschieht, ich halte zu dir«, hatte Mona am Abend vorher gesagt. Sie war unerschütterlich.

Aber Isak konnte letztlich von ihrer Kraft nicht leben.

Auf Frauen ist kein Verlaß, dachte er.

Der Gedanke erstaunte ihn so sehr, daß er eine Weile neben seinem Fahrrad stehen blieb. Was war nur mit ihm los, hatte er nicht all die Jahre Karin gehabt, auf die er sich felsenfest hatte verlassen können?

Nur hätte der Tod sie ihm irgendwann fast genommen.

Isak, sagte er zu sich selbst, ein Mensch hält sein Versprechen auch wenn er krank wird. Und Mona war, das wußte er mit seinem ganzen Wesen, wie Karin, eine Grundfeste.

Er schämte sich.

Maria setzte ihm ununterbrochen zu, seine Träume zu erzählen und sich an eigenartige Gedanken zu erinnern. Er träumte nicht, aber jetzt hatte er zumindest einen eigenartigen Gedanken vorzuweisen, dachte er, als er sich an der Fährenstation aufs Rad schwang und heim zu Karin und Erik fuhr, um ihnen zu erzählen, daß er den Arbeitsplatz bekommen hatte.

An der Karl-Johans-Gata änderte er aber die Richtung und radelte der Stadt zu. Ruben, sein Papa, sollte es als erster erfahren. Ruben freute sich, aber Isak entging die Besorgnis in seinen Augen nicht, er fragte sich genauso wie Isak selbst: Würde er es schaffen?

»Dort arbeiten nur lauter Männer und sicher herrscht eiserne Disziplin«, sagte Ruben, doch als er das Erschrecken in Isaks Gesicht sah, hätte er es lieber ungesagt gelassen.

»Isak«, begann er wieder und versuchte dem Jungen den Arm um die Schultern zu legen. »Es wird gut gehen, du hast immer geschickte Hände gehabt. Und sollte es zu schwer für dich werden, können wir immer noch auf Chalmers Technische Hochschule überwechseln. Wenn du die absolviert hast, kannst du ohne weiteres ... weniger harte Arbeit bekommen.«

Isak zog den Arm seines Vaters von der Schulter.

»Papa«, sagte er. »Lügen ist bei uns nicht üblich. Du weißt sehr wohl, wenn ich das hier nicht schaffe, ist es aus mit mir.«

»Nein!« schrie Ruben auf.

Aber der Schmerz in den Augen des Jungen traf ihn sofort. Isak sah es und fühlte sich unmittelbar schuldig, machte auf dem Absatz kehrt und rannte durch das Kontor hinaus zu seinem Fahrrad.

Mona hatte das ganze Wochenende, das zwischen Isaks Frage und dem bedeutungsvollen Montag stand, im Krankenhaus Dienst. Das war ihm recht, er wollte allein sein. Er nahm sein Boot, lag zwischen Vinga und Nidingen am Wind, reffte nicht, obwohl es außerhalb des Schärengürtels auffrischte.

Ohne konkrete Gedanken hielt er Ausschau nach einem Boot mit dreieckiger Flagge, hielt Ausschau nach Simon. Aber es war, so weit das Auge reichte, von Militär nichts zu sehen, und in verbotene Gewässer wagte Isak sich nicht.

Ich bin kindisch, dachte er. Das alles ist nur meine Sache. Zum ersten Mal im Leben muß ich mich allein zurechtfinden.

Achtern tauchte Bylunds Gesicht auf der Wasserfläche auf, der schniefende Rüssel, die bebenden Nasenflügel, doch schon im nächsten Augenblick dachte Isak, er werde direkt auf den Leuchtturm von Bödö zuhalten und einen Bogen fahren.

Er wußte, daß die Brise zu steif war, daß Erik mit ihm geschimpft hätte, aber er bewältigte das Manöver, und als er das Boot wieder am Wind hatte, dachte er, er werde es wohl schaffen, selbst wenn Egon Bergman ein ähnlicher Typ wie Bylund sein sollte.

Die Welt war für ihn jetzt ganz wirklich, und was ihm salzig übers Gesicht lief, war nur Meerwasser, dachte er, als er bei Långedrag einlief und vertäute. Er machte auf seinem Boot bis in den letzten Winkel klar Schiff, niemand sollte etwas anderes sagen können, als daß alles an seinem Platz war. Seemannsmäßig, makellos und schmuck.

Als er heimkam, rief er Mona im Krankenhaus an: Doch, es ging ihm gut, nein, er sei nicht aufgeregt.

Sie hatten schon gegessen, aber Karin wärmte ihm die Frikadellen auf, er aß hungrig wie ein Wolf und ging bald ins Bett.

Er schlief die ganze Nacht durch.

Um sechs Uhr weckte Erik ihn, Karin schmierte Brote, drängte ihm eine halbe Tasse Kaffee auf, packte die Brote, den Blaumann und feste Schuhe in einen Rucksack. Um halb sieben stellte Isak sein Fahrrad beim Werk zu tausend anderen Rädern, und zwanzig vor sieben stand er als einer von hundert wie die Ölsardinen zusammengepferchten dösigen Männern in einem Kahn, der die große Werft auf der anderen Seite des Flusses ansteuerte.

Schon im Kahn meinte er so etwas wie wortlose Freundlichkeit zu spüren. Aber er wagte nicht daran zu glauben.

Die Werft tauchte vor ihm auf, löste sich aus dem Frühnebel. Am rechten Küstenstreifen sah er die Helligen, wo die riesigen Schiffe heranwuchsen, und neben diesen konnte er die beiden Docks erkennen, eines davon unfaßbar groß.

Eisenbahnschienen, Werkstätten, Magazine, ein Wirrwarr aus großen und kleinen Gebäuden.

Wie sollte er sich da zurechtfinden?

»Ich will zur Maschinenhalle zwei«, sagte er zu dem langen Kerl, der neben ihm stand.

»Hinter der Tischlerwerkstatt über die Schienen«, antwortete der Mann mit den noch nicht ganz wachen Augen.

»Du kannst mit mir kommen«, sagte ein anderer. »Ich arbeite dort. Neu?«

»Ja, ich fange als Lehrling bei Egon Bergman an.«

»Onsala«, sagte der Mann, der groß und dick war.

Isak mochte nicht fragen, was damit gemeint war, aber er sah dem andern, als der Kahn an der Brücke anlegte, ins Gesicht, und traf auf zwei blaßblaue, in Fettwülste eingebettete, neugierige und etwas belustigte Augen.

»Mich nennen sie hier Kleiner«, sagte er.

»Lentov«, stellte Isak sich vor.

»Dreherlehre?«

»Ja.«

Isak merkte, daß man hier mit Worten sparsam umging. Er trabte hinter dem Dicken her an der Tischlerwerkstatt vorbei in die Maschinenhalle und erhaschte einen Blick auf eine endlose Welt aus

Stahl und Maschinen, ehe sie über eine Treppe zu einem Umkleideraum kamen. Er bekam einen Spind, zog rasch den Blaumann über, und in dem Moment als sie über eine andere Treppe zur Werkstätte kamen, ertönte die Werkspfeife.

Mehr als fünftausend Männer fingen gleichzeitig mit der Arbeit an. Isak hatte für einen Augenblick das Gefühl, in dem Lärm unterzugehen.

»Du siehst fast schon erwachsen aus«, begrüßte ihn Onsala.

»Unsereins ist eher an Kroppzeug gewöhnt«, meinte er dann. »Fünfzehnjährige, die ihre Finger nicht zu gebrauchen wissen.«

Er hatte sehr blaue Augen, die tief in einem schmalen, intelligenten Gesicht lagen. Dann und wann huschte ein Lächeln darüber, ließ es von innen aufleuchten. Aber nicht oft.

Er war achtundzwanzig Jahre alt, passionierter Revolverdreher, stolz auf seinen Beruf, berühmt für seine Präzision, seine Fähigkeit eine maximale Toleranzgrenze von einem tausendstel Millimeter zu erreichen. Jetzt bekam er Lohnzulage für die Ausbildung von Lehrlingen, aber er hatte sich bestimmt nicht wegen des Geldes für diese Aufgabe entschieden. Er unterrichtete gerne und konnte ein stilles Glück empfinden, wenn er ab und zu einen Jungen erwischte, dessen Intelligenz in den Händen steckte, und dem auch diese besondere Leidenschaft für das Exakte zu eigen war.

Als Isak nach etwa einer Stunde die Drehbank selbst einstellen durfte und die Maschine seinen ersten Flansch lieferte, wußte Onsala, daß er dieses Mal Glück gehabt hatte.

Die Maschinenhalle 2 war eine Landschaft, unübersichtlich und chaotisch. Aber Onsala und seine Drehbank und sein Lehrling sorgten bald für einen Kreis von Faßbarkeit, ja geradezu Sicherheit.

An diesem ersten Morgen mußten sie schreien. »In der Montagehalle findet ein Probelauf mit einem Diesel statt«, schrie Onsala. »In zwei Stunden ist das vorbei, dann können wir wieder wie Menschen reden.«

Isak nickte.

»Wie heißt du noch?«

»Lentov.«

»Lehmtau?«

»Nein, Lentov!« schrie Isak, denn er wollte den jüdischen Namen, der noch dazu stadtbekannt war, nicht weglügen.

»Toff, fast so wie bei Töfftöff«, schrie er so laut, daß es durch den Lärm bis zu den Männern an den anderen Drehbänken drang.

Einige lachten, andere brüllten.

»Hallo, Töfftöff!«

Da huschte ein so seltenes Lächeln über Onsalas Gesicht, und er sagte: »Das ist diesmal schnell gegangen.«

Aber Isak begriff nicht sofort daß er umgetauft worden war und daß mit dem neuen Namen der Jude weg war.

Eine Woche später hatte er erkannt, daß hier das Judentum keine Bedeutung hatte, weder im Guten noch im Bösen. Hier hätte er ohne die geringsten Folgen Moses heißen und eine Hakennase haben können.

Das begriff er eines Tages, als Onsala ihn beauftragte, in der Gießerei Roheisen zu holen.

»Es ist eine schwere und dreckige Arbeit«, sagte er. »Aber du sollst ja alles von Grund auf lernen, Junge.«

»Frag nach dem Juden!« rief er Isak nach, der mit dem Anforderungsschein schon unterwegs war.

Isak gelang es, seinen Laufschritt nicht zu verlangsamen, und er war froh, daß er Onsala den Rücken zugekehrt hatte.

In der Gießerei stand ein Zweimetermann mit rosiger Haut und schlohweißem Haar über dem jungen Gesicht. Albino, dachte Isak, wie dieser Pfarrer von den Morgenandachten in der Schule.

»Ich soll nach dem Juden fragen«, sagte Isak mit fester Stimme.

»Da bist du an der richtigen Adresse, das bin nämlich ich«, sagte der Mann und zeigte ein breites Grinsen, als er Isaks Erstaunen sah.

Auch Isak mußte lachen, dachte an den Kleinen, diesen fetten Riesen, der ihm am ersten Tag den Weg gezeigt hatte und ein höchst angesehener Karusselldreher war.

Onsala hatte nicht viel für Lob übrig, große Worte waren ihm, soweit bekannt, nie über die Lippen gekommen. Er drückte seine Zufriedenheit durch Grunzen aus, und er grunzte gegenüber Isak gar nicht so selten.

Das Minderwertigkeitsgefühl verging mit der Zeit. Die Angst in seiner Brust war noch vorhanden, und manchmal meldete sie sich, aber tagsüber war für sie kein Platz, und nachts schlief Isak, körperlich ermüdet, tief. An zwei Abenden der Woche ging er zu Maria, sie kamen nicht weiter, aber er mochte diese Stunden.

Nach vierzehn Tagen sagte Onsala: »Aus dir wird ein guter Dreher, ich hoffe, du bleibst.«

Ich werde mein Leben lang hier arbeiten, dachte Isak. Aber dann fiel es ihm ein: »Mein Vater will, daß ich Chalmers besuche.«

»Aber dazu braucht man doch das Abitur«, sagte Onsala.

Isak wußte, daß er eigentlich die Wahrheit sagen sollte, daß er das Abi hatte, und daß das überhaupt nichts Besonderes war, man brauchte nur eine Menge todlangweilige Stunden in einem Schulzimmer abzusitzen. Aber er war froh, daß er geschwiegen hatte, als Onsala fortfuhr: »Mein Gott, Junge, wie gerne wäre ich in die Schule gegangen. Aber du weißt ja wie das ist, es war kein Geld da, und jetzt ist es zu spät. Wenn du auch nur die geringste Chance hast, mach dein Abitur.«

»Chalmers«, wiederholte er, und eine Welt voller Sehnsucht lag in seiner Stimme. Isak schämte sich.

Sonst hatte er beim Reden keine Schwierigkeiten, er kannte die Gespräche in Karins Küche und auf Eriks Werft. Hier wie dort gab es lebhafte und manchmal sogar hitzige politische Diskussionen. Aber hier bei den Göta-Werken gab es wesentlich deutlichere Abgrenzungen zwischen Sozialdemokraten und Kommunisten.

Isak wurde Mitglied bei der Gewerkschaft.

Er kaufte die Bücher von ›Volk im Bild‹ und las sie zu Rubens unerhörtem Erstaunen sogar.

Langsam wuchs in ihm das Bewußtsein um Gewicht und Bedeutung des Geldes. Für ihn war Geld bisher so selbstverständlich gewesen wie die Atemluft, hier unter den Arbeitern bedeutete es leben oder sterben.

Es begann an der Drehbank. Isak hatte in seinem Anfängereifer gewisse Schwierigkeiten, das richtige Tempo einzuhalten. Aber die Kenntnis der Akkordarbeit war ebenso wichtig wie die berufliche Geschicklichkeit, Schande, und nochmals Schande über den, der den Akkord verhunzte. Bald hatte Isak das Tempo wie alle anderen in den Knochen, dreißig Prozent mehr, fünfzig oder manchmal sogar hundert. Er paßte sich an, lernte schnell auf die anderen zu zählen. Es konnte Streit um einen Job geben, wenn der Akkordlohn schlecht und die Arbeit dreckig und schwer war. Aber die Vorarbeiter waren weitestgehend vernünftig und nicht unbedingt kleinlich. Allerdings gab es im Betrieb auch schon mal den einen und anderen weniger beliebten Werkmeister, der sich mit Krawatte und dunklem Anzug hervortat. Aber die meisten wurden von den Männern respektiert.

Bei den großen Karusselldrehbänken, wo Zylinderbuchsen von anderthalb Meter Durchmesser hergestellt wurden, waren Fehler ausgeschlossen. Aber bei den älteren Revolverdrehbänken, wo man Schrauben und Bolzen aller Größen erzeugte, konnte es schon mal ein Mißgeschick geben. Eskilsson versaute eines Tages eine ganze Partie, und Isak war erstaunt über die bittere Enttäuschung, die Wut, die sich in nicht enden wollenden Flüchen Luft machte ...

Als er jedoch erfuhr, daß Helge Eskilsson den ausgefallenen Akkord ersetzen mußte, verstand er vieles besser. Helge hatte zu Hause vier kleine Kinder und mußte dazu noch beträchtliche Ratenzahlungen für ein vor kurzem in Torslanda gekauftes Häuschen leisten.

Während des Krieges ... hieß es oft. Und Isak bekam zu hören, daß alle Drehbänke in drei Schichten gefahren waren, und daß sie Granatenhülsen ausgespuckt hatten. Und er hörte von Schiffen mit Namen wie *Männlichkeit, Ehrlichkeit* und von dem *Panzerkreuzer Oskar II.*, die alle in der großen Werft immer wieder hatten überholt werden müssen.

241

»Herrgott noch mal!« sagten die Männer nur, die es damals beim Auftauchen eines deutschen U-Bootes vor lauter Schreck fast zerrissen hätte.

Eines Tages, es war kurz vor Mittag, überquerte Isak mit einer neuen Zeichnung für Onsala gerade die Gleisanlagen, als er von einem Jungen, kaum älter als er selbst, mit den Worten aufgehalten wurde: »Hej, du, bist du nicht Isak Lentov?«

Isak erkannte den Jungen nicht. Aber der junge Mann, der als Transportvorarbeiter tätig war, folgte Isak zu Onsala in die Dreherei und sagte, daß sie sich vom Militär her kannten, daß er den Ambulanzwagen gefahren und Isak mit seinem gebrochenen Arm in die Sahlgrensche Klinik gebracht hatte.

Während der Mittagspause, in der die meisten Arbeiter in der Baracke aßen, sagte Onsala: »Du hast also das Militär schon hinter dir, Töfftöff?«

Natürlich wurde es deswegen nicht still im Raum, die Frage war schließlich nicht ungewöhnlich. Aber Isak hatte das Gefühl, die Welt hielte den Atem an, die Zeit bleibe stehen, und er dachte an Karins Worte: Nur nicht lügen, niemals lügen, also sagte er: »Nein. Ich bin zwar eingerückt, bin dann aber krank geworden.«

»Dann warten die jetzt, wo du wieder gesund bist, wohl nur drauf, dich wieder in den Griff zu kriegen«, meinte Eriksson.

»Nein, ich bin freigestellt worden.«

»Was hattest du denn für eine Krankheit?« Onsala klang nicht mißtrauisch, eher beunruhigt.

Der mag mich, dachte Isak.

Unaufgefordert und zum ersten Mal freiwillig erzählte Isak die ganze Geschichte, diese ganze traurige Geschichte.

»Nun ja, es ist so, daß ich Jude bin. Ich bin in Berlin aufgewachsen ...«

Jetzt wurde es still in der Baracke, jetzt blieb die Zeit wirklich stehen. Als Isak zum Schluß gekommen war, wie er die Nazis in Bylund, in diesem Feldwebel wiedererkannt, und wie er einen Nervenzusammenbruch bekommen hatte, hätte man eine Stecknadel fallen hören können.

Die Stille erschreckte Isak, o Gott, dachte er, Gott Israels, warum rede ich so viel.

Aber dann spürte er die Atmosphäre, empfand das intensiv warme und starke Mitgefühl hier in der Baracke.

Schließlich sagte der Kleine, dieser große Karusselldreher: »Verdammt, Töfftöff, da, ich schenk dir mein Stück Kuchen.«

Über den Kleinen und sein Freßpaket mit dem vielen Kuchen wurde immer wieder gelacht, aber diesmal verzog niemand den Mund. Der Kleine schien alles gesagt und getan zu haben, was in diesem Augenblick gesagt und getan werden konnte.

Als die Fabrikspfeife zur Arbeit rief, gab manch einer von den Männern Isak die Hand. Und auf dem Rückweg zur Maschinenwerkstätte ereignete sich etwas, das es bisher noch nie gegeben hatte: Onsala legte seinem Lehrling den Arm um die Schultern.

Bei Maria erzählte Isak am Nachmittag von der Mittagspause und wie er unvermittelt über alles gesprochen hatte. Sie freute sich: »Gut, Isak. Das war ein Schritt vorwärts.«

»Die waren so verdammt nett.«

»Ist mir klar«, sagte Maria, aber sie war erstaunt.

»Menschen sind oft sehr nett, wenn man ihnen einzeln begegnet«, sagte sie. »Aber in der Gruppe werden die Leute oft schwieriger, ängstlicher.«

»Nicht in der Maschinenwerkstätte.«

»Wie werden sie denn dann?« fragte Maria. »Ich meine, wie läuft es zum Beispiel bei den Beförderungen ab?«

»Nun, mehr als ein geschickter Dreher kann man nicht werden, und das ist schön, denn man genießt großes Ansehen.«

»Es gibt also keinen Wettbewerb, keine Konkurrenz?«

»Nein.« Isak erzählte vom Akkord und die in diesem Zusammenhang ungeschriebenen Gesetze.

Als die Stunde bei Maria fast um war, erinnerte er sich an den merkwürdigen Gedanken, daß man sich auf Frauen nicht verlassen könne.

»Das war an dem Tag, an dem ich angestellt wurde«, sagte er. »Ich fand es selbst idiotisch, aber es war wie in meinem Kopf festgenagelt, daß alle Frauen unzuverlässig sind.«

»Und was dachtest du später?«

»Ich dachte an Karin und Mona und daran, daß sie zuverlässig sind wie ein Fels.«

»Aber es hat eine andere Frau in deinem Leben gegeben, vor Karin?«

Das Blut unter der Haut flutete heiß, Isak wurde rot.

»Mama ...«

Dann nach einer Weile: »Ich denke nie an sie.«

»Nein, das ist mir schon lange klar«, warf Maria ein. »Aber in deiner Erinnerung ist sie vorhanden.«

»Nein, ich erinnere mich an nichts.«

Maria beugte sich über den Schreibtisch, fixierte ihn: »Warum hat dein Großvater dich geschlagen? Warum wolltest du damals in Berlin ausreißen?« Sein Blick wich ihrem nicht aus, die Frage hatte ihn nicht erregt. Er hat sie sich selbst schon gestellt, dachte Maria.

»Ich weiß es nicht mehr«, sagte Isak.

»Es ist dir bei deinen Großeltern etwas passiert, und ich denke, es ist oft passiert. Diese Wahnsinnsangst, die du hast, gab es schon vor diesem Überfall der Nazis, da bin ich sicher. Du und ich, wir müssen gemeinsam dahinterkommen, verstehst du?«

»Aber ich erinnere mich doch an überhaupt nichts mehr.«

»Du gehst deine Mama nie besuchen?«

»Nein, Mona geht manchmal hin, und sie will immer, daß ich mitgehe.«

»Tu das, Isak.«

Isak wußte, daß er das nicht wollte, daß er es ganz und gar nicht wollte, aber Maria sagte: »Dir fehlt es dazu an Mut.«

»Das ist wahr. Iza, die ich manchmal besuchen muß, ist mir unheimlich genug.«

»Warum das?«

»Hat Ruben dir noch nicht gesagt, daß Iza und Mama sich wie Zwillinge gleichen?«

»Nein«, sagte Maria. »Vielleicht hat er es selbst noch gar nicht erkannt.«

»O doch«, erwiderte Isak. »Papa gehört eben zu der traurigen Sorte Menschen, die immer meinen, an allem schuld zu sein, an jedem einzelnen Unglück.«

Wie scharfsinnig der Junge ist, dachte Maria.

»Simon ist auch nicht anders«, fuhr Isak fort. »Manchmal denke ich, die sind alle viel verrückter als ich.«

»Da hast du vielleicht sogar recht«, nickte Maria. »Aber im Moment geht es um dich. Hast du nie daran gedacht, daß deine Mutter dir schon lange nicht mehr weh tun kann, daß sie nur eine verwirrte alte Frau ist und daß du selbst stark und erwachsen bist?«

Da begann Isak nach einem Taschentuch zu suchen, hatte aber keines bei sich. Maria half ihm mit einem aus, schwieg aber, hatte kein Wort des Trostes.

Als sie sich trennten, hatte Isak sich entschlossen: »Ich werde sie mit Mona zusammen besuchen«, sagte er.

»Gut, und danach kommst du wieder zu mir.«

»Versprochen.«

Sie sagten nichts, weder zu Ruben noch zu Karin, machten sich einfach früh an einem Sonntagmorgen auf, legten den ganzen weiten Weg zum Psychiatrischen Krankenhaus von Lillhagen mit Straßenbahnen und Bussen zurück.

Isak starrte vor sich hin, als sie durch die Korridore gingen, wollte keinen von diesen Irrsinnigen sehen. Olga hatte ein eigenes Zimmer, sie war angekleidet, duftete nach Parfüm, sah elegant aus, und ihre Armbänder klirrten wie eh und je, als sie da so in ihrem Sessel saß und mit Puppen spielte.

Sie zog die Puppen aus, sie zog die Puppen an.

Olga erkannte weder Isak noch Mona, aber darauf war er vorbereitet gewesen. Mona hatte gesagt: »Sie erkennt nur Ruben ab und zu in einem Aufflackern.«

Mona hatte gedacht, Isak werde Mitleid und Zärtlichkeit empfinden, aber er selbst verließ sich auf Marias Worte, daß er keine Angst mehr haben werde. Doch als er Olgas Blick begegnete, unstet wie schon früher, packte ihn eine Wut, die seinen ganzen Körper erfaßte, und die er unmöglich beherrschen konnte.

»Du verdammte Hexe!« sagte er.

Olga verstand vermutlich die Worte nicht, aber sie spürte die Unruhe in der Luft, wandte ihre Aufmerksamkeit einer Puppe zu, riß mit den Fingern daran herum und sagte: »Mein süßer, süßer Knabe.« Ihr Mund lächelte, aber ihre Stimme jammerte, als sie die Puppe an den Haaren zog, sie kniff, aber weiterhin mit dieser eigenartigen Stimme klagend und doch mit innerer Befriedigung vor sich hin lallte.

Isak hatte nur den Wunsch, das Zimmer zu verlassen, er stürzte auf die Tür zu und durch den Korridor hinaus. Er hörte Mona rufen: »Warte im Park auf mich. Ich komme bald.«

Und er saß dort im Gras unter einem Baum, empfand die Gewalt seines Zorns und hielt sich für ein unverbesserliches Miststück, pfui Teufel, sich so aufzuführen, und was Mona wohl dachte und was Ruben wohl sagen würde, wenn er es je erführe. Ganz zu schweigen von Karin.

Als Mona kam, war sie weder böse, noch machte sie ihm Vorwürfe. Natürlich hatte sie traurige Augen, als sie sagte: »Du fährst jetzt auf dem schnellsten Weg zu Maria.«

Maria war zu Hause, Gott sei Dank war sie zu Hause, Isak war unterwegs in die Unwirklichkeit, die Welt begann für ihn zu verschwimmen, und die Angst in ihm war von einer Art, daß er wußte, er würde an ihr sterben, wenn er ihr nicht entkam.

Mona ging mit hinauf und erzählte kurz, was passiert war. Maria freute sich, nahm Isak mit in ihr Sprechzimmer und sagte: »Jetzt sind wir endlich auf dem richtigen Weg.«

Sie hatte seinen Blick so unter Kontrolle, daß er sich nicht daraus befreien konnte, erbarmungslos führte sie ihn Schritt für Schritt zurück nach Berlin und in die frühen Kinderjahre. Isak spürte ihre Kraft und wußte, jetzt würde er sterben oder das Wagnis eingehen.

»Ich habe sie erkannt«, sagte er. »Ich habe das Gesicht wiedererkannt, den Blick und die schniefenden Nasenflügel. Sie gleicht Bylund.«

»Ja.«

»Ich habe so eine Wut gekriegt, ich war wie wahnsinnig und bin durch die Wohnung gerast, und sie hat mich an den Haaren gezogen und mich gekniffen und hat gejammert, aber es hat ihr die ganze Zeit Freude bereitet. Und dann ...«

»Dann?«

»Dann bin ich verschwunden«, sagte Isak. »Ich bin genau so verschwunden wie beim Militär. Aber dann ...«

»Aber dann?«

»Dann kam Großvater nach Hause und hat mich geschlagen.«

»Deine Mutter war ein Scheusal«, sagte Maria.

»Ja!« schrie er auf, denn jetzt war sie wieder da, die große Wut, die alles zur Wirklichkeit werden ließ, und er schrie, er werde ihr die Augen ausstechen und ihr die Brüste abschneiden und ihr einen Pfahl in die Fotze rammen.

Maria stachelte ihn an.

»Gut, Isak, gut! Gib's ihr, Isak!«

Und der Schmerz war unerträglich, war aber doch zu ertragen, und die Welt war vollkommen deutlich.

Isak waren die Augen aufgegangen, endlich.

Flimmernde Hitze lag zwischen den kahlen Schäreninseln. Die Männer, die im Land der großen Finsternis die lange Küste überwachten und die Sonne liebten, lernten sie nun fürchten.

Sie hatten die Sonne immer gesucht, hatten gelernt, jeden Sonnenstrahl auszunutzen. Aber jetzt saßen sie dicht beisammen wie Fliegen auf dem Leim, im Schatten jener Segel, die sie zwischen sich und der Unbarmherzigen spannen konnten.

Jeden Morgen erhob sich die Sonne über dem Land, zur Mittagszeit hatte sie auf dem Meeresspiegel ihre Kraft vervielfältigt und goß besinnungslos ihre sengende Glut über allem aus, heizte Felsen und Anlegeplätze auf, daß es unter den Füßen brannte. Es gab keinen schützenden Baum, nicht einen grünen Halm, auf dem die Augen hätten verweilen können.

Es war August und die Hitzewelle beherrschte alles.

»Bald wird das ganze verdammte Kattegatt kochen«, sagten die Männer, aber das Meer gärte nur so von Quallen. Um kurz baden und sich für ein paar spärliche Minuten abkühlen zu können, säuberten sie eine Bucht von dem schleimigen Getier. Aber das Meer legte sich als brennendes Salz auf ihre ausgedörrten Körper und schmerzte entsetzlich.

An dem Tag, als sie sich die letzte Dose Nivea brüderlich teilten, mußten zwei Rothaarige an Land und ins Lazarett gebracht werden.

Simon hatte es leichter als die meisten, seine Haut wurde tiefbraun und lederartig.

»Du siehst aus wie ein verdammter Wüstenscheich«, sagte eines Abends jemand, und Simons blendend weißes Lachen blitzte wie eine

Überraschung aus all dem Braun. Aber er gedachte seiner uralten Vorväter und deren Wanderungen durch die Wüsten des Sinai unter einer Sonne, die unbarmherziger war als diese schwedische hier, und an die lederne Haut, die sie entwickelt hatten, um zu überleben.

Zum Erstaunen seiner Kameraden las er abends in der Bibel, was ihm den unverdienten Ruf einbrachte, religiös zu sein. Doch dann kam von Ruben ein Paket mit der von Bendixon verfaßten zweibändigen Geschichte Israels. Und so verbrachte Simon die Abende mit Jesaja, Jeremia, Esra und Nehemia im fruchtlosen Versuch, zwischen Mythos und Geschichte zu unterscheiden.

Doch seine Träume waren erfüllt von Bäumen, von rätselhaften irdischen Riesen, deren Kronen Schutz und Schatten gewährten. Hohe Espen zeichneten ihre Spitzenmuster in den Himmel, alte Eichen schenkten Kraft und Weisheit, und weit ausladende Nadelbäume luden zum Verweilen in Vogelgezwitscher und Waldesrauschen ein.

Als er vom Schreien der Möwen und den Flüchen der Kameraden geweckt wurde und sah, wie die Sonne ihre bedrohliche Wanderung über den Himmel begann, dachte er, sobald er Urlaub bekäme, würde er durch die Wälder an dem langen See entlang wandern, an dem Ingas kleines Bauernhaus sich auf einer Anhöhe an den Hang schmiegte.

In der Nacht, die das Gewitter brachte, waren sie alle wie närrisch, rannten nackt aus den Baracken hinaus auf die Klippen, standen dort und ließen Haut und Haar, Lippen und Augen trinken. Sie gaben sich dem Wolkenbruch hin und blieben stehen bis sie froren und einer von ihnen sagte, verdammt, wie wunderbar, nie wieder werde ich mich über Kälte und Dunkelheit beklagen.

Es war eine Aussage, die er dann im Dezember oft genug zu hören bekommen sollte, als es schon nachmittags um drei stockfinster war, das Meer tobte, und der eisige Wind die Kleider bis auf die Knochen durchdrang.

Simon hatte inzwischen zweimal Urlaub bekommen, der erste war das reinste Fest gewesen, und Karin hatte alle seine Lieblingsgerichte gekocht. Er hätte an einem Samstagvormittag kommen sollen, hatte aber die Gelegenheit wahrgenommen, schon am Freitagnachmittag an Bord eines Bootes zu gehen, das zur Neuen Werft mußte. Er fand Karin mit einer Schüssel Erbsen auf dem Schoß allein in der Küche vor, und er ging ohne Zögern auf sie zu und legte seinen Kopf in ihre Schürze, sog ihren Duft ein und fühlte ihre Hände über seinen Nakken streichen.

Da dachte Simon, daß dieses sich Zurücksuchen in die Kindheit doch auch seinen Reiz hatte. Zumindest für ganz kurze Zeit.

Denn dann schauten sie einander genauer an, und er sah, daß sich viel verändert hatte, daß sie kleiner war als er sie in Erinnerung hatte, älter und mitgenommener. Große Zärtlichkeit überkam ihn. Ein fast schmerzliches Bedürfnis, sie zu behüten und zu erfreuen.

Vogel der Trauer, dachte er, der gute Vogel der Trauer.

Und Karin sah, daß der Junge, der da vor ihr stand, jetzt erwachsen war, daß es da eine Härte und eine Kraft gab, die sie einschüchterte.

Ein Mann, dachte sie, und in dem Gedanken lag Entfremdung und Trauer.

Doch dann besann sie sich, sagte sich, daß sie nicht ganz bei Trost sei, was hatte sie denn erwartet, und hatte sie sich nicht immer gerade dafür eingesetzt, daß Simon erwachsen und selbständig würde?

Am Wochenende nach dem schweren Gewitter erfüllte sich Simon seine Träume, rief Karin von der Landungsbrücke in der Nähe der Kaserne an und sagte: »Hör zu, Mama, ich hab vor, Inga mal zu besuchen.«

Er merkte der Stille am anderen Ende an, daß Angst dahinter steckte. Doch dann kam die Stimme zurück, voll Zuversicht wie immer. »Tu das, mein Junge.«

»Ich kann mit einem Kameraden fahren, der in dieser Gegend zu Hause ist und von seinem Bruder mit dem Auto abgeholt wird.«

»Was für ein Glück, Simon.«

Dann nach einem weiteren Schweigen: »Was meinst du, soll ich eine Vorwarnung durchtelefonieren?«

»Ja, das wäre wohl nicht schlecht«, antwortete Simon.

Er stieg hinter der Gemischtwarenhandlung aus, dort, wo der Waldweg zum See von der Landstraße abzweigte.

»Findest du hin?«

»Gar keine Frage.«

»Wir holen dich Sonntag so gegen fünf wieder ab.«

»Gut, tschüs und danke!«

Dann ging er unter den Laubkronen weiter und fand Ruhe unter den großen Bäumen.

Sein, nicht tun, dachte er.

Er sah, daß die Hitze den Bäumen zugesetzt hatte, so manches abgefallene Blatt leuchtete schon golden im Moos. Die lange Vorbereitung auf den Winter hatte begonnen, die Bäume stellten allmählich ihren Säftekreislauf ein, um in Schlaf zu versinken und nur in ihren Träumen zu leben.

Er kam zu einer Lichtung, einem Kahlschlag im Wald, wo man aus Respekt vor Größe und Alter eine Eiche hatte stehen lassen. Es war warm, Simon zog die Uniformjacke aus, rollte sie zu einem Kissen zusammen, legte sich hin und sah in die Krone hinauf, die immer noch dunkelgrün war, fast undurchdringlich.

Der Baum hatte Frieden mit sich selbst geschlossen, die Art von Frieden, der allen lebenden Geschöpfen zuteil wird, wenn sie sich dem Rätselhaften ergeben.

Er schlief eine Weile in dem grünen Schatten, ehe er zum See und dem Haus weiterging, in dem Inga ihn erwartete. Sie hatte aufgeräumt, alles schön hergerichtet, sie wurde glühend rot, als er am Waldrand auftauchte, und sie sagte nur: »Du willst sicher Kaffee haben.«

Inga hatte schon vor Monaten erfahren, daß Simon über alles Bescheid wußte, und sie hatte sich viele Bilder von dem Augenblick ausgemalt, wenn er durch den Wald kommen und sie beide zusammentreffen und endlich über alles würden sprechen können.

Während all seiner Kinderjahre hatte sie Abstand zu ihm gehalten, ängstlich hatte sie den quecksilbrigen Jungen aus den Augenwinkeln beobachtet. Als aber Karin und Erik im Frühjahr hier gewesen waren und Inga bei dieser Gelegenheit erfuhr, daß Simon nun alles wußte, hatte sie ihr Abstandnehmen niedergerissen wie man einen alten Zaun niederreißt, wenn er keinen Schutz vor dem Sturm mehr bietet.

Sie war dankbar für die Monate, die Simon hatte verstreichen lassen, sie hatte die Zeit gebraucht, um sich eine Vorstellung davon zu machen, was jetzt geschehen sollte. Aber sie hatte sich nicht vorgestellt, daß er so erwachsen war, so gut aussah und dem Spielmann so ähnlich. Das Gespräch beim Kaffeetrinken drehte sich zäh ums Wetter, die Hitzewelle und den Regen, der viel zu spät gekommen war. Inga hatte ihre Kühe verkauft, das konnte sie erzählen. Und Arbeit in der Schule gekriegt, bei der Schülerspeisung.

»Da hast du einen weiten Weg«, meinte Simon.

»Ja, aber eigentlich gar nicht so schlimm.« Sie konnte, bis der Schnee kam, mit dem Rad fahren, dann würde sie den Tretschlitten nehmen. Der Schneepflug machte den Weg befahrbar.

Ihm war bewußt, daß sie über die Arbeit froh war, weil sie dadurch mit Menschen zusammenkam und Gemeinschaft erlebte.

Bei Inga gab es keine Bitterkeit und auch keine Traurigkeit wie bei Karin. Eher eine Art Verwunderung in all dem Erdgebundenen.

Wolken zogen auf und die Winde brachten eine Ahnung von der Kühle des Herbstes mit. Sie gingen ins Haus.

»Es wird schon alles gelb«, sagte Inga. »Ist dir das aufgefallen?«

»Ja.« Er dachte an das falsche Gold im Moos und lachte sein neues weißes Lächeln in all der Bräune. Dann holte er tief Luft, und er nahm all seinen Mut zusammen für diese Frage: »Sehe ich ihm ähnlich?«

»Ja, bei Gott«, nickte Inga. »Wenn er hier neben uns stünde, hätte man Mühe, euch auseinanderzuhalten.«

Dann aber dachte sie, das sei wohl nicht wahr. Simon war derber, größer, besaß mehr an Kraft und weniger an Traum.

Es war zwischen ihnen jetzt eine gewisse Spannung entstanden. Deshalb war es eine Erleichterung, daß er das zu benennen gewagt hatte, worüber sie sprechen mußten. Inga versuchte ihrer Unruhe in einer gewissen Geschäftigkeit Luft zu verschaffen, sie spaltete Kleinholz, machte Feuer im Küchenherd.

»Hier ist kalt, findest du nicht? Ich habe einen Hefeteig angesetzt, da kommt die Herdwärme gerade recht.«

Simon fror nicht. Er sah sich in dem kleinen Haus um, als sähe er alles zum ersten Mal, spürte die Geborgenheit und das Wohlbehagen, das es unter niedrigen Dächern in alten Häusern immer gibt. Er dachte erstaunt, daß es hier schön war allein schon durch das Licht, das durch die kleinen Fenster drang und die bunten Flickenteppiche auf den breiten Bodendielen zum Leben erweckte.

Inga machte, wie es schien, aus lauter Tatendrang auch in der großen Stube Feuer im Kachelofen. Jetzt wurde es so warm, daß Simon die Uniformjacke ausziehen mußte, in Hemdsärmeln im Schaukelstuhl saß und fragte: »War er oft hier im Haus?«

»O nein«, erwiderte Inga. »Hier lagen Vater und Mutter im Sterben. Wir sind nie ins Haus gegangen, wir haben uns am Bach getroffen.«

»Es war ein so wundervoll warmer und schöner Frühling«, fuhr sie fort, und bei diesen Worten überkam sie eine tiefe Ruhe, sie konnte sich an den Tisch setzen und mit dem Erzählen beginnen.

Sie fand die richtigen Worte, sie fielen, wie sie sollten, und wie sie es sich den Sommer über ausgedacht hatte, als sie auf Simon gewartet hatte.

Schließlich war sie beim letzten Abend angekommen.

»Ich wußte, daß er sich verabschieden würde, denn seine Geige klang an diesem Abend besonders traurig. Darum war ich gar nicht so verwundert, als er nicht wiederkam.«

In ihrer Stimme lag Wehmut wie ein dünner blauer Ton.

»Auch nicht traurig?«

»Doch«, sagte sie. »Aber weißt du, ich hatte es ja die ganze Zeit gewußt. Wir beide waren nicht für einander geschaffen. Er war zu fein für mich.«

Simon sah es vor sich, wie sie sich zur Erde gebeugt und das Joch aufgenommen hatte, wie es bei den Bauersfrauen durch alle Zeiten der Brauch gewesen war, demütig und dankbar für das Vergangene.

»Er war nicht richtig von dieser Welt«, sagte sie. »Irgendwann später habe ich mir eingebildet, ich hätte das alles nur geträumt. Aber dann bist du in meinem Leib gewachsen.«

»Hat es lange gedauert, bis du gewußt hast, daß du ein Kind erwartest?«

»Ja, lange. Ich habe es wohl nicht zu begreifen gewagt. Ich war schon im November, als Karin kam, dick und schwer, und eigentlich habe ich es wohl erst begriffen, als sie es aussprach.«

»Du kriegst ein Kind, Inga«, hatte Karin gesagt. Noch heute klang es ihr in den Ohren, und sie konnte noch immer die gewaltige Angst von damals im ganzen Körper spüren, als sie sie annehmen mußte, diese Schande wegen des Kindes, das in ihr wuchs.

Verleugnet, dachte Simon. Aber er war nicht erstaunt, er konnte sich von seinen Kindheitsträumen her daran erinnern. Verleugnet und dann verlassen zwischen den gekachelten Wänden des weit von den Bäumen entfernten Krankenhauses, fern vom Rauschen der Kronen und dem Licht über dem See.

»Später bekam ich einen Brief«, sagte Inga.

»Ich weiß, aber Erik hat dich im Krieg dann gezwungen, ihn zu verbrennen.«

»Erik konnte mich doch dazu nicht zwingen«, sagte sie unerschütterlich wie der Boden, auf dem sie stand.

»Er hat im Frühjahr 1940 ganz hysterisch angerufen und ich dachte bei mir, wenn die Deutschen kommen, habe ich Zeit genug, den Brief im Hohlraum der Eiche hinter der Scheune zu verstecken. Aber die Deutschen kamen nicht. Der Brief liegt also noch im Sekretär, wo er immer gelegen hat.« Simon bekam Herzklopfen.

Inga nahm einen Schlüssel zur Hand, schloß den alten Sekretär auf und entnahm einer Schublade eine verdeckte Messingdose.

»Ich habe den Brief damals in die Dose getan, als ich dachte, daß ich ihn vielleicht würde in der Eiche verstecken müssen«, sagte sie.

Sie konnte den Deckel nicht öffnen. Sie mußte in der Küche ein Messer holen, um ihn zu lockern.

Deutsche Briefmarken, abgestempelt am 4. März 1929 in Berlin. Geöffnet, nie gelesen.

»Ich habe die Sprache ja nicht verstanden. Wir haben nie miteinander reden können«, sagte Inga und Simon dachte, warum ist das Leben nur so unbegreiflich, so unfaßbar traurig.

»Ich habe die Bodenkammer für dich hergerichtet, dir oben das Bett gemacht«, sagte Inga, und Simon dachte, daß sie seit Karins Anruf eine Menge erledigt hatte. Sie hatte saubergemacht, ihr schönstes blaues Kleid gebügelt, einen Hefeteig angesetzt, in der Bodenkammer das Bett überzogen.

»Geh nach oben, da bist du allein«, forderte Inga ihn auf. »Du mußt allein sein, wenn du den Brief liest. Kannst du deutsch?«

»Ja«, sagte Simon und ging die Treppe hinauf, die unter seinen Schritten knarrte. Er legte sich mit dem Brief auf dem Bauch der Länge nach auf den gehäkelten Überwurf. Herrgott. Sein Mund war trocken, er ging in die Küche zurück, um sich einen Becher Wasser zu holen, blieb lange stehen und sah Inga zu, wie sie das aufgegangene Hefegebäck in den Ofen schob.

»Du hast nicht zufällig ein Bier?« fragte er.

»Ach nein«, sagte Inga. »Du wirst verstehen, ich hatte ja gar keine Zeit in den Laden zu gehen, und schon gar nicht habe ich daran gedacht, daß du ein Mann geworden bist, der ein Bier brauchen könnte.«

Darüber mußten sie lachen. Dann holte Inga Saft, den Saft aus schwarzen Johannisbeeren, die sie im letzten Sommer geerntet hatte. Also hatte Simon den Geschmack der Kindheit im Mund und den Duft der Kindheit nach frisch gebackenem Milchbrot in der Nase, als er sich oben in der Kammer überwand, den Brief zu lesen.

Es war ein Liebesbrief voll romantischer Worte. Waldfee, meine Waldfee, nannte er sie. Er hoffte, im Herbst wiederkommen zu können, hatte sich erneut um einen Lehrerposten an der Volkshochschule beworben. Aber er mußte sicher sein können, daß sie auf ihn wartete, daß ihre Sehnsucht nach ihm ebenso groß war, wie die seine nach ihr. Ob sie wohl schreiben, ein Lebenszeichen senden wolle. Tausend Küsse. Simon Habermann und eine Adresse in Berlin.

Simon spürte unmittelbar nichts als Enttäuschung, obwohl er sich fragte, was er denn eigentlich erwartet, was er erhofft hatte. Der jüdische Spielmann konnte nicht wissen, daß seine Liebe Frucht getragen hatte, daß es da einen kleinen Jungen gab.

Simon legte sich das Kissen übers Gesicht und ließ die Tränen kommen. Sie versiegten nach einer halben Stunde, aber er empfand eine Wehmut so groß wie das Meer.

Als er zum Waschtisch ging, um sich das Gesicht abzuspülen, sah er, daß das Wasser in der Kanne gelb und abgestanden war. Inga hatte die Kammer schon vor langer Zeit vorbereitet, sie hatte ihn seit langem erwartet.

Inga saß in der Küche. Sie hatte rote Flecken auf den Wangen, aber sonst war sie blaß, sehr blaß sogar. Simon setzte sich zu ihr und begann den Brief zu übersetzen.

»Mitt skogsrå…«, begann er. »Ich bin mir nicht ganz sicher, ob das der richtige Sinn des Wortes ›Waldfee‹ ist, aber es wird ungefähr hinkommen.«

Dann folgte all das von Sehnsucht, Liebe, Küssen. Und die Bitte um eine Antwort.

»Aber warum ist er nicht gekommen?« Ingas Stimme war kaum hörbar, sie hatte die Hände vors Gesicht geschlagen, doch Simon erkannte an ihren Schultern, wie das Weinen in Wellen über sie kam.

»Er hat auf Antwort gewartet«, sagte Simon.

»Aber er wußte doch, daß ich nicht verstehen konnte, was er schrieb.«

»Er hat wahrscheinlich angenommen, daß du zu jemand gehst, der den Brief übersetzen kann.«

Simons Stimme war voll Bitterkeit, als er weiterlas: »Schreibe mir, gib mir ein Lebenszeichen, damit ich sicher sein kann, daß es Dich gibt, daß Du nicht nur ein wilder und schöner Traum bist.«

»Gott im Himmel!« stöhnte Inga. »Zu wem sollte ich denn gehen? Begreif doch, daß niemand es wissen durfte. Die Schande, Simon, ich wäre vor Scham gestorben.«

»Meinetwegen«, murmelte Simon.

»Ja«, erwiderte Inga, und als Simon sich erhob und aus dem Haus lief, rannte sie ihm rufend nach: »Du verstehst das nicht, Simon, du wirst nie verstehen können, wie das früher war!«

Er blieb stehen, wandte sich halb um und sagte: »Nein, das kann ich wohl nicht verstehen.«

»Du hast es doch so gut gehabt, Simon, du hast es dort bei Karin und Erik doch so gut gehabt!«

Karin, dachte er in wildem Zorn, Karin hätte den Brief übersetzen lassen können, hätte nach Berlin schreiben und von dem Kind berichten können. Doch im nächsten Moment wußte er, daß sie das nie gewollt hatte, daß sie den Brief ungelesen haben wollte, während sie sich um ihr Baby kümmerte und daß sie so wenig wie möglich an den Vater des kleinen Jungen mit den unglaublich dunklen Augen erinnert werden wollte.

»Ich geh ein bißchen in den Wald, bin zum Essen wieder da.«

Seine Stimme war lauter als beabsichtigt, war aufgeladen mit dem Zorn, der nicht Inga galt, sondern Karin, und er versuchte zu lächeln, um es zu vertuschen. Aber Inga war schon ins Haus zurückgegangen.

Er kletterte durchs Geröll hangaufwärts, setzte sich hin und blickte über den See, dessen tiefes Blau ganz mit seiner Wehmut übereinstimmte. Aber die Bäume schwiegen, blieben stumm, und er wußte genau, daß ihr Friede nicht für ihn da war, daß seine Heimat die tausend unruhigen Fragen waren, die vergeblich nach Antworten suchten.

Auf dem Rückweg dachte er, wenn Habermann es mit seinem Brief ernst gemeint hätte, wäre es ihm immerhin möglich gewesen, ihn seinerseits übersetzen zu lassen. Es hatte in den zwanziger Jahren eine Menge Schweden in Berlin gegeben.

Im Haus erwartete ihn Inga mit einer Fleischsuppe, die er, wie sie wußte, besonders gern mochte, mit frischem Brot und Bier. Sie war mit dem Rad den weiten Weg bis zum Kaufladen gefahren und hatte ein paar Flaschen Bier geholt.

Er trank gierig, aber es war nur alkoholarmes Leichtbier und verschaffte ihm keine Entspannung.

Keiner der beiden hatte in dieser Nacht wohl besonders viel geschlafen.

Beim Frühstück sagte Simon: »Den Brief kannst du behalten. Er ist ja an dich gerichtet. Ich schreibe dir die Übersetzung auf die Rückseite.«

Aber Inga meinte: »Ich habe die ganze Nacht nachgedacht, und ich weiß genau, daß du mich auslachen wirst. Aber gesagt will ich es haben, daß ich nämlich zu dem Schluß gekommen bin, daß das alles nur deinetwegen geschehen ist, damit du auf die Welt kommst.«

Die ist verrückt, dachte Simon, aber er lachte nicht, und so fuhr Inga fort: »Ich bilde mir ein, daß du dir uns ausgesucht hast. Aber wir zwei, der Spielmann und ich, waren ja so unvereinbar. Hätte er mit mir reden können und verstanden, was für ein einfacher Mensch ich bin, hätte er sich nie in mich verliebt, hätte mich nicht einmal angeschaut. Wir gehörten verschiedenen Welten an, Simon.«

Das ist wahr, dachte er, sie hat recht. Sie hätten nie zu einer Familie werden können. Aber dann verhärtete sich sein Blick wieder und er dachte, hättest du ihn geheiratet, dann hätte er überlebt, wäre gerettet worden, wäre Hitler und dem Vernichtungslager entkommen.

Aber er sprach es nicht aus, und er erinnerte sich an den Mann im Traum, der mit seiner Geige den Hügel hinauf gegangen war, dem Tod entgegen, weil er sterben wollte.

»Du hättest verstanden, daß er auf der Erde nicht richtig heimisch war, wenn du ihn hättest auf seiner Geige spielen hören«, sagte Inga, als hätte sie Simons Gedanken belauscht.

»Das war keine Bauernmusik, Simon, kein solches Gefiedel, nach dem man bei uns herumhopst. Es kam wie aus dem Himmel. Ich hatte nicht einmal geahnt, daß eine Geige so klingen kann.«

»Weißt du etwas darüber, welche Musik er gespielt hat?«

»Ja, einmal habe ich seine Musik im Radio gehört, und ich habe mir eingebildet, daß er mitgespielt hat, denn es war ein Orchester aus Berlin. Der Mann, der die Musik geschrieben hat, war aus Finnland, aber seinen Namen habe ich inzwischen vergessen.«

»Sibelius«, sagte Simon.

»Ja!« sagte sie, und Simon hätte jetzt alles für eine Geige gegeben, um sie in ihr wieder zum Klingen zu bringen, diese wilde, sehnsuchtsvolle Musik von Sibelius.

Aber er hatte keine Geige, und er konnte nicht spielen.

Er umarmte sie vor dem Weggehen lange und herzlich, blieb winkend am Waldrand stehen und dachte, als er den Waldweg entlang rannte, um das Auto nicht zu verpassen, das ihn an der großen Landstraße aufnehmen wollte, daß Inga ihm den erstaunlichsten Trost mitgegeben hatte, den er je gehört hatte: Ich glaube, das ist alles nur deinetwegen geschehen. Du wolltest auf die Welt. Du hast dir uns ausgesucht. Vielleicht werde ich wirklich verrückt, dachte er. Ein so wahnwitziger, unglaublicher, lächerlicher Gedanke.

Aber er war tröstlich.

Simon blieb auf der Brücke mit dem Telefon nur wenig Zeit, bis das Boot zum Abholen kam, also rief er Ruben an und sagte: »Er hat Simon Habermann geheißen.« Und dazu bekam Ruben noch die Berliner Adresse. »Kannst du da nachforschen, Onkel Ruben?«

»Ist doch klar, Simon. Du hörst von mir.«

»Danke.«

Ich weiß doch, wie sinnlos es ist, weiß, daß er in den Öfen gestorben ist, dachte Simon. Aber er mußte dem Rationalen immerhin eine Chance geben.

Die jüdischen Gemeinden der ganzen Welt arbeiteten unermüdlich daran, ein Netz zwischen den Toten und den Überlebenden zu knüpfen. Schon nach einer Woche hatte Ruben Bescheid. Simon Habermann, Geiger beim Berliner Philharmonischen Orchester, war im November 1942 zusammen mit seiner Schwester deportiert und im Mai 1944 in Auschwitz vergast worden.

Die Schwester war schon früher an Entkräftung gestorben.

Er war unverheiratet gewesen, nähere Verwandte waren nicht mehr am Leben.

Simon war sechzehn, als dieser Mann starb, dachte Ruben. Im Lauf von sechzehn Jahren hätte der Musiker immerhin erfahren können, daß er einen Sohn in Schweden hatte. Zumindest hätte er ein Anrecht darauf gehabt.

Zum ersten Mal empfand Ruben einen Groll auf Karin. Sie hatte Anteil an einer Ungerechtigkeit, dachte er.

In der Baracke im äußeren Schärengürtel wartete ein Brief mit einem Poststempel aus Stockholm auf Simon. Er wußte, daß dieser Brief von Iza kam, und daß sie jetzt die Fänge nach ihm ausstreckte.

Ein Foto lag bei, sie war schlank, schön, zurechtgemacht wie ein Filmstar, und sie sah ihn aus Augen an, die vor Hunger brannten.

»Was für eine Braut!« sagten die Kameraden. »Was für ein heißer Feger! Wo, zum Teufel, hast du die versteckt?«

»In Stockholm«, gab Simon Auskunft und merkte, wie er in der Achtung der anderen stieg.

»Wirst du sie besuchen?«

»Ja, sie schreibt, daß sie es gerne möchte.«

»Wirst du dich mit ihr verloben?«

Simon sah die anderen lange und eindringlich an und sagte es dann, wie es war: »Ich hoffe, das bleibt mir erspart.«

Wie immer konnten sie ihn nicht begreifen, schüttelten die Köpfe. Der helläugige Bengtsson, der so viel Sehnsucht in sich trug, grinste verlegen: »Wenn's dir erspart bleibt, könntest du's einem andern vielleicht sagen. Hier ist nämlich einer, der gerne für dich einspringt.«

Gelächter dröhnte durch die Baracke, und Simon hatte keine Möglichkeit für eine Erklärung.

Wenn es da etwas zu erklären gegeben hätte.

Simon stand vor Rubens Bücherregal und las in ›Schwedisches Nach-
schlagewerk‹, erschienen in Malmö 1935, über Spinnen nach: ... *ge-
kennzeichnet durch eine Verdickung des Hinterleibes, der stielartig mit
dem Bruststück verbunden und mit vier oder sechs Spinndrüsen ver-
sehen ist ... Die Beine enden klauenartig /Fig. 2/, an den Spitzen
befinden sich die Mündungen der Giftdrüsen ... Die vier Beinpaare
haben kammähnlich gezahnte Klauen ... Die Hauptpartien des Nerven-
systems bestehen aus Gehirn ... die Ausführungsgänge der paarig
angeordneten Geschlechtsorgane vereinen sich zu einem Kanal, der
in den Hinterleib mündet ...*

Er sah sich Fig. 2 an und schüttelte sich vor Ekel.

Nachttiere, las er. *Raubtiere.* Gifte unbekannter Zusammensetzung.
Die in Schweden vorkommenden Arten sind alle ungefährlich.

Doch es gab eine europäische Art, die Tarantel, deren Biß für den
Menschen gefährlich sein konnte, selbst wenn die Giftwirkung auf die
nähere Umgebung der Wunde begrenzt war.

Kein Wort darüber, daß die Weibchen die Männchen nach der
Paarung auffraßen.

Er wartete auf Isak, der inzwischen den Führerschein gemacht hatte
und Simon mit Rubens Auto zurück in die Unterkunft bringen wollte.
Es war Herbst, gelbes Laub wirbelte draußen von den Bäumen, und
am Meer war die Luft würzig und glasklar.

Die meisten Rekruten hatten Ernteurlaub oder, wie es hieß, aus
familiären Gründen Sonderurlaub gehabt. Simon ging zu Kapitän
Sjövall: Haltung annehmen, Meldung machen ... aber es lag eine

leichte Scherzhaftigkeit über dem Ritual, als er um drei Tage Sonderurlaub aus Familiengründen ansuchte.

»Was ist denn mit Larssons Familie?« fragte Sjövall.

»Ich habe ein Mädchen in Stockholm«, sagte Simon.

»Kein Urlaubsgrund«, sagte Sjövall.

»Sie ist krank«, meldete Simon, und das stimmte ja irgendwie. Kranke Verlobte, schrieb Sjövall, und damit war die Sache geklärt.

Simon verriet zu Hause niemandem auch nur ein Sterbenswörtchen, und am Mittwochmorgen saß er im Schnellzug nach Stockholm und versuchte sich an das zu erinnern, was er über Spinnen gelesen hatte.

Das Bild hatte seinen Reiz verloren.

Daran ist Isak schuld, dachte Simon und erinnerte sich an den Streit im Auto. Es hatte damit angefangen, daß Simon fast beiläufig erwähnt hatte, er werde am nächsten Wochenende zu Iza nach Stockholm fahren.

Isak hatte sich fürchterlich aufgeregt, hatte Simon angeschrien, er sei wohl übergeschnappt, daß er mit offenen Augen ins Verderben renne.

Simon hatte nicht nur wegen dieses Ausbruchs, sondern vor allem wegen des Fahrtempos Angst bekommen, denn binnen weniger Minuten hatte Isak Rubens alten Chevrolet auf fast Hundert gebracht, und Simon hatte geschrien, beruhige dich schon, sonst bringst du uns beide noch um.

Da hatte Isak das Tempo zurückgenommen und wie eine Mauer geschwiegen, und sie waren immerhin zehn Minuten zu früh in normalem Tempo auf dem Parkplatz vor der Kaserne angekommen. Und Isak hatte diese Minuten gut genutzt, er hatte sich Simon zugewandt und von Olga erzählt, und was Mona und er festgestellt hatten.

»Du kannst immerhin jetzt noch frei entscheiden, ob du wie Ruben ein Leben mit einer verrückten Frau leben möchtest, einer Frau, vor der Ruben erst seine Ruhe hatte, als sie in die Irrenanstalt eingeliefert wurde«, hatte Isak gesagt. Und dann hatte er hinzugefügt: »Aber du hast, verdammt, nicht das Recht, Kinder mit einer Mutter in die Welt zu setzen, wie Iza eine werden würde.«

Isak war dem Weinen nahe gewesen, und Simon hatte wie vom Blitz getroffen neben ihm gesessen.

»Ich will sie, zum Teufel nochmal, doch nicht heiraten!«

»Wenn die dir ein Kind anhängen kann, tut die das. Sie hat wenig Chancen zu heiraten, denn sie schreckt jeden normalen Mann ab. Wenn die dich in die Klauen kriegt, läßt sie dich nie wieder frei.«

»Klauen mit Giftdrüsen an den Spitzen«, hatte Simon geantwortet.

»Simon, wirst du jetzt auch schon verrückt? Vielleicht solltest du mit Maria reden, die schreibt dich vielleicht krank.«

Simon hatte Isak angesehen und zu lachen versucht.

»Ich werde daran denken ... an alles, was du gesagt hast. Und danke, daß du mir von deiner Mutter erzählt hast.«

Simon hatte gefühlt, daß das schwierig gewesen war. Aber inzwischen war es Zeit geworden, in die Kaserne zu gehen.

Jetzt saß er in der Eisenbahn und versuchte das alte Bild von der bösen und wirklichen Iza heraufzubeschwören.

Aber dann fand er das kindisch. Einer, der mit Gefühlen spielt.

Isak ist erwachsener als ich, dachte er, als der Zug in Skövde hielt. Einen Augenblick überlegte er, ob er aussteigen und auf die erstbeste Verbindung nach Süden warten sollte. Aber er blieb sitzen. Ich muß sie besiegen, dachte er.

Mein Bild von ihr besiegen, verbesserte er sich und schämte sich so, daß er rot wurde. Ein Mädchen, das ihm gegenüber saß, machte ein erstauntes Gesicht, und Simon mußte auf die Toilette gehen und sich Gesicht und Hände waschen, und danach ging er in den Speisewagen Kaffee trinken. Dort blieb er lange sitzen und sah die Landschaft vorüberfliegen, als würde sie vom Zug aufgefressen.

Iza holte ihn am Stockholmer Hauptbahnhof ab, unverändert, sie war genauso wie immer. Der berühmte Analytiker in der Schweiz hatte ihr nichts anhaben können. Sie zeigte Simon die Stadt, als wäre sie ihr Eigentum.

»Gegen das hier ist Göteborg ein Loch«, sagte sie, und Simon mußte, als er am Fenster in Izas Wohnung stand und auf Stockholm hinunterblickte, zugeben, daß die Stadt prachtvoll war, großartig.

Ruben hatte Iza auf den Anhöhen des Stadtteils Söder eine Wohnung gekauft, und es lag Sonne über dem Strömmen, dem Schloß und den tausend Dächern, obwohl sich der Oktober schon fast dem Ende zuneigte. Simon dachte, wie merkwürdig, daß in Göteborg nie jemand von Stockholm sprach, von der Hauptstadt, und davon, daß sie schön war. Aber gleichzeitig meinte er die Stadt recht gut zu kennen, obwohl er noch nie hier gewesen war, dachte, daß er sie durch August Strindberg und Hjalmar Söderberg kannte und aus Hunderten anderen Büchern, die er gelesen hatte.

Mehr als alles andere wollte er auf Entdeckungsreise gehen, wollte die Drottninggata entlang bis zu Strindbergs Blauem Turm gehen, den Strandvägen entlangschlendern, mit der Fähre hinüber zum Tiergarten fahren und die berühmten Eichen sehen. Aber Iza sagte: »Jetzt wollen wir uns lieben«, und Simon sah ihr ins Gesicht und dachte an die Spinnen: Hab ich dich erst im Netz, freß ich dich auf. Das steigerte die Verlockung nicht, und übrigens hatte er sich im Liebesleben der Spinnen einigermaßen geirrt.

»Ich habe Hunger«, sagte er. »Hast du was zu essen im Haus?«

Iza, die nie warten konnte, wurde wütend, stampfte mit dem Fuß auf, fluchte, machte, als das nicht half, eine dramatische Szene, weinte: »Jetzt warte ich schon seit Monaten auf meinen Geliebten, und dann will er nichts als essen.«

Aber Simon war schon draußen in der verwahrlosten Küche, öffnete den Kühlschrank und fand eine Dose Corned beef und ein paar Scheiben Knäckebrot.

»Komm, laß uns essen.«

Dann fragte er boshaft: »Seit wann bin ich dein Geliebter?«

Da strömten die Tränen wie ein Wasserfall, und Simon merkte mit Erstaunen, daß es ihn nicht berührte. Sie sah seine Kälte, hörte jäh zu weinen auf, und mit Augen voller Entzücken sagte sie: »Ich habe eine Flasche Wein gekauft.«

Sie aßen und tranken fast gut gelaunt, fast wie Freunde, bis Iza mit dem üblichen fieberhaften Eifer in der Stimme sagte: »Du bist also nicht hergekommen, um mit mir Liebe zu machen?«

»Nein, vor allem bin ich gekommen, um mir die Stadt anzusehen, und auch um nachzusehen, wie es dir geht.«

»Du machst Witze.«

»Vielleicht.«

»Ach, du bist grausam«, stöhnte sie und ihre Augen wurden schmal vor Erwartung und ihre Lippen wurden feucht vor Lust.

Simon trank seinen Wein aus, und dann waren sie im Bett, und er, der nach Monaten in den Schären ganz liebestoll war, hatte ihr viel zu bieten, wie er selbst meinte. Er brauchte sich nicht zurückzuhalten, sie wollte keine Zärtlichkeit, nur Ausdauer und zupackende Hände.

Aber er konnte sie nicht befriedigen. Sie wollte von ihm geschlagen werden, und er dachte an die Ausführungsgänge der Spinnen, die im Hinterleib münden, und er konnte nur schwer zuschlagen, und als sie, jetzt wild, in der Garderobe eine Peitsche holen lief, verlor er nicht nur die Lust, sondern auch seine Potenz.

Ihm war übel, er ging hinaus in ihr Badezimmer und übergab sich, redete sich ein, daß die verspeiste Konserve verdorben gewesen war, fühlte aber, daß sein ganzer Körper von Abscheu ergriffen war. Als der Magen seinen Inhalt von sich gegeben hatte, wusch Simon sich, zog sich die Hose an und ging wieder zu ihr.

Sie lag sehr still auf dem Rücken und sah mit leerem Blick an die Decke.

»Du bist nichts als ein kleiner Dreck, Simon Larsson«, sagte sie.

Da kannst du recht haben, dachte er, aber er sagte nichts, denn er hatte ihre Verzweiflung erkannt. Er kroch wieder ins Bett, legte sich dicht zu ihr.

Und ihre Hoffnung entzündete sich wieder, brannte bald mit verzehrender Kraft, und er ließ sich von ihrem Feuer mit Haut und Haar verschlingen.

Drei Tage und Nächte hielten sie durch, haßliebten sich, weinten, schliefen zwischendurch kurz, standen manchmal auf, um zu essen. Er lief ins Milchgeschäft, holte Brot und Butter, sie machte nicht einmal einen Ansatz, zu bezahlen, und er dachte, bald werde sein Geld zu Ende sein.

Sie saugte ihm das Blut aus, drang in sein Mark ein, und er ließ es geschehen, empfand es wie das Bezahlen einer alten Schuld, und sie stieß nicht auf Widerstand.

Dafür haßte sie ihn, alles sollte er haben, alles, was sie hatte ausstehen müssen. Sie erniedrigte ihn, schlug ihn, quälte ihn, und er hatte nichts entgegenzusetzen, erduldete alles, und sie schrie ihre Verachtung laut heraus.

Als am Samstagnachmittag die Dämmerung über die Stadt hereinfiel, schlief er über seiner eigenen und auch ihrer Verzweiflung ein. Da weckte sie ihn mit der Peitsche, schrie: »Schlag mich!«

Aber er konnte nicht schlagen, stand nur aus dem Bett auf und war frei, war mit allen fertig, mit Karin und Inga, der Ågrenschen und Dolly, er war ihnen allen begegnet und wußte, daß sie nicht zu besiegen waren.

Iza lag im Bett wie am ersten Tag, unbeweglich, den leeren Blick an der Decke.

»Geh«, sagte sie. »Geh jetzt, ich will dich nie mehr wiedersehen.«

Er duschte und zog die Uniform an, ging geradewegs hinaus in die fremde Stadt, in der es kalt war und dunkel. Fünf Kronen und fünfundsiebzig Öre hatte er in der Tasche, er wußte es, denn er hatte im Milchgeschäft nachgezählt. Das würde für ein Hotelzimmer nicht reichen.

Er hatte eine Rückfahrkarte, er konnte sich zum Hauptbahnhof durchfragen und den ersten Zug nach Göteborg nehmen. Als er aber den Katarinaberg hinunterging, dachte er, daß er die Stadt auf jeden Fall ansehen wollte, zumindest die Altstadt. Es gab noch keinen Frost, also konnte er die Nacht ruhig einmal im Freien verbringen.

Er überquerte die Schleuse, ging die Skeppsbron entlang und dann hinauf in die Gassen der Altstadt. Eisige Winde quälten sich zwischen den müden alten Häuserzeilen hindurch, Simon fror, fror ganz erbärmlich, als er auf dem großen Platz am Stortorget stand und dem Flügelschlag der Geschichte nachzuspüren versuchte, aber er fror.

Ich habe kein Herz mehr, dachte er, in meiner Brust gibt es keine Pumpe, die das Blut antreibt und warmhält.

Doch seine Beine bewegten sich Richtung Kornhamnstorg, wo die Cafés billiger aussahen. Er blieb lange vor einem stehen, las die Speisekarte im Fenster und rechnete aus, daß er für zwei Kronen und zwanzig Öre zwei Käsebrote und warmen Kakao bekommen konnte.

»Junge, Junge, du bist aber blaß«, sagte die Kellnerin in norrländischem Singsang, und Simon sah, daß sie Mona ähnelte, aber älter und noch mütterlicher war.

Er versuchte sie anzulächeln, aber es gelang nicht ganz.

Das Wichtigste war im Moment, daß er hier bei seinen Käsebroten eine Stunde im Warmen sitzen konnte.

Er biß nur kleine Stücke von dem Brot ab und kaute umständlich, trank den Kakao schlückchenweise und langsam. Allmählich kam sein Herz wieder in Gang, die Wärme drang vom Magen aus in die Füße, von wo sie auf Umwegen schließlich bis in den Kopf fand.

Als das Gehirn zu arbeiten begann, war diese Erleichterung, die er in Izas Schlafzimmer empfunden hatte, wie weggeblasen, und seine Gedanken waren von allerschlimmster Art.

Gott im Himmel, was war er nur für ein Ekel. Jahrelang hatte er von dem Mädchen phantasiert, die das Böse und ihn wirklich machen sollte. Er wollte sie, diese tausendmal Mißbrauchte, ebenfalls mißbrauchen um ihrer Wirklichkeit teilhaftig zu werden und sie begreifbar zu machen.

Denn er wollte sich die Bosheit zu eigen machen, hatte es aber, aus freien Stücken, selbst nie gewagt sie zu entwickeln.

Er dachte an die Ågrensche in den weit zurückliegenden Jahren seiner Kindheit, wie er sich zu ihr hingezogen gefühlt hatte, um hassen zu lernen, ihr die Brüste abschneiden und die Augen ausstechen zu können. In seiner Phantasie, immer nur in der Phantasie.

Jetzt rebellierte sein Magen wieder, wenn er sich nicht beruhigte, würde er das Essen nicht bei sich behalten können.

Bylund. Lange dachte er an Bylund und kam zu dem Schluß, daß sie einander eigentlich recht ähnlich waren, daß aber der Feldwebel der Ehrlichere war.

Es kamen keine Tränen, und dafür mußte er eigentlich dankbar sein, jetzt, wo das Café sich mit Menschen zu füllen begann. Er würde bald bezahlen, aufstehen und gehen.

Bylund hätte es geschafft, Bylund mit den bebenden Nasenflügeln hätte Iza all das geben können, was sie haben wollte. Er konnte Phantasie in die Tat umsetzen.

Aber er, Simon, hätte Bylund fast totgeschlagen.

Die Erinnerung stärkte ihn ein wenig, er konnte den nächsten Bissen schlucken, und der blieb im Magen, wie es sich gehörte.

Simon versuchte sich zu erinnern, wann es begonnen hatte, daß er sich zu Iza hingezogen fühlte.

Er hatte im Sanatorium das dicke, häßliche Mädchen angesehen und gedacht, daß er in ihr dem ersten Menschen begegnete, der in allem was er tat und sagte bedingungslos ehrlich war.

Das stimmt, so ist sie.

Dann erinnerte er sich, daß er die Ziffern auf ihrem Arm angestarrt hatte und daß die Zeit stehengeblieben war.

Sie ist im Besitz der Wirklichkeit, hatte er gedacht.

Inzwischen gab es viele Berichte aus den Lagern, geschrieben von Menschen, die überlebt hatten. Sie erzählten nicht nur von dem Bösen und von den Leiden, sie sprachen auch davon, wie das unfaßbare Geschehen alles unwirklich gemacht hatte.

Dort überlebte man nicht, indem man dem Mitleid Raum gab, schrieb einer. Aber ohne Mitleid wurde die Welt unwirklich.

Sie nehmen die Schuld der Henker an den Verbrechen auf sich, hatte Olof gesagt.

Iza?

Nein, er glaubte nicht, daß sie Schuld empfand. Aber für ein echtes Gegenwärtigsein mußte sie gequält werden.

Ich werde versuchen, ihr zu schreiben.

Was denn? Was sollte in diesem Brief stehen?

Wirkliche Menschen sind liebenswert, dachte er, Wirklichkeit ist, zu wissen, daß man sich auf einander verlassen kann. Wie Karin und Erik. Ruben, Inga, ja, auch sie besaß die Wirklichkeit.

Nicht dieser schwärmerische Musikant, der im Wald ein paar Wochen lang liebte und dann verschwand, um ein Jahr später mit einem albernen Brief von sich hören zu lassen.

Tausend Küsse.

Pfui Teufel, geradezu ekelhaft.

Lange dachte Simon an seinen Traum vom Spielmann, der der Vernichtung entgegenging.

Dieselbe Triebkraft wie seine eigene hin zum Bösen?

Ich habe es in den Genen, dachte er, es ist ein Erbe genau wie die Musik.

Tod?

Ich kann zum Bahnhof gehen, irgendein Gleis entlangtraben, und mich vor die Lok eines Schnellzugs werfen.

Aber er wußte genau, daß er das nicht tun konnte. Wegen Karin.

Er haßte sie dafür.

Dann dachte er, daß er gar nicht sterben wollte.

Das einzige, was er wirklich wollte war, geradenwegs zu ihr in ihre Küche zu fahren, ihr den Kopf in den Schoß zu legen und alles zu erzählen.

Aber das durfte er nicht.

Er mußte mit dem, was geschehen war, allein bleiben.

Allein, das war es, was Erwachsensein bedeutete.

Zum ersten Mal erkannte er, daß er erwachsen war, und der Gedanke war unerträglich.

Du siehst zum Erbarmen aus.«

Am Tisch saß ihm jetzt ein Mann mittleren Alters gegenüber. Er hatte etwas schräggestellte freundliche braune Augen.

»Du solltest was Richtiges essen«, bemerkte er.

»Ich habe kein Geld.«

»Einen Teller Suppe kann ich dir schon spendieren«, meinte der Mann, und die Kellnerin, die Simon schon lange mitleidig beobachtet hatte, kam fast angeschossen mit einem Teller voll dampfend heißem Essen. Simon aß voll Dankbarkeit, und der Mann, der ihm irgendwie bekannt vorkam, sagte: »Andersson.«

»Larsson.«

Sie schüttelten einander die Hände, der Mann hatte eine seltsam breite und kurze Hand, warm und trocken.

»Du bist nicht etwa vom Militär durchgebrannt?«

»Nein, nein. Ich fahre morgen nach Göteborg zurück. Ich hatte Urlaub.«

»Und bist in Stockholm gewesen und hast über die Stränge geschlagen, kann man ja verstehen.«

»Tja«, machte Simon mit einer Grimasse, mußte aber über den Schalk in den braunen Augen lachen.

»Ich habe eine Rückfahrkarte«, sagte er.

»Du kannst mit mir fahren. Ich fahre heute nacht mit einem Lastwagen nach Göteborg.«

Simon dachte, das sei mehr als er verdient hatte.

»Mein Vater hat viele Jahre einen Lastwagen gehabt«, sagte er. »Wahrscheinlich kommst du mir deswegen bekannt vor.«

»Ja, wir haben uns wohl manchmal gesehen, als du noch klein warst«, sagte Andersson und bezahlte nicht nur die Suppe, sondern auch die Brote. Dann bestellte er noch zehn Käsestullen. »Nein, lieber fünf mit Käse und fünf mit Leberwurst.«

»Wir brauchen Reiseproviant«, erklärte er und holte aus seiner Tasche unter dem Tisch zwei Thermosflaschen, die er mit Kaffee füllen ließ.

»Also, auf geht's!«

Sie gingen bergauf Richtung Schleuse, bogen zum Südbahnhof ab, wo Anderssons Lastwagen beladen und abfahrbereit wartete. Es war gegen zehn Uhr abends und die Straßen waren voller Menschen, ein rastloser Strom ohne Anfang und Ende.

»Stockholm fängt an, eine Stadt zu werden, die nachts nicht mehr schläft«, sagte Andersson.

Simon nickte, aber Stockholm interessierte ihn nicht mehr, ihn interessierte nur noch, so nah wie möglich bei dem Fernfahrer zu bleiben, der erstaunlich klein war, einen ganzen Kopf kleiner als Simon.

Ein grüner Dodge wartete auf Andersson, die Persenning war stramm über die schwere Last gespannt. Hinter dem Fahrerplatz befand sich eine knapp einen halben Meter breite Kabine mit einer dünnen Matratze, ein paar alten Decken und einem erstaunlich großen und weichen Kopfkissen.

Anderssons kurzer Daumen deutete auf das Lager.

»Du brauchst Schlaf, Larsson. Ich wecke dich bei Tagesanbruch irgendwo in Mittelschweden.«

Und Simon schlief gut wie ein Kind, eingehüllt in freundliche Träume von rauschendem Gras und lichter Geborgenheit.

Er wachte in der Morgendämmerung auf, als sie die Autobahn verließen und nun der Straßenbelag aus Schotter statt aus Asphalt bestand. Ihm wurde bewußt, wo er sich befand, er setzte sich irgendwo mitten in der Ebene von Östgötland auf, begegnete den schrägen Augen im Rückspiegel und fühlte sich gut aufgehoben.

»Ich habe mir gedacht, wir machen einen Abstecher Richtung

Omberg und essen auf dem heiligen Berg unser Frühstück im Grünen«, sagte Andersson.

Es war nicht mehr ganz so grün, aber eine milde Herbstsonne ging über der östgötischen Ebene auf. Es raschelte unter den Rädern, sie fuhren über einen Teppich aus dunkelrotem Gold.

»Buchenlaub, die Bäume werfen grade die Blätter ab«, sagte Andersson, und Simon betrachtete die säulengleichen Stämme am Weg. Er hatte in seinem Leben noch nie eine Buche gesehen, kannte sie nur aus Büchern.

»Was meinst du damit, daß der Berg heilig ist?« fragte er.

»Omberg«, sagte Andersson. »Er ist einer der acht heiligen Berge der Erde, seit Urzeiten in den geheimen Schriften erwähnt.«

»Du bist ein Ostgöte«, lachte Simon.

»Schon möglich«, sagte Andersson, und Simon dachte, die sind wahrscheinlich noch schlimmer als die Göteborger.

»Ich habe viele Beweise«, sagte Andersson und mußte auch lachen. »Schau dich mal in östlicher Richtung um, schau hinein in die Ebene.«

Simon gehorchte. Ein paar typisch rote Häuser standen dort, deren Fenster verschlafen in die Sonne blinzelten.

»Dort draußen hat Königin Omma vor langer Zeit über ihr Sumpfvolk geherrscht«, fuhr Andersson fort. »Es war ein magisches Volk, das das Geheimnis des Todes kannte und es bei Mondwechsel mit großen Festen feierte.«

»Das dichtest du dir jetzt aber zusammen«, lachte Simon, aber dann fiel ihm ein, daß er von den Ausgrabungen bei Dags Mosse gelesen hatte, einer seltsamen Pfahlbautensiedlung aus dem Neolithikum.

Andersson nickte: »Sie haben mehr als tausend Pfähle ins Moor getrieben und Böden darübergelegt«, sagte er. »Das war keine besonders schwere Arbeit, denn damals sind noch Riesen auf zwei Beinen über die Erde gegangen.«

Simon konnte es vor sich sehen, wie die Riesen die gewaltigen Buchen von Omberg ohne große Anstrengung aus der Erde gerissen, die Wurzeln abgeknickt und die Stämme zwischen Daumen und Zeigefinger durchgezogen hatten, um die Äste zu entfernen.

»Unsere Pinkelpause legen wir bei den alten Mönchen ein«, schlug Andersson vor, und schon sah Simon die Ruinen von Alvastra im Morgenlicht auftauchen.

Andersson hielt den schweren Wagen sanft an, schaltete den Motor ab, zog die Handbremse.

»Man muß sie pfleglich behandeln«, sagte er. »Sie ist nicht mehr allzu jung und hat ihre Mucken, die Karre.«

Sie gingen auf die Ruine zu und befreiten ihre Blasen, den Rücken einem Gedenkstein zugekehrt: Dem Beitrag der Könige Oskar II. und Gustav V. zur Geschichte des Klosters. Simon sah die schrägen Sonnenstrahlen sich durch die Gewölbe des Mittelschiffs schleichen und spürte die Flügelschläge, die er am Vorabend in der Stockholmer Altstadt vermißt hatte.

»Stell dir das mal vor«, sagte Andersson. »Stell dir eine lange Reihe französischer Mönche vor, die durch Europa trotten, Mann für Mann wie aufgefädelt. Sie haben alle Arten von Samen für Heilpflanzen bei sich, Stecklinge von Apfel-, Birn- und Kirschbäumen, die alle zu Ahnen der Pflanzungen hier in diesem alten heidnischen Land werden sollen.«

»Stell dir das mal vor!« schwärmte Andersson weiter. »Stell dir vor wie sie die Urwälder von Småland durchdringen und jeden Morgen zu ihrem Gott beten, ihn bitten, diese Wildnis möge vor dem Abend ein Ende finden, bevor die Wölfe zwischen den Bäumen zu heulen beginnen.«

Simon stellte es sich vor.

»Und eines Tages sind sie dann angekommen und fangen an, eine Kirche und ein Kloster zu bauen«, fuhr Andersson fort.

Simon konnte sie zwischen den Ruinen des Kapitelsaales schwach erkennen, graue Zisterziensermönche, Männer des heiligen Bernhard.

»Welch ein Mut«, sagte Andersson. »Das einzige, woran ihre Hoffnung hing, war der Brief eines Satansweibes, das Ulfhild hieß und schon mehrere Ehemänner umgebracht hatte und trotzdem von Sverker dem Alten geheiratet wurde und nun als Königin hier im Königshof saß.«

»Sie haben vermutlich Gott vertraut.«

»Ja. Dein Wille geschehe. Das ist es, was man Vertrauen nennt und was Wunder vollbringt.«

»Was die Materie besiegt und Berge versetzt«, fügte Simon hinzu.

Aber Andersson lachte als er sagte, es seien wohl etliche Pferde und Menschen dabei draufgegangen, als die Mönche aus den Kalksteinbrüchen von Borghamn Berge hierher versetzten, um ihre Kirche zu bauen.

Die beiden Männer wuschen sich im Baptisterium im nördlichen Kreuzgang die Hände, wo auch die Mönche sich einst die Hände gewaschen hatten.

»Ich wüßte gerne«, sagte Andersson, als er den ersten Gang einlegte und sie, vorbei an dem reichlich mit allerlei Schmuck versehenen Touristenhotel langsam bergauf krochen und Simon fast die Luft wegblieb bei dem Blick über den Vättersee, der sich ihm darbot, »ich wüßte gerne, ob es bei Ulfhild das schlechte Gewissen war, daß sie die Mönche kommen ließ.«

»Es war vermutlich Politik«, meinte Simon, der sich von der Schule her an die Werke des schwedischen Dichters Werner von Heidenstam erinnerte. »Es war nicht nur Gott, der demjenigen Macht verlieh, der sich gut mit der katholischen Kirche stellte.«

In Anderssons Gesicht zeigte sich ein Lächeln, das bedeutete, daß er mehr zu erzählen hätte, es aber lieber verschwieg. Weil es keine Worte dafür gab. Oder ganz einfach aus Freude an dem Geheimnisvollen.

Er gleicht einem alten Chinesen, dachte Simon, als Andersson fortfuhr: »Wie auch immer, es dauerte nicht lange, da hallten die Kirchenglocken über den Berg und vertrieben Königin Omma und auch die Riesen.«

»Wohin sind sie gegangen?«

Simon liebte diesen Augenblick, den Mann, den Berg, die Aussicht, das Gespräch. All das legte sich wie eine Arznei über die Qualen des gestrigen Tages.

»Sie gingen ein in eine andere Wirklichkeit, und dort haben sie es gut«, erwiderte Andersson mit so sicherer Stimme, als hätte er ihnen erst kürzlich einen Besuch abgestattet.

»Schön zu hören«, freute sich Simon, und dann mußten sie beide lachen.

»Links unten hast du die Höhle von Rödgaveln, die der Eingang zum Palast des Bergkönigs war«, erzählte Andersson weiter, aber Simon sah die schwindelerregenden Hänge nicht, denn der Lastwagen rollte schon bergab auf die Wiesen von Stocklycke zu, die von mächtigen Eichen umsäumt waren. Hier gab es auch Lärchen, jetzt in der Zeit des Nadelabwurfs flammend rotgelb. Bei der Touristenhütte bog der Fahrer jäh nach links ab und der Wagen begann wieder zu klettern, vorbei an Pers Sten und hinaus zur Landzunge von Älvarum. Auch hier blieb der Laster nicht stehen, er fuhr über Örnslid hinaus zur Steilküste, von wo man die Wände des Westens sehen konnte.

Hier hielt Andersson an, er sagte: »Du hast hoffentlich keine Höhenangst?«

Simon schüttelte, stumm vor Bewunderung, den Kopf. Wie der Felsen von Gibraltar dem Mittelmeer begegnet, begegnete der Omberg dem Vättersee, bewaldet zwar, norrländisch eindrucksvoll. Der See zeigte sich in strahlendem Türkis, die Sonne spiegelte sich im Wasser und hüllte die niedrigen Berge in blaugrünen Schimmer.

»Was für ein Licht«, staunte Simon.

»Keine Worte«, bat Andersson und nahm die Proviantdose und die Decken mit bis ganz hinaus zur Steilwand.

Ich werde ihm mein Gedicht vom Meer schicken, dachte Simon, als sie dort saßen, die verschwenderisch belegten Brote aßen und ihren Kaffee tranken.

Als Andersson den letzten Bissen gekaut hatte, sagte er: »Das Wasser ist so grün, weil die Riesen ihre dreckigen Unterhosen drin waschen.«

Bei Simon explodierte die Freude in einem großen Gelächter, das im Bauch begann, sein Echo aber in Ommas kilometerweit entfernter uralter Burg fand.

Andersson setzte sein geheimnisvolles Lächeln auf, die Sonne wärmte jetzt, er streckte sich auf seiner Decke aus, zog sich die Schirmmütze über die Augen und sagte: »Ist es nicht komisch, daß alles Wissen, das von außen kommt, dich glauben machen will, daß du nur ein Fliegenschiß im Universum bist? Aber das, was aus dir selber kommt, sagt dir nachdrücklich und eigensinnig, daß du alles bist und alles hast.«

Simon hatte darüber noch nie nachgedacht, überlegte eine Weile und meinte dann: »Irgendwie ist es wohl biologisch bedingt, ein Überlebenstrieb, der dir einredet, daß du ganz unerhört wichtig bist.«

»Nicht doch«, hielt Andersson dagegen. »Auf dieses Wissen kannst du dich verdammt mehr verlassen als auf die ganze Wissenschaft.«

Er schob die Mütze in den Nacken, stützte sich auf die Ellbogen und sah Simon lange an. »Mach die Augen zu, Junge«, sagte er. »Schalte dein Hirn ab und geh nach innen, in die Halle des Bergkönigs in deinem eigenen Herzen. Dort wirst du die Wahrheit darüber erfahren, daß du nicht vergebens geboren wurdest.«

Dann legte er sich hin, schlief ein, und Simon tat, wie er gesagt hatte, schloß die Augen. Zu ihm kam der zweite Satz der Symphonie Fantastique und fast unmittelbar trat er hinter die Bilder und hinaus in das Weiße ...

Er wurde von Andersson, der ihm die Hand auf die Schulter legte, wieder zurück in die Welt geholt. Es war eine Berührung voller Zuneigung.

»Wir müssen weiter, Junge. Na, hast du die Wahrheit vernommen?«

»Vielleicht nicht gerade vernommen«, erwiderte Simon. »Eher empfunden.«

»Gut, dann fahren wir also.«

Von Borghamn aus ging es Richtung Autobahn. Als die Räder keinen Lärm mehr machten, weil sie wieder auf Asphalt liefen, fing Andersson zu pfeifen an. Simon biß die Zähne zusammen, wie immer war er auf Mißtöne vorbereitet, aber nichts störte die Harmonie, als Andersson das Leitmotiv des zweiten Satzes von Berlioz pfiff.

Es war ein Morgen so voller Wunder gewesen, daß Simon sich schon über gar nichts mehr wundern konnte. Alles war wie es sein sollte, und dazu gehörte auch, daß Andersson die Musik vernommen hatte, die Simon dort oben auf dem Berg durchbraust hatte.

Als sie Jönköping hinter sich gelassen und das småländische Hochland erklommen hatten, bekam Andersson die Geschichte mit Iza zu hören, die ganze Geschichte.

»Ist dir klar, was für ein mieser Kerl ich bin?«

»Wie man's nimmt. Ich würde eher sagen, du bist einer von diesen armen Teufeln, die durchs Leben gehen, um alte Schulden abzubezahlen. Damit mußt du aufhören, denn diese Schuld gibt es nur in deiner Einbildung.« Simon schwieg lange Zeit, so erschrocken war er. Aber dann faßte er alles in einer Frage zusammen: »Der Versuch, abzubezahlen, ist also sinnlos?«

»Ja, denn es geht nicht«, erklärte Andersson. »Es gibt keine gängige Valuta. Ist doch selbstverständlich, wenn es keine Schulden gibt, kann es ja auch nichts geben, womit sie zu bezahlen sind.«

»Ich verstehe, was du meinst«, antwortete Simon. »Aber ...«

»Du bist phantastisch!« lachte Andersson und Simon hörte heraus, daß er sich über ihn lustig machte. »Meistens dauert es das ganze Leben, bis man mit den Ratenzahlungen quitt ist.«

Es war lange Zeit still im Wagen. Simon schaute hinaus in die Moorlandschaft von Bottnaryd und dachte so scharf nach, daß sein Gesicht ganz faltig wurde. All das Schwere in seinem Inneren, dieses viel zu Empfindliche und Verwundbare, das er Schuld zu nennen pflegte, gab es also gar nicht.

»Dann ist es wohl Traurigkeit«, sagte er wie zu sich selbst.

»Traurigkeit«, meinte Andersson. »Traurigkeit ist meistens nichts als Selbstmitleid.«

»Jetzt reicht's aber!« wetterte Simon, mußte aber lachen, denn im Moment stimmte es ja, in diesem Augenblick hatten Anderssons Worte Gültigkeit.

»Es gibt immer nur den Augenblick«, erklärte der Fernfahrer.

»Du Lieber Gott . . .«, stöhnte Simon.

»Ganz richtig«, sagte Andersson. »Gott ist der Gott des Jetzt, wie er dich vorfindet, so nimmt er dich an. Er fragt nicht danach, was du gewesen bist, sondern wie du jetzt in diesem Augenblick bist.«

Er ließ den Wagen bei Ulricehamn bergab im Leerlauf fahren und setzte fort: »Du bist wohl auch einer von diesen Narren, die glauben, das Leben unter Kontrolle halten zu können. Darum fühlst du dich zu dem, was du das Böse nennst, hingezogen, bildest dir ein, wenn du begreifst, wie es funktioniert, kannst du dich dagegen wehren und brauchst keine Angst zu haben.«

Simon holte tief Luft, das stimmte, er wußte es, und es tat ihm gleichzeitig weh und auch gut.

Dann war Anderssons Stimme wieder da, milder jetzt. »Wovor fürchtest du dich denn, Junge?«

»Ich weiß es nicht«, antwortete Simon, aber im nächsten Moment wußte er es, eine alte Angst rührte sich tief unten in seinem Bauch.

Er erzählte von Inga, von dem Gefühl der Verlassenheit bevor Karin kam.

»Der Körper hat seine eigenen Erinnerungen«, nickte Andersson.

Sie näherten sich Borås, wo es wie üblich regnete. Andersson kurbelte die Scheibe hoch und bekam nach einigen Versuchen die Scheibenwischer in Gang.

»Es ist etwas Eigenartiges mit Säuglingen«, sagte er. »Mit ihrem Bewußtsein. Hast du schon mal einem Neugeborenen in die Augen geschaut?« Nein, das hatte Simon nicht.

In Sjömarken hörte der Regen unversehens wieder auf und Simon fragte: »Hast du Kinder?«

»Eine ganze Reihe, verteilt über die ganze Welt.«

»In Amerika?«

»Ja, in Amerika auch, und sonst noch da und dort.«

»Du hast also keins mehr bei dir zu Hause?«

»Doch, ich habe einen Sohn in Schweden«, sagte Andersson und das rätselhafte Lächeln war sonniger denn je, als er hinzufügte: »Einen verdammt feinen Kerl.«

Es waren sechs Stunden vergangen, als sie im Glanz der Nachmittagssonne aus Richtung Kallebäck auf Göteborg zurollten. Aber für Simon war die Fahrt kurz wie ein Atemzug gewesen, er hätte mit Andersson bis in alle Ewigkeit im Wagen sitzen können.

»Das war's also«, sagte der Fahrer und hielt vor dem Hauptbahnhof. »Steig schnell aus, mir wird die Zeit schon knapp.«

»Du gibst mir doch wohl deine Adresse?« Simon stotterte vor lauter Hast, als er sah, wie Andersson schon die Wagentür wieder zuzog.

»Wir sehen uns wieder, Junge. Wir sehen uns, nur keine Bange.«

Andersson mußte mit seiner Ladung zum Hafen, die *Britannia* sollte bis spätestens fünf Uhr fertig beladen sein, und Simon sah den Wagen in Richtung Kaianlagen verschwinden.

Er fühlte sich unglaublich verlassen. Aber er betrat den Bahnhof, zählte sein Geld nach, es waren immer noch fünffünfundsiebzig, und fischte ein paar Zehnöremünzen heraus.

Karin war am Telefon.

»Hallo, Mama, bei mir ist alles bestens. Ist Isak in der Nähe?«

»Nein, er ist mit Mona im Kino.«

Simon versuchte zu denken, gewann Zeit durch die Frage: »Und dir geht's gut?«

»Absolut prima.«

»Du, Mama, kannst du Isak bestellen, daß ich es geschafft habe, daß es jetzt vorbei ist.«

»Wovon redest du, Simon?«

Er hörte die Besorgnis in ihrer Stimme und dachte, verdammt. »Ist nur ein Scherz, Mama, eine Wette.«

»Ach ja«, die Stimme klang jetzt eine Spur gekränkt, Karin glaubte ihm nicht.

»Mama!« schrie Simon. »Meine Münzen sind gleich alle, aber mir ist es im ganzen Leben noch nie so gut gegangen, hörst du!«

Das glaubte sie ihm, lachte, und dann war die Verbindung weg.

Als er am darauffolgenden Samstag in die Stadt kam, ging er stundenlang von einer LKW-Zentrale zur andern, von Fuhrwerker zu Fuhrwerker, und fragte nach Andersson, einem kleinen Mann mit braunen Augen, der einen grünen Dodge fuhr.

Nein, keiner kannte Andersson.

»Wird irgend so'n Einzelkämpfer sein«, hieß es. »Davon gibt es in unserer Branche eine Menge.«

Erik brachte Karin morgens den Kaffee ans Bett. Erst hatte sie das verlegen gemacht, aber bald war es zur Gewohnheit geworden. Ein Bedürfnis geradezu, mit frisch aufgebrühtem Kaffee und den oft neuen und guten morgendlichen Gedanken die Bettwärme noch eine Weile genießen zu dürfen.

In diesem Spätwinter kreisten ihre Gedanken häufig um Simon, der fröhlich und ausgeglichen war, obwohl es draußen auf den Inseln bei Kälte und Wind nicht unbedingt erheiternd sein konnte.

An einem Februartag, als es draußen schneite und sie die Nachttischlampe ausgeknipst hatte, um im Licht des anbrechenden Tages den Schneeflocken zuzusehen, klopfte Mona an ihre Tür.

Ach ja, dachte Karin, heute ist Mittwoch, da hat das Mädchen frei.

»Darf ich mich ein Weilchen zu dir setzen?«

Mona kroch ans Fußende des Bettes und wickelte sich in eine Decke. »Möchtest du Kaffee?«

»Nein, danke, ich habe schon gefrühstückt.«

Und dann, sehr schnell, als wolle sie es hinter sich bringen: »Karin, ich krieg ein Kind.«

Karin spürte, daß ihr Herz sich eine Weile seltsam benahm, aber das war sie ja gewöhnt und machte sich nicht viel daraus. Gedanken rasten ihr durch den Kopf, widersprüchliche Gefühle kämpften in ihr, uralte Frauenängste vor der Entbindung, Zärtlichkeit für die junge Frau, Freude, Besorgnis und, von allem am schwersten, das alte Leid ihrer eigenen Kinderlosigkeit.

Neid, dachte sie, ich bin neidisch.

Aber dann durchzuckte es sie, ich werde ein Enkelkind haben.

Das stimmte zwar nicht ganz, und doch war die Freude darüber das stärkste von allen Gefühlen.

»Herrgott, wie schön!« sagte sie.

Und dann laut lachend: »Da hätte man ja selbst drauf kommen können, so viel Liebe in einem so engen Bett und dann nur ein kleines Gummisäckchen als Gegenwehr!«

Mona hatte von ihrem Pessar erzählt, es der verwunderten Karin gezeigt, die gemeint hatte, zu so einem dünnen und schlotterigen Gummiballon hätte sie niemals Vertrauen.

Mona hatte sich damals stellvertretend für das Pessar gekränkt gefühlt, aber jetzt konnte sie einfach nicht sagen, wie es sich wirklich verhielt, daß sie es schon lange nicht mehr benutzte, weil sie die Hochzeit wollte. Und Kinder.

Und ganz besonders wollte sie von der Krankenpflegeschule loskommen.

»Jetzt wirst du Oma, Karin«, sagte sie.

»Jedenfalls sowas Ähnliches.«

Dann verloren sie sich in richtigem Frauengeschwätz von dem kleinen Jungen, nein Mädchen, sagte Mona, ich bin fast sicher, daß es ein Mädchen wird.

»Sie wird Malin heißen.«

»Wieso das?« fragte Karin. Sie fand den Namen altmodisch und nicht schön. Ihrer Meinung nach haftete ihm Armeleutegeruch an.

»Meine Mutter hat so geheißen«, sagte Mona, und da gab es nichts hinzuzufügen.

»Weiß Isak es schon?«

»Nein, noch nicht.«

»Ihr müßt heiraten.«

»Mmmm, hast du gehört, daß Frisörs in die Stadt ziehen wollen, die halten es mit dem Gerede über Dolly wohl hier nicht mehr aus. Und da habe ich mir gedacht, wir sollten die Dreizimmerwohnung im ersten Stock bei Gustafssons mieten.«

»Nicht schlecht«, nickte Karin und dachte, das Leben sei doch wirklich gut gesinnt, Mona und Isak würden ihre nächsten Nachbarn werden. Und das kleine Mädchen, ja, Karin hatte an das Ungeborene schon als an das kleine Mädchen zu denken begonnen.

»Vielleicht könntest du bei Gustafssons anrufen und dich erkundigen?«

»Ja, gerne«, erbot sich Karin.

Aber dann brachen alle Bedenken über sie herein. Wegen Isak und Chalmers.

»Wir können ein Studiendarlehen beantragen«, sagte Mona. »Das klingt albern, wenn man an Ruben denkt, aber trotzdem, wir werden das schaffen.«

Sie schaute Karin bittend an, die aber schüttelte den Kopf. In den Göta-Werken war Isak die Bedeutung des Geldes für das eigene Selbstwertgefühl bewußt geworden. Er bezahlte bei Karin und Erik ganz gewissenhaft für sich. Zu Ruben hatte er gesagt, für Marias Honorare wolle er selbst aufkommen. Das war eine große Ausgabe und ihm war längst bewußt, daß er noch Jahre zu ihr in Behandlung würde gehen müssen.

Das Geld war bei den beiden manchmal so knapp gewesen, daß Mona sich bei Karin etwas für die Straßenbahnfahrt borgen mußte.

Karin wußte sehr wohl, daß Isaks Haltung für ihn selbst wichtig war, aber manchmal tat ihr Ruben leid.

Jetzt hockten die beiden Frauen also im Bett und zählten im Kopf zusammen: Bettwäsche und Handtücher, Kissen, Decken, Betten, Möbel, Kochtöpfe, Teller . . .

»Alles so schlicht wie möglich«, sagte Mona. Und als Karin meinte, sie wollten doch erst einmal im Keller nachsehen, was dort abgestellt war, mußte sie die Augen vor Monas Zorn niederschlagen: »Es kann nicht viel sein«, fügte Karin schnell hinzu, denn sie erinnerte sich, daß sie, als sie das Haus umbauten, die meisten Sachen weggeworfen hatte.

»Schade um deine Ausbildung«, sagte sie, denn sie hatte sich auf Monas Krankenpflegediplom gefreut.

»Pah«, machte Mona. »Ich möchte gar nicht Krankenschwester sein.«

»Aber du weißt, daß eine Berufsausbildung viel wert ist, wenn etwas passieren sollte«, entgegnete Karin, dachte aber im nächsten Augenblick, daß Rubens Familie nie in Not geraten konnte.

Trotzdem seufzte sie, ohne zu wissen, weshalb.

Als Lisa kam, hatte Karin schon bei Gustafssons angerufen, nein, sie hatten die Wohnung noch nicht vergeben, doch, doch, das würde schon in Ordnung gehen.

Während Lisa das Haus aufräumte, machten Mona und Karin einen Spaziergang am Strand. Es hatte zu schneien aufgehört, eine bleiche Wintersonne wagte sich heraus und färbte das Eis rund um die Bootsstege goldgelb.

»Es ist wichtig, daß Isak es bald erfährt«, sagte Karin.

Gegen Nachmittag fuhr Mona in die Stadt, stand am Kai und sah den Kahn mit den Männern der Göta-Werke über den Fluß kommen. Isak war gleich im ersten, freute sich, war aber doch ein wenig beunruhigt, als er sie sah: »Du mußt Onsala noch begrüßen.«

Mona schüttelte dem langen Revolverdreher die Hand, dann aber stand sie mit Isak allein am Kai und sah die Frage in seinen Augen.

»Gehen wir«, sagte sie. Isak schob sein Fahrrad und versuchte gleichzeitig, Mona einen Arm um die Schultern zu legen.

»Es ist hoffentlich nichts passiert?«

»Doch«, sagte sie. »Wir kriegen ein Kind.«

Isak ließ gleichzeitig sie und das Fahrrad los, das auf die Straße schepperte, während er sprachlos da stand und die Freude in sich einströmen ließ. Dann sagte er genau wie Karin: »Mein Gott, wie wunderbar.«

Nach einer Weile brachte er sein Fahrrad zur Gesenkschmiede, schloß es dort für die Nacht an, nahm Mona bei der Hand und sagte: »Jetzt gehen wir erst mal zu Papa.«

Sie schwebten förmlich durch die Stadt, die Füße spürten das Pflaster erst wieder, als sie sich Rubens Haustür näherten und Mona in die Wirklichkeit zurückfand.

»Was wird er sagen?«

»Er wird sich freuen.«

Trotzdem staunte Isak über Rubens Freude, als sie beide sehr jung und etwas furchtsam vor ihm standen und Mona es aussprach: »Wir erwarten ein Kind.«

Es war eine Freude, die aus den tiefsten Tiefen tausendjähriger Quellen emporstieg, eine Freude des Blutes, Familienfreude.

Mona schien es zu empfinden, denn sie sagte: »Es wird ein jüdisches Kind werden, wir werden in der Synagoge heiraten und ich werde euren Glauben annehmen.«

Da tat Ruben etwas Unerwartetes, entzündete die Kerzen auf dem siebenarmigen Leuchter, legte seine Arme um Mona und Isak, und sie standen vor den ruhigen Flammen und Ruben sprach ein langes Gebet auf Hebräisch.

Das alte Gebet drang in sie alle, und auch in das lauschende Kind ein, die Worte waren nicht zu verstehen, aber in ihnen war ein Friede, der allen Verstand überragte.

Etwas später rief Ruben Karin an und fragte, ob sie nicht heute abend zum Essen kommen könnten, er habe etwas Wichtiges zu berichten. Er hörte das helle Lachen in ihrer Stimme, als sie sagte, sie und Erik wollten es versuchen, aber erst als Ruben den Hörer aufgelegt hatte, begriff er, was das bedeutete.

Sie wußte es wohl schon, seine kluge Schicksalsgöttin.

Beim Essen sagte Isak: »Nun, Papa, ich möchte eigentlich bei den Göta-Werken bleiben. Was mich betrifft, lasse ich das Studium bei Chalmers gerne sausen.«

Mona senkte den Blick, um ihre Gedanken zu verbergen, aber Eriks Augen glitzerten neugierig und eine Spur boshaft. Jetzt würde sich zeigen, wie weit die Klassenlosigkeit reichte, die Ruben so gerne an den Tag legte. Nie würde er damit einverstanden sein, daß sein Sohn ein gewöhnlicher Arbeiter wurde, nicht, wenn es ums Ganze ging.

Aber Ruben sagte: »Ich habe das erwartet, Isak. Du fühlst dich dort ja wohl.«

Dann wandte er sich an Erik und gab fast schon ein wenig an: »Isak arbeitet schon an seiner eigenen Drehbank, das ist eine unerhört komplizierte Maschine.« Erik staunte, aber dann schlug er mit der Faust auf den Tisch, daß die Gläser klirrten: »Zum Teufel . . .«

»Nicht fluchen«, mahnte Karin, und Erik kam fast aus dem Konzept, denn Karin war, was Flüche anbelangte, auch nicht von schlechten Eltern. Aber vielleicht dachte sie an das Kind in Monas Bauch . . .

»Isak«, sagte Erik. »Du hast keine Ahnung davon, wie es mit der Zeit wird, wie man sich verausgabt und Rückenschmerzen und Rheuma kriegt. Gar nicht zu reden von den Gehörschäden und den schlechten Löhnen. Ich habe das selbst mitgemacht, ich weiß Bescheid. Auf die Dauer hält man den Dreck und den Lärm nicht aus.«

»Und die Unfreiheit«, fügte er hinzu. »Die ist das Schlimmste.«

Isak wollte einwenden, er habe inzwischen eine ganze Menge gesehen, wolle aber lieber die körperliche Belastung auf sich nehmen, als so ein scheißvornehmer Ingenieur werden. Aber Karin kam ihm zuvor: »Isak braucht Praxis, auch wenn er später noch in Chalmers studieren sollte. Es kann nie schaden, wenn er ein paar Jahre im Werk bleibt, damit sein Leben wenigstens in einigermaßen geordneten Bahnen verläuft, solange das Kind klein ist.«

Dann erzählte sie von der Wohnung bei Gustafssons.

»Ist die nicht zu unbequem?« warf Ruben ein.

»Nein, es gibt dort inzwischen Zentralheizung und Bad.«

Isak dachte, Gott ist gut, und er wollte Gustafssons noch am selben Abend aufsuchen, aber Mona und Karin dachten nur an Bettwäsche und Leinen, Möbel und Matratzen, Teller und Tassen und andere Notwendigkeiten.

Doch keine von beiden sprach es aus, und als Ruben mit Karin anstieß, erkannte sie an seinen fröhlichen Augen, daß ihm etwas Bestimmtes vorschwebte.

Mona erzählte, daß sie zum jüdischen Glauben konvertieren wolle. Erik machte ein erstauntes Gesicht, aber Karin nickte. Sie konnte es verstehen.

Keiner widmete dem Fischhändler auch nur einen Gedanken.

Alle brachen zeitig auf, denn Isak wollte Gustafssons doch noch aufsuchen. Er kam nach einer halben Stunde heim und sagte, alles sei abgesprochen, er werde den Mietvertrag am Samstag unterschreiben.

Es würde teurer werden als er gerechnet hatte, er nannte eine Miete, bei der Karin das Kinn herunterfiel.

»Da nimmt Gustafsson sich aber gewaltig was raus«, sagte Erik, als er später mit Karin allein war. »Hat sich wohl gedacht, der Sohn vom reichen Lentov kann zahlen.«

Karin nickte, meinte aber, bei der heutigen Wohnungsnot müsse man trotz allem dankbar sein.

Am nächsten Tag ging Mona zur Leiterin der Krankenpflegeschule und meldete sich ab. Sie sagte geradeheraus, daß sie schwanger sei, und die barsche Dame bekam mit gespitzten Lippen gerade noch heraus: »Dann würden Sie sowieso von der Schule verwiesen, Mona.«

Während die junge Frau die notwendigen Papiere ausfüllte, sprach die Leiterin von der Verwahrlosung der Jugend, und ob es für das Kind einen Vater gebe, ach so, es werde eine Hochzeit geben, und durfte man fragen, wer der Glückliche sei?

Mona lächelte nachsichtig: »Ja, es ist der Sohn von Ruben Lentov.«

»Die Alte hat ausgesehen, als würde sie ersticken«, lachte Mona, als sie es Ruben erzählte. Der lächelte und dachte, da habe ich nun endlich ein Kind, das stolz auf mich ist. Sie aßen, wie am Vorabend ausgemacht, in einem Restaurant zusammen zu Mittag.

Dann sagte Ruben Karins und Monas Sprüchlein in etwas umgekehrter Reihenfolge auf, das Sprüchlein von Möbeln und Teppichen, Porzellan und Silber, wie er sagte, und Mona liebte ihn allein schon wegen der schönen Wörter.

Er nahm ein Kuvert aus der Tasche: »Dies ist ein Geschenk an meine Schwiegertochter«, sagte Ruben.

»Und Isak«, ergänzte sie.

»Isak hat mit deiner und meiner Freundschaft nichts zu tun«, stellte er klar, und seine Augen funkelten.

Mona lächelte, als sie den Umschlag in ihre Handtasche steckte.

Während der langen Straßenbahnfahrt hinaus zu Karin widerstand sie der Versuchung, den Brief zu öffnen, dachte aber bekümmert, er sehe etwas dünn aus, und sie brauchten doch so viele Dinge. Teppiche, hatte Ruben gesagt. Sie wußte ein Geschäft, wo es wunderbare handgewebte Teppiche gab.

Bei Karin zu Hause nahm sie das Kuvert aus der Tasche, es war noch dünner, als sie es in Erinnerung hatte: »Mach du's auf«, sagte sie zu Karin. »Ich trau mich nicht.«

Karin nahm energisch ein Messer zur Hand und schlitzte den Umschlag auf, der nur ein Stück Papier enthielt.

»Das wird ein Scheck sein«, meinte sie, denn sie hatten beide bisher noch nie einen gesehen.

»Da steht Zehntausend drauf«, stellte Karin fest, und Mona mußte sich setzen, um nicht vor Freude in Ohnmacht zu fallen.

Sie versuchten sich bei einer Tasse Kaffee zu erholen, ehe sie sich die Wohnung anschauen gingen, in der die Frau des Friseurmeisters gerade zu packen angefangen hatte. So viele Rosen, dachte Mona, wie häßlich. Aber die Zimmer waren schön, groß und hell, und die Küche war ebenso geräumig wie die Küche bei Karin.

»Sieh mal«, sagte Mona, als sie am Schlafzimmerfenster standen und zu Larssons hinüber schauten. »Wir können einander zuwinken.«

»Schreckliche Möbel und entsetzliche Tapeten«, bemerkte Mona, als sie wieder zu Hause waren. »Wir werden in jedem einzelnen Raum die Wände weiß anmalen.«

Karin, die die Friseurfamilie nie hatte leiden können, stets aber deren Wohnung mit den Stilmöbeln und den Kristalleuchtern bewundert hatte, war erstaunt. »Wie wollt ihr's denn einrichten?«

»Weiße Wände, weiße Möbel, weiße Vorhänge«, antwortete Mona.

»Das klingt ... hell«, fand Karin.

»Wenige, aber teure Möbel«, sagte Mona. »Massenhaft Grünpflanzen.«

Sie war in Träume versunken, und Karin erkannte, daß sie diese schon lange gehegt hatte.

»Es soll aussehen wie in einem Pfarrhof auf dem Land«, sagte Mona. »Und die Küche soll so sein wie deine, mit vielen Flickenteppichen auf dem Fußboden. Und nur keine Kristalleuchter und solcher Firlefanz.«

Karin war bewußt, daß sie sich geschmeichelt fühlen sollte, also verschwieg sie, daß sie sich schon sehr lange einen Kristalleuchter gewünscht hatte.

Dann hörten sie Isak in der Auffahrt pfeifen, falsch wie immer, und Mona sah wie das verkörperte schlechte Gewissen aus. Er merkte es sofort: »Was hast du denn Schlimmes angestellt?«

Es sollte ein Scherz sein, aber er erschrak, als Mona vorschlug, lieber hinauf in ihr Zimmer zu gehen, um miteinander zu reden.

»Wenn du Hilfe brauchst, ruf mich«, murmelte Karin, die auch ein bißchen besorgt war.

Eine Weile später hörte sie aber Isaks Gelächter durch die Decke hindurch, und kurz darauf rannte er die Treppe herunter, nahm Karin in die Arme und imitierte Rubens etwas schleppenden Tonfall mit dem leichten Akzent: »Schöne Grüße an Isak, Mona, der hat mit deiner und meiner Freundschaft überhaupt nichts zu tun.«

»Mein Vater ist doch wirklich ein verdammt schlauer alter Jude!«

Isak war erleichtert und Karin und Mona begriffen beide sofort, daß er für sich das Sprüchlein auch immer wieder aufgesagt hatte: Bettwäsche, Leinen, Möbel, Porzellan.

Einige Wochen später kam der Samstag, der als ein Tag, an dem alles passierte, in die Familiengeschichte eingehen sollte.

Was Ruben anbelangte, fing der Tag nicht besonders gut an.

»Herr Direktor, Ihre Nichte ist am Telefon.«

Ruben verbiß sich eine Grimasse und sagte müde: »Sie ist nicht meine Nichte, sondern die Nichte meiner Frau.«

Er merkte, daß er lächerlich wirkte.

Die Stimme war wie immer fieberhaft, fordernd. Sie wollte mehr Geld.

»Ich bin am Verhungern«, sagte sie.

Aber Ruben war durch die Jahre bezüglich Iza abgehärtet, und er dachte an Olof Hirtz, und daß er dem Mädchen Grenzen setzen mußte, und so sagte er: »Du weißt, daß du mit der Unterstützung zurechtkommen mußt, die du bekommst.«

Sie schnurrte am Telefon wie eine Katze, als sie erwiderte: »Simon hat eine Woche bei mir gewohnt, er hat wie ein Löwe gegessen und wollte die Stadt kennenlernen und auf großem Fuß leben und so.«

Ruben wurde das Herz schwer, aber seine Stimme war ruhig, als er fragte: »Wann war das?«

»Es ist schon eine Weile her.« Und jetzt versagte ihr die Stimme und Ruben wußte, daß sie log, aber wohl doch nicht in jeder Hinsicht.

»Ich schicke einen Hunderter«, sagte er. »Wie geht's dir in der Schule?«

»So lala«, sagte sie. »Danke, lieber Onkel.«

Das war am Samstagmorgen, er rief Karin an und fragte, ob Simon wie üblich Wochenendurlaub habe. »Ja, wir erwarten ihn.«

»Dann hole ich ihn beim Regiment ab.«

Ruben war verärgert und wußte, daß er zornig war, weil er Angst um ihn hatte und ihn schützen wollte. Also versuchte er sich so gut es ging im Zaum zu halten: Verdammter Junge.

Simon stand auf der Anlegebrücke und wartete auf das Boot, das ihn zum Festland bringen sollte. Der Wind kam von See, aus Nordwest, und war beißend kalt, hatte die Stadt also nicht gestreift und brachte folglich auch keinen Hauch von Rubens Zorn mit.

Simon war gut gelaunt.

Er hatte in der Nacht am tiefschwarzen Meer Wache geschoben. An den eintönig sich hinziehenden Dienst war er inzwischen gewöhnt. Anfangs hatte er manchmal den Wunsch nach einem Krieg verspürt, feindliche Schiffe am Horizont, Eindringlinge auf den Schäreninseln, um schießen, Alarm schlagen und Bewegung in die Sache bringen zu dürfen, damit endlich einmal alles drunter und drüber ginge.

Es gab Wehrdienstleistende, die hatten etwas in dieser Richtung probiert, waren von Sjövall eingesperrt und noch Wochen danach von den Kameraden gehänselt worden, weil alle durch den Alarm aus den Betten gescheucht worden waren und vor Schreck Bauchschmerzen bekommen hatten.

Simon hatte in der vergangenen Nacht lange zu den kleinen Inseln hinübergesehen, hatte gedacht, sie wüßten, daß er sie beobachtete. Ihm war bewußt geworden, daß das Leben dieser Inseln in der Ewigkeit verankert war, daß nichts auf sie eingewirkt hatte, seit das Inlandeis vor zehntausend Jahren geschmolzen war. Dann aber kam ihm der Gedanke, daß für sie wohl eine andere Zeitrechnung galt, und er hatte sich mit einem Atomphysiker unterhalten, der ihm erklärte, daß im Inneren der Steine so etwas wie ein Tanz stattfinde.

»Ich glaube dir«, hatte Simon gesagt und versucht, sich den Tanz im Granit vorzustellen, den Rhythmus, der nichts von Angst wußte.

Dann war er abgelöst worden und hatte noch ein paar Stunden schlafen können, bis die Zeit für Waffenreinigung, Uniformpflege und Landtransport gekommen war.

Ruben sah den Jungen auf sich zu kommen, groß und fröhlich, weiß das Lächeln im wettergegerbten Gesicht, Intensität in den Bewegungen, im Handschlag. Er ist erwachsen und hat ein Anrecht auf Privatleben, dachte Ruben, aber es war schon zu spät.

»Du bist wütend auf mich«, stellte Simon fest.

»Naja«, zögerte Ruben. »Los, steig ein.«

Simon machte es ihm nicht schwer, er war seit eh und je offen wie ein Buch, das gelesen und verstanden werden wollte und nichts dafür konnte, daß sein reicher Inhalt kompliziert war.

»Iza hat angerufen«, sagte Ruben, legte den ersten Gang ein und blinkte in Fahrtrichtung.

Simon wurde feuerrot, dann zog er sich in sich selbst zurück, und es wurde still im Wagen. Er fühlte sich bloßgestellt, als hätte Ruben ihm alle schützenden Verkleidungen heruntergerissen und sein Innerstes entblößt, seine innersten und heimlichsten Phantasien offengelegt.

»Warum bist du hingefahren?«

»Weil ich kindisch bin, weil ich mir selbst Gefühle vormache.«

Wieder langes Schweigen: »Ich hatte mir eingebildet, sie schafft mir eine Wirklichkeit«, sagte er dann.

Und später: »Es ist absolut mißlungen, ich habe für sie alles nur noch schlimmer gemacht.« Er versuchte von den Spinnen zu erzählen, von der Sogwirkung der Vernichtung, kam aber davon ab, hörte selbst, wie angekränkelt das klang.

»Es gab ja auch eine Menge Schuldgefühle«, gestand er. »Idiotische Phantasien, Anteil an ihrem Schicksal haben zu können.«

Dann war es wieder still, er suchte nach Worten: »Ich konnte nichts für sie tun.«

»Nein, Simon, das kann niemand.«

»Das ist schrecklich.«

»Ja.«

»Ich schäme mich wie ein geprügelter Hund.«

»Du wirst nicht wieder hinfahren?«

»Nie im Leben.«

Ruben war so erleichtert, daß er innerlich zusammensackte. Er mußte Simon ein bißchen hochnehmen: »Aber du hast bei ihr gegessen und hast in der Stadt auf großem Fuß gelebt und ihr ganzes Geld verpraßt.«

»Das ist eine Lüge«, fiel Simon Ruben ins Wort und erzählte, wie er mit fünf Kronen und fünfundsiebzig Öre in der Tasche auf der Straße gestanden und sein Geld gezählt hatte, um überhaupt den Mut zu haben, in ein Café zu gehen und ein paar Käsebrote zu bestellen.

Ruben lachte.

»Können wir einen Moment stehenbleiben, ich muß dir was erzählen«, bat Simon, und Ruben fuhr bis zur nächsten Bushaltestelle, um dort im vorderen Bereich zu parken.

Nun folgte die Geschichte von Andersson, von Omberg und Alvastra und den Riesen, die ihre Unterhosen im Vättersee wuschen.

»Er hat die phantastischsten Sachen von sich gegeben, weißt du. Seit ich ihn kennengelernt habe, bin ich der fröhlichste Mensch.«

Ruben wurde fast eifersüchtig, aber dann ließ er sich von der Geschichte vom Saal des Bergkönigs im eigenen Herzen mitreißen, die jedem Menschen das Bewußtsein schenkt, nicht vergebens zu leben. »Aber das beste, was er gesagt hat, ist das von der Schuld«, berichtete Simon. »Er hat gesagt, daß es die Schuld an sich nicht gibt, daß es dabei um nie begangene Verbrechen geht, die somit nie gesühnt werden können.«

»Das habe ich auch schon manchmal gedacht«, sagte Ruben. »Aber es ist nicht wahr, jeder Mensch hat immer wieder einmal etwas verraten oder verletzt oder unterlassen.«

»Du auch?«

»O ja. Ich habe Isak verraten, als er klein war. Ich habe Olga verletzt, indem ich sie heiratete, obwohl nicht sie es war, die ich haben wollte. Ganz zu schweigen von meinen Eltern, bei denen ich nicht ernsthaft darauf gedrungen habe, mit mir nach Schweden zu kommen.«

»Wie hättest du sie denn zwingen können?«

»Es wäre gegangen, wenn ich wirklich gewollt hätte.«

»Andersson hat gesagt, Gott ist der Gott des Jetzt, den nur kümmert, wer man gerade in diesem Moment ist.«

»So leicht kann ich es mir nicht machen«, überlegte Ruben, doch Simon hörte nicht zu, er suchte nach anderen Aussagen von damals im Lastwagen.

»Wie dem auch sei, eine Verrechnung ist nicht möglich, es gibt keine Währung, um Schuld zu bezahlen.«

Ruben sah Simon lange an. Das ist wahr, dachte er, es ist ekelhaft wahr. »Was hat dieser Mann noch gesagt?«

»Daß die meisten Menschen ihr ganzes Leben hindurch immerzu sinnlose Abzahlungen probieren und daß ihnen nicht in den Kopf will, warum die Schuld immer gleich groß bleibt.«

»Diesen Andersson würde ich gerne kennenlernen«, sagte Ruben.

»Das geht nicht«, antwortete Simon und berichtete, wie er bei allen Fuhrunternehmern der Stadt nach diesem Fahrer gesucht hatte.

»Kein Mensch kennt ihn.«

»Merkwürdig.«

»Ja.«

Sie sahen einander kopfschüttelnd an und setzten ihre Fahrt Richtung Stadt fort.

»Wie geht's Mona?«

»Bestens«, antwortete Ruben und bekam zu hören, daß Andersson gesagt hatte, man müsse Neugeborenen in die Augen sehen, denn dabei könne man eine Menge lernen.

Als sie über die Torgny-Segerstedts-Gata Richtung Långedrag fuhren, fragte Ruben: »Du hast gar nicht mehr so lange bis zur Freiheit?«

»Noch sechs Wochen bis zur Entlassung. Wir zählen schon die Tage.«

»Ich werde Ende April nach Amerika fahren und zurück dann über London und Paris. Ich hätte dich gerne dazu eingeladen, wenn du Interesse hast.«

»Was heißt hier wenn?« schrie Simon. Doch dann sagte er: »Warum willst du mich mitnehmen?«

»Weil es mir Freude machen würde ...«

Simon lachte laut auf, es stimmte, sie beide konnten sich miteinander freuen. Es ging hier nicht um eine alte, noch offene Rechnung bei Karin, hier ging es um ihn, Simon.

Ruben strahlte wie die Sonne als er sagte: »Ich stelle nur eine Bedingung. Und das ist, daß du dieses ärgerliche Onkel ablegst. Dafür bist du jetzt zu alt.«

»Und du bist zu jung, Ruben«, meinte Simon, und da waren sie auch schon an der Auffahrt zum Haus bei der Werft.

Eine große, bunt zusammengewürfelte Mahlzeit erwartete sie, Frühstücksmittag nannte es Karin, denn hier gibt es keinen, der Zeit hat, mehr als einmal am Tag etwas zu kochen. Das Schöne Zimmer hatte sich in eine Werkstatt und Nähstube verwandelt, am einen Ende des Zimmers umwogten Wolken von weißem Musselin Karins alte Nähmaschine und am andern Ende stand der Tisch mit maßstabgerechten Zeichnungen, Farbmustern, Möbelmodellen aus Papier und Stößen von Zeitschriften.

»Brautkleid?« fragte Simon und sah Mona in all dem Weiß erstaunt an.

»Nein, du Spinner«, sagte sie. »Vorhänge.«

Simon machte einen Kniefall vor ihr, der Jungfräulichen. »Du bist ja gar nicht verheiratet«, sagte er. Doch dann legte er ihr den Kopf auf den Bauch, sagte: »Hallo, du da drin!« und schaute zu Mona auf.

»Ein Mädchen«, stellte er fest.

»Ja«, sagte Mona. »Klar ist es ein Mädchen.«

»Die zwei sind nicht bei Trost«, erklärte Isak.

»Schwangere Frauen sind immer ein bißchen verrückt«, meinte Karin.

»Ist mir klar. Und Simon hat ja immer gesponnen.«

Sie aßen im Stehen, eine Stehparty also, und mitten in all dem Durcheinander sagte Simon fast nebenbei, ich fahre nach der Entlassung mit Ruben nach Amerika.

Erstaunen und Jubel. Aber Karin warf ein, das bringe sie um, wäre es etwa nicht genug mit einer Hochzeit und einer neuen Wohnung und der Entbindung, müsse da auch noch eine Amerikareise dazwischenkommen?

»Aber Mama«, klang Simon etwas ängstlich. »Um meine Reise brauchst du dich überhaupt nicht zu kümmern.«

»Simon«, entgegnete Karin. »Ich weiß, das Kleid unseres Königreichs hat etwas Magisches an sich, es wächst im Gleichschritt mit den Jungs, die drinstecken, mit. Aber hier zu Hause können wir nicht in ähnlicher Weise zaubern. Ich bin sicher, du paßt in kein einziges früheres Kleidungsstück mehr.«

Sie lachten, sie hatten Samstag für Samstag über Simons Versuche gelacht, sich zivil anzuziehen und sich in Pullis zu zwängen, deren Ärmel nur knapp über den Ellbogen reichten und in Hosen, die aussahen, als hätte jemand sie an der Wade abgeschnitten. Nicht zu reden von den Sakkos, die vor lauter Schreck geplatzt wären, wenn er versucht hätte, sich hineinzupressen.

»Es wird sicher zwischendurch ein paar Tage geben, um die Kleiderfrage zu lösen«, erklärte Ruben. »Ich brauche nur deinen Paß, Simon. Hast du überhaupt einen?«

Simon nickte, er hatte ihn sich kurz vor dem Abitur in dem Gefühl beschafft, daß sich ihm die Welt wieder öffnete und daß vielleicht …

»Ein Glück!« Ruben atmete auf und dachte an McCarthys Geist, der in den Vereinigten Staaten ebenso über der Paßbehörde wie über allem anderen schwebte.

Dann wurden Simon und Isak zu Gustafssons in den ersten Stock geschickt, um diesmal in der Küche Maß zu nehmen. Simon stand lange da und besah sich Dollys altes Kinderzimmer, und Isak sagte, von hier aus kann man direkt in den oberen Stock zu Hause gucken.

Simon nickte, ja, das konnte man.

Die Räume waren schon gestrichen, alles war weiß, wie Mona es beschlossen hatte. »Unsereins hat überhaupt keine Chance, seine Meinung zu äußern«, bemerkte Isak, als Simon meinte, man sei ja geradezu geblendet.

Sie gingen wieder zurück in das große Wohnzimmer.

»Du, Isak«, begann Simon. »Da ist etwas, was ich dir sagen möchte.«

»Noch was«, stöhnte Isak mit gespielter Furcht, sie hatten von Iza und dem Besuch in Stockholm gesprochen, so daß in dieser Hinsicht alles zwischen ihnen geklärt war.

Aber das Schweigen bezüglich Bylund hatte Simon belastet.

Er setzte sich mit ausgestreckten Beinen auf den Fußboden. Isak tat es ihm nach. »Du mußt es wissen«, fuhr Simon fort. »Ich habe Bylund fast totgeschlagen.«

Isak bekam runde Augen, rote Erregung breitete sich in seinem Körper aus. Er wollte alles wissen.

Als Simon zu den Schneidezähnen kam, die im Korridor in einer Blutlache gelegen hatten, konnte Isak nicht mehr stillsitzen, stand auf, schwankte wie ein Betrunkener und begann durch das leere Zimmer zu tanzen.

»Du weißt, ich bin bei Schlägereien immer gut gewesen«, bemerkte Simon gespielt kleinlaut, und Isak blieb mitten im Tanz stehen und erinnerte sich an sein erstes Zusammentreffen mit Simon irgendwann in fernen Kindertagen, als der kleine Junge den langen Grafensohn auf dem Schulhof fertiggemacht hatte.

Er hätte gerne zugegeben, daß er Simon liebte, begnügte sich aber mit: »Teufel noch mal!« Das allerdings voll Bewunderung.

Als sie zurückkamen, meinte Mona, sie hätten ja gewaltig viel Zeit gebraucht, und Karin sagte, es sei für Simon aus Stockholm ein Brief in einem braunen Umschlag gekommen.

Simon erschrak, er hörte es selbst, als er viel zu schnell fragte: »Wo ist er?«

»Ja, wo ist er?« wiederholte Karin. »In all diesem Durcheinander.«

Sie wühlten in den weißen Wolken, krochen unter Tisch und Nähmaschine herum, aber der Brief blieb verschwunden.

»Irgendwann wird er schon zum Vorschein kommen«, tröstete Karin, und Simon stöhnte, aber nur innerlich. Verdammt, jetzt hat Iza sich offensichtlich auf den Kriegspfad begeben.

Er wechselte einen Blick mit Isak und sah, daß auch er an die Worte im Auto dachte: Kann sie dich mit einem Kind festnageln ...

Inzwischen sind fast vier Monate vergangen, dachte Simon. Da ist es wohl nicht mehr gut möglich.

Aber er war beunruhigt und verdrückte sich, ging hinaus zur Werft, wo er Ruben und Erik in einer Holzbude fand, die als Büro diente. Erik machte ein bekümmertes Gesicht, das war Simon schon vorher aufgefallen, und er vergaß seine eigene Besorgnis, als er fragte: »Ist was los, Papa?«

»Erik hat es schwer«, übernahm Ruben die Antwort. »Alles läuft bei ihm ein bißchen zu gut.«

Da mußte Erik lachen und berichtete von den Bestellungen, die sich auf der Werft in fast nicht zu bewältigenden Mengen anhäuften, und daß diese somit weit über das zur Verfügung stehende Areal hinausgewachsen war.

»Ich will nicht vergrößern«, sagte Erik. »Dieser Gedanke, daß alles ständig wachsen muß, hat etwas Krankhaftes an sich. Warum soll ich es nicht bei drei oder vier Booten im Jahr bewenden lassen wie bisher?«

»Weil dann deine Kunden zu einem Konkurrenten mit größerer Kapazität und kürzeren Wartezeiten überlaufen werden«, überlegte Ruben, wie er und sein Rechtsanwalt es im Lauf des Winters schon öfter getan hatten. Erik war darüber jedesmal gleich wütend geworden.

»Es gibt doch da draußen bei Önnered noch Land genug«, warf Simon ein.

»Ja, zum Donnerwetter, ich habe doch in Askim schon ein Seegrundstück an der Hand«, erwiderte Erik. »Aber das wird ein solcher Betrieb, Simon, massenhaft Leute und Buchführung und Papiere und Sorgen.«

»Du mußt einen Direktor einstellen«, riet Ruben.

»Ruben Lentov!« begann Erik. »Wir kennen einander jetzt seit ...«

Aber Simon unterbrach ihn: »Papa«, sagte er. »Stell Isak an, der hat Rubens Geschäftssinn im Blut.«

Erik vergaß, was er hatte sagen wollen, und alle drei dachten daran, wie sie schon früher immer wieder über Isak und seine Fähigkeit gelacht hatten, billig einzukaufen und teuer zu verkaufen, leere Gläser und Flaschen, Sammelbildchen in Schokoriegeln und solche Sachen.

»Glaubt ihr, er will?« zögerte Erik.

»Er braucht vorher eine Ausbildung, Handelsschule«, warf Ruben ein.

»Chalmers«, ergänzte Erik.

Aber da sagte Simon, daß die Technische Lehranstalt von Chalmers Eriks Traum für Isak gewesen war, und niemals Isaks eigener Traum.

Erik mußte lachen: »Du bist ein Genie, Simon.«

»Ja«, meinte Simon. »Ich bin nicht unbegabt.«

Ruben war zufrieden. Wenn alles gut ging, konnte er, sobald Eriks Selbstwertgefühl dies zuließ, seinen Kapitalanteil an der Werft auf Isak überschreiben. Dann wäre der Junge abgesichert.

Aber alle drei saßen sie da und dachten an die Göta-Werke, die die Grundlage für Isaks Selbstbewußtsein bildeten.

»Wir müssen ihn selbst fragen«, schlug Erik vor.

»Ich gehe ihn holen«, erbot sich Simon.

Isak kam, war unerhört erstaunt und ebenso interessiert.

»Das ist ein ganz erstaunlicher Tag«, bemerkte er. »Wird mir Bedenkzeit gewährt? Ich muß das mit Mona besprechen und so.«

Aber er hatte sich schon entschlossen, und ehe er ging, fragte er: »Wie lange dauert diese Handelsausbildung?«

»Ich denke, du schaffst das in einem Jahr«, antwortete Ruben.

Es war schon spät, als Simon hinauf in sein Zimmer kam, und dort der Brief ordentlich auf seinem Schreibtisch lag, ein großer brauner Umschlag, genau wie Karin gesagt hatte.

Er riß ihn auf, fing zu schreien an und raste jubelnd die Treppe hinunter. Ruben war zum Glück noch da, und Simon warf sich ihm in die Arme und brüllte: »Es ist angenommen! Sie geben es heraus, das Gedicht vom Meer!«

Karin mußte sich auf die Küchenbank setzen, ihre Wangen brannten und ihre Augen leuchteten vor Stolz.

Ihr Junge war Schriftsteller geworden, es würde ein Buch herauskommen mit seinem Namen auf dem Umschlag. Er hatte ihr das lange Gedicht vorgelesen, sie wußte, daß es schön war, daß es vom Meer sang und ebenso unbegreiflich war wie dieses.

Auch Erik strahlte vor Stolz.

Doch Ruben, der das Gedicht ins Reine schreiben und dem Verlag hatte zusenden lassen, war längst nicht so erstaunt.

»Darf ich mir den Vertrag mal ansehen«, verlangte er.

Simon sollte vierhundert Kronen Honorar bekommen, und das war das erste Geld, das er in seinem Leben selbst durch Arbeit verdient hatte.

Für neue Kleider reicht es, dachte er.

New York, New York, das Herz der großen Stadt pochte, und Simon genoß den Pulsschlag. Alles war darin enthalten, Leben und Tod, Weinen und Lachen, Angst und Zuversicht, Grausamkeit und Mitleid. Aus dem Rhythmus löste sich eine Melodie, stieg in die Wolken, bezog aus dem Klopfen des großen Herzens ihre Kraft, wurde unanständig, übermütig, lachte über den Dächern.

Ein junges Lied voll Hoffnung, New York, New York.

Es gab Augenblicke, da fühlte der jetzt zwanzigjährige Simon sich alt wie ein abgekämpfter Fremdling aus einer gealterten Welt. Doch meistens war er im Einklang mit der Stadt, die das Lebensgefühl auf Touren brachte. »Es ist phantastisch«, sagte er beim Mittagstisch im Hotel zu Ruben, und dieses Urteil galt allem, auch dem Essen.

Ruben nickte zustimmend und freute sich innerlich darüber, wie phantastisch seine Reise dank Simon geworden war. Schau!, sieh mal!, hast du je . . ., horch! koste! – alles wurde neu, auch für Ruben, der ein Mann konservativer Gewohnheiten war und, wäre er allein gewesen, alle berühmten Kunstsammlungen besucht hätte und höchstens noch das Metropolitan Operahouse.

Er war vor dem Krieg hier gewesen, und der Lärm, das Gedränge, die schamlose Prostitution und die große Armut mitten in einer Welt größten Überflusses waren ihm eine Qual gewesen. Jetzt konnte er, wie Simon, mit all seinen Sinnen genießen, ertappte sich dabei, die geschäftlichen Besprechungen lieber schwänzen, ja sogar Begegnungen mit alten Freunden aus der Verlagswelt eher meiden zu wollen.

»Schon richtig«, bestätigte Simon. »Und es stimmt auch wieder nicht. Du mußt wissen, ich war auch schon hier.«

Er erzählte von der Schule und der Langeweile, die aus allen Ecken kroch, und wie er gelernt hatte, all dem zu entfliehen.

Er schilderte genau, wie er geübt hatte, den Schnittpunkt von zwei Linien in der rechten Hirnhälfte zu finden, um sich zwischen Schläfenbein und Schädelknochen davonmachen zu können.

Ruben lachte.

»Ich bin oft hierher gefahren«, erzählte Simon. »Es hat im großen ganzen so ausgesehen wie jetzt, aber das Wesentliche blieb mir vorenthalten: die Intensität, der Rhythmus.«

Ruben stieß mit ihm an, es war ein vollmundiger, für seinen Geschmack etwas zu süßer kalifornischer Wein, schlug sich den Gedanken aus dem Kopf, für Simon eine Rede zu halten und ihm dafür zu danken, daß er die Reise für ihn so erlebnisreich gestaltet hatte.

Sie waren mit der *MS Stockholm* herübergekommen, es waren für Ruben acht Tage voller Ruhe und behaglichem Luxus gewesen. Doch Simon hatte überall bei Kommando und Mannschaft Freunde gefunden, war im geräuschvollen Herzen des Schiffes untergetaucht und hatte Maschinisten und Mechaniker mit seinen Fragen geplagt.

Während der ganzen letzten Nacht hatte er auf der Kommandobrücke gestanden, die für Passagiere ein verbotener Bereich war, und voll gespannter Erwartung der berühmten Skyline mit Freiheitsstatue und Wolkenkratzern entgegengesehen, und in der Morgendämmerung hatte er Ruben geweckt: Das mußt du miterleben!

Ruben hatte geschwiegen und nicht gesagt, das habe ich doch schon gesehen, er war mit dem Jungen gegangen und hatte sofort erkannt, daß er es so wirklich noch nie gesehen hatte.

Die letzten Tage zu Hause waren durch Simon, der nach dem Militärdienst neu ausgestattet werden mußte, schnell vergangen, Mona hatte ihn als Modeberaterin, wie sie es nannten, von Geschäft zu Geschäft begleitet. Alles wurde so angeschafft, wie sie es bestimmte, und es war ihr Verdienst, daß Simon sich während der ganzen Reise immer passend gekleidet fühlte.

Selbst hätte er sich zu einfache oder zu großspurige Sachen gekauft.

Hochzeit hatten sie auch gefeiert, eine schlichte Zeremonie in der Synagoge und danach ein Essen in Henriksberg. Niemand aus Monas Verwandtschaft hatte der Trauung beigewohnt, doch beim Essen führte Ruben eine Schwester ihrer Mutter zu Tisch. Karin als Gastgeberin nahm sich des Fischhändlers an, und auf beiden Seiten fand man notgedrungen immerhin spärlichen Gesprächsstoff.

Danach hatte man das neue Heim besucht, die Dreizimmerwohnung bei Gustafssons, und dort war alles so gediegen und gemütlich, daß Simon aufhörte, Mona wegen ihres Einrichtungsfimmels zu nekken, und Ruben sagte:»Ich frage mich, ob in dir nicht eine Künstlerin steckt, Kleine.«

Am letzten Abend in New York fuhren Ruben und Simon mit dem Lift hinauf auf das Empire State Building und schauten auf den Riesen mit den tausend Geräuschen und den abertausend Lichtern hinunter. Der Abschied stimmte Simon wehmütig, doch ließ er sich damit trösten, daß sie morgen über den Atlantik fliegen würden.

Die Flugreise war jedoch eine Enttäuschung, Simon mußte Ruben recht geben, daß Fliegen die langweiligste Fortbewegungsart der Welt war.

»Noch langweiliger als Fußmärsche«, lachte Simon, der Spaziergänge verabscheute.

London, die etwas gebrechliche aber freundliche, zuverlässige und intelligente alte Dame mit den vielen Narben aus dem Krieg, empfing die Ankömmlinge mit Sonnenschein.

Als die beiden sich in einem Hotel im Embankment gründlich ausgeschlafen hatten, erwachten die Lebensgeister wieder, sie nahmen ein üppiges, wunderbares Mahl zu sich, und Ruben sagte:»Hier in dieser Stadt habe ich viel zu tun und nur wenig freie Zeit.«

»Ich komme schon zurecht«, erwiderte Simon.

»Die Stadt ist nicht ganz so bieder wie sie scheint, Simon. Sie ist groß und gefährlich.«

»Ich fahre mit dem Bus zum British Museum«, erklärte Simon, tat es, und sah danach nicht mehr viel von London. Nach vier Tagen war er bei den Aufsehern in den historischen Sammlungen bestens bekannt, the Swedish boy, den man immer irgendwo aufstöbern mußte, wenn die Besuchszeit zu Ende war.

Ruben bekam abends Simons ausführlichen Bericht über die gewaltigen Schätze, die unglaublichen Sammlungen aus Griechenland und Rom, Ägypten und dem Zweistromland zu hören.

»Tja, mein Lieber, vor Plünderungen sind die englischen Imperialisten nie zurückgeschreckt«, lachte er.

»Nun, darüber kann man geteilter Meinung sein«, konterte Simon. »Im Moment bin ich jedenfalls heilfroh, daß es das alles hier, an einem Ort vereint, zu sehen gibt.«

Dann fuhren sie über den Ärmelkanal, der Frühling machte sich rundum bemerkbar, es war warm, fast heiß in der Eisenbahn, und Rubens Augen glänzten, als sie nach Paris hineindonnerten. Paris war auch eine ältere Dame, äußerlich vornehmer, eleganter und pikanter als London, aber auch sie war ausgezehrt und mitgenommen vom Krieg. »Paris war die Stadt meiner Jugend«, sagte Ruben. »Die Stadt meiner Träume, wo ich fast alles kennenlernte, was für mich entscheidend werden sollte, Musik, Kunst, die großen Geister.«

Rebecca, dachte er, in einem Frühling haben wir uns hier getroffen.

»Strindberg«, sagte er, und als er Simons Verwunderung sah: »Nicht persönlich, aber die deutschen Ausgaben seiner Bücher habe ich an einem Stand am Seinekai billig erstanden.«

Am nächsten Tag mußte Ruben zu Besprechungen gehen, und Simon besuchte den Louvre. Sie wollten sich um drei Uhr nachmittags im Foyer des Museums wieder treffen. Ruben kam auf die Minute pünktlich, aber Simon hielt die Zeit nicht ein.

Als es auf vier Uhr zuging, bekam Ruben es mit der Angst zu tun: Ich hätte ihm sagen müssen, daß diese Stadt gefährlicher ist als London.

Dann aber kam er, und Ruben sah schon von weitem, daß etwas passiert war, daß Simon bleich war, als hätte er ein Gespenst gesehen.

»Onkel Ruben!« rief er. »Du mußt mitkommen.«

Als Ruben hinter Simon her die Treppe hinauf und durch die langen Galerien lief, dachte er, daß der Junge zum ersten Mal während der ganzen langen Reise in die alte Gewohnheit zurückgefallen war und Onkel gesagt hatte.

Simon machte in einem der frühgeschichtlichen Säle vor der etwa einen halben Meter hohen Statue eines kleinen Mannes halt, der die Besucher mit der unergründlichen Weisheit weit zurückliegender Jahrhunderte anblickte.

Gudea, las Ruben, sumerischer Priesterkönig, 22. Jhdt. v. Chr.

»Das ist er«, sagte Simon. »Der Mann, von dem ich erzählt habe, der Mann, den es meine ganze Kindheit hindurch gegeben hat, und der in der Symphonie von Berlioz wieder zu mir gekommen ist.«

Ruben spürte, wie die Härchen an seinen Armen sich wie bei einem Urmenschen sträubten. Er dachte wieder an Strindberg, den Schriftsteller, der in ihm das Interesse an Swedenborg und Schweden geweckt hatte. Aber nicht einmal Swedenborg hätte Verständnis für das gehabt, was sich hier ereignete.

Ruben schaute von Simon zu der Statue, von den ängstlichen Augen des Jungen zu den orientalischen, souverän ruhigen.

Schließlich sagte er, doch seine Stimme war nicht so fest wie er es gern gehabt hätte: »Wie immer es sich auch mit dem Unbegreiflichen in unserem Dasein verhalten mag, wir sind jetzt hier, Simon. Sind anwesend in diesen unseren Körpern, die der Nahrung und der Ruhe bedürfen.«

Zu seiner Erleichterung sah er, daß der Junge lachen konnte.

Sie aßen schweigend, konnten jetzt das gute französische Essen in dem teuren Restaurant an den Champs Elysées nicht würdigen. An sich hatten sie noch eine Rundfahrt Paris by night mitmachen wollen, gingen aber in stiller Übereinkunft in ihr Hotelzimmer, und Ruben war froh, daß sie nicht die zwei bestellten Einzelzimmer bekommen hatten, sondern ein großes Doppelzimmer.

Sie duschten, zogen ihre Schlafanzüge an, Ruben trank noch einen Kognak, doch nicht einmal der konnte Ordnung in seine Gedanken bringen. Oder in seine Unruhe wegen Simon, der immer noch blaß war.

Als sie aber längere Zeit dagelegen und an die Decke gestarrt hatten, kam die Logik in Rubens Gehirn wieder in Gang.

»Mir fällt eine bekannte parapsychologische Studie ein, in der ich geblättert habe«, begann er. »Ausgangspunkt waren Menschen, die sich unter Hypnose an Dinge aus einem früheren Leben zu erinnern glaubten. Unter ihnen befand sich ein Mann, der ein tadelloses Latein sprach.«

»Ja?« machte Simon, setzte sich auf und knipste die Lampe an. Gott sei Dank, er zeigte Interesse.

»Es waren lange Texte, immer dieselben. Aber es war trotzdem erstaunlich, denn dem Mann fehlte jegliche klassische Bildung.«

»Ja?«

»Nun, man hat versucht, das Leben des Mannes genau aufzuzeichnen, alles, was er erlebt hatte, kleine und große Dinge. Irgendwann erinnerte er sich, daß er anläßlich einer dramatischen Auseinandersetzung mit einer Frau, die er liebte, völlig verzweifelt immer wieder viele Stunden in einer Bibliothek zugebracht hatte. Um ungestört zu sein, hatte er ein Buch entlehnt, es aufgeschlagen und, ohne wirklich hinzusehen, auf zwei Seiten gestarrt, die genau jenen Text enthielten, den er während der Hypnose auswendig aufgesagt hatte. Dieser Text hatte bei ihm das Bewußte passiert und sich in das Unbewußte eingeprägt.«

»Ja«, sagte Simon.

»Ich möchte meinen«, fuhr Ruben fort, und seine Stimme klang immer fester und überzeugter, »daß etwas Ähnliches auch dir passiert ist. Irgendwann, als du sehr müde warst oder noch so klein, daß du dich nicht mehr erinnerst, hast du ein Bild dieser Statue aus dem Louvre gesehen.«

»Und das Bild hat auf mein Unbewußtes großen Eindruck gemacht, meinst du?« Simons Stimme war voller Zweifel.

»Ja«, sagte Ruben und erzählte, daß er erst kürzlich das Bild des Gudea in einem Buch gesehen hatte, einem deutschen Buch über

Archäologie von einem Autor namens Ceram, das gerade ins Schwedische übersetzt wurde.

»Hast du dieses Buch?«

»Ja, die deutsche Ausgabe, ich kann es dir leihen, sobald wir heimkommen. Was ich damit sagen will, es ist eine vielfach abgebildete bekannte Figur. Hast du dir den Katalog mit den prähistorischen Sammlungen des Louvre besorgt?«

Ruben war ganz aufgeregt, Simon sprang aus dem Bett, holte den Katalog. Trotz spärlicher Französischkenntnisse lasen sie gemeinsam über den französischen Diplomaten Ernest de Sarzek, der die Statue bei Ausgrabungen in Lagash am Fuß eines Hügels fand und per Schiff in den Louvre verfrachtet hatte.

Die Statue hatte seinerzeit sehr großes Aufsehen erregt, denn sie war die Bestätigung dafür, daß es eine Kultur gab, die älter war als die der Assyrer, ja sogar älter als die ägyptische.

»Wann hat dieser de Sarzek gelebt?« wollte Simon wissen.

Es stand nicht in der Broschüre aber Ruben nahm an, Ende des 19. Jahrhunderts.

»In den achtzehnachtziger Jahren, würde ich meinen. Wenn du ein bißchen warten kannst, will ich versuchen, mich an Angaben in Cerams Buch zu erinnern.«

Das Schweigen dauerte nur kurz, denn Ruben hatte ein gutes Gedächtnis.

»Es verhielt sich so«, begann er, »daß man aufgrund wissenschaftlicher, vor allem sprachlicher Indizien annehmen durfte, daß es vor den semitischen Hochkulturen im Zweistromland, vor Sargon, ein unbekanntes Volk gegeben hatte. Der Fund des Gudea war der Beweis, und so traten die Sumerer in die Geschichte ein.«

Simon war ganz Ohr, er hatte wieder Farbe bekommen, und erinnerte sich plötzlich an die Schulzeit, an den merkwürdigen Tag, als der Krieg ausbrach und der junge Lehrer gesagt hatte: Die Geschichte beginnt mit den Sumerern.

»Was ich damit sagen will ist«, sagte Ruben, »daß die Statue sehr bekannt ist und bestimmt in schwedischen Zeitungen im Zusammenhang mit dem einen oder anderen Artikel oder einer archäologischen Reportage auf der Kulturseite abgebildet war. Du hast so ein Bild gesehen, und weil du bist, wie du bist, hat sie deine Phantasie angeregt, und damit gleichzeitig deine Träume und nach und nach auch dein Innenleben.«

Er befand sich jetzt auf sicherem Boden, und seine Sicherheit übertrug sich auf Simon. Als sie am nächsten Morgen aufstanden, um zum Flughafen zu fahren und die Maschine nach Kopenhagen zu nehmen, hatte das Rätselhafte seine Macht über ihre Sinne verloren.

Wieder zu Hause, las Simon das Buch von Ceram, das er unglaublich spannend fand. Bald darauf lud Ruben ihn zusammen mit Olof Hirtz zum Essen ein. Die Geschichte von dem wiedergefundenen Priesterkönig seiner Träume in einer Dioritskulptur im Louvre war schnell erzählt.

Olof schien sonderbar überrascht, Ruben glaubte zu sehen, wie sich auch ihm die Haare sträubten. Doch dann legte Ruben seine Theorie von dem Bild dar, das sich in Simons Unterbewußtsein eingenistet hatte, und Olof nickte erleichtert.

Fast enthusiastisch.

»Schreibe darüber, Simon«, sagte er. »Schreibe ein Gedicht oder, warum auch nicht, eine Novelle über einen Tag in deiner Kindheit, einen vollkommenen Tag, wie geschaffen dafür, in den Gefühlen des Kindes ein Muster von Bestand zu formen. Die Sonne leuchtet, es liegt Sanftmut in der Stimme der Mutter, sie nimmt das Kind bei der Hand, schlendert am Strand entlang und kauft am Kiosk eine Wochenzeitschrift. Die beiden setzen sich in den Sand, die hohen Gräser am Ufersaum schwanken im Wind, und die Uferwiese ist in den Augen des Kindes ohne Ende. Die Mutter genießt die Wärme, blättert zerstreut in ihrem Journal und sieht dem Jungen zu, der Kanäle in den Sand gräbt und Meerwasser einleitet.

Sie döst vor sich hin, als der Junge zu ihr zurückkehrt, er sieht die Zeitschrift mit einer Reportage aus dem alten Mesopotamien aufgeschlagen neben ihr liegen. Er kann noch nicht lesen, aber die Bilder verzaubern ihn, die Löwen mit ihren Männerköpfen, die Kanäle,

Tempel und Türme überragen das Gräsermeer. Am intensivsten sieht sich das Kind das Bild des Gottkönigs mit dem eigentümlichen runden Hut und dem gütigen Gesichtsausdruck an, der mit dem Frieden dieses Tages übereinstimmt. Der Junge ist noch so klein, daß er bislang keine Erinnerungen in seinem Gehirn gespeichert hat, alles lagert sich im Unbewußten ab, gewinnt Farbe aus der Schönheit des Tages, aus der Liebe der Mutter und dem warmen Licht über dem Strom.«

Simon mußte lachen:

»Schreib's doch selbst!« meinte er. »Wenn du so sicher bist.«

»Aber ich bin kein Poet.«

»Doch, das hast du schon bewiesen«, sagte Ruben, und sie lachten alle drei.

Aber Simon dachte, daß er diese Novelle nie schreiben werde, auch wenn der Entwurf gut war und die Erklärung einleuchtend, ja geradezu glaubhaft.

Mein Freund der Fernfahrer, Andersson, würde das nie gutheißen.

Der Professor war ein kleiner Mann mit wachen Augen und einem Lächeln, das in seinem unschuldsvollen Gesicht flink hin und her huschte. Das Historische Institut in Göteborg war für Vitalität bekannt.

Es hieß, die Studenten würden dort gescheiter als sie von Natur aus seien, und vielleicht war etwas dran an dieser Behauptung. Jedenfalls wurde hier neben Intelligenz auch Phantasie vorausgesetzt, und die meisten Studierenden entwickelten sich den Erwartungen entsprechend. Studenten, die ein großes Bedürfnis hatten, sich hervorzutun, verschwanden oft schon nach einem Semester zu den Skandinavisten, wo die Möglichkeiten, beachtet zu werden, größer waren.

Simon führte ein kurzes Gespräch mit dem Professor und sagte, er wolle sich nach dem Magister auf Keilschriftforschung spezialisieren. Der Professor lächelte und sagte: »Das ist erfreulich, die meisten hier sind auf Asen und Wikinger fixiert.«

Doch dann verging das Lächeln wieder: »Schweden ist ja nicht gerade der beste Boden für Assyrologen«, fügte er hinzu. »Vielleicht wäre irgendwann London besser geeignet.«

In Simons Träumen tanzte Apollon durch die elysischen Gefilde.

Sein Bett stand bei Ruben in Isaks altem Zimmer. Es hatte deswegen und auch wegen des Geldes zu Hause Auseinandersetzungen gegeben. »Papa, ich werde ein Studiendarlehen aufnehmen.«

»Verdammter Quatsch. Meine Kinder brauchen sich kein Geld zu borgen, solange ich sie versorgen kann.«

In der Küche stieg die Temperatur, hier ging es auf beiden Seiten um mehr als Geld.

»Es wird viel teurer werden als das Gymnasium.«

Aber das Gemecker von damals hatte Erik schon lange vergessen.

»Ewig Dank schulden, wie das immer gewesen ist«, sagte Simon zu Karin, als sie später allein waren.

»Es ist dumm, sich unnötig zu verschulden«, antwortete sie, und als Simon ihren traurigen Blick sah, schwieg er. Ein wenig mußte er das ja zugeben, besonders seit Ruben in die Diskussion mit hineingezogen worden war und nun auf Eriks Seite stand.

»Man kann seine Selbständigkeit auch auf andere Weise wahren als mit Geld«, sagte Ruben und dachte daran, wie sehr er die Hilfe seiner Familie in Anspruch genommen hatte, als er sein Unternehmen in Göteborg aufzubauen begann. Bald aber erkannte er, daß dies ein jüdisches Erbe war, so selbstverständlich wie die Luft zum Atmen.

Simon behauptete sich, indem er verkündete, er werde von zu Hause ausziehen.

Erik war außer sich, er war der Meinung gewesen, jetzt, wo der Junge die Schulbank wieder drücken wollte, werde alles bleiben wie bisher. Aber Simon, der sehr wohl wußte, daß man, solange man an Eriks Tisch saß, dies und jenes immer wieder aufs Butterbrot geschmiert bekam, blieb bei seinem Entschluß. Er bekam unerwartet Hilfe von Karin.

»Du scheinst vergessen zu haben wie das war, erwachsen zu sein und zu Hause bei deiner Mutter zu wohnen«, sagte sie zu Erik.

»Es gibt schließlich Unterschiede zwischen Müttern«, konterte Erik. »Außerdem habe ich mich selbst versorgt und Geld abgegeben, das sie verdammt gut brauchen konnte.«

»Da hast du's«, sagte Simon.

Aber Karin meinte, jetzt reiche es, und die beiden Männer erkannten gleichzeitig, daß die Tränen nicht mehr weit waren. Also verschwand Erik mit gesenktem Blick, und Simon blieb, um zu trösten, aber im Grunde genommen war nichts geklärt.

Alles blieb wie es immer gewesen war.

Nun gab es aber keine Wohnungen in Göteborg, und die Untermietzimmer, die von der Hochschule vermittelt werden konnten, gingen an Studenten von auswärts. Es war Ruben, der vorschlug, Simon solle bei ihm ein Zimmer mieten, und der, als Erik vor Zorn rot anlief, ein Machtwort sprach: »Das ist nicht mehr als gerecht. Ihr habt dafür Isak jahrelang bei euch wohnen gehabt.«

Ausnahmsweise schwieg Erik.

Ruben, der von Monas Art der Inneneinrichtung begeistert war, ließ seine Wohnung renovieren. Alle Wände wurden weiß gestrichen, Samt und Plüsch wurden rigoros entfernt, und an die Fenster kamen ebensolche weißen Wolken wie bei Mona.

Sogar die alte Sitzgruppe mit den großen Ledersofas wanderte unbarmherzig auf die Sperrmülldeponie, wo ein überraschter Bediensteter und seine Frau vor Glück fast einen Herzschlag bekamen.

Auf grazilen Füßen hielten in Rubens Wohnung hellblaue Sofas im Stil Carl Malmstens, weiße Eßzimmertische und anmutige Stühle Einzug.

»Hier sieht es jetzt aus wie auf einem Herrenhof in Värmland«, stellte Karin fest, die in ihrer Jugend irgendwann einmal Selma Lagerlöfs Mårbacka besucht hatte.

Die chinesischen Teppiche durften bleiben und prangten wie Schmuckstücke auf den frisch abgezogenen Parkettböden. Und die verglasten Bücherschränke waren nie in Frage gestellt worden.

»Bald wird jeder erkennen, wie viele echte Kunstwerke du besitzt«, stellte Simon fest, als Ruben und Mona nach nicht enden wollenden Diskussionen die farbenfrohen Bilder an die strahlend weißen Wände hängten.

Simon erzählte, wie er als Kind vor den unbegreiflichen Gemälden gestanden und sie mit dem Herzen zu verstehen versucht hatte. Jetzt gelang es ihm zumindest manchmal.

Als seine Musiktruhe kam und an die weiße Wand im großen hofseitigen Zimmer gestellt wurde, fand Mona sie schauderhaft.

»Mir ist bisher nie aufgefallen, wie häßlich das Ding ist.«

Aber Simon lachte: »Das verzeihe ich ihr gerne.«

Insgeheim war er froh, daß er bei Ruben wohnen durfte.

In einer Vorlesung über wissenschaftliche Methodik hatte er einen rotgoldenen Pferdeschwanz vor sich. Die strahlende Sonne ließ den Mädchenkopf Funken sprühen. Simon konnte sich nicht erinnern, diese Haare schon früher gesehen zu haben, wartete also gespannt darauf, daß das Mädchen sich umdrehen würde. Als sie es tat, war er enttäuscht, langer Hals, unverhältnismäßig hohe Stirn über schmalem Gesicht, blaß und sommersprossig. Trotzdem lächelte er sie ein wenig an, als sie sich nach der Vorlesung erhoben, und er feststellte, daß sie fast so groß war wie er, einen großzügigen Mund hatte und große graugrüne Augen.

Umgekehrt war Simon Klara Alm schon am ersten Tag aufgefallen. Sie hatte festgestellt, daß er gut aussah, daß da aber auch noch etwas anderes war, eine gewisse Unruhe, nicht die der nervösen Art, sondern als wäre er ständig mit den Rätseln des Lebens beschäftigt und erwarte, daß die phantastischen Antworten sich im nächsten Augenblick offenbarten.

Wie gewöhnlich waren ihr zwei Gedanken gleichzeitig gekommen: Das ist ein Don Juan.

Er wird mich nie beachten.

Im ersten Punkt irrte sie sich. Es scharten sich zwar am Anfang Mädchen um Simon, er war freundlich zu allen, mehr aber nicht. Der hat ja nicht einmal genug Verstand, sich geschmeichelt zu fühlen, hatte Klara erstaunt festgestellt.

Aber der zweite Punkt stimmte. Er beachtete sie nicht.

Als er sie jetzt anlächelte, dachte sie, mein Gott, hat der eine Intensität. Dann befürchtete sie einen Schweißausbruch, hatte Angst, nasse Flecke unter den Armen zu kriegen und schlecht zu riechen.

In den nächsten Tagen fragte Simon eines der Mädchen über Klara aus und erfuhr, daß sie Ärztin werden wollte.

»Sie ist schon cand. med.«, teilte ihm das Mädchen mit. »Wahrscheinlich sucht sie momentan nur ein bißchen Entspannung in den humanistischen Studien und macht dann mit Medizin weiter.«

Simon wunderte sich, Klara schien jünger auszusehen als sie war. Aber das Mädchen plapperte weiter: »Sie ist unheimlich begabt, hat das Abitur schon mit sechzehn extern gemacht. Du weißt schon, so eine von diesen eiskalten Intelligenzbestien.«

Simon hielt das für ein Fehlurteil, Klara Alm ist nicht kalt, er hätte nur gern gewußt, wovor sie Angst hatte.

Dann vergaß er sie, bis er sie eines Tages an dem roten Nachmittagskaffeetisch wiedertraf, an dem Direktor Nordbergs zungenfertiger Sohn wie üblich Hof hielt und von der Unerläßlichkeit marxistischer Geschichtsauffassung schon hinsichtlich der alten Griechen sprach.

Klara wurde vor Zorn flammend rot, erhob sich so jäh, daß die Kaffeetassen überschwappten und sagte: »Du machst es dir ein bißchen zu leicht. Ich finde, du solltest zwischen der privaten und der politischen Revolution einen Unterschied machen und mit deinem Vater eine verspätete pubertäre Auseinandersetzung führen.«

Dann ging sie, viele lachten, Nordberg nannte sie erbost eine blöde Zicke, doch auch Simon verließ die Runde und ging Klara nach.

Als er sie in der Diele einholte, sagte er: »Du fürchtest dich wohl vor gar nichts.«

»Nein«, antwortete sie. »Aber ich bin dumm. Die stempeln mich jetzt als Rechte ab.«

»Und das bist du nicht?«

»Nein, im großen und ganzen bin ich mit ihnen ja einer Meinung. Aber dieser Mensch ist so unverschämt selbstsicher, und das auf Pump, wenn du verstehst, was ich meine. Er plappert Marx nach und reichert ihn mit seiner kindischen Aggressivität an.«

»Die neuen Revolutionäre pflücken die Früchte der Bürgerlichkeit vom Baum der Erkenntnis und bezahlen mit Geldern, die ihre kapitalistischen Väter auf mehr oder weniger ehrliche Art verdient haben«, lachte Simon.

»Du bist ja richtig intelligent«, sagte sie.

»Warum sollte ich das nicht sein?«

»Du weißt doch«, erwiderte sie. »Schöne Männer . . .«

»Irrtum!« unterbrach er sie. »Schöne Mädchen haben nichts im Kopf.«

»Ach ja, das hab ich vergessen«, erwiderte Klara. »Wie du vielleicht schon gemerkt hast, bin ich sogar sehr intelligent.«

»Soll das eine Warnung sein?«

»Schon möglich.«

»Nicht notwendig«, sagte Simon, und sie dachte, daß sie längst wußte, daß ihn nur ganz allgemein ihre Bosheit amüsierte. Aber Simon setzte das Geplänkel fort: »Weißt du, ich bin nämlich ein Genie, mich kannst du nicht einschüchtern.«

Sie freute sich sehr, und hielt ein Lachen für angebracht, aber das verstand er nicht.

Als sie zu den Fahrradständern gingen, erzählte Simon von seinem Vater.

»Er war Lastwagenfahrer, politisch enorm hellsichtig. In jeder Hinsicht, ausgenommen was die Sowjets betraf. Jetzt, wo man die Augen nicht mehr davor verschließen kann, daß das Arbeiterparadies ein Polizeistaat ist, hat er das Interesse an der Politik völlig verloren.«

»Du kommst also aus der Arbeiterklasse?« staunte Klara.

»Ja. Das heißt manche Dinge haben sich etwas verändert«, erklärte Simon. Und als er die Neugier in ihren Augen sah, mußte er weiterreden: »Mein Vater wurde wie so viele andere arbeitslos, als es nach dem Krieg mit dem Bereitschaftsdienst vorbei war. Da hat er angefangen Boote zu bauen, Segelboote. Inzwischen hat er eine Werft und eine Menge Angestellte und Sorgen.«

»Vom Kommunisten zum Kapitalisten. Das schafft wohl auch politische Hohlräume«, überlegte Klara.

»Mmmm. Er ist ein guter Mensch«, antwortete Simon, selbst etwas überrascht.

»Das war wohl vorauszusetzen«, sagte Klara. »Daß du einen prima Papa hast, meine ich.«

»Wieso?«

»Nun, du bist doch ein so ungewöhnlicher Junge ohne Bedürfnis sich hervorzutun oder sich aufzuspielen.«

Simon war unerhört erstaunt.

»Klar bin ich genial«, sagte er. »Aber ich kenne mich mit diesem psychologischen Jargon nicht aus, und darum komme ich hier nicht ganz mit. Gehen wir ein Bier trinken, damit du mir Nachhilfeunterricht geben kannst?«

Als sie hinunter zur Allee radelten und dann weiter zum Rosenlundkanal und der Fischerkirche, wo es in der Nähe ein Bierlokal gab, nahm sie sich vor, jetzt alle ihre Kräfte aufzubieten und nett und ganz sie selbst zu sein.

»Erzähl von dir«, bat er, als sie beide ein Glas Bier vor sich stehen hatten und einander über den Tisch hinweg ansahen.

Und sie hörte sehr wohl, was er wissen wollte: Wer bist du?

»Mein Papa hat ein Sägewerk in Värmland«, sagte sie. Sie nannte einen Ort. »Meine Mama ist mit einem anderen Mann durchgebrannt als ich elf war, und es tut immer noch weh. Aber ich kann sie verstehen, denn, nun ja, er ist schwierig, mein Papa, aber super.«

Simon versuchte ihren Blick festzuhalten, aber sie nahm ihn zurück und er schien sich in diesen graugrünen Augen ganz zu verlieren.

Simon bemühte sich, nachzuempfinden, wie es für ein kleines Mädchen sein mochte, wenn es von der Mutter verlassen wurde, und er dachte an Karin, und wie böse er auf sie gewesen war, als sie ihm fast weggestorben wäre. Aber er sah sehr schnell ein, daß das überhaupt nicht zu vergleichen war.

Bald begann Klara von ihrem Studium zu erzählen, und ihr Blick überwand die Einsamkeit und begegnete dem seinen wieder, sie vergaß ihre Angst und Simon dachte, Herr im Himmel, sie ist ja schön.

»Ich habe vor, mich auf die Psychiatrie zu spezialisieren«, sagte sie. »Aber momentan bin ich ganz auf die alten Mythen versessen, weil ich denke, sie hatten noch einen tieferen Sinn. Daß sie eine psychologische Funktion hatten, fast eine therapeutische, verstehst du?«

»Ja«, bestätigte Simon, und sie sah sein intensives Interesse, als stünde er kurz vor einer der phantastischen Antworten, die er immer suchte.

»Ich habe viel über die Volksmärchen nachgedacht«, erläuterte Klara. »Von wie vielen schwierigen Gefühlen sie erzählen, die Kinder so haben, ohne darüber jemals sprechen zu dürfen. Du weißt schon, grausame Phantasien und Gewalt und so etwas.«

Simons Herz schlug jetzt ganz heftig, dieses Mädchen schenkte ihm ein Stück von jener Wahrheit, die ihn freier machen würde, aber das konnte sie nicht ahnen. Sie fuhr fort: »Ich habe vor, mich auf den griechischen Parnaß zu konzentrieren und zu versuchen, Zusammenhänge zwischen all diesen Göttern und den verbotenen Phantasien der Menschen zu finden.«

Simon saß sehr still auf seinem Stuhl. Das ist mein Mädchen, dachte er, und für einen Augenblick glaubte er zwischen den verfliesten Wänden der Bierhalle das Gelächter des Fernfahrers Andersson widerhallen zu hören.

Dann sagte Klara, daß schon viele Menschen vor ihr solche Gedanken verfolgt hatten.

»Dichter?«

»Ja, aber auch Wissenschaftler«, erklärte sie und erzählte von Carl Gustav Jung, dem kollektiven Unterbewußten und den Archetypen, dem Helden, dem weisen alten Mann, der großen Mutter, dem heiligen Kind.

»Er hat in den Mythen geforscht und fand in allen Kulturen gemeinsame grundlegende Wesenszüge«, fuhr Klara fort. »Wenn man etwas über den Menschen erfahren will, muß man sich mit seinen Mythen befassen«, meinte sie.

Das habe ich immer gewußt, dachte Simon.

»Ich kann dir ein paar Bücher leihen«, bot Klara ihm an.

Irgendwie brachten sie es fertig, daß zwei Bier für eine ganze Stunde reichten, dann bestellten sie noch zwei und dazu vier belegte Brote. Als sie endlich aufbrachen, sagte Simon, daß abscheuliche Väter etwas Seltsames an sich hätten, sie bekämen nämlich wunderbare Töchter.

»Ich kenne da noch eine, sie ist mit meinem besten Freund verheiratet«, sagte er, und Klara dachte, jetzt falle ich gleich in Ohnmacht.

Sie trennten sich in der Allee, es war schon dunkel, als sie beide, mit dem Gefühl ein gemeinsames Geheimnis zu haben, jeweils in eine andere Richtung radelten.

Ruben war verreist, und darüber war Simon froh. Er mußte nachdenken.

Und die Gedanken kamen, ein vernünftiger und klarer Gedanke nach dem andern. Das hier war keine Liebe, nicht annähernd mit dem verwandt, was er zwischen Isak und Mona beobachtet hatte. Klara war nicht von Licht umflossen, sie beide würden nie aus sich heraus leuchten.

Sie war ein boshafter Mensch, das hatte sie selbst gesagt, und er hatte es gesehen und auch gehört. Böse, borstig, das wurde sie, wenn sie den Blick zurückzog. Und häßlich. Lang und flach wie ein Brett, und dann all diese widerlichen Sommersprossen im Gesicht und auf den Armen, ja, sogar auf den Händen. Die schön und geheimnisvoll waren, schlanke Finger und weiche Polster auf den Handflächen mit tief eingefurchten Lebenslinien.

Und wenn sie lächelte ...

Nein, er wollte alles vergessen, es war einfach, denn es gab nichts zu vergessen.

Trotzdem war sein letzter Gedanke vor dem Einschlafen, zusammen mit ihr bin ich bei mir selbst.

Er träumte, daß er am Strand entlang ging, und das Leben kam auf ihn zu und hatte goldrotes Haar und es trug in der langfingrigen und sommersprossigen Hand einen Apfel.

Am nächsten Tag sagte Simon, als er sich in der Vorlesung neben sie setzte, daß sie bestimmt gerne Musik höre. »Ja«, sagte Klara.

»Ich habe für Samstag zwei Karten für das Konzerthaus. Gespielt wird die Meeressymphonie von Nystroem.«

Er hatte keine Karten, aber die würden noch zu beschaffen sein.

»Möchtest du mitkommen?«

»Ja, gerne«, sagte Klara und hielt die Augen geschlossen, um ihn nicht sehen zu lassen, wie sehr sie sich freute.

»Ich habe seinerzeit die Uraufführung gehört«, berichtete Simon.

»Die Symphonie hat solchen Eindruck auf mich gemacht, daß ich ein langes Gedicht darüber geschrieben habe.«

Da schlug Klara die Augen auf und sah ihn erstaunt an, und er konnte der Versuchung nicht widerstehen: »Der Verlag Bonniers wird es veröffentlichen.«

Und schon begann die Vorlesung.

In der Einzimmerwohnung in Haga sah Klara ihre Garderobe durch und stellte fest, daß kein Kleid gut genug war. Es war erst Samstagmorgen, und sie konnte noch in die Linnégata gehen, wo sie vor dem Schaufenster einer Boutique schon oft von einer anderen und schöneren Klara geträumt hatte.

Jetzt kaufte sie sich dünne Nylonstrümpfe, denn sie hatte hübsche Beine. Und die ersten hochhackigen Schuhe ihres Lebens, denn Simon war ja doch um einiges größer als sie. Dann fiel ihr ein Jüngling aus der Anatomie ein, der gesagt hatte, sie habe einen netten Po, also probierte sie einen Rock, der sich eng an ihr Hinterteil schmiegte.

»Er sitzt wie angegossen«, sagte die Verkäuferin und holte eine grüne Seidenbluse mit weiten Ärmeln und einem Schluppenkragen, der den Hals umspielte.

»Aber ich habe keinen Busen«, bemerkte Klara, die sah, wie die Seide den Körperlinien folgte und alles enthüllte. Und sie haßte diese Frau, die sie gezwungen hatte, diese Peinlichkeit auszusprechen.

Aber die Verkäuferin lächelte nur und meinte, das sei leicht zu beheben, und ehe Klara nachdenken konnte, hatte sie einen BH mit einer spitz zulaufenden Einlage gekauft.

Ich bin verrückt, dachte sie.

Als sie sich zu Hause die Haare gewaschen und über ein Handtuch gerollt hatte, um eine schöne, weiche Pagenfrisur zustande zu bringen, mußte sie daran denken, daß sie oft unter den Armen schwitzte. Sie benutzte deshalb Aluminiumchlorid, aber das half bei Angst wenig.

»Klara Alm«, sagte sie laut zu sich selbst. »Heute abend wird dich keine Angst überkommen.«

Ehe sie sich ankleidete, überzog sie das Bett frisch. Ganz zum Schluß färbte sie sich die Wimpern, sie waren von Natur aus lang. Als sie, wie abgemacht, um halb sieben zum Treffpunkt kam, strahlte Simon vor Freude: »Du siehst wunderschön aus«, sagte er, und sie dachte, jetzt wäre der richtige Moment zu sterben, ehe alles wieder zunichte war.

Aber dann lächelte sie: »Du mußt wissen, daß die Leute zu Hause immer gesagt haben, die häßliche Tochter vom Sägewerker hat das garstigste Maul im ganzen Dorf.«

»Jetzt ist sie nicht mehr häßlich«, sagte Simon. »Vielleicht wird das Maul dann auch artiger.«

»Das ist die Frage«, sagte Klara und sah aus, als würde sie gleich zu weinen anfangen.

Da küßte er sie.

Aber sie kamen dennoch rechtzeitig ins Konzert, und die Musik umfing sie mit ihrem Zauberring. Klara schwieg auch danach.

Sie gingen durch die Stadt, und Simon erzählte ihr von den Indianerfrauen, die ihre Kinder in der Quelle des Flusses wuschen, und von der Woge, die über den Atlantik wanderte, um an den Klippen von Bohuslän zerschlagen zu werden.

»Als ich die Symphonie das erste Mal hörte, dachte ich, die Woge kann nicht sterben, denn sie wird nie zur Person. Verstehst du?«

»Ja«, sagte sie. »Ich glaube auch, daß Persönlichkeit meistens nur Abwehr ist. Darum ist meine auch so stark und ausgeprägt.«

Da küßte er sie wieder, mitten auf den Mund und mitten auf der Straße.

Simon hatte nie geglaubt, daß ein Mädchen sich ihm mit solchem Vertrauen hingeben würde. Sie war so willig und unschuldsvoll, so nackt und kindlich offen, daß er am liebsten geweint hätte. Aber er konnte sie mitnehmen und ihr Genuß und Befriedigung schenken.

Sie blutete nicht, er verstand und fühlte, daß auch das ein Geschenk war.

Es war zwei Uhr nachts, als Klara in die Küche ging, um sich unter dem Kaltwasserhahn zu waschen, und als sie in einem blauen Bademantel zurückkkam, sagte sie: »Eigentlich möchte ich jetzt sterben. Aber vorher will ich dir noch etwas vorspielen.« Sie holte eine Flöte, und Simon wollte rufen, nein, tu das nicht, kleine Klara, laß es sein.

Aber sie setzte sich ans Fußende des Bettes und spielte Carl Nielsens Flötensolo, in dem die Nebel sich hoben und sich auflösten, etwas zögernd zunächst, als wäre sie ungeübt, doch bald immer sicherer, gehaltvoll und mit Wärme.

Simon lag danach so lange still im Bett, daß sie fragen mußte: »Du bist doch nicht etwa eingeschlafen?«

»Wie kommst du darauf!« entgegnete Simon. Und dann: »Das ist aber mehr als nur ein Hobby, oder?«

»Ich habe die beste Ausbildung genossen, die man in Värmland bekommen kann«, sagte sie und erzählte von dem jüdischen Flötisten in Karlstad, der vor seiner Flucht nach Schweden Berliner Philharmoniker gewesen war und sich später als Musiklehrer durchschlug.

»Er war wunderbar«, sagte sie. »Ihm habe ich zu verdanken, daß ich nach dem Verschwinden meiner Mutter überlebte.«

Simon dachte an geheime unergründliche Zusammenhänge.

»Ich habe meine Mutter behalten dürfen. Vielleicht habe ich deshalb nie Geige spielen gelernt.«

»Wolltest du denn?«

»Klara, das ist eine unglaublich lange Geschichte, und ich habe sie vermutlich bis heute nicht verstanden.«

Aber er dachte an Simon Habermann, den ehemaligen Geiger bei den Berliner Philharmonikern und fragte: »Lebt er noch, dein Lehrer in Karlstad?«

»Ja.«

»Irgendwann werden wir ihn besuchen fahren«, sagte Simon, und dann schliefen sie ein.

Bis zwölf am Sonntagmorgen schliefen sie, und sie waren, als sie aufwachten, sehr hungrig und fanden im Hafen eine Kneipe, die sonntags geöffnet war, und es gab Hering als Vorspeise und dann gepökelte Rinderbrust. Simon bestellte zwei Klare, und als sie mit dem scharfen Getränk angestoßen hatten, sagte Klara, daß sie in ihrem ganzen Leben noch nie so etwas Gutes auf der Zunge gehabt habe.

Vierzehn Tage lang waren sie weit offen für einander und noch immer wie im Paradies. Dann fiel Simon ein, daß er auch eine Familie und Ruben und Isak hatte, und daß Klara mit ihm nach Hause kommen und Karin kennenlernen mußte.

Er sah, daß sie erschrak, aber er wußte nichts von den Dämonen, die sich jetzt von ihrem Herzen lösten und unerbittlich kopfwärts stiegen und dort sofort das Regiment übernahmen.

Als er dann sagte, ich hole dich also am Samstag ab, und meine Mutter lädt uns zum Essen ein, fühlte er eine Mauer zwischen ihnen wachsen.

Simon mußte Karin anrufen und von seinem Mädchen erzählen. Aber er scheute sich vor dem Gespräch und schob das auf Klara und ihre Unruhe. Am Freitagvormittag, zwischen zwei Vorlesungen, überwand er seine Unlust und wählte die wohlbekannte Nummer, hörte Karins herzliche und erfreute Stimme: »Das ist aber lange her, Simon. Wo bist du nur gewesen?«

»Ach, weißt du, Mama, ich hab ein Mädchen kennengelernt.«

»Soso.« Die Stimme schien von weit her zu kommen, und er wollte erklären, wollte sagen, weißt du, Mama, das ist ein so seltsames Mädchen, zerbrechlich und doch stark und häßlich und schön, und ich glaube, ich liebe sie, was immer das heißen mag, aber sie hat so ungeheuerlich große Angst vor dir.

Aber natürlich sagte er das nicht, sondern nur: »Ich möchte morgen mit ihr zu euch kommen, damit ihr sie kennenlernt.«

»Ihr seid herzlich willkommen, mein Junge.«

Das war auch nicht das, was Karin hatte sagen wollen, aber sie war froh, es über die Lippen zu bringen und auch darüber, daß ihre Stimme ganz normal klang.

»Sie ist Ärztin«, fügte Simon hinzu. »Das heißt, sie ist fast schon fertige Ärztin.«

»Allerhand«, hauchte Karin, und dann war es wieder still, bis sie zum Glück endlich ganz normale Worte fand: »Wir essen um zwei, wie immer am Samstag. Ich werde Steinbutt besorgen und etwas wirklich Gutes kochen.«

»Dann kommen wir also. Tschüs bis dann.«

»Tschüs.« Sie wollte noch etwas sagen, aber es fiel ihr nichts ein.

Auch er hatte etwas anderes sagen wollen, aber es wurde nur »Grüß Papa« daraus.

»Mach ich, Simon.«

Schlecht gelaunt und daher wütend auf sich selbst ging Simon zurück in den Hörsaal. Karin legte den Hörer auf, lehnte sich in der Diele an die Wand und dachte an ihr Herz.

Aber das schlug ruhig und sicher.

Entschlossen.

Sie hatte doch gewußt, daß das irgendwann passieren würde. Früher oder später mußte Simon einem Mädchen begegnen, er genauso wie Isak, und Karin suchte nach tröstlichen Gedanken. Es konnte ein Mädchen wie Mona sein.

Aber bei diesem Gedanken mußte Karin in die Küche gehen, sich auf die Küchenbank setzen und ein ernstes Wort mit ihrem Herzen reden.

»Also jetzt!« sagte sie. »Also jetzt immer schön mit der Ruhe, jetzt schlagen wir, wie sich's gehört, langsam und stetig.«

Das Herz gehorchte, und Karin wies den Gedanken an Mona zurück, der so weh getan hatte, weil ihr dabei bewußt geworden war, daß sie Mona verabscheut hätte, wäre sie Simons Mädchen gewesen.

Sie sah sich in der Küche um, die ihr so große Zuversicht gab, und erinnerte sich an eine andere Küche, kleiner und dürftiger, deren Wänden Armeleutegeruch angehaftet hatte, dieser bösartige Geruch, der davon kam, daß man in den Spülstein pinkelte, weil der Abort drei Stockwerke tiefer im Hof des kommunalen Wohnbaues lag. In jener Küche saß eine andere Frau und preßte die Hand aufs Herz, als wolle sie es am Zerspringen hindern, und vor ihr stand Erik, den Arm um die Schultern eines jungen Mädchens gelegt.

Es war ein schönes Mädchen, dessen ebenmäßige Nase fast in die Wolken zeigte, und dessen braune Augen blitzten, als es sagte: »Das ist ja der eigentliche Sinn, daß die Alten sterben müssen, um den Jungen Platz zu machen.«

Alles hat seinen Preis, dachte Karin, aber die Erinnerung an die

Schwiegermutter half ihr. Nie würde sie werden wie Eriks schreckliche Mutter, sie hatte auch ihren Stolz. Nein, sie wollte die beste aller Schwiegermütter werden, so wie sie die beste aller Mütter gewesen war, und niemand würde je auch nur ahnen, was es sie kostete.

Das Herz schlug, kaltgehämmert, Eis war in der Brust entstanden.

Als Lisa kurz darauf kam, hatte Karin Kaffeewasser aufgesetzt, und brachte es über die Lippen: »Kannst du dir vorstellen, daß Simon ein Mädchen gefunden hat?«

»Ist das aber schön!« begeisterte sich Lisa, und ihre aufmerksamen Augen, die immer auf der Jagd nach Staub und Heimlichkeiten waren, glänzten vor Neugier.

»Wer ist es?«

»Sie ist Ärztin«, erwiderte Karin, und damit war es heraus, und sie konnte Lisas Verwunderung ein wenig genießen und über die spitzen Worte lachen: »Na danke. Aber er ist ja immer ein bißchen was Besseres gewesen.«

Karin war sich bewußt, daß ab jetzt in den Nachbarhäusern der Eitelkeitswalzer wieder die Runde machen würde, diese ewige Leier von Larssons mit ihren jüdischen Freunden, ihrer Werft und dem Jungen, der das Abitur gemacht hatte und jetzt auf die Universität ging, um Frühgeschichte zu studieren ... Sumerer, sie konnte das Gekicher hören und mit ihnen fühlen, wenn sie sagten, Simon sei verwöhnt und glaube, das Leben sei ein Kindergarten.

»Wie heißt das Mädchen?« fragte Lisa.

»Himmel noch mal, das habe ich ganz zu fragen vergessen. Weißt du, ich war dermaßen verblüfft.«

»Ja, du hast wohl gedacht, du kannst den Jungen für den Rest deines Lebens für dich behalten«, meinte Lisa und lachte ein bißchen, um der Bosheit die Spitze zu nehmen.

Karin wurde rot vor Zorn und stand auf, wollte Lisa nicht die Genugtuung geben, ihren Zorn zu sehen. Sie ging zur Werft, fand Erik im Zeichenbüro und sagte ganz schnell, um es hinter sich zu bringen: »Simon hat ein Mädchen kennengelernt, eine Ärztin. Sie kommen morgen zu uns.«

Erik fiel nicht nur der Zeichenstift, sondern auch der Zirkel aus der Hand, und er nahm die Brille ab: »Das ist eine erfreuliche Nachricht, Gott im Himmel, Karin, wie schön!« rief er aus, und sie sah, daß seine Freude ganz echt war.

»Ist er verliebt?«

»Ich nehme es an«, sagte Karin, und sie lächelte breit und fast natürlich.

Erik ging zum Kaffee mit ins Haus, so etwas mußte gefeiert werden, und er sprach ununterbrochen davon, wie das Leben so spielte, wenn man jung und verliebt war, und auch davon, wie er sich von ganzem Herzen gewünscht hatte, daß Simon sich verlieben würde.

Dann lachte er laut und meinte, er habe sich doch immer einen Arzt in der Familie gewünscht. Der Teufel soll's holen, aber Erik Larsson kriegt, was er will. Wenn der Junge kein Doktor werden will, dann beschafft er sich eben einen. Großartig.

Karin stimmte in sein Lachen ein, aber es schwebte ein eiskalter Engel durchs Zimmer, als sie Eriks Freude sah und an das Mädchen dachte, das er einmal geliebt hatte, das Mädchen, das von der Schwiegermutter verscheucht worden war. Erik hatte vor Traurigkeit die Schwindsucht bekommen und lange im Sanatorium gelegen.

Dann ließ Karin sich ihren Entschluß, eine gute Schwiegermutter zu werden, durch den Kopf gehen, konzentrierte sich so sehr darauf, daß ihre Gesichtszüge starr wurden.

»Ist ja schrecklich, wie ernst du aussiehst«, sagte Erik. »Du bist hoffentlich nicht eifersüchtig?«

»Nein, weißt du«, erwiderte Karin, und ihre Augen schossen Blitze, so daß er sich schnell aus der Affäre ziehen mußte: »War doch nur ein Scherz«, sagte er, und sie konnte lächeln, ein ungewohntes und unechtes Lächeln.

Eifersüchtig, das war ein häßliches Wort, dachte sie, als sie ihren gewohnten Spaziergang machte. Es war nicht der richtige Ausdruck für die Trauer, die sie empfand, und die einer anderen Trauer nach einem Verlust vor langer Zeit ähnelte.

Petter, dachte sie, er war vernünftig genug gewesen, zu sterben.

Simon hingegen hatte sie enttäuscht. Trotzdem konnte sie ihn nicht hassen, sondern nur das Mädchen. Nein, auch das Mädchen nicht.

Plötzlich dachte sie daran, wie sehr sie Ärzte immer verabscheut hatte, diese Übermenschen mit ihrer Macht über Leben und Tod.

Sie ging in die Fischhandlung in Tranered, bekam ihren Steinbutt und leistete sich, um es richtig luxuriös zu machen, dazu noch ein halbes Kilo Krabben. Es sollte für das Mädchen ein fürstliches Willkommensessen geben. Niemand sollte Karin etwas nachsagen können.

Auf dem Heimweg wich sie den Eichen aus, wollte an diesem Tag keine Wahrheiten hören. Hingegen kam ihr der Umweg durch den alten verwilderten Garten gerade recht, in dem sie mit Simon gespielt hatte, als er noch klein war, und wo sie gedacht hatte, daß niemand ihn jemals würde so lieben können wie sie.

Beim Abendkaffee wirkte Erik nervös. Ob Karin meinte, das Mädchen stamme aus der Oberschicht? Stell dir vor, sie ist aufgeblasen! Sollten sie etwa zum Umgang mit der idiotischen Familie eines Großkaufmanns verpflichtet sein?

»Ich weiß nicht«, sagte Karin. »Aber Simon hat an sich ein gutes Urteilsvermögen.«

»Urteilsvermögen hat doch nichts mit Verliebtheit zu tun!«

Erik schrie es fast heraus, und weil er noch nie ausgehalten hatte, etwas nicht zu wissen, rief er bei Simon an. Er war nicht zu Hause, aber Ruben war am Apparat und wußte wenigstens ein kleines bißchen mehr, obwohl er das Mädchen auch noch nicht kennengelernt hatte.

Als Erik zu Karin zurück kam, hatte er sich zumindest ein wenig beruhigt. »Das Mädchen heißt Klara Alm, ist Tochter eines Sägewerksarbeiters, der Geld geheiratet und das Sägewerk in Värmland übernommen hat.«

»Das klingt doch gut«, fand Karin.

»Naja«, meinte Erik. »Möglicherweise trinkt der Vater. Es hat eine Scheidung gegeben. Klara soll einen sehr hellen Kopf haben, aber leicht hat sie es nicht gehabt.«

Das Mädchen nahm jetzt deutlichere Formen an, Karin gefiel das nicht. Doch dann berichtete Erik, Ruben habe gesagt, Simon sei vierzehn Tage lang kaum zu Hause gewesen und verliebt wie ein alter Kater.

Erik lachte zufrieden, er war so von Freude erfüllt, daß er gar nicht merkte, wie Karin erstarrte und wieder diese verflixte Kälte ausstrahlte.

Klara hatte die ganze Nacht über gegen die Dämonen angekämpft. Und hatte verloren. Das erkannte sie in dem Augenblick, als Simon sie holen kam, in der Tür stand und die ganze Abbruchwohnung mit seiner Energie erfüllte.

Sie war ganz derselben Meinung wie die Dämonen, von denen der eine sagte, es sei lachhaft, daß sie so einen Mann kriege, und der andere flüsterte: Gott wird sich deinetwegen schämen.

Klara hatte einen schwarzen Pullover angezogen, der sie noch blasser machte als sie ohnehin schon war. Die Sommersprossen leuchteten in dem weißen Gesicht, und unter den Augen hatte sie Ringe, Ton in Ton mit dem Pullover. Sie sah, daß Simon sie am liebsten gebeten hätte, etwas Hübscheres anzuziehen, war aber dankbar dafür, daß er es sein ließ. An dem schwarzen Pullover würde man den Achselschweiß nicht sehen.

Sie gingen zum Järntorget und stiegen in die Breitspurbahn nach Långedrag. Simon versuchte, als sie daran vorbeifuhren, von der Schule und von anderen interessanten Dingen auf der Strecke zu erzählen, die lange Jahre hindurch sein Schulweg gewesen war. Aber Klara hörte nicht zu. Sie dachte, wie sie es die ganze Nacht getan hatte, an all das, was er über seine Familie und diese wundervolle Mutter erzählt hatte, und Klara haßte sie schon jetzt. Schließlich wurde Simon böse und sagte, du siehst aus, als würde ich dich zur Schlachtbank führen. Aber sie gab auch darauf keine Antwort, dachte nur, das ist erst der Anfang, jetzt tu ich ihm weh, weil es eben sein muß.

Auf dem Weg von der Haltestelle hinunter zum Fluß versuchte er es noch einmal, erzählte von Äppelgren, seinem Retter, wenn er sich als kleiner Junge verlaufen hatte. Es kam eine kurze Rückmeldung, Klara hatte zugehört und fragte jetzt: »Und warum bist du ausgerissen?«

»Ausgerissen?« überlegte er. »Damit hatte das nichts zu tun, ich bin einfach losgezogen, wie neugierige Kinder das so machen.«

Doch es klang erstaunt, Klara merkte, daß er sich diese Frage selbst nie gestellt und sie jetzt die erste Kerbe in das Bild von der wunderbaren Kindheit geschlagen hatte, und daß sie jetzt sofort auf dem Absatz kehrtmachen und verschwinden sollte, bevor sie ihm zuviel kaputtgemacht hatte.

Alles lief genau so schlimm ab, wie Klara es sich vorgestellt hatte, sie stand wie eine Hopfenstange in der Küchentür, als Simon Karin begrüßte, und Klara hatte den Eindruck, daß das Band zwischen Mutter und Sohn so stark war, daß es sie eigentlich beide erdrosseln müßte, und sie schaute Karin an und sah zu ihrer Verzweiflung, daß diese nicht nur gut, sondern etwas noch viel Schlimmeres war.

Schön!, dachte Klara. Und intelligent, dachte sie, als die klugen Augen sie ansahen, durch sie hindurch sahen und alles ablehnten.

»Willkommen«, sagte Karin, aber dann wurde auch für sie alles unnatürlich, dieses häßliche rothaarige Mädchen mit der feuchtkalten Hand und Simon mit dem ängstlichen Gesicht.

Verrückt, dachte Karin, mein Junge, und dann dieses ...

Doch dann kam Erik mit einer Rolle Zeichnungen unter dem Arm in seiner üblichen Natürlichkeit von der Werft: »Du bist mir aber mal ein großes, prächtiges Mädchen!« sagte er, sah sie aus fröhlichen Augen an, die Versteinerung wich, Klara konnte lächeln und war jetzt richtig hübsch, und Simon umarmte seinen Papa, lachte erleichtert und tat sich groß: »Sie ist mit dem Medizinstudium fast fertig, Vater.«

Das hätte der Wendepunkt sein können, denn Erik sagte, potzblitz, und dabei noch so ein junges Mädchen, und Klaras Lächeln wurde breiter. Doch dann sagten die Dämonen, Simon schämt sich so, daß er dich mit deiner Ausbildung entschuldigen muß, und im nächsten

Augenblick kam Isak und erschrak so vor Klara, daß er sie gleich verabscheute und es nicht verbergen konnte.

Er verschwand mit Eriks Zeichnungen Richtung Werft, rief über die Schulter, ich fang gleich an, Erik. Komm, sobald du Zeit hast.

Sie mußten dringend planen, was vor der Verlegung der Werft noch zu erledigen war.

Erik schien erstaunt, ging Isak aber bald nach, und nun waren die drei wieder allein in der Küche, wo Karin mit einem frisch gebügelten Tischtuch und dem feinsten Porzellan aufgedeckt hatte.

Das Steinbuttgratin mit Krabben schmeckte gut wie immer, aber Klara kaute, als wäre es Stroh, das Schlucken fiel ihr schwer, und sie spürte, wie ihr der Schweiß ausbrach.

Zu Mona sagte Isak daheim später, da hat Simon aber eine seltsame Braut angeschleppt, lang wie ein Kran, häßlich und steif und einge-bildet wie der Teufel. Mona ging also hinüber um Zucker zu borgen, sie war schöner und birnenförmiger denn je, und hätte einem Renais-sancebild der hoffenden Gottesmutter entstiegen sein können.

Klara verabscheute sie wegen der lieblichen Mutterschaft, und auch, weil sie so freundlich und natürlich war. Aber Mona ging zu Isak nach Hause und sagte, daß Klara nicht eingebildet sei. »Sie fürchtet sich nur, das sieht doch jeder.«

Nein, Isak konnte das nicht sehen, und außerdem war das idio-tisch, hier gab es doch nichts zu fürchten.

»Ich würde Todesängste ausstehen, wenn ich Simons Mädchen wäre und Karin das erste Mal gegenübertreten müßte«, erklärte Mona.

Nach dem Mittagessen nahm Erik Klara mit, um ihr die Werft zu zeigen, das half ihr ein wenig. Hier war es zugig und kalt, so daß der Schweiß trocknete, und Erik war stolz auf seine Werft, und Klara meinte ganz aufrichtig, daß die fast fertigen Küstensegler, die bald vom Stapel laufen sollten, einmalig schön seien.

In der Küche wandte Simon sich verzweifelt an Karin: »Sie hat Angst, Mutter, siehst du das nicht?«

»Freilich sehe ich das, aber was kann ich machen?«

»Nimm sie mit auf den Berg, Mama, zeig ihr die Aussicht und rede mit ihr, du kannst doch sonst immer ...«

Als Klara also von der Werft zurückkam, sagte Karin entschlossen: »Möchtest du vielleicht ein Stückchen mit mir spazieren gehen, Klara?«

Klara nickte, ging mit, als wäre sie unterwegs zu einer Gerichtsverhandlung und fest entschlossen, alle Verbrechen einzugestehen und jede Strafe gerecht zu finden.

Sie saßen auf dem Felsen, Karin zeigte auf die Festung, sprach vom Meer und daß es auch seine Schattenseiten hatte, so in seiner Nähe zu wohnen. Schließlich hielt Klara es nicht mehr aus: »Warum machst du das alles? Warum sagst du nicht gleich, daß du mich abscheulich findest und daß ich zur Hölle fahren soll!«

»Na hör mal«, entrüstete sich Karin.

»Ich bin mit dir einer Meinung, ich finde, ich bin Simon nicht wert, und ich weiß, daß ich sein Leben zerstören werde.«

Karin mußte ihren inneren Jubel unterdrücken und sagte: »Ich kann doch einen Menschen nicht gleich mögen, den ich zum ersten Mal sehe.«

»Das klingt einleuchtend, aber inzwischen hast du vermutlich genug gesehen«, erwiderte Klara, die sich jetzt zweifellos ganz den Dämonen überließ.

»Liebe Klara«, sagte Karin. »Du solltest vielleicht mal ein bißchen von dir selbst erzählen.«

»Ich«, sagte Klara. »Ich bin die häßliche Tochter des Sägewerkers, die das abscheulichste Maul von ganz Värmland hat.«

»Wie bist du das denn geworden?«

»Vielleicht war es, als meine Mutter in meiner Kindheit mit einem neuen Mann verschwand. Aber ich weiß nicht, wahrscheinlich bin ich von Natur aus häßlich.«

»Hast du nie mehr was von ihr gehört?«

Es war eine Routinefrage, es machte Karin Schwierigkeiten, allein schon ihrer Stimme die innere Befriedigung nicht anmerken zu lassen. Es gelang ihr schlecht, das fühlten sie beide, aber trotzdem antwortete

331

Klara höhnisch lachend: »Nein, vermutlich hat nicht einmal sie mich lieben können, denn ich habe nie ein Lebenszeichen von ihr erhalten.«

»Dann wirst du sie wohl jetzt, wo du erwachsen bist, aufsuchen müssen«, sagte Karin, als wäre das die einfachste Sache der Welt, und die junge Frau dachte an die Telefonnummer in ihrem Notizbuch, die sie eigentlich schon seit drei Jahren wählen wollte.

»Das ist ein guter Rat«, sagte sie.

»Du scheinst dich selbst ganz und gar nicht zu mögen, wenn du so böse auf andere bist«, bemerkte Karin.

»Stimmt«, erwiderte Klara. »In der Fachsprache nennt man das Projektion.«

»Versuchst du mir zu imponieren?«

»Nein, ich weiß ja, daß das nicht geht.«

»Ich habe so meine Schwierigkeiten mit Menschen, die sich selbst nicht mögen«, erklärte Karin. »Sie lassen andere das teuer bezahlen.«

»Stimmt«, sagte die junge Frau. »Ich begreife sehr wohl, daß du Simon ein besseres Schicksal gegönnt hättest. Da sind wir uns einig. Verlaß dich auf mich, Karin, du große Mutter. Es wird jetzt bald zu Ende sein, das kurze Liebesmärchen.«

Sie verwandelte sich in eine starre Säule, die aus weitsichtigen Augen übers Meer schaute ohne etwas zu sehen, und Karin, die genau wußte, daß dies die Art des Mädchens war, die Tränen zurückzuhalten, bekam ein schlechtes Gewissen und wurde wütend. »Versuchst du mir die Schuld zuzuschieben?«

»Nein«, erwiderte Klara. »Die gute Mutter ist immer ohne Schuld. Sie muß es sein, um überleben zu können.«

Das ging unter die Haut, das tat weh, das traf das Lebensgefühl messerscharf, aber es gelang Karin, mit fester Stimme zu sagen: »Du bist der boshafteste Mensch, den ich je kennengelernt habe.«

»Das habe ich doch gesagt«, erwiderte die junge Frau, aber sie bekam ein ängstliches Gesicht, als sie Karin ansah und feststellen mußte, daß diese bleich wie ein Gespenst war und die geballte Hand fest aufs Herz drückte. Simon hatte ihr von dem Infarkt erzählt.

Als die beiden den Berg hinuntergingen, wußte Klara, daß sie schnell von hier weg mußte, ehe sie noch mehr Porzellan zerschlagen konnte. Kaum kamen sie in die Küche, die jetzt voller Leute war, ging sie von einem zum andern und verabschiedete sich, bedankte sich für das Essen und bedauerte, nach Hause zu müssen, um für die Abschlußprüfungen zu lernen. Zu Karin sagte sie leise: »Verlaß dich auf mich.«

Ruben Lentov war da, Klara reichte ihm eine schlaffe, verschwitzte Hand.

Simon begleitete sie zur Straßenbahn, sie wechselten unterwegs nicht ein Wort. Doch als die Bahn kam, sagte er: »Ich komme morgen gegen fünf zu dir zum Essen. Vielleicht haben wir uns bis dahin beide beruhigt.«

Den ganzen Sonntag ging Klara in der dunklen Einzimmerwohnung in Haga auf und ab und dachte an das Versprechen, das sie Karin gegeben hatte, und sie war dabei so traurig wie ein Mensch es nur sein kann. Um halb fünf öffnete sie eine Dose Champignonsuppe, belegte ein paar Käsebrote, und genau auf den Glockenschlag kam Simon.

Er versuchte sie anzulächeln, sie zu umarmen, aber sie stieß ihn weg.

»War es so schlimm?« fragte er.

»Nein, gar nicht«, antwortete sie. »Es waren doch alle genauso nett, wie du es vorausgesagt hattest. Erik ist lieb und Isak freundlich und Mona unglaublich hübsch. Ganz zu schweigen von deiner Mama, die einfach phantastisch ist. Die große Mutter, die sich in ihrem in eine bescheidene Küche verwandelten Tempel huldigen läßt.«

»Halt die Klappe«, sagte Simon, doch Klara konnte sich nicht zurückhalten: »Sogar der reiche Mann war da, bereit den Boden zu küssen, über den die große Mutter schreitet«, fügte sie hinzu.

»Von wem redest du?«

»Von Ruben Lentov, diesem typischen Vertreter des kultivierten jüdischen Kapitalismus.«

Simon saß sehr ruhig auf seinem Stuhl. Aber seine Augen brannten: »Ich habe nie begriffen, wie du Psychiater werden kannst«, sagte er. »Du hast, was Menschen betrifft, ja nicht die geringste Ahnung. Und ich habe auch nicht gewußt, daß du Antisemitin bist.«

In ihrem Gesicht war jetzt etwas, das um Schonung bat, doch es war zu spät.

»Immer schön eins nach dem andern«, erklärte Simon. »Karin ist keine große Mutter, denn sie hat nie eigene Kinder bekommen können. Das ist der Kummer ihres Lebens, oder zumindest ein Teil davon.«

Dann fuhr er sehr langsam fort: »Ich selbst bin adoptiert worden. Als jüdisches Kind. Mein Vater ist ein typischer Vertreter der in Auschwitz vergasten Juden. Wo du übrigens unter den Henkern gute Figur gemacht hättest!« schrie er, ging und knallte die Tür hinter sich zu, ohne daß erstaunlicherweise das alte Gebäude in sich zusammenfiel.

Klara nahm vier Schlaftabletten, um sich zu beruhigen.

Als Klara am nächsten Morgen aufwachte, war ihr schlecht und sie hatte rasende Kopfschmerzen. Das war gut, war um vieles besser als Angst.

Sie rief im Historischen Institut an, meldete sich dort ab, bekam einen Rüffel, erfuhr, daß sie die Semestergebühren nicht zurückbekomme.

Dann wählte sie die Nummer des Dozenten in der Sahlgrenschen Klinik und fragte, ob sie ihre Famulatur jetzt antreten könne.

»Sie haben einen Monat nachzuholen, Fräulein«, erwiderte der Dozent trocken. Aber er mochte sie ihrer raschen Auffassungsgabe wegen, fügte also hinzu, daß es sich vermutlich machen lasse.

»Ist ja schön zu hören, daß Sie sich die psychologischen Phantasien aus dem Kopf geschlagen haben«, meinte er.

Den ganzen Montag verwendete Klara auf das Schreiben eines Briefes: »Simon. Ich bin ein schrecklicher Mensch, und Du kannst froh sein, daß es zwischen uns aus ist. Aber ich bin keine Antisemitin, und ich glaube nicht, daß ich unter den Henkern von Auschwitz gewesen wäre, wo Dein Vater starb.

Will sagen, ich hoffe das zumindest. Denn wer kann eigentlich wissen ...«

Dann geriet ihr alles durcheinander, aber das war jetzt egal. Sie schickte den Brief nie ab, und am Dienstagmorgen stand sie bei der Visite auf der Inneren Abteilung am äußersten Ende der langen Schlange von Studenten, und ihr Blick war mehr denn je in die Ferne gerichtet.

Doch sie hörte zu, und zum Glück war es bei ihr so, daß ihr Gehirn aufnahmefähiger wurde, je mehr sie ihr Herz verschloß. Die Dämonen waren nun für lange Zeit auf ihre Kosten gekommen. Sie schwiegen.

Simon hatte es nie für möglich gehalten, daß es in seinem Körper so weh tun könnte, es war ein physischer Schmerz in seiner Brust. Die Luft war klar, die helle Septembersonne leuchtete freigiebig über der Stadt, aber seine Welt war grau. Das konnte er ertragen.

Aber der Schmerz, der dort saß, wo die Schuldgefühle ihn in seinen Jugendjahren immer gequält hatten, war unerträglich.

Dieses Mal ist es kein Schuldgefühl, sagte er sich. Er bereute nicht ein Wort von dem, was er gesagt hatte. Im Gegenteil. Das einzige, was Linderung bot, war das Ausdenken noch schlimmerer Dinge, böserer Worte, die er eigentlich hätte aussprechen sollen. Faschistenschwein.

Manchmal dachte er, es sei an ihm irgend etwas verkehrt, etwas in seinem Verhalten gegenüber Frauen. Erst Iza und dann jetzt dieses Weib, das noch viel bösartiger war.

Er erinnerte sich an seine Phantasien über das Böse, die aus seinem Leben eine Wirklichkeit machen sollten. Jetzt steckte das alles in seiner Brust, und das Dasein war für ihn nie so unwirklich gewesen wie jetzt. Ruben sprach mit ihm, aber Simon konnte nicht zuhören. In den Vorlesungen war es genauso. Dieser verdammte Schmerz in der Brust machte ihm das Hören unmöglich.

Er versuchte ununterbrochen nicht an Karin zu denken.

Ruben rief bei Erik an und sagte ihm, daß er sich wegen Simon Sorgen mache.

»Daran stirbt doch keiner«, antwortete Erik. »Aber krank werden kann man.«

Ruben erinnerte sich an etwas, das Erik einmal gesagt hatte, daß er nämlich nach einem Liebeskummer in der Jugend Tuberkulose bekommen hatte. »Wir müssen etwas tun, Erik.«

»Keiner kann etwas tun. Aber es ist verdammt schade, es war ein prima Mädchen, etwas Ungewöhnliches.«

»Was ist passiert, Erik?«

»Ja, was ist passiert?«

Nach vierzehn Tagen bekam Simon Fieber, jetzt konnte vor Karin nichts mehr vertuscht werden. Sie kam fast gleichzeitig mit dem Arzt, den Ruben hergebeten hatte, und der bei Simon eine Lungenentzündung feststellte.

»Das ist heutzutage ja nichts Gefährliches mehr«, sagte der Arzt und spritzte Antibiotika. Aber sicherheitshalber wollte er den jungen Mann doch ins Krankenhaus schicken.

Karin fuhr im Krankenwagen mit.

Dann lag Simon auf der Sahlgrenschen Klinik und träumte wieder, daß er im Grasmeer einem Mädchen nachlief, sie war langbeinig und schlank, launisch wie ein Sonnenstrahl, er bekam sie zu fassen und wußte, daß es Klara war, doch als sie sich umdrehte, war es Iza, die ihn auslachte. Da hörte er eine Flöte und sah, wie der Nebel sich über dem Fluß lichtete, aber er wollte dort nicht hingehen, wollte nicht sehen, daß es Iza war, die spielte und ihm mitten ins Gesicht lachte.

Karin wachte die Nacht hindurch an Simons Bett und bat zum ersten Mal in ihrem Leben Gott um Schonung und um Vergebung. Doch als das Tageslicht kam und er ruhiger atmete, versuchte sie zu denken, daß es gut war, wie es gekommen war. Und daß sie, Karin, frei von Schuld war.

Alles war gut, besonders als die Ärzte nach einer Untersuchung versicherten, Simon werde wieder gesund. Sie verließen sich ganz auf die neuen Medikamente, und dieses Vertrauen war greifbarer als die nächtlichen Hinwendungen an den unbekannten Gott, an den sie nicht glaubte.

Karin bekam Kaffee und ihr kam der Gedanke, das Mädchen könne nicht normal sein und habe Simons Leben zerstört, und daß es wirklich gut war, so wie es gekommen war.

Sie selbst war zu Klara so freundlich gewesen, wie man es nur verlangen konnte.

Doch da begann Simon im Schlaf zu schreien, und danach glaubte Karin, er habe zu atmen aufgehört, und ihre Angst war gewaltig und nur Gott, der zu Beschwichtigende, war da, und sie hörte ihre Mutter krächzen: Leid tun, leid tun, und sie sah sich selbst als junge Frau in der Küche der Schwiegermutter, als sie sagte, die Alten müßten sterben, um den Jungen Platz zu machen, und sie wußte, daß sie mit diesen Worten einen Pakt mit dem Teufel geschlossen hatte, und daß er jetzt gekommen war, um sein Recht einzufordern.

Der Teufel ist nicht persönlich gekommen, dachte Karin. Er hat ein Mädchen geschickt, eine Hexe, die mein Selbstvertrauen zerstört hat, von dem der Junge lebt. Darum mußte er jetzt sterben.

Karin schrie in wilder Verzweiflung auf, und Ruben war da und Erik, und sie sagten, sie müsse sich schonen, und dann kam ihr alter Herzdoktor, den Ruben gerufen hatte. Er untersuchte Simon und konstatierte, daß er bald wieder auf den Beinen sein werde, daß das Sulfonamid gewirkt habe und das Fieber gefallen sei, und dann gab er Karin eine Spritze, und sie konnte sich später nie erinnern, wie sie nach Hause gekommen war, aber nach vierzehn Stunden wachte sie in ihrem eigenen Schlafzimmer auf und Erik brachte ihr Tee ans Bett und berichtete, daß Simon die ganze Nacht fest durchgeschlafen habe und nun fieberfrei sei.

Sie verdöste den Vormittag im Bett und dachte an den Gott, an den sie nicht glaubte, und daran, wie wunderbar groß seine Macht war. Was den Teufel betraf, so war ihr klar, daß sie ihm in ihrem eigenen Herzen begegnet war, daß es ihn bei ihr gab wie bei allen anderen Menschen, nur eben immer wieder verleugnet und beschönigt.

Sie erinnerte sich daran, wie der Friede sie krank gemacht hatte, als all das Böse in diesem schrecklichen Frühling vor vier Jahren offenbar wurde.

Und es kamen ihr alle Träume in den Sinn, derentwegen sie in der Herzklinik geweint hatte. Lange verweilte sie bei der Erinnerung an ihren Vater Petter und an die Nacht, in der er ihr im Traum erschienen war. Er hatte ihr etwas sagen wollen, aber sie war zu müde gewesen, ihm zuzuhören. Ich wollte nicht, dachte sie.

Denn sie wußte jetzt, daß es bei dem, was Petter ihr hatte sagen wollen, um das Böse ging, das in jedem Menschen steckt, und das erst durch Erkenntnis verstanden und bekämpft werden kann.

Da stand sie auf, suchte die Nummer von Klara Alm im Telefonbuch und rief bei ihr an.

Die Stimme der jungen Frau überschlug sich, und das nicht nur vor Erstaunen.

Freude, dachte Karin.

»Ich weiß, daß es zwischen euch aus ist, und ich denke, du magst in vielem recht haben, was du über gute Mütter gesagt hast«, begann Karin zusammenhanglos. »Aber nun verhält es sich so, daß Simon sehr krank ist, und ich dachte mir, daß du als Ärztin vielleicht ...«

»Simon ist krank!« Klaras Stimme war schrill vor Angst.

»Er liegt im Sahlgrenschen«, Karin ratterte Abteilung und Zimmernummer herunter.

»Ich fahre sofort hin. Und ich rufe dich an.«

Klara nahm ein Taxi, bereute es aber, es wäre mit dem Rad schneller gegangen. Aber schließlich kam sie doch hin. Weißer Mantel, und das richtige Gesicht aufgesetzt. Die Stationsschwester war höflich, blieb aber auf Distanz bis Klara sagte, sie wolle aus privaten Gründen wissen, wie es stand, und dabei ein Gesicht machte, als würde sie gleich weinen.

Die kleine Medizinerin ist verliebt, dachte die Schwester nicht gerade unfreundlich und holte das Krankenblatt.

Lobulärpneumonie. Das Antibiotikum hatte gegriffen, er war nach dem Abklingen des Fiebers geröntgt worden. Keine Flecken auf der Lunge.

»Sie können kurz nach ihm sehen«, sagte die Schwester, und Klara wurde mutiger, als die Pflegerin hinzufügte, er werde wohl schlafen, und daß man sicher nicht zu betonen brauche, daß er nicht geweckt werden dürfe.

Er lag privat in einem Einzelzimmer, gottlob, und er schlief, wie die Schwester gesagt hatte, und, mein Gott, wie schön er war.

Klara blieb lange bei ihm stehen und sah ihn an, und es war, als spüre er ihre Nähe, denn er öffnete unvermittelt die Augen und sagte: »Zum Teufel mit dir, Faschistenschwein.«

Als sie sich umdrehte, um wegzulaufen, stieß sie mit Ruben Lentov zusammen, der sie schon eine Weile beobachtet hatte und Simons Worte gehört haben mußte.

Jetzt kam das Weinen, sie rührte sich wie üblich nicht vom Fleck um es zu unterdrücken, aber es half diesmal nichts, die Augen quollen über, und eine Flut von Tränen spülte ihr übers Gesicht. Das große Taschentuch, das Ruben herauszog, war ihr kaum bewußt, aber sie fühlte seine Wärme, als er ihr das Gesicht abwischte und sie zu trösten versuchte: »So, ja, kleine Klara, so ja.«

Da nahm sie sich zusammen, versuchte etwas zu sagen, versuchte es noch einmal und brachte schließlich heraus: »Würden Sie Simon bitte Grüße bestellen und ihm sagen, daß der einzige Mensch, den ich seit dem Verschwinden meiner Mutter geliebt habe, und der sich um mich gekümmert hat, ein Flöte spielender Jude war.«

»Ich werde es nicht vergessen«, sagte Ruben. Aber er war wütend auf Simon, Klara sah es, als sie weglief. Sie kam nach Hause, versuchte sich zu beruhigen, rief Karin an: »Ich bin dort gewesen«, sagte sie. »Ich habe das Krankenblatt gelesen. Er schwebt nicht in Gefahr, er wird in wenigen Tagen entlassen werden.«

»Danke«, sagte Karin. »Danke, meine Liebe.«

»Ich bin sehr unglücklich«, sagte Klara, und ihre Stimme schwankte, hielt aber durch. »Ich bitte dich, mir zu verzeihen ... das, was ich gesagt habe ... über gute Mütter, und daß ich dich traurig gemacht habe.«

»Du brauchst es nicht zurückzunehmen«, sagte Karin. »Ich habe darüber nachgedacht, es steckt ein Körnchen Wahrheit darin. Trotzdem sind Mütter notwendig, oder etwa nicht?«

»Karin, ich werde sie anrufen.«

»Tu das und laß von dir hören, wenn du reden möchtest.«

»Aber Simon ...«, sagte Klara.

»Mit dieser Sache hat Simon überhaupt nichts zu tun«, bestimmte Karin. Und schnell, als fürchte sie, es zu bereuen: »Simon ist schon immer ein schwer begreifbarer Mensch gewesen. Er wird nie ein hübsches und anschmiegsames Mädchen finden, wie Schwiegermütter es sich erträumen.«

»Dann würde ich ja passen.«

»Ich glaube, ja«, sagte Karin. »Ich habe inzwischen die Einsicht gewonnen, daß du sogar verdammt gut zu ihm passen würdest.«

Ihre Stimme vibrierte vor Zorn, Klara hörte es und verstand.

»Das ist nicht gerade leicht für dich, Karin«, sagte sie.

»Nein«, gestand Karin. »Das Leben ist überhaupt schwer zu begreifen. Und, Klara, da ist noch etwas, was du von Simon nicht weißt. Er gibt niemals auf.«

»Mich hat er doch aufgegeben«, meinte Klara. »Ich bin in diesen Tagen total durchgedreht, weißt du.«

Karin legte den Hörer auf und spürte, daß sie dieses Mädchen immer noch haßte, obwohl es etwas Großartiges an sich hatte. Sie ist von allen Menschen, die ich kenne, die einzige, die meinen Teufel erkannt hat, und die ich nie werde hinters Licht führen können, dachte sie.

Klara nahm sich nicht die Zeit, nachzudenken oder auch nur den Mantel auszuziehen. Sie meldete ein Gespräch nach Oslo an.

Eine warme norwegische Stimme, Klara erkannte sie sofort, und ihr Herz flatterte wie ein eingesperrter Vogel. Aber sie sagte: »Könnte ich bitte Frau Kersti Sörensen sprechen?«

»Am Apparat.«

»Guten Tag. Hier ist Klara.«

Es wurde still, als wäre die Erde zum Stillstand gekommen, weder in Oslo noch in Göteborg gab es ein Auto, das einen Mißton beisteuerte. Gott hält die Zeit an, dachte Klara. Dann hörte sie ihre Mutter weinen.

»Ich habe immer gehofft, daß du Kontakt zu mir aufnimmst, all die Jahre habe ich davon geträumt.«

»Und warum hast du nicht angerufen?«

Dann stand die Erde noch einmal still, bis die Stimme der Mutter wieder da war: »Ich habe es nicht gewagt. Aber ich weiß, daß du in Göteborg Medizin studierst. Ich bin so stolz auf dich.«

»Mama, warum hast du nie etwas hören lassen, als ich klein war und dich gebraucht hätte . . .«

»Aber ich habe doch geschrieben, Klara. Ich habe ganze Berge von Briefen geschrieben, die dein Vater ungeöffnet zurückgeschickt hat. Ich habe um das Sorgerecht gekämpft, ich habe mein ganzes Erbe für Anwaltskosten aufgebraucht. Aber damals war es schwer, ich hatte keine Chance, den Ehebruch hatte ja ich begangen.«

»Mama!« Das war ein Aufschrei.

»Das Ergebnis war, daß wir deinen Vater zwingen konnten, zumindest, meinen Anteil an dem Sägewerk und am Kapital auf dich zu überschreiben. Gegen die Zusicherung, nie wieder etwas von mir hören zu lassen.«

»Mama.« Klara weinte jetzt.

»Du warst ja so intelligent, Klara, ich wollte deine Ausbildung absichern, denn ich wußte doch, wie geizig er ist.«

»Aber ich habe um jedes Öre betteln müssen und studiere jetzt mit einem Studiendarlehen.«

»Rufe Rechtsanwalt Bertilsson in Karlstad an, tu das, Klara, und bitte, gib mir deine Adresse, damit ich dir die alten Briefe schicken kann.«

»Du hast sie aufgehoben?«

»Ja, ich dachte ... sie ergeben doch ein Bild davon, wie es abgelaufen ist, was ich empfunden habe, weißt du.«

»Fünf Perioden«, schaltete sich die Telefonistin dazwischen.

Klara gab ihre Adresse an. »Wir sehen uns, Mama. Ich werde dich zu Weihnachten besuchen.«

»Mein Gott, wie schön!«

In den nächsten Stunden bedeuteten Wut und Zorn für Klara Alm so etwas wie Glück. Sie erwischte den Rechtsanwalt in seiner Wohnung in Karlstad, und er bestätigte verwundert, daß es ein Konto auf ihren Namen gab, und daß dieses seit der Scheidung ihrer Eltern bestand.

»Wieviel ist es?« fragte Klara.

»Rund fünfundzwanzigtausend«, mutmaßte der Anwalt. »Es hat Zinsen getragen, wie es sich gehört, vielleicht sind es inzwischen sogar schon dreißigtausend.«

Klara rief den Sägewerker an, hörte schon an der Stimme, daß er betrunken war.

»Du bist ein ganz gemeiner Schweinehund«, rief sie in den Hörer und legte auf.

Doch dann vergaß sie das Sparbuch, auch der Stimme ihrer Mutter zuliebe, in der sie jeden Tonfall wiedererkannt hatte, und in der so viel Schmerz und Liebe gelegen hatten.

Ich habe eine Mutter, dachte sie. Auch ich, Simon, habe eine Mutter, der ich etwas wert bin.

Zwei Tage später trafen die Briefe aus Oslo ein. Klara meldete sich an der Klinik telefonisch krank, eine Herbstgrippe, behauptete sie.

Dann las sie die Briefe und weinte. Und las.

Bis sie jeden einzelnen auswendig konnte. Danach rief sie Karin an und erzählte.

»Das finde ich wunderbar«, sagte Karin. Und Klara hörte, daß ihre Stimme wieder die alte Kraft hatte.

Als hätte auch Karin Genugtuung erfahren.

33

In Rubens Wohnung saß Simon im Lehnstuhl und dachte, das Schlimmste sei jetzt überstanden, die Verliebtheit hatte sich mit der Lungenentzündung ausgeheilt. Er konnte sich nicht mehr richtig freuen. Freude ist nur für die Unschuldigen da, dachte er.

Doch eines Abends sagte Ruben, er habe zufällig mitgehört, was Simon an jenem Nachmittag im Krankenhaus zu Klara gesagt hatte.

»Das war im Traum«, meinte Simon.

»Leider war es das nicht«, entgegnete Ruben, und Simon sah, daß er ganz aufgebracht war.

»Es war im Fieberwahn.«

»Du hast sie eine Faschistin genannt. Nach allem, was geschehen ist, ist es unverzeihlich, mit solchen Wörtern um sich zu schmeißen. Hier geht es um Anständigkeit, Simon, um Respekt vor den Toten.«

Simon schnappte unter Rubens zornigem Blick nach Luft. »Teufel nochmal, du weißt doch gar nicht, was sie gesagt hat.«

»Ich weiß, was sie zu mir gesagt hat, als du wieder eingeschlafen warst, und das reicht. Sie hat mich gebeten, es dir auszurichten, und es ist so wichtig, daß ich es mir sogar Wort für Wort aufgeschrieben habe.« Er nahm seine Brieftasche heraus, fand die Notiz, las: »Der einzige Mensch, den ich als Kind geliebt habe, und der sich um mich gekümmert hat, war ein Flöte spielender Jude.«

Simon dachte, jetzt fängt das wieder an.

Es war lange still, bis er sagte: »Der Mann hat meinen Vater gekannt.«

»Simon Habermann?«

»Ja.«

Simon hatte eigentlich nur einen Gedanken, daß der Schmerz in der Brust trotz allem aus Schuld entstanden war. Seit jeher ein Wissen um Schuld gewesen war.

»Ich werde ihr schreiben und sie um Verzeihung bitten«, sagte er.

»Tu das«, nickte Ruben.

Simon brauchte zwei Tage für den Brief, der Papierkorb war bis oben voll mit Entwürfen. In dem letztlich abgeschickten Brief stand: »Klara. Ich bitte Dich um Verzeihung wegen der häßlichen Dinge, die ich zu Dir gesagt habe. Natürlich weiß ich, daß Du keine Faschistin bist. Simon.«

Er bekam eine Antwort: »Simon. Danke für Deinen Brief. Ich kann Deine Reaktion verstehen, denn selbst war ich ja auch mehr als niederträchtig. Klara.«

Das war gut, aber es minderte Simons Qualen nicht. Das Schuldgefühl nagte an ihm, und es gab Augenblicke, wo er zu ahnen meinte, daß es jemand anderem als Klara galt. Doch das schlug er in den Wind.

Jeder für sich arbeiteten sie sich durch den Herbst, verbissen und fleißig, wie immer. Simon begann sich für Politik zu interessieren, für die unendlichen Diskussionen um den neuen Staat Israel, die unter Rubens Freunden entbrannt waren.

Manchmal dachte er: Ich fahre hin.

Aber er war den Papieren nach kein Jude, und für seine lächerliche akademische Ausbildung hatte man in einem Land, das ums Überleben kämpfte, keine Verwendung.

Als die Weihnachtsferien kamen und Mona ihr Töchterchen zur Welt brachte, empfand Simon zum ersten Mal seit vielen Monaten wieder Freude. Er saß in der Gebärklinik und las, wie Andersson es ihn gelehrt hatte, in den Augen des Neugeborenen. Sie waren unergründlich und unbegreiflich wie Simons eigener Gedanke: Ich habe eine Schwester bekommen.

Am Tag vor dem Heiligen Abend bestieg Klara das Flugzeug nach Oslo. Sie hatte die Reisetasche voller Geschenke für ihre Mutter und auch für die kleinen Geschwister, die sie nie gesehen hatte.

Es waren keine einfachen Weihnachten, Kersti holte Klara auf dem Flughafen Fornebu ab, und sie hatten keine Worte für das, was sie einander sagen wollten. Tagelang suchten sie nach Worten, kamen aber nicht weiter als zu Gesprächen über die Besetzung Norwegens durch die deutsche Wehrmacht und um wievieles besser es trotz allem mit dem Essen geworden war und ähnlichem.

Die kleinen Geschwister erzählten in ihrem klangvollen Norwegisch, es habe immer geheißen, Klara sei merkwürdig.

Ihr war klar, daß sie den Erwartungen der Kinder nicht entsprach.

Auch der neue Mann ihrer Mutter war Alkoholiker, aber umgänglicher, nicht so zerstörerisch wie der Sägewerker. Doch Klara sah, daß Kersti es nicht allzu leicht hatte.

In den Tagen nach Weihnachten meinte Kersti, Klara müsse etwas für ihre Haare tun, dieses schöne Haar. Kichernd betraten sie einen eleganten Salon in der Innenstadt, und Klaras Haare wurden geschnitten und gedauerwellt und bekamen den Schwung, den sie sich schon immer gewünscht hatte.

»Du bist nicht wiederzuerkennen«, sagte Kersti, und Klara betrachtete erstaunt ihr Spiegelbild in den Schaufenstern und überall dort, wo sich sonst noch Gelegenheit bot.

Sie trafen mit Kerstis Freunden zusammen: »Meine Tochter. Sie studiert in Göteborg Medizin.«

Die Mutter war stolz, das tat Klara gut.

Am Tag vor Silvester flog sie heim, saß in der Maschine und ihr wurde bewußt, daß sie fast die ganze Woche nicht an Simon gedacht hatte. Sie hatte an Neujahr Klinikdienst, auch das war ein gutes Gefühl.

Aber nach Hause zu kommen war schwierig, mein Gott, wie sie diese Abbruchwohnung haßte. Eiskalt, muffig, düster.

Ein Rattenloch.

Ein Päckchen wartete auf sie, sie erkannte die Handschrift auf dem Umschlag sofort: Doktor Klara Alm.

Er treibt seinen Spott mit mir.

Aber sie öffnete das Päckchen, es war sein Buch, und auf dem Vorsatzblatt stand: Der Geliebten.

Sie fluchte ausgiebig und lange und hemmungslos gemein.

Aber der Zorn wirkte nicht, es war, als hätte sie ihn in Oslo liegen lassen. Also blieb sie mit dem Buch auf dem Bett sitzen und dachte, daß sie es vielleicht die ganze Zeit gewußt hatte, daß es von dort keinen Weg nach draußen gab, und daß sie Simons wegen nach Oslo hatte reisen müssen.

Um ihn nicht auszulöschen.

Schließlich fror sie so sehr, daß sie zitterte, machte Feuer im Küchenherd und vertrieb die naßkalte Luft aus der Wohnung so gut es ging.

Packte ihre Tasche aus, ging in den Laden um die Ecke und kaufte Brot und Butter, Kaffee, machte einen Bogen um den Fisch, der sie mit Augen ansah, die schon viel zu lange tot waren, und kaufte vier Schweinskoteletts, um über Neujahr versorgt zu sein.

Ununterbrochen dachte sie, er hätte dieses Wort nicht verwenden dürfen, daß dieser Ausdruck nicht stimmte. Sie hatten nie von Liebe gesprochen. Jetzt war es gesagt, jetzt stand das Wort wie ein Haus in dem Buch und machte das, was gewachsen war und froh gemacht und gequält hatte, zur fordernden Wirklichkeit. Zwingend.

Jetzt mußten sie hinein in dieses Haus, mußten dort leben und wohnen.

Sie brauchte zwei Stunden, um die Wohnung soweit warm zu bekommen, daß sie ins Bett kriechen konnte. Aber sie war trotz aller Decken gezwungen, Handschuhe anzuziehen, um das Meergedicht lesen zu können.

»sieh doch endlich ein,
daß die wahrheit nur im ungesagten zu finden ist . . .«

Ganz richtig, Simon Larsson, daran hättest du denken sollen, bevor du deine Widmung geschrieben hast. Worte machen alles endgültig.

347

Wirklichkeit ist etwas anderes, ist stete Bewegung, unmöglich einzufangen.

Sie las das Gedicht immer und immer wieder. Ehe sie einschlief, dachte sie noch, das könnte sie selbst geschrieben haben.

Wenn sie hätte schreiben können.

Und damit war auch ein Wissen in Worte gefaßt, das bisher im Unbewußten ungehindert hatte wachsen können, daß nämlich Simon und sie sich sehr ähnlich waren.

Sie schlief die ganze Nacht durch, und als sie am nächsten Morgen im Herd Feuer machte, dachte sie, daß das, was sie jetzt empfand, Glück war, nur dieses und nichts anderes.

Es war vorbei mit dem Zwiespalt.

Es mußte das sein, was die Leute Frieden nennen, dachte sie und erinnerte sich daran, wie mißtrauisch sie diesem Wort immer gegenübergestanden hatte. Sie hatte es nie verstanden. Aber sie erkannte das Gefühl wieder, sie mußte es früher gehabt haben.

Als Kind, bevor ihre Mutter verschwand.

Und in der Musik, einem Leben im Inneren der Töne, wenn man loslassen konnte und die Flöte wie von selbst spielen durfte.

Klara bewahrte auch beim Telefonieren Ruhe. Ruben Lentov war am Apparat, sie sagte ihren Namen und bat mit Simon sprechen zu dürfen. Sie hörte, daß Ruben sich freute und bezog es bedingungslos auf sich. Doch Simon war nicht zu Hause, er war draußen bei seinen Eltern, um die Silvesterfeier vorzubereiten.

»Ach.« Klara war enttäuscht, sie wollte dort nicht anrufen.

»Du würdest nicht mit mir zu Mittag essen wollen? Ich möchte schon so lange gerne mit dir sprechen.«

Ruben klang verlegen. Klara wunderte sich.

»Das mache ich gerne«, antwortete sie, dachte aber, es gäbe doch eigentlich gar nicht mehr viel zu reden.

»Kann ich dich abholen?«

»Nein, um Gottes willen!« Klara fiel fast in Ohnmacht bei dem Gedanken an Lentov hier in dieser Wohnung in Haga.

»Ich komme zu Ihnen«, sagte sie.

»Nimm ein Taxi, dann suchen wir zusammen ein Restaurant, das heute offen hat.«

»Was mich angeht, ist das Essen nicht so wichtig«, erwiderte Klara.

»Für mich auch nicht. Dann geben wir uns eben mit ein paar belegten Broten aus meinem Kühlschrank zufrieden.«

Sie bürstete ihre neue lockige Frisur bis es knisterte und suchte den Rock heraus, den sie angehabt hatte, als sie mit Simon ins Konzert gegangen war. Griff nach der grünen Seidenbluse, bügelte sie. Als sie sich die Wimpern tuschte, dachte sie, und heute werde ich nicht heulen. Erst als sie im Taxi saß, fiel ihr ein, daß sie ihre Achselhöhlen zu pudern vergessen hatte, fand aber, daß das nichts ausmachte. Heute wollte sie auch nicht schwitzen.

Ruben machte selbst auf, und als sie ihm in die Augen sah, erinnerte sie sich daran, wie lieb er im Krankenhaus zu ihr gewesen war. Sie bedankte sich noch einmal für das Taschentuch, er lächelte und ließ sie wissen, wie wütend er auf Simon gewesen war, und daß er ihre Nachricht übermittelt hatte.

»Das war mir klar, als ich seinen Brief bekam«, sagte sie.

Dann schwiegen sie eine Weile etwas betreten, bis Klara begann: »Ich habe das Meergedicht gelesen. Und mir ist dabei bewußt geworden, daß Simon und ich einander sehr ähnlich sind.«

Da nickte er und Klara wußte endlich, welche Eigenschaft Ruben Lentov ganz besonders auszeichnete.

Menschliche Nähe, dachte sie.

»Darüber wollte ich mit dir sprechen«, sagte Ruben. »Und dann natürlich über dieses Unbegreifliche, was Liebe genannt wird und so schwierig ist.«

»Ich fürchte mich vor diesem Wort«, erklärte Klara.

»Pfeif auf das Wort. Sprechen wir darüber, wie selten sich das ereignet, was man Liebe nennt, denn die allermeisten Menschen halten schon ihre unbefriedigten Bedürfnisse dafür.«

»Ich nicht«, bekannte Klara, und als sie sah, daß Rubens Mund-winkel zuckten, fuhr sie trotzig fort: »Ich meine, wenn ich die Fähigkeit hätte, meine Unzufriedenheit mit Liebe zu verwechseln, wäre ich pausenlos verliebt.«

Darüber konnten sie beide lachen, und Ruben dachte, sie ist wirklich ein ungewöhnliches Mädchen, genau wie Erik behauptet hatte. Und Klara dachte, daß Ruben ein wunderbarer Mensch war, und wie gerne sie den Mut hätte, es ihm zu sagen.

Und dann sagte sie es: »Sie sind ein wunderbarer Mensch, Direktor Lentov.«

Er wurde rot wie ein Schuljunge und meinte, das Fräulein cand. med. Alm möge ihn ab sofort Ruben nennen, damit er sie auch weiterhin mit Klara ansprechen könne.

Er bot ihr einen Sherry an, ging in die Küche und holte die belegten Brote.

Danach sagte er entschlossen: »Ich würde dir gerne etwas erzählen, was ich bisher noch nie einem Menschen gegenüber erwähnt habe.«

Er mußte zunächst nach Worten suchen, als er Rebecca schildern wollte, das Mädchen, das er geliebt und dessen Schwester er geheiratet hatte.

»Rebecca und ich waren für einander bestimmt«, sagte er. »Vielleicht sehe ich es zu romantisch, nein, das tue ich nicht, wir waren für einander vorgesehen. Aber sie wollte aus dem Judentum heraus, und ich, der ich ihre große Sehnsucht nach Freiheit erkannte, ließ sie gehen. Zu einem deutschen Offizier mit einem adeligen Namen, der ihr einen Platz im Reich der Arier sichern sollte.«

Klara legte ihr Brot auf den Teller zurück.

»Ich habe mich in allem geirrt«, sagte Ruben. »Der vornehme deutsche Name half ihr nicht, als die Gestapo kam. Sie starb mit zwei ihrer Kinder im Konzentrationslager.«

Klara merkte, daß sie keine Wimperntusche hätte auflegen sollen, aber auch, daß ihr die schwarzen Streifen im Gesicht egal waren.

Ruben erzählte, wie er sich heimlich mit Rebecca in einem Restaurant in Paris getroffen hatte, in der Stadt, die er liebte.

»Ich hatte so edle Gedanken«, sagte er, und dann mit plötzlichem

Nachdruck: »Pfui Teufel, wieviel Schlimmes hat dieser Gedanke doch bewirkt, dieser idiotische Entschluß, auf sie zu verzichten und wider Gott und die Natur zu handeln. Für sie, für ihre Schwester, die ich mit hierher genommen habe, und die vor Angst und aus Mangel an Liebe den Verstand verloren hat.«

»Für dich selbst«, flüsterte Klara.

»Ja.«

Jetzt mußte Klara ins Badezimmer gehen, um sich das Gesicht zu waschen und mit kaltem Wasser zu erfrischen. Als sie zurückkam, war Ruben ruhiger, sagte: »Ich möchte nicht, daß du das weitererzählst, nicht einmal Simon.«

»Das verspreche ich«, sagte Klara.

Dann tranken sie noch ein Glas Sherry, bis er sagte: »Ich soll so um fünf draußen bei Larssons sein. Ob du wohl genug Mut hast, mitzukommen?«

»Ja«, sagte sie. »Ich trau mich.«

Auf dem Weg dorthin erzählte er im Auto, daß er Großvater geworden sei, erzählte von dem neugeborenen Kind, von dem behauptet werde, es sehe ihm ähnlich.

»Hier bin ich«, sagte Ruben. »Und ich bringe eine große Überraschung mit.«

Karin starrte Klara an, als traue sie ihren Augen nicht, doch dann kam die Freude, kamen Verzweiflung und Zorn, und dann wieder Freude. Klara konnte sehen, wie die Gefühle Karin durchwogten und sagte etwas beunruhigt: »Wir sollten dich solchen Schocks wohl besser nicht aussetzen.«

»Freude kann doch wohl keine Gefahr bedeuten«, konterte Erik und umarmte Klara so fest, daß es weh tat, und Klara dachte, ich muß in Erfahrung bringen, was es mit ihrem Herzen auf sich hat.

Simon und Isak waren mit Eriks Auto unterwegs auf einer Probefahrt. Mona stand mitten in der Küche und kümmerte sich um das Essen und deckte den Tisch und überwachte den Truthahn, der im Ofen schmorte und herrlich duftete.

»Nimm das Kind und verschwinde, damit hier ein bißchen Ordnung reinkommt«, und schon stand Klara mit einem neugeborenen Säugling in den Armen da, schaute von dem kleinen Gesicht zu Ruben, sagte mit großem Ernst: »Es stimmt, sie sieht dir ähnlich.«

»Jetzt haben wir die ärztliche Bestätigung«, stellte Mona fest.

Dann gingen Karin und Klara in das frühere schöne Zimmer, das jetzt auch weiße Wände und an den Fenstern weiße Wolken hatte. Die alten Eichenmöbel waren stehengeblieben und sahen in all dem Weiß irgendwie fehl am Platz aus.

Klara erzählte Karin von ihrer Mutter, von deren neuem Mann, und daß er auch ein Trinker war.

»Kannst du begreifen«, fragte Karin, »warum das Leben so schwierig sein muß?«

»Nein«, erwiderte Klara, und beide sahen das Kind an, das unkompliziert und gut war.

Doch dann hörten sie draußen ein Auto und Karin wurde nervös.

»Klara«, sagte sie. »Simon kann der Schlag treffen. Lauf nach oben, damit wir ihn ein bißchen vorbereiten können.«

Klara übergab Karin das Kind, sie hatte jetzt spürbares Herzklopfen, aber ihre Angst war frei von Dämonen, als sie die Treppe hinauflief.

»Die rechte Tür!« rief Karin ihr nach.

Klara betrat Simons altes Kinderzimmer, fühlte, daß hier alles von ihm durchdrungen war, und ihre Knie zitterten so sehr, daß sie sich aufs Bett setzen mußte.

Als Simon in die Küche kam, verstummte Karin, sah nur das magere Gesicht und darin die vor Qual brennenden Augen, und dachte, Gott im Himmel, was sagt man bloß.

Aber Erik, der fröhlich war wie ein Spielmann, fand Worte: »Hör mal, Simon. Dieser phantastische Ruben Lentov ist nochmal mit einem Weihnachtsgeschenk für dich hergekommen. Es wartet oben in deinem Zimmer auf dich. Sei auf das Schlimmste gefaßt, denn das jetzt ist noch viel schöner als die Musiktruhe.«

Simon mußte lachen, sagte dann zu Ruben, hör endlich auf mit

deinen Weihnachtsgeschenken, und außerdem hab ich ja schon eins
gekriegt. Er ging auf die Treppe zu, aber Karin hielt ihn zurück.

»Vielleicht solltest du vorher ein Schnäpschen trinken, Simon.
Angeblich beruhigt das.«

Ruben wußte nicht, ob er lachen oder weinen sollte, Mona zog vor
zu lachen, doch Simon sagte: »Du bist nicht ganz bei Trost, Mama.«

Dann verschwand er und das Haus hielt den Atem an, aber obwohl
es so still war, konnten sie kein Wort hören.

Nur eine Tür, die geschlossen wurde.

»Jetzt vergessen wir die zwei bis das Essen fertig ist«, sagte Mona,
und fing wieder an mit den Töpfen zu klappern.

Simon stand in der Tür und sah das Mädchen auf dem Bett an.

Dann machte er die Tür leise zu, ging zu ihr hin und begann ohne
ein Wort, sie auszuziehen, die schöne Bluse, den engen Rock, die
Nylonstrümpfe, den BH, alles.

Als er fertig war, legte er sich neben sie aufs Bett und liebte sie, wie
er es im letzten halben Jahr in tausend Träumen getan hatte, stark und
ernst.

»Danke«, sagte sie hinterher, aber er legte ihr den Finger auf den
Mund und fragte: »Hast du deine Flöte dabei?«

»Nein.«

»Morgen«, sagte er. »Morgen wirst du für mich spielen.«

»Ja.«

Sie dachten, es sei nur ein Augenblick vergangen, als Mona an die
Tür klopfte und sagte, man könne nicht nur von der Liebe leben, und
daß sie nun schon seit fast zwei Stunden mit dem Essen warteten.

Da lachte Simon.

Ich hatte vergessen, welch ein gewaltiges Lachen in ihm steckt,
dachte Klara, als sie sich anzog.

Sie kamen Hand in Hand die Treppe herunter und sprachen den
ganzen Abend fast kein Wort, und es war schwierig, sie anzusehen,
denn sie waren so bis in die Tiefen ihrer Seelen nackt und bloß. Nur
Karin wagte einen langen Blick auf Simon, und dieser Blick sagte ihr,

was sie schon wußte, jetzt hatte sie ihn verloren, und jetzt war er glücklich.

Als die Uhr zwölf schlug, erhoben alle das Glas auf das Wohl der beiden: »Auf eure Liebe«, sagte Erik. »Hütet sie von jetzt an gut, verdammt nochmal.«

34

Um sechs am nächsten Morgen hätte Klara das schlafende Haus fast zu Tode erschreckt:»Du liebe Zeit, Simon, ich habe Journaldienst, ich muß vor sieben in der Sahlgrenschen Klinik sein und ich habe keine Schuhe und fährt schon eine Straßenbahn?«

»Du wolltest doch für mich Flöte spielen«, unterbrach Simon sie, aber dann erkannte auch er den Ernst der Lage und weckte Erik, der grunzend die Hose über den Pyjama zog und das Auto aus der Garage holte. Karin suchte ein Paar bequeme flache Schuhe aus, meinte: »Was für ein Glück, daß wir die gleiche Größe haben.«

»Karin«, sagte Klara, die sich wegen des Trubels schämte. »Sag's nur gerade heraus, daß du zornig auf mich bist und mich für leichtsinnig hältst, weil ich Krankenhaus und Job und einfach alles vergessen habe.«

»Ich bin schon neugierig, wie lange du noch bestimmen wirst, was andere denken«, erwiderte Karin. »Könnte ja sein, daß ich dich für dumm halte, weil du nicht verstehst, daß nach einem Abend wie dem gestrigen jeder den Kopf verlieren kann.«

»Ich bin nicht ganz sicher, ob ich meinen schon gefunden habe«, meinte Klara.

»Am meisten werden darunter die Kranken zu leiden haben«, lachte Erik, der mit dem Wagen vorgefahren war.

In der darauffolgenden Woche zog Klara aus der Abbruchwohnung in Simons Zimmer bei Ruben. Sie redeten und redeten, und bis zum Dreikönigstag hatten sie so viel geredet, daß es hätte für ein ganzes Leben reichen können.

Wie Simon das ausdrückte.

In den Osterferien flog er mit nach Oslo, um Klaras Mutter zu besuchen. Er ist nicht das kleinste bißchen ängstlich, dachte Klara, die sicher war, daß er Kersti im Sturm erobern werde.

Was er auch tat.

Als der Frühling erblühte, machten sie einen Kurzbesuch beim Sägewerker, vor allem, damit Klara die Werksstraße auf und ab flanieren und Simon vorzeigen konnte. Er verstand das und blieb willig ab und zu dort stehen, wo die meisten Fenster nebeneinander lagen, um Klara zu küssen.

Der Vater war schlimmer als Simon es sich vorgestellt hatte, rüde in der Ausdrucksweise und mit gehässigem Blick. Wie vom Teufel geritten, zerschlug er jeden Versuch einer Annäherung.

Simon bekam es mit der Angst zu tun, er hatte so etwas schon erlebt.

Sie fuhren mit dem Auto, denn jetzt hatte er einen Führerschein, und Erik hatte ihm seinen Wagen zur Verfügung gestellt. Auf dem Weg nach Karlstad sprach er es aus: »Es ist das Spiel deines Vaters, das du spielst, wenn die Dämonen hinter dir her sind.«

Sie kamen zu Joachim Goldberg, Klaras altem Flötenlehrer. Sie hatten den Besuch vorbereitet, hatten geschrieben und angefragt, ob er sich an Simon Habermann erinnern könne.

»Jetzt ist die Nervosität bei mir«, sagte Simon, als sie in dem Mietshaus die Treppe hinaufgingen, wo Frau Goldberg mit Kaffee und Kuchen wartete und der alte Mann Klara mit großer Wärme empfing. Zu Simon sagte er: »Ich fürchte, ich muß dich enttäuschen.«

Im Berliner Philharmonischen Orchester hatte es mehr als 30 jüdische Musiker gegeben, Goldberg konnte sich nur vage an einen scheuen Geiger namens Habermann erinnern.

»Er hat zu den Gutgläubigen gehört, die geblieben sind und nicht wahrhaben wollten, daß das möglich sein konnte, was ununterbrochen um uns herum geschah«, sagte Goldberg.

Auf dem Heimweg besuchten sie Trollhättan, betrachteten von

oben die stillgelegten Wasserfälle und befanden sich bald mitten in einem widersinnigen Streit über alles und nichts. Schweigend fuhren sie durch das Flußtal weiter.

Sie heirateten zu Mittsommer 1949 in Oslo, wo Kersti eine Hochzeit ausrichtete, die größer und prächtiger war als es jeder von ihnen haben wollte, Simons Familie war mit dabei, Karin mochte Klaras Mutter vom ersten Augenblick an und blieb ein paar Tage in Oslo, um auch die eigenen Kusinen zu besuchen, denen sie den ganzen Krieg hindurch Lebensmittelpakete geschickt hatte. Sie erkannte bald, daß diese sie ablehnten, sie, die Reiche aus dem von deutscher Besatzung verschonten Nachbarland.

»Man konnte nicht ein Gespräch mit ihnen führen, ohne daß einem die deutschen Eisenbahntransporte in den Rachen geschoben wurden«, äußerte Karin sich Mona gegenüber, als sie nach Hause kam.

Karin saß mit einem Topf auf dem Schoß in der Küche. Er war nie ein besonders schönes Stück gewesen, und inzwischen war er nach jahrelangem Gebrauch zerbeult und aus der Form geraten. Ein Henkel war abgegangen.

Sie sah den Topf fast erstaunt an und erinnerte sich daran, wie sie sich einst über ihn gefreut hatte, wie sie in dem Geschäft in der Övre Hamngata gestanden und von all den guten Suppen geträumt hatte, die sie darin kochen würde.

Vermutlich hatte sie diese Suppen in den vergangenen Jahren auch wirklich gekocht, aber der Mensch merkt nur selten, wenn Träume sich erfüllen.

Das dachte Karin und sagte: »Na dann tschüs.«

Dann steckte sie den Topf in den großen Müllsack, der vor ihr stand.

Es war ein so warmer Nachmittag in dem heißen Spätsommer 1955, daß man sich unmöglich im Freien aufhalten konnte. Die Küche war kühler als der Schatten unter den Bäumen, zumindest wenn man ein wenig Durchzug machte. Aber auch das war nicht leicht, denn die Luft stand still. Karin fiel das Atmen schwer.

Sie war mit Lisa übereingekommen, daß sie die warmen Nachmittage dazu verwenden wollten, die Schränke aufzuräumen und alles wegzuwerfen, was ausgedient hatte.

Karin hatte immer ihre Schwierigkeiten gehabt, Sachen auszumustern. Jetzt machte es ihr fast Vergnügen. Ein altes Eßbesteck mit schwarzen Griffen, blecherne Suppenlöffel, die ihr immer zuwider gewesen waren, das verrückte geblümte Kaffeeservice, das sie zur

Hochzeit von ihrem Bruder bekommen hatte, alles wanderte in den Sack, den sie mitten in die Küche gestellt hatten.

Lisa seufzte hin und wieder, machte sich auch schon mal Luft. Als das Kaffeeservice samt Sahnekännchen und allem was sonst noch dazugehörte in den Sack gesteckt wurde, konnte sie sich nicht mehr zurückhalten.

»Na, dann nimm's doch, wenn es dir gefällt«, sagte Karin und hielt einen Augenblick inne. Aber dann seufzten sie beide, denn sie wußten ja, wie voll auch Lisas Schränke schon waren.

Die Anderssons hatten auch an dem neuen Überfluß teil und hatten nicht die geringste Ahnung, wie sie damit umgehen sollten.

Am Donnerstagnachmittag sah der Himmel endlich ein, welche Qualen die Erde litt und wie sehr sie seiner Barmherzigkeit harrte. Gewitterwolken türmten sich von Blitzen zerrissen, und mit Donner und lautem Getöse stürzte das Wasser auf Land und Meer nieder. Die Erde trank, schlürfte sich begierig voll.

Ohne die geringste Dankbarkeit.

Wie es die Erde immer tut, dachte der Himmel, und voll Eigensinn wurde er kalt und grau, gab kein Wasser mehr her, obwohl der Boden sich bei weitem nicht sattgetrunken hatte.

Am Abend nach dem Wolkenbruch wollte Karin nicht zu Bett gehen, sie blieb im Garten sitzen, atmete die kühle Luft ein und warme Luft wieder aus bis sie fror und merkte, daß sie ausreichend erfrischt war, um gut schlafen zu können.

Auch am nächsten Tag trotzte der Himmel, aber Karin freute sich, jetzt konnte sie wieder durch die Landschaft streifen, wie sie es gewohnt war. Etwas schuldbewußt stahl sie sich an der Rückseite des Hauses den Fußpfad bergauf, ängstlich daß die Kinder sie sehen könnten und mitgehen wollten.

Heute wollte sie mit Hügeln und Meer, dem Fluß und den gelben Wiesen allein sein. Sie ging dem alten Badeplatz zu, stand auf der Klippe und dachte, es ist noch gar nicht so lange her, daß Simon hier den Kopfsprung gelernt hat.

Die Zeit zerrinnt einem zwischen den Fingern, desto schneller, je älter man wird, dachte Karin.

Jetzt konnte hier niemand mehr baden, das Mündungswasser des Flusses stank, war braun und ölverseucht. Karin sah die neuen Häuser, diese Kisten, die sich eitel auf die Hügel gesetzt und es in wenigen Jahren geschafft hatten, die Konturen jener Landschaft zu zerstören, die Meer, Strom und Berge in Jahrtausenden geschaffen hatten.

Nie hatte Karin geahnt, daß gestiegener Lebensstandard sich so häßlich auswirken konnte. Wie hatte sie von jener Zeit geträumt, die nach Fertigstellung des Volkshauses kommen und die Menschen von dem Druck befreien würde, den die Armut schafft. Jetzt war diese Zeit gekommen, allen Menschen ging es besser, das war gut, das war wunderbar. Die Angst vor dem Morgen vergällte das Leben nicht mehr, und die andere Angst, die es in der Tiefe immer gegeben hatte, konnte vorläufig mit allerlei Krimskrams beschwichtigt werden. Tausende von neuen Begierden, von denen früher niemand etwas geahnt hatte, schufen sich plötzlich Raum, und fast jede dieser Begierden konnte von dem neuen und häßlichen Überfluß zufriedengestellt werden.

Ich habe Gedanken wie ein alter Reaktionär, sagte sich Karin und wies ihre Gefühle zurecht. In diesen häßlichen Kästen, die die Landschaft zerstört hatten, lebten die Leute in gut geplanten Wohnungen als freie Menschen, die sich nicht zu ängstigen und vor niemandem zu erniedrigen brauchten, und für die Warmwasser und Kanalisation eine Selbstverständlichkeit waren. Die Abwässer wurden auf kürzestem Weg ins Meer abgeleitet und mischten sich dort mit dem Unrat der großen Industrien am Strom.

Sie wandte sich vom Strand ab, nahm den schmalen Pfad durch die Wiesen, wo bald Grundstücke für Reihenhäuser abgesteckt werden sollten, und dachte, dann brauche ich wenigstens die Kisten da oben nicht mehr zu sehen. Was sie wirklich damit meinte, wußte sie selbst nicht, doch als sie zu den Eichen kam und eine Rast einlegte, hatte sie plötzlich das Bedürfnis, von dem Topf zu erzählen.

»Ihr müßt wissen«, sagte sie zu den Bäumen. »Es war ein alter Topf,

der ausgedient hatte. Er fraß außerdem furchtbar viel elektrischen Strom und hatte auf dem Herd keine Standfestigkeit mehr.«
Die Eichen lauschten und verstanden.

Als Karin aber weitererzählte, wie häßlich der Topf geworden war, wie verbeult und uneben, und daß er einen wackligen Henkel hatte, waren die Bäume nicht mehr einer Meinung mit ihr. Der Kochtopf war von einer alten, verläßlichen Schönheit gewesen, fanden die Eichen, und Karin mußte ihnen wohl oder übel ein wenig recht geben.

Dann sprach sie, wie es ihre Gewohnheit war, von Simon und den anderen Kindern, wie gut es ihnen allen ging und für wie vieles sie selbst dankbar sein mußte.

Schon im vierten Jahr studierte Simon an der Londoner Universität, und es mußte ja etwas Bedeutendes sein, womit er sich beschäftigte, wenn er dafür staatliche Fördergelder bekam. Jahr für Jahr flossen Stipendien, die es ihm ermöglichten, zu den seltsamen Zeichen auf den alten Tontafeln aus Mesopotamien zurückzukehren.

Karin verstand nicht, was es Wichtiges mit ihnen auf sich hatte oder warum man bestrebt war, eine Sprache zu begreifen, die schon seit vielen Jahrtausenden niemand mehr sprach.

Es war ein ähnliches Rätsel wie der hohe Lebensstandard und die sich daraus ergebende Häßlichkeit.

Ich werde wohl langsam alt, sagte sie zu den Eichen, die darüber die Köpfe schüttelten. Und Karin mußte irgendwie zugeben, daß das nicht stimmte, sie war letztes Jahr fünfzig geworden, und das war kein Alter mit dem man angeben konnte.

Sie solle lieber an Dinge denken, die sie begriff, meinten die Eichen, und da freute sie sich eine ganze Weile darüber, daß Simon es mit Klara gut getroffen hatte, die jetzt in der Schweiz war und mit ihrer langen und gründlichen Ausbildung bald fertig sein würde.

Die beiden konnten nicht viel beisammen sein, aber das war für die Liebe wohl eher förderlich.

Karin blieb in Gedanken bei Klara hängen, dem Mädchen, das mehr über sie wußte als jeder andere, die ihr aber trotzdem nie nahestehen würde. Respekt, gegenseitiger Respekt, das war es, was zwischen ihnen bestand.

Sie schämte sich schon lange nicht mehr für das, was geschehen war, als Klara das erste Mal zu ihnen kam. Es war eine schwierige Zeit gewesen, in der Karin oft allein durch die Hügel gegangen war und einsehen mußte, daß sie ihrer eigenen Schwiegermutter vielleicht gar nicht so unähnlich war.

Das Wichtigste in Karins Leben, sogar wichtiger als Simon, war ihr Bild von sich selbst als der Guten und Klugen. Der großen Mutter, wie Klara das genannt hatte. Karin konnte inzwischen fast darüber lachen und dachte, das sei ja eigentlich kein übles Bild, besser als das, das Frauen normalerweise wegen ihrer Unzulänglichkeitsgefühle von sich schufen.

Wie auch immer, man strebt schließlich danach, die Vorstellung, die man von sich selbst hat, wahr zu machen, und die gute und kluge Karin war für die Kinder schon nicht schlecht gewesen. Was für sie selbst dabei herausgekommen war, stand nicht zur Debatte, denn sie hatte hart gearbeitet und war für ihre Jahre viel zu gebrechlich und verblüht.

Ähnlich dem Topf, den sie weggeworfen hatte.

Klara hatte einen Beruf, sie besaß das, was Karin immer hatte haben wollen. Sie war nicht von einem Mann abhängig, um leben zu können.

Trotzdem war sie viel mehr abhängig von Simon als Karin es je von Erik gewesen war.

Das war erstaunlich, aber es war bei Mona und Isak nicht anders, denn die Ehe stellte große Anforderungen. Sie wollten alles miteinander teilen, den anderen immer verstehen.

Das führte zu Enttäuschungen und unausweichlich auch zu Kränkungen. Karin konnte es bei Isak und Mona deutlich beobachten, wie auf beiden Seiten die Verzweiflung zunahm, bis neue Versuche zu neuen Streitigkeiten führten, wenn sie sich näherkommen wollten. Statt es bleiben zu lassen, dachte Karin, die nie die Ansicht geteilt hatte, daß Mann und Frau sich von Grund auf verstehen müßten.

Sie hatte versucht, es Mona zu erklären: »Wir kommen aus unterschiedlichen Welten.«

Aber Mona hörte nicht zu, selbst wenn sie eine Zeitlang ihre Ansprüche herunterschrauben konnte, wenn sie daran erinnert wurde, wie unsicher der Boden war, auf dem Isak stand.

Malin kam die Böschung hinter dem Haus herunter auf Karin zugesprungen. Geliebtes Kind, du, dachte Karin wie fast immer, wenn sie das kleine Mädchen mit dem tiefen Ernst und der großen Freude erblickte.

Simon nannte Malin seine kleine Schwester, aber das konnte wohl nicht darauf zurückzuführen sein, daß sie einander glichen. Wo er einen Feuereifer an den Tag legte, war das Mädchen ruhig wie die Bäume, wo er vor Fragen fast platzte, war sie voll reichem Wissen.

Karin setzte sich auf den Felsen, um das Mädchen in die Arme zu schließen.

»Malin, sechs Jahre, und Freude meines Herzens«, begrüßte sie die Kleine fast feierlich. Dann machte sie es wie immer, flocht die Finger in das dichte braune Haar und hauchte dem Kind in den Nacken. Es hatte einen kräftigen, eigenartigen Duft.

»Du riechst, als kämst du vom Himmel«, freute sich Karin.

»Ich habe dich gehen sehen und wollte dir nachlaufen«, sagte das Kind. »Aber dann wußte ich, daß du allein sein möchtest.«

»Das war gut«, nickte Karin. »Aber jetzt möchte ich nicht mehr allein sein, jetzt will ich mit dir zusammensein.«

»Worüber mußtest du denn nachdenken?«

»Ja, was war es nur?« Karin überlegte eine Weile und dann sagte sie, selbst erstaunt: »Über einen alten Kochtopf, den ich gestern weggeworfen habe. Ich dachte, das muß ich genau durchdenken.«

Malin fand das nicht erstaunlich, sie teilte Karins Gefühl von Verlust. »Hättest du ihn nicht mir geben können? Ich hätte in der Sandkiste damit spielen können.«

»Aber du hast doch so viele hübsche Sandeimerchen.«

»Trotzdem liebe ich alte Töpfe«, sagte Malin und Karin gab sich Mühe, nicht zu lachen.

Dann gingen sie Hand in Hand den Berg hinunter und hinaus in den großen neuen Garten.

Der Garten, ja. Trotz des grauen Himmels breitete er sich in Pracht und Reichtum vor ihnen aus, die würdevollen Morellenbäume, die Erdbeerbeete, die für dieses Jahr schon abgeerntet waren, der weiche Rasen, der sich so schön an alle Bäume heranmachte, die Eschen ganz unten am Felsen beim Fluß, und die Fichtenhecke, die noch nicht viel hermachte, in einigen Jahren jedoch Schutz vor dem Wind bieten würde.

Karin setzte sich in den alten Liegestuhl auf dem Holzsteg am Teich und betrachtete die mannshohen Schwertlilien mit den umgestülpten dunkelvioletten Kelchen, die ihre feuerfarbenen Staubgefäße frech emporreckten. Es würde nicht mehr lange dauern, bis sie Samen bildeten, und Karin würde an den zierlichen Samenständen, die man trocknen und im Haus in Krüge stellen konnte, den ganzen Winter hindurch ihre Freude haben.

Malin saß schweigend zu ihren Füßen und versuchte den Marienkäfern die Blattläuse schmackhaft zu machen.

»Laß den Tieren ihre Freiheit«, sagte Karin. »Setze die kleinen Käfer bitte wieder auf die Rosen.«

»Später«, sagte das Kind und sah zu den dicken Rosen am Teichrand hinüber, die unter Hitze und Wolkenbruch arg gelitten hatten.

Als Karin den Kopf zurücklehnte, konnte sie die Apfelbäume an der Grenze des alten Gartens sehen, den sie mit Erik einst zu Anfang hier angelegt hatte. Es waren Åkerö-Äpfel, die knorrigen altehrwürdigen Bäume versprachen reiche Ernte.

In diesem Jahr werde ich sie nicht ernten. Mona kann sich nehmen, was sie braucht, den Rest überlassen wir den Vögeln.

Malin verhielt sich ganz still, als glaube sie, Karin wolle auch in diesen Augenblicken mit ihren Gedanken allein sein, die jetzt von fröhlicher Art waren und sich um den Garten und all das rankten, was sie ihm zu verdanken hatte.

Heimliche Freude zu Anfang, bis dann die Zeit der Werftverlegung kam und sie mit Mona ihre Idee entwickelte. Den ganzen Vorfrühling lang, als das Baby Malin noch von Arm zu Arm weitergereicht wurde oder auf einem Kissen auf der Küchenbank schlummerte, hatten sie beide herumphantasiert und Pläne gezeichnet. Mona hatte von einer richtigen Wiese mit Margeriten und Akeleien geträumt, von Kornblumen und Klatschmohn in der südlichen Ecke. Auf einem großen Küchengarten mit Erdbeeren und Himbeersträuchern als Abschluß hatte Karin bestanden. Zu den Felsen hin wollten sie bodendeckende Polsterpflanzen und Primeln als Frühlingsfreude setzen, und blauen Enzian für den Herbst.

»Hauswurz«, hatte Karin nüchtern vorgeschlagen.

»Weißt du«, hatte Mona hinzugefügt, »daß es zwanzig verschiedene Anemonenarten gibt, weiße und lila und gelbe. Und sogar gefüllte weiße, die wie Röschen aussehen.«

Nein, das hatte Karin nicht gewußt. Sie war immer der Meinung gewesen, daß weiße Anemonen Buschwindröschen genannt wurden und während der kurzen Zeit, die ihnen geschenkt war, überall im Land blühten.

Die beiden Frauen hatten von Ruben Gartenbücher bekommen, und damit bekamen die Träume neue Nahrung, wuchsen ins Uferlose.

Dann war es darum gegangen, Erik zu überzeugen. Es war fast das Schwierigste von allem gewesen.

»Du wirst dich totarbeiten«, hatte er gesagt. »Außerdem brauche ich das Kapital, das in diesem Grund und Boden steckt.«

Da war Karin böse geworden.

»Du redest wie ein unersättlicher Kapitalist, du Blutsauger«, hatte sie so wütend geschrien, daß ihr die richtigen Worte abhanden kamen. Erst später war ihr eines eingefallen: Ausbeuter.

Erik war auch in Rage gekommen, da Karin inzwischen aber herzkrank war, hatte der Zank sich nie richtig ausgewachsen, und Erik hatte sich samt seinem Zorn wie üblich in die Werkstatt zurückgezogen.

Nur bei Isak hatten die beiden Frauen anfangs Unterstützung gefunden, er hatte ihre Meinung geteilt, daß ein Garten bis ganz hinunter zum Fluß etwas Großartiges wäre, Ruben hatte den Kopf geschüttelt und eher zu Erik gehalten, denn wie sollten Karin und Mona einen Garten von so riesigen Ausmaßen besorgen können. Er hatte wohl auch an die Besitzverhältnisse gedacht und daß Isak und Mona bei Gustafssons Miete zu bezahlen hatten.

Niemand weiß, wie es geendet hätte, wären die beiden Gustafssons nicht gerade zur richtigen Zeit gestorben, erst der Mann und dann nach einigen Monaten die alte Frau, die sechzig Jahre lang auf ihrem Mann herumgehackt hatte, es aber nicht schaffte, ohne ihn zu leben. Ihre Erben hatten in dem verwinkelten Haus mit Erkern und zahlreichen Sprossenfenstern nicht wohnen wollen. Es würde ein Vermögen kosten, das Gebäude zu modernisieren, gerade Wände einzuziehen und Kippfenster einzubauen.

Die Erben waren also froh, als Isak ein angemessenes Angebot machte. Mona jubelte laut, Karin nur still in ihrem Herzen.

Im ersten Sommer waren sie nicht besonders weit gekommen, hatten jedoch Leute und Maschinen aufgetrieben, die nach Verlegung der Werft Ordnung schufen und das Gelände planierten. Ladung für Ladung wurde noch rechtzeitig vor dem Frost Humuserde herbeigeschafft. Noch vor dem Winter, den sie brauchten, um Gustafssons Haus umzubauen, wurden Bäume und Büsche gepflanzt.

Im Haus hatte es ursprünglich acht Zimmer und zwei Küchen gegeben, jetzt waren es nur noch sechs Zimmer, denn Mona gehörte nicht zu denen, die sich davor scheuten, Wände umzulegen und Licht und Luft in ihrer Umgebung zu schaffen.

Die alte Küche im oberen Stock war jetzt Webstube, Mona hatte einen Kurs besucht und weben gelernt, und Karin hatte während dieser Zeit Malin gehütet.

Als der Garten angelegt wurde, war Mona wieder schwanger gewesen, hatte dick und unförmig im künftigen Steingarten gearbeitet, und der Bauch war dem Setzholz immer im Weg gewesen. Und Erik hatte einen Mann eingestellt, einen alten Gärtnermeister, der weiterhin einen Tag in der Woche kam und die schwereren Arbeiten erledigte.

Im nächsten Winter waren die Zwillinge auf die Welt gekommen, zwei grundverschiedene Jungen. Der eine schwarz wie die Nacht, jüdisch, introvertiert und nachdenklich. Und der andere blond, fröhlich und, wie es schien, einfach und unkompliziert.

»Wie der Fischhändler«, hatte Mona gesagt.

»Jetzt halt aber den Mund«, hatte Karin ganz erschrocken gerufen, doch Mona hatte nur gelacht, das Flachsköpfchen an sich gedrückt und gesagt, daß sie den Fischhändler ja trotz allem liebe, und daß er ein bißchen verschroben sei, habe mit den Erbanlagen nichts zu tun.

»Weißt du«, hatte sie hinzugefügt. »Meine Großmutter hat irgendwie der Teufel geritten.«

»Genau wie meine Schwiegermutter. Ich wüßte nur gerne, durch was diese Frauen so geworden sind.«

Goldene Jahre, schwer von Süße und mit derselben Art von Selbstverständlichkeit wie damals, als Simon noch klein war, dachte Karin.

Dann nahm sie Malin mit ins Haus, Lisa war für heute schon gegangen, und die beiden beschlossen, für den Abendkaffee eine Torte zu backen, rührten Eier und Zucker, verstreuten Mehl auf dem Küchenboden, schlugen Sahne und hatten viel Spaß.

Sie vergaßen den Kuchen im Ofen, darum war er ein bißchen angebrannt, doch waren sie sich einig, daß er genießbar wäre, wenn man die Ränder wegschnitt.

»Den Fußboden mußt du kehren«, sagte Karin. »Ich bin ein bißchen müde, weißt du.«

Und Malin kehrte, und da sie nun einmal war, wie sie war, machte sie das auch gründlich.

Als sie heimging, meinte sie, jetzt bist du wohl nicht mehr traurig wegen deinem Kochtopf, und Karin antwortete, nein, nein, das bin ich nicht mehr.

Gerade richtig zum Sonntag hatte der Himmel seine schlechte Laune überwunden, fegte die Wolken weg und ließ die Sonne ungehindert mit Bäumen und Menschen spielen. Ruben war gekommen, um bei Mona und Isak zu Mittag zu essen, wie es sonntags der Brauch war. Im

Garten unterhielt er sich mit Karin, und sie erzählte noch einmal von dem Topf, den sie weggeworfen hatte und der ihr nicht aus dem Kopf gehen wollte.

»Ist doch eigenartig«, sagte sie. »Ich habe den Topf seit Jahren nicht mehr in der Hand gehabt, also kann ich ihn doch gar nicht vermissen.«

Ruben erzählte von einem Rabbiner, der gesagt hatte, daß man Tag für Tag so leben solle, als nähme man Abschied von allem, allen Dingen, die man besaß und allen Menschen, die man liebte. Vermöge man dieses zu tun, dann sei das Leben geprägt von Wirklichkeit, hatte der Rabbiner behauptet.

Karin, von den Worten ergriffen, sah Ruben lange an. Und er spürte so etwas wie einen Schatten in seinem Inneren, und er bereute seine Worte ohne recht zu wissen, weshalb.

An diesem Abend dachte Karin vor dem Einschlafen, daß es vielleicht dieses war, was sie zu lernen versuchte, nämlich sich freizumachen von den Bindungen an Menschen und Dinge.

Der Topf war nur ein Anfang gewesen, und daher hatte er sich in ihren Gedanken eingenistet.

Und vielleicht war ihr Leben nach dem Wolkenbruch wirklicher geworden, möglicherweise wuchs etwas Neues in ihr. Nein, nicht Neues, es war wohl immer vorhanden gewesen, jedoch von den Sorgen um die Kinder und all dem Unberechenbaren, was das Leben immer mit sich bringen konnte, verdeckt worden.

Sie schlief nachts wie ein Kind, tiefer und besser als seit langem. Und ihre Streifzüge durch die Hügel waren unbeschwerter, sie hatte weniger Erinnerungen und mehr Freude an ihren Beobachtungen.

»Ich glaube, ich höre allmählich auf zu denken«, sagte sie eines Tages zu Malin.

»Das ist aber gut«, sagte das Kind. »Die Gedanken machen alles meistens nur schwieriger.«

»Da könntest du recht haben«, meinte Karin und betrachtete diesen neuen Menschen, der gerade zu denken begonnen hatte, statt einfach nur zu sein.

Karin saß lange unter den Eichen und bedauerte, daß sie sich immer zu einer Gehetzten gemacht, daß sie in ihrem Leben alles immer getan hatte, um es hinter sich zu bringen. Und was hatte sie dann mit der Zeit getan, die sie herausgeschlagen hatte?

Daran konnte sie sich nicht erinnern.

Doch die Eichen trösteten sie wie gewöhnlich, sie wußten ebensogut wie Karin, daß es dumm ist, das zu bedauern, was man nie wieder ungeschehen machen kann. Auf dem Heimweg war sie wieder ohne Erinnerungen und fühlte sich seltsam frei.

»Du bist so still«, bemerkte Erik. »Du bist doch hoffentlich nicht krank?«

»Nein«, lachte Karin. »Ich habe mich nie gesünder gefühlt, es ist nur so, daß ich aufgehört habe, mich zu sorgen.«

»Willst du damit sagen, es gibt nichts mehr zu bereden?«

»Ja, und wenig zu bedenken.«

»Man könnte sagen, daß es ja auch höchste Zeit war, daß du aufhörst, dir Sorgen zu machen«, erwiderte Erik, doch Karin glaubte so etwas wie Mißtrauen in seinen Augen zu erkennen.

Aber auch das kümmerte sie nicht.

Soll er es nehmen, wie er will, dachte sie.

Erik und Isak wollten Ende November nach Amerika fahren, um Kleinbootwerften zu studieren. Sie fürchteten sich beide vor der Reise, in erster Linie Erik, der die Sprache nicht kannte und Unterlegenheit nicht vertrug. Aber das konnte er ja nicht einmal sich selbst eingestehen.

Er wollte Karin mit dabei haben, aber sie sagte es, wie es war, daß ihr nämlich eine so weite Reise zu anstrengend sei, und gedacht hatte sie, du kannst nicht dein Leben lang an meinem Schürzenzipfel hängen, Erik Larsson. Es ist an der Zeit, daß du auf eigenen Beinen stehst.

Der September war verregnet, doch der Oktober brachte einen milden, goldenen Altweibersommer. Karin hatte am Strand eine Stelle gefunden, wo das Schilf so hoch stand, daß es alles verdeckte außer den Himmel und den Fluß. Sie konnte lange dort sitzen und nur schauen.

Sie war nie so klarsichtig gewesen wie jetzt, wo sie sich freigemacht hatte von allen Überlegungen, was das Leben eigentlich bedeuten sollte.

Jetzt wußte sie, was das Leben war, und wie man es leben konnte.

An diesem Tag, einem Dienstag, kamen die Seidenschwänze angeflogen, eine ganze Schar, unterwegs in den Süden. Sie ließen sich ganz in Karins Nähe nieder, und sie betrachtete die sonnengelben Binden an den Schwingen und die lustigen Köpfe mit den eigenwilligen Schöpfen. Und wieder hörte sie diesen eigentümlichen Gesang, der zwischen Freude und düsterer Trauer lag.

Sie war dennoch erstaunt, als ihr bewußt wurde, was sie erkannt hatte, und sie verstand, daß es dieses war, worauf alle Anzeichen hingedeutet und die große Freiheit vorbereitet hatten.

So leise sie konnte, um die Vögel nicht zu stören, legte sie sich hin und machte es sich bequem. Sie lag ruhig im Schilf und beobachtete aufmerksam, wie sich ihr Herzschlag verlangsamte und nach und nach ganz aufhörte.

36

Mona schüttete den abgestandenen Tee weg, der zu lange gezogen hatte und schon kalt geworden war. Es ist idiotisch, sich Sorgen zu machen, sagte sie laut vor sich hin.

Doch dann kam Malin weinend an und schluchzte, sie sei mindestens hundertmal auf dem Berg gewesen, weil sie Karin entgegengehen wollte. »Warum kommt sie nicht, Mama?«

Da beschloß Mona, die Besorgnis des Kindes ernst zu nehmen, rief Lisa an und bat sie, eine Weile zu den Kindern zu kommen.

Dann ging sie los, im wesentlichen kannte sie ja die Wege, die Karin besonders liebte, war ihrer Sache also sicher und anfangs auch ganz gelassen.

Wahrscheinlich sitzt sie irgendwo, ist vielleicht eingeschlafen, ich muß langsam machen, darf sie nicht erschrecken.

Doch bald war Monas Vernunft am Ende. Sie lief zu den Eichen, lief über Hügel und Wiesen, den Strand entlang. Es dauerte eine Stunde, es dauerte zwei, doch nirgends war eine Spur von Karin zu entdecken.

Als Mona sich wieder auf den Heimweg machte, hatte sie eine vage Hoffnung, daß Karin wie gewöhnlich mit Malin im Garten sitzen werde. Aber eigentlich wußte Mona ...

Isak war zu Hause, Gott sei Dank. Erik war noch auf der Werft, das war gut. Sie bat Lisa, noch zu bleiben und lief mit Isak zum Strand: »Ich habe überall gesucht, vielleicht ist sie ins Wasser gefallen.«

Isaks Augen waren schwarz vor Angst. Gemeinsam liefen die beiden am Flußufer entlang und hinein in den dichten Schilfgürtel. Und dort lag Karin dann ganz friedvoll, als schliefe sie.

»Karin!« rief Isak, in seiner Stimme schwang Erleichterung mit, doch als Karin nicht antwortete, schaute er Mona an und verstand. Er wollte es nicht glauben, packte sie an den Schultern, schüttelte sie und sagte: »Mona, das darf nicht wahr sein. Sag, daß es nicht wahr ist.«

Aber das war es. Sie standen dort und hielten einander an der Hand wie Kinder, keiner hatte Tränen, doch als Mona sich frei machte und ein paar letzte Sommerblumen pflückte, um sie Karin in die Hände zu legen, und beide erkannten, daß sie schon starr war, schrie Isak sein Entsetzen laut heraus. Es war nicht Verzweiflung, denn die hatte ihn noch nicht erreicht, und die große Trauer, die ihm bevorstand, konnte er in diesem Augenblick nicht einmal ahnen.

Doch Mona, die bis in die Lippen weiß wie Schnee war, sagte jetzt: »Isak, wir müssen ganz ruhig sein, einer von uns bleibt hier und hält Wache, und der andere geht heim und ruft einen Arzt.«

»Ich bleibe«, sagte er, denn nachdem das Entsetzen sich freigemacht hatte, wollte er es, wollte eine Weile allein bei Karin sitzen und mit ihr sprechen, wie er es all die Jahre immer getan hatte, wenn ihm schwer ums Herz war.

»Herrgott«, stöhnte Mona. »Wann wird Erik kommen?«

»Er saß über einer Zeichnung als ich ging und wollte sie noch fertigmachen«, erklärte Isak.

Mona rannte los, erst nach Hause, um Lisa zu bitten, die Kinder ins Bett zu bringen und bei ihnen zu bleiben. Malin schaute sie mit großen Augen an: »Sie ist fortgegangen, Mama? Das ist sie doch, ja?«

»Ja«, antwortete Mona. »Malin, Liebes, du mußt jetzt ein großes und vernünftiges Mädchen sein.«

»Ja.«

Mona rannte zu Larssons Haus, zu ihrer Verzweiflung sah sie Eriks Auto in der Auffahrt stehen.

»Ich habe mir Sorgen gemacht, als Karin nicht ans Telefon ging«, erklärte er, aber er sah nicht beunruhigt, sondern wie immer fröhlich aus, und Mona dachte, was sage ich jetzt. Hilf mir, lieber Gott.

»Karin ist ... krank«, begann sie. »Wir müssen einen Arzt rufen.« Und sie rief den Arzt an, den alten Hausarzt, der sich all die Jahre um sie alle gekümmert hatte, und sie hielt Eriks Hand ganz fest, als sie zu dem Arzt sagte, er müsse sofort kommen, sie werde an der Straße vor dem Haus warten, um ihn dorthin zu bringen, wo Karin lag.

»So laß mich doch endlich los, Mona!«

Erik schrie es zornig, aber sie ließ seine Hand nicht los, führte ihn zur Küchenbank und kniete sich vor ihn hin: »Sie ist tot, Erik.«

Dann erkannte sie, daß er ihr nicht glaubte.

»Er wird gleich kommen, der Doktor, er hat Spritzen bei sich.«

Im nächsten Augenblick war der Arzt da, es ging schnell, alles ging jetzt schnell, und Erik warf sich ins Auto und rief dem Arzt zu, die Spritze bereitzuhalten, und als die Straße zu Ende war, lief Mona voraus, und der Arzt sah gleich auf den ersten Blick, daß alles zu spät war. Aber Erik sah es nicht, warf sich über Karins Körper, schüttelte sie, schrie wie wild: »So wach doch endlich auf, Mensch!«

Es war schrecklich. Isak mußte alle seine Kräfte aufwenden, um Erik von der Toten wegzuziehen und ihn ins Auto zu befördern, wo der Arzt schon eine zweite Spritze vorbereitete, um sie Erik in den Arm zu stechen, dessen Zorn in Dunkelheit unterging.

»Wir bringen sie nach Hause«, entschied Mona. »Wir werden so lange Totenwache bei ihr halten, bis Simon aus England da ist.«

Und so war es dann auch, Mona überzog das Bett mit Karins feinstem Leinen, Isak hielt Wache bei Erik aber auch am Telefon.

Zuerst Ruben. Isak konnte hören, wie er am anderen Ende der Leitung schrumpfte, verschwand. »Papa!« schrie er. »Papa, wir müssen jetzt stark sein. Du mußt Simon verständigen. Und Klara.«

Die Stimme kam aus dem Niemandsland zurück, sie war spröde, sagte aber: »Ich übernehme das und komme dann zu euch.«

Und Ruben funktionierte, konnte denken, diese Nachricht sollte Simon nicht telefonisch erreichen, er meldete ein Ferngespräch nach Zürich an und hörte Klaras ruhige Stimme.

Eiskalt in dem Bemühen, die Traurigkeit einzudämmen, sagte die Stimme, sie werde bestimmt einen Platz in der Abendmaschine nach London bekommen. Von dort werde sie mit Simon am nächsten Morgen den ersten Flug nach Torslanda nehmen.

»Sei behutsam mit dem Jungen«, legte ihr Ruben ans Herz.

»Gott im Himmel, wie soll ich das fertigbringen!« schrie Klara, und das Eis war aus der Stimme gewichen, und die Angst brach sie in Stücke.

Sie bekam wirklich einen Platz im Flugzeug. Vom Züricher Flugplatz aus telegrafierte sie an Simon: Komme abends Heathrow stop 23 Uhr Deine Klara.

Das Telegramm wurde telefonisch durchgegeben, Simon freute sich und hatte nicht viel Zeit zum Nachdenken, erst als er im Flughafenbus saß, ging ihm auf, daß es Klara gar nicht ähnlich sah und daß ihr etwas passiert sein mußte.

Dann, als sie ihm in der Halle entgegenkam, sah er es, sah, daß sie den Blick zurückgenommen hatte wie immer, wenn etwas schwierig war. Aber ihre Stimme war ruhig, als sie sagte: »Du wartest am Laufband auf meine Tasche, die rote, du weißt schon. Ich besorge inzwischen Flugkarten für morgen.«

»Du fährst morgen schon wieder?«

Aber sie gab ihm keine Antwort, saß nur fest an ihn gedrückt im Taxi nach London, und zu dieser Zeit wußte Simon schon, daß sie etwas unfaßbar Großem voll von Verzweiflung entgegenfuhren.

Er hatte Angst. »Klara, so sprich doch endlich.«

»Simon, nicht hier.«

Als sie aber hinauf in sein Zimmer gekommen waren, sagte sie es, es konnte nicht aufgeschoben und nicht behutsam getan werden. »Karin ist heute nachmittag gestorben.«

Danach sah sie sehr wohl, daß auch er starb, zwar aufrecht vor ihr stand, aber von Minute zu Minute mehr erstarrte. Bald fing er zu frieren an, sie zwang ihn ins Bett und legte sich neben ihn. Nicht ein Wort sprach er, aber irgendwann in der Nacht merkte sie, daß er weinte, und ihre Anspannung ließ ein wenig nach.

Am Morgen zog er sich mechanisch an und folgte ihr wie eine Marionette zum Taxi und zum Flugzeug. Nachdem sie die Sicherheitsgurte angelegt hatten, machte er zum ersten Mal seit dem Vorabend den Mund auf: »Hoffentlich stürzen wir ab.«

»Es wird schon alles gut gehen«, sagte sie. »Wir müssen. Erik zuliebe.«

Da konnte Simon an Erik denken, und seine Gedanken führten ihn aus der Versteinerung heraus, zumindest ein wenig, zumindest für kurze Zeit.

Das Flugzeug setzte in Torslanda mustergültig auf, und Ruben erwartete sie im Auto mit einem seiner Angestellten als Fahrer.

Göteborg war schamlos unverändert.

Im Garten am Fluß hatte Erik einen Tobsuchtsanfall bekommen. Seine Wut war so groß, daß er Bäume ausreißen und Felsen ins Wanken hätte bringen können.

Es durfte nicht wahr sein, kein verdammter Mensch durfte ihn auf diese Art behandeln.

Isak war die ganze Nacht an seiner Seite geblieben, hatte versucht, ihn in den Arm zu nehmen, wenn die Verzweiflung am größten war, und in der Morgendämmerung war der Arzt mit Medikamenten gekommen.

Ruben und Mona hatten bei Karin Totenwache gehalten. Und auch Malin, die in ihrem weißen Nachthemd gegen drei Uhr herübergekommen war, hatte sich zu ihnen gesetzt und Karin nur angeschaut.

Sie war es gewesen, die gesagt hatte, was sie alle schon wußten, daß Karin seit dem Regen und nachdem sie ihren Topf weggeworfen hatte, unterwegs irgendwohin war. »Sie wollte allein sein«, sagte das Kind.

Lisa kam und kochte den Morgenkaffee, sie müßten ja trotz allem essen, sagte sie. Und Mona kaute an einem Butterbrot, hatte aber Schwierigkeiten mit dem Schlucken, doch Ruben trank eine Tasse schwarzen Kaffee nach der anderen und war unnatürlich wach, was seine Qualen vermehrte.

Für kurze Zeit ging Mona heim zu ihren Kindern, sie würden heute mit Tante Lisa zusammen sein, sagte sie mit solchem Ernst, daß keines mit Einwänden kam.

Dann ging sie wieder hinüber, Erik schlief zum Glück noch, und der Arzt hatte gesagt, wenn er aufwache, bestünde immerhin die Möglichkeit, daß er alles verstehen und sich damit abfinden werde.

Der wird sich nie damit abfinden, dachte Mona. Jedenfalls nicht in der Tiefe seiner Seele.

Dann war Simon da. Und Klara. Endlich noch ein erwachsener Mensch, dachte Mona, als sie Klara umarmte und sie beide weinen konnten, und sie Klara ins Ohr hatte sagen können, daß hier alle übergeschnappt seien und daß es mit Erik am schlimmsten sei und er fast den Verstand verloren habe.

Simon ging sofort zu seiner Mutter, saß bei ihr bis die Kerzen niedergebrannt waren, und was er gedacht oder zu ihr gesagt hatte, erfuhr nie ein Mensch.

Als Erik aufwachte, war er ruhiger, nur als er Simon sah, überkam ihn für einen Augenblick erneut die Wut, er wiederholte, was ihn schon die ganze Nacht gequält hatte, nämlich daß es ungerecht sei und daß niemand die Familie so behandeln dürfe.

Und Simon tobte genau wie Erik, schrie, daß Erik, verdammt nochmal, recht habe, und Klara seufzte erleichtert auf.

Gegen Mittag wurde Karins Leichnam abgeholt, und der Weg, den der Wagen mit dem Sarg nahm, war gesäumt von weinenden Nachbarinnen und schweigenden Kindern. Ruben wollte nicht zusehen, wie Karin weggetragen wurde. Er saß steif im Garten und hatte nur einen Gedanken: jetzt war sie tot, die zweite Frau, die er geliebt hatte, und daß ihm auch diesmal das Recht zu trauern verwehrt war.

Dann entschloß er sich, heimzufahren, in seiner eigenen Wohnung würde er vielleicht, wie Erik, alles herausschreien können.

Klara sah ihn auf das Auto zugehen und fühlte, daß Ruben Unrecht geschah. Sie zögerte nur einen Augenblick, dann rief sie Olof Hirtz in der Sahlgrenschen Klinik an.

Auch er war von Karins Tod erschüttert. Und um Ruben besorgt versprach er, ihn aufzusuchen, sobald er die anfallenden Arbeiten hinter sich gebracht hatte.

»Juden nehmen sich nur selten das Leben«, schloß er, doch wenn er beabsichtigt hatte, Klara damit zu trösten, verfehlte es die Wirkung. Sie legte den Hörer auf und versuchte den Schrei zu unterdrücken, der sich aus der Tiefe ihrer Seele zu befreien drohte.

Nach und nach entwickelte sich dann aber alles ganz normal. Jeder war für eine Woche mit all dem beschäftigt, was vor einer Beerdigung erforderlich war. Alles lief so großartig ab, daß Karin sich geschämt hätte, dachte Klara, als sie in der Kirche stand und die freudlosen christlichen Worte hörte: *Von der Erde bist du genommen, und zur Erde kehrst du zurück.*

Simon verharrte noch immer in seiner Wut, hielt das alles für unwahr, hielt es für eine verdammte Lüge, denn ein Leben war doch so unendlich viel mehr als ein paar Schaufeln voller Erde.

Inga war unter den geladenen Trauergästen, was Klara auf die Idee brachte, sie unter vier Augen zu fragen: »Könntest du dir vorstellen, daß du eine Zeit bei Erik bleibst, bis er über das Schlimmste hinweg ist?«

Inga konnte.

Mona setzte durch, daß Isak und Erik, wie vereinbart, nach Amerika fuhren. Als Erik zurückkam, war Inga in das Haus am Fluß eingezogen und hatte die Tür zur Hütte am See hinter sich abgeschlossen. Sie und Erik waren Cousine und Cousin und hatten einander immer gemocht. Jetzt wurde Inga seine Haushälterin, hielt das Haus sauber und Erik vom Branntwein ab.

Sie war duldsamer als Karin, entgegenkommender. Durch sie kam bei Erik langsam das Gefühl zurück, sein Leben unter Kontrolle zu haben.

Aber froh wurde er nie mehr, diese kindliche Freude, die die Götter Erik in die Wiege gelegt hatten, war an einem Dienstag im Oktober unten am Fluß abhanden gekommen.

Aus der Luft sahen sie, wie sich die Konturen der norwegischen Küste im blauen Meer abzeichneten und Simon sagte: »Es ist merkwürdig, daß auch im Chaos Kraft liegt.«

Klara, die gerade gemerkt hatte, wie müde sie eigentlich war, mußte wieder aufmerksam sein. »Du bist erstaunt?«

»Ja, weißt du, ich habe immer geglaubt, wenn Karin nicht ist, gibt es auch mich nicht. Aber irgendwie habe ich auch gemerkt, daß es nicht der richtige Ausruck dafür ist ...«

Er schwieg.

»Wenn Karin stirbt, wird Simon auch sterben?«

»So ähnlich, und das habe ich nicht nur gedacht, sondern eher für ebenso selbstverständlich gehalten wie unsere Erde oder die Nacht.«

»Und war es nicht so?«

»Anfangs schon, als du kamst und es ausgesprochen hast. Aber jetzt nicht mehr.«

Klara blieb eine Woche in dem Studentenheim am Queen Boswell, war Simon schweigend nahe, während er an seiner Dissertation weiterarbeitete. Sie saß neben ihm in dem riesigen Lesesaal der British Library und dachte an Karl Marx, wie er es wohl empfunden haben mochte, als er Tag für Tag hier saß, um seine Forschungen zu betreiben. Vielleicht war für nichts anderes Platz gewesen, als für *Das Kapital*, vielleicht hatte er seine schlechte finanzielle Lage, seine betrogene Ehefrau und die armen Kinder vergessen.

Klara sah Simon an und beneidete die Männer um die Fähigkeit, die Dinge der Reihe nach zu erledigen und ganz darin aufzugehen.

Eines Abends, als sie in einem der kleinen indischen Restaurants im Studentenviertel aßen, setzte Simon das Gespräch fort: »Es ist wie neu geboren zu werden«, meinte er. »Unter großen Schmerzen.«

Klara stöhnte und trank Wasser, weil ihr von dem stark gewürzten Hühnchen fast die Tränen kamen.

»Mir ist bewußt geworden, daß das, was alles verändert, einzig und allein du bist«, fuhr er fort. »Ich bin dieses Mal nicht auf mich allein gestellt.«

Klara blickte in die Ferne. Er sah es und lachte: »Hallo, du, komm raus aus dem Stein!«

Und da tat sie es, und die Tränen in ihren Augen konnten ebensogut von den scharfen Gewürzen kommen.

»Ich habe da so eine Idee«, sagte sie. »Aber ich fürchte mich ein bißchen davor, sie auszusprechen.«

»Versuch's trotzdem«, forderte Simon sie auf.

Da erzählte Klara von einem kleinen Wagen, den sie gesehen hatte, einem Volkswagen mit roter Karosserie. Sie hatte ihn sich am Nachmittag angesehen, während Simon in der Vorlesung saß.

»Es ist ein Gebrauchtwagen und gar nicht so teuer. Und Geld haben wir ja.«

Sie hatte ein langes Gespräch über käuflich erworbenen schnellen Trost und andere komplizierte Dinge befürchtet. Daß Simon oft überraschend praktisch war, hatte sie vergessen.

»Ich hätte nie den Mut, in London Auto zu fahren.«

»Wir können es doch morgen versuchen.«

Am nächsten Tag machten sie in dem roten VW eine Probefahrt, und Simon mußte sich sehr konzentrieren, um sich im Dschungel der Millionenstadt zurechtzufinden. Es machte Spaß.

»Nun?« Mehr äußerte Klara nicht, als sie wieder beim Autohändler vorfuhren, und Simon sich den Schweiß von der Stirn wischte.

»Doch«, antwortete er, und sie sah, daß er sich freute.

»Du kannst ihn wirklich brauchen, hier sind ja immer die Entfernungen so groß.«

»Meine Überlegung ist vor allem, daß ich dadurch leichter hinaus aufs Land komme«, sagte er. »Du weißt, für mich sind Bäume in Parks nicht ganz das Wahre.«

Das Auto verlieh den Tagen Glanz, die ihnen vor Klaras Rückkehr nach Zürich noch blieben. Es ist verrückt, meinte Simon, eigentlich müßte ich mich ja schämen, daß es mir Spaß macht. Klara sprach nicht aus, was sie dachte, daß nämlich nicht der Wagen als solcher ihm Befreiung schenkte, sondern daß es die Notwendigkeit absoluter Konzentration beim Fahren war.

Dann reiste Klara ab, und Simon war nicht vorbereitet auf die Einsamkeit und die Schuld, die ihm im Zimmer des Heimes auflauerte. Beides hatte sich nur eine Weile zurückgezogen, hatte bis zu Klaras Verschwinden gewartet.

Die Fragen näherten sich ihm zurückhaltend, um ihn nicht gleich zu Tode zu erschrecken: Warum war ich nicht zu Hause? Ich hätte mit Karin am Ufer spazieren gehen und sie im Leben halten können. Beim ersten Mal hat sie doch für mich weiterleben wollen.

Anfangs war noch Vernunft zugegen. Sie erklärte genau wie der Arzt: macht das Herz einmal Schluß, dann ist eben Schluß.

»Im übrigen«, stellte Simon sich der Schuld lauthals entgegen. »Im übrigen ist vieles gar nicht wahr. Ich konnte Karin keine Lebensfreude schenken, zumindest nicht immer. Eigentlich sogar eher selten, denn vieles machte sie mir nur vor, das weißt du so gut wie ich.«

Mit diesen Worten hatte er sich der Schuld jedoch ausgeliefert, die ihre Angriffsmöglichkeiten direkt im Herzen des Kindes fand.

Es war mein Fehler, daß sie nicht froh war.

Dann überfielen sie ihn, die tausend alten Gedanken von all dem Bösen, das in ihm steckte, und das seine Mama immer traurig gemacht hatte. Als seine Gedanken alles in Worte gekleidet hatten, verfielen sie in Schweigen, und ein Abgrund tat sich auf. Simons Entsetzen war so groß, daß sein Mund trocken wurde, ihm der Schweiß ausbrach und das Herz so heftig zu schlagen begann, daß sein Pochen von den Wänden widerhallte.

Im Bücherregal stand noch eine halbe Flasche Wein, er trank sie aus und bekam immerhin soviel Abstand zum eigenen Entsetzen, daß er wieder denken konnte. Vergiß nicht, daß Klara gesagt hat, es läge eine Packung Tabletten in der Schreibtischschublade.

»Nur wenn es unerträglich wird«, hatte sie gemahnt.

Jetzt war es soweit, er schluckte zwei Tabletten und schlief so schnell ein, als hätte man ihn bewußtlos geschlagen. Wachte morgens auf, in seiner Brust, wo die Schuld hauste, war es still, und das war weitaus wichtiger als die stechenden Kopfschmerzen.

J. P. Armstrong trug vor, begrüßte Simon mit einem Kopfnicken, sagte: »Mein Beileid.«

Damit nahm er an Simons Verlust teil, sehr britisch doch absolut ausreichend, und Simon konnte fast lächeln, als er sagte: »Danke, Sir.«

Am Abend rief Klara an und hörte sofort, was los war: »Du darfst nicht jeden Tag Tabletten nehmen, Simon, hörst du.«

»Du hast ja keine Ahnung, wie es ist.«

»Ich komme wieder zu dir«, tröstete Klara.

»Nein!« schrie Simon und warf den Hörer auf die Gabel.

Er haßte sie wie er Karin haßte, diese Frauen, die einander nur ablösten, einen ermahnten und wieder verließen.

Doch eine Stunde später meldete er ein Gespräch an, brachte heraus: »Verzeih mir, aber ich muß da allein durch.«

»Da hast du sicher recht«, bestätigte Klara. »Aber versprich mir, daß du anrufst, bevor du wieder Tabletten schluckst.«

»Das werden teure Pillen«, sagte Simon, und darüber konnten sie beide lachen.

Als er in sein Zimmer hinaufging, dachte er, daß ich mich schlecht gegenüber Klara benommen habe, hat diesmal nichts mit dir zu tun, du elende Schuld.

Er erschrak, als er sich aufs Bett legte und ihm sein plötzlicher Haß auf Karin und Klara bewußt wurde. Hatte in ihm nicht immer finsterer Haß geschwelt?

Hatte Karin das erkannt?

Klar hat sie das, sagte die Schuld und drehte an der Messerklinge, die jetzt tief in seinem Herzen steckte.

Er schlief in dieser Nacht überhaupt nicht, aber die Vernunft versetzte der Panik einen Schlag, und es gelang ihr, sie einigermaßen in den Griff zu bekommen.

Morgens setzte Simon sich an den Schreibtisch und nahm seine Aufzeichnungen vor. Keilschrift, Sumerer, eine untergegangene Sprache, die wiederentdeckt werden wollte. Wie idiotisch, wie unglaublich idiotisch. Daß ein erwachsener Mensch sich mit solchem Nonsens befassen konnte, das war doch verrückt.

Er fing an zu lachen, lachte bis er zu weinen begann, mußte sich wieder aufs Bett legen. Als die Schuld die Klinge noch einmal umdrehte, gab er alles zu: Mama, ich weiß, daß es dich gefreut hätte, wenn ich im Leben etwas Vernünftiges geworden wäre. Ich hätte jetzt Arzt sein können, Mutter, und Herrgott, wie stolz wärst du gewesen, wenn ich als Chirurg in der Sahlgrenschen Klinik Menschenleben gerettet hätte. Da hättest du das Gefühl gehabt, daß auch dein Leben etwas wert ist.

Vielleicht hättest du dann gerne weitergelebt?

Es waren keine einfachen Gedanken, aber die Nacht hatte Simon gelehrt, daß Gedanken weit besser sind als wortlose Schuld, weit besser als sich vom Abgrund verschlingen zu lassen. Diese Erkenntnis beschäftigte Simon schließlich so sehr, daß er sich aufsetzte und fast seine Ruhe vor der Schuld hatte, weil er so intensiv nachdenken mußte.

Er hatte sich oft genug mit der Beschränkung auf Wörter beschäftigt. Jetzt brauchte er die Worte, um überleben zu können. Simon erkannte die Wahrheit in dem schwedischen Sprichwort: Nenne den Troll beim Namen, und er wird platzen. Vielleicht waren Worte der Trolle wegen notwendig.

Als Klara anrief, erzählte er von seinen neuen Erkenntnissen. Sie lachte: »Was meinst du, was Psychotherapie anderes ist! Mein Job ist ein ständiges Suchen nach Worten, die einen Menschen befreien können.«

»Ich bin oft fürchterlich dumm«, gestand Simon.

»Nein«, sagte Klara. »Aber du bist nur immer so absolut.«

Er verstand nicht, was sie damit meinte, versicherte ihr aber, daß er sich besser fühlte.

Nach dem Gespräch kehrte er zu den Abgüssen der Tontafeln auf seinem Schreibtisch zurück, Fragmenten, die angeblich darauf hinwiesen, daß das große babylonische Gilgamesh-Epos auf die Sumerer zurückging. Es war knifflige Kleinarbeit, aber Simon erschloß sich die Tontafeln Stück für Stück und war hingerissen von der Geschichte vom Huluppibaum, der von der Göttin Innana davor bewahrt worden war, im Euphrat zu ertrinken. Sie verpflanzte den Baum in ihren Garten und pflegte ihn sorgsam, denn wenn er groß genug wäre, wollte sie sich aus seinem Holz ein Bett zimmern.

Als der Huluppibaum jedoch seine volle Höhe erreicht hatte, konnte er nicht gefällt werden. An seinem Fuß hatte die Schlange, die niemand beschwören konnte, ihr Nest gebaut, und in seiner Krone wohnte Lilith, die Dämonin, die auch in den Legenden der Juden als die böse Frau bekannt ist.

Er übersetzte, wie Innana bittere Tränen darüber weinte, was ihrem Huluppibaum zugestoßen war, wie Gilgamesh ihr dann zu Hilfe kam und die Schlange tötete und Lilith in die Flucht trieb. Und Innana zimmerte sich kein Bett aus dem Baum, sondern baute aus seinem Holz eine Trommel.

Das klang eigentümlich und trostreich.

Namen für die Trolle, dieser Gedanke beschäftigte Simon. Ihm fiel Samuel Noah Kramer ein, der Amerikaner, der in London Vorlesungen gehalten hatte.

Simon suchte seine Mitschriften heraus.

Frühe sumerische Aufzeichnungen bestanden aus Listen, langen Aufzählungen von Vögeln und Tieren, Pflanzen und Bäumen, Gesteinen, Sternen. Alle dargestellt durch ihre sichtbaren Eigenschaften. Im Universum der Sumerer herrschten Ordnung und Methode, auch die Götter, die in der Kunst veranschaulicht wurden, hatten ihre bestimmten Aufgaben.

Alle transzendenten Qualitäten fehlten ihnen, hatte Kramer betont. Es war eine sachorientierte Kultur gewesen, und doch die religiöseste, die die Welt kannte.

Das alte Volk, das sich selbst als Schwarzschädel bezeichnete, hatte geglaubt, daß es die einzige Möglichkeit sei, die Welt und ihre unfaßbaren Kräfte zu beherrschen, wenn man all das benannte, was ihr innewohnte.

Am Anfang war das Wort, es schuf die Welt und besiegte das Entsetzen.

Aus dieser Erkenntnis wurde die Magie geboren, dachte Simon. Und dann nach und nach die Naturwissenschaften, die im Großen gesehen dieselbe Funktion hatten.

An diesem Abend schrieb er einen langen Brief an Klara und erzählte ihr, was die Schuld von ihm hielt, von seinem Verrat und seinem Unvermögen, Karin glücklich zu machen. Er schrieb wie ein Kind, hielt nichts von Formulierungen und dachte, daß er auch von einer Antwort nichts hielte. Aber er bekam Herzklopfen, als der Antwortbrief eines Tages vor ihm lag.

Simon, ich habe am Telefon gesagt, daß Du in allem so absolut bist, besonders wenn es um Karin geht. Aber Du hast doch die Vernunft eines Erwachsenen. Siehst Du nicht, wie kindisch und egozentrisch Dein Verhältnis zu ihr ist? Der Freudianer würde es einen unbewältigten Ödipuskomplex nennen.

Kannst Du nicht einsehen, daß Du in ihrem Leben nicht alles gewesen bist, vielleicht nicht einmal das Wichtigste? Was ihren Kummer anbelangt, so gab es ihn lange bevor Du zur Welt kamst ...

Er las nicht weiter.

Ausnahmsweise überkam ihn der Zorn sofort, er schoß wie glühendes Eisen durch seinen Körper und explodierte im Kopf in weißglühender Raserei.

Er hatte nicht um eine Diagnose gebeten. Er hatte der Psychologie schon lange mißtraut, obwohl er von den Deutungen fasziniert gewesen war, von der souveränen Bereitschaft, Dinge in Worte zu fassen, von denen niemand etwas wissen konnte.

Was wußte Klara denn, was konnte sie wissen, fühlen, verstehen von dem Verhältnis, das zwischen Karin und ihm bestanden hatte! Sie verhielt sich gegenüber dem Unbegreiflichen wie so viele andere Menschen auch, wartete mit ein paar Phrasen auf und distanzierte sich.

›Früh und unbewußt hast Du die Schuld an ihrem Schmerz auf Dich genommen ...‹ Jawohl. Auf der Bewußtseinsebene war mir seit vielen Jahren klar, daß es ihren inneren Schmerz lange vor mir gegeben hatte. Aber diese simple Tatsache verändert in der Tiefe nichts.

Wie konnte Klara etwas ahnen von dem feinen tausendfädigen Netz aus Trauer und Schuld, das zwischen ihm und Karin immer bestanden hatte.

Immer, dachte Simon. Es war uralt, schicksalhaft, in Jahrtausenden geflochten.

Karin redete nie viel, sie wußte, daß man von den wichtigsten Dingen im Leben nicht reden konnte.

Er knallte den Brief in dem Gefühl, daß er in seiner Hand Funken sprühte, auf den Schreibtisch, hörte das Telefon im Foyer des Studentenheimes klingeln, dachte, jetzt ruft sie an, mein Gott, wie ich sie hasse. Aber das Gespräch war nicht für ihn, das verschaffte ihm Bedenkzeit. Er mußte aus dem Haus, ehe Klara anrief, diese Klugscheißerin von einer Psychoanalytikerin, die überhaupt nichts kapierte.

Er rannte zur New Oxford Street, bei der Tottenham Court Road erwischte er einen Bus und einen Fensterplatz in der oberen Ebene und hatte Aussicht auf die Stadt mit den betriebsamen Menschen, über der die Dämmerung hereinbrach.

Er sah ohne zu sehen.

Doch als er aus dem Bus stieg und von der Menge aufgenommen wurde, diesem nie versiegenden Strom von Menschen, kam sein Bewußtsein wieder in Fluß. Tausend Schicksale liefen da ihrer Vollendung entgegen, tausend Wege, Leben, die gelebt und nach einem unbekannten Muster beendet wurden, einem Muster, das nur erahnt werden konnte.

Vor dem Kaufhaus Harrods in der Brompton Road stand ein großgewachsener Inder in grauem Überrock und mit dunklem Gesicht und dunklen Augen, die wie gebannt in eine ausgestellte Kücheneinrichtung mit Töpfen und Schneidbrettern, Messern und Toastern starrten. Er war ganz versunken und verwundert, als glaube er, die Dinge im Schaufenster sprächen eine geheime Sprache und hätten Kenntnis von der Seele des abendländischen Menschen.

Simon hätte den Mann am liebsten wachgerüttelt, hätte ihm gerne gesagt, es gebe da nichts zu begreifen, alles sei nur Schein.

Hast du schon einmal von unbewältigten Ödipuskomplexen gehört, hätte er ihn fragen wollen. Ohne sie zu begreifen? Ja? Dann kann ich dir nur sagen, daß es da nichts zu begreifen gibt, sie unterscheiden sich in nichts von den Küchengeräten.

Simon fühlte sich immer wieder zu dunkelhäutigen Menschen hingezogen. Eine Gruppe schwarzer Jungen stand vor einem Kino Schlange, Simon stellte sich hinten an, blieb in ihrer Nähe wie auf der Suche nach einer Kraft der Menschen, die noch wußten, daß sie Träger des großen Schicksals waren, das unter der Haut keinen Platz hatte und vom Menschen nicht beschrieben werden konnte.

Das weiß aufblitzende Lachen der schwarzhäutigen Männer wußte mehr vom Leben als jeder verdammte Psychologe, dachte Simon, machte an der Kinokasse kehrt und rannte wieder in die Stadt zurück. Er wollte nicht irgendwo stillsitzen und sich von seiner Wut ablenken lassen.

Er selbst war Wirklichkeit.

Wie Karin es immer gewesen war, dachte er. Ihre Traurigkeit hatte ihr Wirklichkeit verliehen, hatte ihr Mut gemacht, nie nach befreienden Worten zu suchen. Sie hatte immer gewußt, daß das Leben nicht erklärt, sondern nur gelebt werden kann. Und durchgestanden.

Sie hatte gewußt, daß das mühsam war.

Er ging ohne Umschweife auf ein Straßenmädchen zu, blieb vor ihr stehen, sah in das weiße Gesicht mit dem roten zu einer Wunde der Verzweiflung geschminkten Mund, versuchte in ihren Augen zu lesen, in das Wissen vorzudringen, das sie gewonnen hatte, indem sie ihr Schicksal erfüllte, das darin bestand, bis auf den Grund zu gehen, in die Tiefe der Schande abzusinken, der Schande der Millionenstadt, die sie sich aufgeladen hatte, und die ihre Vernichtung wollte.

»What a nice boy«, sagte sie und es war unmöglich, die Verwunderung mißzuverstehen, aber er war entschlossen. Heute nacht wollte er mit ihr untergehen.

Er übersah alle Details in dem schäbigen Zimmer, die erschlaffte Haut des alternden Körpers, die Absurdität der Situation. Alles nur Schein. Er wollte diese Frau zur Verzweiflung bringen, wollte sich davon versengen lassen.

Natürlich gelang ihm das nicht, er lächelte, sie lächelte, sie schliefen miteinander, fast kühl. Er bezahlte, ging, wollte sich waschen, wies den Gedanken aber von sich, tief in den Dreck, das wollte er doch, Wirklichkeit wollte er.

Er betrat das nächste Pub, soff sich voll, und hatte nicht die geringste Erinnerung daran, wie er anschließend doch nach Hause gekommen war. Als er zu seinem eigenen Staunen am nächsten Morgen in seinem eigenen Bett aufwachte, fand er zwei Zettel vor, auf denen stand, daß Zürich ihn um 19 Uhr und um 21.35 Uhr zu sprechen gewünscht hatte. Klara war jetzt bestimmt beunruhigt, und das geschah ihr ganz recht, dachte er.

Aber in der Universität hatte er dann doch ein ungutes Gefühl und rief nach der letzten Vorlesung bei ihr an.

»Danke für den Brief«, sagte er. »Er ließ jegliches Einfühlungsvermögen vermissen und war außerdem dumm.«

»Simon, ich appelliere an deine Vernunft. Du mußt . . .«

»Ich muß gar nichts«, schrie er, konnte aber, ehe er den Hörer auf die Gabel schmiß, gerade noch sagen: »Ich schreibe.«

Und das tat er, noch immer im Zorn, aber das Eisen war erkaltet.

Ich bereue, mich Dir geöffnet zu haben, und meine, Du kannst dir alle Deine schönen Worte über Ödipus in den Hintern stecken. Du hast nichts kapiert, weder von mir, noch vom Ödipusmythos . . .

Das war gemein, aber er fand es witzig, schickte den Brief also ab und fühlte sich am nächsten Tag, als er Klara anrief und sie bat, den Brief ungelesen zu zerreißen, nur noch miserabler.

Das werde sie nicht tun, sagte Klara, aber könnten sie nicht miteinander über weniger wichtige Dinge in einem Ton sprechen, der ihnen die Gewißheit gab, daß zwischen ihnen alles so war wie es eigentlich sein sollte?

In dieser Nacht träumte Simon, daß er schwerelos in seinem Bett liege und abhebe, durch die Decke und den über London liegenden schmutziggrauen Nebel hindurch ins Blau fliege.

Tagsüber war er intensiv mit dem Ursprung der Sumerer beschäftigt, dem Rätsel, das nur über die Sprache zu lösen war. Doch diese Sprache glich keiner anderen, weder den indogermanischen noch einer der semitischen. Er war fasziniert von den Schriften der Hethiter, den ersten Indoeuropäern im Mittleren Osten. Durch sie bekamen die Inschriften auf den Tontafeln einen vertrauten Klang, obwohl die Wörter lang und unverständlich waren. Aber es gab da etwas, einen Rhythmus, eine zu ahnende Melodie, die ihm selbst vertraut schien.

Anfang Dezember kam Ruben zur Buchmesse nach London. Er blieb über das Wochenende, sie fuhren in dem roten VW aufs Land und fanden ein Coaching Inn mit einer langen Geschichte und gemütlicher Einrichtung. Am Sonntag durchstreiften sie die Landschaft, liefen über Felder und durch entlaubte Wälder. Es war nebelig.

»Ich würde gerne über Karin sprechen, darüber, wie sie in der letzten Zeit war«, begann Ruben.

Das war hart, aber Simon hatte das Bedürfnis, soviel wie möglich darüber zu erfahren, wie sie gedacht und gefühlt hatte.

Ruben erzählte von dem Gespräch über den alten Kochtopf, und wie er damals zum ersten Mal geahnt hatte, daß etwas Neues in Karins Gedankenwelt Form anzunehmen begann.

»Ich habe einen alten Rabbiner zitiert, der zu predigen pflegte, daß man jeden Tag leben soll, als nehme man Abschied von allem, von

Menschen und Dingen. Das hat unerhörten Eindruck auf Karin gemacht.« Simon schaute Ruben erstaunt an.

»Dann hat mir Mona erzählt, daß Karin für ihre Spaziergänge immer mehr Zeit gebraucht hat«, fuhr Ruben fort. »Das hat mich ein wenig beunruhigt, und eines Tages habe ich sie gefragt, woran sie während all dieser Wanderungen denke. Da sagte sie, daß sie völlig unbelastet sei von Gefühlen und auch von Gedanken.«

Simon mußte stehenbleiben, um richtig aufnehmen zu können, was Ruben da erzählte.

»Sie strahlte etwas Seltsames aus, etwas Neues«, sagte Ruben. »Als ich an diesem Abend zu mir nach Hause kam, versuchte ich es zu verstehen, den Ausdruck in ihren Augen zu deuten.«

»Ja?«

»Ich kam zu dem Ergebnis, daß Karin glücklich ist«, betonte Ruben. »Dieses Neue war Glück, zum ersten Mal seit ich sie kennengelernt hatte, war sie ohne Trauer. Es wird dir auch aufgefallen sein, daß sie eine gewisse Traurigkeit in sich trug?«

»Mehr als alles andere in ihrem Leben«, pflichtete Simon bei.

»Ich habe das gemerkt.«

»Glaubst du, sie wußte, daß sie sterben wird, daß das der Grund war?«

»Ich weiß nicht, sie wußte es vielleicht, aber nicht mit dem Verstand. Ich glaube nicht, daß sie darüber nachdachte.«

Simon kamen die Tränen, aber das fiel im Nebel nicht auf, und Ruben fuhr fort: »Ich habe viel darüber nachgedacht, daß es einen tieferen Sinn im Tod gibt, mehr als nur das Vergehen des Körpers, daß es darum geht, psychisch zu einem Schluß zu kommen. Alles was ich gelebt habe, all mein Wissen, mein Glück und mein Leiden, meine Erinnerungen und Bestrebungen müssen auf ein Ende zulaufen. Das Bekannte, die Familie, die Kinder, das Zuhause, die Ideen, Ideale, alles womit du dich identifiziert hast, mußt du hinter dir lassen.«

Simon dachte an die Woge, die an den Klippen von Bohuslän gestorben war und alle ihre Erfahrungen an das große Meer zurückgeben mußte, ehe sie wiedergeboren werden konnte.

»Das muß es sein, was Tod bedeutet«, überlegte Ruben. »Dieses Verzichten. Und gerade diesem gilt wohl auch alle Todesangst, meinst du nicht?«

»Da magst du recht haben.«

»Ich wollte, daß du es erfährst«, begann Ruben wieder. »Weißt, daß Karin frei von allem starb, sie hatte alles hinter sich gelassen und war glücklich, als sie von uns ging.«

Als Ruben abgereist war, kam die Trauer zu Simon. Sie war groß und voller Wehmut. Aber wo die Trauer war, konnte die Schuld nicht sein, sie schlossen sich gegenseitig aus.

Schließlich dachte er, Karin habe ihm ihre Trauer als Erbe hinterlassen.

Das ist ihr Land, dachte er, hier hat sie gelebt und gewirkt. Es ist groß und einsam aber nicht unerträglich. Man kann hier wohnen und leben und die täglichen Pflichten mit Sorgfalt erfüllen.

Klara und Simon fuhren zu Weihnachten nach Hause, trafen sich in Kopenhagen und setzten ihre Fahrt mit der Bahn fort.

Es waren keine einfachen Feiertage. Die Tage bewegten sich nur mühsam von der Stelle, häuserschwer, endlos wie die Karl-Johan-Gata. Aber die Menschen nahmen es auf sich, gaben den Kindern zuliebe ihr Bestes, wie sie das ausdrückten.

Klara und Simon übernachteten bei Erik im früheren Kinderzimmer. Er haderte nicht mehr mit dem Schicksal, war aber gealtert und geduldiger geworden. Simon war entsetzt, er wollte einen starken und aufbrausenden Vater.

Isak und Mona waren sehr still geworden.

Klara hatte ihre Studien in der Schweiz beendet und hatte eine Anstellung an der Psychiatrie der Sahlgrenschen Klinik in Aussicht, die ihr keine Gelegenheit bieten würde, das Wissen zu verwerten, das sie sich bei den Jungianern in Zürich erworben hatte. Simon mußte nur noch zwei Abschlußprüfungen in London hinter sich bringen. Schon im März würde er wieder zu Hause sein und seine Doktorarbeit fertigschreiben.

Er und Klara waren bei der Behörde für eine Wohnung vorgemerkt, doch Ruben hatte ein wachsames Auge auf die Dreizimmerwohnung einer neunzigjährigen Dame in seinem Haus in Majorna geworfen.

An einem regnerischen Tag Ende Februar bat J. P. Armstrong Simon um ein Gespräch. Er wurde sogar gebeten, in dem schönen Raum Platz zu nehmen, in dem der Professor Bücher und Abgüsse von assyrischen Löwen sammelte. In seiner Jugend hatte er bei Sir

Leonard Woolley an den berühmten Ausgrabungen der Königsgräber von Ur teilgenommen, war jetzt aber auf die Assyrer spezialisiert.

»Die Universität von Pennsylvania unternimmt zur Zeit Teilausgrabungen in Girsu. Es geht um den Eninnu-Tempel.«

Er lächelte, als er Simons Interesse wahrnahm.

»Jetzt ist dort ein Mann erkrankt, ein Schriftexperte. Man hat sich an uns gewandt, um schnell einen Ersatzmann zu bekommen, und nun möchte ich Sie fragen, ob Sie Interesse hätten.«

Nicht einmal wenn der sumerische Sonnengott aus seinem Himmel herabgestiegen wäre, um mit ihm zu sprechen, hätte Simon erstaunter sein können. Und wenn Innana selbst ihn auf ihr Liebeslager gebeten hätte, wäre er nicht glücklicher gewesen als jetzt.

»Sie sind hier bei uns ja praktisch fertig, ich gratuliere übrigens zu den Ergebnissen. Es würde Ihnen vielleicht Vergnügen bereiten, das Ganze aus einer eher handfesten Perspektive zu betrachten«, sagte der Professor.

Vergnügen bereiten, dachte Simon.

Hier ging es um den Fünfziggöttertempel der Gudea bei Lagash, und ›Vergnügen bereiten‹ war ein sehr britischer Ausdruck für den Jubel, der ihn erfüllte.

»Ich bin wirklich sehr dankbar, Sir«, antwortete Simon, und das waren fast schon unnötig viele Worte, doch der Professor lächelte gnädig.

Dann ging alles sehr schnell, Visum, Geld, Tickets. Simon konnte gerade noch seine Dissertation verpacken und nach Schweden schikken. Sein Auto mußte stehenbleiben, wo es stand, nämlich im Hof des Studentenheimes. Er telefonierte mit Ruben, der sich aufrichtig freute, mit Erik, der verstand, daß man zu einem so abenteuerlichen Angebot nicht ›nein danke‹ sagen konnte, und mit Klara, die traurig war.

»Es sind ja nur ein paar Monate, die Ausgrabungsarbeiten werden unterbrochen, sobald die Hitze kommt«, beschwichtigte Simon.

»Paß gut auf dich auf«, bat Klara und Simon dachte zornig, die wird Karin immer ähnlicher, legt einem die Last der Schuld auf.

»Du wirst doch verstehen, daß ich eine solche Chance wahrnehmen muß.«

»Selbstverständlich verstehe ich.«

Sagt sie jetzt ›mein Junge‹, werde ich verrückt, dachte Simon und fühlte, daß er dieses persönlichkeitsvernichtende Verständnis immer gehaßt hatte. Doch dann war Klaras Stimme wieder da, zornig: »Ich werde wohl ein Recht haben, enttäuscht zu sein«, bemerkte sie.

Da war es vorbei, und sie konnten zusammen lachen. Aber das letzte, was sie ins Telefon schrie, war dieses verflixte: »Paß gut auf dich auf.«

Er flog nach Basra, einschließlich Zwischenlandung war er 13 Stunden unterwegs gewesen, und er schlief fast ein, als er sich in dem englischen Kolonialhotel eintrug, das wie eine Theaterkulisse am Ende des Flugplatzes lag. Hinter dem Gebäude gab es einen Park, und Simon war klar, daß das, was vor seinem Fenster raschelte, der Wind war, der durch die Kronen der Palmen wehte. Aber für mehr an Eindrücken war er zu müde.

Am nächsten Morgen um acht riß David Moore mit Getöse die Tür auf und rief, jetzt, my boy, beginnt der Ernst des Lebens.

»Er wartet draußen in Gestalt eines alten Jeeps auf dich«, verkündete er und war so amerikanisch, daß er einem Western hätte entsprungen sein können.

»Darf ich noch duschen?«

Simon hörte, wie britisch er klang und sah, wie Davids Augen vor Abscheu schmal wurden, als er sagte, Gott allein wisse, wie die Klempner Ihrer Majestät der Königin Viktoria ihre Arbeit hier in diesem Mausoleum überhaupt hatten bewerkstelligen können, aber vielleicht gäbe es ja doch noch einen Wasserstrahl aus irgendeinem verrosteten Rohr. Simon lachte, sprang aus dem Bett und streckte dem andern die Hand hin.

»Larsson«, sagte er. »Simon Larsson. Ich bin Schwede, du kannst mich also nicht mit Imperialismus, Kolonialhotel, Gentleman-Getue und anderem, was so typisch britisch ist, ärgern. Ich bin unschuldig, verstanden!«

David Moore mußte sich vor Lachen in einen alten Korbstuhl schmeißen, der erschrocken ächzte.

»Ein Schwede. Von der University of London. Hatten die sonst niemand?«

Der Gedanke freute Simon.

Sie nahmen ein ausgiebiges englisches Frühstück zu sich und dann wurde Simon samt Koffer und allem Zubehör im Jeep verstaut. David zog vorsorglich die Jalousien herunter und verklebte eine Ritze an Simons Tür mit Papierstreifen.

»Besteht Gefahr, daß wir erfrieren?«

»Du wirst es gleich merken«, erwiderte David.

Binnen einer halben Stunde hatten sie die Stadt verlassen, folgten der Straße nach Norden, und Simon erinnerte sich an Grimbergs Worte: ›Ein Land des Todes und der großen Stille ist Mesopotamien, schwer ruht auf ihm die rächende Hand des Herrn.‹

Wüste, so weit das Auge reichte, unberechenbare Hügel aus Sand. Hier und dort verlor sich die Straße in den Wanderdünen, aber der Jeep fuhr nur kurz durch unwegsames Gelände und fand den Weg jedesmal wieder.

»Schneeverwehungen gar nicht so unähnlich«, meinte David. »Daran bist du wohl eher gewöhnt?«

Simon mußte lachen und bekam dabei Sand in den Mund. Der heiße Wind fegte Sand in den Wagen, in Augen und Mund, unter den Hemdkragen, über Rücken und Bauch und vermischte sich dort mit dem Schweiß, daß es am ganzen Körper zu jucken begann.

Sie machten Rast in einem Lokal am Rand der Sumpfstadt Al-Shubaish, spülten sich den Sand mit schmutzigem Wasser aus dem Gesicht.

»Glaub ja nicht, daß du hier ein Bier kriegst«, sagte David. »Hier bestimmt der Prophet Mohammed die Trinksitten, aber spül dir den Mund vorher mal lieber mit Wasser aus. Du kriegst hier nämlich Coca-Cola zu trinken.«

Es war eine armselige aus Schilf erbaute Hütte, die aussah, als wolle sie demnächst den Geist aufgeben. Aber die Cola war gar nicht so übel, sie war einigermaßen kühl und beseitigte vor allem das lästige Knirschen zwischen den Zähnen.

»Hier bringe ich gerne die jungen Milchgesichter her«, berichtete David Moore. »Es ist ein so heilsamer Ort für romantische Narren. Du kriegst hier nämlich ein Volk zu sehen, das noch unter den gleichen Bedingungen lebt und haust wie zu Zeiten der alten Sumerer.«

Mit einer ausladenden Handbewegung wies er auf den Kai, und Simon sah die spitz zulaufenden Kanus des Sumpfvolkes, die noch genauso gebaut waren wie das berühmte Silberkanu im Grab des Meskalamdug in Ur. Doch vor allem sah er die stakenden Männer und deren ausgemergelte Kinder in den Kanus. Ihre Augen waren mit Fliegen bedeckt.

»Hier gibt es alles«, erklärte Moore. »Malaria, Aussatz, Tbc, Bilharziose. Du kannst es dir aussuchen. Zur Lebensweise gehört auch die schreckliche Unterdrückung der Frauen mit Grausamkeiten verschiedenster Art, Blutrache und die betörende Sitte, den Frauen die Schamlippen abzuschneiden.«

Es war Simons erste Begegnung mit der Not, und er war nicht vorbereitet auf das Schamgefühl, das ihn überkam, die bedrückende Erkenntnis, wie groß und wohlgenährt, wie gepflegt und gut ausgebildet er war.

»Nicht weit von hier liegt der Garten Eden«, erzählte David Moore. »Nichts versetzt mich mehr in Erstaunen, als die Fähigkeit des Menschen, zu lügen.«

Simon schaute weg, als am Kai eine Frau an ihnen vorbeiging, scheu wie ein Tier, und so mager, daß der schwangere Leib grotesk wirkte.

»Bist du Christ?« fragte Moore.

»Den Papieren nach bin ich Lutheraner«, antwortete Simon. »Aber in Skandinavien hat das Christentum ziemlich an Bedeutung verloren.«

»Macht das irgend etwas besser?«

»Ich weiß nicht. Vielleicht sind wir dadurch handlungsfähiger.«

»Hier saßen über Jahre die Engländer. Aber meinst du, die haben etwas anderes getan, als Chinin in ihre Getränke zu mischen und die Ölleitungen bis zum Meer zu bewachen?«

Sie mieteten ein Kanu, und Simon schämte sich, als der grüne Eindollarschein den Besitzer wechselte und er erkannte, daß dies das Größte war, was diesem Sumpfaraber je widerfahren war, der so seltsam milde lächelte.

»Apropos Chinin«, nahm David das Gespräch wieder auf. »Hier gibt es auch die eine oder andere entzückende Anophelesmücke.«

»Was ist das denn?«

»Sie überträgt die Malaria.«

Es war eine eigenartige Welt, durch die sie sich vorwärts stakten, eine Welt, die schon vor Tausenden von Jahren von Menschen aus dem Lehm des Deltalandes erbaut worden war. Hier und dort standen Häuser des gleichen Typs wie auf alten sumerischen Reliefs, Schilfbündel zu Gewölben gebogen.

»Hier müßte man Bulldozer einsetzen und das Wasser ableiten, müßte wie verrückt DDT sprühen, die Kinder in Schulen schicken, Krankenhäuser bauen und den Frauen den Schleier herunterreißen«, schimpfte Moore. »Das wäre sinnvoller, als in der Wüste in alten Ruinenhaufen zu stochern.«

»Warum bist du Archäologe geworden?«

»Weil ich ein ebensolcher Spinner war wie du.«

Als sie wieder im Auto saßen und vor lauter Sand nicht reden konnten, versuchte Simon die Bilder von den Kindern zu verdrängen. Er mußte an die etwas unverständliche Frage nach seiner Religion denken, hatte Moore den Juden geahnt?

»Was hast du eigentlich für eine Religion?« fragte Simon.

»Ich«, sagte David Moore. »Ich bin ein von Herzen gläubiger Jude.«

Als sie auf der Brücke über den Euphrat fuhren, um dann in Richtung Tello nach Norden weiterzufahren, verkündete David: »Der Alte sieht deinem Kommen mit großen Erwartungen entgegen. Unser kleiner Professor aus Pennsylvania heißt Philip Peterson und glaubt vertrauensselig, daß alle verdammten Tonscherben, die wir hier finden, große Geheimnisse enthüllen werden.«

»Welche denn?« fragte Simon erschrocken.

»Na, zum Beispiel, wo die Hauptstadt von Akkad lag, dieses vielbesungene Agade. Immerhin haben wir eine Chance. Unsere liebe Gudea war doch vermutlich daran beteiligt, es dem Erdboden gleichzumachen.«

»Wohl kaum«, entgegnete Simon. »Das haben die Bergvölker getan, die Gutier.«

»Wo es um Mesopotamien geht, kann man sich nie sicher sein. Jemand setzt irgendwo in der Wüste den Spaten an, und schon verändert sich der Lauf der Geschichte.«

»Ja«, bestätigte Simon und dachte an die Bilder vom großen Krieg, die er vor seinem inneren Auge gesehen hatte, als er das erste Mal die Symphonie von Berlioz gehört hatte.

Dann waren sie am Ziel, Moore stellte vor.

»Um allen Mißverständnissen vorzubeugen«, sagte er. »Das hier ist Simon Larsson, ein Wikinger aus Schweden. Er hat London nur einige Jahre mit seiner Anwesenheit beehrt.«

Alle lachten, Peterson offensichtlich erleichtert. Er war ein stämmiger Mann um die fünfzig. Simon mochte ihn vom ersten Augenblick an.

Sie waren dabei, das Viertel der Schreiber freizulegen, es sah aus, als hätte ein verrückter Riese zertrümmerte Mauern auf den Mond geworfen. Um all die Tonscherben zu sortieren, die zutage gefördert worden waren, hatte man ein Zelt errichtet.

»Ich hoffe Sie nicht zu enttäuschen, Sir«, sagte Simon.

»Meine Güte, ich heiße Philip«, sagte der Professor. »Wie darf ich das verstehen? Du bist doch Sumerologe, Schriftexperte?«

»Ja.«

Simon bekam eine Schüssel Suppe, dicke amerikanische Suppe aus der Dose, und dann brauchte er nur noch in das Zelt zu gehen, wo die Scherben ordentlich aufgereiht lagen.

Das meiste waren Listen von Lagerbeständen, das wußten sie

schon. »Aber wer weiß«, lächelte Peterson. »Fang halt mal an, mein Sohn.« Simon konnte also nur einen kurzen Blick auf die Ruinen des Eninnu-Tempels werfen, ehe er im Zelt saß und dachte, so heiß kann's ja nicht mal in der Hölle sein.

Sie hörten erst auf und setzten sich alle zusammen, als der Himmel schwarz wurde, urplötzlich, als hätte jemand eine Lampe ausgeknipst. Peterson sah Simon hoffnungsvoll an, aber der schüttelte den Kopf: »Was ich bisher gesehen habe, ist nur das Übliche.«

Ein Mann, der beim Essen nicht dabei gewesen war, tauchte auf und grüßte: »Thackeray«, sagte er. »Engländer, Enkel des Schriftstellers. Ich bin der Arzt in diesem Cowboylager. Du hast dich hoffentlich nicht von diesem verdammten Moore im Sumpf rumschleppen lassen.«

»Hatte ich eine andere Wahl?« fragte Simon.

Thackerey stöhnte und sagte: »Ich hoffe, du bist ein Mann, der viel Glück hat. Bist du das nicht, hast du ungefähr zehn Tage Zeit.«

»Wovon sprichst du?«

»Malaria.«

Er gab Simon eine Packung Tabletten, Chinin. »Du löst morgens und abends je vier Tabletten in abgekochtem Wasser auf«, sagte der Arzt und ging.

»Es ist keine gefährliche Krankheit«, erklärte der New-Yorker Tischnachbar mit dem semmelblonden Schopf und der beruhigenden Ausstrahlung, der Blondie genannt wurde. »Aber fünf Mann hat es bisher erwischt und sie sind mit mit hohem Fieber heimgeflogen worden.«

»Das ist ja verrückt«, meinte Simon.

Der Mann am Tisch gegenüber lachte und sagte, dies sei der Ort, den ein berühmter Krieger gemeint habe, als er sagte, die Überlebenden müßten die Toten beneiden.

Nach einigen Tagen in Hitze und Sand wußte Simon, was der Mann damit gemeint hatte.

Es wurde davon, daß Simon Philip Peterson Tag für Tag enttäuschen mußte, nicht besser. Die Laune der Gruppe wurde an dem Tag besser, als Simon neue Scherben erhielt und sofort feststellen konnte, daß dies etwas anderes, weitaus Interessanteres war. Mit klopfendem Herzen übersetzte er, Philip Peterson hing an seinen Lippen: ›Er kappte die Enden der Schnüre an Peitschen und Gerten, ersetzte sie durch Wolle von Mutterschafen. Die Mutter rügte ihr Kind nicht, das Kind widersetzte sich der Mutter nicht, niemand lehnte sich auf gegen Gudea, den guten Hirten, der Eninnu erbaute.‹

Fast gleichzeitig erkannten sie alle den Text auf den berühmten Zylindern im Louvre wieder. Was sie gefunden hatten, waren Kopien oder möglicherweise Entwürfe.

Peterson war untröstlich.

Zweimal erklomm Simon die Mauern des Tempels, gewaltige tote Ruinenhaufen. Stumm, ohne ein Lebenszeichen, kein zu erahnendes Flüstern Gudeas.

Simon wußte nicht recht, was er erwartet hatte, aber seine Enttäuschung war ebensogroß wie die Petersons.

Spät am Abend des zehnten Tages, Simon war allein in seinem Zelt, überkam ihn der erste Schüttelfrost. Er wußte, daß er jetzt nur noch eine Stunde Zeit hatte, bis das Fieber ihn ganz in seiner Gewalt haben würde, und da rannte er zu der Ruine, kletterte die Mauer hinauf bis zur Krone.

Es war eine Mondnacht.

»Gudea«, sagte er. »Um des barmherzigen Gottes willen.«

Er fror, daß die Zähne aufeinanderschlugen, aber er bekam, was er wollte. Es stand ein Mann auf der Mauer und erwartete ihn.

Das rätselhafte Lächeln war nur zu ahnen, es war vor allem die Andeutung der milden Weisheit und deren Verstärkung in den halbmondförmigen Augen, die hervorstach.

Als Simon die Frage stellte, über die er seit seiner Kindheit nachgegrübelt hatte: »Was tust du in meinem Leben?«, wurde das Lächeln breiter, wuchs sich zu einem Lachen aus, das zwischen den Mauern erklang und von einem Echo vervielfältigt wurde. Simon fühlte, wie das Fieber seinen Körper eroberte und wollte vor Wut und Verzweiflung schreien, denn er war jetzt doch schon ganz nah, fast angekommen bei der Antwort auf das Rätsel, mit dem er sich sein Leben lang beschäftigt hatte, das er wegen dieser verdammten Malaria aber nicht würde lösen können, der er sich nicht mehr widersetzen konnte, und die bald sein Bewußtsein trüben würde.

Er fühlte, wie er fiel, fühlte daß er sich während des Falls entlang der Mauer verletzte und auf einem Vorsprung liegenblieb, wo der Wüstenwind das Fieber kühlte, den Schmerz im Bein aber ins Unerträgliche steigerte.

Im nächsten Augenblick streckte Gudea seine Hand aus, Simon faßte sie, eine kleine Hand mit auffallend festem Druck. Leicht, als wäre er eine Daunenfeder, hob die Hand ihn über die Mauerkrone, und im selben Augenblick stand der Tempel wiedererrichtet vor seinen Augen.

Die goldenen Stiere bekleideten die Wände zwischen den Säulen auf dem großen Platz, und die Zikkurate verliefen himmelwärts, gleichzeitig schwer und leicht, ein gewaltiges Zeugnis der Vereinigung des Menschen mit Gott.

Es war hell, die Sonne überflutete den Tempel, als wäre er eine ganze Stadt, verlieh all diesem Großartigen Glanz, löste Reflexe in blauem Lazulith, schwarzem Diorit, weißem Alabaster aus. Aber vor allem in dem vielen Gold, das Dächer und Wände bekleidete, diesem warm schimmernden Gold.

Simon war sich entfernt bewußt, daß jenseits der Mauern Nacht herrschte wie schon vorher in der Wüste, und daß Steven Thackeray, der Enkel des Schriftstellers, Simons Körper fand, Leute und Bahre herbeiholte, das gebrochene Bein schiente und alles tat, was zu tun war. Doch Simon vergaß Dunkelheit und Wirklichkeit über den schwindelerregenden Gesichten dort in der Tempelstadt, und dies vor allem wegen des Mannes, den es schon in seinen Träumen gegeben hatte, und dessen geheimnisvolle Liebe Simons Sinne jetzt erfüllte.

»Wie hat die Sprache geklungen, die das Leben zurückgab?« Gudea lächelte dieses kaum zu ahnende Lächeln, und Simon glaubte zu erkennen, daß darin jetzt ein Anflug von Trauer lag.

»Es ist nicht so, wie du glaubst«, sagte er. »Es ging nicht um die sumerische Sprache an sich, sondern um etwas viel Größeres. Das Sumerische gab es ja in Schriften und Gebeten, aber meine Träume drehten sich um den Ursprung. Es gab eine uralte Sprache, die älteste der Menschheit, in der mit Tieren und Bäumen gesprochen werden konnte, mit Himmel und Wasser.«

Gudea seufzte, und es bestand kein Zweifel mehr, es lag Trauer in seinem Lächeln, als er fortfuhr: »In dem gesprochenen Sumerisch, in der Sprache des Volkes, gab es noch Reste der ersten Sprache. Ich dachte, ich besäße den Schlüssel dazu, könnte sie erschließen und die Verbindung wieder herstellen. Aber es war zu spät, der Weg zu der großen Wirklichkeit war versperrt, und unsere Lieder konnten ihn nicht wieder öffnen. Die sumerische Sprache hatte ihre Macht verloren, sie mußte beim Akkad Wörter und Ausdrücke entlehnen, die wir in alten Zeiten nicht brauchten, als alles noch einfach und heil war.«

Er fügte hinzu: »Es war vielleicht der letzte große Versuch, der auf der Erde unternommen wurde, um den Menschen wieder Anteil haben zu lassen.«

Doch dann lachte er: »Jetzt gibt sich der alte Gott mit jedem Kind, das geboren wird, doch noch Mühe und versucht, die Ganzheit wieder herzustellen. Am Anfang eines jeden Lebens kann sich der Mensch noch immer mit allem, was lebt, verständigen, auch mit den Flüssen und dem Himmel. Doch dann geht das meiste verloren.«

Gudea streckte die Hand aus, und auf dem großen Platz wuchsen die Eichen, Simons Eichen aus dem Land seiner Kindheit, und vor ihnen stand ein kleiner Junge mit zornig flammenden Augen und schrie seinen Abschied heraus, nahm Maß, beurteilte, bewertete und benannte die Bäume.

Simon schrie vor Schmerz und irgendwo stach man eine Nadel in seinen Arm und die wilde Qual wich.

»Du beginnst ja doch zu erkennen«, sagte Gudea, »daß, wer beurteilt, die Wirklichkeit verliert, und daß, wo immer ein Urteil gefällt wird, sich die Ganzheit entzieht.«

Dann nahm er Simon bei der Hand: »Wir müssen unsere Wanderung mit einem Gruß an den Gott beginnen, der in unseren Herzen wohnt und der nie in seinem Bestreben ermüdet, die Verbindung wieder herzustellen.«

Simon sah, daß die Trauer jetzt aus Gudeas Gesicht gewichen war, und daß die Halbmondaugen voll Zuversicht waren.

Sie gingen am Fuß des Turmes in den Tempel, und Simon erschrak vor der Größe und der Kraft des Raumes. Doch als er seinen Blick dem Gott zuwandte, der sie ganz vorn in der Halle erwartete, hielt Gudea ihn zurück.

»Keiner kann ihn ansehen, ohne vernichtet zu werden. Ihn darfst du nur in deinem eigenen Herzen schauen, in dem Tempel, in dem er immer auf dich wartet, und der grenzenlos ist.«

Dann fielen sie beide auf die Knie, Seite an Seite, und die Welt verging, sowohl die große Wüste rund um die Ruinen, als auch der goldene Tempel in der Sonne. Simon verharrte, bis Gudea ihm die

Hand auf die Schulter legte, eine leichte Berührung voll Zärtlichkeit, die Simon wiedererkannte.

»Jetzt wirst du Nin-alla, die Tochter des Ur-Babu, begrüßen, die die Oberste Priesterin des Mondgottes und meine Gemahlin ist.«

Simon folgte Gudea, der einen Kopf kleiner war als er, die breite Treppe der Zikkurate hinauf zur ersten Ebene, von wo er die leuchtende Tempelstadt überblicken und hinaus in die Dunkelheit schauen konnte, die sich schwarz hinter den Mauern türmte.

Doch Gudea führte ihn noch hundert Stufen weiter, bis sie an der Spitze den Tempel des Mondgottes erreichten, hoch oben, als schwebe er über dem Erdboden.

»Die Priesterin schläft und darf erst beim nächsten Entfachen wieder geweckt werden«, sagte Gudea. »Sie braucht all ihre Kräfte, um das Silberschiff über den Himmel zu lenken.«

Simon verneigte sich vor der Schlafenden, die er kannte, gut kannte, und deren rotes Haar zu einem schönen Kranz um die hohe Stirn geflochten war.

Auf dem Weg die Treppen hinunter hörten sie Geigenspiel, eine Melodie von wilder Schönheit, und Gudea sagte: »Ja, du mußt unserem Geigenspieler lauschen, den du selbst wie den Wind jagst, dem du jedoch nie begegnen wirst.«

Und da wußte Simon, daß es Habermann war, der da spielte, und er lief dem Klang nach, doch der Geiger trieb Spott mit ihm, verschwand zwischen den Säulen des großen Palastes. Nur ein einziges Mal, für einen kurzen Augenblick, bekam er den Rücken des Spielmanns zu sehen, und er war ganz so, wie Simon ihn aus seinem Traum kannte, scheu, ausweichend.

Jetzt bin ich verloren, dachte Simon. Ich finde nie aus diesem Palast ohne Anfang und Ende heraus. Und er schrie seine Furcht hinaus, und im selben Moment beugte sich der lange Aron Äppelgren über ihn, genau wie es zu sein hatte, und er wurde auf das Fahrrad gehoben.

Sie gingen wie immer zu Hause über die Wiesen, und Aron machte alle Vogelstimmen nach und ärgerte die großen Möwen, und Simon lachte wie damals als Kind und machte in die Hose wie damals, als er noch klein war.

Dann fiel ihm ein, wo er war und er rief: »Gudea!«

»Aber ich bin doch immer hier«, sagte die sanfte Stimme in seiner Nähe, und Simon wußte, daß es wahr war und daß es nichts zu fürchten gab.

Jetzt standen sie in einem Beduinenzelt, der schwarze Stoff fraß das Licht auf und es dauerte eine Weile, bis Simons Augen sich soweit an die Dunkelheit gewöhnt hatten, daß er die Frau sah, die sich in der Mitte des Zeltes vor ihnen verneigte.

»Ich war kinderlos«, sagte sie. »Das ist in unserem Volk schlimmer als der Tod. Du wirst also meine Freude verstehen, als Ke-Ba, die Priesterin, eines Nachts kam und mich bat, mich des Jungen anzunehmen, den sie heimlich geboren hatte.«

»Du weißt ja«, fuhr sie fort. »Weißt, daß die Priesterin des Gatumdu nicht schwanger werden kann, daß ihr Schoß vielen Männern dient und den Auserwählten große Wollust bereitet, daß der Same aber der Göttin gehört und im Leib der Priesterin nicht wachsen kann.«

»Als Ke-Ba schwanger wurde, wußte sie also, daß das Kind dem Gott gehörte, und wagte nie, es Akkads Priestern zu sagen, die das heilige Kind vernichtet hätten.«

Simon nickte und sie fuhr fort: »Darum durfte Gudea hier bei mir aufwachsen, und er schenkte meinem Leben Wert und wurde zum Segen für sein ganzes Volk.«

Simon sah die Frau lange an, es gab auch bei ihr etwas, das er wiedererkannte.

Aber erst beim Abschied, als er bemerkte, daß die Wände des Zeltes dem großen nordischen Wald wichen, erkannte er, daß es Inga war, die zu ihm gesprochen hatte, und daß da der lange See war, blau und kühl in der endlosen Wüste.

Aber schon waren sie wieder in der Tempelstadt und Gudea sagte, ich möchte auch, daß du meine Mutter, die große Ke-Ba kennenlernst.

Und er führte Simon in ein weiteres goldenes Gemach mit leuchtend blauen Wänden und einer goldenen Decke.

Eine Frau wartete in der Mitte des Raumes.

»Ich lasse euch allein«, sagte Gudea.

Und Ke-Ba, die das Kind geboren hatte, es aber nicht hatte behalten dürfen, wandte sich langsam um, braune Augen voll Wärme begegneten seinem Blick.

»Mama«, sagte er. »Karin, geliebte Mama.«

Sie lächelte ihr altes breites Lächeln und er dachte, Gott, guter Gott, ich habe vergessen, wie schön sie ist, und er erkannte jeden Ton in der festen Stimme, als sie sagte: »Simon, mein Junge.«

Sie standen einfach da und hielten einander bei der Hand und die gemeinsame Freude war so groß, daß sie die Wände des Raumes sprengte. Dann sagte Karin mit all der alten eindringlichen Kraft in den Worten: »Ich mag diese Schuld nicht, mit der du dich abquälst. Du warst mir im Haus am Fluß jeden Tag eine Freude. Nichts, was du getan hast, hörst du, hätte anders sein dürfen.«

»Mama!« rief er. »Warum bist du gestorben?«

»Ich hatte beschlossen zu gehen, sobald mein Teil vollbracht war, Simon. Es war ein gutes Leben, aber ich wollte nicht als alter Mensch im Weg stehen.«

Er öffnete den Mund, um zu widersprechen, sie sah es und lachte: »Ich scherze, Simon. Da war etwas, das du nicht wußtest.«

Sie erzählte ihm von Petter und den Seidenschwänzen, und er erkannte nun endlich die Quelle der Trauer im ihrem Herzen.

»Das Leben ist groß, Simon«, sagte sie. »Viel größer als wir ahnen.«

Er schaute sich um und die Unendlichkeit der Ebene traf auf die des Meeres, und hinter Karin lagen die Wälder, die tiefen Wälder, und über ihnen ein Himmel ohne Ende.

Doch dann überkam Karin Unruhe, und sie sagte, wie sie es all die Jahre getan hatte, Simon, es ist höchste Zeit, du mußt dich beeilen.

»Lauf«, drängte sie und hängte ihm den Rucksack mit den Schulbüchern über die Schultern. »Du kommst noch rechtzeitig«, versicherte sie. »Los geht's im Sauseschritt!«

Er nickte, er war sicher, sie sorgte für ihn, wie sie es immer getan hatte. Er würde rechtzeitig an Ort und Stelle sein.

Aber er drehte sich an der Küchentür um, wie immer, und sie stand, wie es zu sein hatte, am Herd und sagte lachend: »Beeil dich, mein Junge.«

40

Und er war rechtzeitig dort und schlug an einem normalen schwedischen Nachmittag die Augen in einem grauen Krankenhauszimmer auf und hörte Stimmen vor der Tür, beglückende schwedische Stimmen.

Ich bin zu Hause, dachte er, und eigentlich war er gar nicht erstaunt, denn irgendwo gab es ja auch hinter Spritzen und Bahren, Flugzeugen und weißen Kitteln ein Bewußtsein, Klaras Gesicht über ihn gebeugt, ihre kühlen Hände, die das Kissen umgedreht und seine Stirn getrocknet hatten, Ruben mit besorgtem Blick, Erik voll Angst.

Simon war traurig, er wollte nicht zurück in die Wirklichkeit, die so viele Menschen für die einzige hielten.

Karin hat mich betrogen, dachte er.

Aber im selben Augenblick wußte er, daß sie getan hatte, was sie hatte tun müssen.

Nach einer Weile wurde ihm klar, daß die Stimmen vor der Tür über ihn sprachen.

»Das kann so nicht weitergehen. Es scheint ein Zustand der Verwirrung zu sein, der mit der Malaria nichts zu tun hat«, sagte eine junge Stimme.

»Gehirnerschütterung und Fieber, das erklärt alles.«

Er war eine ältere Stimme, die fortfuhr: »Seine Angehörigen haben doch versichert, daß er psychisch stabil ist, kein neurotischer Typ. Und seine Frau ist selbst vom Fach und keineswegs beunruhigt.«

»Aber er halluziniert seit vierzehn Tagen, auch zwischen den Fieberanfällen, wo er eigentlich ruhig hätte sein müssen.«

Das war wieder die junge Stimme, und Simon verabscheute sie.

Er hatte keine Angst, aber er ahnte Gefahr, und er hatte Zeit zum Nachdenken, denn die Stimmen entfernten sich jetzt. Ich muß den Bildern standhalten, ihnen nicht mehr nachgeben, dachte Simon.

Los geht's im Sauseschritt.

Im nächsten Augenblick wurde ihm bewußt, daß eines seiner Beine eingegipst war, und vage konnte er sich daran erinnern, daß er es sich beim Fall von der Mauer gebrochen hatte.

Er versuchte zu schlafen, die Bilder kamen, aber er trieb sie in die Flucht und wachte auf, bevor er noch mitten in ihrem Fluß war. Es gab eine Klingel neben dem Bett, er läutete, eine Nachtschwester kam.

»Könnte ich eine Schlaftablette bekommen«, bat er. »Ich kann nicht einschlafen.«

Er sah ihre Verwunderung, dann kam ein abgehetzter diensthabender Arzt und fühlte ihm den Puls, ordnete an, den Tropf am Arm zu entfernen und dem Patienten einen Becher Brei zu verabreichen.

»Willkommen in der Wirklichkeit!« sagte der Arzt und war schon wieder verschwunden. Simon lächelte.

Und schluckte seinen Brei und nahm seine Tablette, verbrachte eine traumlose Nacht in ausgiebiger, schwarzer Ruhe.

Am nächsten Morgen war der Stationsarzt da, der Mann mit der jungen Stimme, und Simon stellte fest, daß sie einander kannten, Studienkollegen gewesen waren. »Hallo, wie geht's dir?«

»Doch, danke, halt müde.«

Per Andersson sah sich die Fieberkurve an, die nach unten zeigte, fühlte den Puls, horchte das Herz ab, und Simon verstand, daß das alles nur die Neugier des Arztes vertuschen sollte.

Er sprach eine Weile über die Malaria, daß die Besserung jetzt schnell fortschreiten werde, und daß das Bein heilte, wie es sollte.

»Du mußt so schnell wie möglich mit einem Training anfangen. Möglichst schon heute«, sagte er.

Dann mußte er gehen. An der Tür drehte er sich aber noch einmal um. Er konnte seine Neugier nicht mehr zügeln: »Wer ist Gudea?«

»Ein sumerischer König, einer der letzten.«

»Und was ist so besonders an ihm?«

»Nun, er hat einen großen Tempel gebaut und versucht, die sumerische Sprache wieder zu beleben, die schon fast vergessen war. Sein Name bedeutet ›Der Gerufene‹. Aber warum, zum Teufel, interessiert er dich?«

»Du phantasierst seit fast vierzehn Tagen von ihm.«

»Ach so?« sagte Simon und seine Verwunderung verlieh den Worten Inhalt. »Aber vielleicht ist das gar nicht so komisch«, überlegte er. »Ich schreibe meine Dissertation über ihn, und ich hatte ja hohes Fieber.«

»Wir haben das schon komisch gefunden, lange andauernde Halluzinationen gehören nicht zum Krankheitsbild.«

»Ach so«, sagte Simon wieder.

»Ich habe schon gedacht, du bist besessen«, sagte Per Andersson lachend.

»Besessen«, sagte Simon, und jetzt war seine Verwunderung echt. »Glaubt die ärztliche Wissenschaft an sowas?«

»Es gibt viel zwischen Himmel und Erde«, antwortete der Arzt und verschwand. Er wirkte fast enttäuscht.

Simon blieb im Bett liegen und dachte, daß er es geschafft hatte, daß er es wohl in Zukunft auch schaffen werde. Aber der Sieg brachte ihm keine Genugtuung, er verspürte kaum Freude.

Klara kam und, ja, er freute sich, als er sie sah.

»Du kannst einen ganz schön erschrecken, Simon«, sagte sie leise.

»Das wollte ich nicht«, erwiderte er.

»Bist du ihm begegnet, deinem Gudea?«

»Ja, zumindest in den Träumen«, sagte Simon und fürchtete, Klara könnte von Jungschen Archetypen anfangen oder von irgend etwas anderem Ermüdendem, gegen das sich zu wehren er nicht die Kraft hatte.

Doch sie saß nur bei ihm und hielt seine Hand während er einschlief.

Am dritten Tag mußte sie fragen: »Er hat dir doch hoffentlich nicht den Lebenswillen genommen, Simon?«

Da sah er, daß sie weinte, aber er konnte ihr nicht erzählen, daß es nicht um Gudea ging, sondern um Karin, die ihn dazu gebracht hatte, aus der Küche zu laufen.

Erik kam kurz zu Besuch, erkannte aber, daß Simon sogar zum Sprechen zu müde war, blieb also nur mit feuchten Augen neben ihm sitzen: »Ich habe mir so verdammte Sorgen gemacht.«

»Das war nicht nötig, Papa. Du hast mir ja beigebracht, wie man kämpft.«

Sie konnten sogar ein bißchen lachen.

Ruben kam mit Blumen und Büchern, er hatte die Kleine dabei, Malin, und es tat gut, sie zu sehen.

Im Korridor sprachen sie davon, Antidepressiva einzusetzen, aber Klara lehnte ab.

»Er schafft es ohne, er braucht nur Zeit«, sagte sie, aber Simon wußte, daß sie sich Sorgen machte.

Ein paar Tage später sagte Per Andersson, der Stationsarzt: »Wir kriegen einen Engländer, einen Lord Sowieso, der auf Malaria spezialisiert ist.«

Bei der Visite am nächsten Tag waren mehr Leute anwesend als gewöhnlich, es wimmelte nur so von weißen Kitteln. An der Seite des Chefarztes stand ein kleiner Mann, der The Queen's English sprach.

Per Andersson erstattete in etwas holprigem Englisch Bericht über den Fall: »Wir haben uns einige Zeit Sorgen um den Patienten gemacht, er hat mehrere Tage fast ununterbrochen halluziniert.«

»Das kommt manchmal vor«, sagte der Lord. »Excuse me.« Er zog Simons Augenlid hoch und leuchtete mit geübter Geste einen Augenblick mit einem Lämpchen in die Pupille.

»Keine Anzeichen von Dauerschäden«, sagte er und ersah aus dem Krankenblatt, daß es sich hier vermutlich außerdem um eine fieberhafte Gehirnerschütterung handelte.

Ein Zucken durchlief Simon, sein ganzes Wesen sammelte sich, als er die Hand erkannte, die Berührung. Er starrte die kurzen Finger an, wagte den Blick dem Gesicht entgegenzuheben und sah in die Augen mit dem geheimnisvollen Lächeln.

Ich bin verrückt, dachte Simon.

Alarmglocken läuteten, sei auf der Hut, paß verdammt noch mal auf!

Doch als die ganze Gruppe gehen wollte, besiegte Simons Bedürfnis, noch etwas mehr zu erfahren, seine Angst, und er fragte: »Entschuldigen Sie, Sir. Sind wir einander nicht schon begegnet?«

Sein Englisch war fast ebenso nasal wie das des Lords, er hatte nicht vergeblich vier Jahre an der London University studiert. Er wußte, daß seine Stimme fest war.

Der Engländer drehte sich auf dem Absatz um und ging an das Bett zurück, schaute Simon und dann die Fieberkurve mit dem Namen an und sagte überaus erstaunt und fast heiter: »Simon Larsson, natürlich. Ich erinnre mich sehr gut an den Morgen in Ohmberg.«

Ohmberg, sagte er, es war nicht anzunehmen, daß die Herumstehenden den Namen in der Geographie orten konnten, aber alle wirkten überrascht, und der Chefarzt sagte, wie es in solchen Fällen üblich ist, daß die Welt klein sei.

Simon fühlte das Lachen in sich aufsteigen, direkt aus dem Bauch, und er fragte: »Glauben Sie immer noch, daß die Riesen ihre Unterhosen im Vättersee waschen, Sir?«

»Of course«, nickte der Lord mit glitzernden Augen, und das Lachen sprang aus Simons Körper heraus und explodierte im Raum. Es war so gewaltig, daß Simon dachte, es halle, wie schon einmal, bestimmt in Königin Ommas Burg wider.

Alle lachten, die meisten unsicher, und manche dachten, dieser typisch englische Humor sei in all seiner Unbegreiflichkeit einfach unwiderstehlich.

Aber der Lord wandte sich an seine Kollegen und sagte bedauernd: »Sie müssen wissen, ich verbrachte einen ganzen Tag mit diesem jungen Archäologen, um ihm in jeder nur möglichen Weise klarzumachen, wo in der Welt er nach der Halle des Bergkönigs zu suchen habe. Aber denken Sie, er hat auf mich gehört? Nein, er mußte auf kürzestem Weg in die Malariasümpfe des Irak und in die Ruinen-haufen von Lagash.«

Alle nickten, keiner begriff, das Lächeln wurde immer angestreng-ter, aber Simon ließ nicht locker: »Wie geht es Ihren Kindern, Sir?«

»Ich hatte einigen Kummer mit einem meiner Söhne, aber das ist jetzt so gut wie vorbei«, antwortete der Lord. »Und dann habe ich noch ein Töchterchen dazubekommen.«

»Ich gratuliere.«

»Danke.«

Die kurze Hand des Lords lag auf Simons Schulter, sie verströmte Kraft, und er sagte: »Wir sehen uns wieder, Simon Larsson.«

Und weg war er, aber im Zimmer zurück blieb seine Freude und eine große Sicherheit, die in Simons Herzen Wurzeln schlug, mitten in der Halle des Bergkönigs.

Er wurde erstaunlich schnell gesund, aß wie ein Löwe, schlief wie ein unschuldiges Kind mit sanften und freundlichen Träumen.

Klara kam am Tag seiner Entlassung, um ihn abzuholen.

Draußen stand sein Wagen, der rote VW, der aus London mit dem Schiff herübergebracht worden war.

»Ich werde fahren, wenn dir dein Bein Schwierigkeiten macht«, bot Klara an.

»Tu das nur.«

Es machte Freude, die Welt zu betrachten, die voller Erlebnisse war, voller Wirklichkeiten, sie zu genießen. Im Haus an der Flußmün-dung erwarteten ihn die andern, er nahm Malin in seine Arme und flüsterte: »Ich kann dir Grüße von Karin bestellen.«

Sie nickte, nicht im geringsten erstaunt.

Der gedeckte Tisch wartete bei Mona und Isak, Simon humpelte durch den großen Garten und sah, daß der Frühling schon am Werk war. In aller Bescheidenheit hatten die Leberblümchen ausgeschlagen und wetteiferten unter den Eschen in ihrer Bläue mit den Trauben-hyazinthen.

Als sie sich an den Tisch setzten und die Gläser erhoben, sagte Simon: »Wir stoßen auf Karin an, auf die Erinnerung an sie.«

Und das taten sie auch, und Simon fühlte, daß die Trauer ihren Schmerz jetzt verloren hatte. Bei ihnen allen.

In der Dämmerung ging Simon den Hügel hinauf und über die Wiese zu den Eichen der Kindheit – um seinen Bund mit ihnen zu erneuern.

Marianne Fredriksson
Hannas Töchter
Roman. 384 Seiten. Gebunden

Als Anna ihre fast 90jährige Mutter Johanna im Pflegeheim besucht, ist diese nicht mehr ansprechbar. Anna ist zugleich traurig und wütend. So viele Fragen möchte sie noch stellen, so vieles möchte sie noch wissen über das Leben ihrer Mutter Johanna und ihrer Großmutter Hanna. Wie ist es gewesen vor fast 100 Jahren auf dem Land, als Hanna mit ihrem unehelichen Sohn Ragnar den Müller Bromann heiratete? Wieso konnte sie sich später nie an das Leben in der Großstadt Göteborg gewöhnen? Wie hat sich ihre Mutter gefühlt, als der Vater starb, und warum hat sie niemals rebelliert gegen ihr tristes Hausfrauendasein? Jetzt ist es zu spät, all diese Fragen zu stellen. Anna – Tochter und Enkelin – begibt sich allein auf die Reise durch das Leben ihrer Mutter und Großmutter und findet mit Hilfe ihrer Aufzeichnungen Zugang zum Leben ihrer Vorfahren und vor allem auch zu sich selbst. Anna, Hanna und Johanna – drei Frauen, drei Generationen, eine Familie. »Hannas Töchter« ist die sensibel und zugleich kraftvoll erzählte Lebensgeschichte von drei Frauen, die die Entwicklung der schwedischen Gesellschaft über zwei Jahrhunderte atemberaubend und einfühlsam nachvollziehen läßt. Marianne Fredriksson hat ein warmherziges Buch über die Liebe in den Zeiten des Umbruchs geschrieben.

»Ein Buch zum Verschlingen ...«
Borje Isakson, ›Dagens Industri‹

Wolfgang Krüger Verlag